King of NOD

SCOTT FAD

some things never die

Hooded Friar Press
Nashville

Hooded Friar Press is a small, traditional publishing house dedicated to publishing high-quality books by new authors. We believe in the importance of creative collaboration between writers, editors, and designers. In the spirit of that collaboration, we strive to treat every author as we would like to be treated with honesty, trust, and respect. We love books, and we believe that, in order to make books the world will love, the publishing process must be inspired.

KING OF NOD: SOME THINGS NEVER DIE
Published by Hooded Friar Press, Brentwood, Tennessee

For information regarding permission, write to:
Cold Tree Publishing, 214 Overlook Court, Suite 253, Brentwood, Tennessee 37027.
www.coldtreepublishing.com

Printed in Canada

Grateful acknowledgement is made for permission to include the following copyrighted material:
Face Behind the Moon by Samuel Easterman. Copyright © by Samuel Easterman. Used by permission.
Changeling by R. Gustavius Creek. Copyright © by R. G. Creek. Used by permission
Selected by Limon Cevreaux. Copyright © by Limon Cevreaux. Used by permission.
Dark Rooms by Candice Chance. Copyright © by Candice Chance. Used by permission.
The Deathbird by Harlan Ellison. Copyright © by Harlan Ellison. Used by permission.

Publisher's Cataloging-in-Publication data

Fad, Scott.
   King of Nod : some things never die / Scott Fad.
   p. cm.
   ISBN 978-0-9817609-0-2
1. South Carolina—Fiction. 2. Science Fiction. 3. Supernatural—Fiction. 4. Islands—Fiction. I. Title.

PS3556.A32 K5 2008

813.54—dc22   2008934695

First Edition: November 2008
10 9 8 7 6 5 4 3 2 1

For Miss Virginia Wood

King of Nod

Prologue
Early Lessons

He was a little white boy, but he crawled onto the old black woman's lap as if she were his very own mother—or, more likely, his grandmother or even his great-grandmother, for she was certainly old enough. A frog's foreleg was snatched in the round puff of his right fist. The rest of the animal dangled, lifeless and pungent as a stalk of seaweed rotting on the beach.

He presented the frog to her chin. "Lookit, Miss Laylee! Lookit what I done killed."

"Why look at that, Mr. Boo! You kill him all by yourself—or you find him dead?"

"Myself. Hit 'im with a stick."

She examined the frog with doctorly interest. Her jowls, butterscotch pudding, sagged. "Oh well now," she said and tapped the frog with a yellow pad of flesh, sending a dozen tin bracelets clattering to her elbow. Then, blazing for a miraculous instant, bluish sparks fizzled from her fingernail. In the boy's knuckles, abruptly, a mossy knee flexed. "I don't see as that jasper's really dead."

The boy was used to her jokes. And her magic. He slung the frog close to his eyes, frowning and uncertain. "He a'sleepin?"

"Naw, he ain't sleepin."

He waggled his fist. "He pre*tend*in?"

The boy's words curled tartly around the edges—the salt of Carolina low country. Oak leaves fallen and left to broil in the sun. The old woman's voice was a sweet lyric of songbirds and Baptist hymns. The boy came from one of the wealthiest families on the island. The old woman lived in a shack.

She stroked a gnarl of brown sticks through his hair. "Mr. Boo, I ever tell you the story 'bout this ol frog I come 'cross one day?"

The boy was still eyeing the dead animal mistrustfully. He shook his head.

"Don't figure you wanna hear 'bout him..."

"Tell me!"

She shifted his slight frame around to ease the stab against her hip. Then she told him the story the way it actually happened, and it had happened a hundred years ago (or maybe it was two hunert, she guessed), about a little frog who had once approached her from Pigg's Creek.

Ice crystals glittered, melted in her eyes. She was made of cinnamon and molasses, burnt wood, rusted bedsprings, pine soap, cypress hides. Her dress was the rag she used to mop floors.

"Come hippy-hoppin right up to my garden where I'se pullin weeds. Well, I look at him. An' he look at me. Then you know what that jasper went an' done?"

The boy lowered the frog and watched her closely.

"Why, Mr. Boo, that ol frog get to *talkin*. Jes open his little mouth and *talk*, plain as you talkin to me. An' he say, 'Is you the guffer doctor?'"

And since it had been some considerable time since she had come across a talking frog, she had dropped her load of weeds in surprise and nearly squashed him. When she didn't answer him right off, the frog asked his question again. (She rocked-creaked her chair gently, petting the boy's small back.)

"'Why yes, I suppose I *is* the guffer doctor,' I says to him.

"Then he say, 'Thank gawd, cause I got a black whammy on me that needs fixin.'"

So she had picked up the talking frog and carried him inside her little house. (Passing through the very same tottering porch where she and the boy now sat, looking over the very same garden. Pigg's Creek was beyond the garden, beyond a field, slogging somewhere behind oak and ficus and magnolia.)

The frog told her, "Witch put that whammy on me, turnt me into this here frog. 'Fore that...well, it been so long, I don't hardly remember. Seem to figure I was a *prince* once, a ways back."

(The dead frog curled into a rancid green pickle on the boy's naked legs.)

So, she had gathered up some stump water (so she told the boy) and some bellis petal and some teneka root and dry cricket wings and pennywort and the two fattest beetles she could find along with all the other magic flotsam it took to untangle a witch-spell. It went into a skillet over a low flame...she chanted...she spit...set light to four candles...snipped a sprig of her hair and chucked it in the flame (not the skillet, mind you, boy, but the flame—an' my, wasn't my hair jes as black-pitch as crow feathers in them days?)...recited the twenty-second Psalm (only the beginning part— *My God, my God, why hast thou forsaken me? Why art though so far from helping me, and from the words of my roaring?*)...dappled in some sour mash...poured the lumpiness into a wooden cup...then set the concoction under the house to cool.

The frog, as instructed, gulped it down.

"Well, Mr. Boo, you know what happen next?"

The boy rocked his head slowly, mouth open.

"Why that little frog, he turn into a *slug*. A slimy ol gray *slug*." Her wrinkles wadded into a scowl of distaste, and the boy, watching her, scowled too. "'You ain't no prince,' I says. An' that slug, he look up at me with them slimy eyes, an' he say, 'Oh, *that's* right, I'm gettin to remember it all now. That wasn't no black whammy that witch put on me—it was a *white* one.'"

The old woman cackled and rocked the chair.

The boy scrunched his lips; a tuft of chestnut hair fell across his brow. One eye closed, he considered the green sack of jelly in his lap. "Not a prince..." he said thoughtfully. The dead frog suddenly squirmed. It sat up and looked at him with dull accusation.

The boy yelled out and then laughed. The old woman's pigtails reared back, and she laughed with him.

That was the first lesson.

❖   ❖   ❖

They attacked from all directions.

He raced them (they were gooks; he was an American pilot) from the beach to the Indian shell mound, whipping through brambled hedgerows, tip-toeing gator-infested sloughs, pounding sun-baked lanes—arriving ahead of them all, breathless, giggling. He fell to his rump, heedless of the broken-edge oysters and clams that bit him.

From behind, still struggling through the brush, their complaints: "You cheater; you cheater!"

He laughed and scrambled up the great pile, planted his legs on top and shouted at them. "King of the island! I beat you all!"

His father said Seminoles made the pile; they traveled to the island in canoes and dug in the sand and mud for shells and came to this place to feast on them. So many shells, a billion shells, piled up over centuries as the Indians came and made this a sacred place. After the red men were murdered or exiled, it was the runaway slaves who escaped here and topped off the peak. Built over centuries, and now he claimed the summit. A mountain of dinosaur teeth and mastodon tusks and whalebones and aborigine skulls all pounded into sharp little white-gray flakes and daggers. He could see every compass point across the island: down into South Patch and north toward his own house. He saw the fuzz of mainland trees in the west across the Yamawichee Sound. He saw the Atlantic in the east, a bolt of slate-blue silk stretching to other worlds. He stood atop the mound, and he was lord of it all.

Then realized someone had been there before him—for perched alongside him at the peak was a burlap doll, its apple head carved into a grimace of pain and anger. It was a face from the carvings of African masks. The boy bent to study this unexpected discovery when Dewey Fitch appeared from the scrub, saw him standing high above, and pointed at him. "Boo Taylor, you cheated! You took a shortcut!"

He quickly forgot the doll. "There ain't no shortcut, boy. I'm king of the island!"

Then Lester Meggett stumbled into the clearing. Then Ashford Marchant, pushing up his thick glasses.

"You boys look awful small down there!"

At last, Hoss Beaudry burst through: his shirt ripped, thorn scratches making an Indian tattoo across his cheek.

"King of the island!" Boo Taylor jumped up and down, crushing Cro-Magnon ribs and brontosaur legs. "Try and get me down!"

They came after him, and he easily pushed them away one after the other until they came up from different sides. They circled him, and he circled to face them, laughing, breathless. Then they yelled out and jumped him—so many arms and legs pushing and grabbing and kicking, the doll was decapitated and eviscerated under their feet—and in a big ball they all tumbled, boys and their burlap victim, sliding down the sharp, petrified shards of mammoth spine and dragon tail and whale jaw, laughing and falling and being gobbled alive by a pile of dead bones. Not yet seeing the ancient, dark giant who lurked just a few feet away in the brush, the thing that would terrorize their lives. Its shadow was already moving against them, preparing to make itself known, preparing to leap, to scream.

"King of Sweetpatch Island!"

That was the second lesson. When the beast finally did spring a few moments later and a child was left shredded in pieces (not unlike a burlap doll), they ran shrieking and were changed forever.

April 4, 1968

It wasn't until he was nine-going-on-ten when the lie was finally exposed—thrust into harsh sunlight where it roasted like week-old roadkill on playground blacktop.

"Liar!" was the word he hurled at it.

The word was followed by his fist.

The other children were a yellow-jacket swarm around the two boys, fearful and enthralled, agitated by the feuding swelter of Atlantic salts and marsh stink, and now gasping as a single being.

The punch caught Wade Dutton square in the mouth. The big boy teetered: a road sign in the teeth of a hurricane. And then he fell backward, hard.

In the dizzying heat, Boo Taylor hitched deep breaths, T-shirt sweat-plastered to his skinny ribcage. Tall oaks dripping Spanish moss hemmed the ball court. Beyond trees and children, cicadas rattled in scrubby fields and the ocean pounded sands. From somewhere else, amid the jangle of children sounds, a band of Negro girls chanted at jump rope:

> *Who dat comin when de sun get low,*
> *Snatchin dem childrens when dey moves too slow?*
> *Who dat comin from de swamptree shade?*
> *It's grandaddy comin wit de butcherman's blade.*

He watched Wade Dutton strike the ground. Watched sweat fleck off the red crew cut. Watched Neanderthal dullness cross Wade's face. "Why, you little bastard!" Wade spat, and there was blood in it. "You little *fourth-grade bastard!*" The wide-eye surprise narrowed to furious slits. Wade shuffled to his feet. But the nine-year-old fist swung out again, and Wade Dutton went down again.

From the spectators, another collective sigh. "Oh good Lord, Boo Taylor," someone whispered, "you're crazy!"

From under the basket, Gussie Dutton—Wade's little sister—shrieked: *"Git that boy, Wade!"*

The game, forgotten as the basketball pinged into the grass, had begun under the glow of spring blossoms. The boys of Mrs. Wiltbank's fourth grade had razzed and clowned up and down the court with routine, after-school good cheer.

Until Wade Dutton bullied onto the court and the glow bleakened under a passing fat cloud. The others avoided him, were cautious and ingratiating and anxious for the game to end so they could be rid of him.

All but Boo Taylor who had pitched himself against the older boy in a battle of honor.

It was an unforgivable perversion of accepted schoolyard order. The Duttons were a motherless clan risen from the dark romance of poverty to assume a brutal redneck lordship over the island. Wade was the youngest of the four Dutton boys—two years older than Boo Taylor, although just one grade separated them. (Gussie, the only Dutton girl, pug-ugly and carrot-haired, was Boo Taylor's age.) Their father was a drunkard who scuttled his shrimper on Cedar Knee Hammock in '62. As the youngest son, Wade had honed supreme skills in intimidation through years of abuse at the hands of his father and famous brothers. The children of Sweetpatch Island knew this—and knew that on playgrounds, nine-year-old boys did not block Wade Dutton's shots, did not steal the ball away from him, and did not weave lithely past him with the ball and score points.

Aghast, the other boys—Hoss Beaudry, Ashford Marchant, even half-retarded Lester Meggett—shadowed Boo between shots to whisper their cautions. Boo did not acknowledge them.

It was the stubbornness that, under other circumstances, merited their admiration. For if Wade Dutton was the last son of a generation of terror, Boo Taylor (the only son of the island's only white physician—*royalty* by the standards of Sweetpatch Island) was the blue-eyed prince of a nobler dynasty. By the age of nine he had already distinguished himself as hero and eccentric, equally welcomed in the home of the mayor and the humblest Negro shanty. His natural charm kept him in good favor with the gentry despite his pagan restlessness and his occasional wanderings down to the dilapidated schoolhouse in South Patch where he sat in on class with the colored children and their flustered schoolmistress. His proficiency with his daddy's .22 and with a skiff salvaged from the Pittman Boatyard had birthed legends of daring adventures through the inlets and creeks and swamps that tangled the western coast of the island: downing marsh deer and ducks, gallantly offering these kills to neighbors and strangers, landing hammerheads and skewering gators and slitting them open in search of human remains.

Boo Taylor's father was the esteemed Dr. Silas Barnwell Taylor, a local boy educated in the finest schools of the North; his mother was the refined lady of Beaufort, Miss MaeEllen LaCharite. Antagonism was not presumed of young Robert E. Lee Taylor; it was the province of bohunk trash like the Duttons. His rampage against Wade Dutton on the playground was not only suicidal, it showed poor manners.

The boys on the basketball court had shied away as Wade Dutton hurled his brawn, shoving and grabbing at Boo's shirt, tripping and spitting. Boo's knees and elbows were skinned raw, his neck and arms cross-hatched from Wade's ragged fingernails—but he accepted the abuse mutely, played grimly, and had shown at least enough wisdom to keep from shoving back or complaining. Wade called for the ball but time and again was flustered by Boo's darting hands. Each time Boo Taylor touched the ball, he danced around his clumsy rival, slid to the basket and—with or without an elbow in his ribs—logged another two points.

Wade Dutton, to his credit, had remained true to his nature. He could rough Boo Taylor around the court, but to flat out strike him would be an admission of defeat, and he could not conceivably admit defeat to a scrawny nine-year-old rich boy. Not with his bratty sister watching and just slavering at the chance to blab it to his brothers. Nevertheless, he saw the futility of the brute-force tactic, and so he had called upon another celebrated Dutton talent, one he could wield with equal proficiency.

And the taunting began.

"Hear your momma's laid up with a gin hangover again. Why, your momma surely loves the bottle, don't she, boy?

"You still nursin on that ol nigger housemaid, rich boy? You suckin her teaties?"

Wade probed as the ball worked up and down the court. Boo ignored him, and Wade's frustration ballooned.

It was Dewey Fitch who supplied the lethal indignity. Dewey, who lived in rabid terror of Wade Dutton under all other circumstances, now supposed a certain kinship since they were on the same team. Having fallen into the hypnotic rhythm of Wade's taunts, Dewey soon blurted his own: a vague bit of rumor picked from an overheard conversation.

Wade Dutton recorded Boo Taylor's flinch at the words and called time-out for a consultation. The story was stammered out; the game resumed, and Wade Dutton had his weapon.

"You're a liar!" Boo yelled.

"No I ain't neither. Ain't that right, Dew-boy?"

"Right as rain, Wade. My momma said so."

"*Liar!*"

The taunting was relentless—it was all lies, all of it; Wade Dutton and Dewey Fitch were two liars and nothing they said could be true.

When Wade Dutton went down the second time, he did not pause for words or to examine his spit. He tore to his feet bellowing. Boo saw the fat right hand coming but did not bother to duck it. It crashed into his cheek and sent lightning bolts through his head. He crumbled into clouds. . .

. . . *rising breeze-tossed like a feather. . .like a dry leaf. . .like a cotton burst of dandelion. . .the girls at jump rope, making witch incantations:*

> *Queenie, Queenie gots two daughters,*
> *Hated one and likes the other.*
> *One was black, and one was white,*
> *One was day, and one was night.*
> *One is milk and silk and spice,*
> *The other ain't so very nice.*

. . . *higher. . .finding at last the old woman, wrapped to her waist in bean shoots.*
"*Miss Laylee!*"

She straightened up and raised one dirt-gnarled hand to her eyes; a dozen tin bracelets slipped to her elbow. Her other hand clutched an apron-load of weeds to her hip.

"Miss Laylee! Is it true? Is what those boys said true?"

Sprigs of wispy steel wool fluttered in a tidal draft, framing a delicate portrait of wrinkles. A million broken-glass wind chimes jangled, sent out a million white-hot needles.

Why wouldn't she answer? Oh, his head hurt, pounding and swelling as though he were wearing a too-small football helmet, and why couldn't he move his arms?

"Miss Laylee, is it true?"

Her lips moved, a single word, but it was lost in a sough.

"...what did you say? Miss Laylee, you got to tell me."

Again she moved her lips; again the word was...

"Bastard!"

Stung, his eyes fluttered.

He stared into a denim crotch.

His arms were pinned under massive knees. Somewhere above that, a broad ape torso. And even higher, a smeary pig's face squealing a blue-ribbon stream of curses.

Caged, armless, Boo attacked again and clapped a sneaker into Wade Dutton's ear, making him howl.

"God*dammit*, Boo Taylor, you *quit* it!"

Wade tugged a swatch of Boo's hair, and Boo cried out, kicking and kicking until the burn in his scalp and the hot ache in his gut wore at him. His limbs slackened, and he wailed in frustration.

Wade Dutton was a hound now, barking spittle in his face. "Say you're sorry!"

"No! You're a liar; you're a *liar!*"

Gussie Dutton had shouldered her way through the boys, and her orange head now hovered over her brother's. "Make him say it, Wade! Make him say he's sorry!"

Wade tugged Boo Taylor's hair, and Boo groaned. "Say it!"

"No!"

Another tug. "*Say* it!"

"Make him *say* it! Make him *say* it!"

"No! No! You're a fat liar!" Kicking again, knees thumping Wade Dutton's back until Wade reared back and cannoned a punch at his nose.

Boo's skull smacked the ground. Sun flares erupted, and all kicking ceased.

Blood welled from his left nostril.

Gussie Dutton shook her head. "Boo Taylor, you don't got the sense God gave a turnip. Wade, you make that boy say he's sorry."

Warmth trickled a snail's trail over Boo's cheek, into his ear. His braincase pulsed kettledrum rhythms. When he squirmed again, a big fist materialized an inch from his nose, a wad of grass splayed like green hair through sweaty knuckles.

"You say you're sorry, or I'll make you eat this," Wade said.

Instead, Boo hockered deep in his throat and spit.

Another round of gasps.

Then, iron bars fell on him. Wade was spitting back, slamming grass at his mouth;

"*Eat it,*" growling, "*eat it, eat it, eat it! Goddamn little fourth-grade rich boy, you spit on me!*"

Boo clenched his teeth, pitched his head under the fat hand, skull grinding into dirt and loam while Gussie Dutton shrieked gleefully, "Make him *eat* it, Wade!" and the grass and thick fingers wormed over his gums until something bitter leaked into his throat. He coughed and spit, his head hammering against hardpan.

Iron bars lifted. Tears dripped down each side of Boo Taylor's face.

"Now, say you're sorry."

Choking, sputtering green saliva: "I *hate* you, you fat liar."

"My brother ain't no liar, Boo Taylor," Gussie said.

Wade Dutton wiped the remaining grass across Boo's shirt. "I ain't lyin. It was Dewey's momma who said it, and Dewey's momma ain't no liar. *Dewey!*" he called out, "Is your momma a liar?"

Boo craned his neck and watched Dewey Fitch cringe. "No, Wade," Dewey answered softly, "she ain't no liar."

"Well, your girlfriend here says your momma's a liar. But ol Boo Taylor never did have no sense, did you rich boy?"

Gussie's red face bobbed in agreement. "Don't have the sense God gave a turnip."

Wade breathed a sigh and shook his head sadly. "Called me a liar an' spit on me."

"And he socked you when you weren't lookin!" Gussie offered.

"That's right. You socked me when I weren't even lookin. Now, you just say you're sorry, rich boy, and I'll let you up."

"No. Get off me."

Wade's hand came forward and grabbed hold of Boo's ear. "Say it," he bellowed, and coiled the ear.

"Get *off!*" Boo cried. "You're a *liar!*"

Wade twisted, and Boo screamed, and Gussie clapped and laughed. The other boys shuffled nervous glances to each other.

"Say it you little bastard!"

"You're a big fat *STINKY LIAR!*" With the roar, Boo Taylor heaved a sudden, violent jerk, and his right arm pulled free. He marveled for an instant. In the next instant, he jammed the hand into Wade Dutton's throat. Wade gagged, and now the ear was freed, too. The meat slab above him faltered. Boo Taylor yanked the rest of himself clear, then stomped Wade's broad stomach.

Wade rolled away, and Boo sprang to his feet. The swarm disassembled. Dewey Fitch lit off for the safety of the schoolhouse.

Gussie Dutton gaped at Boo Taylor. "Get up, Wade," she said weakly.

Wade Dutton was cradling his belly and gulping for breath when Boo Taylor landed on him: a wildcat down from the hills, a hailstorm of lead fishing weights.

"Get up, Wade," Gussie said again, then hollered angrily, "Wade, you *get him;* you get up and *get* that *rich boy!*"

Boo Taylor's ropey arms flailed wildly. Mud and bits of grass sprayed filthy rain from his back. Wade Dutton, still gulping for air, cried for Boo to stop punching him and curled into the ground.

"Wade, you *get up* or I'm tellin Harley an' Petey, an' they'll *tan your hide!* Now you *get up!*"

When Wade Dutton began sobbing, Ashford Marchant called out, "Let him up, Boo!" and after another few punches Boo Taylor stopped.

He stood. Ribcage rising, falling. Rabbit's heart tripping. He swung his eyes around to meet the stares of the other boys and girls. He shot Gussie Dutton a quick glance, fearing an attack from her. But she was standing behind her fallen brother and looking at Boo Taylor with astonishment.

"You let that little boy whup you," she said. "Boo Taylor, you whupped him good."

Boo stepped away from the crumpled bull on the ground, and the swarm parted for him. They watched him and saw someone different than they had known: this boy in the T-shirt slopped with dirt and blood and grass, his wary eyes sweeping over them with dangerous intent. Boo Taylor looked like a Dutton.

"Boy's a liar," Boo whispered at them. And then he tore away.

❖   ❖   ❖

Where Pigg's Creek made ready to spill into the brown marsh flats of the Yama-wichee Sound on the south end of Sweetpatch Island, a cottage massed of scavenged timber, tin, clapboard, and tarpaper sagged on squat stilts with a mean leeward pitch. By its looks, a stiff wind might knock it over. It had, however, survived several hurricanes and nor'easters and one memorable blizzard, all contributing to the eerie romance of the old woman who lived there. The old woman herself was in the garden, wrapped to her waist in a patch of bean shoots as the sudden, certain feeling of the boy came to her, running *(hopping)* reckless like the boy *(like a little frog)*. She straightened into the shadow of a scarecrow and looked toward Old Sugar Dam Road. Not yet within sight, of course, he was still Up Island where the white folks lived along the cobbled roads in their fine homes far from the scrubland trailers and shacks of the South Patch coloreds and the marsh-side white trash.

He was still there, but he was coming to her.

She clutched an apron-load of weeds to her hip. A large gray dog hovered nearby; he had sniffed the scent of whatever had caught the woman's attention, and so he moved closer to her to protect her from its threat.

Cicadas rattled in the sage, and no-see-ums swirled about her stubby pigtails. As she stared toward the north and a hot breeze bore a marshy whiff from the Yamawichee, a fish crow took wing high above her head and shrieked her name. She glanced at the bird.

Liar! she heard.

Bastard!

Then the sun exploded. The garden tilted; the island itself shifted like a boat running aground. She felt her legs buckle but caught herself as she reached high and snagged the crow in her free hand, not even dropping her load of weeds.

It was an old trick, and one of her favorites.

She flew north as the black feathers fitted themselves into her flesh. She closed her eyes and let the wings carry her.

She flew at last to Carriage Avenue where oaks grabbed handholds across the center of the cobbled lane to construct a miles-deep cavern of wizards and faeries. She found Boo Taylor pelting through this tunnel, arriving at a wide lawn buried under overgrown azaleas, swinging across the grass, up steep porch steps, dashing into the white Victorian that soared high among the others in the Up Island antebellum quarter.

The crow swung down and perched on a windowsill.

"Boo sugar, is that you?"

It was the boy's mother, her words sinking like a liquid fog from her second-floor bedroom along with Debussy piano chords from her turntable. Both crow and boy pictured her: exquisitely beautiful but languid and blurry on her bed, washcloth on her forehead, pulp romance split open in her lap.

The boy crept noiselessly over the polished floorboards and past the stairway.

"Robert E. Lee Taylor, if that's you down there will you please answer me?"

Yes, he heard. No, he would not answer; he ignored the call with house cat aloofness. He eased through the door that separated the doctor's suites from the rest of the house and slipped through the first door to a stark white hallway.

The crow hopped to another window to follow him.

The boy was crouched at the door of his father's office, hovering there to listen. Doctor Silas Barnwell Taylor was in an examination room across the hall. Mumbling and a faint sob—some patient was in there with him, eyeing a big needle in the doctor's hand. Boo Taylor leaned around the doorframe and saw his father turned three quarters away. The doctor's jet-black hair was slicked back precisely until it got to the rough dark spokes along his neck. The boy could see only a small part of his father's face but had no trouble making out the sharp features—the hooked nose, abrupt angles of cheekbones and jaw, the thin black mustache lining the upper lip.

What do you see, boy? the crow whispered.

But the boy would not answer her. He withdrew from the doorframe, slipped into the office and glared at his own face in a cabinet mirror: tousled red-brown hair, ruddy flesh tones, blunt and round features. As he watched, without realizing it, his hands curled into fists.

What are you thinking, boy?

For a moment, again, he would not answer, then whispered back to the crow— whispered about the time his mother called his father *handsome, like a European nobleman*, something she had gathered from one of her romance stories. *Mama, will I look like a nobleman?* But she had laughed at him, saying, no of course not, that he would be *rugged and beautiful, like a ship's captain. Or a cowboy.* But he would not look like a nobleman. Not like his father. This is what he whispered to the crow as he remembered his mother's words and as the bully's words slugged him like a fist in the gut. The crow flinched as it felt his pain.

No, you're a liar.

The boy watched his round cowboy features and flexed his thick ship's captain fists and now understood that the liar was not Wade Dutton after all.

He punched the mirror. The crow blinked and then disappeared in a puff of black feathers.

❧   ❧   ❧

The dog was at her hip, nudging her.

She looked around, coming back into the land of flesh and blood. Then down to the nuzzling animal.

"Shamus, looks like Mr. Boo's comin," she told the dog. The dog flapped his tail and licked her hand.

The sun, real now, as was the ground beneath her feet and the stink of the marsh, swept its heat over her in the sway of the trading tides. Still clutching an apron-load of weeds, she started her slow shamble out of the field.

Inside, she made ready for the boy's visit, muttering and humming about her kitchen; she pulled two mason jars from the cupboard and drew a milk bottle filled with yauponberry wine from the icebox. She filled the mason jars with the reddish-black liquid and sneaked a sip. This particular batch was a bit sugary to her liking, but the boy favored it sweet. After a moment's thought, she picked a sprig from one of the herb-bundles that dangled like sleeping bats from her kitchen ceiling. She dropped it into the boy's glass, and stirred it with her finger.

The cottage was dark. She'd had electric lights since the power company finally ran lines into South Patch back in '63, but she didn't use the lights much. They heated up the place like an oven; without them, the house stayed cool on even the most blistering of days. She attributed this to the newspaper she had packed into the walls, which made for good insulation and was widely known to keep out ghosts.

The pain in her left knee growled for her to hurry off to the porch and find a place to sit. Dr. Taylor had wrapped the knee after she hurt it slipping on a freshly mopped floor two weeks back. He had even offered her a bottle of white pills for the pain, but she had waved him away. Instead, she had boiled up some adder's tongue and crowley root and chickweed, swaddled it all in buckram, and slid it inside Dr. Taylor's knee-wrap. She had no doubts Dr. Taylor was a fine doctor or that his pills were good medicine. But she had her own medicine and had lived by it since before Dr. Taylor was a baby. The coloreds and the white trash knew old Laylee, the guffer doctor, and they came knocking on her porch door when they had a touch of the swamp air, or their bowel was running hot-and-cold, or some young mother wanted the herbs and spice to help carry her child, or they needed a root-cure to help with the pains in their joints. She supposed Dr. Taylor knew as much. Supposed he had gotten used to such things on this backward little island where the poor marsh-side whites and the poorer South Patch blacks thought it funny that their guffer lady and midwife scrubbed floors for the fancy Up Island white doctor.

Wind chimes jingled a greeting to her when she made it through the screened door with the two jars of wine. She settled into a battered wicker rocker. From inside, her radio rolled staticky, angelic choruses. Her hound, Shamus, joined her on the porch, scattering a half-dozen chickens in the yard where she and the boy—when he was younger, at least—sometimes took stark-naked showers under rainstorms.

She looked west, to the sun falling and setting fire to the mainland. In the place between, the staggering orange rim of the ruined Chaliboque Mansion reared from the swampland. The house was now inseparable from the oaks and cypress and vines and bog creatures that clung and rooted to its corrupted hulk—so that house and swamp had become a single creature unto itself: half inanimate and dead, half desperately and violently alive. And in this burning at the brink of day-lost and night-gained, the house-creature stretched for her with shadowy skeleton fingers, trying to catch hold of her to drag her into nightfall. It was no accident that her porch was aimed at that old, ruined place. She had to keep watch over it; that too was part of her curse.

The place had once thrived with field hands and Sea Island cotton and old-world wealth. No more. The Chaliboque house, which had survived two burnings, did not survive a third. The shifting sands had pushed Pigg's Creek back on itself until the house was now mostly wrapped by marsh, and anybody who wanted to poke through the old place would need a boat to reach it when tide was in. The plantation went bust, and the Sladeshaws (who inherited it from the LaValle family) were long gone from Sweetpatch Island. And the black flesh that bled for the Chaliboque crop was gone too; only the ghosts and a scrap of colored poor remained.

Eulahlah Colebriar, now looking over those same fields from her own house where she tended her own crop, had survived it when the rest had gone extinct. It was a victory of sorts, but surely a bitter one. And one among a dismal few.

From its perch over the garden, the scarecrow turned with the breeze. She followed its gaze to find the boy, at last, coming on the dirt trail that spiked off Old Sugar Dam Road. The frog-hop was gone from his step, head drooped, hands shoved in trouser pockets. His sneakered feet dragged and raised dusty roostertails.

"Shamus, go fetch that jasper 'fore it gits too dark."

Sad gray eyes considered her, tail thumping porch floorboards.

"Gwon," she urged.

And the dog trotted off to the boy. She watched as dog and boy met and made their way finally to the foot of her tiny porch. The boy would not look at her; he ruffled the dog's shoulders, kicked absently at the chickens. Close up, she could see his bruises and scrapes and his shorn, dirt-smeared clothes.

At last, she said, "Why, Mr. Boo, you been out wrasslin gators again?"

The boy shrugged. A grown-man face on skinny, little-boy limbs. She thought of a marsh deer. Or a just-hatched egret.

"You been fightin, boy?"

He shrugged again. Then he nodded.

"Lordy, Mr. Boo, I never knowed you to fight nothin that didn't have four legs an' a big set of teeth. What you been after this time?"

After a moment, he offered, "Wade Dutton."

"Gawd, ol Hank Dutton's boy?" she asked, feigning great surprise.

"Yes'm."

"Well, no wonder you look like a hog that's been through the slaughter house. That boy's twice your size an' three times as ugly."

That made him smile a bit despite himself.

"Now, why don't you git on up here so's we can have us some wine an' watch that fine sunset the Lord saw fit to give us this evenin. And ol Laylee can give them bruises a lookysee."

"Don't need no lookysee."

"Naw, course you don't," she said, exaggerating a nod, "you jes too almighty hard in the head. Now you git on up here."

"Yes'm," he said, and he climbed the three porch steps with Shamus behind him and sat on a bench next to her chair.

The old woman cupped the boy's chin in her ringed fingers and examined the blood and grass that streaked his face. "Mm, mm, *mm*. Ain't you jes hard in the *head*, Mr. Boo." She spit into her apron and wiped his cheeks and eyes and all the way back to the ears, her bracelets jangling.

"Does your face hurt, boy?" she asked, very serious.

"Only a little."

"Well, it's killin me," she said, and cackled. It forced another reluctant smile.

When she brought the apron away, the corner of it was soiled with his wounds, and the boy's face was raw. "Don't believe nothin too serious got broke. 'Spect you gonna live to a ripe ol age if you can steer your way 'round them Dutton boys."

"Yes'm."

Her fingers probed the puffy red swell under his left eye. "I believe you need a poultice for this eye, Mr. Boo."

"Don't need no poultice."

"Ain't no trouble!" she exclaimed, giving him her finest pickaninny act. "Got me some ginger root right here in my kitchen. And some cooter bones, and some smelly ol bat dung—"

"Miss *Laylee!* I ain't in no mood for *teasin!*"

"Aw, now I forgot how all growed up you was," she said. "N'how danged hard in the head. Well, your daddy's sure to raise a ruckus when he gits a look at that shiner."

He jerked his face from her hands, blurting, "He ain't really my daddy."

In the plum-orange glow of sunset, she watched his jaw tremble.

"Did you know?" he asked.

She made a sing-song voice of disbelief, saying, "Lordy, what make a boy ask such a thing?"

"That's what Wade Dutton says, and that's what Dewey Fitch's momma says. I'm a *bastard!* I'm *adopted!* And everybody heard it! Momma and daddy lied—and *you* knew it, too! Didn't you?"

"Why Mr. Boo, you—"

"Didn't you?" His eyes lashed at her, and she was stung. She tried to match his bold little-boy glare, but inside she was an old nigger field hand and he was the master, and despite herself, she cowered a bit.

Gently, she asked, "You ain't spoke to Miss MaeEllen or your daddy 'bout this, has you?" Rigid on the bench, he shook his head. "Well, you best speak with them first, Mr. Boo. Lest you want ol Laylee t'get whipped for speakin when it ain't her turn."

He glared a moment longer. A plum-orange glitter rimmed his eyes. When it spilled over, he looked away and was once again her little boy. In the quiet, she offered him his jar of the yauponberry wine. He glanced at it briefly, then took it from her, needing both hands.

The radio played "Revive Us Again," and the melody seeped unbeckoned and sweetly high from her throat. She rocked the chair, allowing Boo Taylor his quiet turn to taste the wine and still his stormy waters. The last of the sunset was dying over the mainland. As the ground cooled, the ocean-breeze gave way to the land-breeze. She took turns watching the evening's first stars and watching her boy fidget with his jar, drawing pictures in the dew of the glass. From the fields came the first signs of night: crickets chattered, frogs chirped, wallerwops groaned, graves trembled. The rustle of bats on the wing flitted close to the house, then far away, and then close again. Lightning bugs sparkled in the nighttime air, and she remembered a bit of folk wisdom she'd been told as a little girl.

"Mr. Boo, you know what some folks says 'bout fireflies? They says if you git the light from a firefly in your eye, you go blind."

After a moment, his voice came to her from the darkness, "You already told me that one."

She chuckled. "Did I? Well did I ever tell you what some folks say 'bout skeeters?"

"If a skeeter bites you," he dictated back, bored, "hold your breath so it can't fly off. Then you can kill it. Yes'm, you told me already."

She clapped her hands on her knees, bracelets clanking, and chuckled again, "Well, Mr. Boo, I s'pose I need to tell my stories over and over so's I can keep 'em all straight. Did I tell you what folks say about snakes? What happens when their tails gets broke? Lord, I must'a told you that one."

She waited for him to respond, but for a while he said nothing. Then, in a very quiet voice, she heard him say, "I remember the story 'bout that frog. The one who thought he was a prince."

She sighed.

Lesson learned.

(Inside the shack the radio-song of angels came to an end, replaced by a frightened man's voice . . . the man choking out some news about the doctor—interrupted by thunderburst crackles—or about the king . . .)

Into the gloaming, she said, "You best be on your way home, Mr. Boo. If your momma knew you was out on ol Laylee's porch this time a'night, she'd whip us both. And tell your daddy to fire me *skit-skat*."

(. . . terrible news . . . a rifle, shots fired . . . a balcony . . .)

"She ain't my real momma," the boy said plainly. "And he ain't my real daddy. I don't know who my real momma and daddy are."

(...Memphis?)

Before she could say something of comfort, the boy stood and climbed down the porch steps. Shamus, who had crawled under the house, scrambled out to follow him up the dirt track as far as the trees.

(*The king-doctor*, the scared man said...*shot dead*, and cities were burning; the beasts were raging in the streets.)

She watched him go, the tiniest jumble of stick arms and legs poking from a dirty T-shirt and ragged shorts, becoming lost beyond the deepening purple veil where monkeyshine creatures, seen and unseen, rustled silk wings, giggled, and breathed low, husky sobs. Just a pup and easy prey to the haunted and brute fiends loose in the winds of this night.

She called out to him, "Mr. Boo, don't you go crossin that ol troll-bridge this time a'night! You go Church Street, you hear?"

A faint call in return: "...*okay*."

"An' you stay to the middle of the road, boy!" she called again. "And steer clear a' them spooks!"

Eulahlah Colebriar leaned forward in her hand-me-down wicker rocker, waiting for the boy's answer. But he had vanished.

(The king is dead.)

That was the third lesson.

Part One
Long Live the King

Whiskey nor brandy, ain' no friend to my kind,
Dey kilt my po' daddy, an' dey trouble my mind.
                                        —*Old Rhyme*

Hurricane Joseph was born angry off the west coast of Africa—more vapor than substance in those infant moments; nevertheless, a conspiracy of terrible forces that could neither be circumvented nor mollified. He gathered corpus in all the timeworn patterns on his deliberate and steady crossing of the Atlantic, drawing from the depths and summoning from the heavens and spinning electric turbulence in an ever expanding arc.

Making landfall on the Indies, greatly fattened, he paused to gorge on the steaming gulf surge before veering north. By the time he slammed into the Carolinas, spilling forth the great accumulation of his rage, he was a monster.

He rained devastation and death.

Then shifted again, moved now north up the coast, sending out watery tentacles, feeling, searching, sniffing, drawn toward his destined end, plunging into the Delaware as land masses shattered him, diminished him. He slipped into the Brandywine and Christina, searching and closing in, seeping into the Red Clay and White Clay, into a hundred feeder streams and creeks and rivulets and gutters, until at last he found his place to die.

All cyclonic phenomena, by definition, repeat. Concepts of beginning and ending are meaningless.

two

Would she have judged him a decent man?
He wondered.

three

Boo Taylor watched the storm through the window of a dingy Texaco station.
I thought I killed him.
Rainwater dribbled down the sides of his face, mingling with his sweat. The rainwater and sweat were collecting in his collar, the discomfort not registering as it should have had he not been preoccupied with the thing outside. He stared through the streaked and grimy glass into the downpour. A dim grey shape was out there, a

grey just a shade darker than the grey of the storm, wavering in and out of perception, taunting. The harder he focused, the more indistinct the shape became.

"You a ball player?"

The attendant was calling to him from behind the counter.

"You look like a ball player."

Boo answered without turning. "I'm a brick layer," he said. He continued to gaze through the window, trying to will the shape out there into clarity. A remnant shiver passed through his shoulders, tremors after an earthquake.

The man behind him was mumbling. "Look like a ball player."

It was midafternoon, but the sky had vanished behind a pulsing dark veil that hovered at lamppost height. Traffic was rumbling by on the water-choked lanes of Route 13, headlights glaring, wipers whacking madly. The Tahoe, safe and dry by the pumps, was the only vehicle in the station. Boo Taylor had checked the front fender and grille for dents or some other sign of a collision, was surprised and relieved to find none, and then pumped the truck full. The attendant had shadowed up to the shop door to watch as he got on his hands and knees before his truck to look for evidence of whatever beast he'd just murdered on the highway. When he went inside to pay, he and the attendant were the only two people in the place.

He could still feel the impact, the solid *thud* against the truck, that first spike of panic.

"S'cuse me, mister brick layer." The attendant was calling to him again. "Need your signature by the old X when you're ready."

Boo turned from the window and went to the counter. He bent to scribble his name, dripping water on the counter. The attendant was looking at Boo Taylor's calloused and scarred right hand as he wrote, drops splattering from his sleeve. The hand was minus two fingers.

"How'd you get so dang soaked?" the man asked.

Boo glanced outside again, still seeking that shape in the gloom. "Thought I hit something a ways back," he said. "Dog or something."

"Ouch!" The attendant held up Boo's credit card. "Kill it?"

Boo Taylor looked at the attendant: gap-toothed grin and twinkling eyes. *Rudy* was embroidered over the heart of his black shirt in blood-red letters. "Couldn't say," he told him. He plucked the card from the man's hand. "Got out to look, but I couldn't find anything."

Or maybe whatever he hit was standing out there now, waiting for him.

"Ouch!" Rudy said again, smile widening. He was taking in Boo's suit, all sopping wet wool, chafing and obviously uncomfortable. Yes, the suit was expensive, double breasted charcoal gray with pinstripes. Boo Taylor owned just three suits; they were all expensive, and now the Armani pinstripe was ruined.

"Give you credit," Rudy told him, "gettin out in this bitch. If it was me, I'da gunned it the hell out'a there, high and dry. Fuck the dog for gettin in my way, see? Say, you mind me askin what happened to your hand?"

Boo glanced at the scarred mass of his hand, at the remaining fingers holding his card. "Cut myself shaving," he said.

The attendant snorted. "Reason I ask is, used to be a fella with three fingers that pitched for the college up the road."

Boo arched an eyebrow.

"Helluva junkballer. Christ, that must be close to twenty years ago." The man squinted at the credit card receipt. He frowned. "Fella had a funny name. Sure as hell wasn't *Robert*. Heard he went pro."

Boo Taylor watched as the man glanced back and forth between him and the receipt.

"Reason I ask is, that fella looked somethin like you."

He handed Boo the receipt, and Boo tucked it into his wallet along with the card. "Well, you know us three-fingered fellas," he said, turning to leave, "I guess we all look alike." The attendant snorted again. When Boo touched the door a flare of lightning suddenly blasted the day apart, and the sky above the gas station splintered into pieces. The building trembled. A can of something wet fell from a shelf and crashed on the floor. Then the lights of the station sputtered and blinked out.

The attendant was muttering as Boo Taylor pushed his way through the door. Outside, the storm was battering the tin overhang, and the world was a roar. As he approached his truck, he watched scattered motes of substance gather, specks of lightning and flecks of molecules accumulate and thicken with each step to summon, at last, the very definite shape of a man.

The man stood just beyond the protection of the roof, not more than five feet from the Tahoe's right fender. Clothes clung like wet leaves on wide, rawboned shoulders. Drops of rain dappled a shaggy afro, capturing glints and sparkle to make a silvery halo. The man was cradling his left elbow in his hand.

(Some things don't never die, boy.)

The words swam to him through the mist, across distant Southern swamplands.

(They jes change shapes.)

Boo Taylor shrugged sodden wool over his flesh. He picked out the ignition key and continued toward the truck, and when he reached the truck's door, he stopped. He flicked his eyes to the elbow and the hand that clutched it. "You hurt?" he called out.

Up close, he could now see the face: craggy and weathered like driftwood, only so much darker; eyes like the halves of seashells, glowing mutely, with a hundred thread-thin bloody veins shot through them. The man could be thirty or sixty.

"Gwine naut."

The sound was startling, the slogged boil of a garbage disposal. Boo Taylor realized he hadn't expected the man to speak.

"What was that?"

The old-or-young face didn't change. The graveled words dribbled out again. "Naut. Gwine up naut."

For another long moment the words remained gibberish. Then Boo heard the familiar rhythm from his childhood, the Gullah cadence of black-water swamps and tin shanties and shady porch stoops. Eye to eye, he saw now that he and the man were almost exactly matched in dimensions—height, thickness—each the negative image of the other.

I know you, he said in his mind. *I know you...don't I?*

The tiniest crack curled the corner of the man's heavy lips. "Doan b'lee suh."

Don't believe so?

Through the veil of rain, blood-soaked seashell eyes shimmered back at him.

From the highway, the sudden blare of an eighteen-wheeler. Boo Taylor turned to watch a VW Beetle squeal out of the big truck's way like a turtle scooting from the path of a barreling gator. He felt the man's gaze piercing him between the shoulder blades like an ice pick.

When he looked around again, the man with the seashell eyes hadn't moved. Even the faint smile lingered. After another unsure moment, Boo Taylor slipped out his wallet. He thumbed out a five dollar bill and held it out to the man. The man looked back—then looked down at the bill and the mangled right hand that held it.

"They've got coffee inside," Boo told him. "And sandwiches."

The man glided forward and lifted his wounded left arm. His fingers uncurled like snakes, then curled again around the bill. "Gwine up naut," he said, locking the seashell eyes back onto him.

Boo Taylor looked away. He nodded toward the shop. "There's coffee inside," he said. Then he climbed into the truck and pulled away.

four

Forty minutes later he was settled in a leather booth. The Armani jacket was a puddle in the seat next to him. Across the table, brown hands held an old magazine, open to a page near the middle.

"This is you?"

Boo took a sip of ice-cold vodka and nodded. He couldn't see the man across from him, just a pair of thick forearms and rough hands. The candle in the center of the table cast the man's flesh in a dusky rose. All around him, candles at the other tables flickered like stars in the night. The hurricane had knocked out the lights.

The rough, rose-lit hands pushed the magazine closer to the flame. "How old were you?"

"Seven, I think. Maybe eight. Where'd you find that, anyway?" Boo rubbed at the sparse brown hair at his thinning temples, thinking how old and grizzled and thick-shouldered he was now and how young and spindly that boy in the picture had been.

In black and white, rows of ragged Negro schoolchildren sat at simple, wooden desks. All were looking up with an expression of casual interest—the pleasant continuity abruptly interrupted by that single Caucasian face. The photographer had cropped the white face upper-left like a star on a flag. The white boy was reaching up to clasp the hand of a smiling black man in a dark suit.

"*I* didn't find it, Stoney had it—and I lost ten dollars over it, 'cause there's no way this is real. You tellin me you went to a black school down on that cracker island?"

"Sometimes," Boo answered. "We had a white school, too. I guess I took turns for a while."

A waitress, glowing in a white tuxedo shirt, hovered past. Boo Taylor caught her by the arm and ordered a cigar and another vodka.

"So, you're saying that kid in this picture is actually you." The voice beyond the candle was incredulous.

"Yes," Boo answered. He felt weary. A wet collar chafed his neck; he tugged his tie loose and unbuttoned the collar.

"And you met Martin Luther King Jr."

"Yes."

"You actually met him."

Now at last the first tendrils the vodka were seeping into the capillaries of his brain, making wavy echoes of the tinkling glass and disembodied whispers swirling about the darkened tavern. He wondered that people felt the need to speak in whispers: was it in reverence to the hurricane or simply a reaction to the darkness?

"He was visiting the island," Boo said—and realized that he, too, was whispering. "I had no idea who the man was at the time. That picture didn't come out until after he was killed, and that was probably two years later. Where did Stoney find that thing, anyway? I haven't seen it in twenty-five years."

The November 1969 edition of *Harper's* was now rolled up next to the candle; the photograph and article inside had caused a sensation on tiny, impoverished Sweetpatch Island when first published. The whites were unhappy the island's brief chance at fame was dominated by a Negro image. And the blacks resented a rich white boy commandeering their champion.

The caption: *Little Robert Lee Taylor welcomes Reverend King to the Palmer Washington Schoolhouse on Sweetpatch Isle, SC.*

Boo glanced around at the random firefly glitter of candles and the useless glow of emergency lamps. Doors gasped open, inhaling a new party into the bar, unseen in the gloom but stomping feet and clattering umbrellas.

(He felt the thud shuddering solidly through the front bumper, through his bones. A moment before, some blackness had streaked across the storm-blinded highway. What had that been? What in God's name had he killed?)

He swallowed the rest of his drink.

Almost immediately, the waitress appeared out of the dark again with his second vodka and the cigar. Boo Taylor promptly pinched the end off the cigar. "By the way, Elgin," he said, rolling and crinkling the cigar in his fingers until a fragrance like old books rose from the dry leaves, "crackers come from Georgia. I'm pure South Carolina."

He lit the cigar with the candle, momentarily brightening the flame and sending dark plumes into the air. (*Something burning; something dead,* he thought in an obscure flicker of a memory.)

A second waitress came into view and caught sight of the man in the booth across from Boo Taylor. She made a quick spin about. "Elgin? Elgin Highsmith? When'd you get here?"

From across the booth, a brown, bald head slid into the candlelight—momentarily, the man was identical to the vagrant at the gas station—then shadows shifted, and the resemblance was gone.

The girl bent to the table and gave the man a kiss on the lips. Her hair was a purple crew cut. The sparkle of at least four hoops dangled from her left ear and another from her left nostril. "Isn't this just wild! Doesn't it look like *Phantom of the Opera* in here?"

"Miss Burke," Elgin said, "have I ever introduced you to my boss?"

The girl extended her hand. Boo raised his own heavily scarred right hand; she glanced at it briefly before accepting it. "I know you," she said happily. "Vodka on the rocks, right? Where's that pretty wife of yours tonight?"

"She's not—" Boo started, but the girl startled him by moving behind him to go to work massaging his shoulders. He glanced at Elgin who was now smiling widely.

"Your muscles are tight," the girl said.

To Elgin's obvious delight, Boo Taylor was now squirming uncomfortably on the leather seat.

Elgin asked her, "You got any news on the lights?"

"Maybe a few minutes; maybe a few hours," she answered, "that's all they keep saying." She burrowed a knuckle at the base of Boo's neck until something popped. "Nobody knows. They say the wind knocked over a main or something out on Smiths Bridge. Wow, your muscles are *tight!* Hey, if you're Elgin's boss, does that mean you lay bricks, too?"

At this, Elgin barked a laugh. "Boo Taylor lay bricks? This here's the man himself, darlin. Taylor Builders. Too important to get down and dirty with us common folk anymore."

Boo smiled dryly. "Mr. Highsmith is lead foreman. He stacks more paper than block himself these days."

Somewhere beyond the girl, another group entered the bar, and a purplish light shone briefly through the open doorway. A wide-shouldered silhouette flickered and was gone.

(Rain slashed the Tahoe; his surviving fingers gripped the steering wheel like white iron. Engine ticking. Heart ticking. Wiper blades ticking. On the side of the road, time passed but somehow stood still. Should he get out? Get out and see. . . what? A dog? A man?)

I am a decent man, he told himself.

The girl's hands were relentless. Boo Taylor's upper body was wobbling under a thorough kneading. "I hope you take good care of Elgin," she said. "We go *way* back. What happened to your fingers anyway?"

Boo took a draw on the cigar. "I was making cookies, and they got caught in a blender."

She looked doubtful. "Boy, are your muscles ever *tight*. You could use a full-body massage. I can do it, you know—I took classes." She hauled her face close to his and smirked. "Or are you a coward?"

Elgin Highsmith coughed into his fist.

Boo made himself grin. "The world's *biggest*, ma'am."

At last she released him, though her gaze and the smirk lingered. Then she leaned to Elgin and gave him another kiss on the lips, a final squeeze on the arm, and she was gone.

Boo watched her vanish into the steady shifting of shadow-bodies. "What the hell was that?"

"Temptations," Elgin said, mocking Boo's drawl, "they will be our ruination."

"Speak for yourself, boy—I am a pillar of virtue." Boo took another long swallow of vodka. The alcohol was working its magic; a light fog circled his eyes. "I am a rock amid a storm of impropriety and a sea of legal misadventure. And between the two of us, *you* are the one who's married."

Elgin was laughing happily. "So where *is* that pretty wife of yours tonight, anyway?"

"She'll be along soon enough. And there is very little chance Sandy Baker or anyone else is going to be Mrs. Taylor anytime soon."

(When he got out, it was like stepping into the ocean: waves of ice-cold sea-water drenched him in sheets, threatened to drag him on a riptide course toward oblivion. Was there something, or someone, with him under the waves? Some tentacled creature, wounded and furious? Some mossy, drowned thing, watching with dead fish eyes?)

Boo Taylor blinked again at the darkness. He fidgeted the cigar through his incomplete right hand, not liking the darkness at all, worrying what it concealed.

And told himself: *I am a decent man.*

And heard his voice echoed back: *a coward.*

Sandy Baker, an impossibly pretty, young tax attorney at Flickinger, Kipp & Diamond, had inserted herself very neatly into his life not long after Boo's own lawyer, Allen Noble, introduced them at the firm's Christmas party eight months ago. *She's seen you around the office and wanted to meet you. I suppose she's into cavemen.* She was not his wife, and never would be, though she seemed to have claimed right of first refusal. That kind of presumption was initially charming, but was now becoming tiresome and even a little creepy. *I told her you're not exactly the reliable type, but she was persistent. I think she has plans to reform you.*

Elgin Highsmith leaned forward. "So, you gonna tell me how your meeting went?"

A college in Chestertown was building a new stadium and wanted to give it a stone façade. Taylor Builders came highly recommended. The job would fill his winter calendar.

"They liked the bid," Boo answered. "They're *considering*."

"Boo, that's a five million dollar job."

"Not anymore it isn't. I had to cut your take."

"You're kidding. Right?"

"I mean, I only drove through a damn hurricane to meet with these guys. You'd think that would count for something."

Elgin tapped the magazine against the table impatiently. "Boo. Are we gonna get the thing or *aren't* we?"

Boo checked the luminescent dials of his watch then glanced around the dark room, wondering where Sandy and Allen might be; they were going on twenty minutes late. "I had to trim a few corners, Elgin. I told them you'd be willing to work for minimum wage."

"You *are* kidding."

Before them, the candle sputtered. The flame made a few despairing last jigs and then died. The only light in the booth now was the red glow at the tip of Boo Taylor's cigar.

Boo looked at the place were the flame had been, and asked, "You don't have a flashlight on you, do you?"

An invisible voice floated back: "What am I, a hardware store?"

They sat in silence. In the dark. Then Boo broke out laughing, and soon Elgin joined him.

After a minute passed and they settled down a bit, Elgin called out, "Hey, Boo?"

"Elgin?" he answered, groping. "Elgin *Highsmith?* Is that *you?*"

This sent them into another bout of laughter.

When they settled again, Elgin asked, "Hey, man, you okay?"

"I'm fine, Elgin. It's just been a lousy day," Boo answered, and then thought, *the day's not over*. He exhaled a heavy bolt of unseen smoke into the room and closed his eyes, listening to the hushed and fluid babble, the clink of glasses (*like wind chimes*, he thought), the occasional sharp laugh, his own breathing, and, outside, the dying rumble of the storm.

He hadn't seen it coming.

Blackness flashed out of nothingness, suddenly solid and tearing into view.
Then, the thud.
Just a dog?
He thought, "I killed him," and felt the solid thump of cracking ribs and splintered skull and ruptured sinew. The thud struck him, too, shoving him back in the seat, and for just an instant he hesitated as the sick terror of it swept through his heart and took his breath away because it was done and couldn't be taken back—and in that instant he wanted to slam the accelerator to the floor and race away, get home to a snug blanket, warm and dry, "easy enough," the notion crooned.
No. No running away.
Instead, he wrestled the furious rains for control of the wheel and pulled onto the shoulder to face what lay behind.
It was just a dog; it had to be.
And he hadn't seen it coming.

Alone, the rain pelted the Tahoe, a thousand roaring, vicious pebbles unloaded from the heavens; great gusts rocked the cab. He reached a trembling hand to flip off the wipers, to flip on the hazards.

Where had it come from? A dog—surely that's what it was, that's what his mind had first made of the mass bolting into the headlights. It was too sudden and too close, but...then, something in the last shattering moment as it wheeled to confront him—and suddenly those weren't the eyes of a dog blazing up at him at all.

Something from his past. Dark limbs pulled free of a swamp grave, crawling northward over miles and miles, over years and years, from beyond time and space to make this dripping-wet rendezvous.

"Gwine up naut."

Please, not a man—the thought numbed him, sending acid churning through his belly. It couldn't be a man—it was too quick; the shape was all different, and...

He got out of the truck, and the storm slapped at his face, whipped at his clothes. He squinted and leaned into it, using an arm to steady himself against the truck. When he reached the edge of the truck, he pushed off, trotting along the open shoulder to the spot of impact. Clutching the lapels of his coat together, he scanned the side of the road, waiting for the carcass to reveal itself. The wind flailed the tail of his coat like an unraveled spinnaker. Water flooded his shoes. It was just a dog; he would find a dog, and it would be dead by the side of the road, and what was he supposed to do then? He tracked back; there was nothing, so he kept going—going farther back than it could have been. Nothing.

He crossed to the low concrete median and studied the southbound lanes. A car crawled past him, wiper blades thwacking madly, the driver, ghostlike through the window, gaping and accusatory. Nothing.

He crossed back to the shoulder, backtracking and slipping down the grassy bank, kicking through scraps of newspaper and candy bar wrappers and beer bottles, his shoulders at street level. Still nothing. Just a dog; that's all it was, and it had limped off somewhere.

Ahead, the Tahoe's lights blinked an amber beacon through the storm. He worked through the gully, finding nothing. Closer to the truck, he dared a glance beneath it and saw nothing. He climbed up to the truck; the maelstrom dancing wickedly about him. Nothing. Nothing. And then he turned, and the man was standing near the woods. Holding his arm. Staring at him.

"I dreamed of him again, Miss Laylee."

"Did you? Why, that ol' man, he in the tide, boy. He come, an' he go. An' he most always leave somethin to rot on the beach."

The man stepped back into the tress and...

Suddenly, hands, cold and slippery, grabbed his face and yanked him backward. His first terrified thought—*the dead man's got me!*—as someone screamed, "Boooooo!" into his ear from inches away. Light ruptured his eyes and shrieks rose from everywhere. He ripped at the cold, wet thing on his face, sending a tumbling arc of cigar sparks across the table. He turned under the harsh, unexpected lights of Buckley's Tavern and saw Sandy Baker standing over him.

"Wow, the lights are back," she shouted over the crowd's jubilation. "Did *I* do that?"

Elgin Highsmith, who had obviously seen Boo's moment of terror, was bent over the table in a fit of laughter.

Sandy brought her gaze down from the ceiling lights and looked innocently at Boo. "Oh honey, did I scare you?" she asked.

This sent Elgin into another furious gale.

Behind Sandy, Allen Noble stood awkwardly with two umbrellas. "Guess we timed this perfectly," he said. "The lights coming on, I mean."

Sandy ran a hand down Boo's shirtsleeve. "How'd you get so *wet?*" she asked and eyed Elgin who erupted again and nearly collapsed off his seat.

Boo, his heart settling, turned to Elgin's convulsions and couldn't quash the smile that crept over his face.

"Go on," Elgin urged him, "*tell* the girl. How *did* you get so wet?"

"I thought I hit something. On the road—a dog or something, and I got out to check."

Sandy's expression melted to concern. Her eyes scanned his body for injuries. Allen Noble looked interested. "Are you okay?" she asked.

"I'm fine. The truck's fine; everything's fine."

"What about the dog?" Allen asked, and Boo gawked at him.

"What about the *dog?*" Elgin repeated, struggling to pull himself back to the table. "What about the *dog?* What do you *think* happened to the dog? Our boy's got him strapped to the hood of his truck, like any good redneck!"

five

Boo Taylor swirled ice in his glass and tried to replay the number of vodkas he had ordered over the course of the evening. Sandy Baker was occupying the booth at his side, leaning too close so that he was now sitting on his damp suit jacket. He felt her impatience. Across the table, his foreman and lawyer were hunched over the article in *Harper's*. "Well now, this is interesting," Allen Noble was saying.

Sandy was uncharacteristically aloof. She had given the photograph a cursory glance before ordering a glass of pinot grigio.

"Really, *very* interesting," said Allen, glancing up. "Boo, I had no idea." He returned to the article, his blonde hair flipping forward like fingers massaging his forehead. It was a head of hair Boo Taylor marveled over—how any man's hair could grow so thick and precise, so *disciplined*. (His own hair, thinning away from his temples, was a scraggly red-brown nest he kept very short out of convenience.) Allen and Sandy would make a fine couple, Boo thought, with their precise blonde hair and delicate faces and humorless lawyer garb. Almost brother and sister, although Allen's sallow complexion lacked Sandy's glowing athleticism. Sandy Baker was perpetually tan—or, by comparison to Allen Noble (and himself, for that matter) her olive tone would always be shades darker. And where Allen was delicate in a way that sheathed dagger instincts in the courtroom, Sandy was a fragile and compelling sculpture, severe blonde hair and blazing white eyes wrapped in elegant, tanned gossamer that concealed no threat. Boo had laid in wait for an aggressive side to betray itself, a lawyerly combativeness. But if it was there, she kept it secret. Even her voice was innocent—a soft and baby-like whisper. Sandy, he had come to understand, worked her magic by drawing you into her vulnerable sweetness with those doe eyes and pixie features until you were disarmed by it all, could not take advantage of it; you submitted to it.

"I think you should make a copy of this page," Elgin Highsmith was telling Allen. "And frame it."

Allen Noble smiled uncertainly.

Elgin pressed. "For your office wall. Impress all your black clients. You got some of those, right?"

He shared a wicked grin with Boo.

"Well maybe . . ." Allen said. "Sandy, you could have one in your office, too."

"That's wonderful idea." She smiled at Boo. He smiled back.

Making love to her for the first time felt like a violation.

The slow dissolution of her spell over him started nearly a month back in a moment that remained clear in his mind. It was a Sunday morning. She had been standing behind him as he shaved, the mirror catching both of their images. Her eyes locked onto the reflection of his. "Boo, don't you think we'd make beautiful babies?" And suddenly there was another reflection, in her eyes, caught there by the morning sunlight: a desperation, a *craving,* and—deeper than that, in a barely perceptible flash—a shadow of some awful creature lurking inside her. Something restless that wanted to be fed. The image had startled him so badly he'd cut himself.

Children?

A line of blood trickled down his neck as a familiar ache thrummed through him for the first time in a decade—like a healed wound opened and bleeding. Over his shoulder, she had still been watching him, still smiling hopefully; the beast within had disappeared, but his revulsion remained.

We don't belong together, he thought then.

Now, tipsy with drink, he looked at her to see if he could find evidence of that dark shadow slinking behind her eyes.

She saw his gaze and mistook it for affection.

The waitress with the piercings arrived with another round, giving Boo Taylor a furtive wink before disappearing. Sandy's hand was on his thigh. She was looking at him closely; now an unreliable expression of hurt or concern behind a delicate smile. "What?" he asked her.

Her smile became more timid. "I thought you were cutting back," she said.

He looked at the glass. "This is only my second, I think."

She nodded at the cigar in his hand. "I meant smoking."

"Oh."

We don't belong together.

He consulted his watch but saw only a blur. Then excused himself to go to the men's room. Unsteadily, he negotiated the endless flotsam of bodies on the saloon's tides. Business suits criss-crossed the floor; casual-Friday slacks lounged on barstools. Images flickered mute rainbow dances on wide television screens.

Lightning flashed, and he flinched.

Soaking wet shirt? Driftwood limbs?

The crowd shifted, refocused.

Nothing.

Just patrons shuffling across the room like crabs on a beach; waitresses flitting table-to-table like humming birds to flowers. Drinks were served. Cigarettes were smoked. Joking. Talking. Laughter. Nothing.

Until a low, painful moan rose from the floor as the lights faltered, winked, stuttered—and the world once again plunged into darkness.

six

Sometime later, he awoke and found himself riding along in a car that was struggling through the last throes of the storm—and a moment later realized he was driving it.

seven

Six hundred miles south, in a land of endless summer, the sky was stark and white-hot, and no one had reason to think of storms. Though even at that great distance, the tiniest ripples of Joseph's voltage shuddered the thread-fine antennae of certain small insects—evidence that the consequences of any meteorological event, no matter how far removed, traveled the globe's ceaseless and complex currents to eventually disturb atmospheric conditions world-wide.

Thus, however subtly, Joseph was felt by, and altered forever, every life on the planet.

Wilbursville, Georgia was a collection of clapboard homes and tin-roofed shacks that had fixed itself like a tick just past the South Carolina line on Route 157, feeding from the slow trickle of life that bled from the big road. The off-ramp dumped into a lane of weeded lots and gas stations. To the man who pulled his exhausted and badly rattling Mercury Monarch into town, Wilbursville was a welcome site. It had been a long day's flight across the flat, muggy Southern highways.

The distance between Wilbursville and Sweetpatch Island didn't appear far on a map. But appearances, he knew, could be deceiving.

In fact, appearances were notoriously unreliable.

She had told him this. It was one of the things she preached.

The man driving the Monarch had never been to Wilbursville before, but he had seen a picture of it in a newspaper article. The article was about an historic church, the Fair Weather Baptist Church, its peeling gray spire rising from some bone-dry back lane amid the corn rows and bean fields of this tired little hamlet. An old-time Baptist church, built in 1927 and still standing, having survived all manner of calamity through the generations, those man-made and those rendered by God Himself. *She* had shown him the article, put her finger on the picture and smiled at him, and told him what he had to do. And after driving those same bone-dry back lanes, circling and circling, scattering crows and lifting storm clouds of red dust, he at last found the church. It looked just like the picture in the newspaper. The church would suit just fine.

A can of gasoline sloshed in the Monarch's trunk.

He lit a cigarette.

Plans were being put into motion. Traps were being set. Ancient hurts were being summoned home. *Everything in its season, she had told him, and every season takes its turn—life ain't nothin but a great big wheel.*

Now, at the turn of this new season, certain rituals needed to be performed. Come nightfall. Then it would begin.

He pulled into the shade of an old oak to wait out the sun. The Monarch settled into deep ruts left by a tractor. The man closed his eyes. He closed his eyes and tried to invoke images of *her*, somewhere waiting for him, lounging like a panther in satin and cooing her dark promises. He closed his eyes and tried to make this image appear.

But images could be deceiving, and instead he saw pictures from his youth.

Here was a boy traveling the sandy trails of Sweetpatch Island, in a time before his great corruption, before the great dark clouds took over the sun, just a boy enjoying the beaches, the swamp, the shell pile, the docks...salt winds upon the waves...

The church was waiting. The gasoline in the trunk was waiting. Somewhere, *she* was waiting.

But when he drifted to sleep, his dreams were of being a boy again, home, surrounded by his friends and floating in the surf.

❖   ❖   ❖

Boo Taylor was dreaming.

He was drifting in the ocean, buoyed by waves toward a starless night and watching the shore where a fire was swirling around a steeple, a castle tower, and single demon danced and hooted with delight. Both the demon and the fire looked familiar, something from a distant past—perhaps even a past life, because the image seemed timeless; he imagined the scene being played out over and over again to the amusement and horror of a hundred generations.

Vengeance is the Lord's job.

The words came from the lacerated, brown lips of the oldest and wisest living human on earth—he saw her, not dead at all, but blind with age and held captive in decaying, burning ruins.

Seems folks keep forgettin that, keep tryin to set things right on their own. Seems like all the world's hurt comes down to that.

As the wave swelled, he reached for the old woman...reaching, stretching...until the swell slid away and the demon and his fire were snuffed by an endless blackness.

Folks' job ain't vengeance, it's forgiveness. Forgiveness is the only way to stop that wheel from turnin. You got to remember that, boy.

She was supposed to be dead; they'd found her bones. He reached for her, but he was falling, falling through the water.

You remember that, or you be lost forever.

In the blackness beneath him, something cold and slick caressed his leg. There were things in the water with him. He sobbed and heard his sob deflected, close.

A hand touched his back.

Another clutched his thigh.

Another palmed his cheek.

Another slipped along his stomach and reached down between his legs where the pulsating—fire-and-ice, fire-and-ice, fire-and-ice—hands tugged his slick skin, warring for possession, moaning for attention, urging and caressing him, removing his clothes and stroking relentlessly, (your muscles are tight!) kneading, coaxing, and the ocean became sheets and a pillow. The night sky became his bedroom ceiling. The eager hands lowered him on a mattress, and a thick wetness slowly slipped over his erection; the weight now settling there as hands continued to run over him, as a tongue found his neck. A breast, hard and soft, prodded his ribs.

He struggled against the body (not many, but one) as it groped, nibbled, tasted, slung skin around him. The hands pinned him to the bed, and one hand reached into his chest and squeezed his heart *oh God it hurts* laughter *it hurts* fingers clamping cruelly, pressure building, vessels rupturing; the pain was immense; it was a bright, white-hot light in this black place.

Temptations of the flesh, boy...

Yes. Yes. Please let me go.

...will be your ruination!

Fingers and tongue and breasts and legs and lips and pulsating fire-ice, fire-ice flesh wrapped around him, slid up and down the length of him. He spasmed, bucked his hips uncontrollably. The voices surrounding him roared laughter at this.

...come be with us!

He knew they were dead, knew she was dead, but she was at the window, and he reached for her

...come join us!

and, seeing his agony, heard her calling his name.

"Boo!"

He thrashed in a tangle of sheets, pushing away from the body that had him pinned to the bed. Sandy Baker straddled him; she was gripping a handful of his chest hair. She was looking not at him but toward the bedroom window. Moonlight was urging a velvet glow into the room.

His breath came in rasps, his heart was pounding, and his head felt like it had been split open by an axe.

Sandy whispered urgently. "There's someone out there."

He wiped the sweat from his eyes.

Then, her flesh pulled away from his; he sensed the cool emptiness in the bed, like a refrigerator cleaned out, door left open. He turned his head to see a lifeless heap of comforter dragged to the foot of the mattress, along with various bits of clothes. He rose, sitting up, looked about the room.

At first he didn't see her; she was another rigid shadow in the gloom. Then he realized the shape, abrupt and misplaced, was Sandy standing naked and gazing silently through the picture window.

"What is it?"

Her shoulders pivoted an inch to acknowledge she heard. But she didn't take her eyes from the window. Then her voice hissed back to him. "Someone's out there," she said. "I think."

His breath was coming easier now. He pressed the heels of his palms to his eyes to try to quell the throbbing.

"Who is it?"

"Who *is* it?" she whispered. "How should . . . I heard something scratching at the window and I looked up, and someone was there. I think he was looking in."

"Someone was scratching?"

Now she looked at him. "You didn't hear it?"

Sandy's body was ghostly in the moonlight, and whoever was out there was getting an eyeful. Then he remembered the ghost-man in the rain, and he slid out of bed and padded to her side. The wide picture window framed the woods that crowded against the back of his house. Joseph had passed, clearing away the clouds as he went, and now a lopsided chunk of moon exposed limbs twisting and swaying in a vestigial breeze. The world glistened with the evidence of the storm's passage.

"He was looking in the window," she said. "But. . .well, it seemed like he was back in the trees."

The window was a good seven feet off the ground. Boo judged the angles; from bed, she couldn't have seen a man if he was back in the trees. Unless he had climbed up one of them.

Gwine up naut.

Can't kill a dead man, boy.

He cleared his throat again. "There's nothing out there," he said firmly. "And I'm going back to bed."

She tensed again. "You don't. . .you don't want to go out and look?"

"And do what?" he asked, looking down at himself. "Beat him with my dick?"

"Oh, funny. Take a bat or something. Just to scare him off."

"Sandy. . .I'm going back to bed," he said. He started away—then turned to her again. "Sandy, did we just. . .?"

Now she looked either embarrassed or irritated. "Did we just *what?*"

He felt a remnant burn of fire-and-ice on his flesh as he watched her for a moment longer. Then he walked toward the bathroom. He flicked on the lights. Red eyes glared back from the mirror. Beneath the unforgiving fluorescents, the heavy muscles of his chest and shoulders were slick with sweat, and the scars on his thigh and ribs were stark pink ridges.

He opened the medicine cabinet, found a bottle of Excedrin, and dropped three into his palm. He swallowed them with a glass of water. When he got back to bed, Sandy was already under the sheets and asleep.

..eight

Ringing. (A dog's growl.)

Ringing. (A boy's scream.)

Ringing. (A witch's laugh.)

Ringing. His eyelids parted heavily, and he saw blurry red-glow numbers from his alarm clock.

4:04 a.m.

Sandy Baker was reaching over him. "Don't answer," he grunted.

"I have to," she answered groggily, "it's been ringing on-and-off for ten minutes."

An apple-sized breast dangled in his face, and he resisted a sleepy urge to bite it.

"Hello?" Sandy slipped the rest of the way over him and sat at the side of the bed. He listened to her voice but was not listening to her words. It was a little-girl's voice.

She snapped on the light, and he blinked. Her eyes burrowed into him as she listened intently. Her face was distress and confusion; seeing this, he quickly sat up and rubbed his face to clear his head. He heard the electric tone ramble through the line.

Then he realized: four o'clock in the morning?

"Sandy, who is it?"

After another few seconds, Sandy broke away from the phone. She held out the receiver. "It's your mother."

She's not my mother, he thought automatically and took the phone from her.

"Boo, I'm so sorry," Sandy was saying in her comforting, commiserating, endlessly aggravating baby's voice—making him angry with her, making him hate her frail, helpless beauty and wanting to be rid of it. "But she...well, I think she said your father is dead."

Something Burning, Something Dead ~ May, 1971

The pier thrust like a defiant skeleton arm straight into the belly of the Atlantic. Boo Taylor sat on the very edge, dangling bare feet above the swelling-falling waters, daring sharks to take him.

It was the cool glow before dawn, when the rest of the island was listless in doze: half-dreaming, half-waking, reaching back, slightly desperate to grasp a faded dream, peering ahead, slightly dour to consider a day's routine. Gulls laughed, lamented. Willets peeped and paraded in the surf. The tide unfurled salt-foam carpets onto ghostly sand ballrooms.

He was the only person in the world awake.

He stared at the horizon: rose-flush sky over rosy-blue sea, the glow heightening and steadily blanching away the ink of nighttime. He was waiting.

May was the month, perhaps the very best of months. Partly spring but mostly summer. Waiting, yes. But by May, even the wait could be savored because the prize ahead was certain now, rising blazing hot—not yet seen but felt on dusty and sweltery weekend ball fields and tugged at from the end of after-school fishing poles: once those morsels of freedom were tasted, it was known—*known*—the feast would surely follow. School weeks broke apart like log rafts unraveling in strong surf nearing landfall after a long journey through chill seas. School bells could be tolerated, their meanness mocked, their threat scoffed at and ignored like an old-lady teacher's wagging, liver-spotted fist. By May, nothing could hold it back: summer, *true* summer, freedom that stretched on forever.

Somewhere behind him, across the beach and a reedy slough, an orange pup tent sagged in the backyard of his parents' house, sheltering dew-grass, sleeping bag, *Archie* comic books, flashlight, bag of marshmallows, canteen of lemonade, half-eaten turkey sandwich, sneakers, and socks. He had not slept there, as he told his parents he would. There were jungles to explore, beaches to capture. Dead silent streets to roam in secret. Selfless acts of heroism that could be performed only at night, only by boys, and only alone.

He had heard once that when you turned thirteen, they could try you in court as an adult, so last night had been his last shot at innocence.

In this limbo between night and day, spring and summer, the ocean tangs were bruised by two alien smells: whiff of campfire and whiff of rot. Something burned, something dead. (*Hated one; liked the other*—wasn't that the way the old rhyme went?)

No, he hadn't spent the night in that orange tent. In the hours before dawn and the line that marked his thirteenth year he had wondered: At what point do you recognize wrong from right and stand by it, when the rule of the land is more than just what adults lectured but something decided on your own? At what point do you *really* take ownership of a life that, up till now, was directed by a mother and father and teachers and all the others who gladly told you *their* way? When was it time to stop hiding behind skirts?

He had wondered at night, then decided, then took action—and so whatever it looked like in the light of day would be his and his alone.

Now, he watched his shark-bait toes, watched the swirling, dancing light show beneath, almost like flames, timeless and fluid. When the time was right, he looked up again and watched the mythic continents beyond the horizon. Waiting...

It was coming...(He spread out a boy's hands, urging.)

Waiting...

Coming...

There! Fire, first glimpsed, coral red and blazing—just the slimmest fingernail curl rising, burning zigzag patterns in his retinas. The change scorched through him: cells exploding, bones shuddering and lengthening. He flexed new muscle and felt it harder now than it had been only an instant before. Freedom.

He un-spread a man's hands, satisfied.

When the sun was fully risen and beginning to blind him (and the change was already losing its glamour) he stood and turned to land, seeing two things now he did not expect. Two things that had been hidden from him in the dark of night. *(Queenie, Queenie had two daughters; hated one and liked the other.)*

The first was the bloated carcass of a dolphin washed among the gray stumps of the pier.

The second was a burlap doll—stick limbs and a wrinkled apple face sculpted in ghastly malevolence—sitting, as he had been sitting, oak-twig legs perched over the edge of bleached planks. He picked up the doll and felt-heard the dry rustle of its viscera. Black, lifeless, and lightless eyes glared secret witness to his crimes. A coldness ran through him.

Then, his name was being called from somewhere ashore. Hoss Beaudry, who lived two blocks north, was hustling red-faced, gracelessly onto the pier. "Boo! Hey, Boo, happy birthday! Oh wow, that's some smell!" (Whiff of campfire or whiff of rot?) Hoss charged over to the dead dolphin, jarring tremors along the pier's spine. The corpse's gray smile was unpeeling from its face.

Boo swung the doll behind his back.

In the distant yard, grainy beyond a thin haze of campfire soot, a shadow on four legs scampered away.

two

By the time Hank Dutton arrived in an outboard to haul away the dead animal, the carnival in the backyard was at full pomp and frolic—balloons bounced, crepe flags fluttered and snapped, and the island gentry trampled the grass. (The pup tent was folded away in the garage, and the burlap doll was tucked in the bottom of Boo Taylor's bedroom closet.) Bright tablecloths covered card tables borrowed from the Methodist church, laden now with bowls of potato salad, pans of peach cobbler, mounds of red velvet cake, and tall stacks of fried chicken. MaeEllen Taylor—pretty and pastel in the glaring brightness of the afternoon—was astounding all with her ability to balance fury and embarrassment with her drippy sweet, mint-julep charm.

A cloud of spoiled meat breathed over the lawn on the ocean breeze.

"Oh, can you just imagine? A fish! That dreadful ol *fish* decides on this very day of all days to swim up and die on my beach. Why, I hardly think that's fair at all!"

Boo escaped the carnival to stand on the beach by his father. Out of respect for MaeEllen the other guests did not join them, although certainly every man and boy among them wanted to. Hank Dutton was soaked up to his round and droopy waist in the sloshing surf, wrapping a chain around the cadaver's tail. Fillets of putrefying flesh loosened and pulled away in his strong hands. The stench was enormous.

Further out, his flaking boat bobbed alongside the pier where it cradled a few sullen Dutton boys.

"Whaddayah s'pose happen t'this feller, Doc?" the elder Dutton bellowed. He rocked drunkenly; his T-shirt was dazzling with grease and fish guts and golden patches of old sweat.

"Couldn't say, Henry. Maybe he ate a bad flounder."

"Ha!" Hank Dutton slapped at his thigh, splashing himself.

Squinting, Boo asked him, "What are you gonna do with it?"

"*Do* with it?" Hank Dutton ran a thick forearm across his brow. "Why, I guess I'm gonna take him home an' eat him!"

Boo looked at him, horrified, and the man barked another laugh.

"Naw, I'm teasin. Hey Doc, whaddayah figure—haul him down south a ways and let 'im wash up on Sadfellers Beach somewheres? Let the crabs and niggers have him?"

The doctor smiled thinly and nodded.

From this spot on the sand, Boo Taylor could look to the north and find the trawler that a drunken Hank Dutton famously ran aground on Cedar Knee Hammock back in '62, its hull splayed like the ribs of a dead whale. He glanced in that direction while; from the lawn behind him, his mother's elegant voice rose above the chatter. Boo was thinking, *not my mother, not my real mother,* when he was suddenly blinded by a flash of spun copper and sun fire. He blinked, brought his hand to his eyes to fend off the glare.

Gussie Dutton stood up in the boat, rising above the corpse-smell, and Boo saw through the boy-disguise: her hair, flames, deceptively gathered back and tamped beneath a cap, her legs long and naked and a different, even more pleasing shade of copper. She was a flame atop a tall, slim candle.

"Think that about got her," Hank Dutton was grumbling, but Boo barely heard him—was instead all netted up in that candle-flicker web of hair, that face chiseled in splendid profile; expressionless (or a trace of disdain)?

Had she been looking at him?

Of course she had, but for how long?—and he had never acknowledged her.

That was Wade in the boat with her, he now realized, and he hadn't acknowledged him either.

"Guess we'll let you folks get back to your comp'ny."

Too late now to extend offers, to say hello, to wave or make invitations to the party... and Lord, what must she think of him?

Festival sounds rolled over the slough, cold-hearted derision for the white-trash Duttons. At his side, the doctor was more polite: "Henry, thank you kindly for coming 'round so quickly. You have surely made MaeEllen very happy."

A roiling wet laugh. Was his father going to step forward and shake that plump hand? No, Hank Dutton was backing through water. Boo was backing over sand. From the boat, Gussie was glaring green daggers at him, stabbing him for his snub, and he looked away.

Hank Dutton slung his belly over the side of the boat. Wade went to haul him in, and doughy mounds of flesh and a black, hairy crease rose from the sea.

The motor sputtered, and Boo Taylor had backed all the way to the nutgrass. At last the boat was furrowing out to sea—shocking copper pennant at the prow. The dead body slapped the surf in its wake.

The rot hung over the party even after the offending beast had been removed. A trace of the campfire smell also remained, as if a weeks-dead pig had been barbecued. Or as if someone had set fire to a swamp.

Boo Taylor worried beneath the warring odors, sitting at a picnic table with his two best friends, Ashford Marchant and Hoss Beaudry. Ash, slim and easy with sunlight burning the rims of spectacles that magnified the sharp and clever eyes beneath. Ash Marchant was water-bug quick with his glove and a tough out on an infield grounder. Hoss, in counterpoint, was all bleached and round. His pale hair matched his pale skin, and his paleness went with his bloatiness, and the bloatiness was aggravated by a chronic logjam of snot in his sinuses. The overall package was reminiscent of the Pillsbury Doughboy—which had, in fact, been his nickname until Boo tagged him "Hoss," short for Horace (and in honor of the middle Cartwright son), and then championed the name until it stuck. Hoss Beaudry had never beaten out an infield grounder in his life, but he had developed a surprising ability to hit the long ball.

"Still stinks," Hoss said.

Boo looked at him, wondering how any smell could get through his packed nostrils.

"That was Gussie out in that boat, wasn't it?" Ash asked, and now Boo was stung by a bit of fire.

"Gussie and Wade," Hoss answered.

"That Gussie sure is fillin out, all right."

"Boy, you said it."

"So what'd y'all figure stinks worse, that dead fish or ol Hank Dutton?"

Two boys laughed at that; Boo wasn't one of them. He glanced miserably to the disappeared wake of the south-bound skiff, hoping for another peek of copper pennant.

With school out soon, he might go a whole summer without seeing Gussie Dutton. He had maybe a few weeks to catch her in class, speak some apology about the party she missed, if he could even make the words sound right—somehow, words got tangled up around Gussie Dutton. The last time they spoke he bungled it when he asked if the stories about her oldest brother, Henry Ray, who Boo had heard was recently shipped back from Vietnam all inked up with Chinese tattoos, were true. Had he really asked if her brother had smuggled home a collection of human ears?

"So where's that smoke comin from, anyway?" Hoss was saying, and suddenly the other ballplayers arrived to answer his question.

"Hey, did y'all hear what happen?" Dewey Fitch and Lester Meggett rushed at them through the party. Boo saw MaeEllen wrinkle her nose as they bounded past—as if blaming them for the stink. Both boys were products of the same, squalid marsh-side neighborhoods as the Duttons.

"The colored school down in South Patch got burnt down!" Dewey told them. He was smiling, showing his bad teeth. Greasy black hair hung in his eyes.

No one believed him.

"No, I swear to God! My daddy's on the crew this mornin, an' he got the call. Too damn late to do nothin, he says. Place was burnt right to the foundation."

(Whiff of campfire.)

"To the foundation," Lester echoed. Lester's hair also hung in his eyes, but it was a dirty blond; he smiled, but it was a dull, compulsory act on his bland face.

Ash Marchant challenged, "Did *you* see it?"

"Naw, it's what my daddy says. Says they figure somebody went an' set fire to her."

"Well, that old place *was* a tinderbox," Ash said.

Boo looked away and saw Eulahlah Colebriar shambling through the crowd, carrying a steaming pot of baked beans. She was pretty in a new gray dress and a sparkling white apron. Matthew Dufette, the family lawyer, walked with her in his seer-sucker suit and bow tie. He said something that made both of them laugh—Laylee's cackle riding like a bird song over the rest of the carousing.

"Hell, y'all know what that means," Ashford Marchant was saying. "That means the Negroes are coming to our school next year."

"Like hell!"

"No way!"

"Ain't no way that's gonna happen—they got to build themselves another school, is all."

"Dew, there's no way they're gonna build another school," Ash told him. "And you know what? I bet somebody *did* burn that ol school down on purpose. I just *bet* they did."

"What for?" asked Hoss.

"You ain't makin no sense," said Dewey.

They huddled around Ashford, and he explained it to them: "See, a while back the Federal District Court ordered the local school board to integrate all the schools by nineteen-sixty-nine, remember? Then, the board got all up in arms, and the court gave 'em a two-year extension."

"Hey, I remember," Hoss said. "All the parents yellin about it. Then that extension thing come along. Y'all remember?"

"Federal government don't have no say in it," Dewey said.

"Anyway," Ash continued, "that extension comes up end of the school year. *This* year—next month. School board's been trying for another extension, say they need more time and more money to expand the white schools."

"Course they do. Ain't no room for all them colored folks."

"But *now*...argument's blown, see? Colored school's burned down, so they *got* to integrate. Can't build another colored-only school. Not now."

"Somebody must'a figured that out," said Hoss.

Ash nodded. "Somebody put a match to it, I bet."

"So, some nigger did it," Dewey said.

Boo growled, "Dewey, watch your damn mouth," and got a look in return that was honestly puzzled.

"Now, for me," Ashford Marchant continued, "I'm against the integration. See, my daddy explained it to me. Says it's got nothing to do with us and the Negroes. He says it's the damn Washington government telling the South how to run its business. My daddy says it's the same as what started the States' War." Ash's daddy, Garson Marchant, had accumulated fortunes in building supplies and was the second wealthiest man on the island behind Osgood Satterfield, so his opinion was generally accepted on matters of business and politics.

"I bet I know who did it," Hoss offered, and they all looked at him. "I bet it was that Solomon Goody."

"Why, sure," Ash said, nodding. "Sure he did; y'all know how he is."

And that was true; they all knew how Solomon Goody was. For four years, colored children on Sweetpatch Island had the option of attending the white school or their own. Several made the attempt—and abandoned it shortly later, patchworked with plum Dutton bruises, red-orange tomato spoils, white talcum makeovers. Only Solomon Goody had lasted: a hard length of black rail with a provocative foot-wide afro and surly insect-dark sunglasses. He was the very image of the Black Panthers they all saw on television. By now, he was a junior in the high school, and no one—not even the Dutton boys—gave him much trouble anymore.

"Solomon Goody..." Dewey said, considering.

"Why'd a nigger boy go an' burn down a nigger school?" Lester asked.

"Les, watch your mouth," Boo told him.

Ashford tried to explain it again, and an argument ensued. Points of logic were debated. Ignorance and brilliance were tossed about with equal conviction.

While the matter of Solomon Goody and the burned schoolhouse was argued, Boo looked off for Laylee Colebriar again, finding her gathering empty glasses near a broad cloud of lavender azalea. Below her new gray dress, billows of nylon pooled at her ankles. Her black-and-white saddle shoes were scuffed, pigeon-toed, and two sizes too big. A happy smile lingered across her face, on the verge or the heels of a good laugh. Somebody watching her (*he* was that somebody, he realized) would believe she was carrying on silent conversations with the flowers and birds.

Then MaeEllen breezed by her. She looked up to see his mother—all lace and ruffles, hurrying—and the smile cowed a bit as his mother flung a bit of acid. His mother, MaeEllen Taylor, was the prettiest woman in the yard—on the whole island, probably—but her smile was painted on and cracked around the fringes. She came to stand next to the doctor, preening. Had his mother said "happy birthday" to him yet? No, but she had commanded the day, from the call to Hank Dutton to the selection of his clothes. It was, he understood, *her* party, not his; he was an ornament. As he watched his parents (*not* his parents!), he watched two strangers. It had seemed that way more and more since the day he learned he was adopted: their differences widening, their similarities narrowing. Perhaps, that was just an aspect of growing up—or perhaps it was that covert fear he'd now identified in his mother, her revulsion at wondering what pagan blood flowed through her adopted son's veins.

"Hey you boys," Boo said suddenly, brightly. "Let's ditch this party and go on down to the shell pile and play some ball."

"We only got the five of us," Hoss pointed out. "That's not enough."

"We'll get the Standish brothers to come."

Dewey grunted. "Hell, I ain't playin with them. Them boys is *Yanks*."

"I'll pitch both ways," Boo offered.

"Ain't none of us can hit you anymore," Lester said dully.

"I'll throw easy."

three

The shell pile was on the border of Up Island and South Patch at the very eastern tip of Soap Water Creek. The baseball field nearby was stamped out of a white-dust yard behind an abandoned brick building. It was the second best ball field on the island. The best was at the white high school, but that was claimed by the Duttons and their friends the Deeg brothers, Murphy Ransome, and the other older boys.

They took toward the field on their bikes.

Boo and Ash, swift and easy on their new ten-speeds.

Hoss, wobbling, still on a Sting-Ray, though he never got the knack of the wide handle bars, yellow tassels trailing in a shriek.

Sherman and Billy Standish, recruited to round out the game, on matching five-speeds, grunting to keep up.

And Dewey Fitch pumping at a dinosaur scavenged from the Pofoksgo Street junkyard—once metallic green and now speckled with rust, missing spokes, lopsided tires scraping the guard in a steady *whuff-whuff-whuff-whuff-whuff* like a small motor. Lester Meggett was perched suicidally on the handlebars because Lester did not own a bike.

"Those guys are crazy," Billy Standish said when the Dewey-Lester machine barreled at jet speed into Polk Road traffic, Dewey howling and Lester shouting, *"Push her, Dew-boy, you got her."*

"Won't live to see high school," said Ash.

"Dewey's crazy, and Lester's a few eggs shy of a dozen," said Sherman Standish.

"I'll say," said Hoss.

"Catch 'em!" Boo yelled.

It was, as always, a race—weaving down roads both dirt and paved, trespassing on grass boulevards, skinnying through dank alleys, marauding forests, dodging indifferent cars and ducking low branches, whizzing from blasting sunlight to slippery black shade. They knew their trails and the many man-made and beastly hazards along the way.

They knew, but did not always expect...

From shadow—four legs scrabbled from a densely weeded ditch by the road. It was suddenly there, vaulting the palmetto fans, huge and boiling with ferocity. Then, just as suddenly, it slipped back into shadow.

"Did you see that?"

"What the hell was it?"

"Some big dog is all."

"A dog my hairy dixie ass. That was the *Mamie Stuvant!*"

More rustling on the roadside, leaves parting, and the shadow was emerging again, drab, thick as a tree and just as dark and hard-limbed. She was toting a burlap gunnysack pregnant with poison sumac and dead squirrels, marking them all with a yellow grin. *Looking right into me,* Boo Taylor thought with startling panic. That burlap sack squatting, that wrinkled apple face glaring right into him from the pier.

"Oh man, keep goin—everybody just keep goin!"

"What for? It's just an old lady." Sherman and Billy Standish were new to the island, and of course they didn't know, couldn't know.

"Shut up, you damn Yank, an' keep pedalin!"

"Why?"

"Cause she's a *witch,* that's why!"

Mamie Stuvant, prowler of roadsides, was a witch.

four

But the Standish brothers didn't know, so the story had to be told. The Standish family had arrived on the island only months earlier. Because the family came from New York and had named their oldest son after the man most loathed in the Confederacy, the boys had been widely censured. Sherman made matters worse by insisting on wearing a New York Yankees cap on the playground. Sherman had survived his first encounter with Wade Dutton, but his hat had not.

The storytelling was done after the game, on the beach, in the soft light of dusk and bonfire. Dewey and Lester did most of the talking and, between them, botched the job thoroughly.

"See, Mamie Stuvant, she's supposed to be the ghost of Joker Tribbit's wife," Lester said.

"Who's Joker Tribbit?" asked Billy Standish.

The others groaned. "Jee-zoo, you Yanks never heard tell of *Joker Tribbit?* Of the *Beast?*"

The two boys shook their heads, and Dewey scowled. "Aw, you guys don't know *nothin!* The Beast, see, he's kind'a like this ghost of a nigg—I mean, this colored man named Joker Tribbit. He got hung and fed to the dogs about a hundred years ago."

"It was nineteen-thirteen," Ashford told them.

Dewey tried to do the math in his head.

"Naw, they burned him *up*, is what they did," Lester said.

"*Hung* him."

"*Burned* him."

"*Dogs* ate him."

"Anyway, they lynched him, see? And now he's a ghost. Sometimes he's this big dog—the *Beast*, see, on account of this dog what ate him up."

They made seven pits in the sand to accommodate seven bodies, circling the bonfire and staring at it with ritual, heathen lust. Hoss Beaudry sweated as if rotating on a spit. Dewey and Les lit cigarettes, and Sherman Standish joined them; their smoke and the smoke of the bonfire banished the worst of the mosquitoes. Pelican-shaped driftwood floated on the quiet Atlantic, wavering in and out of sight. Tropic trade winds huskily rattled the palmettos. Stiff, twisted oak limbs, salt-sheared, cowered back from the ocean so severely that the trees appeared to be gnarled old men running inland to safer ground.

"This all happened around here?" Billy Standish asked.

"Down south further, near that old Chaliboque Mansion. He used to be a hand there, they say. That's where folks see him sometimes. That's where they buried him."

"Buried him alive."

"Couldn't a' buried him alive, you numb nuts, if they already hung him and burned him."

"Oh."

Cigarette coals swirled in their hands like bottled fireflies.

"An' his wife, they say she was a real live witch. She's the one what said he was gonna have to wander 'round the island forever."

"Sheba was her name."

"Joker was his. Joker Tribbit."

"Caught him stealin money from Mr. LaValle, the rich man who owned Chaliboque and most of the island back in them days before Dr. Taylor and Ash's daddy and Mr. Satterfield all come along and started buyin everything up."

"Stole his money is what they say, so they lynched him. Hung him from this big ol tree."

"Cut down now."

"Yeah, tree's all cut down now. But that's where it happened, right down near the Chaliboque house."

Hoss Beaudry said, "Naw, it was near Bluff Beach."

"Same fuckin difference, fatty!" Dewey raged.

"Cause ol Joker Tribbit went an' stole this white man's money or burned up his house or somethin."

"And them men what lynched him fed his body to the dogs!"

"Turned the dog into some monster. The Beast."

"Roamin the Patch ever since. Just like Sheba, too. She come back, too, as a ghost."

"Mamie Stuvant."

"Yeah—Mamie Stuvant, she's Sheba's ghost they say. Lives in a shack down past the bridge on Soap Water Creek."

"Off Rue Duck Lane is where it is—hidden back a ways. And she's the one what keeps the Beast and makes him come out."

"We saw him once," Hoss said.

Dewey and Lester looked at him, now grave and nervous.

A stray bloodsucker found Boo Taylor's throat. He smacked his neck, and the others jumped.

"You...saw him?" Billy asked, curling into himself.

"Real close to here," said Dewey.

"By the shell pile," said Lester.

Sherman eyed them dubiously, but Dewey and Lester did not waver from their solemnity. A gnarled, oaken arm was fed to the flames.

Dewey Fitch dragged at his cigarette and gulped. "We was playin there, years back."

"Years back. King of the hill."

"And comin off, we see this *thing*."

"It was a *dog*."

"No, the *Beast!*"

"Well, what it was—well, we figure it was Joker Tribbit. This big ol...*thing* with red eyes. Standin in the shadows, an' he been watchin us."

"Just the biggest damn thing there ever was."

"Not sayin nothin."

"But maybe *growlin*, kinda. Like maybe it *is* a dog."

Lester and Hoss nodded.

"Don't know what he was doin so far north, you know? Folks say the Beast stays put down in South Patch, but once you get north of the Soap Water you're in Up Island. Everybody knows that."

"*She* brings him," Hoss said. "Mamie Stuvant—cause she's supposed to be *her* ghost—Sheba's ghost, only a different kind'a ghost, I guess."

Quietly, Dewey flicked his cigarette into the fire.

"...what did it do—the Beast?" Billy Standish asked. "What did it do when you saw it?"

"Said somethin," Hoss answered.

Dewey Fitch rumbled, "*Maybe* said somethin," and they all remembered how upset Dewey was because he hadn't heard it, had instead been hightailing it for safety before the rest of them.

Hoss said, "Well, he—*it*—had this real spooky voice. Deep. Kinda like that dog growl. He said, 'I'll kill you dead.'"

"Thought he said, 'I see somethin dead.'"

"Aw, that don't make no sense."

"Anyway, whatever it was, it just lay back there in them shadows, twitchin an' growlin. Then it moves off—nothin there all of a sudden, but the leaves and branches and stuff, they all move."

"Like somethin just run off—but you couldn't really *see* it run off."

"So we got out of there, too."

"You bet we did."

"Then we hear this scream."

"Like somebody's gettin murdered back where we was. Back where *it* was."

"Oh Lord, we ran."

"We ran."

The Standish brothers looked instinctively to Boo Taylor for validation of the story. Boo shrugged and gestured to Ash Marchant.

Ashford, arms folded, grinned; the firelight made flat orange circles of his glasses. "Here comes the worst part. What happened to that boy, Timmy Duff."

Slowly, looking from face to face before settling on Ashford, Billy Standish asked, "Who's Timmy Duff?"

Ashford almost answered, then caught himself. His smile faltered, smugness melted. He bowed his head as Boo and Lester and Dewey and Hoss did the same. The Standish boys, urged by electric voltage, blazed as the others went dim.

"Who is he?" asked Sherman. "What happened to him?"

After a moment, Boo Taylor looked up to see that nighttime was closing its noose around them; oak shadows that once fled to the shore now turned into hundred-arm monsters groping seaward. He suddenly wanted to be far away from this place, away from these boys. When he glanced to Ash he saw a stranger in the dark, just one stranger in a circle of strangers. "Mamie Stuvant got the Beast to kill him," Boo said. "He was the one we heard screaming."

Yes we ran, Boo remembered. We all heard that scream, back in the scrub, or decided now looking back that we did. Just like we all now remember seeing that darkness, that place absent of light in the vertical stripe of tree shadow with two coal fire dabs of eyes. We all—except for Dewey—now decided that we heard it speak, too.

But what it really said (Boo's version) was: *The king is dead.* Though he was coming to admit memories sometimes grew and twisted a bit like a vine, and friends comparing versions by a fire were the water that fed the vine's wandering course.

Joker Tribbit had been lynched by white men.

That much, at least, was historical fact.

Boo had been hearing the story before he was old enough to drink from a glass, and so it was for every other child of Sweetpatch Island, a patch in the tapestry of lore and legend and tedium and despair they gossiped at each other on playgrounds or over campfires—its place in the canvas slit to pieces and rewoven, reworked, and stitched back and forth in an endless construction and unraveling. Joker Tribbit had been murdered and now haunted the island's shores. He sometimes took the form of the *Beast*, a dog-like monster, at the bidding of Mamie Stuvant who was supposed to be his wife's ghost. Although, according to island chatter, she didn't always need the Beast to do her killing. There were rumors of poisonings, whispers of death curses. A boy named Timmy Duff was killed six years ago, another fact—Mamie Stuvant was implicated by innuendo only and, by cunning, had escaped conviction.

They had all seen her, had all run from her. Just a glimpse from across the road in the light of a streetlamp at night, or in the shockingly harsh flare of noonday sun—and those maniac eyes and fierce gator's mouth were enough to make a boy believe the stories were incomplete, that there was something even more ghastly about her.

But he was not a boy any longer. Time to put aside the ghost stories, wasn't it?

Again, Dewey and Lester did the telling:

She was a witch. She gathered the ingredients for her potions from alleyways, garbage cans, low-tide detritus, the unholy cold places in the swamp—from roadside culverts where tire-squashed animals got kicked. She was a big colored woman. *(No she was white! No she was mixed!)* She lived alone in a creepy house off Rue Duck Lane. *(No she had a big dog! No, fatty, that was the Beast she sometimes conjured!)* Six years ago, a ten-year-old white boy named Timmy Duff *(No he was twelve!)* who was known to throw rocks at Mamie Stuvant's house, and who was rumored to have a grandfather in Joker Tribbit's lynch mob, was found ripped to pieces *(No the Beast got to him!)* less than a mile from Mamie Stuvant's decrepit little shanty, and when they found him, parts of his body were missing *(His hands, his ears, his fingers; no, fatty, not his fingers—his balls!)* and the police didn't arrest her because they were afraid of her.

"Did you guys see it? Did you see his body?"

"No, but I swear we heard screams right after we saw that big ol black thing in the weeds. And it was next day they found him, and I can tell you my momma wouldn't let me come 'round the shell pile for two whole months after."

"They found him around here?"

"No—found him off by Soap Water Creek. By the bridge. Must'a been dragged there."

"And *she* did it—everybody knows, 'cause he was always teasin and lookin in her windows. And she's Sheba Tribbit's ghost."

"Yeah, she's her ghost."

"But she's real, too. Flesh and blood."

"Flesh and blood, all right—more like a witch than a ghost."

Full dark now, a night heron quawked at them from above. A million creatures seeped out of sodden sand burrows to claim the night beach. Something large lurched wetly in the slough behind them.

"So what is she," Sherman asked, "a witch or a ghost?"

"Both. Nobody says you can't be both."

Flames unraveled, danced.

"She's a skin-stealer," Boo Taylor said quietly, and the suddenness of his voice commanded their attention. They watched, waited. He had no intention of continuing until Ash nodded solemnly at him.

"Skin-stealer," Boo said. "Miss Laylee told me all about them. Never told me that's what Mamie Stuvant was, but I sort'a figure that's it."

Why, use t'be whole race of us folks livin on this island knowed about skin-stealin, Mr. Boo. Nowadays, ain't but a couple left who remembers the secret to it.

Just a trick, she'd told him. Play with light, play with shadow—like blowing smoke in someone's eyes was all it came to. Let it creep in through the nose, the ears, the eyes, fog the mind and find the shape in there that suits the person.

Turn old to young, small to big. Turn the ugliest foulest thing to the most sweetest an' prettiest.

Could it turn a person into an animal?

Why sure! An' the other way 'round, too. Take the skin of somethin close by, long's you been invited in—though, when you done, the skin's used up an' there ain't nothin left for the poor critter to come home to.

Just a trick. Just a little touch of magic.

"So you have to be a witch to do it?" Billy Standish was asking him.

Boo nodded. "I guess."

"So she's a witch, too."

"And a ghost," said Lester. "Ghost, witch, and skin-stealer."

Billy thought a moment, then looked at Boo earnestly. "Did Miss Laylee ever say if Mamie Stuvant is really Sheba's ghost?"

"No, but old Fish Hook who runs the High Spot down in South Patch told me once that Mamie Stuvant was Sheba and Joker's daughter. He also said that story about Joker and Sheba Tribbit was true. They did lynch him. Burned him and fed his body to the dogs."

"And she cursed them men?"

"Guess that'd only be fair. He called it 'Sheba's Curse.'"

"But what about that Mamie Stuvant?" Billy asked, stricken. "Did she really have the Beast kill that boy?"

Boo thought, then said, "Of course she did."

In the silent spell that followed, Boo Taylor stared at the fire, tumbling into it and feeling the years of his life stacked one upon the other like thirteen tall steps leading him to this time and place. He stirred his haunches in the sand for a comfortable seat, inhaling ashes (whiff of campfire)...

Thinking of angry Solomon Goody, who was the obvious person to blame for the fire at the colored school.

Worrying about a burlap sack asleep or awake on his closet floor.

Dreaming of spun-copper hair perched on a boat's prow like an enemy's pennant.

And bringing forth a boy's version of a memory: a shapeless darkness as it coalesced into an identifiable figure from his nightmares whispering threats from the shadow:

The king is dead.

five

That night, he dreamt of his mother again.

Faces shattered, shattering glass. Night winds wailing like a newborn infant. Blood and saltwater everywhere.

And...shadow coming to life, reaching, reaching down to the wails, shadow arms reaching...

He woke up not sure if he really remembered any of it.

six

Another day, another carnival. This time, the canvas was not blue Carolina sky but the vaulted, sun-parched timbers of the Cavalry Baptist Church deep in South Patch where Boo Taylor sat (not a boy, but a strapping young man—they all said so) aside Laylee Colebriar.

A grain of salt in a pepper shaker.

"Who this you brung along t'day, Eulahlah? Can't be Dr. Taylor's boy—he too *big*."

Too big to fit inside the shelter of her wing anymore.

Pastor Leroy Hatchel—salt-and-pepper himself—magician and showman, one gaudy golden tooth, catapulted to the pulpit and razzed the shaker, brandishing a floppy black brick in his fist, started in on his once-a-week jamboree. His shoes attacked the quivering planks beneath; his voice attacked the quivering planks above. He found his cadence and exhorted the choir and audience to find it within themselves, to pick it up, to follow him.

"Fire!" he bellowed.

"Amen!" they returned.

"Sal*va*tion!" he roared.

"Hallelujah!" they shouted.

He paraded and bowed, whirled about, stomped, joked, wept.

"Man's own sin heft on the back of God's own Son."

"That's *right!*"

"Hefted on that big ol cross."

"Yes!"

"*Big* ol cross."

"Big one!"

"Big as a bus."

"Big!"

"Big as a New York skyscraper. Big enough to carry a million poor souls."

"Big!"

"Gawd, ain't we lucky the Lord's Son got Hisself such a *strong* back?"

Then a sermon (Boo rarely listened to the sermon) about Cain slaying his brother Abel—the first and most famous murder in all of history, brother killing brother. ("Ain't there been enough brother against brother ever since? Why, I guess that's all it's been: jealous over God; one thinkin he better than the other. 'Am I my brother's keeper?' he ask. 'Why, yes you is,' said the Lord. 'Yes, indeed you is.'") At last the choir was rising into "Family of God" to the sprinkle of a tinny piano, and over his own froggy voice lilted Miss Laylee's sweet birdsong. All around him the air lifted, filling the church and stretching walls and roof beams; the old wood was just too tired and small to hold onto such a sound. By the third verse, he stopped singing and only mouthed the words so he could listen—imagining the hymn through the ears of some passerby: all that music trembling, stirring sawdust clouds, and pouring glitter through the open windows.

After "Family of God" it was "Amazing Grace" (too much like funerals) and after that the prayer requests:

Jesus help Mavis Jefferson's baby girl, Candy, with that bad kidney that put her in the hospital in Savannah.

Jesus bring peace to Enoch and Alma Lovett who lost a child in miscarriage.

Jesus give Lucas Ash (Lucas stand up for everyone to see!) the strength to fight the bottle.

Glistening faces enthralled as popsicle fans flapped the late-spring sweat, recycling it. While calamities and jubilations rolled along, Boo Taylor searched for Solomon Goody's kinky black halo among the pews but never found it.

Afterward, among cars and hunched skeletons on the gray-dust beach, he shook very old hands.

"Gawd, Boo Taylor, if you ain't gittin big."

"Eulahlah, you remember when that boy was jes a little jasper, used to crawl 'round 'neath the church?"

"Lord, he git his good clothes an' his face so dirty he look like a little colored boy. Wonder Miss MaeEllen didn't whip a few inches off his hide."

They regarded him with great sun-flash, yellow-white smiles. He recalled names as best he could. They all knew *his* name, knew his daddy and pretty Miss MaeEllen.

He walked with Laylee Colebriar, back toward her house and the lunch she promised him. He reined the springs in his thighs to keep pace with her gentle shuffle. She used a cane now. Not always, and Boo decided it was more of a prop than a necessity. She poked the stick along in front of her, making craters in the dirt, feeling the ground with her blunt antenna, and reading the secret tremors transmitted from the earth's core. Above them, lost in a bearded oak, a mockingbird complained about their slow passage. Somewhere in South Patch, little girls jumped rope and chanted about ancient murders.

They came to the High Spot, a shanty market and pool hall populated on Sunday mornings by the men whose women populated the church. Boo Taylor went in by himself to buy a Dr. Pepper and, for Miss Laylee, a cream soda.

Old Fish Hook smiled at him from behind stacks of cans and bowls of jerky and mounds of fish. "Why, hey there, Mr. Boo," he said in his whispery voice. "How's your daddy doin?"

"Fine, sir."

Boo took two bottles from the glass refrigerator. In the adjoining pool room, cue sticks tensed and altered their tangents amid lazing cigar smoke as a dozen or more sets of eyes considered the boy-man who had intruded. Boo Taylor felt the eyes as fingers, regarding the muscle in his shoulders and calculating the threat bunched in the fiber.

In the front room, on spindly chairs, old men with rheumy docility nodded and smiled weakly at his glance. Somehow, that was even worse than the electric tension buzzing fitfully from the young men at the tables.

He approached the counter with his money. Behind him, twenty eyes examined the ruddy complexion of his neck.

Fish Hook alone was smiling, but that might just be the scar curling up from his lip. "That be all today, Mr. Boo?"

"Yes sir."

"You gittin big, ain't you?"

"I guess."

A chair lurched, sending a brusque screech through the air. In the pool room, someone mumbled, and others chuckled.

"You got Miss Eulahlah out there with you?"

"Yes sir, we're coming from church."

More chuckles. Boo turned to see who was talking. Some eyes turned away and others bobbed cool contempt.

"Why, you tell Miss Eulahlah I said howdy," Fish Hook whispered as he handed over change. He shot a mean look at the young men. "And do the same for your momma and daddy."

"I will."

Boo looked at the men as he left. It occurred to him that a great many things must have gone on in the years before the thirteen of his life.

The bell chimed his departure. He joined Laylee Colebriar outside while inside cue sticks relaxed.

seven

Why, that little frog is you, Mr. Boo.

The only time it had ever snowed in Boo Taylor's lifetime was the Christmas when he was ten-going-on-eleven.

Sitting at Laylee Colebriar's kitchen table, watching the flaming-hot sun explode inside a glass bauble at her window, he remembered that season—already long ago—and how it had begun typically enough. The day after Thanksgiving he followed routine by cajoling MaeEllen until she let him haul the Christmas boxes down from the attic. Ten was old enough to be embarrassed by his enthusiasm, but not embarrassed enough to restrain it. The boxes, deceptively light considering the treasures contained therein: ropes of barbwire lights, misshapen plastic wreathes, frail glass bulbs for the tree. A special box for the stockings that hung from the mantel, limp on December first, swollen to life with magic heels and toes by the twenty-fifth. Another box held the nativity pieces, a mishmash of at least three different sets—one ceramic, another plastic, and a third made of some kind of clay sculpted onto wire skeletons. Laylee guided him as he stationed the pieces on the mantel, tutoring him on the different characters and their role in the miracle. The conglomeration boasted two Marys, two Josephs and no less than seven wise men—but not a single baby Jesus. At Laylee's suggestion, they substituted with a ceramic lamb.

On the morning of their expedition to the mainland to chop down a tree, frost laced the grass and a strong nip stung the air. December frosts were rare on Sweetpatch Island. Laylee made a thermos of hot chocolate; MaeEllen made him wear a pair of her gardening gloves—which he took off as soon as they bundled westward.

Over the next few days, the chill remained and dominated talk in the school hallways as students counted down toward the holiday. A nor'easter was rumored to be slouching down from the Maine coast—and might hit the Carolinas near Christmastime. The possibility of snow was suggested but generally scoffed. The doctor, who had lived his whole life on Sweetpatch Island, claimed that to his knowledge there had never been a snowfall of any consequence in all those years. A few dustings that blew off like confetti, but nothing more. Laylee Colebriar told him about a terrible February storm in the mid-twenties that blanketed the island shore-to-marsh for over a week, massacring yuccas and sea myrtles and sand dollars by the thousands. Boo knew of no one else old enough to confirm the story.

By Christmas Eve, the weatherman on TV was skeptical. A warm front was moving up from the gulf to overrun the high pressure system that had been sitting on them for the last week. The front would collide with the nor'easter overnight. It would be a wet Christmas. Not a white one.

"Mr. Boo, how many a' these you gonna eat? Two?" She was flattening grilled cheese sandwiches in a blackened skillet. Butter, burnt mercilessly, strangled the kitchen under gray billows.

He blinked away from the sunburst at the window. "Can I have three?"

She cackled happily. "You gonna be able to eat that many?"

"Sure I can."

She leaned all of her scrawny weight into the spatula. "You have yourself a nice birthday, Mr. Boo?"

"Yes'm."

"You get a lot a' presents?"

"Yes'm, a *lot*."

She smiled through a greasy haze. "Figure you might want one more present?"

The present is a gift, she told him once—or, more likely, she told him several times, though he never got that particular joke. His life had been full of gifts—an orphan boy wailing himself into consciousness in a fine doctor's house, *that* was maybe the first, and there had been a whole stream of them ever since, piled high (as a New York skyscraper) around him without being asked for. Like the stolen baby Jesus (turned into a lamb) awaking to strangers approaching his cradle, laden with gifts. For what? For being born beneath a star—right place, right time?

When he thought of the Christmas morning two years and five months earlier— waking up to find an apocalyptic white hurricane waltzing beyond his bedroom window: lawn, bushes, trees, streets disappeared beneath a blank canvas—it was Laylee Colebriar's face he painted there.

As soon as he could pull on clothes he flew downstairs, did not pause to admire the giant spruce he'd chopped down with his father now dressed up like a birthday cake in the parlor and surrounded by wrapped boxes, did not notice the stockings freshly stuffed above the fireplace, did not consider the variant players of the mantel-top Christmas miracle. He blasted outside and into the swirling, crystal dance, laughing and whooping and kicking his feet at the stuff. He put his hands into it, and it was *cold*. All along Carriage Avenue, neighbors in various states of dress poked dubious nostrils through front doors and toed the alien substance that had gotten on their doorsteps. The other children along the lane were soon out on the street with him, sliding and falling. A snowball fight swept up from the storm, and a few parents joined in; it was fought without teams, a free-for-all as snowballs mashed together by inexperienced hands joined the snowflakes to fill the morning sky. Boo found his parents stationed at the door in their robes, watching the celebration with smiles that conveyed a rare satisfaction with the God's ability to construct actual moments of absolute, uncompromising perfection.

A gift. The present.

Only when his hands were burned raw and his parents called to him did he finally leave the snow. Fire blazed in the fireplace, and never had flames seemed more appropriate in that house. He opened his presents, watched impatiently as his parents opened theirs; but his hands were already warm again, and the snow outside whimpered for his return. "After you eat something," said MaeEllen; instead of the elaborate Christmas breakfast she planned, he shoved frozen waffles into the toaster.

He was halfway through the meal when a knock bounced off the front door. "Now what are you knocking for?" his father's voice sounded through the house. "Goodness, this is a surprise! Merry Christmas!"

The sing-song reply: "Oh, wouldn't fit to jes walk in on special family days. And Merry Christmas yourself."

Then skinny, hunched-over Eulahlah Colebriar was shuffling into the kitchen, snow clustering on the shoulders of her ragged sweater and the peak of her knit cap. "Merry Christmas, Miss MaeEllen, Mr. Boo." There were no busses on Christmas; she had walked through snow all the way. "Lord, that ain't no breakfast! Miss MaeEllen, shame on you. Where's my skillet?"

She scrambled eggs, fried strips of bacon, boiled a batch of grits.

"I was coming to fetch you this afternoon," his father said.

"Afternoon's apt to be too late."

They ate her breakfast, coaxed her as best they could to sit with them at the table, but she refused and cleaned the pots and pans while they ate. When the meal was over, she said, "Mr. Boo, I believe I saw somethin out on the front step might belong to you. You best git it 'fore the wind carry it off."

He walked with her to the front door. His parents trailed, looking as confused as he felt. When he opened the door, he saw it propped against the porch railing. He had never seen one for real before, but he knew what it was.

"Ain't no hills hereabouts, but I hear tell they shut down the causeway. I reckon that might do."

Finally, he choked: "It's a sled!"

The gift.

Two copper pipes for runners, curled up on the ends and bolted into a rectangle of plywood. A length of two-by-four and rope for a handle, a red-and-green bow tied to the rope. The entire contraption was painted bright blue.

Calls to Ash Marchant and Hoss Beaudry, and then everyone piled into the Caprice wagon, and they slip-slided to the foot of Dedmens Causeway, which was indeed closed. They took turns climbing the causeway's steep pavement—up as far as they dared—and then flew down in a shriek of wind and snow, laughing and shouting, hugging the blacktop and bouncing so hard it jarred their bones. They raced on and on down to Sandpiper Boulevard, slowing at last or colliding with a palmetto. The doctor watched for traffic, shooting the all-clear sign before each new flight down the slope. The women watched from inside the car.

After a dozen runs, the rope came loose. They made a few attempts to tie it back on, then abandoned it and carried the sled by its handle. The handle itself started to jiggle after Hoss rammed into a parked car. Boo and Hoss tried going down together and tumbled off before they were halfway down. Ash tried it standing up, made a few wobbly few yards, came up smiling proudly through a bloody nose. They urged Dr. Taylor to take a turn, but he claimed to have better sense. They exhorted MaeEllen and Laylee to watch when they rode no-handed or on their knees.

Finally, one of the copper tubes cracked where it was bolted to the plywood, and it broke in two. The boys counseled with the doctor to assess the damage. There was a failed attempt to splice the two pieces together by shoving a stick through the tubing. Someone suggested pulling off the handle and turning the sled upside down. They tried that, but the flat plywood only ground against the street and would not gain momentum. By then, the snow was giving over to a rainy drizzle anyway. So they piled back into the car, hauling the battered sled with them.

The present.

They drove through the rainy mist—mist that was something magic only hours earlier—down into the poor streets of South Patch.

"Mr. Boo, you know what they says about snowflakes? They says every little snow-flake is an angel, come flyin down to pay a call on us earth folks. So when it snows, why it's like steppin into heaven!"

How did you know it would snow?

She *knew*.

Because she could make magic as easily as she could grill cheese sandwiches (which she did now) and boil tea (which she did that Christmas night, always picking at the various leaves and sprouts from the forest that hung upside down from the ceiling, dabbing the right spice and proper leaf and necessary root to summon enchantments).

"How'd you make that sled? Who helped you?"

"Mr. Boo, sometime askin 'bout a thing spoils a thing."

Later, settled under a blanket on her parlor sofa with Shamus rolled into a large, furry ball on the floor where Boo could pet him (the room was a box no wider across than the length of the old sofa), it struck him like a dagger in the heart that Laylee Colebriar had no family. She was alone in her tar paper shack—and beyond that was only her work scrubbing floors at the doctor's house, and those gentle people at the church. He pictured a hunched skeleton picking through scraps in the junkyard on Pofoksgo Street, studying a picture of a sled shorn from a magazine—shriveled lips chewing on nothing in effort to balance a hammer and nails; walnut-knurled, old lady fingers trembling bolt and nut through copper pipe. He saw a lonely seven-mile hike on arthritic knees, dragging a homemade sled with a bow on it, snow crusting her shoulders and cap, and the red rim of cold wounding her eyes.

Merry Christmas, Mr. Boo!

What had he ever done to deserve it? What had he ever given her in return?

His Christmas gift to her was one of those little glass figurines she liked, bought with allowance money. On the year of the snow, it was a glass frog. She made a great show of placing the frog on the sill of her kitchen window where he could see it.

"Why, that little frog is you, Mr. Boo. Think I'll keep that rascal right here so's I can talk to you all I want when I make my bacon in the mornin. Why, I believe that ol frog even look like you some, 'round the eyes."

Two years and five months after that Christmas, on the day after his thirteenth birthday—the first full twenty-four hours of being a *man*—she presented him with another gift.

For his birthday. For being born.

The house was filled with the lingering smoke of his grilled sandwiches—a fine Sunday smell. The box she handed him (shifting weight as he shook it) was wrapped in Sunday funnies. He stripped the paper, lifted the lid.

Stupefied, he gazed up to her merry cackling.

"Dirt?"

Her laughter rolled through the house like loose marbles, went on helter-skelter for a full minute while his gaze went back and forth: taut, elfish wrinkles to crumbling pile, nearly identical shades of brown. He sniffed at the box, seeking enchanted scents—root charms…spice hexes…perhaps even gold—but believed the only foreign ingredient he could nose from the heap might be blood.

"What do I do with it?" he asked her.

She laughed harder for a moment. "Why, gosh boy, you *tend* it!"

"Tend it?"

"It's yours," she told him. "When you turn eighteen—when you git to be a full-growed man."

His heart plummeted; his blood sailed. *But I'm already a man,* he thought.

"Talked it over with your daddy, an' he give it his blessing. Set it up through his friend, Mr. Dufette. Give it to you five years from today. This here boxful ain't but a *deposit.*"

He stared at the box that offered no explanation, stared up at the window where the glass frog winked sunlit wisdom at him. Past the frog's head, an oak swayed in a breeze from the distant sea.

Just for being *born?*

"Folks say the soil on this island ain't good for growin nothin but scrub grass an' gravestones, but I guess I proved that wrong, now didn't I? It run from the knob of them trees up toward the Old Sugar Dam. To the tree line east. To Pigg's Creek west. Walked off, it counts for thirty-seven full acres. Ain't worth much now, even less when I bought it—but maybe someday."

"You're giving me…your *place?*"

"My property. For when you turn eighteen—sooner if somethin was to happen—"

"*Nothing's* gonna happen!" he yelled at her. Suddenly, he didn't want to be a man anymore; he wanted to wind it all back.

She smiled, gently now, and laid warm sticks upon his wrist. "Oh, Mr. Boo, I reckon somethin bound to happen some time. Ol Laylee been 'round a long while. Longer than you know. 'Round *too* long, I figure. Don't got the back I used to, an' pullin weed takes a good back—an' Gawd, you know how I hate to see a garden go to weed."

He looked away from her, despising the tears he saw and the ones he felt.

"Lot a' things happen on this ground since the sea give birth to it, an' I guess I been 'round t'see most of it. Lot of evil blood been spilt into this ground. Lot of good blood, too. Mr. Boo, maybe you been 'bout the best thing done happen on this ground in a while. You is a *fine* boy. You gonna be a fine man, too…*some*day."

"Not yet," he said.

She laughed, smacked brown flesh against white. "We still got us some time left, I guess. Jes so's you know, I s'pect you to tend t'my garden when I see fit t'leave it. An' you tend to ol Shamus, too. Figure you may curse me for it someday. 'Cause pullin weeds is a tough job. An' it keep goin on forever."

He shoved the box at her. "I won't take it."

Her eyes, yellow, wet: "Oh, yes you will."

After lunch, he pedaled away from her, north. Leaving his bleary eyes and the *deposit* where it belonged, little box of dirt within a little box house.

..eight

He pedaled to the ball field.

He found grass-colored baseballs in the dirt, dirt-colored bats in the grass. Gloves scattered like dismembered hands, fattened and squashed. Bikes toppled to their sides like shot buffalo. The ball field was a graveyard exploded, littered with long-dead parts—or a barren Martian landscape, strewn with the wreckage of a lost rocket ship—or an Egyptian desert, sands blown away to reveal mummy limbs and dusty relics.

(Longer than you know.)

But no living person.

He swung off the bike and left it with the other dead buffalo. He picked up a ball, fingering the grass-polished leather for a clue. He squinted into the sun, searching...

And heard the echoes of war.

Gooks and American pilots, on the other side of windrow brambles, both sides laying claim to the hill. Grinning, he dropped the ball and chased after them. *"King of the hill!"* someone was bellowing, and it had been *years* since they played that game. So, maybe the tight clock springs *had* unwound, releasing his heart back to boyhood, and they would all be there: his friends made small, innocent, trusting. He ran, laughing, letting thorns cut into his boy's arms and spill his boy's blood (*best thing*) into the ground as he dodged a cottonmouth's tail in the slough.

He heard their call: *Come join us!*

"I'm comin!" he called back.

Broomsedge slapped his ankles; sea oats slapped his cheeks. He sloshed through dead water, dug over the bank, racing the sun. He heard his name (*King of Sweetpatch Island*) and chased after it, claiming it...

...and broke through the last stand of bramble.

Not a pretend war. A real one.

Dewey, Les, and Hoss. And four other boys.

Thrashing through the petrified shark's teeth of the shell pile.

Lester, locked up with a rail-thin tangle of iron.

Thick-armed Dewey pushing around two others. It had been his voice: "This here's *our* place!"

The biggest of them was on top of Hoss Beaudry.

(He never hesitated, and later he wondered over that. He assessed—as the men in the High Spot had assessed him only hours earlier—and identified his tribe, immediately, instinctively. Immediately and instinctively, he attacked.)

He grabbed the boy on Hoss, threw him off. The boy's knuckles came around and pounded hard into his ribs. Boo's breath faltered. But he grabbed the fist before it got away, then swung out with his own, clobbering the boy in the very instant he recognized the face.

Because he knew these boys, too. Had been to their church.

Then why wasn't it the same?

The boy got up and rushed him, but Boo stepped away, rapped him in the ear, and sent him sprawling into brambles. Then he dragged one of the other boys off Dewey and held him around the neck.

"You boys get out of here," he said, facing the first one again and holding this smaller one before him as a shield.

The bigger boy was getting up from the thicket. He identified Boo Taylor, looked unhappy and slightly mystified. He threw a brown finger toward Dewey Fitch. "*He* started it. We weren't doing anything." Blood dripped from the boy's lip.

"Fuck you, nigger!" Dewey roared.

"Shut up, Dewey!" Boo roared back. His ribs ached.

Hoss, whimpering, drew to his knees.

Boo released the small boy, shoved him away. The others drew to opposite sides so that eight sets of eyes could regard enemies and eight sets of lungs could heave oxygen back into depleted blood streams.

Boo said, "You boys, go on."

"This isn't just *your* place," the big one told him.

Boo put a hand to the throb inside his ribs. "Just get goin."

"Yeah, get goin, nigg—"

"Dewey!"

Silence.

(You is a fine boy.)

(Ain't there been enough brother against brother ever since? Why, I guess that's all it's been.)

Boo looked around at the boys behind him—his friends—wishing Ash had been there; Ash would have kept Dewey from it. Boo felt finger muscles curling bone into fist, wanting to pulverize Dewey Fitch. Les did whatever Dewey said. Hoss went along so he wouldn't be ragged.

Boo Taylor did what he was born to.

Turning back to the others he said, "Just...*go*."

Quietly, angrily, they did.

*C*nine

He thought about a stolen baby Jesus appearing like a ghost from nowhere, deposited anonymously at the door of Sweetpatch Island's only white doctor—then skin-changing to a lamb and getting presents just for being born under a star.

After dinner, remembering he had one last present yet unopened, he dug through the bottom of his closet and exhumed the burlap corpse.

He beheaded it, tossed the apple glower into the trash.

He dismembered it, chucked stick arms and legs out the window.

He gutted it, spewing dusty offal across his desk.

He inventoried:

...old newspaper stained with tea...clumps of Spanish moss...dried frog eyes... sumac leaves...threads of fingernails...animal fur (*rat* fur, he decided)...snail husks...shark's tooth...gator's tooth...infant-sized femur bone...a crumpled page from Genesis (most of chapters IV through VI)...clipped end of a cigar...aluminum beer tab...

Trash?

No. He sniffed the pattern to the ingredients. *Frog eyes, snail husks*. Essence of Laylee Colebriar. *Sumac leaves, gator's tooth*. But *not* of Laylee Colebriar. Mixed together in all the wrong proportions and all the wrong combinations. Nothing of *goodness* in all this, it was poison.

Un-wadding the ball of the newspaper stuffing, he read two headlines, then read the stories. A woman, unidentified, found drowned and washed ashore near the Cause-way. *Something dead.* And three Negro girls burned to death when fire swept through a church in Slocomb, South Carolina. *Something burning.*

He packed the guts back into its burlap skin, knowing just exactly what to do to kill the spell.

Through the house, sneaking past MaeEllen and the doctor. Outside, across the lawn. Onto the planks of the pier. Sea air smelling like the coming month of June ruffled his hair and filled his lungs as the planks bobbed beneath him and the ocean bobbed beneath the planks and the last glow of a westering sun revealed a bleakened horizon in the east.

Spring was ending; summer was coming. And summer was a boy's season.

Heaving doll guts to the sea, a ghost pain pulsed against his ribcage. *(I hit that boy. Why did I do that?)* He turned, afraid, and beneath a bleeding sky, caught a glimpse of a four-legged shadow slouching over the land.

Part Two
Sightings

I have never killed a man, but I have read many obituaries
with great pleasure.

—*Clarence Darrow*

*T*he heat was something he'd forgotten: the pure hell-fire of the Carolina sun
unchecked by any shade, boiling the island's beaches and marshes until the air
was a hot, thick soup. *Sweat patch* they called it as boys. And now sweat slid over
him in torrents, soaking his shorts, his socks, making deep salt rivers in the creases
of muscle as he ran the island streets. Even at this early hour, the pavement was
blistering the thin soles of his running shoes.

A delivery truck passed; he edged closer to the curb and inhaled exhaust.

The heat was the same, yes (something burning), and so was the stink of saltmarsh
(something dead). MaeEllen Taylor, virtually comatose with grief, was the same. The
house was the same. Everything else, however, was different.

He hadn't stepped foot on Sweetpatch Island in nearly twenty years, and the
change was startling. He drove his rented Buick over Dedmens Causeway to an alien
landscape of golf courses and condominiums; roads had been widened and paved and
were bustling with tourist traffic. Streets were lined with gift shops and seafood restaurants. He got lost, made wrong turns, stopped at red lights where intersections never
existed. He passed a sign pointing to some place called the *Sing Satterfield Wildlife
Refuge,* another for an oddity called *Gator Beach,* and strangest of all, red-white-and-
blue billboards announcing *Solomon Goody for U.S. Congress.* Everywhere, people
clogged the roads and spilled over the sidewalks, all strangers—nobody knowing or
caring that Boo Taylor had finally come home.

At Carriage Avenue he slowed to a jog, then to a walk. A *Taylor Dufette Realty* sign
was posted in a lawn two doors from his parents' place; it was the third he'd passed
this morning.

When he reached the doctor's house, he made his way across the grass lawn, then
over the dunes to the pier. A voice from the beach yelled at him. "Hey, can't you read?
That's private property."

A sign had been nailed to the pier's railing; he hadn't noticed it earlier.
Private Jetty. No Trespassing.

The man who had spoken was wearing a pink Izod shirt over plaid swimming
trunks, his face was beet red and his legs were bone white. He seemed to be studying
Boo's sweating torso.

Boo shrugged. "I won't tell if you won't," he said. The man grumbled at him and walked away. Boo paced to the end of the pier and sat down, dangling his running shoes above the surf as dead bits of flotsam rippled beneath him like debris from a shipwreck.

He sighed, gathering his wind.

He in the tide, boy.

Behind him, childhood echoes peppered the beach. Little boys splashed the surf on commando raids. Mothers laughed inanely or shrilly after them. A little girl cried over and over for "Stingo."

He come an' he go.

Behind the tourist crowds, beyond the reedy, saltwater slough, a tall and remarkably unaltered white house rose to confront sun and sea. His mother was in there, mourning and melted in an upstairs bedroom. Sandy Baker was in there, too. And some woman named Bess Pope who was latest in a quarter-century line of replacements for Eulahlah Colebriar.

An' he most always leave somethin to rot on the beach.

The doctor, of course, was not inside. He was laid out in a shadowy back room of Duckett & Sons Funeral Home a half-mile away on Loggerhead Street, and the horrible shriek that had been engraved across his forever-silent face would by now be ironed smooth and powdered.

Sweat crept around Boo's shorts and into a dark web through the sun-parched wood grain. From the sky, gulls called. From the beach, willets answered. He brought his hands together and stared at them, palms touching, as if reading a book.

The lost fingers made a hole, like missing pages. The other fingers, thick and scarred, heavy and yellow with calluses, wrapped his hollow space.

His right ring finger halted abruptly in a stub at the first knuckle. The top of the stub was flat and hard. It had always, from some odd association of his childhood, reminded him of Boris Karloff's flat scalp in the Frankenstein movies. The skin on top was worn smooth, a shade more red than the surrounding skin, and the rim was hard, like plastic. He could pinch the top of the stub and feel the abbreviated bone within, waving free inside thick sinew. He was prone to jab the stub of his ring finger against doorjambs and table tops, and when he did, the fleck of bone inside would jab its flesh-and-muscle cushion. He had become familiar with that unique pain—the pain atop the monster's head. It was sometimes so precise, like a needle prick, that it could bring tears to his eyes.

The smallest finger of his right hand was completely gone. A remnant of bone was locked in the still-functioning socket, and he could make the flesh there wiggle—but there was otherwise no evidence a finger had ever been there at all.

Beneath the knuckles, an intricate macramé of pinkish scars, as if the flesh there had survived a long-ago encounter with a meat grinder.

He put his hands back down on the plank and expelled a breath.

The ocean rose and fell beneath him.

No, his father was not in that house—nor had he died there, apparently;

although no one had yet explained to Boo precisely *what* had happened to the doctor. Just whispers and worried looks from the revolving-door well-wishers the previous evening, all in painful deference to the wounded Miss MaeEllen.

He plucked a dried bit of seaweed from the wood and dropped it into the sea where it floated amid the other bits of detritus, carried by an outgoing tide toward distant lands in the east.

Toward Nod, he mused. East of Eden.

Then: *I am in Nod. And I have come back.*

two

When he opened the back door, MaeEllen Taylor's voice dripped like fog from her upstairs bedroom. "Boo sugar, is that you?"

A shift of floorboards over his head and Sandy's childlike voice answering: "Can I help with anything, Mrs. Taylor?"

"Why, you are a can of peaches, girl, but if you call me 'Mrs. Taylor' one more time, I swear I will find my hairbrush and whip your pretty little backside with it."

"Miss MaeEllen, then. Can I get you something?"

Boo listened, recalling the impressive tapestry of emotion his mother had woven last night for the steady flow of neighbors and friends: valiant tears, then bizarre laughter, then sickly sweet charm, and on to apocalyptic wailing. *You must forgive me,* she pleaded in her more rational interludes, *I am simply not myself; I'm sure you understand.* Surely, it was an award-winning performance.

In the kitchen, Boo pulled on his T-shirt and opened the *Patch Caller*. He ran himself a glass of water from the tap and sipped at it as he leafed through the paper.

"Boo Taylor! Are you pretending not to hear me?"

MaeEllen shouting again, and Sandy's comforting voice. Boo set the paper down and headed toward the steps to rescue Sandy, dodging a forest of flower arrangements in the foyer. He followed his mother's complaints to discover Sandy Baker leaning over his parents' bed, holding a glass of water. Her deep tan was startling in a pale pink sundress, her effortless beauty surprising him as it sometimes did.

Beyond Sandy, MaeEllen Taylor was a deflated heap of gray cloth beneath a single, lavender sheet. The straps of a slip hung loosely over her shoulders. "Why, I just knew I had a son someplace. Look how you make this poor little girl wait on your mother."

Boo leaned on the doorframe. "She's not a poor little girl. She's a lawyer, and she makes more money than I do."

MaeEllen's eyes were empty of humor. The fine debutante face was still there, hardened in some places, slackened in others. Scowl lines marred her forehead and the bridge of her nose. Curls of brown hair were clamped between flat metallic clips that circled her face like silver roaches.

"Well, I suppose that makes it okay, then," she said to him, and then to Sandy, "It's okay dear, you are a lawyer and you make more money than my son does. You may feel free to dote upon me."

Sandy smiled and set the glass down next to a bottle of pills that Boo now noticed.

MaeEllen trembled a heavy sigh. "Well, I suppose I should be getting ready, shouldn't I?"

Boo glanced at his watch then back at the withered woman on the bed who was making no effort to get up. They were due at Duckett & Sons in an hour. "You should stay here, Mom," he said. "I'll take care of the arrangements. I suppose about everything has already been decided anyway."

"Would you, darling?"

"Of course he will," Sandy put in. "I'll go with him."

Boo was acutely irritated at this. Sandy Baker had insisted on accompanying him to the island. The presumption had caught him off guard, so when he tried to talk her out of it and was met with dewy eyes, glowing with the promise of some cataclysmic emotional storm, he had given in too easily.

MaeEllen was wrinkling her forehead. "I really should be there, don't you think? I just don't know if I'm up to it."

"We'll take care of everything," Boo said.

"But if you both go, then I will be *alone*." More wrinkles appeared. She turned her appeal to Sandy.

"We'll wait for Bess," Sandy told her. "We won't leave until she's back from the store. Boo needs to get a shower anyway. Would that be okay?"

"Well yes, I suppose," she said to Sandy and then back to her son. "Now Boo, you must be careful with those Ducketts; they'll insist on throwing in those outrageously expensive extras, and Silas would never approve of that. The Ducketts have been robbing three generations of grieving families on this island, and Simon Duckett is certainly no better than his daddy *or* his granddaddy."

Boo smiled patiently. "We'll leave the credit cards here."

"I am serious, Boo Taylor! If you're not careful, that old bandit will have you buying a coffin with solid gold handles and cashmere lining."

"You have nothing to worry about, Mom. If I ever bought gold coffin handles in some weakened moment of grief, I can assure you I'd be back to dig them up later."

They locked eyes for a moment. She turned uncertainly to Sandy. Then she closed her eyes. "You are an awful son," she lamented. "Always a joke." She brought the back of her hand to her forehead as her chin began to quake.

Sandy slid to the mattress and picked up MaeEllen's damp hand. "You raised a cad, didn't you?"

"No, I did not—*I* didn't raise him at all. He saved all of his affection for the housekeeper."

And then she wept freely, twisting her face away. Sandy held her hand and waited. Boo shouldered off the doorframe. The house was all at once intolerably hot and airless. When the worst of MaeEllen's sobbing ebbed and she hitched and sniffled, Sandy handed her a tissue from the nightstand, nearly knocking over a stack of Victoria Holt romances.

Boo motioned for Sandy who joined him at the door. "We'll be downstairs until Bess gets back," he said.

"Mom," MaeEllen called from across the room. "When did *mom* start? When you were a little boy, you called me momma. Then when you were older it was mother; around your friends it was always mother—you got too big for momma. Now it's just plain old *mom*."

"What would you prefer?" Boo asked. "How about 'Miss MaeEllen?'"

She glared at him dully. "This from a grown man who calls himself *Boo*. You only accepted that name because Eulahlah gave it to you. But I should know by now I cannot win with you, can I?"

"That's not true. You always win with me."

"You're smirking. You don't think I can see it, but I can."

He sighed. "I am not smirking."

"You are!"

He sighed again and took Sandy by the arm. "We'll be downstairs."

They fled softly to the kitchen. In the refrigerator, Boo found a pitcher of iced tea behind the stacks of covered dishes that had been stockpiling from neighbors ever since their arrival. He poured a glass for himself and Sandy, and they sat at the kitchen table.

"Boo, I don't know why you act like you dislike your mother so much," Sandy said. "I don't think you really dislike her; I think it's just an act."

"She was never my mother."

"She raised you."

"No she didn't; you heard it straight from her majesty's mouth."

"That's nonsense. She *raised* you."

"Thank you, counselor, I was there."

Fault lines quivered at her lips. "Don't get mad at me."

"Don't make judgments, then."

"Boo, stop it!"

I told you not to come. He looked at the frost dribbling a circle from his glass onto the table; he looked away from Sandy and his anger and impatience and the things he had no desire to explain to her. *Told you not to come,* and yet here she was.

He felt her sulk bearing on his chest like a lead weight. He picked up the glass and let himself cool with a swallow of iced tea. The tea was thick with sugar and lemon. The way Laylee Colebriar used to make it—the way his mother liked it, he supposed, and the way she must have taught Bess Pope to make it.

Silently, he grumbled.

"You look nice in that color," he said.

"Do you like this?" she asked. He looked up and saw she was grateful, and the ease of her gratefulness demeaned her. "I was thinking I might buy a hat today. Can we go shopping after we're done at the funeral home?"

He heard the bed creak upstairs. And the whisper of a moan.

three

At just after 2:00 that afternoon he saw the ghost.

He was standing outside of a gift shop, paging through the book he'd just bought. He looked up, and the ghost glided past, indifferent to him, not seeing him at all, a mystical bob of copper-spun fire, of swishing white legs, of trembling breasts. A sharp, fiercely beautiful profile drifting out of the masses, drifting into view, floating closer (a faint smile on her lips?), now floating past, receding, slipping into the churning chaos of the marina, his heart slipping into the breeze to follow her— while the rest of him remained bolted to the bricks and could do no more than let her fade from view.

He took a step toward her. Someone crashed into his back; he distantly registered this as he stared into the crowd, thunderstruck, distantly registered the cry of *"Wup, wup!"* from behind him.

The ghost was swirling like a crimson dragonfly, in and out of view.

There, a lick of red-gold flame.

Now disappearing again.

Behind him, barely heard, a man squawked, "Gosh, I'm sorry!" Then, a woman, "Merle, you weren't watching!" Cold fingers tapped and probed his back. Not wanting to, he turned away from the vision to attend to the commotion behind him. A man was pointing an empty Styrofoam cup at him. Next to the man was a woman wearing a shocking yellow turban. Both gaped at him.

"I *was* watching," the cup holder said. "He stopped. You stopped, fella—I didn't see you."

"Look at this!" The woman with the yellow turban snatched the back of Boo's shirt. "Merle, give me that napkin." She plucked a napkin from the cup holder's hand and attacked the tail of Boo's shirt. "Oh, this is *aw*ful!"

"Don't blame me," the man complained to her, "he stopped!" To Boo, he accused, "You shouldn't stop like that. I'm awful sorry, but you shouldn't stop like that in a crowd."

(*Not a ghost*, he thought, trying to twist back to the fading vision, deciding he needed to follow her. Needing to follow—but she was slipping further and further away...)

...and this aggravating woman had him by the shirt. He lifted his arm away from her and craned to look at his back. A great brown foam was splashed over the light blue of his golf shirt and bled to the seat of his khaki pants. "What the hell is *that?*"

"Mocha-chocolate milkshake," said the man.

"It's not coming off," said the woman.

Boo growled, "Of course it's not coming off." He tried another glance into the shifting and rearranging curtain of bodies. A hint of scarlet fire burned a brief flicker off in the direction of the footbridge.

The man argued, "Well, you can't stop like that in a crowd!"

"It's going to stain," said the woman.

"It's okay," Boo said. The urgency to follow the girl was building toward panic. "Look, it's my fault. It's okay, now."

The woman was still swiping at the small of his back when he started away. "Put some seltzer on it!" she called after him.

Sandy was somewhere trying on outfits while he was exploring the shopping village that had once been the battered and slightly dangerous old docks of Mermaids Head. Dock Street had become the southern leg of a horseshoe now known as *The Harbor District*. Across from Dock Street was Merganser Boulevard, and connecting the two lanes was a boardwalk footbridge that spanned the bored, brackish flow of Mermaids Head Creek. The loop of shops and restaurants enclosed the old marina where pleasure craft and fishing boats rocked indolently in their slips. The old Pittman Boatyard was completely gone, paved over. A lifetime ago, he had scavenged his first skiff from that weeded graveyard of old hulls.

Growing up, the docks at Mermaids Head had been noteworthy for their complete and unapologetic masculinity. No women nor any sign of their influence could be found there—except for the names painted to the sides of boats. The place held little regard for appearances or cleanliness. A simple hosing was a thorough enough washing for a boat deck. Paint faded and flecked without regard. Awful smells were encouraged. Fish guts were allowed to fester in the sun, and gulls were free to pick at them. Nothing like this charming shopping village where the entire lengths of Dock and Merganser were now cobbled with an antique, herringboned brick, and an insect swarm of tourists and street vendors scuttled over the walkways.

He had let himself be carried by the tourists to the water's edge where he could look at the docks themselves. When he reached the railing, he stopped to watch a man on one of the older vessels, tugging at nets and mumbling profanities. The man and the boat were throwbacks. Sleeveless, the man was all ropey, sunburned arms, stained gray clothes, long beard. The stub of a cigarette was pinched in his lips, and a skull tattoo shriveled with age on one shoulder. The man momentarily set the nets down and wiped sweat from his brow with a forearm. He looked up to find Boo Taylor watching him and stared back through slit eyes. An immense hatred emanated from the man that, rather than turning him away, actually *drew* Boo Taylor. They stared that way at each other for several seconds until at last the man on the boat spit into the water and went back to his nets.

Boo watched the man for a few moments longer. Then he turned back to the bustling tourist crowd.

After more wandering, he came to a bookstore window and a display announcing a collection of titles of local interest. He found himself laughing. Royal Goody, younger brother of the famous Solomon Goody, had written a slim, paper-back text called *Blood on the Beach: A Folk History of Sweetpatch Island*. The book had a homemade look with its smeary print and xeroxed, overly dark photographs. Boo went inside and bought a copy.

The picture on the back cover confirmed the author was the same boy Boo Taylor had once fought at the shell pile. *(He started it!)* Beneath the picture was a brief biography. Royal Goody, an amateur folklorist, still lived on the island with his wife and children and was Vice Principal and head football coach at Sweetpatch Island High School.

He took the book outside to read in the shade of the bookshop awning:

An Island Born

The assembled clay and sand that conspired to become Sweetpatch Island were introduced ten thousand years ago when the ice masses of the Pleistocene epoch retreated inland. The ice melt flooded the seas and stranded several obstinate crops of highlands that went on to become the long chain of barrier islands that hug the North American Atlantic coast. Over the centuries, these islands-in-the-making were hammered mercilessly by waves on their ocean sides. This pounding led to the formation of their sand beaches. On their mainland sides, rivers expelled silt onto the island's banks. This process continues today. The barrier islands are constantly formed and reformed by the great natural forces that gave birth to them.

Sweetpatch Island, as a case in point, is continuously crawling ever northward under the barrage of feuding flood and ebb tides. The island's rusted southern bluffs are being clawed to pieces by the relentless waters, and their remains are being dragged and discarded on the northern shore. The island is, in effect, leapfrogging itself to the north. As the old southern heights crumble, the northern beaches rise and reach ever northward.

In our own century, the bluffs at the southernmost point of the island have lost over sixty feet, and the dunes of North Beach have gained nearly one hundred feet. In World War II-era photographs, Cedar Knee Hammock can be seen as a distant fuzz off of North Beach in the Yamawichee Sound. Today, the tiny island is merely a short walk away through knee-high water, and on Spring ebb tides, the islet connects to the main island by a sand bridge. In the south, Pigg's Creek grows wider and deeper. During spring flood tides, the creek has been known to breach the low marsh flats to touch the Atlantic, and in this fashion makes a temporary island of the old Chaliboque Plantation.

He flipped several pages forward until he came to what he was searching for.

Sheba's Curse:
The Legend of the Beast of the Patch

Of all the odd folktales birthed on the shores of Sweetpatch Island, "Sheba's Curse" or the legend of the "Beast of the Patch" is perhaps the most famous (or infamous). Every child who has grown up on the island in this century has heard the story, from older children or their parents or their grandparents. Over the course of time, "The Beast" has served handsomely as the island's very own version of "The Boogeyman," and it is certain many a Sweetpatch Island child has been cautioned to come in after dark "or the Beast will get you."

My sources for this story are many. Mavril Pickett's *Sweetpatch Folklore* (Lee Island Press, 1947) includes an interesting, if somewhat abbreviated version of the tale. Additional sources include original stories in the *Patch Weekly* (now your *Patch Caller*) graciously shared by Mrs. Hedda Coppelson (a xeroxed copy is now accessible at the Sweetpatch Island Public Library), original stories in the *Beaufort Gazette,* and interviews with Miss Irma Lynn Preston and Mrs. Dorothea (Dotty Mae) Jackson. I also had the privilege of reading the original journal of Mrs. Margaritte Sladeshaw LaValle, granddaughter of the Honorable Permanence Trappe Sladeshaw, Secretary of State under President Andrew Jackson. Mrs. LaValle features prominently in this story, and a collection of private Sladeshaw family documents is kept at the library at Georgia Southern University.

I should also give thanks to the number of remembered and unremembered boys and girls and aunts and uncles of my childhood who first introduced me to "The Beast."

What we know to be the facts of this story, and even what we suspect to be fancy, have a great deal to reveal about the island's history of racial brutality. The facts of the story are as follows:

In the early 1800s, the Beauchamp family bought Sweetpatch Island in its entirety (please refer to the chapter "Early Modern History"). Toward the time of the Civil War, the remaining Beauchamps (headed by Mr. Wallaston Beauchamp), having sold several parcels of land on the northern part of the island, now owned only the land south of Cabot Trail. (Cabot Trail is now called Dedmens Road, and the land south of it, as the reader may know, is today commonly referred to as South Patch, or Black Patch, or sometimes Brown Patch.) In the Beachamps' time, this land was the site of the family's plantation and the family mansion, both known as Chaliboque. Only weeks prior to the shots fired on Fort Sumter just a few miles up the coast heralding the beginning of the Civil War, Wallaston Beauchamp sold his remaining property on Sweetpatch Island to a Mr. Victor Ballantine LaValle, the son of a prominent Georgian planter. Such remaining property consisted of land, mansion, and slaves. Mr. Pickett's account says the sale of Chaliboque took place after the war; however, a mention in the "Society's Ways" column of the July, 1862 *Beaufort Gazette* would dispute this. In any event, a post-war sale would seem unlikely.

As one can guess, Mr. LaValle's timing, with regard to establishing a profitable plantation on the island, could not have been worse. The same events that doomed so many Southern property owners, as a result of the Civil War and the Reconstruction period that followed, dealt him a devastating blow. Serving to his benefit, however, was Sweetpatch Island's relative isolation. For the most part, the former slaves had neither the means nor the opportunity to travel to the mainland and little opportunity waiting for them there should they attempt it. Most chose to stay on the island and went back to the fields and kitchens to perform the same work as freed men and women as they had as slaves.

They found conditions little changed. Wages were room and board and little more. The whip was still used, mostly by Negro overseers. The hours in the cotton fields were still long and grueling under the harsh sun. And there were other acts of brutality against the workers. For years after the war, life on the plantation proceeded much as it had before.

In time, however, the free Negroes of Sweetpatch Island gained additional opportunities. The ports brought new prosperity to the communities north of Cabot Trail and the need for workers—in oyster processing factories mostly—as well as the chance to secure work and passage with sea merchants. Such opportunities threatened the continued prosperity of the LaValle family and its plantation.

Just prior to his death, Victor LaValle attempted to secure the preservation of Chaliboque by marrying off his grandson, Samuel, to Margaritte Norville Sladeshaw, the granddaughter of his old friend (the previously mentioned Permanence T. Sladeshaw), who's family had prospered considerably through Reconstruction in the railroad business.

When Victor died in December, 1901, the plantation passed along to Samuel and Margaritte LaValle.

It is clear that despite the infusion of capital his marriage served to secure for the family business, Samuel LaValle inherited serious labor difficulties when he inherited Chaliboque. Victor LaValle had been considered a strict lord of the manor and was, to say the least, not well liked by the Negro workers. The many stories of Victor LaValle's atrocities against his workers might have been the basis of their own legends had they not been so overshadowed by the singularly horrible crime perpetrated by his grandson.

In any event, due to the senior LaValle's reputation and the new opportunities available to Negroes on the island, it became increasingly difficult for Samuel to persuade his black field hands to continue at the plantation. This despite the more attractive pay offered as a benefit of the Sladeshaw purse strings. The reader should note that by the turn of the century, two fully mature generations of African Americans had been born to freedom. The old ways of the whip were dying quickly, even on Sweetpatch Island.

This is where fact ends—as we can verify it through documentation—and where fancy begins, though much of this is reported by reliable witnesses.

By some accounts (the *Patch Weekly* and the journals of Mr. McDougan and Mrs. Beauchamp), Samuel LaValle was a rakish fellow, very handsome, an excellent and enthusiastic hunter, an innovative businessman, and quite popular among islanders, both black and white. By others, notably the journals of Margaritte Sladeshaw LaValle, he was a mean-spirited, spoiled young man who maintained several adulterous affairs and who may have been slightly mentally retarded. We can guess that the truth may fall somewhere in between. We know he inherited Chaliboque at the age of twenty-one and that he made frequent trips to the mainland without his wife (he is mentioned frequently in the society pages of the Charleston and Savannah papers). He was reported to be a heavy drinker.

In Samuel's employ as an overseer at Chaliboque was an Negro named Joseph or Jojo Tribbit (today, he is sometimes referred to as Joker Tribbit; however, I could find no reference to this name in the accounts of the day). By all accounts, Mr. Tribbit was a man of commanding presence. He was also frequently accompanied by a large and fearsome hound (this is an important point as the reader will soon come to understand).

The following are a few passages from the day, taken verbatim, that include descriptions of this remarkable man:

From a 1906, September 4-10 letter from Mr. Corviasse McDougan to his wife, Emily:

"That great black oversear (sic) Tribbit of LaValle's took into Kasselman's with that hound of his demanding a load of bale wire and cloth. I made mention to Perry Byrd regarding the unnatural girth of the man's shoulders, and Perry speculated it was the part bear in certain breeds of negroe. One of us must have spoke too loud, for the man turned upon us at once. There I swore our apologies, negroe or no, for neither Perry nor me would no more anger that big man than we would stick a finger in a terrapin's maw. When poor Kasselman's new boy gave him a holler, Tribbit gave the lad an icy look. The boy jumped to his own apologies. Tribbit left with his parcels, and Perry and I took the opportunity thereafter to give the boy council (sic) regarding the nature of LaValle's man."

And my personal favorite from the May 8, 1904 entry of Margaritte LaValle's famous journal:

"There is the aura about him that hints of a great nobility, as one might assume of an African chieftain, which may very well have been his birthright were he not orphaned on these shores. The aura collapses, however, once the brute opens his mouth to speak, upon which his guttural efforts are more reminiscent of a great jungle beast. A lion comes to mind, so proud and so ponderously male, or, rather a leopard (black of course) padding stealthily along tree limbs in shadow. I might permit myself to be afraid within my own house to have such hulking savageness tread so freely were it not for the uncommon gentleness so evidenced in Mr. Tribbit's devotion to his strange wife and sweet child and, for whatever obscure purpose, to my husband. Further, he remains a gentleman to me at all times, to the circumscription of his deficient ancestry."

Another important and intriguing figure in this drama is Mr. Tribbit's wife, Bathsheba. She is believed to be his common-law wife, not uncommon for the times. In fact, tales (not documented, alas) report Joseph Tribbit was already married when Bathsheba entered the scene to bewitch him and squeeze out the first Mrs. Tribbit. Another variation has Bathsheba poisoning her predecessor to have the great Chaliboque overseer for herself. Legend informs us that Bathsheba was a voodoo priestess.

While we can expect that Joseph Tribbit was among the first generations of free Negroes born on Sweetpatch Island we are led to believe that Bathsheba appeared on the island after a childhood in the Caribbean (Haiti according to some, Barbados according to others), presumably securing passage aboard one of the many merchant ships that now frequented the island's ports.

She purportedly bragged about her many powers, including "skin-changing," an ability to slip into the skin of other people and even animals. It was a power many witches of the day claimed. The concept is familiar to cultures throughout the world. Variations include the lycanthrope in Eastern Europe and the Wendigo of the Native Americans. Bathsheba Tribbit claimed to be over two hundred years old, having stolen the skins of younger women as she aged, thus achieving immortality.

It is interesting to note that some islanders believed Mrs. Tribbit was a Caucasian or at least half white. This is what was reported to me by both Miss Preston and Mrs. Jackson. Mr. McDougan's letters describe her as a "sand-skinned devil with copper hair and eyes as dark as his (Tribbit's)." Mrs. LaValle's journals, however, use the word "negroe" to describe her in at least three different passages.

Here then, you have the three major characters of our story. Samuel LaValle, the beleaguered plantation owner; Joseph (or Jojo) Tribbit, the fearsome overseer; and Bathsheba Tribbit, the mysterious voodooer. The legend continues:

Somewhere around 1910 or so, with the continuing loss of able-bodied Negro hands to work his plantation, Samuel LaValle struck an extraordinary deal with Jojo Tribbit. He would offer full partnership in Chaliboque in return for Tribbit's management of the workers. Apparently, Tribbit was so respected among the African Americans living on Sweetpatch Island that knowledge of his co-ownership would help to erase the years of enmity the plantation earned under the harsh rule of Victor LaValle's lash. Times must have indeed been desperate for Samuel LaValle. Whether or not this alleged deal actually transpired is not known. There has never been found any record of a change in property ownership. We do know, from references in Mrs. LaValle's journals to "the partnership," that at least the appearance of such an astounding arrangement was announced publicly. And, we may infer from a number of sources that the arrangement, real or not, was successful. At least for a time.

Tragedy struck Chaliboque when Mrs. LaValle died giving birth in April of 1913. She had never been a healthy woman and had suffered a number of prior miscarriages. On this occasion, she had traveled to the home of Mr. LaValle's aunt in Aiken with a trusted housemaid where conditions were not so primitive as they were on the island. The child, a daughter, survived.

Shortly after Samuel returned to Sweetpatch Island with the child, he and Jojo Tribbit had a falling out. Allegations emerged at this time that Joseph Tribbit had raped Margaritte LaValle and bore complicity in her death. This is highly unlikely; in fact, it is almost too cliché to warrant consideration. Also, Mrs. LaValle's journal, which was current almost to the date of her death, gives no hint whatsoever of anything of the sort and in fact is consistent in representing a respectful, if distant, relationship with Mr. Tribbit. Her writings only suggest a rather frail woman who was looking forward with great pleasure to becoming a mother, however ambivalent her feelings toward her husband.

Whatever the reason for the falling out, the consequences were dire for all parties. Charges against both men swept like fire across the island, dividing black and white. Black islanders, hearing Joseph Tribbit was to be arrested for rape, urged him to go into hiding or leave the island. Mr. Tribbit, however, maintained his innocence and refused to leave.

On July 8, 1913, it was not the police but a lynch mob who showed up at the Tribbit house on Sadfellers beach.

The mob was led by Samuel LaValle.

The reader should note that during this period of the South's history, grisly tales of Negro lynchings abound. Many communities throughout the area, tragically, have similar such bloody chapters in their histories. And, as a result, legends bearing remarkable similarities to "The Beast of the Patch" are found throughout the region. Some may have their own origins; others may owe their roots to the savagery and madness that struck Sweetpatch Island over July 8th and 9th of 1913 and the weeks that followed.

This is how it ended for Joseph Tribbit according to legend and the testimony of Miss Preston and Mrs. Jackson, both of whom were alive at the time. (Although neither claimed to have seen the lynching in its entirety, as one would assume no Negro could have.)

As the great hound howled (presumably chained), the mob dragged Joseph Tribbit from his house. Bathsheba was either dragged out with him or followed the mob on her own. The mob beat Joseph and Bathsheba. Tribbit was then hanged from the limb of an oak tree. The tree, not far from Sadfellers beach, became known as "Joker's Gallows" and stood until 1958 when it was cut down by persons unknown.

Following the hanging, the lynch mob built a bonfire nearby. They threw Joseph's body into the fire. Stories say either the mob or Bathsheba then dragged out his body, and Joseph's dog was then set free to eat his remains. Another version has the dog attacking Bathsheba as she tried to stop the desecration of her husband's body. The dog was then shot and thrown into the same fire.

The only witnesses to the actual lynching, other than Bathsheba, would have been members of the lynch mob themselves, and certainly none of them ever stepped forward publicly to describe what happened. The details, we can assume, were either spun out of fantasy or are the result of the quiet talk of the participants passed through the years, or some combination of both.

In the weeks that followed the death of Joseph Tribbit, Samuel LaValle was purportedly haunted by his ghost. According to Negro witnesses, the shade of Mr. Tribbit or his hound or both (somehow magically combined into one frightening monster) was frequently seen wandering Sadfellers beach at night during this time. Mrs. Jackson reports having a personal encounter with "Joker" Tribbit one week after he was killed.

> "Had my baby brother, Beanie, by the hand. Just fetched him off the Soap Water. He was fishing back there. Momma sent me down to fetch him, cause it was getting toward night, and some folks had seen old Joker by then. So Momma was scared for Beanie and made me go after him. We were walking along the bluff, and it was already mostly dark. Moon wasn't up yet. A man come walking up from where the water come up on the sand. Big man in raggedy clothes, and I knew right off it was Joker. I'd seen enough of him when he was alive to know who he was dead. Well sir, I can tell you I was just too scared to do a thing, to run or jump or drop dead myself. Same for Beanie, except he had such

a hold on my hand I thought he was gonna pull it off. Old Joker walked himself right up to us, just as real as you sitting there. Thought he was gonna reach out and take the two of us with him. Then he said to me 'Gimme that child.' It was old Joker's growling voice, too. A body ain't likely to forget that voice. Only he sound sad, and I ain't never heard big Joker Tribbit sound sad when he was alive. Beanie screamed and run off, and that got me to running, too."

On April 26th, a little more than two weeks after the lynching, Samuel LaValle also died. Already known to be a heavy drinker, his drinking had apparently become even heavier (from guilt perhaps? or the nocturnal visits of the Joker?). It is believed he drank himself to death, although it is certainly possible he was poisoned by a vengeful member of his house staff or Bathsheba herself.

He was found in the morning by a housemaid. According to legend (this was not mentioned in newspaper accounts of his death, for obvious reasons) his body had been partially eaten by the mysterious "Beast" during the night.

Not long after Samuel LaValle's funeral, a fire swept through the Chaliboque Mansion, destroying a good part of it. We can only guess how the fire was started. It was likely an act of arson carried out by another vengeful individual; however, legend prefers to believe it was Joseph or Bathsheba performing one last fiery act of revenge.

Shortly afterward, Bathsheba Tribbit disappeared from the island altogether with what remained of her family. She emerged several years later on the mainland in the rural town of Kowe, South Carolina, where she began a ministry, which she ran until her passing in 1946.

Ownership of what remained of the Chaliboque Plantation passed to the Sladeshaw family in Statesboro, Georgia. The property was later sold to the Savannah law firm of Campion & Saachs and eventually divided and sold in parcels.

That might be the end of the story were the ghost of Joker Tribbit willing to rest so easily. But the frightening circumstances of his death and the conveniently soon-to-follow demise of Samuel LaValle made too big an impression on an already superstitious local population. Stories abound during this period of people running into the ghost of Joker Tribbit (similar to Mrs. Jackson's account). Large dogs or packs of dogs were seen in the night, supposedly animated by the spirit of Joseph Tribbit. Scarce is the local child on the island today who does not have a great aunt or uncle claiming to have seen one of these specters.

Tales specifically about "The Beast" or "Sheba's Curse" became more prevalent after 1934 (twenty-one years after the lynchings and Samuel LaValle's death) when a wild animal attacked several people over the course of two months in South Patch. Accounts in the *Patch Weekly* report that six people were injured and one killed by "The Beast." Of course, many of the superstitious locals believed this was the spirit of Joker Tribbit, joined in crime by his skin-changing wife. During this time, several mongrel dogs and a few alligators were shot by locals during ad-hoc hunting forays scouring South Patch for "The Beast."

In the years since, "The Beast" has been sighted any number of times, in any number of forms, and in any number of places throughout the island. As recently as 1971, a mauling death was attributed to "The Beast."

As of this writing, what is left of the Chaliboque Mansion still stands (or, to be more correct, crumbles) on the bluffs overlooking Yamawichee Sound. The older locals still...

And then, for no conscious reason, he picked that moment to look up from the pages, and he saw the ghost passing.

~four

By the time he made the footbridge, the girl was gone. His wrestling match with the crowd brought back a sense of normalcy. It wasn't a ghost he was looking for anymore; it was just a girl. Curiosity, he told himself; he just wanted another look—a better look this time, so he could be certain. He picked off his sunglasses, making lighthouse turns and craning to see over sunburned heads. On Merganser Boulevard he picked around more milling and perspiring bodies. Still not seeing her, he decided to work toward the line of shops.

By the time he entered The T-shirt Palace, the chase had gone stale and his sense of urgency faded. The shop was a stadium of shirts looming in rows several tiers high. *Over 2,000 Iron-Ons—You Choose.* A faint burnt-plastic odor rode a mechanical breeze.

"Looks like you could use a new shirt!"

He turned—a teenager was smiling her braces at him. A tag was pinned to her blouse: *Sheryl Hennessey.*

"Know where I could find one?" he asked.

The girl hesitated, then freed the glinting silver and giggled. "Oh, I sure hope so! What do you like?"

She gave him a tour through the shop. Boo looked at the onion skin sheaves of decals papering the walls and draping the ceiling from strings. The selection over his head was devoted to various cartoon hot rods. Dewey Fitch, he remembered, had worn a shirt with a roadster decal day after day one summer until it disintegrated off his back. Something about a purple people eater, he seemed to recall—and then a brilliant golden-red flashed two aisles away.

The ghost, at first in profile, turned briefly toward him, eyes glistening. Vacant, without recognition. A dispassionate wet luster that shivered through him. And then the eyes swept on somewhere else.

His breath returned.

It was the same girl who had dreamed past him on Dock Street. But it was *not* the girl he had supposed she could be. Of *course*, she wasn't that girl.

At his side, the clerk waited. "Maybe this one?" she offered and shuffled to a navy blue shirt on the rack. As he half-glanced again at the red-haired girl two aisles over (also a teenager; and yes, see the differences?) Sheryl held up the T-shirt for him. Stick Jamaican figures struck various poses of dance. *Jam'n on the Patch* in big letters, *Sweetpatch Island, S.C.* in smaller ones.

"It's fine," he said.

"Is the color okay? It comes in other colors."

"The color's fine."

The girl across the aisle turned again to profile. The rich, scarlet-gold hair was the same, but the jawline was a rounded compromise. The nose too slight. The lips too thin. Not the same.

"This is a medium; you couldn't get it over your head. Are you a large or an extra large?"

Boo coughed, looked down again. "Extra large, I guess."

"Take both." Sheryl pulled two shirts from the rack and held them out to him, then sent him off toward the changing booths at the back of the shop.

In the booth, he slipped off his ruined golf shirt, drew a few deep breaths, and looked in the mirror. *His* face in the glass, *his* scarred right hand. He could see the thrum of his heartbeat beneath the heavy muscle of his chest. *Nothing is wrong*, he chanted silently, *nothing is wrong*. He looked at his shirt, damp with sweat and stained chocolate brown. Then, he crawled into the extra large T-shirt, inhaling the tang of new cotton and dye, the stiff fabric scratching his skin.

He left the booth and went to the cash register, searching for the young clerk. He spotted her chatting with another customer and was about to call for her when a voice spoke from his side. "May I ring you up, sir?"

It was the red-haired girl, coming toward him.

She smiled at him, her eyes on him, and it *couldn't* be her—these eyes, though very pretty, were brown, not green.

But the smile had the same brilliant, effortless allure. And the skin glowed with the same copper-penny shimmer. And now he was confused again. She slipped behind the counter and he followed the curve of hip, the slope of shoulder, the sway of hair and tried to believe it was not her. He handed her the price tag.

"Fourteen fifty," she said; the voice was deeper but curled with the same low-country tartness. "You want me to bag that old thing—or burn it?" She nodded at his blue golf shirt, and again that smile.

"Bag it, I guess," he said, unable to help his own smile. He reached for his wallet and handed her a credit card. The girl turned to the register, then quickly turned back—and now it was her turn to stare. She flapped his card up to his face.

"Robert Lee Taylor—you're not *Boo* Taylor, are you!"

"Yes."

"Oh my Lord, I *thought* I recognized you from somewhere! I saw you on the street and I thought—why, I've seen *pictures* of you. From when you were a boy."

"You . . . " and then he saw the name tag.

Georgia Ransome.

"Oh," he said. He stared at her again and registered all the compromises in the girl's features. This was, he decided, much worse than a ghost.

"I just *knew* it. You know, Momma talks about you all the time!"

He smiled awkwardly at the girl across the counter. And as she handed the card back to him, and as he realized for the first time the perfect face before him was not scarred—the only evidence he ever needed to know this really wasn't Gussie Dutton. The girl sweetly asked him, "Lord, what on earth happened to your hand?"

He took Sandy to an early dinner at a restaurant on Dock Street. She was in a new outfit: lime green blouse and white skirt. Shopping bags were piled next to her chair. Their table overlooked the mouth of Mermaids Head Creek where the sun was in its decline and flood tide was peaking.

"Where's a good place to watch the sunset?"

He dimly registered her question. "Here, I suppose," he managed. She was suddenly a complete stranger.

"No, I mean someplace without so many people. Someplace *private*."

Over her shoulder, he now saw the letters. They had been there all along but only now came together in his mind. On the old concrete sea wall.

PLEASE I STIL LOVE YOU

Thick letters brushed in black paint a foot high. The words, lonely, were just above the high-water line as if they had slithered up for air from the soft mud bottom of the creek, like one of the shapeless dark things that crept there and could make it no further in the harsh light of sun.

Desperate and haunted. Pleading.

Please, I still love you!

Drips of black paint running like blood or dark tears into the water. Words from a Don Henley song came to him, mournful but still managing to be angry, something about a desperate lover leaving his mark on some solitary rock. *Baby I've changed, please come back*. . . Come back.

Please come back. . .please, I still love you!

His heart ached and throbbed with the certainty the words were left there for him.

Carefully, Sandy asked, "You okay?"

"Sure. I'm thinking."

That's how it felt, he was thinking. *That's how it felt to be with her. How could you have forgotten that?*

five

(Thud! Shuddering up the bones of his arms. I killed it!)

He couldn't sleep. Sandy's heat and the persistent, half-slumbered dreams made the bed a shrimper's net of constraining, brine-soaked sheets. He kicked himself loose and set his feet on the floor.

He rubbed his temples.

Sweating, his flesh coiled under layers of copper-spun flame.

He tottered to his feet and left the room.

He wandered downstairs into his father's office and sat in the heavy, leather chair.

The desk lamp cast an inadequate light against the quiet and loneliness of night. *Your father is dead.* Had that really been just two nights ago? The world was playing tricks with him, cutting and pasting time in nonsensical patterns. A phone call *(a thud in a rainstorm)* two nights ago was ancient history. A flicker of a girl's red hair erased an entire quarter-century. Yesterday had become the summer of 1971, and that left today in utter confusion.

His let his hands roam over the mahogany surface of the desk, picking at various items in a semiconscious effort to discover clues to his father's life and death. An old coffee mug brimming with leaky pens. An empty ashtray and empty pipe. A sixties-era rotary phone, dull black and heavy as a brick—clumsy and incongruous beside a new computer. He could smell the man here, in the fragrance of wood and leather, in the musty medical texts, in the surface of these objects.

He trundled open desk drawers and dug through the forty years of bric-a-brac, stirring more of his dead father's musty essence into the room. Files of old documents, many age-yellowed and brittle. Anonymous keys. Book after book of blank checks. Several items he could not explain: a collection of porcelain thimbles, a *Carter-Mondale '76* button (the doctor had been a steadfast Republican since the sixties), a soft-core porn paperback, and an expensive looking set of pearl earrings.

In the lowest left drawer were hundreds of photographs, stacked neatly on edge. Some were only months old. Some were ancient, sepia-toned blurs. He picked through the photographs and caught glimpses of his youth.

He withdrew one creased square to study under the desk's spotlight. Laylee Colebriar, standing before a great magnolia tree. An empty clothesline ran over her head. Her eyes were on the grass. (She never looked into a camera, she once told him, because pictures took a bite out of your soul and were a frequent ingredient in black magic.) A clean white apron wrapped her waist. Bangled bracelets, dozens on each wrist. Saddle shoes, two sizes too big, bent clumsily inward. Sweat gleamed from her sweet, butterscotch face, her neck.

He slipped the picture into his shirt pocket. Then he shuffled again through the stack. Here was ten-year-old Boo Taylor standing like a shy midget next to a sad mountain giant, both squinting into an unseen sun and holding a string of silvery fish. He remembered a long-ago trip with the doctor to the Smokey Mountains. A gentle old giant lived there in a cabin next to a stream. Old Ben was the giant's name. Old Ben had shown him how to tie a fly, *tried* to show him how to tease the fly over the ice-cold water's surface with poetic, slow-motion waves of his magic fishing rod.

He tucked the picture of himself and Old Ben into his shirt pocket, and it slipped neatly beside the photograph of Laylee Colebriar.

A light blinked on from somewhere at the front of the house. He looked up to see a weak amber light filling the frame of the office door. Another light, closer, clicked on, and the glow at the door brightened. Slippered feet shuffled toward him, dusting the floor. Then a shadow touched the wall outside the office.

"If that's a thief in there,"—his mother's voice—"I think you should know I am carrying a very large pistol."

"Mine's bigger," he called back.

MaeEllen Taylor appeared in the door in a rumpled and stale robe, her hair dry and lopsided.

"Mom," he said cheerily and noted her frown, "You've got your days and nights backward. Bess is gone, but I can whip you up some eggs if you want breakfast."

"The only breakfast I require at the moment," she said flatly, "is a glass of Knob Creek and some ice." She shuffled the rest of the way into the office.

"Wrong room for the liquor cabinet. You were looking for the liquor cabinet, weren't you?"

She settled into one of the armchairs across from him. In the antique yellow of the desk light, her skin was dull paste, her eyes were raw and glazed, drooping like a sad dog's. "I am guessing that is another cleverly disguised, smartass insinuation," she said. "Believe me, I know very well where the liquor cabinet is. And I am equally well acquainted with the many interesting bottles of pills your father keeps in his cabinets back here."

"I'm sure you are," he said.

She glared back, challenging him with her bruised, watery eyes. "He kept the pills locked, but I have my own personal key," she said. "I had it made in secret. Your father knew about it, of course, but he was gentleman enough to not mention it. I keep it tied to a little string around my neck so I will be sure to find it in emergencies. Would you like to see it?" She grinned fiercely at him, trying to show him some of her old iciness, but all he saw was the warm droop of her eyes.

"No thank you," he said. He flipped through the stack of photographs and plucked out a serrated rectangle. He tossed it across the desk—a much younger MaeEllen Taylor, dressed in her Sunday finery, standing beside slim, handsome Dr. Taylor. Boo watched his mother take in this image, watched the fleshy lines sag. She sighed.

"We have to talk about your finances," he said. "Eventually. I'm meeting with Matt Dufette on Thursday if it's okay with you. I'll tell him no, if you'd rather I didn't."

"By all means, please go ahead." she said and waved the back of her hand at him. "When Matthew Dufette starts talking about money, I do not understand half the things that come out of that man's mouth. I had the same problem with your father, for that matter."

"You're a millionaire," Boo told her. "Several times over, in fact. Seems the doctor became a real estate baron while I was gone."

"It was mostly Matt's doing; your father just went along for the ride," she said and smiled wistfully. Then, with sudden interest, "Millions? Exactly how many?"

Boo pursed his lips. "Somewhere between twelve and fifteen, as near as I can figure it." The enormity of this fortune was still boggling his mind. "I guess the tourists can thank Matt and the doctor for all those golf courses and gift shops."

MaeEllen wagged a hand at him. "They can thank Osgood Satterfield for most of that. He wound up owning two-thirds of the island before Matt got wind of what he was up to and talked your father into retiring so those two scoundrels could snap up whatever Osgood hadn't gotten his greedy little hands on yet."

"Taylor Dufette Realty," Boo said. "I suppose the land in South Patch was a particular bargain."

"Did you know," MaeEllen was saying, "your father would go on and on about some girl named Fannie Mae, and I thought he was talking about Martha Whitley's girl, Frances. She's Frances Mae—Frances Mae Butler now; married some farmer." She placed the photograph back on the desk. Boo saw that she left it facing her, and that her eyes didn't leave it. "Deviled me why your father would get so worked up over a forty-year-old girl with buckteeth living in Yamassee."

Boo flipped the photograph of himself and the old man across the desk. "Who's that man?"

MaeEllen's glance was cursory. "I'm sure I have no idea."

"The doctor took me to his place in the mountains once. You remember that time?"

"No."

"We were gone a whole week. You don't remember?"

"Vaguely." She was bored.

"So, who is he?"

"A patient. I don't know." She inhaled, and it sounded mournful. Then glanced at him. "So why aren't you upstairs in bed with that pretty little girl you brought with you?"

Boo smiled and took the picture back. "Mother, I am shocked. You know I would never sleep with a girl under your roof."

"I know nothing of the sort. So what's wrong with this one?"

"Who says there's anything wrong?"

"I do. She is being far too nice to me. She's afraid of losing you, and she is being nice to me to win points. I suppose either of us could tell her how fruitless that strategy is going to be." MaeEllen looked at him, pleased with herself. "So what is it? What's wrong with her?"

"There's nothing wrong with her."

"Maybe she's talking about marriage? Maybe she's talking about children? Or is it some other horror?" MaeEllen was on a roll. She leaned back in the chair, letting her dull hair splay against the backrest. "What do they say that sends you running?"

"You're assuming I'm the one that runs. Generally, it's the other way around."

"Really? I find that hard to believe."

"I tell them I had a damaged childhood and haven't seen my parents in fifteen years. It shows a certain disregard for family and commitment."

"It has been nineteen years," she said, "as I have already reminded you several times. You know, I didn't recognize you when you walked in last night. I thought you were a policeman. You got bigger around the shoulders, and your hair is thinning." She sighed. "At least you didn't get your nose pierced or something dreadful like that."

"I did get a tattoo," he said.

"No, you did not. You would never do such a thing."

"You'd like it; it's a heart that says 'Mom.' It's on my left butt cheek."

She gave him a leaden look. "I see you've become a comedian. I have to assume it was your stellar wit that attracted that pretty young girl. And you haven't answered my question. She looks frail, is that it?"

"She's tougher than she looks. She's an orphan, did I tell you?"

"How tragic."

"You think I'm joking."

"I *know* you are joking. Where is she from?"

"I don't know."

"You don't know," she said dully.

"Originally, somewhere in the South, I think. She slips into a very nasty drawl when she gets mad."

MaeEllen was incredulous. "You don't know where she's from?"

"She doesn't like to talk much about her childhood. I suppose we have that in common."

MaeEllen ignored this. "So you don't know where she's from; what *do* you know?"

Boo considered changing the subject. He glanced down at a boyhood photograph of himself and Hoss Beaudry, arms slung companionably about each others' naked shoulders before a glaring Atlantic background. One tall and sturdy, one pasty and plump. *Hated one and liked the other,* he recalled. "Her parents died young," he said, "so she was raised in foster homes. She got through law school by working as a stripper."

MaeEllen Taylor made a contemptuous sound in her throat. "And where did she go to school?"

"I don't know. Somewhere in New York, I think—or New Jersey."

"You don't—"

"I didn't *ask* because it isn't important to me. And to be perfectly honest, *she* isn't as important to me as she likes to pretend."

"So, it isn't serious?"

"That depends if you're using her definition or mine."

MaeEllen closed her eyes and shook her head lightly, a hint of a sarcastic smile stretched her lips. "That," she said, "is a shame. You two should make a fine couple. Two orphans. Two stray kittens. I am sure you have a lot in common." She appeared ready to push up from the chair and then stopped herself. Her mood suddenly softened. "You know, Boo, you could certainly stay here and look after your father's business. I am sure there's quite enough to keep you busy."

"Is that what you want?"

"It's what I just suggested, isn't it?"

"What do I know about real estate?"

She grimaced. "What do you think your *father* knew? He hired *people* for that—and just looked over things, I assume to keep them honest. You can do that."

Boo carefully placed the photograph of Hoss Beaudry back on the desk. "I have my own business, thank you. Anyway, I'm sure Matt Dufette will make a generous offer to buy you out."

"Matthew Dufette will not live forever, either—and I may not choose to sell. And have you considered the fact that you are also a millionaire? That money has always been yours, too."

"No," he said flatly.

"What are you saying 'no' to?"

"I'm saying I don't want a job. Or your money."

MaeEllen looked at him closely, her rheumy eyes glistening with hurt and anger. The house made a few settling tics. A floor fan rattled from one of the front rooms.

Then she clenched her lips, sending angry, old-lady ripples across her mouth. "I see your sense of gratitude has not improved with age," she said, and this time she did finish pushing up from the chair. "Now, if my bitter, smart-ass of a son doesn't mind, I am going to get my drink."

She clutched the front of her robe together and shuffled to the office door. Boo watched her fade past the dim circle of light at the desk. The room felt suddenly empty. Boo sat at the desk for what he thought was a long time, the night around him as still and silent as before—yet seemingly filled with some clanging vibration, as if MaeEllen's departure consisted of the aftereffect of the gong of a giant bell. Looking around, he now didn't like the look of the darkness surrounding him. He realized he was sitting in a dead man's seat, in a dead man's chambers—and in the barrel-bottom of night, perhaps that wasn't the best place to be.

At last, he got up and gathered the remaining photographs from the desktop. He stacked them together and tucked them back in their place in the drawer.

He found MaeEllen in the kitchen.

The bruised eyes considered him for a moment with fear—as if she expected an attack—then with a tired and frigid sort of surrender. She was leaning against the counter and holding a medium-sized glass filled with ice and what Boo presumed was bourbon. Watching her stand there in her bed-crumpled robe, she looked like a part of the house, and he felt more and more detached from it. He must look like an intruder to her, he thought, a gangster from the North come to spoil her simple Southern world.

"How did he die?" he asked.

She took a slow drink, her bleary eyes gleaming at him above the rim of her glass. He wondered if she would answer. "Heart attack," she said at last, words like a knife scraped over rock. "I'm sure I told you that."

"But when did it happen? Where was he?" Not in this house, he knew—and saw again the silent, eyes-squeezed scream echoing from the cool shadows at the funeral home.

"One of his properties," she answered. "On Culpepper Road. I told him not to go down there, that ugly place."

"What place? What are you talking about?"

"One of those *homes* he rented," she said listlessly. "Not much better than a tenement. Did you know we have tenements now on Sweetpatch Island? Well we do, and your father became a slum lord."

"I never heard of Culpepper Road," he said. "In South Patch?"

She nodded and swirled the ice in her glass.

"What was he doing down there?"

"Some woman. She owed back rent, I suppose, and skipped out." She took another swallow. "One of the neighbors called the office late Friday afternoon to report a prowler. Silas assumed it was the tenant and went down to see for himself."

She set her drink on the kitchen countertop. Boo watched the palsy shudder of her hand, the violent tinkling of ice, and was reminded that his mother had truly become an old woman.

"So who found him?"

"I told him not to bother," MaeEllen continued. "It was getting late, and I did not like him going down there with all of those…when it's so *late*. A sixty-nine-year-old white man in South Patch at night, all alone, can you imagine? We have people to do those things, I told him. That's what we *pay* them for."

She closed her eyes. Boo waited for her to continue.

"When it got late, I called Augusta Ransome and she called the police. They said—"

Boo started—"Why would you call Gussie Ransome?"

MaeEllen Taylor was momentarily drawn from her memories. "You didn't know, did you?" she asked quietly. "She is your father's office manager—for the last ten years at least. I suppose she runs the place as much as anyone does."

Boo scowled at this. Then he realized his mother was watching him closely. He sighed heavily. "Okay. You called Gussie."

"And she called the police," MaeEllen continued. "The place was a horrible mess, they said. Broken furniture, food left out for days. They found Silas in an upstairs room."

She stopped to fight off a sob, the lines of her forehead and between her eyes folding deeply with the effort. The sob escaped her anyway. Boo quickly moved to pull a paper towel from the rack and handed it to her. MaeEllen dabbed her nose and eyes as Boo tried to picture his skinny, dignified father crumpled like a sack of rags on the floor of some tenement in South Patch.

"He was holding onto a phone," MaeEllen said, pushing herself through her sobs. "Of course the phone was out, like the power. They say he was holding it so tight they couldn't pry his fingers from it. The ambulance people had to do it." Then she looked at him fiercely, challenging him. "And before you hear it from everybody else, he was also stark naked."

Boo flinched—a combination of this revelation and MaeEllen's ferocity. He was about to ask her to repeat what she had said, then decided he had heard her clearly already.

He breathed in heavily. MaeEllen was glaring at him so violently that he averted his eyes. "So you think he was having an affair with this woman?"

MaeEllen exploded: "Boo Taylor, your father was *not* having an affair! Not with some *tenant* and not with *anyone else!*"

Boo glanced up. The glass in her hand was going to shatter if she gripped it any harder. The bags beneath her eyes were shiny with tears.

"Your father," she said evenly, "did not have affairs."

"Of course he did." It was out before he realized it. *You know damn well he did.*

MaeEllen Taylor's entire body was hitching, and he was afraid she would collapse. He tried to put his arm around her, but she pushed him away. He tried again, this time taking her by the shoulder, and she let him guide her to a chair at the kitchen table. When she was seated, he took the glass of bourbon from the counter and placed it before her.

He leaned against the counter and waited. MaeEllen took a short drink. She gazed frantically around the room until her teary eyes rested pleadingly upon him. "Can you imagine that, Boo?" Her voice was shredded and mournful. "Silas all alone—and in pain and dying. In the dark."

Imagine it? Hadn't he seen it in a dream?

MaeEllen was sobbing again. Boo touched her trembling head and gently stroked her hair as he recalled words the doctor once spoke to him: "You might want to consider how heroic she's been."

Some time later, he helped her back to bed.

And an hour after that, he kicked awake again, hearing the phantom ring of a telephone. In a moment of terrified disorientation, he looked around for the glowing red numbers of his alarm clock, then looked across the room, expecting to find Sandy's naked silhouette at the window.

Boo, someone's out there. He was looking in.

But Sandy was in bed next to him, fast asleep.

His heart settled. He was in his parents' house. He was home. He watched the rise and fall of Sandy's breaths and remembered his mother's admonition: *You don't know where she's from?*

You don't know?

He sat up, set his feet on the floor. He held his face in his hands for a moment. Then reached over to the nightstand and picked up the two photographs he had tossed there. In the dim moonglow he could not see the images now, but he remembered them. An old black woman, smiling uncertainly at the ground. An old mountain man holding out a trophy of silvery fish. Was it true, he wondered? Did the camera really take bites out of your soul?

He thought of an old photograph of Martin Luther King shaking the perfect, unscarred hand of a little white boy, and a little while later, he was able to sleep.

six

Mid-October in the Great Smokey Mountains.

An unreliable season in the hills—like high summer during the day, becoming a sneaky winter when the sun went down.

Ben Shallcross, eighty-four years old, had been witness to the turn of the mountain's seasons time and again, seasons of life and seasons of death, cycling over and over and marking the persistent throb of the earth's pulse. He had seen a great many things in that time. A lot of it good. Some of it bad. And a few things that were unspeakable. And in this final season of his long life, Ben Shallcross had begun seeing ghosts.

❖ ❖ ❖

"Say Ben, you old cooter, you fixin to stay hid in these hills forever?"

He had heard that question, or some form of it, maybe a thousand times.

He was about to answer: *No Russ, I'm packin t'night, and Alma says she's leaving your tired old bones and comin with me*—but of course that couldn't be Russ asking. Russell Cooper had died in 1984 when his heart gave out watching a Falcon's game in Sal Marco's bar in Gatlinburg. That was two years after Alma's lingering TB had come to a blessed end.

Just another voice in his head, he thought.

But he turned, and there was Russell's grandson, Elton—and Ben now remembered that Elton had stopped by the cabin to put up the storm windows and was taking the opportunity to fuss at him about moving out of his drafty old cabin. Elton wanted him to move down hill to Packersburg to bunk at the Cooper Ranch with him and Eva and their kids. The ranch was a nice enough place, but Ben knew a young family like that didn't need a doddering old fool messing up their works. Anyway, he'd been on his own for too long to ever feel comfortable calling someplace "home" where you ate supper when someone else told you to, and where you had to shut the door when you wanted to use the toilet.

"Stay hid? Expect I might, Elty, 'less you got a reason why not."

Elton grinned through the thick red puff of his beard. "All kinds'a reasons, old timer. It's a big world out there."

"Is it? Well now, I seen enough of it in my day, I guess. Figure I can see all I want of it from my front porch."

Ben, sipping black coffee from a tin cup, considered the matter further.

Hiding? Was he really hiding?

Quietly—quiet enough so Elton couldn't hear—he mumbled into his coffee, "...sometimes, boy, you just find your spot and hunker down."

He recalled another question he'd been asked:

"Hey Ben, what's worst you ever been afraid?"

He'd heard *that* question only once, years and years ago—and that time, it really had been Russell Cooper who'd done the asking. Heard it just that one time, though he found he repeated it to himself often. It seemed he knew the answer. Because hadn't there been a time...?

The worst he'd ever been afraid?

But for the life of him, he couldn't remember.

❖ ❖ ❖

Late afternoon.

Elton had finished the windows, and now Ben was on a hike across an open field. The day had turned damp, and that was wreaking havoc with the cold that had been clogging his lungs for what seemed like weeks. He moved methodically and delicately, trusting his bulk on the oak staff that bowed under him.

His broad shadow touched the tree line, and he stopped.

He had been watching the ground for tangles of bramble and hadn't dared to look at his surroundings, not even to see the preacher bird who'd been singing to him for the last twenty minutes. But now, coming to this unexpected stand of trees, he looked up.

A black cavern of forest beckoned him.

He turned, pulling the pulpy Stetson from his head and using it to shield the glare of the dying sun as he looked around to the rolling slopes of timothy and bluegrass from which he'd just come. Then back to the trees in a stumbling circle, looking for a color-coded blaze on one of the trunks but not finding one.

He squinted.

Drew his mouth half open as if to ponder a riddle.

None of what he saw looked the least bit familiar.

Ben Shallcross had crisscrossed the paths of these hills day after day since time out of mind. For a time, he did his hiking in a green park ranger's uniform. In those days, his mutt dog, Willie, kicked along at his heels or chased up fowl when he made his rounds. Then Willie died, and soon after Ben left the Park Service for his pension—so now he walked the trails alone. He hadn't kept count of the years he'd spent in the mountains, but it was generally acknowledged in the tiny crossroad burgs speckling the foothills that he knew them better than any man since the last Cherokee was hauled away, kicking and whooping, back in '48. *Ask Old Ben,* the locals would say, *he knows the hills.* Old Ben who knew the quickest way to get from here to there and the ways with the overlooks that made you dizzy, the streams where brookies still wrestled so thick you could pluck one out with your hand, the coves where coons romped alongside of beavers, the bushes with the plumpest blackberries, the springs with water so sweet you'd swear it was honey. Old Ben who knew the spiderweb trails of these hills as well as the spiderweb blue veins on the back of his hand.

And now here was that same old Ben at the mouth of a dark gulf of woods he could swear to Jesus-on-the-cross he'd never seen before.

He peered in. Caught glimpse of a shadow cavorting between birch trunks.

He fixed the Stetson back on his head and started in.

"Gettin feeb, are you, Ben?" he hears Russell Cooper asking him. "Can't tell your rights from your lefts anymore."

"Don't I know it," Ben answers. "Getting worrisome, all that forgettin."

"Forgettin..." Forgetting to put gas in the pickup and having to hitch a ride all the way to Packersburg to collect his pension check. Forgetting his frozen french fries were cooking in Crisco—and nearly burning his cabin to the ground.

There is that kind of forgetting—forgetting to do things...and of course there is the other kind of forgetting.

The other kind he tries not to think about too much because it is just too awful.

How long you been holed up in these mountains, Ben?

Where'd you come from, Ben?

Where's your home?

Hey Ben, what's the worst you ever been afraid?

The worst . . .

He can't remember. Memories lost, torn out of the book and cast to the wind.

His father is a name, but a face he cannot see.

His mother is a vague fragrance of a woman with neither a name nor a face.

How can he not remember them but still have a vivid recollection of his Grandpa Ike—that thunderous elf with his Abe Lincoln beard (he remembers the beard precisely) and whom young-boy Ben had seen no more than a dozen times before he died in 1924? How can he forget the name of the town where he grew up (just the whiff of it, like salt and spoiled eggs) but still see the street number painted in rough, white strokes on the mailbox that was hammered to the front gate? How can he forget how he had gotten that ragged, three-inch scar on his left thigh? Or remember, clear as yesterday, when Eustis Meggett shot his daddy's milk cows one by one on Halloween day back in '28—but be unable to recall a single, blasted Christmas before 1958?

Forgetting.

Memories.

Just those incomplete, floating scraps, like the early-autumn leaves that flick and twirl about him in this unknown stretch of wood—just glimpsed, but not long enough to wrap his fingers around them. Like those leaves, little scraps of dry, dead matter.

And like those leaves, scattered by the chill winds of a dying season.

He had already broken several of the rules he gave to the weekend hikers when he'd been a ranger.

The first rule was to never hike alone. Well, he had been hiking alone for decades and that rule was for the folks who didn't know the trails like he did. Or thought he did.

The second rule was to stay calm if you got lost. Aside from the early grumblings of panic, he thought maybe he was handling that one just fine.

The third rule was to not venture down any trail you weren't sure of. *That* one, he was breaking with every step. He was not at all sure of this trail—certainly, if he'd ever been on it before, he'd now somehow managed to forget it. This far north was still state land, he was fairly sure, and the trails were supposed to be marked with colored blazes. But he hadn't seen a single blaze since stepping off the bald.

Now, he was worrying about the fourth rule:

If you were fool enough to get lost at night, stay put and stay warm.

The dimming light of early evening filtered through the trees and flickered off the wings of the insects scattering before his passage. The canopy blocked too much of the sky to judge the time accurately. And of course, he'd forgotten his watch. Six o'clock? he wondered. Later than that?

Head down, watching his feet, he blundered steadily onward. Small animals pattered in the leaf fall. Somewhere close by, a pair of warblers burred a ruckus. He listened to these sounds, listened to his breath coming in ragged puffs. A tickle rose in his chest on spider legs. He cleared his throat roughly. The tickle rose further, now on bird claws, and he had to hold himself up by his staff while he spluttered a hoarse, painful string of coughs.

He spat and took a moment to catch his breath.

When he looked up again, he found himself in a cool forest grotto, standing on a crest and overlooking a small pond.

Then, a magical thing occurred: the woods came alive. Dead leaves lifted in a thousand orange-yellow-black flutterings, lifting, dancing, gently tapping the air all at once.

Butterflies, he realized. Thousands of them.

Monarchs—it was the time of their annual migration, and they filled this secret forest like a calico rain, like a thousand tropical bird feathers tossed into the air. Microscopic scales on their wings reflected an odd luminescence in the diminishing light, flickering on and off, sprinkling rainbow dust into the trees.

It was as if the woods had caught fire.

He watched, entranced by this silent spell, this private spectacle of floating plumage.

Smiling, he trod softly to a chair-sized grayback that was splattered with lichens and sulfur. He sat on its cool surface to watch the colorful whisper-troupe perform on its pond stage.

Breathing easier now.

Wondering, but no longer worrying, how he managed to find himself in this magical place. The water beneath the butterfly parade was swollen by the untended tangle of an ancient beaver dam; a glittering mist veiled its shore. No empty beer cans here or tire tracks or spray painted rocks. No tourist tents with their port-a-potties and their Coleman gas stoves and their crackling radios. Far away from the signs of man. Unspoiled, like the first-growth wilds he remembered from his earliest days in the mountains.

How long ago, Ben? How long ago was that?

Hadn't he been to this crest before? Though far from certain, he did sense some dim recollection of it. On some other occasion, without this fine flutter-dance of monarchs. Perhaps sometime long ago. Perhaps in another season.

He placed the staff on the rock and kneaded the knots in his thighs. A fit of coughs tore through him; he bent into it; rode it, and at last it passed.

Still, the butterflies danced.

He closed his eyes.

Yes, breathing much easier, now.

Sorting out the puzzle of getting home, taking deep breaths. Listening to the soft strokes of wings beneath him.

" *...hey, Ben...?*"

Hearing, even softer, the tremor of his paper-skinned heart.

" …Ben, what's the worst…?"

Hearing, softest yet, a whispered voice from the past:

"…the worst you ever been afraid?"

That question.

That awful question.

It is Russell Cooper who asks it—in the same tavern where, three years later, Russell will fall over dead in his Lone Star Beer. On this day, however, Ben is leaning over an easy shot at the ten ball, ready to drop it and call the game—and then Russ speaks up with that question, and Ben straightens up to look at him, expecting to see that old boy smiling his big, horsey grin because he found some trick to get Ben to miss a gimme shot.

But Russell is not smiling. Because Alma, his wife of forty-two years, is down in that college hospital in Knoxville at that very moment, dying of tuberculosis. Russell is a little drunk and scared bad himself, maybe the worst old Russ has ever been scared—and that is reason for the question.

But Russell is dour and sad, and Ben has a glimmer of a memory.

Wasn't there something…

It flashes through him then. Like a comet. Large and complete and burning hot and brightly terrifying—and for that horrible instant he remembers it all, every last microscopic, torturous detail…

…and then, gone.

Russell is waiting.

Ben looks away; he can't help it. He mumbles something about the time he set down his rifle to pick up a bear cub and then its momma had come running from behind and he had barely enough time to grab the gun and shoot her before she could rip him to pieces. But even as he tells all this, it does not settle right with him.

Wasn't there something…

…about wildflowers? about stepping onto a bus one dark morning?

Russell is staring at him with his wounded, tipsy eyes. Ben doesn't like that stare. It feels like judgment. So he looks away and bends to line up another shot at the ten ball. A beer-thick sigh rolls behind him. "Hell Ben, there's worse things than momma bears out there."

Worse things.

He figures Russell Cooper knows something about fear. Aside from Alma rotting away in the hospital, Russell had been a boatswain's mate in the Pacific in '44 and '45 during the worst of it. Ben had been a year in Europe, spent most of that time in England (in the rear with the gear) and was never near a shot fired in anger.

His stick strikes the ball. The shot rolls wide.

…not right!

He wasn't sure when he first heard noise below.

It had been there for some time, along with the light-as-air whisper of butterfly wings and the rustle of branches, jangled up with the myriad, unimportant forest sounds serving as background music to his thoughts. It was there well before his mind had clicked upon it and calculated it as something peculiar.

Eyes still closed...he listened to the splashing.

Something was in the pond.

His eyelids butterflied open, and the world tilted.

On instinct, his gnarled fingers gunned for the staff, then went for his chest as he was seized by another furious spasm of coughs. He bent over, gagging, retching, flinging mucus from his lungs and ripping his insides to shreds as he coughed, as he tried to focus on the thing in the swirling pond mist below. The coughing spell consumed him, and a separate mist, a vapor of blood, bloomed inside him.

Slowly, a bit at a time, the coughing died away. He rubbed his eyes, and the mists cleared.

He sighed.

(Somewhere deep within his ravaged breast, the moldering lid of an ancient steamer trunk reluctantly yielded, squealed on rusty hinges...*Oh, how long, how long have you been hiding away in these hills, old man?*)

Below, half-submerged in the dark and chill waters of the pond, was the most beautiful woman in the world. Swimming. Sweeping ballerina strokes across the surface, sending wave after wave, ripple after ripple to the pond's banks. Her skin was pearl white in the mist. Her hair, long and blue-black like the wings of a raven, clung in wet coils over her naked shoulders.

She was...*almost*...familiar.

He sighed again. She moved so gracefully. Drops glitter-danced from her fingertips, like rubies in the purpling dusk. The butterflies, he dimly noticed, had vanished. Had they collected to become this girl? Was her pearlescent moonflesh the accumulation of their wings, their legs, their antennae—all drawn together in some mystical choreography?

He rubbed his eyes again to see if he had been fooled by the faltering daylight and the dark forest mist and his yellowing, eighty-four-year-old eyesight.

But she was there.

And now she stopped her dance to look at him. The ripples stilled.

Smoothly, and with in infinite slowness, she stood, a moonrise of pale shoulders, the sable-hair waterfall freezing in mid-flow. Her breasts rose, buoyed on the water, lifted into the air. She tilted her face to him and caught a stray, blushing ray of sunset.

He sighed for a third time. And had the unexplainable understanding that this maddeningly near-familiar face knew him, knew all about him, knew his secrets and crimes. Those brown-almost-black eyes, blurry with nostalgic tears, were reading the aches and miseries stuffed into the ancient, cobwebby fissures of his soul, reading them and deciphering them all, remembering the things he had forgotten. Here before him, encased in weepy, star-glistened skin, was the repository of all his forsaken memories.

"Come be with me!"

Her voice carried up from the pond like a chorus of night spirits, and he shivered.

The voice? Yes, the voice was familiar, too, and *why couldn't he remember!* He made a fist just as her arms ascended from the water, two trickling, silver-slick angel wings reaching to enfold him.

"Come be with me, Ben!"

She started forward. Floating. Floating toward *him*, he realized, and jolted with sudden, electric fear. He felt himself lurch out of a semi-dream fog. He blinked. Yes, she was there, and yes she was sliding across the pond and coming for him.

He bolted to his feet, sending rusty daggers through his brittle joints. Trembling, groaning, he turned and lurched away.

He sensed her floating behind him, stretching out her arms to gather him in. *"Ben!"*

He stumbled into the forest and back down the lost, dark trail. The October breeze blew after him, whispering his name through the swaying limbs of the trees.

"Ben, don't turn away!"

seven

Until the old man collapsed, it was a properly somber and dignified service, surprisingly well-attended, impeccably organized; even the weather was cooperating (threat of thunderstorms, but not until late afternoon), and all seemed to be proceeding nicely. Matthew Dufette was in the middle of the eulogy when the trembling old man slowly stood from a mid-row pew and struck one palsied finger toward a vacant, shadowy place behind the pulpit—as if about to make a suggestion (or as if pointing at something he'd seen, Boo Taylor later decided). At his flanks, whispers stirred. The whispers, which spread across the congregation like ripples across a gray pond, grew louder—and eventually reached the front pew where Boo Taylor sat between his mother and Sandy Baker.

He turned to watch.

A wispy-haired, bent, troll of an old man stuffed into a rumpled black suit. Pointing. Mouth open, choking out soundless syllables. Eyes wide with some terrible euphoria, with some awful *knowing*.

Didn't he recognize that old man?

Didn't he recognize that silent scream?

A woman seated next to the man tentatively touched his arm and made a quiet inquiry. As if to answer, the man turned and blazed one eye at her while the other went slack, and a thin line of drool slipped over his lip. It ran down his chin and hung there, wobbling in the light of a stained-glass prism. Then the drool snapped loose. The terrified eye rolled up. The trembling legs gave way. And the man crumbled.

The gloomy stillness of the First United Methodist Church erupted with black-costumed motion and shrill exclamations. MaeEllen Taylor clamped onto Boo's shoulder, prohibiting him from taking action. "Oh good Lord, can you believe it?" she breathed furiously, "can you just *believe* it? In the *middle* of your father's funeral!"

❖ ❖ ❖

Back in a suit again.

Not the Armani pinstripe, which had been ruined in Hurricane Joseph. This one was solid black, handmade by a tailor in downtown Wilmington, Delaware. (A breath of a memory there, a poem chanted to him, a woman standing at a backward doorway: *Tailor's mother had a son, and never had another one...*) He felt restless in it. Tied up, like a calf in a rodeo.

The church was a modern structure: an A-frame design of imported sandstone and exposed steel beams and pillars, replacing the old Methodist Church that had burned in the autumn of 1971. An ugly building, Boo Taylor decided—and as a man who worked with stone and knew it could be stark and cold or solid and warm depending on the shapes, the colors, the angle of stacking, and (most important) the shades of city or nature surrounding it. This sterile pile of rock sat too easily with the "new" Sweetpatch Island; it groped for attention with its monumental blandness. From outside, it was more prison than church.

And yet, it filled up with old-time islanders. Dewey Fitch was in that crowd; Boo had seen him step through the church doors holding onto his mother's elbow. And a much heavier Royal Goody with three quiet children and a pretty woman Boo guessed to be his wife. Then Red Prettyman, towing two children of his own. He counted off the faces: Mr. Joyce, his old basketball coach, rounder and more threadbare than he remembered; Wade Dutton, skinny but with same red crew cut, decked in a blue policeman's uniform (who had grabbed Boo's hand, pumped it madly, "Damn boy, look at you, solid as a rock—you still playin ball?"); Lester Meggett, bearded now, in a flannel work shirt with a fat checkered tie; Mrs. Atkins, former next-door neighbor, now widowed and morose; Winston Crowley, former mayor, now hobbling on a cane; Sue Berry, gone plump as Boo always guessed she might. He made these discoveries with brief sweeps of his eyes, glimpsing the spell two decades cast on old friends and enemies: made thick or gaunt, made gray or bald, wizened, taller, wider, expanded, or diminished.

When he caught a flash of scarlet, *not* diminished, dancing like a bright candle flame atop so much somber gray and black, he stopped looking.

And the first tear sprang to his eye.

It came unbidden as he looked upon his father's dead body.

"Forgiveness, Boo Taylor," Pastor Thackery had whispered to him earlier. But, could he forgive? Perhaps he already had and just didn't realize it.

Then that shuddering, gray figure emerged from the pews, ghastly, and lifted his finger. The crowd turned from Matthew Dufette's eulogy, stared, gasped.

"What in the world...?"

"What's wrong with...?"

"Who *is* that...?"

That last was Boo's question, because he *knew* that old man, didn't he? He followed the direction of the quivering, pointed finger to see nothing but a hidden alcove and a sharp slant of shadow. And maybe somewhere in that place was a flicker of movement, a flutter of brown cloth, now retreating.

But MaeEllen was jerking his arm again. He turned back just in time to watch the brittle stack of bones collapse.

The throng flew apart like a confusion of black-winged bats, many flapping away from the man, many more flapping toward him. Wade Dutton was the first to reach him. A woman nearby screamed, others shouted, a few swooned. Matthew Dufette stuttered nonsense into the microphone, and Reverend Thackery raced down the aisle like a terrified Ichabod Crane.

From the middle of the frenzy, Wade Dutton's head popped up like a crew-cut jack-in-the-box. His face was deeply flushed. He shouted, "Is there a doctor in the house!"

Several heads pivoted involuntarily to the casket.

Inside, the only doctor they had known all their lives—"the doctor"—lay as lifeless and uncaring as a ceramic doll.

Do they expect him to crawl out? Boo wondered crazily.

But it seemed they expected exactly that.

eight

After the graveside ceremony, thunderclouds threatened as Boo wandered to a distant edge of the cemetery to smoke a cigar. Wade Dutton caught up to him, lighting a cigarette.

"That was old Mr. Beaudry, wasn't it?" Boo asked. "Hoss Beaudry's father?"

Wade nodded.

"How is he?"

"Dead before he hit the ground."

Boo winced. "Heart attack?"

"Near as I can tell, the old man had the mother of all strokes. Like his brain exploded."

Wade snapped his fingers.

Just like that, Boo thought. "What was he looking at?" he asked.

"What?"

"He was pointing at something behind the pulpit. In the shadows. I think some-one was back there."

Wade shrugged, blind behind dark aviator sunglasses. He pulled on his cigarette, and Boo saw the fragment of a blue-green tattoo peek from beneath his sleeve on one wiry, orange-haired biceps. *Semper Fi.* Wade, like his brothers, had stopped growing in the eighth grade, and Boo stood over him by four or five inches. His police revolver sat on his hip under a complicated series of snaps and leather straps.

"I still can't believe it," Boo said.

"What's that?"

"That the people of this island would actually *arm* a Dutton."

Wade laughed and slapped him on the back. "Needed somebody to keep the *other* Duttons in line, I guess."

"They still need it?"

"Oh my Lord, do they ever. I guess Harley's my best customer—or *worst*. Spends half his days in the drunk tank and the other half fuelin up for it." Wade chuckled and sent a plume of smoke into the air. "How's Miss MaeEllen holdin up?"

Boo looked around, found his mother being escorted by Simon Duckett from the canopied grave site. She was firing instructions as they walked, and the funeral director was nodding agreeably. Sandy Baker and Bess Pope trailed.

"Hell, Wade, you know MaeEllen Taylor. She whimpers and moans for a while, but then she comes at you with a hammer." He sighed. "Actually, she's been kind of heroic today."

Wade nodded while Boo watched his mother. She looked very pretty in her mid-length black dress, her hair a commanding, born-again silver beneath a compact black hat and veil, a string of pearls shining from her lovely neck: a years-younger version of the woman he'd spent the last several days alternately resenting and consoling.

Mourners were weaving around tombstones, softly mumbling about the calamity at the church. In gray and black, they looked like the dispersing elements of a storm. Lester Meggett and Dewey Fitch were huddled with Billy Standish, passing around a single can of beer. Lumbering by them, uttering something that made the three laugh, was Mr. Haufmann who once owned a little grocery on Fulton Street Market.

Boo asked, "What about the doc, Wade?"

"What about him?"

"Were you there when they found him?"

"Oh." He made a small cough. "No, I'd been workin day shift. Call came in around midnight I guess."

Boo wrung a finger through his collar. "Just a heart attack? Nothing out of the ordinary?" He was picturing the silent scream.

"You mean him bein naked and all?"

"Well yes, that."

Wade hung his head. He drew deeply on his cigarette as Boo stared at him. "Jeez, Boo, I don't like bein the one to talk to you about this stuff."

"What happened to him, Wade?" Boo asked firmly. "He wasn't alone in that house, was he?"

Wade made a quick look around to see who was within earshot. He spoke softly. "Well, he was alone when Goose and Freddy found him. But maybe he wasn't alone *before* they found him. His clothes were in another room, stacked up all nice and neat."

Boo blew out burst of smoke. "That's crazy."

"Yeah, no shit."

"In the middle of the night?"

"Right."

"But the tenant had skipped out. There was no *power* on at the house."

"We know."

Boo looked away, tried to picture it, tried to splice this information with his lifelong image of the doctor. "Who was he with?"

"We don't know. Maybe nobody, Boo, and you got to realize that," Wade said earnestly. "Maybe nobody at all."

"Nobody," Boo said. "So he just decided to take a shower, then."

Wade scowled at him.

"What about the tenant that skipped out?"

Wade shook his head. "Ran the name and didn't turn up nothin. Look, this place wasn't exactly the Ritz, and I don't think anybody gets too all fired concerned about IDs and stuff like that when they rent the place. Probably some dumb, broke country girl with three kids who ran back to her folk's place on the mainland."

"You must have found something else."

"Nope. Nothin 'cept some creepy writin on the bathroom mirror, but that could'a been there months for all we know."

"Something creepy like what?"

Wade bobbed his head uncomfortably. "Like, 'He came and he went,' or somethin like that. And, 'How's about that for a joke?'"

These words struck Boo like a wrecking ball. "That's what it said?"

"Somethin like that, I guess. Written in lipstick."

Boo stared into the beetle-green lenses of Wade Dutton's sunglasses. He saw himself reflected back as twins. "Nothing more, then?"

"That's it, Boo," Wade said.

Boo Taylor heard a telephone ringing in his brain, conjured back his dreams— ugly images swirling like detritus in the curl of a wave, glimpses of sickness and night-mares and oceans churning with unclean, groping creatures; his father stumbling on rickety legs, wheezing, spindly muscle dripping like old cheese from his bones. And screaming. Running from...what?

Yes, he was home, summoned back to a land of scrub grass and gravestones. A line from Reverend Thackery's sermon came to him: *The voice of thy brother's blood crieth unto me from the ground.*

And then, in the distance, amid the petrified tombstones, he realized that some-one was watching him. A blubbery arm rose and cheerfully flapped a brown canvas mast in the sea breeze. Dumfounded, Boo felt his own arm rise to wave in return.

Wade Dutton grabbed his arm. "Hey, you all right?"

Boo looked at him sharply, then back to the distant corner of graveyard where he saw nothing.

Overhead, a gull shrieked laughter.

"Fine," Boo said. He drew on his cigar.

Wade was now guiding him to the cars. At the hearse, holding his mother's hand, Sandy Baker was waiting for him. She chilled him with a flash of warm blue ice.

Wade had said something to him but, shaken, he had missed it.

"What's that?"

"I asked," Wade said, "if that's your wife with MaeEllen."

Boo made something that was not quite a smile. "Girlfriend," he said. "Never did get married."

"Sure is a pretty one."

"Yes, she is."

"Looks kind'a familiar."

"You think?"

"Where's she come from?"

He sniffed, frowned. "Wade, you're starting to sound like MaeEllen."

Wade Dutton dropped his cigarette and smashed into the turf with his shoe. Boo heard the next question coming, dreaded it, wanted to pull away, felt the fire sweep across his face. His gaze dropped to the grass as the low clouds rumbled the threat of storm.

Wade asked, "By the way, you seen Gussie yet?"

nine

The limousine pulled up to the Taylor house. Out back, buffet tables were piled with food, and the first guests were log jamming Carriage Avenue as old-time Sweetpatch Island gathered for a particularly quiet party upon one of its most favored lawns.

Lester Meggett and Dewey Fitch cornered him under the mammoth magnolia.

"Helluva thing, old man Beaudry knockin off like that."

"Hoss's dad."

"Christ, boy, you don't think I know that!"

"Like t'scare the hell out'a me."

"What the hell you figure got into him like that?"

"Maybe he saw your face."

"Maybe he smelled your bung hole."

Dewey's tie was draped over his shoulder while he ate. Dewey had gone a little plump; Lester had remained as bone-skinny as he had been at thirteen. Each balanced a beer, a cigarette and a full paper plate.

"Damn, boy," Dewey said to Boo, leering wildly, "*that* one—she could be in the movies." Sandy had just passed by, filling a plate for MaeEllen. Lester watched her dreamily.

Then Royal Goody appeared and swallowed Boo in a bear hug. Lanky Royal Goody had grown a bullish neck and waist and looked every thick inch the high school football coach.

"I bought your book," Boo told him.

"You're kidding!" Royal glowed, showing his pleasure. "My readership just doubled."

"That's some horseshit," Lester chimed merrily. "Everybody on this fuckin island must'a read that little fart of a book. Goody-two-shoes is practically famous."

Dewey said, "Ain't quite as famous as his brother, though."

"No, ain't that famous."

"Who'd ever figure them Goody brothers'd get so famous?"

"On *this* island?"

"Figured they'd get lynched, first."

"*Both* of 'em."

"Can you fuckin believe it? *Senator* Solomon Goody?"

"Not senator, you dumb shit—*congressman*."

"Same fuckin difference!"

"*In*famous, maybe," Royal said. "Not everybody's happy with it."

"Not happy with what?" Boo asked, pleased with this easy smile on his lips, the lightness in his chest. Had he really spent two decades away from these people?

"That little fart of a book I wrote—which, it turns out, ruffled a few feathers."

"Put all the bloody details in there," said Dewey. "Hung out all the dirty laundry."

Lester was shaking his head. "Ain't it a shame? Everybody's a fuckin critic."

"That bit about the docks."

"That black fisherman."

"Captain Narcisse. That was a good one."

Boo vaguely remembered the story of a Negro sea captain beheaded shortly after the Civil War. His head had been mounted on his boat as a warning.

"The town fathers," Royal said, "pretend lynchings never took place here. Worried about the tourists."

"That's some horseshit, too; tourists eat that crap up." Lester Meggett crinkled his empty beer can. "By the way, how'd you get ol BoGat to tell you that stuff, anyway?"

"Mean bastard."

"Meaner'n a hammerhead."

"Thought he'd be dead by now. He was a hunert years old when we was kids."

Royal Goody said, "He was eighty-seven when he died two years ago."

"Smelled like he died *five* years ago."

"Say Boo, did y'all read that part about the Beast?"

Boo Taylor looked at Lester who was gazing back dizzily, a cigarette smoldering from the lips of his bearded, too-skinny face. For the first time, Boo noticed the purple veins of an alcoholic webbing Lester's nose and cheeks.

He realized the others were looking at him. "I did," he said quietly, thinking that Royal's version was actually short on some of the bloody details.

A short silence fell. The others, he decided, were thinking the same thing.

Boo looked toward the beach. Gulls, attracted by the food, were gathering, fluttering among themselves in a parody of the human gathering, looking on in earnest as if deciding how to approach. Above them, the clouds were darkening, jelling. The cool, electric scent of rain breezed in from the waves—and beneath that, a thicker smell, like an animal's breath, like old meat. Had something dead washed under the pier?

"Y'all been down there yet?"

Boo looked around and realized Dewey Fitch was talking to him. "Have I been where?"

"The old Chaliboque place. South Patch."

"No. Not in almost twenty years."

"Well, it's all state land, now. That whole bottom part of South Patch. It's a wildlife refuge: the Sing Satterfield Wildlife Refuge."

Boo seemed to recall arrowed signs along the road. "Who the hell is Sing Satterfield?"

The others chuckled. "Rich widow," Royal said. "*Very* rich widow."

"Osgood Satterfield got married again?"

"Not him, Boo. Old man Satterfield passed back in eighty-eight or eighty-nine. Sing Satterfield was his boy's wife."

"Some kind'a recluse," said Dewey.

Boo calculated in his head. "So you're saying Dalton Satterfield died?"

Dewey nodded.

"Well hell, Dalton was just a few years older than us. What happened to him?"

"Went off to college on the mainland, same's you," Dewey answered.

"Never came back, same's you," said Lester.

"Was livin someplace up north and got married, from what I hear. Then he died, and she gets everything."

"She donated most of the land around Chaliboque to the county," said Royal, "with the condition they make it a wildlife sanctuary."

"*Sing* Satterfield," Boo said, "that's not her real name, I take it."

Dewey laughed. "Who knows? She's some kind'a recluse."

Royal was nodding. "I know she sits on the Sanctuary board, but otherwise she seems to keep a pretty low profile."

"How's that for a laugh?" Ketchup leaked from the corner of Dewey Fitch's mouth. "Old biddy owns half the fuckin island, and nobody's ever seen her."

Lester spoke up. "I seen her."

They all looked at Lester Meggett. His eyes seemed to be locked on Sandy Baker who, at the moment, was bent over a tray of asparagus dip.

"Like hell," said Dewey.

"Have *too*. I work for her, don't I?"

Dewey chuckled, "Yeah that's right, you and half the fuckin island." Then to Boo—"Lester here works for Satterfield Properties, runnin a backhoe. Can you believe ol Les could actually hold down a job?"

Lester made as if to punch him, staggered, dropped a wad of potato salad from his plate. "I *seen* her," he challenged. "She talks to me. She got a big place down on the Atlantic side of South Beach she uses sometimes."

"Sure she does, Les."

"Does *too*. Suck the bone, Dew."

"Suck the *pole,* Les; you ain't seen her." He turned to the others. "Whole fuckin corner of the island is deserted. Now they got hikin trails run through it for the tourists...picnic tables, barbecues. Even got a little tourist museum with plants and stuffed birds. Got a skeleton of a gator in there; kids think it's a dinosaur."

Lester wobbled drunkenly. "I *seen* her!" he grumbled.

"What does she look like?" Boo asked.

Lester Meggett's eyes swam back in his head. Sandy Baker breathed past, waving happily to Boo on her way to another errand, and Lester made no attempt to stop staring at her. "Ugly," he said, baring his teeth. Then he laughed harshly and pointed his beer at Boo Taylor's chest. "Rode hard and put up wet!" He laughed again.

Clouds, dipped in swamp water, their bellies yellow-green and plump, rumbled. Premonitory gusts skittered paper plates and cups through the legs of adults, making fine games of chase for the children.

Boo looked at Royal Goody. "What about Chaliboque?" he asked.

"*That's* still there," said Dewey. "I do some fishin with my boy on the Yamawichee, and you can see it. A wall or two maybe come down, and some of the roof's gone. But it's still there."

Royal added, "Pigg's Creek runs a lot higher now, and the bluffs are falling away. The place'll be collapsing into the swamp before too long."

"Still there," Boo said wondrously.

"Scary old place," said Dewey.

Lester grunted. "Scary? You know what scary is? You see Loretta Hibbits' legs today? Like a couple sacks of potatoes. By God, I used to *worship* them legs."

"Turned into a regular hound, all right."

"Regular dog."

"Regular bowser."

"You'd still give the dog a bone, though, wouldn't you, boy?"

"Aw, you're sick."

It went on.

Boo worked through the crowd, accepting condolences. After a hundred healthy hands shaking his crippled one *(Lord, if you ain't solid as ever, boy; you still playin ball?)*, a thousand wrinkled crone-kisses on the cheek *(My, ain't you grown into a fine lookin young man!)*, ten minutes at MaeEllen's side *(Did you see that awful papier-mâché hat Catherine Prettyman was wearing?)*, and another ten minutes with Sandy *(Don't you want to spend any time with me?)*, he finally shook himself loose, lifted a beer from an ice chest and walked alone to the pier.

Private jetty; no trespassing.

The crowd faded to a muted babble on the lawn far behind him, losing its resonance and significance as he watched the far-flung ripples of the Atlantic. He lit a cigar; it took several attempts with his hands cupped against the stiffening ocean breeze. Through the smoke, a pungent nastiness struck him, and he wrinkled his nose. Something had definitely died beneath the pier. Its smell was rising through the planks, but he couldn't bring himself to look for it. With casual, meandering steps, he made his way to the end of the pier where he looked out and exhaled a long day's worth of exhaustion.

He sipped his beer (ice).

Puffed his cigar (fire).

Inhaled the corpse smells beneath his feet (death).

One of these—ice, fire, death—started his eyes watering again. Or perhaps it was the combination of the three. Or perhaps it was merely the day itself, with all of its surprises and miseries, creeping up behind him on the pier.

Yes, it must be that last, because he felt its footsteps tremoring toward him along the planks, ringing faint reverberations up the length of his bones. He heard its cautious breaths, whispering *(his name?)* from behind, drawing nearer. He *(closed his eyes)* saw it in his mind's eye, closing the distance, reaching for him in broad daylight. Coming to him…as if in a dream.

A light touch on the arm (a butterfly touch).

Tugged him.

Turned him around.

Beckoned him across time and oceans and fields of stars and other worlds, and my God how could he have missed, in that backyard world of dour blacks and grays, such blinding, scarlet-gold brilliance?

"Gussie," he said. His cheeks were tingled by a cascade of hot pin pricks.

Her eyes were sad, tentative, hopeful. Wet and wide as the ocean. Brimming with emerald glitter and fear.

She asked, "Should I be worried about you?"

Beyond her, whatever had been was now blurred and running like rain dappling a watercolor canvas.

"You never have to worry about me," he told her.

A corner of her mouth twisted, only one side, and so it was not exactly a smile. "I do, though," she said. "Always."

She took his hand.

"I'm sorry about the doctor."

Boo dragged on the cigar. He meant to look away from her, but he couldn't. "Your employer," he said. "When did *that* happen?"

Her skin, real, warm-blooded, and smooth, touched his callused palm. And here were infinitesimal lines tracing from the corners of her eyes as proof of the passing years, as if tears had etched a story in her flesh.

"Years ago; I don't remember. You saying you don't approve?"

"I'm saying I didn't see it coming."

"But you don't approve."

"Gussie, you certainly don't need my approval for anything."

Her cheeks burned, her eyelashes dropped and Boo felt his body tottering dizzily over the waves. He wanted to tell her how dangerous it was to be touching her skin again—

—she let go of his hand. "He was very generous, and I *liked* the man."

Boo grunted.

The breeze lifted, and disloyal auburn strands reached across the span separating them. Her hand reached up to catch them. Her fingers neatly tucked them behind her ear—and here was the scar: an angry, pink paraffin snarl creeping from her cheekbone to the lobe of her ear, then lost beneath the fine copper wisps in the cords of her long neck.

"People change, Boo Taylor."

This time, he was able to look away. "No, they don't," he said, thinking: *You haven't. Not a bit.*

"Once trailer trash, always trailer trash, is that it? *You've* changed, you know. Your accent—you sound just like a Yankee, now."

"You mean like a tourist," he said. "Speaking of trailer trash, where's that asshole you married?"

She scowled. "That wasn't called for."

"Yes it was. Is he here?"

"Somewhere, yes; wherever the beer is, most likely. He was hoping he'd get to see you."

"Oh, I'm sure of that."

"He is!"

Boo reared around and gestured to the open sea. "Gussie, if I can just get off this miserable island without running into Murphy Goddamn Ransome I'll consider it the highlight of my week."

From behind her, a child's voice called out, "Momma!" She turned as Boo studied bright teeth revealed by the sad half-smiled twist of her lips. The tip of her tongue rustled through the gap, and he could taste it.

A child stepped forward. A little boy who was watching Boo closely.

"Have you met my youngest?" she asked.

Cigar smoke lifted from his left hand, and the smell of death lifted from the sloshing surf. The needle jabs freckled his face again.

The little boy was gazing at him with suspicious cat's eyes.

"Jeremiah, say hello to Boo Taylor."

The boy stuck out his hand. "Hi." *Hah,* he sounded like a good Southerner. Dark hair and round face, not like her at all; and so serious in his miniature navy blue blazer and stiff, red tie. Boo bent down and took the boy's five fingers in his own three.

The boy gawked happily at the stubs. "How'd *that* happen!"

Boo glanced at Gussie: a spark, a shared painful grin. "I was biting my nails, and I missed," he said, making the boy glare at his hand in amazement. "How old are you, Jeremiah?"

"Five."

"Six next month," Gussie said, straightening a lock of the child's hair as he backed into her skirt. "Such a *big* boy, aren't you?"

The boy nodded emphatically. He hadn't taken his eyes from Boo's hand. "Momma, you said we were goin."

"In a minute."

"You said we were goin *now!*"

"We are. Go find your daddy."

But the boy was not moving, was content to stare at Boo and his scarred hand. Again, Boo glanced to Gussie, flashed a moment of brilliant electric contact, and she put her hands on the boy's shoulders and held him out as a shield.

"It looks," she said, "like I'm working for you now."

Boo was lost. He had to blink his way up from the green ocean depths of her eyes. "What—you're what?"

"Taylor Dufette Realty. I suppose you're the new boss-man."

"No. Everything goes to MaeEllen."

"Oh."

"Although," Boo said expansively, "I am pretty sure that fine gentleman Matt Dufette will be buying her out as soon as Southern decorum permits."

She laughed: "Very good—*that* didn't sound Yankee at all!"

The boy tugged on her skirt. "Momma, we're supposed to be leavin."

"We will when you go find your daddy."

"I don't know where he is!"

"Well go *look*, silly." The boy was still not moving. Gussie rapped him lightly on the rump. "Go on!" she urged him, and he finally turned and scampered away.

Boo followed his progress toward the lawn where activity had slowed considerably. Most of the eyes, he now saw, were upon him and Gussie and the scene unfolding on the pier. There was MaeEllen spying down; and Lester and Dewey shoulder to shoulder; Billy Standish, a hot dog frozen two inches from his lips; Mrs. Kendall, old teacher, mouth poised to catch flies; dozens of others taking in this show.

Boo Taylor watched the multitudes watching him, unable for the moment to turn back to Gussie without the boy as their buffer. So he searched the crowd instead, wondering if a particular set of carnivore eyes might be there, burning him from above a flapping brown dress. Not there, of course—not in the wide open. It was the wrong place to look. Somewhere dark would be better, maybe beneath them right now, cuddled with that smelly corpse and peering through a gap in the boards.

Eyes averted, he was still powerfully aware of Gussie's presence at his side. A shimmery magnetism grazed the hair on his arms.

What are you thinking, Gussie, right now? And what would you say if I told you what I've been seeing?

"She's lovely, Boo."

He turned to her and saw she was making her own scan of the lawn. Boo looked around again to find Sandy Baker in the distance, glowering poison at him over folded arms. Murphy Ransome would be up there too, Boo presumed, perhaps wearing an identical expression.

"She introduced herself to me. She was very charming."

He found the beer and cigar tucked into his left hand and looked at them dumbly, momentarily at a loss to remember how they'd gotten there.

Stepped right out of a hurricane, stepped right in front of my truck, on a highway six hundred miles north of here—now, what would you say...?

"Are you still painting?" he asked.

With a deep breath, she turned back to him. "Every now and then. Not so much."

"I still have some of your paintings. You were very good, you know."

"You're just being nice. How long are you staying?"

"My flight leaves tomorrow night." And because he didn't want to see how she might respond to this, he followed quickly: "I met your daughter."

After a moment's hesitation, she gave him a pleased look. "So I hear. You made quite an impression."

"She looks like you. I thought it was you."

Now an eyebrow arched. She laughed. "Did you?"

A silence followed, ripe with awkwardness. Time beat slowly, much slower than his kettledrum pulse, but still too miserably fast; he kept squandering these moments with her just an arm's length away. Why couldn't he get his lungs, his throat, his mouth to come out with the words? Instead, his brain was pinwheeling with those bizarre suppositions: *if I told you, if I told you, Gussie, what would you say?* Better, maybe, that he couldn't speak.

...and then, not more than two hours ago, watching me across the cemetery lawn...

"Momma, we got to *go!*"

Her little boy again, stomping up the pier, hands on hips. She looked up and called to him, "Okay, honey, I'll be right there!"

She turned a sad smile to Boo.

His distress mounted. Overhead, a low beast-like growl rumbled through the soupy layers of clouds, and the first cold sprinkle of rain struck his forehead.

What would you say...?

The boy reached them. "Momma, come on!"

"Okay, okay, I'm *coming*," she told him and took the boy's hand.

Again, that sad smile pointed at him. "Well," she said. Her hand reached out to briefly touch him on the shoulder, and then she turned away, holding her boy's hand as she walked down the pier.

He followed the course of her flaming hair.

What would you say...

Followed its blazing trail to the entrance of the pier, leaving sparks over solid ground, casting light into the wide lawn...

...if I told you...

Followed it until it was snuffed out in the gray and black tide pool of mourners.

...please, I still love you!

ten

Above, the crowd made an effort not to notice. But they were generations-bred island people, saw visions in the tides, sniffed prophesies in the winds; they heard babies dying in the cries of seagulls, sifted for fortunes in the salt and sands. And they were not at all happy with the spectacle of that solitary figure perched at the end of the pier and all that dangerous ocean swell surrounding him, like an albatross come to rest on the deck of a boat with God-knows-what miseries hitched to his wings. It was the perfect harbinger of calamity. For although, almost to a person, they were glad to see Boo Taylor again, they were nearly as unanimous in their anxiety.

The whispering started.

First, the doctor?

Then, old Charles Beaudry? At the *funeral,* no less?

And now this broad shouldered, slightly broken looking boy-turned-man, friend-turned-stranger who stood alone in the soft drizzle, contemplating the ocean in a pose that portended worse things to come.

Royal Goody, not a superstitious man (though he was a fifth generation islander), excused himself from his wife and strode through the turbulence of bodies toward the pier.

No Trespassing!

He hung at the foot of the pier for a moment, shaken himself by the surety of tragedy held in the forlorn tilt of the man's head—then shook it off, stepped onto the pier and walked its length. With a few strides to go, Boo Taylor dipped his shoulders around to acknowledge his approach, then straightened back to the sea.

Royal clinked his beer bottle against Boo Taylor's. "Better days."

Boo grinned cheerfully around a soggy, dead cigar. "Amen," he said and slung a strong arm across Royal's shoulders.

Royal watched the smile, not believing it, and recalled the first time he had seen that face in the pews of the old Cavalry Baptist Church where it glowed like a cue ball among eights. Not too hard to believe that little boy, always serious and aged beyond his years, would become this big, rough man.

"Martha is quite taken with you," Royal said.

"Who's Martha?"

"My wife!"

"Oh. Sorry. I met her; she was very sweet. Not from the island, is she?"

Royal shook his head as he took another drink. "She says you're a brawny version of Steve McQueen." When Boo looked at him, Royal shrugged. "Martha's a big film buff."

"What's that make you—Sidney Portier?"

He laughed. "Woody Strode when I'm good, Godfrey Cambridge when I make her mad."

Boo Taylor's smile now seemed terribly sad. "Les and Dew think Sandy should be in the movies."

"She *does* look like someone."

"Wade Dutton said the same thing."

"Martha says she's a cross between Yvette Mimieux and Carol Baker."

Boo turned to look upon the Atlantic. Storm clouds rumbled. The drizzle was coming heavier now, and the proximity of those pervasive and increasingly violent waves was suddenly making Royal Goody nervous.

"I'm sending her home tomorrow, Royal," Boo said quietly. "Alone. And that'll be the end of that."

Royal saw a flame of scarlet hair licking in the wind toward a granite-framed Boo Taylor as an island population watched, judged, and worried as black clouds collided and swelled and seas heaved mammoth warnings of catastrophe. "I'm sorry, Boo."

"Oh Lord, I've been through worse." He tried to smile around the waterlogged cigar in his teeth.

Royal nodded at this—nodded but felt Boo Taylor's despair infecting him. "Not that I know her or anything, but are you sure you know what you're doing?"

"What you mean is, does it have anything to do with Gussie."

"Well. Well, I suppose." He coughed. "So, does it?"

A sheen of silvery sea mist was layering Boo's tough-guy, movie-star features. "You know, Royal, there are two kinds of people in this world. Those who ask you what happened to your hand, and those who *think* about asking but don't. Sandy never asked. Not once."

Royal looked at his feet.

"Anyway," Boo said, "I want to ask you something."

"Fire away."

"Do you believe in ghosts?"

"You know I don't," Royal answered.

Boo arched an eyebrow at him. "After everything? You can still say that?"

"There are always explanations, Boo."

Boo Taylor locked his age-old eyes on him as if challenging this statement. Then the unconvincing smile came back as he turned away. "What if I told you," Boo Taylor started, staring straight ahead, "that I saw Mamie Stuvant today."

"Where?"

"At the cemetery."

"I guess I'd tell you it's been a hard day on a lot of people." Royal spoke delicately and with concern. "Boo, you didn't really see Mamie Stuvant—you know that. Right?"

Boo Taylor said nothing for a moment. He plucked the cigar from his mouth and seemed to notice for the first time it had gone out. He pitched it into the ocean. "Then where do you suppose that thing came from?"

Royal Goody followed Boo Taylor's ravaged right hand as he lifted it and pointed toward the splintered piling that held up the corner of the pier. There, a squat, bur-lapped dwarf was wrinkling an apple-faced grin at him.

Conditions on the Coast ~ June, 1971

"Dare you to go into Mamie Stuvant's house."

The words hung in the air, a predator bird hovering over the beach, threatening to swoop and seize one of the boys by the throat, and in the shadow of that floating threat their throats clenched, chatter faded, and they all looked at Dewey Fitch.

Dewey was the one who had flung forth the dare. He was smiling and showing his bad teeth and looking at Hoss Beaudry.

"And she's gotta be there," Dewey was saying, grin widening. "You gotta knock on the door so she lets you in."

Hoss was all slippery whiteness and scorched redness. "Then what?"

Dewey paused to think. "Why, then she *eats* you, boy!"

Boo Taylor leaned back in the sand. Hoss would surely chicken out. And that was okay, except Dewey would rag him for days.

"I'll do it," Hoss said.

A boy's month, June: a thousand bare feet chasing over grass and dust, splashing creek beds and surf foam, shaking tree limbs, sliding into bases. Brick walls tumbled, roofs blew away, and the world became pure sunlight-moonlight—too long spent combed-down, shoe-laced, desk-trapped, book-saddled into place. When June came, it was an explosion of adolescent fury reined in for nine long months: birth of a season—the best season of all. Summer.

But restlessness thus freed became recklessness.

The sky-roof must be tested, gates sought out, borders prodded to determine the electric voltage.

A boy's month, but a reckless one.

June had become a month of dares. And Boo Taylor had started it on the first day of summer vacation.

two

On the first day of summer vacation they had traveled on bikes to a construction site on Sadfellers Beach, hoping to find wet concrete and immortalize their palms. It was Saturday, so the place was abandoned.

"That sign says *Marriott*," Hoss Beaudry announced. "Who'd pay good money to stay on this ratty ol island? 'Specially in *South* Patch."

"Lots of people," Ashford told them. "My daddy says tourist business is gonna hit big around here. Says some folks are gonna get rich."

"Rich?" Dewey scoffed. "Rich off what?"

"Beaches. Hotels everywhere, he says. And golf courses."

"*Golf* courses? In South Patch? Boy, that's just nuts."

A chain link fence circled the site. The site was pocked with puddles and mud. Fragments of foundation and wall, ten feet high in places, framed the perimeter of a long building—easily the biggest thing on any of the island's beaches. Errant cinderblocks and equipment littered the incomplete shell.

Then, Boo Taylor saw an abandoned plank spanning a wall corner and a ladder slanting all the way from ground to top. He conceived the dare, never guessing where it could lead reckless, summer-gorging boys.

He said, "Hey Ash, dare you to walk the plank."

It was meant as a joke, but he toppled the first domino and doomed a hundred others stacked innocently behind it.

Ashford Marchant only laughed at him, and that *might* have been the end of it.

"I'll do it!" Dewey Fitch answered.

And Dewey sprang wildly off his bike, the others watching as he scrambled under the fence, entered the foundation shell, cautiously, stepping through the ruptured lumps of sand and clay and the tossed-about construction trash.

"See anybody comin?" he yelled back. He was in the shadow of the wall, moving the ladder through the muck, positioning it to the plank.

"Nobody!" Lester shouted.

"Well, keep a lookout! Make sure the coast is clear!" He went up the ladder.

Sherman Standish called out, "Awful high, ain't it, Dewey?"

"Sure it's high, you Yank pussy! Wouldn't be a good dare if it wasn't high."

Sherman looked at Boo. "You gonna stop him?"

"Stop him?"

"He'd stop if you told him, Boo. Heck, that's awful dangerous."

Dewey placed a sneaker on top of the wall. He pulled up the other foot, pinwheeled his arms for balance, and stepped onto the board.

Stop him? Hoss and Ash and Billy Standish were watching Boo now, too. But why stop Dewey Fitch if he wanted to break his neck?

The plank was a foot wide, maybe twenty long. Ten feet up, and it would look like a skinny rope from that height, Boo thought, and he expected Dewey would climb down when he saw this for himself along with the broken blocks and other lethal things beneath.

But Dewey stepped carefully away from the edge.

Lester bellowed, "That board slippery, Dew?"

Dewey tottered. When he regained his balance, he hissed, "Shut up, you damn retard!"

Moving again, delicately, keeping his arms wide. After a half-dozen baby steps, he began to slide his feet along rather than pick them up. He looked like an ungainly species of bird, wings spread, making its way along a wire.

"Hope nobody drives by," Billy Standish said.

"What if somebody sees?"

"What if somebody yells?"

"And then he slips——"

"Shhh!"

Dewey was barely a third of the way across when the plank sank sharply.

He stopped. Seven boys made calculations to determine how much worse the sag would get. The soft rumble of surf and faraway gull screams were the only sounds on the beach.

"Dewey, why don't you come on back?" Boo called out gently. "Board may not hold."

Dewey swayed over the foundation. His arms, no longer held victory-high, drooped low in front of him. He bent his legs as if preparing to kneel.

"Come on back!" Sherman called.

"Yeah!" said Billy.

After a few more moments of hesitation, Dewey doused their concern: "Get bent, you pussies!"

He slid forward. The plank bowed deeper and deeper as he moved. Dewey Fitch wobbled, marble-kneed and solitary, trembling forward, approaching dead middle. There was a sudden rasp, wood scraping concrete, that split the day wide open. Dewey froze.

"Holy gosh, it *moved!*" Hoss whispered.

The board had lurched several inches along the edge of the block wall and now threatened to fall away.

Boo Taylor leapt off his bike and clambered under the fence, muddying his shirt. He slogged quickly across the site as boy shouts followed him from the safety beyond the fence.

"Hold on there, Dew."

"Boo's comin, Dewey."

"Don't look down!"

Dewey, still frozen on the plank, was staring at the pile of concrete shards and rusty iron bars and the wheelbarrow tilted on end just beneath him. Boo quickly climbed the ladder, and when he reached the top grabbed the plank and pinned it to the ledge. "Dewey, I'm just gonna hold the board steady, okay?"

Lumber vibrated in his hands—it was Dewey's violently shaking legs.

"Okay, Dew?"

Several seconds later Dewey answered in a small voice, "...okay..."

Boo watched Dewey's back, still locked at mid span.

"Dew, you gotta get moving." The board was gray, old, and splintery. The bow in it looked even steeper up close.

Still no movement.

"You want to kneel down, maybe? Crawl the rest of the way?"

Boo waited.

"Dewey?"

"No."

Boo waited again. He felt the others behind him, silent now, but mounted on his shoulders, expecting him to make everything all right. He wondered if he should climb out on the plank to help Dewey across. No good, he decided, the thing was nearly breaking under Dewey's weight alone.

"Try givin her just one step," Boo called. "I got a good hold down this end. She'll hold steady enough."

Still, Dewey didn't move.

Then, cautiously: "...you sure?"

"Hey, no sweat."

More waiting.

The vibrations under Boo's hands went wild. Dewey was bending his left knee... lifting it...

His left foot slid three inches forward.

His knee straightened, and the trembling quieted.

"Hey, that's good," Boo told him, cheerfully.

Dewey called back, "You see all that shit down there?"

"Hell no. All I see is this here board and the other side."

Dewey's head bobbed. He had been looking at the scrap below, and now he was looking at the far side of the wall.

"See that?" Boo called. "Boy, you're already halfway there. If you made it the first half, you can make the second half. Right?"

He waited again. Then again, the board shook as Dewey's leg rose and he slid a sneaker forward. Wood creaked; splinters popped.

"You got it, boy," Boo said. "Let's see a couple more like that."

Dewey moved the right foot again. It shook madly. Then the left foot. The tendons in Boo's wrists were on fire.

"You're doin it, Dew."

Another agonizingly slow shuffle. Another. The plank bobbed with Dewey's shifting weight, but the creaking steadily lessened.

From behind them, Lester shouted, "Almost there, Dew!"

Then Sherman: "You got it, Dewey."

With the end just a few feet away, Dewey's back straightened. The swag in the board eased. Boo loosened his grip, and his forearms came away light as balloons.

"Way to go, Dew!" Lester shouted and let out a whoop.

With his last step, Dewey shot his arms over his head and whooped in return. He knelt to the ledge. Boo scurried to the opposite wall with the ladder; the others—now, finally—came scrabbling under the fence.

"Did the dare! Did the dare!" Dewey bugled.

"You did it, Dew-boy!" Lester trumpeted with him, grabbing him around the waist, and they both fell over in the mud. The others happily called out their congratulations from a distance.

And then Billy Standish asked, "So, what are you guys up for next?"

Dewey, smiling up from the mud, shouted, "Another dare!"

Oh here it comes, Boo thought, already imagining the worst. He looked at Ashford Marchant who was looking back and shaking his head.

Stop him?

Am I my brother's keeper?

Dewey grabbed hold of Lester: "Dare you to steal that wheelbarrow over there!"

"What the hell do I want a wheelbarrow for?"

"Pussy?"

"Nothin pussy about it. Where am I supposed to *put* it?"

"That ain't the point. It's a *dare*."

To Lester Meggett's mind, this logic was sound. His normally dull face bunched at the brow under the strain of intense thought, accepting the dare, yes, and now tracing a path of escape, figuring how to raise a wheelbarrow over the fence...

"Somebody's gotta come with me and make sure the coast is clear," he said at last.

Hoss Beaudry, still in the habit of schoolrooms, shot up his hand. "I will!"

"No," Lester said quickly. He raised his eyes hopefully to Boo Taylor. "I want you, Boo."

Boo sighed. Now imagining being brought before the doctor: *But he asked me to make sure the coast was clear, now how was I supposed to say no?* And for a moment, he believed he heard his father answering, shouting at him angrily.

But it was just a man in a hard hat bellowing from the other end of the construction site.

And they broke for the fence.

Later, safe in Up Island, they stopped and huddled, joked about the man in the hard hat, recounted various moments of Dewey Fitch's walk on the plank. There were still hours of daylight left, and Boo wanted to get back to the ball field.

"I'da done that dare, Dew," Lester said. "If that man hadn't a' come along, I'da done it."

"Aw, youd'a peed your shorts, first."

"No. I'da done it."

Dewey, half-covered in drying mud, grinned and presented a set of gray teeth. "Tell you what, Les—got another dare for you. I dare you to climb the oak outside Miss Corning's house and look in her window."

Miss Corning, the junior high science teacher who wore slinky silk blouses.

Lester Meggett smiled greedily. "Oh hell, that's easy."

"He won't see anything," Hoss said, and he managed to sound jealous.

three

The way Boo saw it, he had two choices:

Go along. (*Come join us!* they shouted.)

Let them to it by themselves.

The draw was sometimes strong. He heard their laughter—mostly companionable, but sometimes mean and sometimes downright *terrible* to one another. He sat in on their storytelling beneath shade trees and before beach bonfires. The sharp edge of their tales fish hooked his flesh and tugged him toward the challenge, toward giggling stunts and madcap getaways, and had he been a year or two younger—or perhaps just younger by a month—he might have yielded to the pull.

But he was supposed to be a man, now.

Or *becoming* one. So, he left them to their child's play and went off on his own. Sometimes Ash Marchant sided with him, but mostly Ash fell in with the others. For the rest, it became a rampage of summer dares. Boo expected as much of Dewey Fitch and Lester Meggett. Billy Standish was a year younger and could declare that alibi. And Sherman was a Yank and couldn't be trusted to show good judgment. Hoss Beaudry was a disappointment, still baby-fat and too pliant, too susceptible to Dewey's goading.

As a group, they still assembled for baseball games at the shell mound and afterward for the telling of tales: dares and otherwise. Still friends and still fun—until, inevitably, the first dare was presented, tossed like a dart, striking and wounding its target, getting tossed back, then back and forth until blood flowed from prick wounds; assignments were determined, strategies debated, and...

...and Boo left them to it while they called after him, enticing him to join, to enjoy, to at least post watch and make sure the coast was clear. But, his choice was made.

four

Miss Corning with the slinky blouses wasn't home on first try but screamed Lester down from the tree on second try, and Lester Meggett became hero of the island for almost ten minutes.

When his minutes were up, Lester dared Billy Standish to swim out to the *Kissy Mae,* BoGat Pederson's boat anchored off the docks at Mermaids Head Creek. After a few strokes of white paint, the *Kissy Mae Butt* was christened, and it was Billy's turn in the spotlight.

Billy goaded Hoss Beaudry into moving the Tarleton's lawn jockey across Logger-head Street to the steps of the town hall. When Hoss got Lester to help, Dewey accused him of cheating.

Hoss dared Lester to dump cold water on one of the high school girls tanning on Atlantic Beach—with the idea that a bikini top might get left in the sand. Sherman took the challenge instead, got punched and chased by Kristy Kressner, and narrowly escaped a worse beating by her boyfriend, Jimmy Earl Deeg.

Lester dared Dewey to steal some beers from the several cases that cooked in his father's garage. With Billy making sure the coast was clear, Dewey nabbed a six-pack of Black Label along with a bottle of Gentleman Jack, and afterward they each drank a warm beer, a few swallows of whiskey, and got mildly sick.

The first weeks passed, sweetened by the ambrosial peril of another dare, another adventure, another chance to best the hand of authority that had bound them so tightly during the first dozen or more years of their lives.

But as tastes refined, the sweetness soured, and dares took on a bitter, cruel flavor.

Billy dared Hoss to pee on Mrs. Tarleton's roses, and when Hoss got Lester to stand by the back door to make sure the coast was clear, Dewey accused him of cheating.

Lester dared Billy to steal several tomatoes out of the Pedicord's garden, and Billy refused, declaring that dares could no longer involve stealing or breaking any other law.

Dewey dared Hoss to swipe a pair of his stepmother's undershorts and claimed it was within the rules since they were in the same family. Hoss refused, and Dewey ragged him badly.

Lester dared Hoss to drop his drawers in front of the girls on Atlantic Beach. No one really expected him to do it, but again, Dewey ragged him.

Billy dared Lester to shave Handley Atkin's decrepit old beagle, Maxie. He would have done it, too, had Boo not caught wind of the plot and stopped him; Mr. Atkins was the Taylors' next-door neighbor.

Dewey dared Hoss to ride his Sting-Ray no-handed for one simple block, knowing Hoss was unable to do it. Then Dewey did it himself.

Dewey dared Hoss to swim to Cedar Knee Hammock at high tide, knowing Hoss wouldn't even try. Again, Dewey did it himself.

Dewey dared Hoss to climb to the peak of the Methodist Church rooftop. Hoss made it no further than halfway, got stuck for half an hour, and finally, crying, made it back down with Lester's help.

Dewey dared Hoss to jump from the first pole at Dedmens Causeway into the Yamawichee, twenty feet high, and Hoss refused. Dewey did it from the second pole— thirty feet high.

Finally, Dewey dared Hoss to knock on Mamie Stuvant's door.

 five

"I'll do it," Hoss said.

And it was, of course, a dare unlike all others. The fall wasn't into concrete shards or angry girl fists or the pea soup Yamawichee waters—nothing so safely *real*. Cuts and bruises and even a broken arm, they all got bandaged up and healed.

But Mamie Stuvant was a...

"You will not," Boo said before he knew it.

Dewey clapped, gamboled. "You heard him! You heard him! Boy said he'd do it!"

Boo shot Dewey a glare, quieting him.

The black pit of dead bonfires claimed the sand before them; the real fire was in the sky, circling west and making summer barbecue of them.

"Hell, she's just an old woman," Sherman said.

Lester bobbed agreement. "That's right, just an old woman."

Billy Standish said, "I thought you guys told us she was a ghost."

"She's a ghost, but she's real, too."

"Naw, she's just an old woman."

"Crazy is all, maybe."

"Murdered that boy, though, didn't she? Sicked the Beast on him."

"Who says? Never got proved, did it?"

"Maybe she didn't, then."

"Maybe that was all just made up."

"She got that mean ol dog, though."

"What dog? *You* never seen it."

"Then maybe there ain't one. Maybe there ain't a Beast at all."

"Maybe not."

"Maybe she's just crazy a bit."

"Maybe she ain't crazy at all. Maybe just poor."

"Maybe folks just pick on her."

"Inside. He has to go *inside;* she has to let him *in.*"

"And then what?"

"And then tell her, 'trick or treat, you wigged-out old biddy!'"

And in all their talk, Boo heard the sham of bravado while the old boyish fears trembled beneath their voices. They could talk, because it hadn't been them to take the dare. Hoss, the one who had, wasn't speaking at all. Mamie Stuvant was a murderer, witch, ghost who slouched in shadows and dark corners and jack-in-the-boxed from roadsides. Who knew what gloomy, bat-cave horrors festered within the walls of that house—dirt floors, skeletons chain bound with ghastly expressions, skittering rats and salamanders, jars pickling human organs, heathen chants and bloody rites...Of all of them, to send cloddish Hoss Beaudry into such a place?

We're too old for this—I'm too old for this.

Then why are we all afraid?

Ash Marchant, who'd been lying back and chomping on a long stalk of broomsedge, now rose to his elbows and threw the force of his expectations upon Boo's shoulders.

Stop him, Ash said without speaking.

Stop him?

"You can't do it," Boo said again.

Hoss looked at him grimly. "Boo, I said I would."

Hoss's gray T-shirt was painted black with sweat circles around his neck and in creases above his belly. His white-blonde hair stuck out in mad, wet spikes. His knee wept from a slide into second base.

"My *man!*" Dewey squealed.

Hoss took a slap on the back and offered a fractured grin in return. Then more slaps of congratulations and encouragement.

"Hell," Sherman said with less enthusiasm than the others, "what's the big deal? She's just an old lady."

The terror bubbling beneath Hoss Beaudry's uneven smile answered that Hoss didn't believe that. Not yet. But how was a thirteen-year-old boy supposed to admit he was afraid of an old woman?

Stop him, Ash demanded silently.

Boo said, "What if she *does* have that big dog?"

"She don't," Dewey said.

"Nobody ever *really* seen it, did they?" Billy Standish asked.

Boo frowned, tried again: "What happens if she gets hold of your daddy on the street? What if she tells him you were out to her house, playin some stupid game?"

Ashford rose to his knees, pressed his glasses up with a finger. "That's right. Like she's always grabbing Mr. Dutton and complaining about Wade and Harley throwing rocks at her house." The Duttons were the only boys they knew crazy enough to provoke Mamie Stuvant.

"That's right," Boo said. "What's your daddy gonna do when he finds out you were foolin around at Mamie Stuvant's house?"

Ash looked around to the others, to Dewey in particular. "Y'all know how his daddy is."

"He won't find out," Dewey challenged.

"But what if he *does?* You gonna take his whoopin for him?"

Momentum and bluster faltered all around.

Except for Hoss who said, "He won't find out. I said I'll do it."

"You don't have to," Boo told him.

"I'll *do* it, Boo." Eyes, pleading, aimed at Boo Taylor—explaining the things a sweat-cursed, swollen oaf could never speak in words to the strongest, most agile boy on the island. Boo blinked away. Comes to me again, he thought, and felt the others watching him.

He'll listen to you, Ash cautioned.

They'll rag me if I don't, Hoss worried.

Boo blinked again, opened his eyes, and it was Hoss's blood-shot wretchedness gazing back. "Hey, I guess Hoss is the man," Boo said.

The expression on Hoss Beaudry's face was unreadable.

Ash Marchant pursed his lips.

Dewey bugled a distorted echo: "Hoss is the *man!*"

The others corrupted the echo still further and stampeded Hoss with smacks to his back. Hoss turned from Boo and made his chest swell. He put on a wide, stupid grin and, still squatting in the sand, bowed clownishly around the circle.

"So when's the man gonna do it?" Sherman asked.

"Today!" Dewey blared. "Let's go out there right now."

Hoss blanched. "Today?"

"Right now! I wanna get me a look at that spook's face when ol Hoss comes bangin at the door."

Hoss's slick brow collapsed on itself. "I don't think I can, today."

"Why the hell not?"

"You ain't turnin fag already?"

"I knew it—I knew he was gonna fag out."

Hoss insisted, "I'm not faggin out." But his expression said otherwise.

"He's not faggin out," Boo declared and then, under all that pale-fleshed anguish, groped for rationales, found one, weak, but used it anyway. "His daddy's home today.

Y'all know how his daddy is. It ought to be a day when his daddy's at work so he won't find out."

"He's home tomorrow, too," Hoss added quietly.

Dewey scowled; clouds rumbled. "Hell, my daddy ain't worked in months, and I don't make excuses out of it. You're faggin out, fat boy."

"Am not!"

"Then, let's get goin."

"But—"

Ash Marchant spoke up, and all attention turned to him. "Your daddy working day after tomorrow?"

Dewey's scowl untethered by a knot.

Hoss considered Ash cautiously. "Tuesday?"

"Tuesday. Day after tomorrow."

Day after tomorrow.

The day after tomorrow was a long time away—uncounted miles and a thousand distractions lay between. A whole day and two whole nights buffered *now* from *then*.

Hoss wiped a hot streamlet off his lip. "Yeah, he's working on Tuesday."

"Good. Day after tomorrow, then," Ash said. "That okay with you?"

Hoss nodded, already regaining some composure.

"That suit you, Dewey?"

Dewey Fitch grunted. Then spread his arms in a gesture of beneficence. "Hey, suits me fine. Long as the boy don't fag out."

"I ain't gonna fag *out!*"

"What about you boys?" Ash asked all around and received murmured assent. Hoss squatted back in the sand. Dewey backed across the fire pit. Ash watched them, nodded. "Day after tomorrow, then." He leaned onto his elbows, plucked a fresh stalk of broomsedge and gnawed it. When the others weren't looking, he turned to Boo and squeezed a self-satisfied grin around the stalk. *There you go. Bought you two days.*

six

"What about Loretta Hibbits?"

"Too much lard in her butt. Saw her out on North Beach last week, and she was jigglin all over the place. I'd take Sue Berry first."

"I'd take Kristy Kressner."

"Naw—Loretta Hibbits."

Boo Taylor and Ash Marchant sucked broomsedge while others puffed cigarettes with varying degrees of competence. Above, seagulls squawked a mimic of the senseless banter.

"Yeah, I'd take Loretta Hibbits, too."

"You think Sue Berry still has her cherry?"

"Hey that's a poem, Les. 'Sue Berry lost her cherry.'"

"You don't even know what a cherry is."

"Sure I do."

"Only cherry you're ever gonna see's the kind that goes in a *pie*."

Cruel laughter, aimed at Billy Standish. Boo Taylor, lost in the imaginary smoke of his thoughts, cleared his throat and spoke automatically. "Lay off him, Dewey."

Oak leaf canopies shaded them; ocean breezes swept coolness off the frosty tops of waves and delivered it to the bluff, chilling passions. Just a few hot coals and smoldering cigarette butts in the pit. Crisis was safely consigned to the mythical era of day after tomorrow, but Boo caught himself brooding over the embers, poking his toe at charred sticks and from time to time caught Hoss doing the same.

Sherman Standish announced, "It's a tie for me. Sue Berry and Loretta Hibbits."

Both girls were high school juniors, which put them several years beyond the reach of Sherman Standish and the rest of them.

"Or maybe Doreen Scanlon."

"Or Lisa June Potter."

"Lisa *June?* Boy, she's got *warts*."

"Well hell, Loretta Hibbits got a nose like a moose."

"Those aren't warts, you idiot—those are moles."

"Same fuckin difference."

"What the hell's a moose nose look like anyway?"

"Looks like Loretta Hibbits."

Hoss, brooding, but faking it well, pitching in his own happy nonsense to compete with the others. Boo worried the stalk through his cheek, fretting over the possibilities of coming face to face with Mamie Stuvant.

Just whispering the name inside his head made him shiver.

And then he heard another name, spoken aloud by Lester Meggett, and a sweltery copper thickness scalded him. Lester Meggett, trying to blow smoke rings, said suddenly, "Hey, I saw Gussie Dutton yesterday."

Boo Taylor's molars clamped the grass stalk, and muddy fluid leaked into his throat.

"Out by the high school field. She was in the stands. Wasn't wearin nothin but the top of her bathin suit."

"No *bottom?*" Hoss Beaudry asked wildly.

"Course she was wearin bottoms, you fat dummy. She had shorts on."

Hoss was crestfallen. "Oh."

Boo squirmed in the sand, which, without warning, had become hot and chafing.

"Thing is," Lester continued, "she was just *hangin* out'a that thing."

"Gussie's got some tits, all right."

"What was she doin?"

"Nothin. Just watchin them boys playin. Some of her brothers and Murphy Ransome and Richie and Jimmy Earl Deeg."

"She wasn't playin ball with 'em?"

"Naw, she don't do that no more. 'Sides, those boys are lots older—they don't want no girl playin with 'em."

"What the hell were *you* doin there?" Dewey asked. "Ain't them boys pounded you enough already?"

"They didn't see me, I ain't stupid. I was hidin in the trees behind the backstop."

Dewey snuffed a cigarette in the sand. "Yeah, and I bet you was greasin your stick, too."

"So that's all?" Hoss asked. "You just *saw* her? She was just watchin them?"

"Naw, she was giving old Les a head job," Dewey said and cracked himself up.

"Dewey," Boo said ominously and Les cowered.

Ashford adjusted his glasses, said, "That Gussie Dutton's all goo-goo eyes over Murphy Ransome, anyway."

Blood steamed to Boo's cheeks. "No she isn't."

Hoss nodded. "That's right. He's gotta be at least four years older. He's gonna be a *senior*. He's got his *license* already."

"Yeah, he's too old," said Lester.

Ashford plucked the stalk from his mouth. "So what? Doesn't stop you boys from getting a high hard one over Sue Berry."

"Besides, Gussie looks older," Dewey said. "She's got bigger tits than most the girls in high school."

Boo Taylor, having endured a full day of Dewey Fitch, was thinking about grabbing a handful of his greasy black hair and laying on a serious beating.

"Loretta Hibbits got bigger ones," Lester said.

"Kristy Kressner has the biggest."

"But Sue Berry—boy, I'd take her first."

The talk moved back to older girls and Boo breathed again.

seven

Until, on the ride home, cruising past the high school, Boo held his breath as the peppery chatter from the baseball field drew his attention.

"Y'all wanna go watch those boys play ball for a while?"

Only Ash and Hoss were with him; the others had gone their separate way home.

Hoss pouted. "If that's Murphy Ransome and the Duttons, then I ain't gettin anywhere near there."

"Hey, they're just playin ball. Won't be any trouble if all we do is watch."

"That's not what you want to watch," Ashford said, grinned, and Boo felt a spike of anger. "But Hoss is right—no sense fooling around with those boys."

Boo gazed dismally toward the bleachers. "Okay, forget it."

At the corner of Pinewood and Carriage, Ash split away, calling, "See you Tuesday."

Day after tomorrow.

Hoss went bloodless.

At the Taylor front yard, Hoss dallied, fidgeted with the tassels on his handgrips, hitched at his shorts. Boo marveled at the pink-and-white checker pattern on his cheeks.

"You don't think nothin bad's gonna happen," Hoss said hopefully.

"I don't know," Boo answered.

"I don't know about there bein a ghost and all—but she's got that dog everyone thinks is the Beast, and she could sic it on me. I never seen it, but..."

"I think the dog story's just made up—and the thing about that boy, Timmy Duff. Somethin else got to that boy, and folks just blame *her* for it, like folks do. The whole thing's just made up." Boo looked at the ground, saying this. "Anyway, you don't have to take that stupid dare."

"Yes I do."

"Only one who's gonna rag you is Dewey, and what Dewey Fitch thinks doesn't mean anything. Hell, you think *he* has the guts to knock on Mamie Stuvant's door?"

"That's just it! Dewey wouldn't have the guts to do it, so if I *do* then he can't rag me anymore. He can't rag me if I do something *he* wouldn't."

"So let him rag. Who cares?"

"*I* care." Eyes sliming over with tears, lip puffing toadishly. "I get ragged all the time. Everybody rags me. You don't know 'cause nobody rags on you. Even if you *didn't* do the dare, Boo, none of those boys'd rag you."

Boo looked away again, said quietly, "I get ragged."

Evening was softening the sky. Next door, Mr. Atkins' sprinkler wagged slowly to and fro, wetting his grass with a private rain cloud. From screen windows up and down Carriage Avenue, dinner scents beckoned.

Hoss sniffled.

Boo sighed. "I was thinkin. Maybe I should go with you—make sure the coast is clear."

Hoss brightened for a moment, darkened a moment later. "Won't work. Won't *count*, then."

No. Boo heard Dewey Fitch chanting, *Needs a babysitter; needs a babysitter!* And other chants for other schemes: faking sick, faking hurt, saying his daddy found out about it.

He sighed again. "Okay, then I was thinkin about *how* you should do it. What you should say. I think you should act like you're tryin to sell something. A magazine subscription or something. Or a raffle ticket."

Hoss was cautiously interested. "Or maybe Burpee Seeds? Like that?"

"Only it has to be something you can fake good."

"Like Burpee Seeds."

"Burpee Seeds, then, fine. But you should be carryin something with you to make it look good. Maybe a catalogue or something. And a notebook with people's names in it and prices—like that."

"She'll think I'm just sellin stuff."

"Right."

"She won't figure it's a joke."

"Why would she?"

"'Course she won't. I bet kids do it all the time."

"Sure they do."

Hoss was smiling. "There's Burpee Seed stuff in the back of comics—I bet I can cut stuff out and paste it on a notebook, like you said! And get some seeds from Dalfields! She won't figure somebody's playin a joke at all!"

And then, miraculously, Hoss was laughing with relief.

eight

Nighttime.

Boo was still doubtful.

To knock on that door.

Ghost of Sheba Tribbit; conjurer of the Beast...every man, woman, and child on Sweetpatch Island knew to steer clear of Mamie Stuvant's house—all except the secretive colored folk who skulked there under cloak of night to invoke some blasphemy: incantations to send spirits down enemy stovepipes, potions to make cheating husbands vomit blood, elixirs to charm a neighbor's wife.

Burlap dolls, stuffed with rubbish? Was that part of her magic, too?

He imagined Hoss Beaudry now two blocks north and at this moment paging through a *Fantastic Four* comic, scissors in hand, paste at the ready.

He was certain no kid had ever gone to Mamie Stuvant's house of horrors to sell Burpee Seeds.

In another room, his mother read about daughters of contessas in torn dresses; his father read about *infectious pneumonococcus.* In another house, Hoss Beaudry read about heroes and villains irradiated with strange powers.

Boo Taylor read the Bible.

Because Laylee Colebriar said it was a cure-all.

Because Pastor Hatchel's sermon, not listened to a month ago, now echoed all the way north from the planks of the Cavalry Baptist Church.

Because, from that same day, a page fed to the ocean along with dry moss livers and newspaper bowels kept washing back to shore, over and over, with all the rotting husks of dead animals. It was that page to which he returned yet again, trying yet again to find the fairness in it.

Abel was a keeper of sheep, but Cain was a tiller of the ground.

("Why, gosh boy, you tend it—when I see fit t'leave it. Figure you may curse me for it someday.")

And in process of time it came to pass that Cain brought of the fruit of the ground an offering unto the LORD. And Abel, he also brought of the firstlings of his flock and of the fat thereof. And the LORD had respect unto Abel and to his offering: But unto Cain and to his offering he had not respect.

(Hated one and liked the other.)

Where was the fairness in that? What did that *mean*? That God was unjust? Mean? Crazy? Or, was something else being kept secret, some cruel game which mere men were not allowed to understand?

And it came to pass, when they were both in the field, that Cain rose up against Abel his brother, and slew him.

(His fist swung around and smashed the face in the moment of recognition. And later, bloody-lipped, the boy pointed, accused: "*He* started it.")

And the LORD said unto Cain, Where is Abel thy brother? And he said, I know not: Am I my brother's keeper?

What was *that* secret—the secret kept from Cain that led to murder, the very *first* murder—and why was it shoved three ways (pastor, doll, and conscience) at a boy-man all on the same day ten thousand generations later on this worthless little island?

Not finding answers (or, rather, none he liked), he folded the pages closed again.

And, much later, sneaked outside: chilling his toes in grass...warming them in sand...rasping them against old board...dangling them in salt air.

He watched the moonglade. Watched it glitter a silver trail, starting from the edge of the world and rippling all across that distance until it presented itself to his feet. *His* feet! Daring him—chosen above all others—to step down, enter silverness, and follow...and see what waited on the other side of the moon.

He swept a gaze up and down the shoreline. Purposeful. The only person in the world awake. Lone and silent sentinel of Sweetpatch Island. Making sure the coast was clear.

$\mathcal{C}$nine

He got up early, loaded up his fishing gear, and pedaled into South Patch. Leaving ahead of Hoss Beaudry who would want to spend the day fretting, ahead of Dewey Fitch who had thoroughly soured him on company.

He crossed the old wood bridge spanning Soap Water Creek where dreary black men leaned on the railing with drooping bamboo fishing poles. They nodded their greetings. Boo nodded back, drifted past them, wound through dirt lanes. He let the morning stillness sluice through him, a baptism of salt marshes and cattails and dragonflies; passing at lengths through prehistoric wilderness, wet under summer dew, dry under summer dust, tall shouldered and shaded; passing at other lengths through boondock hovels crammed with rusted jalopies, flapping clotheslines, broken sofas, and mad dogs on chains. Herons stalked the sloughs, wrens and plovers guarded the sky; beneath him, the wheels took the road, freeing his body to soar with the birds.

He skidded to the ground, briefly, at a blackened badland.

He stepped off the bike.

Palmer Washington Schoolhouse

He tried to recognize the ramshackle timbers—but that was gone now. Instead: charred front doors forever opened to a void, a crispened roof accordioned over the walls, coal drifts buried classrooms. Solomon Goody's handiwork, according to island wisdom, though the boy himself had not claimed responsibility, had not yet been *found* to be questioned about it.

Some said his skeleton was somewhere in the embers.

And then Boo Taylor saw something new, something not there before. Perhaps it was Solomon Goody's skeleton fist stabbing upraised from his grave.

No, it was a hand-painted sign tacked to a post.

Support <u>REV</u> LEROY GIBSON HATCHEL
your friend!
for SCHOOL SUPERVISER
CORRINGTON RIVER DISTRICT
Elections Sep 11 register to vote!

He read. Then climbed back on his bike.

And, yet further south, turned off old Sugar Dam Road toward Miss Laylee's cottage from where a breeze chimed coffee-and-biscuit invitations (because she had Monday mornings off, and he felt her there, inside, humming gospel tunes, puttering through her kitchen) but he skirted the invitation, trundled around her gardens and across lumpy grass fields and into the woods that bordered Pigg's Creek.

He half-pushed, half-carried the bike beneath the oak and cypress ceiling, trying not to catch his rod on the branches.

At last, deep in the woods, he came to Pigg's Point (the name was his invention), a red-clay bluff at a bend in the creek.

He performed the rituals:

Parked the bike, gathered his gear.

Right-ended the skiff he'd beached among cedar roots.

Filled the bottom with a dozen or so small rocks.

Stripped barefoot, climbed ankle-deep in an eddy, scrunched nose-to-nose with his mirrored twin, peering deep in concentration until the crayfish bait were glimpsed, snatched, tucked in a jar.

Then he loaded the skiff and pushed into the creek. Tide was two-thirds risen; he paddled against the current, westward, following the widening creek until it opened into the Yamawichee Sound. He veered for a favorite deep spot halfway between shore and a remote slip of sand, dropped anchor, hooked the first crayfish, and cast.

He waited.

The sun made it over the trees and was broken apart again in a thousand orange shards on the water. He felt a tug on the line. He tugged retaliation. An unseen quarry jigged; he jigged with it. And then he was reeling in the first catch of the morning, mounting it on the stringer, and casting again.

Waiting again. He thought how fine a day it might be if he didn't have to worry about Hoss Beaudry and Mamie Stuvant.

A corner of the old Chaliboque house ogled him with idiot eyes through the cover of forest overgrowth in the distant southeast. Fish crows and swallows flitted there, in and out of the eye sockets of an empty skull. He saw a smaller version of himself paddling a scrap-wood raft across Pigg's Creek on his very first adventure to Chaliboque. How old had he been? Eight years old, maybe? That very first time he snuck off from Miss Laylee, slogging through the ancient swamp—and teetered on little boy legs to look at last upon the broadest, highest thing in the world—so high his neck hurt to look up and see it all. The Chaliboque Mansion. Haunted, of course. Favored dwelling of Joker Tribbit and any number of island spooks.

Even then, known to be one of Mamie Stuvant's hideaways.

He watched that little boy scrabble through a shattered window like he'd found pirate's treasure. So dark inside, jumbles of ruined furniture. Smells—dead animals and long-dead fires. So *quiet*. Someone in there with him? Someone watching?

The King!

Whispers, muskrat scratchings, leathered wings pulsing swamp-water breaths across his little boy flesh. He had gathered up a stick from the garbage, wagged it at the threatening, capering, eager shadows.

Yet he kept exploring. And the house swayed in welcome.

King of the Patch!

Come home, come home at last!

"Not me," he told the house, swinging the stick at a vaporous hand that caressed him, the hand disintegrating into cobwebs.

Yes, boy.

He knew the voice—that old, sweet birdsong voice. Yet the shadow it came from was so small, so young. A delicate thing, backing deeper through crumbled hallways, up the broken spine of a staircase. He followed, but she was quick. "Not me," he told her. Outside now, the clip-clop of horse hooves on brick. Violin music within, swirling with those ghostly whispers. Sunlight filtered through dust and fractured glass and shredded fabric, made cinema shows on the walls—ladies in fancy dresses, men and boys bustling, all smiling and reaching for him.

Mr. Boo!

Look how tall.

Look how handsome.

Come home, boy—come be with us.

Master. Master Boo!

"No. I don't belong here," he told them. But the sweet little one, the delicate familiarity shifting, growing, plucking filth from the floors, gathering stench from the air as it swelled—became tall as a man, became broad as a bull. Then shifted again and became Gussie Dutton, then again to become a beast. *Skin-stealer*, he thought.

Look 'round, boy, the Beast said in a garbled man-voice. *You is home, all right. King supposed to live in the biggest house on the island.*

He tried to say no again, but he could no longer speak. Because the Beast was starting toward him...

...and when he came awake, it might have been a minute or an hour later, he sensed something—a faint rippling in flat water—and instinctively grabbed the rod, wondering if he hooked another whitefish or maybe a channel bass. When it came up slack, he noticed the big gray-green log swimming toward him, sunlight dazzling off dozens of spiked mirrors.

"Yah!" he yelled at it.

He grabbed at the rock ammunition stockpiled in the boat's deck. The gator (about a six-footer, he figured—even longer than the skiff) was cutting lazily for the flip-flopping fish on the stringer.

He pitched the first rock, apple-sized. It plunked harmlessly a foot short.

He pitched a second and clipped the tail. The gator kept coming.

Only a dozen feet away now, Boo Taylor reared back and fired off a third. The rock smacked a protruding yellow eye, and the gator writhed into a violent splash, diving under. Boo grabbed another rock and hurled it into the turbulence. Then another.

The channel clouded with mud.

He pulled in the stringer.

His heart was pounding.

ten

He broke through tree cover, pushing the bike along bearing two whitings, a sea trout and a channel bass in a silvery cluster at the handlebars. By the stub and direction of his shadow, he calculated it to be still an hour shy of noon. He crossed the wide meadow toward Laylee Colebriar's house.

He was nearly to the garden when he saw someone in the shade of the house, standing at the bottom of the porch steps. Miss Laylee, he thought at first and waved—then saw it was not her at all, and, passing string beans and cabbage, let his sun-shocked eyes focus into the deep shade. Not Laylee at all, but a boy—and by the time he was through the garden, the boy was advancing with fists balled at his hips, and Boo saw who it was.

"What the hell were you doin back there?" the boy shouted—same boy he hauled off of Hoss Beaudry a month ago and punched in the mouth. "You got not business in that place!"

Stunned by the anger, Boo responded casually, "Got business there if I want. Didn't figure you owned the creek." He propped the bike on its stand, leaned the pole against it.

They boy took another menacing step. One of his fists rose, and Boo remembered the blow he took to his ribs.

The boy was shouting again: "Don't smart mouth me!"

Boo made his own fist. "You want another bloody lip?"

"What were you doing back there?"

"What do you care?"

"Tell me!"

Dust and flecks of dead grass clung to the boy's clothes and his hair—as if he'd been rolled in sugar (or maybe spent the night sleeping on the ground?) Behind him, seen only by Boo, a gray shape crawled from the shade beneath the house.

"I was just fishin," Boo said and, looking at his fist, made it unclench.

"Where?" the boy demanded, stepping forward again—and then Shamus approached at a trot, growling, and the boy went suddenly liquid.

"Mr. Boo!" Laylee Colebriar's voice sang from behind the screen door, jingling in tune with the wind chimes. "You leave off Mr. Royal an' come on up here with them fish. Did you bring 'em for me, or is you jes showin off?"

The boy watched the dog uncertainly as it circled to Boo's side, nudged its head under Boo's hand, demanded a scratch behind his ears.

Boo called to Laylee: "Thought I'd bring you some lunch."

She stepped through the door, and breakfast scents followed her to the porch. She carried the scents in a towel-covered bucket.

"Well, bring them fish on up here. Mr. Royal, you come git this pail."

The boy mounted the rain-warped steps. Boo, with Shamus hovering at his side, unwound the stringer from the handlebars. He dropped the channel bass for the dog who snatched it up and trotted back to his cave.

The boy was scowling from the porch. "What was *he* doin back there?"

"Aw, don't you mind Mr. Boo. He jes a fisherman is all."

"But this...this is *South* Patch."

"Mr. Royal, a fish don't know the difference, north or south, east or west. Reckon people don't neither—till somebody shows 'em. Fisherman goes where the fish goes. Ol Saint Pete, he was a fisherman, too—did you know that?" She hollered, "Mr. Boo, you know that?"

Boo nodded, judged the boy's mistrustful glare.

She cooed, "See? He jes a fisherman." Then, hollering again to Boo, "You gwon an' git them fish on into the sink an' clean yourself up whilst I set Royal here on his way."

Boo carried the stringer around them and went inside.

"Who is that boy, Miss Laylee?" Boo watched from the parlor window. The boy was plowing buttercups and toadflax on his way to the woods.

From the kitchen, the old woman waved her hand and made a song with the dozens of metal bracelets on her wrist. "Aw, jes some boy lives 'round here."

"Did you make him some food?"

"Why, yes I did. Oh my, we got us two whities and a troutfish. Lord, this whitey's still kickin. That's a good mornin's work there, Mr. Boo."

"Hooked a few eels, too, but I threw 'em back."

"Eel's no good for cookin. Stick him in the frying pan, an' his legs pop out!" She cackled.

"Where's he goin?"

"Who?"

"That boy."

"No place you need to know about."

"What's he doin?"

"Mindin his own business. Like you should."

The boy disappeared behind the trees.

"That's Royal Goody, isn't it? Solomon Goody's little brother."

She didn't answer him.

He turned, and she was standing in the kitchen doorway. In her hand, a sharp, skinny knife sparkled with silver scales and fresh blood.

"Half brother—an' Mr. Boo you leave young Royal be. He's a good boy, but he caught hisself some trouble. Last thing he need is Boo Taylor pokin after him."

From where the boy had vanished, two killdeer burst out of the woods on panicked wings.

"Okay," Boo said.

He followed her into the kitchen.

She cleaned the fish. He sat at the table, sipping lemonade and picking yellow paint chips from a table leg. The window was open wide, letting a marshy breeze rustle the dried herb bundles over Laylee's steel-wool head. A pair of mocking birds tussled and complained to each other from somewhere in the tall oak next to the house. Flies buzzed at the window and among the dewberry and winged sumac that feathered around the window frame like a wreath. Boo marked that the flies would not enter the kitchen. Then he saw a flash of light—the sun sparking life into the glass frog—and daydreamed that the flies feared a leap, a stab of crystal tongue, a swallow.

That little frog is you, Mr. Boo.

Laylee Colebriar was tugging toothpick bones from the trout with knife and thumb. Thin steel cables shifted and coiled under muslin shoulders to the long familiar rhythms of labor.

"Did Mamie Stuvant really kill that boy?" he asked.

Knife and fingers stopped.

After a pause and a breath, she asked, "That woman do anything to you?"

"No."

Knife and fingers went back to work.

"Don't seem to be any concern to you, then, do it?"

"It might be."

"*'Might be'* sounds like you got somethin in mind."

Boo stuck his finger in the jelly jar. "Maybe."

He heard her sigh, watched the cables in her shoulders lift with the breath of it, and he prepared himself for her interrogation. But she changed the subject. "You fond of fish, Mr. Boo?"

He leaned back. "Sure."

"Been eatin fish most of seventy years," she said, "an' I ain't never really found 'em much to my likes. Too much work to fish, and too much work spoils the eatin. Time you through cleanin a fish—cut his gut open, slop out his bad parts, strip off his skin, and pick out his skeleton—ain't a whole lot left for a meal."

Was this supposed to make him feel guilty for having her clean his catch?

"I guess," he said. He watched the knife flash efficient strokes through the flesh. Her fingers were a bundle of knotty old sticks, but she worked them with the grace and purpose of concert pianists, of artists...of magicians.

"Ever see a gator get after a fish?" she asked.

His eyes rose from her hands to her face.

Had she seen?

"Sure," he said.

"Gator jes rip his teeth into that fish. Take the skin and bones and all the bad parts, too. Just rip his big ol teeth right in and take what he get. Always leave some bits around for the other fish to come pick at. You ever see that?"

"Can't go fishin around here and not see that," he answered.

She set the knife in the sink and turned around. The pianist-artist-magician hands were slopped with slime and scales, but she made no movement to wipe them on a dishtowel or her apron.

"Saw a gator get a pintail once," she said sweetly. "Watched that rascal sneak up behind that bird and pick him right off the water, jes like he pickin a berry off a vine. Took him down to the bottom an' drown him an' gobbled him up. Nothin but a couple feathers left."

She shook her head at the memory of it.

Then she stared at him, and he stared at her.

"Mr. Boo, if that Mamie Stuvant was to ever use her teeth on you...why, I s'pose you apt to lose somethin. An' you try throwin rocks at that ol witch, you only make her mad."

Had she seen? Had she followed, watched from the woods? Had she *sent* that gator?

He tried to read the withered, chestnut lines of her face, but they were a mystery of ancient wisdoms. It was a face carved by Stone Age flints from the trunk of a mystical tree, runneled by countless seasons of storms and droughts and brushfires and more storms—so many twists and crags, like trails cut through jungles and desert mountains. Each part of her face worked its separate, cunning magic, and so she could show at the same time (as she was now) concern, admonishment, humor, weariness, a mother's love, and a thousand other blends of grins and frowns.

"She's related to Joker Tribbit, somehow, isn't she? Everybody says she's Sheba Tribbit's ghost, but she's really their daughter."

The mysterious wooden crags softened, reshaped, and added sadness to their collage, then shifted again and hinted anger. "Granddaughter, or so she claim." Her lips twitched. "Though some folks say hogwash—say that claim ain't nothin but good for business. Keep folks scared. Surprised you ain't heard that, Mr. Boo—seein how you always pokin into things."

"Well, what do *you* say?"

"What do I say about *what?*"

"Their *grand*daughter. Is she?"

After a long moment, the old woman said, "I suppose she is."

Boo blinked, leaned forward. "Really? Did you know her?" he asked. "When she was younger, did you know her? What was she like? What happened to her?"

She didn't answer. He watched the kaleidoscope twist, bubble, twirl through another liquid reshaping of expressions. At last, she asked pleasantly, "Mr. Boo, you figure you ever told me a lie?"

"What?"

"Asked you if you every told me a lie."

He shrugged, curled a grin that tried to be sly. "You talkin about any lie in particular?"

"Aw!" she gruffed. She threw her hand at him and rattled a dozen bracelets. "Mr. Boo, I always figured you was a boy who knew how to keep his word. Now I'm askin for your word on somethin."

He studied her doubtfully. "On what?"

"Somethin *important*."

"What is it?"

"Awful, awful important."

"What?"

The ancient crags whirled, jumped, pulsed, fizzled, and eventually settled into an indecipherable maze. "Want your word you ain't gonna go near that Mamie Stuvant."

What's wrong with that woman, Miss Laylee? Are you afraid of her?

The old woman held his gaze. Reading his thoughts, certainly, although hers were still buried in wrinkle-fold crypts. Fish slime drooled down gnarled fingers to her forearms and made him ill.

"You gonna give me your word?"

Flies now buzzed around her hands and lighted on the discarded scales and innards. "Okay," he told her grumpily.

She frowned. Then wiped her hands on the apron, scattering the flies. Shimmery smears of guts streaked the whiteness.

He ate the fish from a plate webbed with scores of slim cracks. "Aren't you gonna have some?" he asked.

She smiled. "Don't seem to have the taste for fish this mornin, Mr. Boo. 'Sides, I got to git goin. Swoozie Horner 'bout ready to drop her baby, an' the bus don't go there, so I got some walkin ahead. You stay a bit if you like. Maybe pull some weeds."

He was mopping bread across the plate for the last scraps when she dropped a red flannel pouch on a string around his neck. He held it up in his fingers. The stuffings rustled like dry leaves, and he thought of the burlap doll and articles about drowned ladies and burned up little girls.

"What's that?"

"Got a lot of names, I guess. I call it a *wongah.* An' don't you be askin me what all it's made of—don't s'pect you really wanna know. An' don't you go pokin at its insides, neither."

"What's it for?"

She laid a hand on his hair. He could not make himself look at her face. At last, her voice came to him sadly. "Maybe it help keep the teeth off your throat," she said.

He let go of the pouch, and it settled near his heart.

..*eleven*

He kept his word for almost three hours.

It was midafternoon when he knocked on Mamie Stuvant's front door. Fist against wood, rebounding down the length of his arm. Distorted. Far away, yet too loud. And too much like glass shattering in his ears.

If she was hiding a big dog, it was silent.

He had scouted this nameless dirt tract near Soap Water Creek for the previous twenty minutes, checking this shabby inland coast, and it was *too* clear. No neighbor or passerby to see him—to *witness* him. At least it was broad daylight, and there was some comfort in that.

The house was a sagging diaper, alone in a grassy cove at the very dead end of dusty lane, with the disconcerting oddity of a doorknob on the left and hinged side of the door—an aberration that tottered him a bit slantways.

Otherwise: slipshod walls of asphalt and wood; flattened tin-can shingles, bleached and peeling; a tar-paper roof drooping like a swayback mare under the fecal stink of marsh gas settling from the west; and cardboard panels blinding several broken panes. The place had no recognizable shape, was instead a heap of odd angles quilted together by an untrained hand.

He stood in the windless shelter of the front stoop, shuffled his feet, waited, counting to ten and no higher than ten.

...four...five...

He looked back at the yard he'd somehow willed himself to cross (would soon cross again, the opposite way...*six...seven...*), seeing the view that must be seen from inside: a deathscape—a movie ghost town without even a breeze to toss the dust—corrupted by a few deranged patches of toadflax and bull thistle, great mounds of rusted garbage, several hundred mostly broken bottles, and an overturned baby carriage. And like a desert, it was all bone-dry.

Everything but his flesh, which was drenched with sweat.

...eight...nine...

Something slumped behind the door.

Boo Taylor's heart frenzied—a turtle trapped in its shell. Within the house, poorly laid floorboards whined protest under an enormous weight. The wrong-sided doorknob rattled, and he braced. Laylee's wongah rustled and pressed against his soaking chest.

A sliver of blackness. His eyes, bruised by the glaring afternoon, saw nothing but shadow. A tang of rancid fruit crept on bitter spider legs through the door, escaping with papery sobs that might be breaths or a lunatic's laughter or the whisper of clothes.

"Mrs. Stuvant?" he asked.

It was the first, safe line. (Simple, yes, but rehearsed and agonized over nonetheless. Should he call her by name? Was "missus" better than "miss"—wasn't that more respectful?)

She's right in front of me!

A voice, unaccustomed to speech, now spoke like the rusty turn of a crank.

Mamie Stuvant said, "Doctor's boy."

Needles jabbed his face.

She knows who I am!

In all the rehearsals, this was never considered. His anonymity was an advantage now conceded; before, he could break and run and hide, and she could never know where to find him, and he could lay hidden for *months* if he had to. But she *knew*. All the rules were thrown in doubt.

Somehow not running, he answered her. He coughed. "Yes ma'am," he croaked.

The door slimmed open by a breath. He imagined a dusky outline of some globular mass much larger than himself. Spoiled fruit smells slithered out more boldly, enveloped him, drew him closer.

The thing inside said, "You ain't one'a them rock throwers is you?"

What did she say? He choked: "I'm a...I'm—"

Miss Laylee's cautions, the gator at Pigg's Creek—first Laylee knew and now Mamie Stuvant knew! June's heat, like a blacksmith's anvil, flattened his chest, and he believed he might suffocate to death right here on Mamie Stuvant's front stoop.

"I'm a—"

He stopped his mouth. Breathed.

She wants to know if you're one of the ones who throws rocks at her house.

"No ma'am, I would never." He swallowed. Did she believe him? Could she see well enough from her bleak cave to know it was the brutal Duttons who did those things?

"Doctor's boy," the rusty voice cranked again. Then a wet stir of gravel: she was chuckling at him. He felt himself being weighed and sized and considered like a slab of pork hung over a butcher shop counter. "What you comin t'see ol Mamie for, boy? Got need for the cure-all? Or maybe the poison? Somebody you want sick, or maybe more you want *love*sick? That it?" The grin widened.

The magazines and spiral notebook puckered in the sweat under his arm—his clever ruse. But that was for later.

"Well, I—" He swallowed again and spoke the practiced line around a desiccated tongue: "First of all, I wanted to introduce myself."

The wet gravel laugh stirred again. "Then jes come on in and introduce yourself, doctor's boy."

Grayness brightening a shade at a time as a thick arm wrenched the backward door open. After thirteen years of unquestioned terror, Boo Taylor got his first good look at Sweetpatch Island's great dark witch.

And saw a sharp, intelligent face.

Thick black eyebrows. Coffee-toned skin, heavily sugared and creamed in patches, other flavors in other patches. She smiled yellow teeth, ripe with secret amusement.

She was backing from the door; he was stepping inside.

Blindingly dark, unnaturally cool. Sickly sweet peaches and a hundred lesser odors wrapped him like a blanket. He steeled for the phantom dog he was sure would erupt from some shadow. But the house was quiet. And apparently empty. In pathetically thin slips of sunlight, he saw garage-sale furniture: sofa, a few chairs, scattered tables—all showing signs of repair with tape and string, but set about in rational patterns. In between were newspapers piled in tall stacks, boxes swollen with scavenged baubles. And, further evidence of her weirdness, glass bottles everywhere, hundreds of them.

Mamie Stuvant was hovering over him, filling up the space around him. "You sweatin like a frog on a griddle, boy. S'pose you could use a dab of sump'n? Sump'n with *ice?*"

That little frog is you, Mr. Boo. Mamie Stuvant knew about the frog too. "Thank you."

She took her eyes from him and began to move away. "Workin in the kitchen. Always workin, boy. Makin work all day, all night—ain't never enough time."

He floated behind, not understanding her babbles, grateful not to be looked at. He watched her back, all fleshiness rippling under a simple brown dress and soiled apron. The dress was sleeveless and revealed heavy shoulders, doughy rolls above elbows. A very long tangle of coarse, black hair snaked down her back, strangled by a red handkerchief at the base of her skull. "S'pose a boy don't know nothing 'bout work, do he?"

"We've got school," he said to her back. "That's like work, I guess."

She barked a laugh. "Got school, he says!"

They came to the kitchen, and the sour fruit smell was like a smack in the face. It was Laylee Colebriar's kitchen—twice the size, but ceilinged in the same bat-dangling bundles of herbs, floored in the same cracked linoleum, stocked with the same second-hand refrigerator and stove. The one remarkable exception was the collection of bottles on every conceivable surface.

Insects must thrive in this place, he thought, although he couldn't see them. And mice. And maybe rats, all waiting for nighttime to slink forth and glut on whatever spoiled fruit she left on her countertops. Peaches—that was today's feast. A peck basket of them sat on a table.

"Set down, boy. Introduce yourself," she told him and busied herself at the refrigerator.

He tiptoed, took a chair at the peach-strewn, bottle-strewn table. He set the magazines and notebook before him, then changed his mind and decided to keep them in his lap, then changed his mind again and put them on the table, hiding them beneath his elbows.

"My name is Boo Taylor," he said, and again the rehearsed line was empty and utterly inane.

"*Boo?* That's what folks be callin you?"

She walked to him from the refrigerator and handed him a jelly-jar glass filled with tea and ice. He noticed a slick brown scar skidding across her right bicep.

"That ain't nothin but a bad joke, boy. They ain't really callin you Boo, is they?"

He looked at the glass. The same comic book squiggles as the jar he drank from just hours ago?

"It's short for Robert."

She made a grumping noise. "Rob short for Robert. Or Robby or Bo even. Boo don't fit. Somebody be havin a laugh at you, boy; somebody makin a joke." Mean humor glinted from her eyes like shards of broken glass. "*Booooooo* Taylor," she said, and laughed. "The Boo don't fit—and you ain't no more a Taylor than ol Mamie is."

She knows I'm adopted? She knows that, too?

He went dizzy, felt he might slip off the chair. The magazines, the practiced speech were abandoned. Moronic. He had the urge to run again, judged the distance to the door, questioned if she had maybe locked it.

"Tailor do his stitchin with needle and thread. Like a doctor. You ain't got no needle, does you?"

"No ma'am."

"And you ain't got no decent thread to you neither, I guess."

"No."

She laughed again. "Heard me a joke once 'bout a tailor. Wanna hear it, boy?"

He nodded dumbly.

She crooned:

> *"Tailor's mother had a son,*
> *and never had another one.*
> *When that child die, without his own,*
> *her granchilds' names was Smith an' Jones."*

She watched him. Toyed her happy ferocity over him. She had not stopped smiling, and the smile was untying his strength.

"Well, boy? You gettin the joke?"

"No ma'am."

"Sho' you is!"

He scratched his chin, tumbling off balance, out of control. The "joke," he knew, was gibberish, and what was he supposed to answer?

"Aw," she uttered with disgust, mock or real. Then she shifted her thickness to the counter where she hefted a weapon the likes of which he had never seen before. A large wooden cone with a handle at the base—a club with a pointed end. She dropped peach slices into a colander. The colander was perched on long spider legs over a bowl. She began grinding the cone against the peaches until a yellowish-orange fluid bled through.

Mesmerized by these acts, imagining poisons, he asked, "What are you making?"

She grunted as her great, floppy arms muscled the cone in a circle. "Bread," she said and stirred her muddy voice with another chuckle. "This here's the way ol Mamie makes her bread."

"Peach bread?"

"*Peach* bread, he says! Boy, I never hear tell of *peach* bread. What it taste like?"

"I don't—I mean, I never had any. I thought that's what you said you were making."

"Said I be makin *bread,* Boo Taylor." She looked up from her work to grin at him. "What the peach say when the man step on it?"

"What did—what?"

She grumbled a laugh. "Don't say nothin, boy—jes make a little whine!"

Her laughter rolled across the kitchen walls.

He looked around, seeing all the bottles: green, brown, clear; all different shapes—some like liquor bottles, some like milk bottles, some just jars. Some empty, others filled with viscous liquids of various colors.

"You make wine," he said. "You sell wine to folks."

"Cawse I do." She plopped more peach slices into the colander. "Queen root for what hurtin 'em, and wine for what ailin 'em. Jes like my grams, makin bread. You ain't partial to Mamie's tea, doctor's boy?"

He looked at the forgotten jelly glass sweating in his hand, green-brown brew within, imagined poisons again—but he sipped anyway.

Just tea. But bitter with unrecognized spices. He glanced at the bundles and pouches dripping from the ceiling and wondered what exotic mix went into this potion before he showed up, wondered also how long it took for poison to work.

"It's good," he told her. "Different."

"Good, he says! *Cawse* it different."

She went back to work, and he studied her: face scrunched with effort, maybe a pretty face once, now blunted by age and too much weight; eyelids and lips stained by tea bags; a few freckles sprinkled across her nose like oil drops.

Mamie Stuvant is just a bootlegger, that's all, and that's how she makes her money, and that's why people visit her late at night. And I'm sitting in her kitchen and talking with her, and she's just a normal person.

He looked at his tea. "What's queen's root?" he asked.

"*Queen* root. Root of the great queen." Her garbled voice rose again in song:

"Find the place where the sparrow done die,
six inch over, six inch down,
that be where the queen root lie."

She started humming; he was used to Miss Laylee's humming, her singing, her mysterious little rhymes. But Laylee's voice was high and like a bird while Mamie Stuvant's was something from the swamp.

"So, you mean you dig it up?"

"Onliest place you find a root, ain't it?"

"What's it for?"

"Queen root good for lotta things. Headache. Constipation. Depend what you mixin with it."

Not much different than Miss Laylee, really.

"Your grams taught you that? About queen's root and how to make cures and things."

"And how t'make peach wine and apple wine and dandelion wine. Grams put ol Mamie through doctorin school *and* liquorin school. Don't s'pose folks be teachin them things at your school, eh boy?"

She picked up a large knife and began slicing more peaches.

Boo let his eyes wander, counting bottles, counting all the same things from Eulahlah Colebriar's kitchen. "Folks say you're related to Joker Tribbit," he said— then immediately froze for letting such a thing slip from his mouth. He eyed her carefully. She was eyeing him back.

"Related, eh? That's what *they* be sayin?"

He nodded dumbly.

"Know what else they be sayin?" she asked, grinning sharply. Boo swallowed. "Sayin *all* us coloreds is related. Say a lotta things, folks do. Well I s'pect half the coloreds on this island got ol Joker's blood in 'em."

The smile shifted. Did it soften a bit?

"Know what Mamie's grams be sayin? Sayin it be a *pig* givin birth t'Mamie." She slapped her knee, rebounding flesh, and laughed. "Found Mamie in the pen out back—suppin at the pig's teat 'long side a regular pig baby that was suppin at the next teat. Say she pull Mamie off screamin for the Devil. Clean the stink off the child and raise'm herself. You believe sech a tale, boy?"

Boo chanced a nod of agreement.

"Well so did Mamie. Till she get t'be 'bout your size—then Mamie hear the truth." She glowered. "Know what she figure?"

Now he chanced a shake of his head.

"Figure she like that pig story better."

Boo waited for her to laugh again, but her face was suddenly blank. Then something like warmth crept back in, and she asked, "Wanna see how Mamie's real family look?" She gestured the knife toward the refrigerator. Boo looked and saw three photographs there. "Gwon," she urged—another shake of the knife—"take a look."

He stood, walked across the room (feeling that knife itching a spot between his shoulders) and examined the three photographs held by magnets to the refrigerator door. Two snapshots with washed-out tones, taken maybe minutes apart, showed a woman holding a fair-haired infant while a dark-haired little girl stood by her side. Only the little girl's change in stance distinguished the pictures from each other. The third picture, black-and-white, was evidently the same woman years younger. The woman looked at him with a cunning smile, a message of recognition. She was very pretty.

"Is this you?" he asked.

Mamie Stuvant laughed, making her awful, sloppy gravel sound. He believed he could actually stop being afraid of her if she just didn't laugh.

"Mamie's own little girl. Girl-childs always been what we doin best in Mamie's family—strong little girls. Boy-childs ain't but a curse."

"Where does she live?"

He waited for her answer but only heard the wet slip of her knife. He turned. She had been glaring into his back, the heavy brows massed to a worried scowl.

She sang again, sadly:

> *"Find the place were the crow done fly,*
> *six feet down, six feet over*
> *that be where my baby girl lie."*

More humming, her eyes still aimed somewhere in his direction but no longer seeing him.

"Married this ignorant white boy off'n the mainland," she said. "Don't know what that boy like more, gittin his ass drunk or beatin my baby. Beatin kilt my baby,"— she scowled, then grinned, and it seemed gnats flew from between her teeth—"and drinkin kilt that ignorant white boy."

Boo glanced at the tea, thought of witch's brew again, then shook it off with man thoughts. *She's a little bit crazy is all. She's an old woman, and her daughter died, and people pick on her because she's strange, and she didn't have anything to do with that boy who got killed.* And, believing this, he started back to the chair, not looking at the big woman with the knife, instead gazing casually at the clusters and sacks on the ceiling, preparing again to launch into his practiced speech when he saw the fingers.

He stopped. Stared.

Two mummified fingers, swaddled together and dangling from a string. Pointing at him. With accusation? Or just targeting him?

Timmy Duff's missing parts.

The well-advised warnings, the tales and rumors, the fireside chills, the shrieking getaways, Laylee Colebriar's cautions and his disregarded promise, the years of terror surrounding the witch—the years he foolishly let slip away while she crooned her lunatic songs at him—now, they all slammed back into his heart.

Without meaning to, he croaked weakly, "Oh, Jesus!"

Mamie Stuvant's eyes slid back into focus. The knife dripped peach nectar into her knuckles. "Ain't Jesus, Boo Taylor," she said slowly. "Jes an ol coon."

A space no wider than the knife's shaft separated him from the witch. Kitchen walls folded in on him. He touched Laylee's wongah beneath his shirt. *What...did she say?* "You're a *what?*"

"Coon paw."

The knife flashed up.

He flinched away, raised his forearm, girded for the first slash.

A twist of her wrist. She snapped the knife across the string and came down with the two mummy fingers.

"Coon?" he asked.

Gray and lumpy, slightly curled, not pointing but beckoning. Fingernails gone black. They might be a thousand years old.

"They're too big for a coon."

She grunted. "Thought an island boy be knowin somethin 'bout the swamp. This here's only medium size for a coon." She pushed the fingers under his chin. "Coon can't hurt you when he dead."

She gurgled her laugh again, and for the first time, he saw how sharp her teeth were.

He picked the fingers from her hand. Light as paper, and just as dry. Knuckles swelled like miniature walnuts. He looked for telltale tufts of fur but couldn't find any.

"What's it for?"

She turned away and went back to her peaches. With the knife out of sight, his breath came easier. "Lotta things," she said. "Specially a bad cold. Grindin it up with saffron and dried up dog shit and stump water."

"Dog shit?"

"Dog shit drawin the fever. Sometimes use a little spit stead'a stump water. Sometime use gator teeth stead'a coon paw."

He stared at the fingers. "And you eat it?"

"Cawse you doz'n eats it—nobody eat dog shit! Les'n they crazy. Wrap it up in black paper an' sleep with it under your neck. You gwine set down, boy, and show ol Mamie what you peddlin?"

After another moment's pause to consider the coon paw, he forced his unreliable legs to carry him back to the table. He dumped the fingers beside a peach and wiped his hand on his shirt.

He sat down, swam through the murky soup his mind had become. Unrelated thoughts careened off each other, spinning them into wild orbits until nothing made sense anymore—burlap dolls, boys socked in the mouth, Gussie Dutton's lustrous green eyes stabbing reproach, Cain slew Abel, a summer of dares. *Dare you to go into Mamie Stuvant's house.* He tried to grab hold of the fiction he'd come to tell her and decided maybe she *did* put something in the tea.

"I'm sellin magazine subscriptions," he said, empty of the enthusiasm he had practiced. "Goin door-to-door. Lots of us kids are sellin stuff this summer."

Mamie Stuvant wiped peach blood on her apron and came to the table. "Magazine, eh?" She sat across from him. The sharp noise of her chair scraping against the floor made him jump. "Be makin work all the time, boy, ol Mamie don't hardly got time to be lookin at no magazine."

But she reached across the table for them. She squinted at Tricia Nixon's round white face and straight blond hair on the cover of *Newsweek*. (The doctor's reception room address had been snipped away from the cover.) She fanned the pages, squinting and frowning. "How much these cost?"

He opened the notebook and recited from the figures he'd written there, finishing by reminding her, "And that's a lot less than the newsstand price."

She picked through the other selections. He was glad her attention was diverted. It had occurred to him that she might actually want to buy a subscription, and he was prepared to take her money and send the order off himself. The longer she read, clucked her tongue, made interested grunts the more he thought that was how it would go. Until she said, simply, "No."

She regarded him over the pages.

"You don't want to buy anything?" He had concocted a sales pitch but no longer had any intention of using it.

"You rememb'ren that joke Mamie tell you, boy?"

"Yes."

"Then say it back."

His brain scrabbled for it, but of course it was tossed out in the seconds after it was given. "I guess I don't remember."

She glowered. "Want you t'be rememb'ren it. Maybe someday you figure it out." She told it again:

"Tailor's mother had a son,
and never had another one.
When that child die, without his own,
her granchilds' names was Smith an' Jones."

"Now, say it back."

He did, but it took some coaching.

Satisfied, she said, "Get the joke yet?"

"No ma'am."

She growled, shifted focus to consider the magazine again. "Don't make no sense t'buy what she git free. Store on Polk always throwin 'way good magazines. Can I keep this here one?" She looked at him hopefully.

"Sure."

She smiled at him, and emboldened, sensing freedom just ahead, he chanced another sip of her bitter tea.

"Guess I should go," he said, standing up. "I got a lot more houses to visit. Guess there's gonna be a lot of us kids out sellin stuff this summer."

She eyed him dully.

"Make some money, you know?"

"Sho' you ain't no rock thrower, Boo Taylor?"

"No ma'am."

"Don't look nothin like your momma, does you?" she said.

Boo was one step away from the table and stopped there. "I...that's 'cause I'm adopted. She's not my—"

But the gargantuan form flapped an arm in disgust. "Ain't talkin 'bout that prissy little drunkard. 'Sides, 'dopted don't mean shit. Don't look nothin like your daddy, neither."

This was almost too much. Boo smiled and nodded uneasily—then, unable to think of what else to do, took his next step toward the door. Mamie Stuvant pushed up from the table and followed him as he walked to the front of the house as quickly as decorum allowed, reached for the knob and for a feverish moment—before he realized the knob was on the wrong side—thought he was forever, hopelessly trapped inside. Then he remembered, grabbed for the opposite side, and came up with the knob.

Sunlight streaked in and brought the afternoon's heat with it. "Sorry I couldn't sell you anything," he said, breathing clean air. "Hope I didn't bother you too much. Hope you don't mind us kids comin around to sell stuff."

"Only thing Mamie be mindin, boy, is them rock throwers."

He stepped through the door and into light.

"Hey boy!" she called out, compelling him to face her again. "That thing 'round your neck startin t'stink some."

His hand went to his heart.

"Buck-powder and guffweed and frog blood. Maybe a drip of grain alc in it, too, if Mamie knows that old toad."

She grinned. Enough light pierced the shadows to glitter across a row of sharp yellow teeth.

"You gwine tell ol Laylee that Miss Mamie says howdy."

He nodded absently, starting down the scorching bright walk and into the dust world beyond. He turned again, regretfully, when her gravely voice, still not through with him, reached out and halted him.

"Come back soon, doctor's boy! Give you a taste a'that peach bread!"

She waved happily and closed the door.

twelve

They met in front of Boo Taylor's house. Woolen clouds arrived from the sea to watch. The clouds robbed the boys of the brightest of the sun's light but not the worst of its heat.

As Boo expected, Hoss was the first to arrive.

"Where'd you go, yesterday? You know how many times I came around? Went to the shell pile. Went to the docks. Went to the beach. Nobody knew where you went. I figured you could, you know, *help* me with stuff. Where'd you *go?*"

"Fishing."

The too-many juices that pumped through Hoss Beaudry's plumpness threatened to boil.

The question was whether or not to tell Hoss the coast was clear. He'd tossed that one around most of the night, swinging his toes above the Atlantic, consulting stars and the tread of the moon for answers. The coast was clear; nothing to worry about. Just a strange lady. Still a *scary* one, of course, but not deadly. No beast lay in the woman's shadows; no murder lay in the woman's heart. No need to fret, Hoss.

He could tell him that.

And, he had accumulated what he thought was some valuable intelligence:

She's not a ghost, but she is Joker Tribbit's granddaughter or something, but don't bring it up. If she asks if you're a rock thrower, tell her absolutely not; you would never think of throwing rocks at her house. If she offers you tea—take it; it's not poison. Don't get spooked if she already knows who you are. Don't tell her bootlegging is illegal. Tell her how pretty her daughter is in the picture, but don't say anything stupid 'cause she died. And don't worry, they're just coon fingers.

He wanted to report all this, but what of Hoss then?

On the brink of proving his courage—to Dewey Fitch, yes, but finally to himself. If Boo told him about his own visit to Mamie Stuvant, then how many more years would Hoss be shackled to the notion that he needed Boo Taylor's guardianship? More years shackled to *me,* he thought and winced at his selfishness—is *that* why I did it? No. I am my brother's keeper. I checked; the coast is clear. And that's enough.

It was enough. Let him sweat just another pint or two, and in a little while, he walks away a pint or two lighter, an inch or two taller.

Coast was clear.

The wongah was still lying next to his heart, and he had ideas about slipping it around Hoss' neck. *Laylee made this, and I don't know if it works or not, but it can't hurt.* But maybe it *could* hurt, if Mamie Stuvant sniffed it out again, sniffed out the prank because of it, and then…

…and then what would she do?

After Hoss, the Standish brothers arrived. After them, it was Dewey Fitch and Lester Meggett wobbling in tandem on Dewey's monstrous bike. Almost at once, Dewey hooted that Mamie Stuvant was going to cut Hoss into little pieces. Boo told him to shut up.

While they waited for Ashford Marchant, Hoss showed everyone the elaborate Burpee Seed presentation he had prepared. Even Dewey was impressed.

Hoss had attacked his collection of comic books in a feverish quest for Burpee Seed ads, found dozens, and carefully snipped out the logos. Then he went to the National Five & Dime to purchase a three-ring binder and a parcel of accounting paper (an official-looking green with official-looking green and red lines that made up a confusing series of rows and columns). Next was a stop at Dalfields Hardware to buy a dozen packets of seeds: six flower and six vegetable.

Back home, he pasted identical Burpee Seed logos on the top of each official-looking page—twenty-two pages worth, using up all the small logos he could find. He pasted a slightly larger version on the twelve seed packets. And he pasted the largest logo he could find on the notebook's cover. In the inside pockets of the notebook, he stuffed the seed packets (vegetables in the front, and flowers in the rear) carefully aligning them so the Burpee Seed logo would show. He completed the notebook by writing names and addresses (taken from the phone book) in the first four pages of the accounting paper, indicating order selections and quantities and moneys collected.

The last touch was the T-shirt. He had meticulously duplicated the Burpee Seed logo on the front of a white T-shirt using pens and magic markers.

"Went through four shirts to get it right. I know it looks fake and all—you know, like a kid did it. But I figure it can't hurt. If she can't see the notebook right off, at least she'll see the shirt."

Boo Taylor thought about the magazine charade he had thrown together and was humbled.

"What about money?" Billy Standish asked. "What if she makes an order and wants to give you money? You got all those names in there, sayin people gave you money. What if she needs change or something?"

Hoss looked at him, horrified.

Boo put a hand on Hoss's damp back. "Hey, I'll get an envelope from the doctor's office. I got a few dollars and some change, and we can stick that inside."

Boo slipped inside and brought back an envelope from his father's desk. Hoss worried that it needed a logo pasted on it, but Boo assured him it would be okay.

Then Ashford Marchant showed up, and they all mounted their bikes for the ride to South Patch and Mamie Stuvant.

They abandoned their bikes in an empty scrub field and scrambled behind the tree line until the house was in sight. Dewey wanted to crowd the yard to watch up close. Boo made him and the rest hide around a rusted pickup that was twenty yards up the dirt lane.

They huddled. Boo took Hoss by the shoulders and stood him up. Now that they were on that anonymous dirt lane and Mamie Stuvant's house was a physical thing, Hoss Beaudry's terror had come wide-eyed awake.

"Jeez," Hoss whispered, staring wetly at Boo, a sopping and quivering weight with no indication of moving anywhere of its own volition.

Boo shot a cautionary glare at Dewey Fitch.

Dewey understood and kept silent.

Stickiness dribbled down the sides of Hoss's face. The Burpee Seed design on his shirt ran multi-colored sweat.

"You ready?" Boo asked.

Hoss said nothing.

"Just an old lady," Boo said. *The coast is clear. No hound, no murderer, no ghost, no witch.*

Hoss squeaked.

Tell him! It's all clear!

"What if she ain't home?" Lester asked.

"Then he's gotta come back when she's here," Dewey said.

Now Hoss spoke quickly, "No, dare's off! It's not my fault if she's not there."

"But you gotta go inside."

"You said *Tues*day *morn*ing!"

"Said on a day when you're dad ain't home, is all."

"No! You said——"

Voices rose. Boo glanced at the house and hushed them. "Don't make so much noise!" he whispered fiercely.

"We'll figure it out if it happens," Ash said softly.

Boo faced Hoss again. "You got everything?"

Hoss made a hurried glance at the notebook. "Yes."

"Look inside; make sure you got all the seeds there."

Hoss did as he was told.

"You know what you're gonna say?"

"Pretty much."

"And we're all gonna be right here."

Hoss's lower lip quivered; the bottom half of his face threatened to collapse.

Boo sighed. "You want me to go with you?"

"That's not fair," Dewey said behind him.

Boo looked at Hoss Beaudry's bloodless face and had a horrible portentous moment when he saw where the blood had gone: dripping in reds and blues and greens and oranges down the front of Hoss's baby-fat gut.

"I'll go," Hoss said. He sucked a tortured deep breath and stepped away from the abandoned pickup.

They crammed at the edge to watch.

He moved gracelessly across the yard, across the dirt street, a puppet animated by an inexperienced marionette. Alone and miserable in the thick heat, vulnerable as a plover chick, white and plump and soft.

"Everybody be quiet," Boo whispered, although no one had spoken.

Hoss made it as far as a single step onto Mamie Stuvant's yard. He stopped.

They waited for him to turn around, to come running back.

"He's faggin out."

Hoss opened his notebook, shuffled through it.

"What's he doin?"

"Faggin out."

"I bet he forgot a pen."

"No, he's got at least five in his pocket."

"Will you guys be *quiet!*"

Hoss looked up...hung suspended, like...a fat...drop on...a tap...

"He's coming back."

...and plunged forward again.

They lost him when he passed a clump of sumac trees, saw him again when he made it to the front stoop. He raised a pudgy white hand and knocked on the door.

Dewey made a wheezing sound. "I'll be shaved naked and cooked on a spit. The boy *did* it."

They waited, waited with Hoss, Boo remembering how it was when he stood on that very spot a day earlier, listening to unwished-for movement beyond the door, whining floorboards, whispery voices, knowing who was approaching.

Just an old lady.

The door cracked—the wrong way.

Hoss stood before a wedge of blackness. They heard the muffled set of tones, exchanging that first, terrifying introduction. Ashford whistled a breath. Lester grunted. Dewey whispered, "Is that her?"

Blackness widened, and they all watched Hoss Beaudry step forward and get swallowed. The door, like jaws, clamped shut.

"I don't believe it; I don't believe it!"

"He's *inside* there. With *her.*"

"Boy's got more guts than me."

"More guts than brains."

"He's *inside* there!"

"Hoss is the man!"

The others watched; Boo Taylor leaned away, let his back sag down the rusted old door of the stray truck while inside that house, bottles stood and fell like glass soldiers, herb bundles (and coon paw) decorated ceilings, and peach clouds blossomed sweet-sour plumes. And Hoss Beaudry dodged shadows to prove his mettle.

Lessons learned: there are no ghosts or witches.

He sighed. And while the self-satisfied breath celebrated that now certain comprehension, another part of him gloomed melancholy. For if Mamie Stuvant was no longer a witch, then Laylee Colebriar could not be one either.

Storm clouds, now fallen much lower than they had been just ten minutes ago, drum-rolled a green caution of rain. Gulls flew off, fleeing, fearful. Somewhere close, or made to seem close—wavering in and out like poor reception on a radio—little colored girls chanted at jump rope:

"Queenie, Queenie had two daughters,
Hated one an' liked the other."

So. It would be a world bereft of magic. The myths so willfully brainwashed into place—only to be unlearned when clock hands met at this fated rendezvous. The price of turning thirteen, it seemed: the undoing of those special thrills, the illumination of all the great dark mysteries.

And what would replace them?

(Green eyes; spun copper hair?)

"Hell, I just thought of somethin."

It was Lester speaking, drawing his head from around the edge of the truck.

"What happens if she wants to order some seeds? Won't he have to come back and deliver 'em?"

They watched him. Considered this.

And a moment later, Boo Taylor laughed; breath bursting forth and freeing days-worth of worry, years-worth of brainwashed fear, expelling it all into the thick, storm-threatening atmosphere. The others joined him, laughing at their own fear— "Just an old woman," they kidded each other, and just a bunch of stupid old stories. And as they laughed, they wondered about the celebration the rest of the day would bring. To the ball field. To the shell pile. Bonfires—a celebration for Hoss, for themselves. They laughed until the first heavy raindrops splatted their skin and some horrible shrieking-laughing thing from inside the storm ripped the day apart.

Boo Taylor's heart locked up in mid-beat.

"What the hell was *that?*"

Another scream; another laugh blasting across the dusty street.

"It came from the house."

"What is it?"

"Is it *Hoss?*"

And still more shrieks, exploding from Mamie Stuvant's house as if a hysterical bomb was set off, hurling its bizarre, fearsome shrapnel upon their heads in a sudden downpour. And beneath that, a savage lupine growling. Boo Taylor lurched to his feet, scrambled to the edge of the truck, pushed the others out of his way. He jammed a knuckle into his mouth and went no further.

The house was dark, still, sagging, and patient; a toad gloating, vapid-eyed, mocking his satisfaction while about its shingled back the storm and sanity unraveled.

Relentless, stuffed inside the toad mouth, Hoss Beaudry bellowed shredded-throat screams. Then, the worst yet, a ragged, tortured, sobbing, *"BOOOOOOO!"*

"...Boo, he's calling you; he's calling you..."

"...what's she doing to him..."

"...killing him, she's killing..."

"...a joke..."

"...no, do you *hear* it..."

"...oh Jesus what's happening..."

"...somebody stop it; she's *ripping him to pieces!*"

A high, wounded-animal wail rose from the midst of the screams, and Boo Taylor heard his name shrieked over and over. He bit down, drew blood. *But...the coast was clear!* The shrieks jagged and choked, staccato, breathless...

Ceased abruptly.

Only the sloppy sheet-falls of the storm.

Six boys, one missing, huddled and shivered.

"What do we *do?*" Ash whispered wildly. He grabbed Boo Taylor by the shoulders and shook him; the others grabbed for him, too. "Jesus, Boo! Jesus! What do we do?"

From the house, a low, gravely laughter gurgled like a flooding sewer. And then came the wet, grunting sounds of a big animal feasting.

Boo Taylor ran.

Part Three
Love Letters

Draped across the sheets, she reaches down beneath.
I take her hand, take her nipple in my teeth.
"Please," says she, "drink all of me,
so we may die this very eve.."
—*R. Gustavius Creek,* Changeling

long, long ways back..." she said.

Boo Taylor stood shin-deep in scrub grass on this, his second visit to a graveyard since coming back: his father first and those others in the Methodist Gardens, now this gray slab far south and alone in the old Baptist cemetery on Church Road. He held a bouquet of wildflowers in his fist.

"Hey old lady," he called to her in a whisper.

He leaned toward her and placed the flowers in the tall grass of her bosom as a cream-winged butterfly joined a pair of yellow jackets flickering in and out of the buds as if two petals had sprung to life. In the far off, the Atlantic pounded the island with constant thunder. Up close, only the feathery stalks of grass, the flowers in recline, the insects at play, and this thick stone fossil.

Eulahlah J. Colebriar
Died 1971

He felt her brittle bones collapsing beneath his feet.

"Got any tricks to show me, today?" he asked. "Any stories to tell?"

He let the whisper sink like liquid oxygen into the ground to wake her.

"Any more lessons?" Feeling the bones stirring now, tickling the soles of his feet. "Seems like I must've missed one or two..."

And, in the hush that followed came the movement again: fingers beetle-scratching the packed grave soil deep, deep beneath. The tremor of his voice had been recognized in that deep, very lonely, very sad place.

Boy?

The barest hint of a sigh.

He rocked backward, heart clogged and lungs caught in an airless bunch in his ribs. "Yes," he answered softly. "Me."

He listened closely, felt the grave give off a tremble, watched the grass sway in contradiction to the breeze. A faint tin clatter of bracelets. A whispery laugh.

He fell to his knees, placed his hands on the ground. The ground was as warm as a body. "Me," he said again, crying now, a seven-year-old boy falling into her lap; her arms circling to take him in, her cheek bending to his forehead. She rocked him, and the delicate hum of her voice vibrated through his flesh.

A long ways. . . she said.

"Tell me," he said, stroking her hair, which had somehow become the texture of uncut grass, "about Mamie Stuvant."

The earth shuddered at the name.

"Tell me the secret," he said.

Which secret?

"All of them. Tell me all the secrets."

Witch secrets? She laughed raucously and slapped her knee. The sound rebounded through the shadowy oaks. Boo looked about quickly. He was alone.

"Stop playing games, old woman, old, old, wonderful woman! Tell me. *Help* me. . ."

He sensed-felt-imagined her considering this, and he waited for her. She smelled like fresh flowers. One of the yellow jackets rumbled past his ear.

At last, another sigh from the body-warm depths beneath him.

But a car was rattling by on nearby Church Road, and the spell was broken. He lifted his head, wiping at the flower petals that glittered multi-colored tears on his cheek. The flowers were crushed, and the grass over the grave was flattened in the shape of his body.

"Secrets," he said.

But she was silent.

Finally, because she once told him it was one of the most potent ingredients in any magic brew, he swiped up a handful of the loose and sandy grave dirt and stuffed it into his pocket. Just in case he might need it.

Then he left her alone again. He started back to his dead father's house because he had calls to make.

two

First call:

Unanswered, after six rings. He hung up and dialed again, feeling braver, until Gussie Ransome picked up slightly out of breath. "Hello?" He hesitated, suddenly unsure how he might possibly respond to that voice. He had a clear image of her gripping the phone and waiting with increasing aggravation as he faltered. "Hello?" she said again.

He surprised himself by hanging up.

Second call:

Allen Noble's secretary cracked the door and peeked into his office. The lights were off. "You didn't get my buzz?"

Allen, in shadows, made an impatient gesture toward the deeper shadows in the corner. "I'm busy."

"Yes. But in case you're wondering, that's Mr. Taylor on the line." She made an attempt to see in the corner but it was too dark. "Are you *in?*"

Allen Noble glanced over the photograph of his wife, disregarding it to see what Sandy Baker wanted him to do. Her wet, crimson eyes glowed from the shadows with such fierce agony he thought she might shatter into a thousand glass fragments before him—or pounce on him and claw his face if he, the next moment, erred and said something other than just the right thing. She was either a dove with a broken wing or a wounded jackal ready to spring.

"Um," he said, and began to stand—then quickly sat again.

He watched the nails of Sandy Baker's small hands dig into their palms.

"No," he said, "I'm in conference. Tell him I'll be available to call sometime in the next few days."

His secretary left as Allen watched the small hands relax.

Third call:

Ringing on Boo Taylor's office desk. Elgin Highsmith answered and smiled when he recognized the voice. "How all you rebs gettin along down in Dixieland?"

"It's salt air and mint juleps on the veranda. Just like old times."

Sunlight slanted through the window. Elgin wanted to be outside, was never comfortable behind a desk, and now Boo Taylor was explaining that he would be held up for a few more days—maybe a week. Could Elgin handle things without him?

"A week?"

"That a problem?"

Elgin considered the folders and call-back slips piled on the desk. "No, I got it covered. How's your mother?"

"Just fine, thanks for asking."

"And Sandy—"

"Gone."

"Gone?"

"I sent her home last week. We had a talk."

Elgin took a breath. "She dumped you."

"It was mutual."

Silence then while Elgin looked at the very pretty face smiling from a frame on Boo Taylor's desk.

"Don't tell me. You ran into one of your old girlfriends."

When Boo Taylor didn't immediately answer, Elgin Highsmith howled. "Oh, I wish I'd seen *that!* Was there a cat fight? Who threw the first punch?"

"Sorry to disappoint you, but it wasn't like that."

"What *was* it like, then?"

"Drop it, Elgin."

"I'm serious! Talk to me!"

A long sigh crackled through the phone.

"Talk to me, Boo."

A few more moments of silence passed. "It was overdue, and you know it," Boo said. "And so did I; I just don't think she did."

"And then the great love of your life got you to make the move."

"I never said she was—"

"I bet you wanted to marry this girl, didn't you?"

"Elgin—"

"But something went wrong, right?"

"You're a pain in the ass."

Elgin was delighted. "This is good stuff! Ladies and gentlemen, we're about to find out why the famous Boo Taylor is a forty-year-old bachelor!"

"I'm thirty-nine."

"So what happened to this girl? How come you two never got married?"

"Elgin—"

"She *is* the love of your life, isn't she?"

When, again, he didn't answer right away, Elgin roared again.

"You think this is funny?"

"Hell yes, it is! Tell me what happened!"

"Knock it off."

"Tell me!"

"All right, smartass, you really want to know?" Boo Taylor's voice was charged with supreme annoyance. "Okay, then. She got me arrested and kicked out of college. Satisfied?"

Elgin fell out of the chair, breathless with laughter. The telephone cord swept a few folders onto the floor.

"I went away to Duke on a baseball scholarship," Boo was saying, "and I guess it spooked her a little since she was stuck back on the island."

Trying hard to control himself, Elgin said, "Can't keep 'em down on the farm once they seen the coeds."

Boo ignored this. "When I came home on weekends, she'd get pissy. She had a fierce temper."

"No doubt."

"Then she started flirting with this old boy she knew I couldn't stand, and she'd do it in front of me."

Elgin had to hold the receiver away from his mouth so he could laugh again.

"So one weekend, I brought a girl from Duke home with me to the island. Debbie Vandercliffe."

"Debbie Vandercliffe, I like that! Debbie the debutante!"

"Actually, I think she *was* a debutante."

Elgin roared again.

"I thought I was making a point, but it didn't go over too well."

"I guess not!" Elgin was having trouble breathing. "What happened?"

"Well..." Boo was silent for another few seconds. "A few days later she stole her brother's car and drove to the campus. She was trying to spray paint some obscenity about me on the dorm wall."

Elgin wheezed; his eyes were clamped shut, and tears started streaking down his cheeks.

"A security guard caught her and tried to stop her."

Now Elgin held his stomach with one hand and gripped the phone with the other, his body wracked and trembling.

"That's about the time I walked in. The guard went for his baton, and I decked him."

"You—"

"Shattered his bridgework and gave him a concussion. So they arrested me, and I was thrown out of school."

Elgin couldn't speak. He lay curled in a fetal lump, jittering with electric hilarity.

A full minute passed before he could gather his breath. He wiped the tears from his face.

"Satisfied?" Boo asked.

Still hitching, Elgin said, "I can't believe you never told me that story! And, now you're gonna win her back!"

"It's not like that. She's married now. And that's not—"

"Not married to that old boy you couldn't stand?"

"Well yes, if you really want to know."

Laughter threatened again, but Elgin held it back.

"And that has nothing to do with why I'm staying on," Boo was insisting.

"Of course not!"

Elgin took in several deep breaths. He gathered the spilled folders from the floor. "What do you want me to say if Sandy calls?"

He heard Boo Taylor's staticky grumbles through the line. "You think this is funny?"

three

Not funny, he thought.

Elgin's laughter still rung in his ears.

It was the least funny thing there was.

He was contemplating another attempt at calling Gussie Ransome, but his irritation with Elgin Highsmith soured him on the idea.

Boo Taylor is a LYING SNOB BASTARD!

She had spray painted it in bright red across the wall in letters two feet high. He still remembered the shock of coming through the stairwell, seeing her tussling with a security guard, seeing those words.

He looked at the phone. He reached for it, then let his hand drop.

Not funny, he thought miserably.

Everything had gone horribly wrong, almost as soon as he had left her and gone off for school, it seemed. And then his fist connected with the guard's jaw, and the world fell to pieces.

He drummed his fingers against the desk, wanting to call her but still not able.

Royal Goody's book, he saw, was lying next to his hand. An outraged black fist thrust to the heavens. Absently, Boo picked it up. He flipped through the pages to the middle and read.

The Haunted Ferryboat

I was first told the following story by my Aunt Nattie (Miss Annette Louise Timmons, who now lives in the town of Bluffton on the mainland) only a few years back...

He skipped forward a few paragraphs.

...proceeded to relate one of the sometimes dissimilar versions of the tale that follows. Aunt Nattie was right about two things: I had never heard the story before, and there is some corroborating mention of it in the *Patch Caller*. I also have the memories of some very helpful islanders to rely upon.

The tale is worth putting in print if for no other reason than it involves as its principals one of the more prominent historical families of the island: the Satterfields. In this case, Mr. Raymond Daggot Satterfield and his wife, Mishelle Tull Satterfield.

I was able to secure some compatible (partially compatible, at any rate) versions of Aunt Nattie's story from the following current and former Sweetpatch Islanders: Mr. Charles Evan McClain, who now resides in Waynesboro, Georgia; Mr. Winston (Fish Hook) Johnson; and Miss Dorothea (Dottie Mae) Jackson. And, I was able to interview Mr. Satterfield himself just before his death. I will provide Mr. Satterfield's version of events at the end and allow the reader to determine what is fact and what is fancy.

Our story begins in July of 1922 when the ferry operating between Mermaids Head and Stono Point sank during a storm, killing all eleven on board. The ferry had been established by Cooper-Stono Boat & Wares, and a round-trip then cost three cents. At the time, Cooper-Stono was owned by Reliance P. Satterfield, a prominent Charleston businessman with extensive holdings on Sweetpatch Island. The story was quite a sensation at the time, appearing in articles as far away as Atlanta. Locally, accounts of the incident seem more focused on the inconvenience of losing the sole mode of routine transport between the mainland than with the loss of life.

It was some weeks before Cooper-Stono was able to restore the ferry service. Shortly afterward, according to my aunt and the other islanders, the ghosts of some of those who perished on the ferry began appearing to passengers.

Miss Jackson explains: "Most folks on the island back then was afraid to step foot on that boat after the last one sunk. White folks 'cause they was scared it was gonna sink again. Black folks 'cause it was haunted. Most of them bodies was never found, and the water ain't a fitting resting place. Especially for some so young. Them little girls was surely stuck out there, crossing back and forth, day after day, and nowhere else to go."

According to Mr. McClain, who was a young boy at the time, he saw three girls sitting quietly, shoulder-to-shoulder on one crossing. He pointed them out to his mother who claimed not to see them at all. When he stepped off the ferry at [[Corrington Landing]] and looked around, the girls hadn't moved, although one looked up and waved at him.

Mr. Johnson tells of the time on a return trip from the mainland when he heard giggling coming from nowhere in particular and then felt little hands touching his arms and shoulders. When he looked around, he saw nothing but small, wet footprints. He tells of others who swear to similar experiences.

According to Mrs. Jackson: "They (the ghosts) wasn't so much a curse as a warning. That's what folks said after what happened to poor Miss Mishelle leastways, and I guess maybe they was right."

In the Spring of 1932, Cooper-Stono was handed down to Reliance Satterfield's children, Raymond Satterfield and his sister, Lucille. The younger Mr. Satterfield proceeded to commission a second ferry and opened an additional route to the mainland at Stono Point. In addition, he operated two oyster processing plants on the island. At the time, his various enterprises combined to be the largest employer on Sweetpatch Island.

Like a number of wealthy Southern families of the day, Mr. Satterfield enjoyed summering on Sweetpatch Island's prestigious North Beach where he and his young wife might enjoy the cool ocean breezes. The Satterfield family had owned a sixteen-room "cottage" on Carriage Avenue since the 1880s and two others on Rain Guild Street since the early 1900s.

Alas, tragedy struck again on the night of April 2, 1936. On a stormy night, the *Sadie June* failed to arrive at Stono Point at its appointed time. A search was mounted. Eventually, the boat was found run aground and still smoldering from a fire on the mainland well north of its intended course on the Yamawichee.

According to the account in the *Patch Caller*, the grounded vessel was found mysteriously empty. This caused considerable consternation since one of the passengers on board that evening was none other than Mrs. Satterfield herself, who was allegedly nine months pregnant at the time.

Eventually, Captain Dag Bailey turned up and claimed he left the wreckage in search of assistance after the boat was grounded. When questioned about the incident, he indicated that a lamp was knocked over in the storm, starting a fire that quickly spread. He then heroically steered the craft to the nearest point of land and was able to bring it onto solid ground safely. In the confusion, the passengers, who were mostly poor blacks (with the notable exception of Mrs. Satterfield), must have abandoned the vessel and either drowned or swam to shore.

Three bodies were eventually recovered when they washed ashore not far from the disabled boat. One of these was Mrs. Mishelle Satterfield.

Mrs. Satterfield, who was only twenty-three at the time, was eventually buried near the Satterfield's home in Charleston.

Soon afterward, stories of what had happened on the night of April 2 apparently began to spread as various "witnesses" emerged.

According to Mr. Fish Hook Johnson, he was told by one survivor that Captain Bailey had abandoned ship shortly after the fire started. The fire itself, he says, was started accidentally by the midwife who accompanied Mrs. Satterfield when the poor woman went into labor.

Mr. McClain also claims Captain Bailey leapt overboard at the first sign of fire. In his version, the fire was started by one of the ghosts from the doomed *Sadie June*.

"Was one of them girls folks was always seein. Spooked folks pretty bad; then that fire got started, and all hell broke loose."

Mrs. Jackson mentions a first-hand account from Captain Bailey himself (she referred to him as "Baylor"). She says that Captain Baylor confided that the fire was started by a "wild girl."

"That girl, he say Gawd, she come from nowhere, wasn't but half-dressed, and she got the Devil in her. Tell me that witch-girl just wail out loud and put a scare into Miss Mishelle and them others, sayin she gonna turn to a wolf and eat all them folks up in her little bit of dress almost falling off. Then she just got lost in the smoke, and he didn't see her after."

(For the record, no one seems to know what became of the Captain. I even checked old Cooper-Stono payroll records and found no further mention of him after 4/2/36. It seems he disappeared shortly after professing his heroism).

Aunt Nattie's account is closest to Mrs. Jackson's, although some of the details vary (for instance, the wild girl becomes another "ghost-girl," presumably a remnant from the earlier ferry tragedy). I believe it's possible she may even have first heard the story from Mrs. Jackson.

In any event, I apologize to the reader for the lack of consistency.

One hears the echoes of "The Beast" legend in Mrs. Jackson's version of events: fiery deaths and even a mysterious "witch." Mrs. Jackson swears to the story's veracity as she not only heard it from Captain "Baylor" but also from the Satterfields' household staff. (At the time, Dottie Mae Jackson was employed by the Shallcross family, the Satterfields' next-door neighbors on Carriage Avenue.)

As the reader may know, it is often the case when researching folktales that the more colorful elements of one story (in many cases, from an entirely different geography) may be "borrowed" to spice up another story (one of perhaps rather ordinary circumstances), thus creating a colorful new tale to toss around the campfire. Most often this is done in perfect innocence. When I playfully asked Dottie Mae Jackson if the witch-girl that Captain Bailey saw might have been the famous Sheba Tribbit, she seized my arm excitedly as if she hadn't considered this before. "Why, I'm sure it was!" she told me. Thereafter during our conversations she repeatedly and casually referred to this figure as "Sheba's ghost."

So, how does such a story (certainly a tragedy by any account) become the wild tale of "The Haunted Ferryboat" whispered across the kitchen some sixty years later?

As I have indicated, I was fortunate to speak with Mr. Raymond Satterfield himself, just before his death at age eighty-seven in 1990. Mr. Satterfield would not let me tape-record our interview; however, he did respond to several of my questions enabling me to rough out a version that is clear on the following:

• Yes, his wife and unborn child were killed in the tragedy. Mrs. Satterfield was accompanied by a nurse on a trip to the mainland where she would be giving birth under more sanitary conditions than could be arranged for on the island.

• He claims to know of at least five survivors, though he could not name them.

• Captain Bailey also survived the ordeal and piloted the boat to safety before going off in search of help.

Raymond Satterfield and his sister sold Cooper-Stono less than a year after the tragedy. Stories of the haunted ferryboat continued to circulate, however, with new ghostly sightings reported up until the company was closed down when Dedmens Causeway was built in 1956. This includes reports of the spirit of the drowned Mrs. Satterfield forlornly looking into the depths of the Yamawichee over the ferry rail, seeking her lost child. There are several mentions of ferry riders seeing a beautiful woman rising from beneath the cold Yamawichee waters, not far from where the old ferry grounded. These accounts occur, invariably, at nightfall. A famous picture of such an alleged sighting was first published in Mavril Pickett's text; however, the image is crude and extremely blurred, and could be presumed a human (or inhuman) figure only by the greatest stretch.

Mr. Satterfield eventually remarried and started a new family. And while he would not discuss all of the details of this story with me, he did graciously give me blessing to proceed with its publication…

Boo set the book down. He realized his foot had jogged open the bottom drawer of his father's desk where the stacks of photographs were stored. His thoughts were still on Gussie. Were there any pictures of him and Gussie in here? Did he really want to see them if there were?

He was reaching in, ready to pull forth a stack when he noticed a lump tucked into the back corner of the drawer. He pulled it out, unwrapped his father's handkerchief from the object and held it in his hand.

A silver pocket watch, heavily tarnished, the engraved letters black and gritty.

SBT

His father's initials. Silas Barnwell Taylor. And within the folds of the handkerchief, a photograph, the hues diluted with age so that the images were ghostly: the doctor, smiling and comfortably happy, arm around the shoulder of a very pretty young woman who was gazing at him with complete adoration.

four

Lester Meggett tipped his glass to the pitcher, letting beer rise to the brim until a few runnels spilled over. "You're a natural!" Dewey Fitch shouted over the honkytonk blaring from the juke. Lester cocked his glass to Boo Taylor and winked over an unshaven cheek before quaffing down a third of the glass. Then he tucked a cigarette back into the corner of his mouth.

Lester Meggett was still grimy in a green *Satterfield Properties* T-shirt and blue jeans. The brim of a threadbare baseball cap was drawn low over his eyes. Dewey Fitch looked scoured raw from a recent shower; his hair was still damp and plastered to his skull.

"Nice you comin out with us, Boo," said Dewey.

"Like old times," said Lester.

"Old place ain't changed much."

"Men got meaner, women got uglier, and food got worse."

"Serve buffalo wings now. You gotta try some."

Boo Taylor sipped his beer and took in the place, filled to the rafters with smoke and rednecks. And at the moment, Lyle Lovett's chords were blasting loud enough to shudder the booth at certain bass lows. "Is Blue Boys still open?" he asked.

A dizzy smile spread Lester's lips. "Naw, that ol dive burnt down few year's back."

"Black folks all go to this place called The Sand Dollar now," said Dewey.

"Down on Calhoun."

"Naw, it's on Ship's Tide."

"Same thing. Hey Boo, you met Dewey's wife yet?"

Boo had noticed the ring on Dewey Fitch's finger, but as Dewey hadn't mentioned a wife, he thought it better not to raise the subject.

"*Ex*-wife," Dewey said.

"Well you're still livin with her."

"I got the kids to think about."

"Anyway," Lester said to Boo, "she's real fat."

Boo waited, but Dewey did not immediately respond. After a moment, Dewey explained reasonably, "She put on a little weight after havin the kids."

"Aw, she was always fat."

"Least I *got* married. Beats chokin the chicken."

"I don't choke the chicken."

"Sure you don't."

"Anyway, you know what Dewey has to do so he can fuck his wife? He rolls her in flour and goes for the wet spot!"

Dewey found this hilarious.

The juke flipped over to a Garth Brooks song, drawing scattered catcalls from the crowd. Boo Taylor shifted in his seat, and a piece of duct tape curled away from the vinyl.

"Hey, lookit there, Boo." Dewey was pointing across the bar. "Your best pal just walked in."

Murphy Ransome loped across the floor to a booth on the far side of the room. He shook hands with a plumpish man in a cowboy hat who already sat there. Eyes narrowed, lips pursed, Boo Taylor hunched over his beer as a mellow and nostalgic dislike settled over him.

"Don't worry about them boys," Lester told him.

"I'm not worried," Boo said.

Murphy was still slim, still in possession of all of his longish dark hair, and he was still good looking. Boo wondered briefly who Martha Goody would cast to play the part of Murphy Ransome. Fess Parker, perhaps. Or maybe Max Baer Jr.

"Wanna invite them boys over?"

Boo now recognized the man in the cowboy hat. It was Harley Dutton. "Hell no."

"Bet you could take 'em both with one hand."

"Ever notice," Dewey said, "how Gussie wound up taller than all her brothers?"

"Know what I think?" Now Lester cupped his hand to his mouth conspiratorially. "I think Clara Dutton got sick of ol Hank's little dick and found herself a backdoor man. They say she was a good looking woman 'fore Hank and them boys used her up."

"That's what you think, is it?"

"Used her up. Used her up, and then she died."

"She died of ovarian cancer," Boo told them. "Two years after Gussie was born."

"Don't mean those boys didn't have a hand in it."

The younger Dutton boys had been like rough older brothers to Boo through the years he and Gussie were together. Harley and Petey (who tolerated him, but not much more) remembered a sickly woman spitting obscenities from a living room sofa; Wade and Gussie claimed not to remember her at all.

Lester was slouched deep in his seat, his head propped on the heel of his palm. His eyes were a happy blur. "Boo, you still playin ball?"

"Oh hell, Les, not for years."

"*Look* like you're still playin ball."

"No."

"Look like you could whip 'em both. You sure?"

"I'm sure."

"Shame," Lester said and shook his head with exaggerated sweeps; the ashes on his cigarette had grown long and curled and threatened to drop into his beer. "Next to Murph, you was maybe the best I ever seen on this island. Maybe you was even better than Murph."

Lester's head began to bow toward the table. His eyes snapped open suddenly and he straightened up.

"How about I give you a ride home, Les?" Boo asked.

"Aw, I ain't ready to leave yet." He fumbled with the pitcher. After he splashed more beer on the table, Boo grabbed the pitcher and held it to Lester's tipped glass.

"That Sandy sure is a fine looking girl," Les said, "You ain't gonna marry her?"

"No."

"Shame. Some bastards got all the luck. Hey, whattuhyuh call a hippy's wife?"

Boo shook his head.

"Mississippi!" He roared laughter. "Get it?"

Boo Taylor excused himself and went to the bar. He got directions to the payphone and maneuvered toward it. He pulled a slip of paper from his pocket as Wynona Judd now came through the juke, singing about girls with guitars. While Boo fidgeted at the phone, thick cigarette smoke stung his eyes, provoking the memory of sneaking, underage, into Oakies for the first time, an island rite of passage, hand-in-hand with Gussie Dutton behind Wade and whatever girl Wade was seeing at the time. They stormed the door, heads down, through a surprising lack of resistance. And discovered this sprawling, dimly lit cavern crammed with sweaty cowboys and bad smells. How old had they been—just sixteen at the time?

He studied the number on the paper. He dropped change into the phone, started to dial—then stopped—then dialed again. He held the phone to one ear and covered the other.

After the fourth ring: "Hello?"

"Gussie?"

She fired back angrily, "You're at Oakies, aren't you?"

"Yes."

"Don't tell me—you've been drinking."

"Well—"

"I *told* you not to call me when you're drinking!"

"Gussie—"

"And don't expect me to give you or Harley a ride anywhere, either!"

"Gussie, it's Boo Taylor."

"Oh! Oh my Lord, Boo. Boo, I'm sorry!"

Her distress put him at ease.

"I can barely hear you over that racket. What on earth are you doing at Oakies?"

"Catching up with the boys," he said.

"Is Murphy there?"

"Yeah, I think I saw him under a table a while back."

"You saw—oh, very funny. What are *you* doing there? I thought you flew home."

Boo slid the phone number back into his pocket. Having Gussie actually on the phone was turning out to be a lot easier than thinking about it. "I have some business to take care of first. And, I was wondering if you wanted to have lunch."

"If I—well sure, I suppose. I mean, if you want."

"How about tomorrow?"

"Tomorrow? Let me think. What day is tomorrow?"

"Saturday."

"Saturday? Okay—I mean, I *can't*. I think I have to work tomorrow; I mean..."

He was enjoying himself now; he hadn't expected her to be so unsettled. "Don't they let you take a lunch break?" he asked.

"Well of course they do—I mean, of course I can." She paused for a deep breath. "Okay, then. Where'd you want to go?"

"It's your island now, you pick a place." He suddenly remembered his lunch with Sandy, the graffiti on the seawall. "Not near the docks, though."

"Are you buying?" she asked.

"Sure."

"Then you're taking me to Del Rey's, and I'm ordering the lobster!"

❖   ❖   ❖

He ordered another pitcher at the bar, and while he was waiting saw Lester slouched back at the table as someone—Murphy Ransome he realized—stood over him and engaged him in conversation. Dewey Fitch had disappeared.

Boo paid for the beer and steered back to the booth.

Murphy smiled at him. "Hey, Boo. See you got the prettiest date in the joint."

Boo set the pitcher down. He held out his disfigured hand, and Murphy shook it. Murphy Ransome was an inch or two taller than Boo and an inch or two less broad. His bronze face was smooth and angular and still rich with lazy good looks and a supreme Southern cockiness.

"Just got off the phone with your wife," Boo said.

"Yeah?"

"We're having lunch tomorrow."

"That so?"

"Del Rey's. Is that a good place?"

Murphy's smile had gone somewhat flat.

"I hear their lobster's good," Boo said and slid into the booth. Lester Meggett was barely conscious, although he still managed to keep a death grip on his glass. Boo grabbed a handful of peanuts and popped a few in his mouth.

"That Harley over there?" Boo asked.

Murphy blinked and closed his mouth. "Harley? Oh yeah, that's him."

Boo leaned over and waved. Harley Dutton frowned and waved back. "You're right," Boo said to Murphy, "my date *is* prettier than yours."

Murphy Ransome was looking at the empty spot next to Lester. He seemed to be debating whether or not to sit there. Finally, he said, "Say Boo, I was sorry to hear about the doc. He was a good old fella. I remember that time he set my arm. You remember that?"

Lester Meggett suddenly came to life. "Broke it! Broke it first half in the Lobeco game."

Murphy brightened. "That's right!"

"Thought you was goin pro, till then."

"You never know, Les," Murphy said, then turned to Boo Taylor. "Say Boo, you never did make it to the Bigs, did you?"

Boo shook his head. "Two months in Triple-A was as close as I got."

"Too bad. Tough luck with your hand bein all fucked up like that, I guess." Murphy was smiling broadly.

"Actually, Murph, I was a knuckleballer, and this thing gave me an edge. Helped with the grip, if you can believe it."

"No shit?"

"No shit."

Lester piped in, "Heard it snap all the way up in the bleachers. Thought you'd go pro."

Murphy was nodding; he placed a hand on Boo Taylor's shoulder. "Things worked out for me okay, though, didn't they? Married Gus, got a family, even started my own agency. What about you, Boo—you got a family somewhere?"

Boo crunched a few more peanuts, deciding he wanted to slam his fist into Murphy Ransome's face. "Not that I know of, anyway," he said.

Murphy chuckled and squeezed Boo's shoulder. "Say, I was wondering... Miss

MaeEllen, she want to make any changes in her coverage you think?"

"I really couldn't say, Murph."

"I mean, as a widow n'all. There's things she ought to consider."

Boo leaned back in the booth. He was waiting for Murphy Ransome to hand him his business card. "That's sweet you should ask," he said. "I'll tell her you were concerned."

"You just tell her to give me a call if she wants to talk."

"You can count on it, Murph."

Lester picked that moment to belch loudly. Murphy chuckled again. "Well listen, Boo, you say hey to Miss MaeEllen." He nodded at Lester. "And you take care of your boy, here."

"Sure will, Murph. And I'll make sure Gussie brings you home a doggy bag."

He offered Murphy a pleasant grin. Murphy grinned back and then sauntered away, leaving Boo alone with a nearly catatonic Lester Meggett.

The Eagles were crooning "Peaceful Easy Feeling" when Boo realized Lester was completely passed out. Dewey had not returned.

Boo waited for the song to end. Then he hauled Lester from his seat, slung him over his shoulder, and carried him outside.

five

12:40 a.m.

Queenie, Queenie had two daughters
Hated one and liked the other
One was milk and silk and spice
The other not so very nice
One got married, one got killed
One laughed hard when the blood got spilled

The little black girls swung their jump rope under the glow of the only working streetlamp on Carp Street. As Boo Taylor's rented Buick Regal glided quietly past the girls, they looked at him, baring their white teeth in shark smiles. The moth-infested light directly above them carved hollow starvation in their cheeks. It was only as the car was almost past them that he noticed the hulking dog that was restlessly circling the girls.

Lester Meggett sagged next to him, beard flattened against the window, and with each snore, the thin line of drool he had started down the glass lengthened. Lester had conveniently woken long enough to inform Boo he lived at number seventeen on Carp Street in Westview Estates. In South Patch, he told him, and the place was crawling with niggers. Then he was back into coma, leaving Boo to wander the streets of a modern South Patch. After twenty minutes of aimless turns down unknown streets, he rolled into the trash-filled glare of a 7-Eleven parking lot to ask directions. A sallow teenager under fluorescents breathed gum on him and explained there was no such thing as Westview Estates or Carp Street, but he could get him to Westview Avenue only a half-mile away.

Boo piloted the car as directed through more unrecognizable roads until he and Lester were creeping down a dark lane bordered by a string of homes identically cheap and depressing. The headlights swept over a sign poking from a patch of scrub, and Boo backed the car up to get another look.

Westview Court

A Satterfield Properties Community

Security Patrolled! No dogs allowed!

Carp Street was the second turn off the main road where mobile homes were stacked against each other like boxes on a shoe store shelf and rusted sedans crammed the spaces in between. The patches of dirt that served as front yards were an abstract aesthetic of garbage bags and plastic toys and glittering broken glass.

Number seventeen was two battered tin homes beyond the girls with their jump rope. A red Mercury Monarch of some ancient vintage with expired tags nested in the sandy tracks next to the place. Looking closer, Boo saw the rear axle was hunkered slightly askew on cinderblocks, giving the car the effect of a large metallic dog straining to take a leak on Lester Meggett's lawn.

Boo stopped the car. When he opened the door, the big dog pealed away from the girls and grumbled toward him at a trot.

Boo jerked back into the seat and slammed the door.

The dog reached the car, and it was enormous. Yellow, bland eyes considered him through the slim pane of glass, conjuring ancient images that burned like flash fire through his memory—myths and legends, roadside ambushes, screaming chases in a storm, a solid thump against the grille.

What did I hit?

His right hand tingled.

A few yards away, one of the little girls laughed.

Another clapped her hands.

The third squealed some indecipherable word, and at this, the dog moved away.

Boo watched as it slinked back to the girls. Then he looked at Lester who breathed wetly on the window.

Carefully, Boo opened the door again. The heavy night heat pressed down on him as he got out of the car and circled to the passenger side. He looked off toward the dog and the little girls.

The dog was two glowing eyes. The girls stared at him dumbly.

Boo opened the passenger door, and Lester spilled out.

"Don't bring that boy 'round here."

The voice gurgled from behind him. Boo Taylor, burdened with the weight of Lester's shoulders, twisted around to see the blank, pitch-black screen of the collapsing porch tacked to the face of number nineteen. Something bobbed in the shadows within.

"Granddaddy don't want that drunken ol white boy 'round no more. Cut him up with his butcher blade...you see soon enough."

A dim silhouette, shoulders and frizzled gray hair, made slow, ocean-rocking motions. The whole world was the dreary, dead circle in gloom beneath a single streetlamp. The little girls grinned sharp white teeth from slippery faces; the hound slouched, dull and brutal; a hundred more eyes taunted from just beyond the crooked boundary of light.

Lord, what did I hit?

Lester grunted a snore. Boo heaved his body from car; Lester's eyes fluttered, pasty and webbed with blood; he mumbled, "Lucky ol' bastard. . ." and went limp again.

"Don't look nothin like his momma, do he?"

Lester Meggett was as skinny as a bag of sticks, but he was all sagging, lead weight, and Boo groaned to half-carry, half-drag him across the dirt lawn and open the creaking screen door.

The front door was locked.

With those hungry, patient eyes on his back, Boo hitched Lester up on his hip, patted his pockets, and dug out a key chain. Sweat ran waterfalls down Boo's face and neck and pooled in his shirt. The third key fit the lock. He pushed the door open and dragged Lester inside. The screen door banged closed behind him. Nicotine and decay smothered him in a hot, wet blanket, stuffed rags down his throat, his lungs. Things on small legs were scuttling in the darkness.

Boo leaned Lester's slack corpse against vinyl paneling that buckled an inch under his weight—then blindly slapped at the wall until he found a plate with two switches. He flipped them on.

The innate wrongness of the place overcame him; the atmosphere was too thick, the walls somehow collapsed inward like a cave. He looked closer at the misshapen dimensions of the room. It took a moment to focus. Then the images emerged, and he was accosted by ricochet vulgarities variously taped and tacked to the flimsy wallboard, the ceiling, even the windows: fur-and-meat splays of female genitalia, centerfold cut-outs of breasts, thousands and thousands of them, carefully clipped and mounted, surrounding him—interspersed with sad-eyed Christs, weepy Madonnas, cadaverous faces grinning from battlefields. It was a vast conglomeration of eyes— tear-drop labia eyes, nipple eyes, empty skull eyes. Patches of faux wood grain showed through the collage, but the images dominated.

Lester's head lolled like a dreamy lover against him and Boo felt his own flesh recoil like a slug touched by salt. He suddenly wanted to drop that sick, dead weight and let it go sprawling into the room.

Instead, he grimaced and dragged Lester deeper into the place, toward an open door he hoped was the bedroom. His foot slipped; he looked with frantic disgust and was relieved to see it was only a discarded pizza box. The floor and furniture, he now noticed, were heaped with soiled clothes and beer cans and ripped-apart newspapers and magazines. A green-blue carpet was pocked with cigarette burns.

The wall-mounted eyes followed his progress.

He tugged Lester into a tiny bedroom and let him drop on a bare mattress. Lester's arm flopped into a TV tray, spilling a ceramic bowl to the floor and lifting a stale cloud of cigarette ash.

Boo wiped the sweat from his forehead. He felt as if he had fallen down a sewer. He considered the limp body. Should he pull off his shoes? Undo his belt? He rejected those thoughts, deciding instead he needed to get out of this place as soon as possible. He left Lester Meggett where he fell, and he stepped quickly out of the bedroom.

Back in the front room he was about to drop Lester's key chain on a rickety table when he saw a familiar name peaking up from a pile of old magazines. He picked a slip of paper from the pile, letting the keys slide away in a metallic clank. The name was pleaded in black ink over and over and over in a pathetic, child's scrawl:

Sandy Baker Sandra Baker Cassandra Baker
Sandy Meggett Sandy Baker Sandra Baker-Meggett Sandra Meggett Sandy
Sandy Baker Sandy Baker Sandy Sandy Sandy

Scribbled on the back of an envelope. On the table, a dozen or so unopened pieces of junk mail; Boo picked up another envelope and saw the same repeated, desperate scrawl of names.

Sandy please spred your legs for me
Please I stil love you

Boo dropped the envelopes. He quickly moved to the front door and struck the light switches.

❖   ❖   ❖

He breathed the remarkably clean air outside where it felt ten degrees cooler. His skin felt coated in slime. From number nineteen, the toad-voiced woman was still speaking as if her conversation was unbroken.

" ...why I told you, granddaddy ain't likely to let such a thing go..."

The little girls had vanished. Boo looked for sign of the big dog and saw none. He started for the car.

"...been searchin from hell to heaven and all stops in between..."

He walked into the street to get to the driver's side door.

"...and he don't take well to rock-throwers, ain't that right, doctor's boy?"

Boo stopped.

Papery wings flitted at the streetlamp.

The shape within the porch shadow continued to bob.

"Them bones you found, boy; they ain't who you think they is."

Insect madness swept across his brain. He took a step for the porch. The streetlamp's pallid flame shimmered the rusty, angular web of the screen.

"Is that you?" he called out.

As he touched the yard, the shadows suddenly came alive and rushed him. He raised his arms to ward off their teeth. They swarmed around him, grabbing his clothes, tugging at his arms, squealing at him, dragging him back into darkness, and he nearly screamed until he heard their little-girl voices.

"We scared a' that ol witch."

"Yeah, we scared."

"She mean; she hurt children."

"She kill a boy."

One of the shadows grabbed his mangled right hand and pulled it. "Take us with you," the little girl whined. She was smiling beguilingly and leaning backward with the effort of tugging him to the car.

"Yeah, take us away from here, 'fore that ol witch get us."

"She say she get us all."

Boo looked from the girls to the screened porch. The shape inside the porch was no longer moving.

"...time is come, boy."

The little girls shrieked; hands flew away from him; stick legs scampered on gravel. Boo watched the girls scramble down the crumbling roadway, watched them as they stopped and turned on the far side of the dismal yellow circle to look at him and break into criminal giggles.

"Take us with you, man," one of them shouted.

"Yeah, we so *scared!*"

They giggled again and ran as a cluster into the night. Boo touched his clothes in the places their hands had been—and realized his wallet was missing.

He looked after the girls. *"Hey!"*

Their laughter faded into the miserable depths of dark roads and alleys. He looked briefly back at the screened porch. Then he broke into a run and chased the three little girls down Carp Street.

They ran across the main road of the Westview Court mobile home park—he saw fleeting, dusky provocations of stick arms and legs—and into the blackish maze of dirt lanes and low, flat buildings

"Take us with you, *please!*"

"Please, we so scared!"

"Yeah, she *mean*, man."

Through an alley between homes, he ducked under a clothesline barbed with wooden pins and crashed into a trashcan. He righted himself and hurdled a low bush. Ahead, the little girls bounced and skipped and scampered across a short, grassy field out of the mobile home park and onto an adjoining street. They were laughing and hooting back to him. He lumbered across the field and into the street.

They brought him into a foreign neighborhood of crowded, ramshackle, two-story houses on stilts. The houses were just as dead and lightless as the mobile homes he'd left. A giggle rode the rancid marsh from behind one of the houses. He trotted off the road and pushed down a rutted dirt driveway, coming to the back of the house. Blackness shifted ahead of him. He darted for it. After a few steps, taloned fingers seized his ankle, and he tumbled.

His hand reached for the claw and wrapped around the slick, rubber ribs of a snake. *"Shit!"* he hissed, and discovered he was holding the prone corpse of a child's bicycle. He pushed to his hands and knees. His left ankle throbbed, and his left elbow was skinned. Panting and letting his sweat drip into the dirt, he listened for another sound from the girls and instead registered the tremors of a guttural rumbling somewhere close behind.

He stood slowly. Turned slowly.

Shadows accumulated from a dozen places, gathering upon themselves as his eyes adjusted and something immense and solid slid from beneath the nearby house. It hovered at a spot a few feet away, wobbling in and out of the remnant glow from distant streetlamps. Boo spread his hands in supplication and made a slow backward step. The shape, shoulder muscles bunching and unbunching, slid a step forward to match his.

Another ghost titter feathered from the street.

Eyes locked to the great shadow-thing, Boo Taylor stepped back again. Again, the shape advanced to maintain the distance between them.

"Git boy!" The disembodied echo of a little girl.

A massive head pivoted toward the street.

"Boy you git now!"

The head bowed; shoulder muscles unbundled. The shadow unfastened itself from the ground and skimmed past Boo Taylor's legs. Boo turned and watched it corner the house at a trot.

He blew out his breath and decided to wait where he was. His elbow was sore, and he rubbed it. He listened.

Nothing but the sounds of night.

After an interval of time passed, and nothing else materialized from the shadows, he limped back to the street.

Houses were dark, shut up for the night. Like Westview Court, the lawns here were crammed on top of each other and crowded with old-model trucks and cars, sometimes three or four deep. The smell of marsh decay was bad; it was always worse, Boo remembered, on the southwest side of the island and especially bad at low tide when the mainland breeze drifted across the exposed mudflats and carried the rot of a million dead sea creatures across the night.

Alert for signs of little girls and large dogs, he followed the unmarked line of the exact center of the street—habit from a superstitious cradle rocked by Eulahlah Colebriar's lullabies:

When you out at night, Mr. Boo, you keep to the middle of the street, you hear me? The very middle.

A car trundled by several lanes ahead—on Westview Avenue, if his bearings were correct—and he was grateful for the company of familiar noise.

White spooks hide on one side, and black spooks hide on the other.

A shadow jerked on his right. He stopped and watched. Trash littered the front yard of the house across from him. A light gleamed green-yellow from an upstairs window.

They like to snatch you up you get too close, either way.

A giggle—purposeful; an invitation to dance—breezed from the open front door. Boo stepped away from the middle of the street. A small, squarish lump in the dirt border of the road reflected the glow of the streetlamp. He walked to it and leaned down to pick it up. His wallet. He flipped through it quickly. His license and credit cards were untouched, but the bills were gone. He looked up at the house.

"We so scared!" a girl's voice called from the front door.

"Take us with you."

"Please?"

He stuffed the wallet into his pocket as a shadow crossed the light in the window. He looked up, but it passed before he could see what made it. A voice—not a little girl's voice—seeped like black ink from the front door, and with it rolled a harsh, dog's-breath stink.

Git boy. Git boy now.

When he retreated, the window went dark.

six

He woke early Saturday morning and punished himself with a long run.

Back at his parents' house, hobbling on a sore ankle, he climbed to his second floor room to shower and shave. The burlap doll from the pier was squatting on the bureau next to his bed, glaring at him with its dead eyes.

"Good," he said to it. "You didn't move."

seven

"My grams called this a *toby*."

Pastor Leroy Hatchel held the burlap doll to the morning sky while Royal Goody and Boo Taylor watched from a picnic table bench on the grounds of the Good Friends Baptist Church.

"What's it for?" Royal asked.

The reverend shrugged. The sun made twin yellow circles of the old man's spectacles and a flame of his gold tooth. "Some kind'a hoodoo. Had an uncle once found one of these on his front doorstep and dropped dead that very night. Boo Taylor, I expect this ain't the first one you seen, is it?"

Boo was still trying to get used to this very old and frail version of Pastor Hatchel. He smiled grimly. "No, it's not," he said.

The old man nodded. "Expect Eulahlah Colebriar knew all about tobies. You ain't opened this one up, has you?"

"Not yet."

Reverend Hatchel gently placed the doll on the tabletop and produced a pocket-knife from his jacket. He glanced at Boo. "You mind?"

Boo waved him ahead.

Slowly, palsied old fingers directed a surgical slice across the doll's belly, then extracted two small wads of newspaper, clumps of Spanish moss, bits of dried plant, several strands of hair, the incomplete label from a bottle of Four Roses, a few small animal bones, a burnt stub of cigar, and what appeared to be the desiccated tail of a rat. Wrapped about this, like a length of intestine, a dingy shoelace that might have come from a small sneaker. "Is there supposed be some formula in this," Royal asked, "or just a handful of trash?"

The pastor grinned. "You tell me. You see anything?"

Royal stuck his finger in the clutter and stirred it around. "Is that a chicken bone?"

"Rat, most likely."

Boo saw patterns, familiar ones. "Read what's on those pieces of newspaper."

The reverend flattened out one of the wads, and Royal did the other.

"From the *Patch Caller,* back in seventy-one," Pastor Hatchel announced, squinting. "'Bout the fire that burned down the old colored school."

"This one's recent." Royal studied the paper closely and clearly did not like what he found. "It's about a church fire in some place called Wilbursville."

"This mean somethin to you, Boo?" the old man asked.

Boo Taylor looked at this old man pastor, seeing in those frail shoulders and wrinkled flesh the shape and run-down curve of Laylee Colebriar's spine. The strength, like hers, was in the eyes, in the grit of his golden tooth, the sermonizing poetry of his voice. He was perhaps the closest thing to her still alive on Sweetpatch Island—and that more than anything, he decided, was the reason he'd sought him out.

"Of course it does," Boo said.

Frowning, the old man asked, "Where'd you find this thing?"

Boo and Royal looked at each other. "Waiting for me at the end of MaeEllen's pier," Boo answered

"And who," the Reverend asked, "do you figure put it there?"

Now Royal Goody looked away, shaking his head. Boo watched this, then turned to look Pastor Hatchel square in the face. "Mamie Stuvant put it there."

An uncomfortable spell of silence followed. The nearby Atlantic rumbled and the crisp green leaves of tall oaks clattered in a light, leeward breeze.

At last, Royal said, "Boo thinks he's seen her."

"I did see her. And that thing"—he pointed at the doll—"didn't get there by itself. Also, there was something written on the mirror at the house where they found the doctor."

"What did it say?"

"I'm not sure, but it certainly had the ring of Mamie Stuvant to it. She's a skin-stealer. Sheba Tribbit stealing skins down through the years, still alive. You even put that in your book, Royal, didn't you?"

Royal scowled. Boo stood to stretch his legs and glanced at the thing lying eviscerated on the table. "As you can see," Boo said to the reverend, "Royal Goody is a skeptic and not much use to me. I was wondering what you think about all this."

The old man looked between the two of them. "Think about what in particular?" he asked.

"Your uncle that dropped dead. What do *you* think happened to him?"

A cloud swept before the sun, making the world a little darker as the pastor bowed his head to blink out the round lights of his eyes and considered the sandy soil beneath his feet. His lips worked like brown taffy as he pondered this question; his hand, still clutching the still-open pocketknife, trembled under the weight of nearly eight decades.

Let's hear a sermon, Boo thought. *An old-time, bible-thumpin rant. I need one!*

And the reverend, after coughing into his fist, obliged.

"I was born on Daufuskie," he started. "Growin up, my daddy's mother was the island's guffer lady. My Grammy Della. You know what a guffer lady is, Mr. Boo?" He looked up, lighting the lenses of his spectacles again.

"I suppose Laylee Colebriar was one," Boo answered. "The local folk doctor."

"Folk doctor, midwife, sometimes a prophet. Some folks figure maybe they was witches; my momma surely thought that way about my grams. But Grammy Della wasn't no witch. Witch is a whole different thing, though I expect they share methods. You think this island changed much since you left us, Mr. Boo?"

The reverend's gaze was challenging; he was warming into his lecture now, gathering brimstone and fire. Boo answered the old man's question with a nod.

"Well boy, you ain't seen *nothin*. You wasn't 'round when most colored folks on this island was livin on dirt floors, with no electricity, and the only plumbing was the ditch out back. Black man was apt to get beat up just for crossin north on the Soap Water bridge; woman was apt to get raped. Nighttime back in such days was pure *black*. Come nighttime, you was all alone and *blind*. Ain't nothin to do but listen to the bugs and the gators and whatever foul spirits creepin around in all that big darkness."

Taffy lips curled into a mean grin; a sliver of gold shone through.

"You be surprised, boy," he said, "what there is t'see nighttimes, settin on your porch when you got no television to watch. You find out then this world don't run on computer chips and hot rod engines. This world—the *real* world—runs on *blood*. Runs on the *tides*, on the settin sun and the risin moon. Runs on faith—on prayer, on curses, on dreams and nightmares, and the good and evil folks do. Runs on the things nobody can see, the things nobody *meant* to see."

He took a breath and closed his eyes.

"I was born on the islands," the preacher continued, "and my daddy was a pastor, and I knew right from my first breath I was born to follow him. I'm a man of God, Boo Taylor, and I'm a man of these islands. I been through every black swamp and shanty crossroad and gloomy shack and coarse jungle up and down this coast, speakin the Word and tendin souls. Been doin it for near sixty years now. Been in most every house on this island, one time or another: mansions and ghettoes and awful dark places no better'n a leaky wood crate. Places where God's Word been set on its head and religion turned black—where folks kiss snakes, sleep with rats, drink stump whiskey and chicken blood while they chant strange languages at their fire. Has this island changed? It *has*, and it *hasn't* at the same time. All that glitz and shine don't change what's underneath."

He reached down and gathered a handful of dirt. He held it up to Boo Taylor's face as proof. No.

"Has it changed? You look at that toby, and you tell me. You visit the swamp, you see it still—tucked deeper back in the shadows, deeper and deeper back as the years go by; but them kind'a folks is still dancin and howlin at the moon with all their dreadfulness. And there's more of 'em than you could guess, and more depraved than you want to think about."

Sweat gleamed his wrinkled, brown face; his fist quivered; his chest swelled.

"Have I seen *witches?* Why, I believe I have. Have I seen *ghosts?* Yes, boy, I seen ghosts, and I seen things a whole lot *worse.* Seen a baby born with its head spun backward; seen another born with horns and a tail. Seen a full-grown cat fall out of a clear sky. Seen a spider once wail like a newborn—sound so harsh and fearful it brought me to tears. Laid a man t'rest once and seen him walkin 'round the next week, his clothes still filthy from the dirt he was buried in.

"I seen a lot a' things, Mr. Boo."

The old man settled back on the bench, suddenly exhausted. His chest shrunk again. He let the dirt spill from his hand to the ground, and the breeze blew it onto Boo Taylor's shoes.

"You ask me what I think happened to old Uncle Rand? Well, Mr. Royal here likely tell you it was *superstition.* Power of *suggestion* and nothin more. And I ain't gonna argue with that."

Boo flashed a glance at Royal Goody who was solemnly watching the pastor.

Wearily, the ancient reverend reached over to pick up a swath of burlap and the small shoelace that held the thing's guts together. He looked at it mistrustfully.

"And you tell me, Boo Taylor, that you seen Mamie Stuvant. Well, I ain't gonna argue with that, neither."

The clouds retreated. The day was moving toward noon and collecting heat.

Minutes passed in silence.

A fish crow fluttered overhead; Boo Taylor followed its dips and flits across the raw blue above until it settled on a power line. It considered its audience below and then let out a single, staccato squawk.

Boo looked at his watch and saw he would be late for his lunch date. To the others, he said, "I saw her."

Royal Goody stood with folded arms and looked troubled. "Maybe you saw someone, but it wasn't Mamie Stuvant." He paused, looking up now to notice the crow. "It wasn't her, but maybe it was Crystal Burne."

eight

Gussie Ransome checked her watch. Then checked it against the clock above the patio bar. She had been going through similar motions for fifteen minutes.

He's not coming, she decided.

Around her, the open air smells of baked bread and olive oil and seafood and the nearby Atlantic, and she realized with true surprise that a large part of her was relieved. The burden of seeing Boo Taylor again almost outweighed the desire.

But, having understood this, it was now the *desire*, the sense of *lost chances*, that overwhelmed her.

No lunch. No conversation. No stroll on the boardwalk. None of the scenarios she had played like movie previews through her mind's eye would be played out for real. Certainly, none of those scenes had her sitting alone at a table on Del Rey's patio accepting the maitre d's increasingly pitying glances.

None of the clever responses she had rehearsed for the obvious questions would be needed. She hadn't needed to worry if she should give him a kiss when they greeted or another when they parted. She hadn't needed to fret over whether or not to hot-roll her hair. The anguish of deciding between the new pastel slip dress with the racy bust line or the reliable yellow knit (which was *not* new and had a stain at the hem if you looked close enough, but *damn* she looked good in that dress) had all been for nothing.

Murphy, at least, would be pleased. Boo Taylor had stood her up, and she would have to face Murphy Ransome's smug reaction to that.

Boo was not coming, and she knew why. He had never forgiven her.

Or maybe he had.

That would be worse, she decided. If he had actually forgiven her. If he was actually healed and had spent his years away not thinking about her at all.

Her name is Debbie-something, and on an early February weekend he actually brings her to the island. And in that sweet, thoroughbred Raleigh face and that expensive, city-cut blonde hair and New-York-bought clothes, she sees all of her small-town, white-trash high school fears coming true. There she is, a college girl straight out of her nightmares—all peaches and cream and parading around the island on Boo Taylor's arm like the princess of the ball. His rich-boy frat buddies have all come with their own pet college girlfriends, and the whole platoon of them have landed on Atlantic Beach where they rent a string of rooms at the Seaside Haven and drink beer and whoop it up, making enough noise so all of Sweetpatch Island knows they've arrived and claimed this pathetic stretch of sand. Enough noise to make certain she can hear them down there on the beach having their great wild party. Retaliation for her behavior last Christmas.

Stupid behavior, that Christmas. Silly.

She had been aloof over the holiday, dramatically so: kisses only perfunctory, excuses when he wanted to make love, fictional engagements with friends when he wanted to see her. "I know what you're doing, Gussie," he tells her. "There's no need for it; we talked about this."

But she only confounds him more. "Why Boo, I'm quite sure I have no idea what you're talking about."

He is seething by the time they arrive at Marty Simington's New Year's Eve party. And she's frustrated because the strategy hasn't worked: he's not remorseful or apologetic for leaving her alone while he's off to college. He's being stubbornly reasonable, and all she's done is waste the short time they have together. She's miserable; he's miserable; he's right; she's wrong. And so he sits miserable and unspeaking behind the wheel, and she decides to ask forgiveness and spend the last days of the holiday in his arms. Out of the car, she reaches for his hand. "I'm sorry," her hand means to tell him, and then she drags him into the dining room, cleared now to make a dance floor, and gets him to shag with her; "I'm sorry; I'm so sorry," her eyes mean to say, and he finally begins to smile. Marty Simington's well-stocked bar loosens him up some more. At her side, holding her hand and wrapped by their friends, he laughs and seems happy again. And when "Unchained Melody" comes on, they slow dance. She feels tears coming when he cradles her body across the floor and her hands clutch the safe and warm muscles of his shoulders and his back, and when he kisses her on the neck she feels she might swoon. "Let's leave," she whispers to him, "now," even though midnight is still an hour away. She slides off of his body to find a bathroom while he goes for their jackets, and on her way back to find him is practicing an apology when she sees Billy Standish blunder up to Boo Taylor and wrap his arm around his neck and shout something that includes the words "college pussy." And instead of walking away, instead of saying or doing any one of a hundred things that would have set her mind at ease, goddamn Boo Taylor just laughs.

In an instant, the fears wash over her like a cold Atlantic wave, shocking the warmth from her body and sending shivers of hurt and rage through her. And when the wave withdraws, at exactly that horrible moment when she is most vulnerable, the very instrument required to salve her uniquely ruptured, booze-weakened ego suddenly steps up behind her.

"Hey there Miss Dutton, you're lookin fine tonight. You wanna dance a few?"

She barely hesitates.

"Why I certainly would. You're lookin mighty fine tonight yourself, Mr. Ransome."

Later, she catches Boo standing in the corner with their jackets watching them. After five songs, during which she dances with Murphy Ransome and flirts with him and rubs her body against his with enough coquettishness to shame even Scarlett O'Hara, she looks back and Boo Taylor is gone.

"Gussie, you waited. I'm sorry"

Boo Taylor swept breathlessly by and filled the chair across from her.

"I lost track of time, and then I got lost. They *moved* Pofoksgo; the damn thing *dead-ends,* and then it picks up again two blocks later."

His presence was sudden and vigorous; it shot a bolt of panic through her. He grabbed a linen napkin from the table and dabbed it to his forehead, and she was breathless herself. There he was, sitting before her, filling up that recently empty place, heaving breaths out of a white shirt that was opened indecently to the third button. Tufts of red-brown hair sprouted there. She felt her cheeks going flush.

"God, you're still good looking!" she blurted.

He laughed, and she felt herself go completely red.

The lines she had practiced scattered like children running from thunder and lightning.

"Did you order?" he asked.

"No, I waited for you."

She watched him, still absorbing the enormity of his presence as he lifted the menu, opened it, leaned back in the chair, drew a deep breath—and it was not really him; it couldn't be.

"What's good here?"

"Just about everything," she answered and forced herself to pick up her own menu though she already knew what she wanted. She blindly scanned appetizers and gathered some semblance of calm.

The waiter arrived. She ordered, and when finished couldn't remember a word she'd just said, just knew that now Boo Taylor was ordering and she couldn't take her eyes from his forearms. The sleeves of his white shirt were rolled to the elbow, exposing cords of muscle and feathery curls of hair. He made a joke with the waiter about sharks in the local waters, and she missed it. She laughed with them anyway.

When the waiter left, removing their menus, the space between them was dangerously empty.

"How's Hank making out these days?" he asked her.

She blinked. "How's who?"

"Hank. Your daddy."

"Oh. He got remarried."

"You're kidding."

"He lives on the mainland now. The Satterfields bought up all the places on Shell Pot and turned the whole place into a Robert Trent Jones golf course." The words were coming easier now. "Daddy took the money and got himself a little place in Corrington."

"Do you see him much?"

"Almost never."

"How about Wade?"

"Oh, Wade's in and out of our place like he owns it." Boo was sipping at his water, and she did the same. "Did you know Wade's a corporal in the police force now? And married, with four boys?"

"I saw him at the funeral," Boo said. "He told me Harley's the town drunk."

"He's not *that* bad!"

She looked at his arms again, noticed how he folded his hands so the fingers of his left hand covered the vacant space on his right. She wondered if she could reach over and take one of those hands in hers.

Boo was watching her closely.

"I have something to show you," she said. She reached into her purse and pulled out several photographs of her children. He accepted these with an expression she couldn't quite read.

After several moments, he finally said, "They're all beautiful."

"Thank you."

"They don't look like Murphy at all."

"Of course they do!"

"No, they don't." He handed the pictures back to her. "They don't look genetically deficient to me. In fact, they all look exactly like you."

She took the pictures and considered him quietly. "Are you going to be surly?" she asked him.

He settled back in the chair. "I don't know. I haven't decided yet. You show me pictures of your children, what am I supposed to think?"

So he wasn't healed. She closed her eyes briefly.

"You should be happy for me," she told him. "My children are the best thing in my life. Really, you have no idea."

He looked away. "No, I guess I don't."

An uncomfortable silence fell. She watched his profile as his eyes followed the flight of a gull over the ocean.

"So," she said.

He turned back to her.

"I hear you have your own company now."

He nodded.

"Tell me about it."

"Gussie, it's not a very interesting story."

"I always wondered. I always wondered how you wound up in Delaware, of all places."

He inhaled, and it seemed he was making an effort to disregard whatever thoughts were occupying him. He made a grim smile. "The coach at Duke knew the head of admissions at the University of Delaware, and he got me in."

"After you lost your scholarship, you mean." Her face started to glow.

"After you got me kicked out of Duke, you mean? Yes. I had to sell Miss Laylee's land to pay for Delaware. Osgood Satterfield was always after me about it once he found out she left it to me. Remember?"

Yes, she remembered; Laylee Colebriar's patch of land near Chaliboque. He had wanted to live there, had planned to build his own place there; Osgood Satterfield was buying up every spare scrap of land, but Boo Taylor was never going to give it up. But he also wasn't taking any favors from his father. So, he'd had no choice.

I'm sorry, she wanted to say, *it was my fault you lost your scholarship. My fault you had to sell Miss Laylee's property.*

He seemed to read these thoughts. He shrugged.

"Anyway, I played college ball," Boo said, "and worked construction in the summers for a contractor. I got an economics degree, too, but it never seemed much use. When I was in the minors, I worked for the same contractor in the off-season."

"I used to look for your name in the paper."

"Where, the obituaries?"

"The sports pages!"

"Well, there couldn't have been much to find," he said. "It turns out I'm a better brick layer than a ball player."

"You were a great ball player, Boo."

"No," he said. "But at least I was smart enough to know it. My heat wasn't hot enough, and my junk was just plain mediocre, so I got out before they cut me. Or sent me back down. I used my savings to buy out the contractor, and I went into business. It was either that, or get into coaching, and I don't know that I would have made a good coach, either."

"I think you could have been anything you wanted."

He shrugged again. "I don't know. Maybe I just wanted to be anonymous."

He leaned back and let the sun light the wistful wrinkles at the corners of his eyes. His ball-player, brick-layer shoulders stretched the threads of his white shirt. He was set apart from the rest of the lunch crowd; anyone walking in would be drawn to him— that boy staring down from the mound with such intensity; even then, he was set apart and surely destined for greater things than Sweetpatch Island could ever offer.

By the time the waiter came back and placed a basket of rolls on the table, she was feeling some sense of herself returning and was glad these awkward preliminaries were behind them. Maybe now they could just talk and enjoy themselves.

She tore a roll in half and was about to speak when she looked up and saw his face had gone dark.

Her hope deflated.

"Gussie," he said quietly.

She put the roll back in the basket. "Don't say it, Boo."

"Don't say what?"

Whatever it is you're about to say. She felt sweat bubbling at her temples. "You know."

He looked at his hands. He spoke softly, a painful grin twisting half of his mouth. "But it's true, you know."

"Boo, please…"

"Why can't I say it?"

"Because."

"Because why?"

"Just *because,* Boo."

He looked up. "Gussie, I was coming back for you."

They are different, are supposed to rise above teenage romance pettiness, are surely under the spell of the powerful force that brought them together when they were still young, yet already fully awakened to the monstrous and benevolent extremes the world offered—when they were both thirteen but really so much older, and she looked into his age-weary boy's eyes and for the first time said the words "I love you."

He will go off to college. They discussed it so sensibly.

Sensible that he will follow his scholarship to Duke, even if it is so far away.

Sensible that she will stock shelves and bag groceries at the new Food Lion on Polk Road and wait for him.

Sensible when all that is still in the future and just imagination. But when he loads into his '72 Vega and actually drives away from her, sensibility is replaced by the dread of being stuck in Hank Dutton's filthy house on Shell Pot Lane without him. Boo Taylor can't know that fear because he'd grown up in the doctor's splendid mansion, not that squalid house of fistfights and drunkenness and perversion and brutal, masculine hatred. He's a Taylor; she's just a Dutton. When he drives away, a lurking shame awakens and works on her. It croons to her as she sleeps. It laughs at her as she labors mindlessly in the grocery stockroom while Boo Taylor gathers education and opportunity in the great world across the water, that world filled with doctors and lawyers and generals and politicians and businessmen—and they don't just have sons, do they?

She lets the shame feed the doubt all that first autumn, when the Vega gives him trouble and he can't make it home every weekend like he promised. And when he finally does come home for Christmas she puts on that foolish display with Murphy Ransome. And, trumping her, here he comes with Debbie the college princess and his invading army of rich-boy buddies.

Sensible. He's just sending a message; just be sensible.

Instead, she steals Wade's '68 Plymouth and makes the drive up I-95 to deliver her own message in person.

Boo Taylor is a LYING SNOB BASTARD!

He does not come back to Sweetpatch Island after Duke officially dismisses him.

The night he spends in jail, she spends crying in Wade's Plymouth in the street across from the police station. The next day, she pleads with Boo as he leaves the station. He refuses to talk, refuses to look at her. He walks by as if she isn't there—so she cries, grabs his shirt, begs him to hear her apology. She throws her body in front of him so he can't get by without throwing her aside.

Finally, he looks at her.

His face is not angry; it is creased as if in deep thought. The muscles of his jaw throb. When he speaks, his voice is calm and sad. "Go home, Gussie. Go on back to the island where you belong." His hand reaches up, touches her shoulder, and gently pushes her out of his way.

He was going to do this.

He was going to make her do this.

"Boo," she said; she looked down and fidgeted with her napkin. "I didn't hear from you for eight months. I was sure you were through with me."

He leaned forward and spoke with quiet intensity. "I was mad, and I needed to cool off."

"For eight months?"

"Gussie, you got me arrested, and you got me thrown out of school. You were driving me completely nuts, which I guess was the general plan. I didn't know what to do."

"I was scared," she said.

"I told you I was coming back."

"I was *scared*."

"You were playing games with me."

Now she looked up and glared at him. "And that college girl you brought down here? That wasn't a game?"

They were drawing uncomfortable glances from the surrounding tables.

Boo leaned back, collecting himself. He spoke softly. "You know damn well why I did that."

Unbidden, her anger started to rise. "Boo Taylor, I was scared out of my mind," she told him. "You were off at school, and I was stuck here, and I was scared you'd forget about me. I know I was stupid, and I know I was playing games, but I was eighteen years old and I was scared."

"We talked about it," he said. "You said you were fine with it."

"Well I guess I was wrong!"

Over Boo Taylor's shoulder she saw the waiter make a step toward them, then reconsider and walk the other way.

Boo said, "Would you rather I stayed here and got a job pumping gas at Finkle's? Would that have made you happy?"

Oh God, yes, she thought, and bit her lip. "Of course not."

"Or maybe I should have knocked on doors selling encyclopedias like good old Murphy Ransome."

Her anger flared. "That's a cheap shot!"

"Is it?"

"You know it is!"

"I wanted to marry you, Gussie."

She was stung. Paralyzed. Tears sprung to her eyes and welled there. The world was suddenly lit by a naked lightbulb of such astounding brightness that everything beyond Boo Taylor's face disappeared.

"Boo," she whispered hoarsely.

She reached across the table for that hand she had been wanting to hold, but he pulled it away.

I wanted to marry you, too.

But she hadn't. Instead, she had gone out and done the one thing, the very worst possible thing she could have done to him.

"And now you show me pictures of your *children?*"

Quietly, she said, "I didn't do it to hurt you."

"I was coming back for you."

"I didn't *know* that."

"How could you *not* know that? I would have walked through fire for you."

Walk through fire.

She placed her hands on the table so she could lean closer. "I didn't hear from you for eight months, Boo. I tried everything, and you wouldn't call. *Eight months*. Do you know how long that felt like? I lived in a low-grade panic twenty-four hours a day, every day, month after month thinking my life was over. I was sick! I wanted to die! And the longer it went, the more I was sure you were through with me."

"Gussie, I wrote you that letter."

"After *eight months,* Boo! By then I was sure…"

He was silent.

Something, maybe the lunch she hadn't had a chance to eat, churned in her stomach. The glass next to her hand, the basket of rolls, the empty bud vase had all taken on a sharp, glaring edge; everything around her seemed suddenly false, like a painting. She reached for the napkin, seeing her fingers shake, and dabbed her eyes.

The chatter at the nearby tables had gotten noticeably quieter.

"Gussie," he said, "I haven't had a relationship last more than six months since you."

"And that's my fault?" The words were out before she could stop them.

A fierce, hurt look crossed his eyes, and she saw his answer there. Her fault? Yes, of course it was. Gussie registered this accusation—he might as well have smacked her across the face.

She stood up sharply. Knowing she was drawing stares. Not knowing what she was going to say. Certain only the acidic rampage tearing through her gut would make it bad.

"Boo Goddamn Taylor!" she yelled. "So this here's why you wanted to haul me off to lunch? So you could sit there and blame *me* for all your problems?"

"Gussie," he said evenly, "I thought it was time to close the book."

"Close the book?" She screeched, her voice broke, and her rage surprised even herself as all measure of control now collapsed in one startling implosion. "Well you go right ahead and *close* your damn book!"—she flung the napkin on the table— "and fly on back to *wherever,* and maybe now you can date somebody for more than a few months!"

Her vision was blurred, keeping her from seeing what Boo Taylor's expression might be or even if he were making any movement to get up. She turned to stalk off, then turned back to him. She wagged a finger in his direction—knowing how foolish this looked while somewhere down in the more rational depths of her mind she thought that no, she had not played out this scenario in all of her imaginings: the cliché of the tossed napkin, of storming away, of firing off the last angry shot.

"You sure became a bitter old man, Boo Taylor," she roared, sobbed, "and I don't even *like* you anymore!"

nine

The uncommonly pretty woman in the yellow dress barged through the crowded patio of Del Rey's, toppling the stares she got like bowling pins. Boo Taylor watched her fade into the fuzzy distance, a ship's speck receding over the horizon.

At some point in his youth, under the tutelage of Laylee Colebriar, he had decided that the earth really was flat, and nothing since had ever convinced him otherwise.

Gussie Dutton (Gussie *Ransome,* goddammit!), who had originally disappeared off the edge of the world a lifetime ago, had miraculously reappeared for a taunting few days. She had certainly just plummeted again back into that dark land of dragons and lost ships.

This world, flat as it was, had been fine again for a glorious moment.

But it had just turned barren once more.

Looking at the linen napkin wadded up in his right hand, he understood that Gussie Ransome was not his only unfinished business on Sweetpatch Island. Hurricane Joseph, the thump against his truck's grill, the phone-call pronouncement of his father's death—someone had been calling him back to attend to matters he had neglected for twenty years. Matters he had conveniently forgotten.

With thoughts of shipwrecked lives and mysterious, screen-hidden voices and apple-faced demons and Sandy Baker's histrionics and young boys torn to pieces by wild beasts—and wondering what he was supposed to do next or if he should just run for the hills—he drew in the ghostly remnants of her scent and felt like doing nothing at all. Because in the end, without her, nothing mattered anyway.

Above him, someone cleared his throat. Boo looked up and saw the waiter. The man smiled at him and asked pleasantly, "Would you care to see the dessert tray, sir?"

ten

Gussie Ransome sat behind the closed door of the den, nursing the lump that was lodged like a burning coal in her chest. It hurt physically, and she had to clamp her teeth against it.

She listened to the muffled play-by-play chatter from the television several rooms away. Murphy was in there, napping. Going past, she'd had to fight the urge to stomp in and kick him in the ribs.

Eight months, she raged.

Eight months, she wept.

Her eyes were closed, but she couldn't stop herself from seeing the accusation haunting Boo Taylor's weathered, grown-up face. He had nursed his own pain, or had picked at the scab of it over the decades, hardening his own scar around his own version of their mutual collapse. That scar would forever numb him from appreciating how hellish those eternal eight months had been: an excruciating, time-crawling span more like eight thousand years, during which she had become weary and old and utterly lost.

Eight months before she finally heard from him again.

I wrote you that letter.

She still had it, although she hadn't read it in almost twenty years. At the moment, it was tucked into the very bottom of her sewing kit, and every so often, when she went into the kit to stitch up one of Savannah's sleeves or the knee of Jeremiah's jeans, she might catch a glimpse of the envelope between rolls of thread.

Eight months.

By the time his letter had arrived, she was already six weeks moved out of Hank

Dutton's home and into Mavis Bergman's boarding house on Polk Road. The letter was among the clutter of loose flyers and junk mail and bills; she had recognized the handwriting on the envelope and reached for it desperately.

As she reached for it now.

Outside the police station in Raleigh, his last words to her are, "Go home." For once, she listens to him. She goes home.

Murphy Ransome is there waiting for her.

Confident and certain of himself, as if he has been expecting her all along; he is relentless, and so she relents to him. "How 'bout a movie, Gus? Nothin wrong with just a movie, is there?" He's a diversion, nothing more; she tells him as much, and he doesn't seem to mind. And so she's not thinking much about the tall, confident man who sits so relaxed beside her in the dark theater; she's fixed instead on the great web of grief she has knitted and spread over her world, trying to find ways to escape it even if just for a few minutes at a time, or maybe the quick two hours it takes to watch a movie.

Murphy is patient with her. It seems to be his way; after all, he has already waited for her for so many years.

As months pass and she becomes more and more certain Boo Taylor is lost to her forever, it is Murphy Ransome who offers solace. He's charming. He treats her well. He's tall and wide-shouldered and handsome. Has a steady job. And most importantly, he is uncomplicated. Murphy Ransome will never be plagued by the ghosts and demons that always haunted Boo Taylor. Murphy is simple and relaxed and confident. He knows what he wants, and he knows it will come to him.

When she finally gives in to his unique brand of laid-back relentlessness, it is as much as anything a confirmation to herself that she is to be forever consigned to the island and its hell of mediocrity. She's just a Dutton, after all, and this is home and where she belongs—just as Boo Taylor had told her. And when his letter finally arrives, after eight months, she is sure his words will confirm it as well.

All those years ago, she had taken the letter with her into the dining room, the place where she sometimes took dinners with the other boarders.

(In the den, she reaches to the bottom of the sewing kit, pushing the clutter aside with her fingers.)

The letter was so small and innocuous, really nothing significant at all. Why did it feel like a lead weight in her hands?

(Her fingers close around one tattered edge and delicately pull it free.)

The envelope had been (is now) vibrating in her hand as if some living thing were inside and trying to make its way out. No, that had been (is now) only her hands shaking.

I would have walked through fire for you.

After several minutes of sitting and looking at the letter and being afraid of it, she finally opened it and lifted out the single page to read the familiar and long-lost handwriting.

Her better nature, it turned out, had been right all along. If she had only weathered the storm of waiting, all would have been well again.

>Dear Gussie,
>
>I miss you.
>
>I want you to read this letter. When you're done, I want you to tell me how much I got right and how much I still have wrong. Does that sound fair?
>
>"Every man is an island" somebody once said and got famous for it (or maybe not if I can't think of who it was). That's probably not true, but I can see now how we make our own islands if we're fool enough. I realize I have been on an island. It's an island I made because I was fool enough to move away and be apart from you. I am surrounded by a sea of people, but I am separate from them. They're all pretty much good people. They like me and we get along just fine. They're not much different from the folks on Sweetpatch, Gussie, except they all talk funny.
>
>What I'm trying to say (and probably screwing it up badly) is that they're all okay, but they're just not YOU. They're not Gussie Dutton. I have come to realize that without you, I am cut loose from the thing that makes me more than just a solitary person. Apart from you, I made myself an island, alone and incomplete. For maybe the first time, then, I know what I put you through when I left Sweetpatch. I should never have done it. I should have either stayed or taken you with me. You knew it. You were always smarter than me. You tried to tell me. You tried to tell me before I left. You tried to tell me in your letters and calls. You tried to tell me last Christmas. You tried to tell me when I got arrested. You kept trying to tell me in all different ways, but I was too much the fool to hear you.
>
>Gussie, you're a hard person to handle, and you're dangerous, and I love you. I feel like I have always loved you. Even when we were little kids and I hated you and you hated me, I still I loved you. Before I was born, and I was curled up inside my mother's womb I think that lovely woman I never met whispered your name to me and promised me what you would be like and told me you would be waiting for me out in that world. And that's the reason why I came out of that warm place. To be with you.
>
>I'm sorry it takes me so long to figure these things out. I wish I had been quicker at it. Maybe I would have saved myself that little time in jail and all this longer time in my island prison. I want to come back to Sweetpatch and be with you, or you to come north to be with me. I doesn't matter which. I just don't want us to be on separate islands anymore.
>
>I love you, Gussie. I know you love me too.
>
>—Boo

She had written her letter in response later that night, sitting in her room at the child's desk that Mrs. Bergman's husband had been nice enough to move out of the backyard shed for her. She sat at that desk, in the trembling wooden chair, letting the lamp on the nightstand cast a yellow witness to her agony. The words came hard, each one a lump lodged deep inside of her that had to be wrenched loose and pulled up through her chest in a cold, metal clamp.

Her letter was much shorter than his. She said what she had to and no more.

> Dear Boo,
> I am marrying Murphy Ransome next month. It would be a horrible mistake if you tried to do anything to stop it. So please, for my sake, don't.
> I wish, as I always have, only the best for you.
> Gussie

She sent the letter off in November, just after Thanksgiving. She and Murphy were married on Christmas Eve. Boo Taylor did not try to stop it, and she was always grateful to him for that. She did not send him a letter when Georgia Mae was born the following July. But she was sure someone would have gotten the word to him.

Hiding in a Glass Box ~ July, 1971

> It's dark out there, so here I hide,
> to find it's worser here inside.
> — *Limon Cevreaux*

She was hiding. Sitting in plain view under the wide-open, high-burning, mid-summer sky, but still hiding her body *(curse? blessing?)* as far away from the monster fish as a small island allowed.

Trapped.

Her body.

Whipcord sunrays flayed her shoulders; bleacher splinters jabbed her legs—far above, a naked candle-top flame shone and fluttered and burned provocative light-house signals, announcing her body for miles around.

July: the month when you remembered how mercilessly hot the summer could get. When the days were blasted wide open by the sun, leaving you stranded and conspicuous under hothouse glass. When the nights were sweltery thick fever-dreams tangled up in damp sheets. And notions of escape were lost in the hazy, glaring distance.

Before her, the high school field was a sandy griddle upon which the boys of her herd broiled, preened, perspired, and blistered insults at one another.

"Damn, Wade, you swing like a pussy!"

"My grammaw hits better'n you, boy!"

"C'mon you Murph, fire it down his throat!"

Their cruelty was purposeful and natural, rival bulls posturing, a herd she was glad to run with because there was protection in their collective brawn.

"Fire that rock, Murph; fire it in there!"

"Rip it down his throat, boy!"

Murphy Ransome, tall and tan and sleekly muscled, was doing all the pitching as he usually did—except when it was his turn to bat, and then Richie Deeg would pitch to him, and you could tell right off how much *harder* Murphy threw the ball.

"Burn it past him, Murph."

She sat alone, watching below and all around, perched in the highest row where every angle of sight was unbroken, where no approach could go unobserved, where no one could sneak up from some corner or shadow to grab hold of her.

And yet, he sneaked up on her anyway.

Not the monster fish, but another.

Harley bellowed, glaring at the third base dugout: *"Hey!"* A gunshot roar that brought the others about-face.

Then, from shortstop, Red Prettyman: "Hey twerp, spectators gotta pay five bucks."

Hearing this, Gussie Dutton—the only spectator—stood up and girded to shout back an insult, but faltered then when she saw who had managed to get by her without being seen.

Boo Taylor was standing alongside his bicycle at the third base dugout—and how did he manage that? She whipped around, panicked because she *hadn't* been paying attention, and maybe the *monster* had come, too.

But the coast was clear.

She relaxed.

"Get back on your little bike an' keep ridin," her brother, Harley, shouted.

She wanted to shout the boy off, too, but her tongue held when she remembered the one time she had actually seen Boo Taylor all summer: North Beach, on the fourth of July, when high-summer celebration exploded world wars across the nighttime sky, and entire families all bedded together on blankets and sand. Island-strong, they cheered on the heavens, all spellbound by the fireworks—all except that one face she discovered by chance, remarkable among the others because the light show was not reflected there but instead was absorbed, dampened, snuffed by inner darkness.

Boo Taylor's face, but it had gotten much older.

And now the same face stared grimly at Harley and Red and Murphy and the rest of the bulls. "Just wanted to watch," Boo told them.

The herd snorted, laughed.

"Go watch somethin else."

"Yeah, go watch yourself."

Harley took a few threatening steps off third, and Boo Taylor took a single step backward.

"Aw, that boy's okay. He can watch." It was Wade, coming up from the batter's box.

Harley spit a stream of Red Man at third base. "Not if I say he can't."

(She looked quickly at Murphy, to whom they all deferred, smiling casually and impartially from a pace off the mound.)

Richie Deeg, drifting in from left field, yelled, "You know that boy, Wade? Ain't he Doc Taylor's boy put a whuppin on you?"

Red barked a laugh. "*That* little peckerwood? That's Doc Taylor's boy?"

"You the doc's boy?" Richie's tone was deceptively charming—and of course this was all an act; they all knew full well who Boo Taylor was. Richie and Red and Harley closed from three sides—not bulls now but wolves, circling a calf.

"Yes," Boo Taylor answered.

"Thought you was. What's your name, boy?"

Boo hesitated. Then said, "Robert."

Harley grunted. "No it ain't. Tell him your *real* name."

Clearing his throat, the boy whose face had gotten so much older answered, "It's Boo."

"Boo?" Richie asked, chuckling, and the others joined him. "You say your name was *Boo?*"

"Yes."

"Boy, that's a nigger name," Richie said and drew more laughter.

The wolf pack was closing in; Boo Taylor stood facing them, not running like he should—he was seconds away from getting his bike trampled, his nose bloodied. Didn't the simpleton know that?

She fired another hopeful glance at Murphy who was still watching with his persistent (and often maddening) amusement.

"Hey, ain't y'all heard?"—Harley again, another two steps closer to the annihilation—"this here boy's a nigger-lover."

"Harley, you don't say. Boo, is that true? You love niggers, do you?"

"Hey sure, I remember. You're the boy with that spook nursemaid."

"Why, he sure is. Even goes to the spookies' church."

"Got his picture took with that famous jig, too. Remember it was in that magazine?"

"Oh, well hey," Richie said thoughtfully. He pushed the brim of his cap back and studied Boo Taylor with great interest. "Them jigs send you here to keep an eye on us, that it? You a spy, Boo?"

They all roared laughter.

"Yeah, niggers sent him up to spy."

"No, FBI sent him."

"No, Malcolm X sent him."

"Why Boo, they hang folks 'round here for that kinda thing," Richie said reasonably. "Ain't you heard?"

Wade trotted the last few steps to reach the dugout ahead of the others, the bat cocked lazily but meaningfully over his shoulder. "Look," he said firmly, "Boo Taylor's okay."

"Boy's on our field."

"Ought'a know better."

Wade wagged the bat to the other shoulder. "He was with that boy got killed by Mamie Stuvant."

The laughter folded up, fell to the dust.

Red Prettyman whistled.

Richie Deeg brought the brim of his cap back down and reverently spit a line of tobacco juice near his feet.

The fireball sun hung over their silence and made dwarfs of their shadows. One by one, they came to identify, as she already had, the doomed, shipwreck-survivor grayness that aged the boy's face and added lead weight to his bones.

Wade broke away from the others, approached the man-boy. "How you doin, Boo?"

"Hey, Wade."

"Sorry about that Beaudry kid."

Boo nodded.

"He was that fat kid, wasn't he?"

Testily: "He wasn't *fat*."

"Hey, okay." Wade knuckled a brown dribble from his chin. He swung around to read Murphy's face, then swung back to Boo Taylor. "See you brung your glove?"

Boo Taylor's baseball mitt was looped over the handlebars of his bike. He reached for it, looked at the others tentatively.

"He can't play," Harley groused. "He's just...a kid."

Wade shot back, "I seen him play, an' he's better'n your sorry ass!"

"I say he can't play."

Red said, "He'll get hurt."

Harley peeled off a Sweetpatch High Yellowjackets cap, wiped sweat from his forehead with one beefy arm. "You're damn right he'll get hurt."

"Liable to get run into."

"Liable to get shot."

More laughter, but the meanness was shamed out of it.

"Hey *Gus!*" Jimmy Earl Deeg called from centerfield, "this ain't the rich boy's got a crush on you, is it?"

She quickly yelled, "You shut up, Jimmy Earl!" and glanced at Murphy, horrified to find him grinning at her.

Red chuckled happily. "Little pecker's full'a surprises, ain't he."

"Well, he ain't playin," Harley said and crammed the cap back over his scalp.

Wade turned, appealed to Murphy Ransome.

"Already got a game goin," Murphy said congenially. "But he can shag balls in right, if he wants."

Harley snarled.

Wade said, "Already got a game goin, Boo. Right field's closed; you want, you can stand out there and shag fouls."

And she watched Boo Taylor accept this supreme compliment quietly, offering only a soft "Okay" as he stole the glove from his bike and trotted onto the sacred field.

The others were returning to their positions, Harley grumbling, "Hell, Wade, why don't you just *blow* the kid."

On his way out to right field, Boo Taylor swiveled his chin over his shoulders and snatched a bashful peek to a place high in the bleachers.

two

She watched Murphy Ransome, sharing only the slimmest bit of her attention for Boo Taylor in closed-off right field and for the monster fish still skulking somewhere in shadows. Murphy, shirt unbuttoned, generaled from the mound, jaw lumped with Red Man, glowering toward the plate. Anywhere else he was nothing but smiles, but on the mound he was fierceness and scowls—*dangerous,* she thought, and liked the way the word thrilled her. An *in-control* kind of dangerous, and it showed in the sunlight glints of his sharp spikes as he whipped his leg around, whipped his oak-board stomach around, his tanned shoulder muscles pulsing sunlight from ripped-away sleeves, and at last snapping his long arm overhead as he unleashed the ball.

They swung and missed, were lucky to nip a pin's width of leather, and celebrated outrageously if they ever caught one full-on and sent it into fair territory. It was Wade's turn now, her hard-limbed brother who otherwise seemed so capable but was, before Murphy, all one-beat-too-late awkwardness.

Wade caught a piece of a fastball, and she cheered. He turned and grunted at her, embarrassed, because it was just a foul.

"Yeah, way to knock her, you pus!" Harley taunted from shortstop.

Next, Murphy offered a changeup as a gift; Wade swung early, checked, caught the ball off the end of the bat and nubbed a lazy pop-up near second base. The ball landed in infield dirt just ahead of Harley's lunging, stocky reach and rolled into the outfield.

"Got me one!" Wade shouted.

Harley roared back, "That was right field, dipshit. You're out!"

"Fuck you, Harley, that's a hit!"

From center, Jimmy Earl Deeg shouted, "Right field, boy."

The game was Round Roscoe, an invention they found useful when there weren't enough for teams. Everyone took a turn at bat and got to swing at every ball pitched from the pile while all the others played the field. With right field closed, any ball hit past the infield on the left side was a hit and worth one run; any ball over the fence was a grand slam worth four runs. Any ball fielded cleanly, fouled, hit to right, or swung-and-missed at was an out. When the pile was empty, the turn at bat was over.

In Round Roscoe, it was compulsory to argue any play that was remotely questionable and exhaust every blue insult until the matter was resolved.

Wade, already scarlet-faced with sunburn, now bloomed shades of purple. "Just cause you're haulin a caboose full a' *lead,* you fat fuck, don't mean it didn't land *fair!*"

"Eat shit and quit your blubberin."

"You can't *field* worth shit!"

"You can't *hit* worth shit."

"Hit it past *your* sorry-ass glove."

Gussie stood up and shouted, "Harley Dutton, that was a hit and you know it!"

"Yeah, Harley Dutton," Red Prettyman sang girlishly.

Jimmy Earl Deeg chanted, "Right field, right field, right field."

Murphy Ransome observed all from the mound, smiling his relaxed, amused smile, swinging his head back and forth between the combatants like a spectator at a tennis match. Finally, he snapped a ball in his glove, spit with authority, and said, "Hell, it was close enough. Give it to him."

"Goddamn, Murph!" Harley yelled.

Murphy looked into the bleachers and smiled at her. "You heard the umpire," he said.

She smiled back, her face suddenly several degrees warmer.

Wade bugled triumph. Murphy spread his arms in an appeasing gesture to Harley who was shaking his head in frustration but obediently stalking back to his position.

"Good cut on that, Wade," Murphy said. "Thought the changer would'a fooled you." He flashed another quick smile into the stands.

Wade hit nothing but air at Murphy's next two pitches. *He could do that every time,* she thought. *He just toys with them.*

Then it was Red Prettyman's turn. Red managed three foul balls, a grounder back to Murphy, and another grounder down the third base line that just squeaked by Richie Deeg for a hit. He swung and missed at Murphy's other pitches.

When it was Murphy Ransome's turn to hit, Richie Deeg took over the mound.

"C'mon Murph, let's take this shitheels downtown."

"Boy ain't got nothin, Murph."

Murphy stood at the plate, offering up his long back to her. The seat of his pants was dusted with sandy dirt where he sometimes wiped off his pitching hand in that gesture that was just so casual to him but made her think of gunslingers. The bat rose from his fists like a defiant finger pointed toward the hot, blue sky. Arm muscles flexed.

Richie Deeg's first two pitches were way outside. His third was in the dirt just before the plate.

"Hey Deeger, how 'bout a strike."

"While we're young, boy; while we're young."

The next pitch was down the middle. Murphy whipped the bat around and roped a line drive into center field. Gussie watched, hands balled into fists, as Jimmy Earl Deeg scrambled toward the ball and was just able to reach it before it hit the ground.

"Tough shot, Murphy," she cried.

He smoked the next pitch into the ground between third and short, and she cheered. The next was a line shot over Wade's head for another hit, and she cheered again. The next pitch was outside, and Murphy lunged with the bat. The ball popped high into right field.

Boo Taylor sprang off his knees as if he'd been stung by a wasp.

Belatedly, he circled under the ball, right hand shielding the sun while his glove fluttered uncertainly. He took two awkward steps sideways. Then three backward. Then rushed forward. At the last second, he lurched backward again.

The ball thudded into the ground. A moment later, Boo Taylor's rump thudded next to it.

The older boys howled laughter.

"Hey there Boo, that's a pretty dance step you got there, boy!"

"Boy, you daydreamin out there?"

"Hey Wade, thought you said your girlfriend could play!"

Boo Taylor sat up and hung his head. When he dragged himself to his feet and trotted after the ball, Gussie wondered if he might just run clear to the fence and hop over it and keep going until he ran all the way back to his fancy home on Carriage Avenue. But he stopped to pick up the ball at the base of the fence. While the others laughed, he flicked the ball once into his glove, shook his head, and then reared back and threw.

It was a perfect missile aimed at the mound. Richie Deeg, who was bent over in his mirth, had to straighten quickly to catch the ball before it slammed into his stomach.

He looked wondrously at the ball in his glove. "Goddamn," he said.

From left field, Red Prettyman shouted, "Little pecker's got an *arm!*"

Before she could catch herself, Gussie stood up and yelled, "Nice *throw,* Boo!"

Murphy looked up at her, and she sat down quickly.

"Try *catchin* the next one!" Harley growled.

Boo Taylor ambled back to the middle of right field and squatted back into his hands-on-knees position. Murphy was watching him now, too, she noticed. He spit a bit of juice on the plate, tapped the bat against his cleats. He faced Richie Deeg again and got into his stance.

With the next pitch, Murphy swung from his heels.

And missed the ball completely.

"C'mon, Deeger," he grumbled (but kept his smile), "how about a strike."

"That *was* a strike."

Red shouted in, "Yeah, Deeger, let's see some strikes or we'll put the *kid* in to pitch!"

"That *was* a strike, asshole!"

Murphy settled into his stance again. The pitch came in; inside. Murphy straightened and caught the ball next to his stomach with an angry bare-handed smack. He glared at Richie.

"Sorry," Richie said.

Wordlessly, Murphy tossed the ball back to the mound.

"Start warmin up, kid!" Red yelled.

The next pitch came down the middle with nothing behind it. Murphy lit into it, ball cracking wood, and then watched Red and Jimmy Earl race into deep left-center. They gave way when they saw the ball would easily clear the fence.

Gussie stood up and clapped and cheered and was vaguely hurt that Murphy did not turn around to acknowledge her.

"Knocked the piss outa her, Murph."

"Good rip, boy."

Over the next few innings, Murphy Ransome shut down the others and piled on runs to his own score. Richie and Jimmy Earl Deeg collaborated in an argument with Harley over a ground ball that Harley clearly bobbled at shortstop. Red stomped and raged that a ball hit down the third base line was not foul. Harley yelled at Wade for taking too many pitches, and Wade threw one of the bats at him. In the fierce tussle that followed, Wade got a bloody lip and Harley's cut-off T-shirt was torn down the front. When the game resumed, Harley's burly chest and stomach hung out of the flapping remains of his shirt, and both brothers were coated in dust and sweat.

Gussie moved from naked sunlight to the shade beneath the corrugated roof of the third base dugout. Between batters, the boys trotted over for her company and a guzzle from one of the water jugs. Only Boo Taylor stayed away, stayed in the heat of right field, a quiet marble-faced eagle (it was always a fine face; she had to admit that even when she was convinced she hated him), slender and humorless, while the others were a circus of braggarts and brawlers. When the occasional ball was hit in his direction, he swooped in confidently, absent of the gawkiness of that disastrous first play. He plucked grounders and snared fly balls, rifled the ball back with remarkable power. *"Damn, that little shit's got a cannon,"* Red mumbled when he threw a perfect strike to Murphy from near the right foul pole.

In the seventh inning, Jimmy Earl Deeg knocked a fly ball into shallow right field. Boo Taylor chased it. At a full sprint, he dove forward spectacularly and the ball fell neatly into his glove. He hit the ground, rolled through a somersault and vaulted back to his feet. Hoots rose from the field.

"Nice catch, Boo!" she shouted.

He tossed the ball in to Murphy, glanced her way, and unfurled his first smile of the day.

"Hey Gus, your boyfriend's showin off for you!"

"Shut up, Red!" she yelled.

When Jimmy Earl's turn was over, Murphy Ransome spit out a lump of chaw and loped toward the dugout.

Gussie straightened out of her slouch. Murphy, smiling, hoisted the water jug next to her. "Hot as hell out there," he said pleasantly.

"Hot in here, too," she said.

Murphy tilted the jug to his lips. She watched his throat throb, watched silver trails of water leak over his chin, drip down his naked chest and hard stomach to disappear into the waistband of his jeans. He brought the jug away and gasped. He faked a belch and laughed, and she laughed with him.

"You like that boy?" he asked.

She hesitated. "Like who?"

He jerked his thumb. "That little rich boy."

"Boo Taylor?" She looked briefly into right field, wishing now she hadn't cheered his diving catch. "That's silly; Red doesn't know anything. I don't even *know* him."

Murphy was still smiling. "He's your grade, ain't he? I bet he's in all the smart-kid classes with you."

"Some," she said—and wanted to say, *but he's just a boy.*

"Well, I guess Wade likes him, if you don't." He took another swig from the jug.

"I didn't say I didn't like him."

"So you *do* like him."

"Didn't say that either. I don't *know* him."

Murphy nodded and capped the jug. "What d'you figure he was doin pokin around Mamie Stuvant's house?"

Gussie considered, then shrugged.

He shrugged back. "Seems like a nice enough boy."

"I guess he's all right," she said.

Murphy's smile widened. He set the jug back on the bench and swaggered back to the field, leaving her with the words *he's all right* echoing in her mind. And that was okay, wasn't it?—she wondered: *he's all right,* that's all; that didn't mean anything.

She replayed the conversation, feeling stupid and not knowing why.

❖　　❖　　❖

Of course Boo Taylor had a crush on her; a lot of the junior high boys did. It was because she was taller than most of them and had grown breasts. And because her Dutton pug face had somehow, miraculously, lengthened and slimmed with the rest of her to become pretty. She *was* pretty, she realized, although she was still sometimes finding that difficult to believe.

That was a discovery made on a day a year-and-a-half ago when she overheard Shermy Standish and Ben Clement saying her name in the library behind a shelf where they didn't see her. She waited for the vicious insult, the kind she had grown up with—something about her drunken father, or her frayed, thrift-shop clothes, or her run-down home—and didn't know what to make of Shermy saying she looked like "Ann Margaret—didn't you see that Elvis movie?"

She wasn't sure who Ann Margaret was but remembered the witch in *The Wizard of Oz* was named Margaret-something, and she was ready to pounce around the shelf and haul off on Shermy Standish when Ben said, "Naw, she's prettier'n that. She's more like Ginger, you know, on *Gilligan's Island*." Shermy went on to argue that Ginger didn't have red hair, but Ann Margaret did, and Ben said Ginger *did too* have red hair, and if Shermy's Yank parents weren't so cheap and bought a color TV then he'd *know* it.

Hank Dutton didn't have a color television in his house either, but Gussie had watched enough grainy black-and-white reruns on the cracked Westinghouse to know who Ginger was. And she was *beautiful*. These boys couldn't be talking about her, she was certain—but there was her name again and an escalating series of fantasies concerning what they would do with Gussie Dutton if they got marooned on an island with her.

After ten minutes, unable to resist, she stepped around the shelf, hands planted on her hips, asked sweetly, "You boys about through with your dirty talk, yet?" and watched their faces go crimson.

The picture of Ann Margaret she later tore out of a *TV Guide* and taped to her mirror did not look much like the other face she saw in the mirror. She looked doubtfully between the two—oh, the hair might be the same color, but Ann Margaret's was perfectly straight and it shimmered; her own hair, even washed and brushed, was like trampled red straw. And Ann Margaret's cheeks were round and they glowed; her nose was tiny; her eyes were incredibly bright against the dark lines of makeup. Her own face was longer, sharper. And even though she was just eleven at the time, her face was more grown-up compared to the doll face in the picture.

She practiced a smile like the one in the picture.

Maybe, with her hair done; maybe with that eyeliner, that lipstick...

But that wasn't about to happen. Hank Dutton wasn't buying his daughter makeup, and she wasn't asking him. And of course, without a mother or even an older sister to turn to, how was she supposed to know how you even put on makeup?

Still, she saw the prettiness, a mystery to her; it was the same face she always saw in the mirror—but not *exactly* the same. She couldn't identify the precise changes, and certainly couldn't figure out how or when they'd happened. About the time her

breasts appeared. About the time she caught the junior high boys looking at her...
and even high school boys.

A blessing?

And then, of course, the monster fish got a look at her.

A curse.

Red's turn at bat was over, and Murphy called out to Wade, "Hey, that friend a'
yours hit as good as he fields?"

"Boo? Sure, I guess."

Harley grumbled from shortstop.

"Think he might wanna take a few cuts?" Murphy asked.

"Sure he would."

As Harley grumbled some more, Murphy cupped a hand to his mouth and shouted into right field. "Hey Boo, you wanna bat?"

Boo Taylor, a statue in another world, didn't move for a few seconds, then snapped
up from his haunches. *"Me?"*

"Yes, *you!* Hurry it up."

And then the youngest player on the field tucked his glove under his arm and
started in. Now the others, except for Wade, grumbled along with Harley. "Murph, it's
hot out here; quit fuckin around," Richie called from left. Jimmy Earl kicked the dirt
at shortstop.

Boo grabbed a bat, gave it a few hard swings and stepped up to the plate. He
feathered a few more swings, and settled into his stance. The bat waggled nervously
over his head. Murphy toed the rubber and faced him.

"C'mon Murph, put the little fucker away."

"Right past him, boy, right past him."

Murphy wound, reared, let the pitch fly.

The ball drilled into Boo Taylor's ribs. Boo grunted and crumbled to his knees.

"Boo!" Gussie called out.

"Goddamn, Murph," Wade yelled from third base.

Gussie realized she had taken three steps out of the dugout and stopped herself,
her eyes flashing between Murphy standing on the mound and Boo Taylor propping
himself back up with the bat.

"Hey boy," Harley shouted, "gotta move when you see it comin."

Boo walked slowly to the ball and picked it up.

Murphy's arms were spread apologetically. "You okay, boy?"

Boo nodded, unable to speak with the air flushed out of him. He tossed the ball
back to Murphy and returned to the plate.

"Take it easy on the kid," Red yelled.

Gussie returned to her seat as Boo returned to his stance. Both faced Murphy
Ransome.

The next pitch came inside again—then curved away; Boo lurched away from the plate, caught himself, and swung wildly. The ball rolled to the backstop.

"Get the little shit outa there!" Harley yelled.

Wade called, "Hang in there, Boo!"

Murphy took another ball from the pile. Boo cleared a divot in the dust, planted his right foot. He swung behind a fast ball and clipped it hard into the first base dugout.

"There's a piece, boy!" Wade shouted.

The next pitch, low and inside. Boo swung at air.

"Stay with him, Boo."

"Fire it by his ass."

Another scorching fastball; Boo pounded a grounder between Wade and Harley.

"Nice rip, boy!"

"C'mon Murph, put some heat on it."

The next pitch was a curve ball, drifting too far outside. Boo lunged and popped it into empty right field.

"Smoke it in there, Murph."

Murphy Ransome wound and threw. Boo Taylor stung the ball hard up the middle, and Murphy had to duck sharply to escape it.

"Good one!" Gussie cheered.

Murphy dusted off his knees, smiling. He grabbed another ball, and Boo dug his feet into the dirt.

Murphy Ransome reared back, whipped forward, and the pitch came in high and hard. Boo Taylor leaned back. The ball followed him, and Boo leaned back farther . . .

The ball struck Boo Taylor's face with a sickening smack.

Gussie screamed.

Boo fell into the dirt.

She sprinted out of the dugout. Wade and Murphy were ahead of her; the others were running in behind. She saw the frightened, guilty looks on their faces and was scared. By the time she reached Boo Taylor, he was up on one elbow and making bleating noises, and she offered a quick prayer of thanks that Murphy Ransome hadn't killed him.

Then he lifted his face and she saw all the blood, and thoughts of thanks seemed premature.

Murphy knelt behind him and lifted his shoulders into his lap. He came up like a rag doll. "Hey, you okay, Boo?"

Gussie skidded into the dust beside them. Blood gushed from Boo Taylor's nose, mixed grotesquely with dirt; his face was masked under a red-black paste. She grabbed his arm. "Boo, can you talk?"

He opened his mouth and spit clods of the paste down his T-shirt. "I can't see," he croaked.

"That's because you have your eyes closed," she told him.

"Oh," he said. His face wiggled, and more grotesquery spilled away. "I don't think I can open them."

She wiped some of the grit from his cheeks and eyelids. He moaned and winced away from her. She ran to the dugout for a water jug, raced back and fell to his side. As gently as possible, she poured water over his face.

"Shit, look at his nose," Wade said from behind her.

Beneath the bloody mess, Boo Taylor's face was lumpy, vari-hued balloon; his nose started straight near the bridge, then cocked right, and then cocked left again.

"Looks broken," Murphy said.

"Of course it's broken, you asshole," Wade shouted, "you *broke* it. What the fuck were you doin?"

Harley was standing behind Murphy. "I told you he was gonna get hurt."

"He was doin fine till Murphy tried to stick one in his fuckin ear."

Murphy glared furiously at Wade, then looked around at the others until his eyes finally fixed on her. "The boy was crowdin the plate, and I was just brushin him back."

"He's thirteen years old," Wade barked.

Harley laughed. "Well, I guess that's old enough to learn how to duck."

"Fuck you, Harley. You couldn't even spell your own name when you were thirteen."

"Don't wise off with me, asshole. You're the one said he could hit."

Wade was coiling back to pounce on Harley when Boo Taylor's creaky voice caught everyone's attention. "My fault," he said. He brought a hand up to his face, fingered away more of the muck while blood continued torrents down his chin. "Figured it was a curve. Damn thing never curved."

Wade continued glaring at Murphy. "C'mon," he said, taking Boo's arm. "We gotta get him to a doctor."

three

"Wade?"

Was the house empty? Seemed empty—but wasn't that a faint spasm in the floating dust motes? Yes she felt, if not saw, the turmoil. A slight banking of sound-waves off a shape that shouldn't be there. A dead silent spot somewhere that drew air and expelled poison. She knew, if not heard, because the tiny hairs on her arms had gone prickly.

"Hey?"

Silence. (Something else?) Smell of rancid food from the kitchen. (Something watching?) Smell of cigarettes and stale beer from everywhere else. Wade had promised. Had promised to be here, because he knew she was afraid to be. . . alone.

Alone?

"Hey, anybody?"

She waited, let the house settle around her, tingling her flesh as every pore, every hair, every cell alerted to the possibility of movement.

She waited. Alone, perhaps, but could she chance it? Still clutching the door-knob, she looked at the wide sunlit space behind her—should she run back there and wait it out?

No. The house was empty. Just her frayed nerves, sensing phantom stirrings and sniffing relic odors. She went inside.

Get a hold of yourself, she forced the command through her brain. *Get a hold. Get a hold.* She exhaled. Inhaled.

How different this house from the one she'd just come from on Carriage Avenue, with its wide, whitewashed stairway lifting high like a pyramid from a lush garden jungle. She had been to that house before but always through the efficient little doorway around back, *patient's entrance,* and that was not much different from stepping into a store. Or, like being ushered through the servant's entrance. The back door was the way poor girls with blood-splattered thrift-shop clothes were supposed to enter the doctor's house. Going in the front door was trespassing. She had no right to go that way. She didn't *want* to go that way—but she *did* want to, and Boo Taylor *made* them do it. And so she had climbed those steps, feeling like a thief even though she and Wade had the prince himself propped up in their arms. She held him, wondered over him as he urged her up the white stairway toward the shaded porch above, and she counted the steps. There were exactly fourteen.

There were only three steps in the front of her own home on dismal Shell Pot Lane. Three steps, and the middle one was rotted through, so she had to stretch over it just to reach the front door. The step had been broken for nearly two years—so long that weeds were poking through it. So long that if Petey ever got around to fixing it (as he kept saying he would) she would probably keep on stepping over it anyway.

Stepping—a creak?

She studied the mute walls, the clutter.

"Hello?"

Junk everywhere—now even more, it seemed, after Boo Taylor's house. She tried to keep up, tried picking up behind them, but there were so many of them and only one of her, and they didn't care how the house looked, anyway.

"Hey, anybody? Anybody home?"

No answer. Harley was probably out with Murphy and the Deegs somewhere, still arguing about the game. Petey was working a roof job with Clyde Jones somewhere down on Oakland Street—although by now they'd have knocked off for the day and were drinking beer and watching baseball in Clyde's trailer. Her father would be down at Dink Potter's house—like Petey, watching baseball and drinking beer. And Henry Ray...

She had no idea where Henry Ray was. And she didn't like not knowing.

Where are you, Henry Ray? She felt him; the tiny hairs on her arm sensed him— slithering like a foul, giant fish somewhere in the shadows.

Where are you Wade? You promised!

Inside the pet shop, the one in the little strip shopping center on Polk Road before it went out of business in 1969. Wade took her there when she was just six, took her past the plastic toys and the squawking birds and the silent, busy rat-things—back into the rows and rows of bubbling glass tanks. Cool and dark back there, the motorized, churning water filling her ears and belching fine mists and taking her into a faraway underwater zoo. In each tank a minuscule zebra herd of bright colors darted from her fingertaps: neon tetras, silver angelfish, black mollies. Her favorites, the fancy tail guppies, such sleek and fragile silver bodies, labored to drag wide, fanned skirts of rainbow. They swam pirouettes about each other, skirts billowing psychedelic waves through the water.

And beside them, a tank twice as large with a single fish.

A mutant. Ugly.

Colorless—so unlike the others fish. A great fat toad of a fish, prowling dark waters, staring with dull, muddy eyes, pulsing water through fat, stupid lips.

The fingertaps didn't budge it. Slow. Mindless. She watched the lumbering ogre, hypnotized and repulsed.

Then Wade plunged his hand into the water next to her, laughing. "Watch this!" And suddenly there was a small splash in the big fish's tank.

A flash of silver and rainbow.

"Wade, no!"

The guppy dragged its wagging rainbow behind rocks before the big fish saw it, hovered there while the big fish turned, cowered there as the big fish nosed its hiding place. The guppy, watchful, sprinted around the stone, swirled into a crevice. The big fish floated close, and the guppy moved again.

For ten minutes, the little fish hid from the giant, always seeking the farthest, safest shadow, always alert to the lumbering movement within the glass box. How long would the darting rainbow keep ahead of the dull-faced monster? Maybe forever, because the big fish was so slow and stupid and the little one was so quick and clever and watchful.

That pretty rainbow, dragged about. Curse or blessing?

The rainbow slipped out of shadow, and there was a muddy flash and roiling water. The big fish moved so fast!

A plump, brown body floated up from the disturbed, pebbly bottom. A tiny flap of rainbow dripped from its thick lips. It gulped, and the rainbow was gone.

"Hey Wade, you here?"

Halfway up the stairway, another plank seeped the faintest dog simper from somewhere in the living room. But she could see the living room from where she stood, and there was no one down there. She started up again, listening between her steps. Listening, and. . .She stopped.

"Henry Ray, is that you?"

A sigh?

She held the banister. She held it for more than a minute.

And then sprinted the last few steps and into her room.

She had her own room at least, and in that had fared better than her brothers. Wade and Harley slept in the room next to hers. Petey had always shared his room with Henry Ray.

Then Henry Ray enlisted in the Army.

Then Henry Ray got discharged.

Her room was the smallest by far. It wasn't even a room until Petey and her father tacked up a new wall and knocked out a doorway. The door they hung never fit right and never closed all the way—she had to prop a trash basket against it to keep it from swinging open.

She hadn't seen Boo Taylor's bedroom but was certain it was five times bigger. Anyway, the rest of the house was *huge:* church-high ceilings, walls as far apart as banquet halls. Room enough for *ten* families. And everything *smelled* clean. And...

Another creak echoed from the hallway.

She pushed open the door, peeked around. The hall was empty. She walked to the stairs. Empty.

Alone.

Damn old house!

She sneaked into the bathroom.

A cubicle dominated by man-things: combs and shaving cream and razors; mismatched towels in a wet heap on the floor. She cleared out a space at the sink, looked up to find a bloody dishrag of a girl in the mirror.

The white halter top was stained with Boo Taylor's blood. And though she had wiped much of it away, there was crisp blood residue in the creases at her elbows and knuckles—even inside her bellybutton.

"I'm sorry, I'm sorry. I thought it was a curveball, but it didn't curve."

"Gussie, your boyfriend's bleedin all over you."

"Shut up, Red."

She stripped out of the halter and saw a reflection of the peach-sized breasts that had bloomed on her chest seemingly overnight, managing to fascinate the boys at school even more than they fascinated her. Blood and grime streaked her flesh in bands above and below the halter lines, as if a giant Band-Aid had been stripped off her chest.

She turned on the shower and stepped out of her cut-off denim shorts and panties. Blood had splattered on them as well, and the dark stain was a reminder of that first unexpected pool of warmth stinging between her legs, the embarrassment because no one ever *explained* what happened to girls when they went through the change.

She climbed into the shower. Water struck her flesh and she closed her eyes, languoring in the warmth that sluiced over her body and washed her clean. She let her hands massage the blood from her skin. It came away in a pink flow down her legs— just like before, only this time it wasn't her own blood, it was Boo Taylor's. She thought of Boo Taylor, living in that big house on Carriage Avenue, so far away from Shell Pot Lane. Maybe he was asleep there now, somewhere within those cathedral heights, dozing through the pain of his shattered nose under the spell of his father's pills. And nursed by two mothers—his own (prettiest woman on the island, she always thought) and that wonderful old colored woman.

The rushing hot water...the drifting thoughts of better places...kept her from hearing the creak of bathroom door hinges.

four

Boo Taylor had been naked to the waist on the ride to Carriage Avenue; his T-shirt, a bloody rag, was wadded over his face (she held it there), giving her the opportunity to examine his chest:

Deep muscle-shadow under his nipples. Unexpected swirls of red, golden, brown hair—a garden just coming to season. The angry stitches sewing his ribs where he took the first pitch. And the flannel sack, dangling against his flesh. She held it in her fingers for a moment: rustle of leaves, twigs, insect wings. The heat and agitation of her touch activated the ingredients, mushrooming plumes of licorice. She breathed it in, wondering over its mystery because this bit of witchery (and she recognized it as such) wasn't something to be discovered around a rich, Up Island boy's neck.

Wade asked, "So they found her just sittin in the kitchen? With him right there dead an' all?"

Boo's face moved under her hand.

Since piling into the bed of Richie Deeg's pickup, Wade hadn't stopped asking about Mamie Stuvant. (Murphy Ransome hadn't volunteered to take them in his truck—had he been afraid?)

Gussie unpeeled the shirt to check Boo Taylor's crooked, eggplant nose. The bleeding had mostly stopped. He watched her through puffy, watery slits. "Wade, leave the boy alone," she said. "He's in pain."

"Hey, I'm just tryin to take his mind off it. So she was just sittin there?"

"Yes," Boo croaked, a boy with a bad cold.

"That's the part I can't figure," Wade said thoughtfully. "How long 'fore the cops showed up?"

Boo suffered to speak, and his words were hard to make out. "Don't know. Twenty minutes, maybe. Wouldn't believe us at first."

"See, that's what I can't figure. She didn't just *disappear* somewhere? Just waited— him all dead an' right *there?*"

Boo blearily nodded.

The *Patch Caller* had reported its own version of what happened to Hoss Beaudry, left out far too much, and the spaces between had been crammed with wild speculation from around the island. A mutilated boy noosed by the feet, a slab of meat gutted like a calf in Mamie Stuvant's kitchen. Went there to sell seeds, folks said. Went there on a dare, said others. There were stories that an animal had gotten to him, that parts were eaten away, that other boys had watched it all happen. The paper never mentioned the other boys by name, but Sweetpatch Island was a glass box and everyone knew which boys ran together.

And word got around that Dr. Taylor's boy had been in that very house the day before the murder. Gussie didn't believe that part of the story until Boo confirmed it.

"They say she had animal parts hangin all over the walls."

Boo Taylor shook his head.

"They say she came after *you* with a knife, too."

"No."

"They say she wrote stuff on the walls in that boy's blood."

He looked glumly at his shirt. "I don't…know about that," he said quietly. "I didn't go back in."

Then the pickup bounced through a turn, stirring dust vapors, and they watched in horror as Boo Taylor's ruined nose snuffled, tickling toward a sneeze. The blast came, and he cried out as he caught yarn-bundles of red mush in his hands.

Around them, oaks thickened and yards broadened. Hints of clean white porches dappled through the greenery. The smell of the land had changed, the marsh clouds were somehow scrubbed clean and sprayed with aerosol salts and summer blossoms. The tires of Richie Deeg's truck rumbled onto worn, antebellum cobbles. They had come to Carriage Avenue.

"So now she's locked up," Wade was saying, shaking his head. "See, now that's what I can't figure—why she just sat there *waitin*."

"Waiting," Boo said.

"An' drinkin *tea*, they say."

Crazy, she thought. Then, because she couldn't help herself, Gussie asked him the question that bothered her the most. "But *why'd* she do it? Why'd she want to kill him?"

Boo Taylor looked at her through swollen, agonized eyes, and a dribble of blood traced down from his nose to his upper lip and ran with his tears. It was hard to tell where one misery began and the other left off.

Richie Deeg stayed long enough to help unload Boo Taylor and his bicycle. Then, flicking nervous glances at the big house, explained he had to get the truck back right away.

"You go on then, Richie Deeg!" Gussie yelled after him angrily. But her anger was really more at Murphy Ransome who had also abandoned them. So it was just her and Wade taking hold of Boo Taylor's arms and leading him across the wide, green lawn. And up those grand steps that led to the front door of the doctor's house. A secret breeze from behind the dark screen door blew a cloud of spice and a jingle-jangle melody. A moment later, out of nothingness, a silver-haired troll appeared.

Trolls are magic, she remembered—and wondered where such a thought came from.

The troll regarded each of them with a smile. Gussie felt helpless to keep from smiling in return.

When the old colored woman (because that's all she was) spoke, it was a high, happy child's song. "Good Gawd, Mr. Boo, what the devil you been into now? Wrasslin gators again?"

Boo answered groggily, "*Big* gators."

The troll-woman pushed open the door, ushering a draft of cinnamon and cloves and offering a face that came from the pictures of angels in Gussie Dutton's Sunday school reader—compassion and sorrow and joy glowing from her all at the same time. The tambourine clatter of a dozen bracelets rang her presence. "Miss Gussie, you hurt too?" The ancient eyes were examining her bloody clothes.

How do you know my name? She traded a quick, sharp glance with Wade.

"N-no ma'am. That's *his* blood. I mean, that's Boo's blood—not mine."

"S'pose he got any left?" she asked and cackled at her. Gussie felt herself smiling again. "Miss Gussie, Mr. Wade, you bring the boy on in. Dr. Silas ain't in jes now, but I'll fetch him by the phone."

She knew *both* their names! And she used them so casually, as if they were all old friends. She looked at Wade again, got the same look of happy confusion in return.

They bookended Boo Taylor inside, following the hunched old woman through cool breezes and clean scents, ogling the high-ceilinged opulence as they wound through hallways and doorways (so big!) until at last they came to the familiar examining rooms at the back of the house.

The old woman, her spice perfumes and wrist clatter filling the room, helped them sit the wounded boy on an examining table. She tilted his head to the lights and scrutinized the damage, and Gussie and Wade stood back to watch her. She was uncannily like one of the troll dolls they sold at the Five & Dime. "Good Lord, Mr. Boo, you gone an busted that nose good. Mr. Wade, you do this?"

Wade blanched. "No! A'course not—I mean, *no* ma'am. He got hit with a baseball."

"Well, whoever done it made a good job of it." She laid her frail fingers like crow's feathers around Boo Taylor's nose, tenderly kneading the plum-ripened flesh. "Does your face hurt, Mr. Boo?"

"Some...I guess."

"Well, it's killin me," she said and erupted another cackle. Boo smiled, and Gussie and Wade laughed with her—and suddenly, her fingers jerked, crunched, and Boo Taylor screamed. He sprang off the table, bent himself in half, covered his face with his hands, wailing.

"Goddammit Laylee! That *HURT!*"

Gussie watched in amazement.

"No reason to take the Lord's name in vain," the old woman said sweetly. "Had to be done sooner or later. Figured you rather it be sooner. Now, straighten up, an' let ol Laylee see if she got to do this again."

She grabbed his wrists, and he tried to tear them back. "You're not doin *that* again!"

"Oh, hush, boy," she said, and she led him back to the table where he sat and submitted to getting his face prodded again. She wiped fresh smears of blood with her brown-leather fingers, wiped her fingers on her apron. The hands went to either side of his nose; he flinched, relaxed.

"Why I believe that nose a'yours looks better now than it ever did, Mr. Boo. Miss Gussie, ain't he a handsome one?"

She took a step forward and peered over the old woman's shoulder. Boo Taylor's face was still swollen and a dozen ugly shades of purple, but the troll-doctor had managed to straighten his nose.

"Yes ma'am."

"Maybe a bit shy a'handsome at the moment," the old woman said. "You a little early for Halloween, Mr. Boo, but that there's a fine mask you got. Time come 'round, maybe you git Mr. Wade here t'clobber you with another ball." She laughed and released his face. "You folks s'pect you can keep an eye on this rascal? See he don't die while I fetch his daddy?"

They told her they could, and she left them.

"That's Miss Laylee," Boo said from the table. Under the harsh light, she was again struck by the round shadow of muscle on his naked torso.

"She your nanny?" Wade asked.

"Hell no—I don't need a nanny! She's...she cleans and cooks and stuff."

"A housekeeper?"

"...yeah, I guess."

Gussie thought the woman seemed awfully old for a housekeeper, but she didn't say anything. She had never known anyone with a housekeeper—for all she knew, all housekeepers were old women.

Blood was running down Boo's lip again. She pulled a gauzy tissue from a box on the counter and swabbed his face. He let her do it—it didn't occur to her to hand the tissue to him; it seemed she had been wiping his face for him for the last hour.

"Thanks," he said puffily.

"That Miss Laylee," she said, "she's funny." Behind her, Wade poked through items on the countertop.

"I guess."

"How'd she know our names?"

Boo Taylor shrugged his boy-muscle shoulders. "She just knows things. I stopped tryin to figure out how she does. She's just real smart, I guess."

She dabbed the tissue to his chin. "Lots of niggers are smart like that."

Boo dropped his eyes. "I guess."

"I mean, smart like *knowin* things."

He looked up and past her, distressed (that grayness that aged him, she thought). Then he saw something over her shoulder and smiled. "Wade, you know that's a rectal thermometer?"

She turned.

Wade spoke around a glass tube. "Just takin my temperature."

Gussie giggled. "*Rectal,* Wade—that means it goes up your *butt.*"

Wade yanked the thing out and gaped at it while Boo and Gussie laughed.

When the doctor came, she and Wade melted away under his disdain.

Would have melted right on down those tall porch steps and away from Carriage Avenue if the old woman hadn't taken their hands and hauled them, grudgingly, to the kitchen for lemonade. She felt—knew Wade felt, too—like a dirty Dutton.

"He thought it was a curve ball," Wade offered lamely as they backed out of the examining room. "And he didn't duck."

So they drank lemonade in the big kitchen that was like the kitchens of television and movies. And Gussie Dutton got her first taste of Miss Laylee's magic—not the lemonade (although it was cold and wonderfully tart) but in the way she inflated them again, tickled them back to laughter, shrunk the cavernous rooms down to coziness.

For several minutes, she even forgot about the monster fish.

Then Wade got up to leave, and she was reminded.

"Told Petey I'd pick up some hamburger at Haufmann's before it closes."

I'm not going back there alone!

Gussie stood to join him, but the old woman looked at her, stricken. "Oh, Miss Gussie, you ain't leavin yet. Mr. Boo be crushed you leave 'fore he git the chance t'see you. His daddy won't take but a bit to finish up with him."

"Hey, I'll be home by the time you get there," Wade said, understanding her distress completely. "Market's close by."

"You promise?"

"Course. Don't worry."

But she made him promise twice more as she and Miss Laylee walked him to the front door.

And then Wade was gone, waving, and disappearing, and it was just Gussie with old Miss Laylee atop the porch steps.

Just the two of them. Why did it feel arranged?

A hand as warm and damp as a dishrag took hers and urged her to sit on the top step. Gussie Dutton, high above the street, fourteen steps high, gazed out upon the row of tall houses. Carriage Avenue was an island inside an island, and it felt good to be in here, standing so high.

She knows I like to watch from up here. She knows things.

"How'd you know my name?" Gussie asked.

Miss Laylee (strange name, it went with the mystery) smiled, spread wide her web of brown wrinkles, and Gussie felt her heart captured there. "Why, Mr. Boo goes on 'bout you all the time, Miss Gussie."

"He does? What's he say?"

"Oh, good things mostly. Said you was pretty, an' I guess he was right enough 'bout that. Said you was smart, an' that ain't hard t'see, neither. Said you was a *tough* one, too."

The damp fingers—not a dishrag, but a salve—clenched, churned up an electric pulse. Gussie felt a spark leap into her hand and catch in her bones.

She's doing magic on me; Gussie understood this with certainty, did not feel compelled to resist.

"So. You s'pose you a tough one?"

Gussie met the old woman's gaze and was taken on a tour of decades, of centuries, spun through time out of mind, sweeping over vast deserts, boiling thick jungles while she clung to this hand, sailing down to lost worlds, then up again to starlit eternity. Magic. She saw islands within islands from a great height, a dozen generations at once fighting the same battles for the same ground over and over, saw the futility in it, the sadness of it.

All of it, inside the old woman's face.

She knows things, Boo Taylor had said.

And that seemed so very true because that rumpled troll face had seen everything and remembered everything and stored all of it away within its spidery stitching.

And now, with a simple gaze, she and the old woman had shared lifetimes.

Gently, guided by the stick-and-leather hand, she settled back into the real—not all the way down, still hovering in this high perch with the trees. Gussie looked at her own hand, caught within the other, fascinated over the residue tingle that fluttered there.

"You a tough one, Miss Gussie?" the old woman asked again.

She knows things.

"Sometimes."

She knows me.

The old face, now familiar after lifetimes shared, nodded—joy, compassion, sorrow. "Ain't easy t'be tough all the time."

A warm breeze ruffled the high fortress trees and touched upon the shade within the porch. Corkscrew strands of Miss Laylee's hair danced.

She knows...

The anguish, deeply buried, was drawn forth. Somehow, the old woman had read the mark of the monster on her.

Warm oceans flooded Gussie's eyes. She bowed her head into the cotton fluff of cinnamon and clove and let the oceans spill over. The magical leather hand lifted and held her neck, held her close.

"Somebody been after you, child?"

She let herself nod into the warm sleeve. The hand made soothing circles on her neck, jingling sweet-sad lullabies.

"Get you?"

She shook her head: no, not yet...but for how long?

"Ain't your daddy is it?"

"No," she mumbled.

"Good." The hands, suddenly forceful, pushed her from the comforting shoulder and held her up so she could look into the ancient smile. "Gawd, Miss Gussie, what blackness run in men's blood sometimes. Surely can make the world a harsh place on folks. What starts it, you figure?"

Gussie shook her head.

"Figure somebody put it there—or they put it there theyselves?"

Gussie dabbed a knuckle to her nose. "Maybe they're born with it."

"Hmph!"

Another spell of silence.

Then, the old sorceress spoke again, her tone brightened. "You trust Mr. Boo?" Her eyes sparkled when the lips formed his name.

Gussie was horrified; she looked toward the house. "Oh, Miss Laylee, I don't want him knowing—"

But the old woman held up a hand to stop her. "Trust him t'do you a special favor, I mean."

Gussie considered. "I don't know him all that well," she said.

Miss Laylee laughed her cackle. "Oh, I s'pect that gonna change soon enough," she said and cackled some more. "Mr. Boo still got some polishin left to be done—but far as boys go, he's about as fine as they get."

"I suppose he is."

"You can trust Mr. Boo—for this favor, leastways, you can."

The coffee flesh above her eyes folded over; she glared meaningfully.

I don't know about Boo Taylor...but, I do trust you. "Okay," she said.

The old woman nodded. "Good. Now, you get Mr. Boo t'bring you 'round my place when he feelin up to it. Ol Laylee gonna brew you up a little somethin. Keep whoever been devilin you clear."

Sparks again, this time within the crone's eyes. Meanness? Did she doubt the troll-woman could make such magic? No—the tingle in her flesh, all the way to the bone, said she could.

But those sparks made her nervous.

"I don't want to hurt anybody," she said.

Laylee patted her hand. "We ain't gonna hurt nobody, Miss Gussie. Just spook 'em off some. I s'pect whoever it is deserves *that* much, leastways."

Yes, at least that much.

"I don't want...Boo knowing...about..."

"Mr. Boo still too young to know such things. You jes git the boy t'bring you 'round my place. Don't think you have much trouble with *that*. Spect he *fly* you down if he knew how." She laughed again.

Gussie tried but was unable to laugh with her this time. She looked at her hands instead. There, she saw Boo Taylor's blood scrawled in hieroglyphs in her knuckles. The sudden fear, the sick *smack,* remembered.

Could Boo Taylor fly?

"Wade didn't do it," she said softly. "The baseball. Wade *likes* Boo. It was... someone else."

After a moment, the cinnamon stick hand reached over and folded over her own hand, and the dried blood disappeared. The old woman breathed. It was a long and patient sigh. "Miss Gussie, I s'pose the boy had it comin."

Gussie looked up, saw a mahogany sculpture pointed to an invisible place in the trees. "Some boys is happy to stroll 'long to whatever clock the Lord put in their heart. Mr. Boo...why, he always tryin to jump ahead, see what ain't ready to be seen yet. Always pokin that nose a bit too far than it's meant t'go. Wonder it took *this* long 'fore it got broke."

The sculpture turned, and Gussie looked into the wells of sadness.

"Guess he lucky it didn't get whacked off by a butcher knife."

five

Propped up by the doctor's hand, Boo Taylor staggered onto the porch. He smiled at her, the idiot grin of a drunk beneath the baroque scroll of his nose. At mid-face, in counterpoint, a single bar of white tape was turned down in a clown's frown.

Gussie cowered a step down the long stairs. Then another. When the doctor horrified her with an offer to replace her ruined clothes, she believed she might flee—but the old woman ushered the doctor away. And then disappeared herself, gray smoke and jingling spice clouds fading behind the screen door, and so it was just Gussie and Boo Taylor sitting together on the top step.

Boo smiled dreamily and swayed like a ship's mast catching a breeze.

"Did your daddy give you some kind of pill or something?" she asked.

"...pills..."

His eyes were heavily lidded above the florid swells. He bumped her shoulder.

She said, "That Miss Laylee's a sweet old lady."

The face worked out of its smile. "...don't call her a nigger."

"I didn't call her that."

"...don't like to be called that."

"I know."

"Then *don't*."

"I *didn't*."

But had she? She tried to remember. That effortless word, tossed about so freely by her brothers, her friends. She looked at the screen door, hoping hard that old Miss Laylee had moved well inside by now.

"I think she's wonderful, Boo. And pretty. How old is she?"

Boo wobbled. "She's a witch. I...ran away."

His handsome eyes, color of faded jeans, were glazed, and she imagined the brain behind those drugged blue marbles making somersaults.

"She's a *witch?*" Gussie asked.

"He was...calling my name. Did you know that?"

He tried squaring his shoulders, rebounded sloppily.

"He...*screamed* for me...awful...to help. But I was so scared. I wouldn't go... in there. So, I ran away. Hey, Gussie?"

She put a hand on his knee to steady him. "Yes?"

"I told him coast...was clear. Coast was clear, but...it wasn't. She was just... *waiting*."

His chin quivered. She took his hand and watched tears fill the gash between his eyelids. A big car rolled down Carriage Avenue, thumping cobbles. Boo looked away and followed the car, his head bobbing with a drunken cadence she knew too well.

"Gussie," he said.

His eyes discovered her chest; he looked there intently. She drew an arm across her breasts.

"That...my blood all over you?" he asked. "Gosh, I'm sorry."

Her cheeks heated. "Wasn't your fault."

"Didn't duck that curve, though. Hey Gussie?"

"What?"

"She wrote my name."

"Who did?"

"In blood. . .Hoss's blood. *Booooooo!* Like a joke, get it?"

"Boo, what are you talking about?"

"I wouldn't go back inside. . .there. They showed me a picture, 'cause I wouldn't. . ."

He leaned to his knees, wrapped his head in his hands. The flannel sack pendulumed near his feet. She heard him sniffle once, painfully, through his shattered nose.

six

She reached for a towel that wasn't there.

Fell to the floor, she thought, pursing shower water from her lips. She pushed back the curtain, looked at the empty rack and empty floor beneath.

Had she put a towel there? She pushed the curtain wider, trying to remember when sudden, mind-shattering fear froze the water to her flesh.

He's here!

And in that moment he *was* there.

Sitting on the toilet.

Shirtless; pants bunched at his ankles; lean, hairy knees splayed. His mouth hung open below his drooping, yellow mustache and slack, unshaven cheeks.

"Hey, little sis," Henry Ray said flatly.

His big hands were cupped behind his close-cropped white head, and he was looking at her with moronic casualness.

She felt her nakedness completely. Drips of water collected icicles on her nipples; welled snow crystals in the new, red hair between her legs; slithered winter tides down her arms and thighs and hips and shoulders.

His nakedness, sweat-glistening slug skin, was a nightmare—an outrage.

An angry skull tattoo flexed on his shoulder, winking at her.

"Get out of here, Henry Ray," she said lowly, evenly, grasping for an illusion of control.

His floppy chest and belly heaved a sick breath into the room. "Well, I would,"— he spoke slowly, and she felt his eyes creeping over her skin on beetle legs—"but I got some business to tend to first." He inched his legs apart, showing her his fat, lazy penis, dangling like a fetal corpse from a nest of hair. "See, this here's the only head in the house."

She snatched the shower curtain with both hands, covering herself—but the curtain was clear as glass! She searched the floor. The closest towel was heaped near Henry Ray's feet. Only her bloody clothes nearby.

"Hey, put that thing down," he told her.

Over the curtain, she judged the distance to her room, questioned if he would chase her. But he *would* chase her. And the door to her room didn't lock. . .

Henry Ray stared through the clear-as-glass curtain with his bland face—always, since coming home after his discharge, that same expression: colorless, remote. She had pitied it at first, saw only dull, listless pain in it. Oh, but it could change; she had *seen* it change—with deceptive, monster-fish ferocity.

(Blackness in his blood)

Languorously, achingly, his eyes drab and sick, he whispered to her, "Let me see it."

"You have to leave," she said, breathing force into her words.

He sighed. Looked regretful. "Not so *soon*," he whined.

"No, Henry Ray, you have to leave. Now!"

"Not so *sooooon!*"

His hand went between his legs. His face took on a breathlessness. A *neediness*. She closed her eyes as Henry Ray started groaning. As long as he didn't come after her like he did before. As long as he just sat there and did whatever sick thing he wanted to do and didn't *touch* her...

Downstairs.

The sound of the front door opening?

"Wade?" she cried out, heard the hysteria in her voice and hoped that if it *was* Wade then he heard it, too.

Henry Ray snapped his eyes around. Suddenly, all languor was gone, and he was a carnivore.

Wade's voice rose up the stairs. *"Gus?"*

"Wade, hurry!" she called, watching Henry Ray's suddenly blazing eyes. "Be *careful!*"

Heavy footsteps bounding up the steps. Henry Ray shot to his feet, his half-erect penis pointing at her accusingly. He tugged at his pants. "You dry hole *bitch,*" he seethed viciously.

Gussie coiled the curtain tighter. "Wade, be careful!"

From the hallway: "Where *are* you?"

"Bathroom!"

In a flurry, Henry Ray got his pants to his waist. He faced the door, was pulling up his zipper when the bathroom door burst open.

Wade, crouched low, sent his bright and terrified eyes sweeping over the tiny room.

A trace of the taunting dullness slipped back into Henry Ray's face as he glared at Wade. Wade looked at him, at the hands still fidgeting with the zipper, then looked away to Gussie and seemed grateful to take his eyes off his older brother.

"You okay?" Wade asked, gaping at the flimsy shower curtain.

"Course she's okay, you little *fuck,*" Henry Ray said, his thick voice dripping disgust. He was a cold steel spring, coiled tight. "You stupid little fuck *asshole;* what *you* gonna do, anyway?"

Wade's face was a deathly gray.

"Said, what you gonna do, *boy?*"

Henry Ray stepped forward.

"What you gonna *do?*" The coil wound tighter. "Want another whuppin? That it, boy? You wanna *bleed*, baby bro, ain't that right?"

Another step. Wade was frozen at the door, one hand locked around the knob.

"Oh, you're gonna bleed, all right. Your gonna bleed from your *ass*, boy, 'cause that's where I'm gonna shove my foot."

She started, "Henry Ray, you leave him—"

He turned on her. Exploded. *"Shut the fuck up, BITCH!"*

Spit flew from his fat monster-fish lips and hung there.

The room trembled; the plastic curtain wavered. His eyes—how could she ever think of them as dull?—were white fire over the charcoal smear of whiskers.

Gussie felt her icicle legs, rainbow curse, totter within the porcelain coffin and threaten to crumble.

What had she done?

Surely, she must have done something; it must be her fault somehow. Her body— the way her body had changed; she had provoked him. Punishment? Yes, because it was her own fault. Her body's fault—the blessing-curse changes it had made.

Yet...even before...when she was an ugly little stick girl, hadn't he...

"Mmmmmmm, if you don't look fit to eat, little girl."

He had ignored her when the others were around, when the beer and back-slaps and shouts had greeted his homecoming and he bragged about back-alley knife brawls with sailors and gooks and the cheap slant puntang and they all roared along with him. "In the rear with the gear," he told them, managing to look unhandsome and cruel in his green uniform, "Homesteaded up the Quartermaster's ass last fucking leg. Sweet time, boy." His voice was slower than she remembered. His eyes never opened all the way (they drooped like his big, bushy mustache, and that was new too), and he never looked her way. And she felt guilty because he was her brother and she wasn't glad he was home and was relieved he didn't seem to see her...

But when he found her alone in the backyard, tying up another trash bag of empty beer cans, she was suddenly trapped under the bestial intensity of his attention. "Damn girl, you growed up good. Ain't you gonna give your big bubba a hug?" She went to him because he was her big bubba, even though he hardly spoke to her in all the years before he left—but she was only ten then, and he was nineteen—and now she was wrapped in his cigarette smoke and beer smells and his hands lingered over her back longer than they should have and slid down her back lower than they should have, and...she remembered that maybe those hands had wandered over her before, when she was younger...bedroom stories and gentle, heated stroking...baby sis, baby sis...and so she had finally pulled away from him, smiling at him but feeling soiled and ill, as if she had been playing in the heat and swampmud all day. She pulled away, and she knew even then to stay away from him, when all he did was hug her a little too long and too hard in the wide open of their backyard...

He came and went like a ghost, sometimes gone for blessed days and sometimes laid up on the sofa, letting empty beer cans bury him under aluminum pyramids. She hoped for the day he would leave them for good; he always talked about it, but it was always in the distance. He had infested the house, and he was too strong and mean to put out, and he wouldn't be put out, had no real notion of leaving. Once, when she thought he was asleep on the sofa and she was gathering his empties, she jumped when his hand licked out to cup her thigh. "How old you gettin t'be, girly-girl?" he slurred at her, and she answered, "Thirteen," and felt sick as he stared at her body—different parts of her body. "Come gimme a hug," and he was reaching for her leg again, but she stepped away, laughed nervously. "Henry Ray, you want another beer?" she asked, not wanting to get it for him, but wanting desperately to leave the room. "Beer ain't what I want," he said, and he kept staring that dull, pasty stare that made her afraid and ill, and so she laughed nervously again and left him...

On a hot May night she awoke from fitful, sweating dreams of brute apes and jungles and blood and Henry Ray's rough hand was sliding up her leg, and when she smelled his nicotine sweat she realized he was lounging on the floor alongside her bed—not dreaming. Not dreaming! The moonlight cast a pale blue glow on his naked, tattooed shoulders—she feared (crazily then—how could she think it!) he was naked below the shoulders, too, naked all the way down. The hard flesh of his hand pressed into her leg. "Let me see it," he whispered, crooned, wounded animal puling, his breath coming in short noxious gasps. "Let me see your red pussy." She was too scared to scream, too scared of the vile danger slopping into her ear. His thick paw drew circles on her hip. "Show it, show it. Let me see it, pleeeeeeeeese!" Voice urgent, haunted. When his finger looped into the band of her panties and he moaned beer and cigarette and rotten-meat fumes on her neck, the terror finally ruptured loose—she slammed his hand away, tore out of bed, out of the room, sobbing as she fled down the dark steps—not screaming, not yelling for her father or Petey or Harley or Wade because this was sickness and she was a part of it. He was naked in her bed, his hand had touched her. Had TOUCHED her!

And it...must be...somehow must be her fault?

...wasn't it?

So she told no one, but she cried at night and didn't sleep and hid in whatever shadow she could find like a feeble rainbow-tailed guppy, hiding from the lurking, fat monster-fish in the glass box that was Sweetpatch Island.

And, on a day in June, after he'd been gone for five days in a row, and she was beginning to dare to hope he might be gone for good or dead in some roadside ditch, she was bringing in the laundry from the clothesline out back when Henry Ray was suddenly on her from behind. She didn't hear him, only felt his breath at her neck and his hands on her shorts. She dropped the clothes basket and screamed, felt his strong fingers digging at her clothes; he spoke restlessly, "I ain't gonna hurt you, I ain't gonna hurt you, oh God, I want it bad, oh it's so pretty, it's so pretty." She screamed and fought against him until he cocked her throat in his is arm and shook her and she thought her neck might snap under all that sweating steel. "Stop it!" he bellowed, his lips smearing her ear. "Stop it, stop it, I ain't gonna hurt my girl!" He had forced a hand down the front of her pants, squirmed the fingers there, groping, clawing lower, and she squeezed her eyes shut and waited for the depravity to happen and conjured the vague suicidal images that would come after. "That's it, that's it," he crooned, his arm relaxing around her neck, "oh God girl, soooo good, you like it, bitch, you love it." His arms fell further slack, and she whipped her elbow into his ribs.

He grunted; she lurched away, screaming again, bolting for the front door. Her foot snagged the clothes basket, and she tripped, flinging shirts and pants and underwear through the living room; screaming, she stumbled for the door under the rain of clothes, fearing the wounded monster-fish, coming up behind, reaching for the rainbow tail—she caught the knob and threw the door open to scalding sunshine and freedom and Wade running up through the yard. "What is it? What?" Wade called as she crumbled into his arms sobbing. Henry Ray came to the door. Wade's eyes locked onto hers, shocked and repulsed and fearful. "What—what's he doin?"

Henry Ray charged.

Wade didn't run (oh, God bless him, she thought) but crouched lower, pushing out from the doorway and slipping beneath Henry Ray's bull chest.

Tattooed arms slung through vacant space, caught nothing.

Then Wade's shoulder and Henry Ray's gut collided.

The brothers collapsed to the floor. *"Fucker! FUCKER!"* Henry Ray roared. Head low, Wade thrashed blindly, pelting his fists at Henry Ray's naked ribs. Henry Ray bear hugged Wade's shoulders, swung him around.

"What the Sam Hill you *doin,* boy? You *hittin* me? I'll tear you *up!"*

And then Henry Ray's big fist came free, and he sledgehammered jabs at Wade's back. Gussie stood, wrapped in a plastic cocoon, watching arms and legs scrabble for purchase, elbows slamming into tile, fingernails clawing through skin and hair, gouging at eyes. Her bloody clothes were tangled up between them. Wade's head bobbed out from under a slimy armpit, his eyes glassy with terror. A moment later, Henry Ray's fist looped across the room and pounded Wade's cheek.

Wade toppled. Henry Ray was on him, pummeling.

Gussie threw aside the curtain and jumped.

She landed on Henry Ray's back and hailed her own sharp knuckles at his shoulders and neck. "Lay off him, lay off him! You're *killin* him!"

Henry Ray bellowed at her, let Wade go, took her arms in his iron hands and flung her across the room.

She landed in the tub, backbone barking against the porcelain rim and sending lightning bolts through her body. The shower curtain popped off the rod in a dozen cap-gun snaps.

She huddled inside the plastic nest, spine pulsing fire, legs tingling numbness. Had he broken something? Wade cringed in a pile near the doorframe. Between them, Henry Ray slouched, breathless and enraged.

"I'll...*kill* you."

Was he talking to her or to Wade? She couldn't tell because his eyes had pasted over again, and she held out the supreme hope he was talking to himself.

Wade, bleeding and dazed and angry on the floor, said, "Get out, Henry Ray. Just go away."

Henry Ray heaved disease through his lungs. He looked down and saw Wade. He blinked. Cleared his eyes with his knuckles. Dabbed at blood on his own lip.

"Get out," Wade said again.

Henry Ray worked his lips and spit a misty spray of blood and saliva on Wade. "Fuck you, boy." He jabbed a short kick at Wade's legs. Faked another one. Smiled.

And then Henry Ray finally left.

For good, she prayed, *for good, let him be gone for good...*

seven

He wasn't gone for good.

Only for two days.

(What had she done? Her fault—it must be!)

"You can't tell anyone, not ever. Just...*please*, don't leave me here alone, okay? He'll go away soon. He's got to go away *sometime*."

Wade frowned through his bruises. "Who says?"

She dreamed about a crack in the glass. What happened, she wondered, when all the water spilled away?

eight

"Find what you're looking for?"

Boo Taylor looked up sharply, saw "Library Aid" tagged to a plaid breast pocket, then recognized the tall and pathetically slim-shouldered teenager who had spoken to him.

"Hey, Dalton."

The teenager grinned pleasantly, and Boo looked down at the paperback he had folded in an effort to hide it. He brought a hand to his nose and lightly fingered the bandage. *Folklore & History of Sweetpatch Island* by D. Mavril Pickett. A persistent ache reverberated through his braincase.

Dalton Satterfield was a friendless mainlander, rarely seen heir to an old money fortune who summered on Sweetpatch Island with his family in a huge antebellum mansion on North Beach. And apparently, like Boo Taylor, sought shelter from the fierce island fire among these dim and lonely shelves.

"Help you with anything, Boo?"

Boo Taylor thought, fidgeted, then answered.

Dalton Satterfield's acned face wrinkled with curiosity. "You're looking in the wrong place," he said. "Here, let me show you."

A half hour later, Boo Taylor was hunched over a thick, yellowwood table in a dim basement chamber, leafing through stacks of old newspapers. Two bare lightbulbs in the ceiling cast crisscross shadows. The smell of the place reminded him of campfires.

Thirteen years earlier the *Patch Caller* was a weekly and its pages were smaller. Boo read about Strom Thurmond's campaign speech on the steps of the Corrington County courthouse. About the grand opening of Dedmens Causeway. About a man shot on Daufuskie when caught stealing a pig.

Boo delicately turned moth-wing pages, picked through editions with varying dates until he found what he was looking for. The next clue in a trail started from the stuffings of his burlap birthday gift.

Unidentified Woman Found Drowned

The body of a white woman found last Tuesday morning just south of the Duty Yellow House off Dedmens Causeway has yet to be identified. The woman is believed to have drowned when her vehicle went off the causeway. Her body was discovered by two local boys who it appears notified the Reverend Leroy Hatchel. County police were then summoned and pronounced the woman dead. County officials have not indicated if they intend to search the sound for the vehicle.

In accordance with county health regulations, if no identification is made within ten days, the remains of the unknown woman will be laid to rest in County Field. Anyone with information…

He put this aside, jumped forward several years, and found at last the article he was searching for.

Kenworth Duff's Boy Killed by Wild Animal

He read the article carefully, read it again, then read more in the stories from the next several editions. He looked for a pen and paper to make notes.

nine

From across the Yamawichee and deep into the mainland eighty-six miles away (as the crow flies), the murderess felt the tremble in the boy's step and heard her name cursed in his mind. This made her smile. Caused her to pause at her task and savor his misery.

At her feet, on the floor of her jail cell, rat bones chewed clean were arranged in meticulous patterns around the carefully placed carcasses of several beetles and one large spider—not the ideal ingredients, but the best available and good enough for the job. Her blood dripped freely among these items. The blood was not needed for the spell, but neither would it interfere. The blood was just for a joke.

Now she heard wings flapping, the black call of death coming near, so she set to finish her task. Scrawling the final letters on the block wall, dipping the rag to her wrist for more of the gruesome ink.

When it was done, she sat on the bench and waited.

The flapping was getting closer.

Darkness seeped into the edges of her vision like a cold fog, summoning a recollection of her first violent days on earth, replayed so many times since and leading up to this long-awaited moment. Birthed by a pig, her grams insisted, suckled by cats, licked clean by snakes, and stealing their skins to wear when needed. Scavenging from shadows. Spying through a thousand different eyes. Ministering to others' sins. Setting things right.

The beat of wings disturbed the fog, warped the vision. The wings drew to the barred window just above her head, and there they settled.

She reached up slowly (she could no longer move quickly) and took the bird in her hands.

It was an exceptionally large crow, and that pleased her.

She brought the bird into her bloody lap. She forced its head toward the wall so she could look through its oil-drop eyes at the joke she had painted there.

Time you got new frends boy
but you lookn in the rong plases

Then she stuffed the bird into her mouth, using her failing strength to force it down deep into her throat.

Setting things right.

She chuckled. It was a good joke.

Satisfied, she leaned back to let the rest of herself leak away. She closed her eyes, grinning widely, black feathers poking from her yellow teeth, knowing what this would look like when they came to find her.

As blackness took over the world, she heard the wings (now reborn) testing themselves in the barred window over her head before setting off in unsteady flight toward her distant island home. Not really a long flight—a good sized crow could make it before nightfall. She wondered where the boy would be come nightfall, anxious for him and that red-hair witch to hear about her joke.

And that was her last living thought.

ten

Still far away, Gussie heard Eulahlah Colebriar—the faint jangle of her bracelets—beckoning to her. The sound was air itself, the light, carefree melody of hope.

You c'mon down t'see me, Miss Gussie. I gots what you need, child. You hurry now.

Hugging Boo Taylor around the chest, she followed the trail south to the old woman's music. When the bike came around a bend in the trail, she saw the place for the first time and realized it wasn't the old woman's bracelets that had been singing to her. It was wind chimes.

Boo stopped the bike, and she climbed off.

The place was tiny. A place where elves and fairies would have lived in times long ago. Somewhere ancient. Somewhere sacred and magic. Ivy toyed with flitting insects, rising, whirling green and moist, hugging the comfortable porch rails, nestling the weathered lattice seat that lifted the whole place high off the ground as if it were weightless as a balloon. The place leaned on a lazy tilt, backward or sideways or frontward; she couldn't tell which; perhaps the wind blew it from side to side, from front to back.

"She actually *lives* here?" Gussie asked, and Boo Taylor nodded casually. Then he pointed.

Rising in the distance, beyond the pirouetting wrens and swallows and thick, harassing clouds of midges, were the fractured battlements she had only heard about in stories. "Is that Chaliboque?" she asked, and he nodded again. "Can we see it? Will you take me there?"

He smiled. The swelling had gone from his face, but his nose was still purple. "Maybe after we see Miss Laylee," he said.

A big hound appeared from nowhere, bounding up the dirt road. *The Beast!* was her first thought, because she was an island girl and certainly knew the South Patch legends, and so she grabbed for Boo Taylor's arm. But he was already rushing ahead. The big dog tackled him, and the two of them—almost identical in size—rolled in the dirt. "Shamus!" he cried, laughed. The dog, gray-furred and sagging with age, its great tail wagging madly until Boo shouted. *"Oowwww!"* He cupped his nose, and the dog backed away, tail stilled.

Boo looked at his hands, held them up for her to see the blood.

"Mr. Boo, don't you go hurtin ol Shamus—he jes an old man!" Miss Laylee's voice lifted high on bird wings from the off-kilter shack. "Why Miss Gussie, if you ain't the prettiest? Mr. Boo, you gwon pick us some beans. Miss Gussie an' me gonna set in the kitchen and chat a spell."

Boo came to the kitchen window twice while they talked and while Miss Laylee lathered up a mix of powders and syrups and rancid twists of hide. Both times, the old woman sent him back: first to shuck corn and peel beans, next to weed the garden.

"But I'm still bleedin."

"Aw!" she said and flapped a hand.

The old woman gave her a jelly glass filled with ice and a yellowish fluid. Gussie drank, expecting lemonade, and gagged on the abrupt tang of alcohol. "God, Miss Laylee, what is this?"

"Dandelion wine," she said, matter-of-fact. "Bit of dewberry in that batch, too."

The house smelled of spice and fresh chopped wood and pipe tobacco, all breezing through the herb bundles overhead and cool earth beneath. And mingling with the scents were the sounds: the jingle of bracelets and wind chimes, dim warble of birds, gospel chants from a plastic radio. And the pleasant lilt of Miss Laylee's voice— humming at times with the radio but mostly chattering lectures about her weird, herbal charms.

She talked of root cures for headaches made with stump water and gator tails. She instructed her on how to treat warts with bacon fat and salt and grain alcohol. She explained how to plug up a man's dung in a knot-hole to give him constipation, throw it in a fire and give him a fever, throw it in water and give him cramps.

"There's no dung in *that*, is there?" Gussie asked, nodding at the brew thickening on the burner.

"Oh Lord, course there ain't. Don't smell like dung, do it?"

Gussie shook her head. Actually, it smelled like burning rubber tires. "What *is* in it?"

"It *works,* child. That's all you got to know. Works *powerful.*"

Powerful. Was it to be a poison, then, dribbled secretly over his food? "Miss Laylee, I really don't want anybody to get hurt."

The old woman turned. She did something to the flame, and then walked to the table and sat down. "Miss Gussie, you been in to see Mr. Boo's daddy when you sick, ain't you?"

"Yes ma'am."

"He give you his medicine sometime? Taste *foul,* don't it?" She scowled. "He give you a shot, it *hurt,* don't it?"

"Yes'm."

Bracelets clanged as the old bones gently kneaded Gussie's hands. "Sometime it's the harsh road that leads to the healin road, you understand?"

Gussie nodded.

(Somewhere outside, Boo Taylor groaned.)

The old woman sighed. She looked toward the window, seeing the trees or something a great distance beyond. "Sometime the way to healin is a blessed short road. But mostly it's a long one, Miss Gussie. Most times, it's a long, long road an' mighty harsh. This here medicine got itself a nasty kick, child. But it's gonna lead to *healin.* So...?"

So... The question, asked on the curve of her leather eyebrows: *you sure you want to go through with this, child?* However this poison worked, it wouldn't be pleasant. Henry Ray would suffer, maybe badly, and it would be on her conscience. So she had to decide.

Could she hurt her own brother?

She looked into the old woman's clever, ancient face and nodded. "Okay, Miss Laylee," she said.

Miss Laylee sat quietly with her for another few moments. Then she got back to her feet, a bone-creaking pain rumpling her face.

"Good. Then let's you'n me get to work."

Gussie stood at the window in the tiny parlor, surrounded by shelved walls cluttered with ceramic and glass figurines. Boo Taylor was kneeling in fresh soil along a row of tomatoes, tugging at weeds with his hands and a metal claw. He was shirtless. She watched his thin muscles, watched the pouch dangling at his sweaty chest. Gussie swirled melting ice cubes in her glass.

It was brave of Boo to come back to the ball field a week after Murphy broke his nose. All the boys thought so; they were as surprised as she was when he rolled up on his bicycle with his glove and cleats and bandaged nose. He took right field again, and they joked with him—not mean jokes, either—about taking another turn at bat. "Bring your football helmet, Boo?" Even Harley hadn't been unkind. Murphy was full of apologies, but Boo insisted it was his fault. "I should have ducked it."

And after the game, he approached her cautiously. "Miss Laylee says I'm supposed to see if you want to come down to her place tomorrow."

Gussie came back to the kitchen and watched the old woman stir a wand through the pot. She was stirring in rhythm to a hymn on the old radio. She may have been humming, too; if so, her voice and the radio voice were in perfect harmony.

"Did Mamie Stuvant really write Boo Taylor's name on the wall?" she asked. "In that boy's *blood?*"

Pursed lips curled to a frown. A fly buzzed around the old face. "That's what they say."

"Do you believe it?"

"Oh, Miss Gussie, I believe that creature bound to do anything."

More flies flitted at the window, and Miss Laylee swatted at them. A glass lump on the sill fired off a needle-glare of sun.

"*Why* would she do it?"

She waited. The old woman was silent.

"They say it's because Hoss Beaudry's granddad was there when they lynched Joker Tribbit. Same with the other boy, Timmy Duff, that got killed a few years back. Do you think that's true?"

She waited again.

"Did you know her? When she was younger?"

Again no answer until the old woman finally muttered into the pot, "*Hateful* woman. That's what she is—don't need more reason than that." Miss Laylee made angry knots with her lips. "All the hate swirlin 'bout this island, years an' years of it all piled up—more years than a child like you could ever guess. All that hate all stuck together with sticks an' mud, that's what that woman is. Hate run through her heart like swamp water. Hate stuck in her bones like a trapped snake. That woman got all the worst of Sheba in her blood, an' none of Jojo."

Then she mumbled something at the pot too quiet to be heard.

"Jojo?" Gussie asked. "Did you know Joker Tribbit?" Gussie was calculating years in her mind, coming to answers that made no sense. Miss Laylee couldn't be *that* old.

The old woman blinked out of her spell, smiled wanly. "Old Joker? Why I use t'see that man 'round plenty 'fore they strung him up. Plenty more, since. Though, Joker ain't his real name. Real name was Joseph, an' he was mostly known by folks back then as Jojo. That other name was give to him after he got killed an' folks need somebody to blame their bad luck on. A pig die, an' they say it was bad luck, bad *joke*. House burn down, boat get sunk. 'Ol' Joker musta paid me a call,' they say. An' the name stuck."

"But you knew him? When...well, when he was alive?"

"Course I did! Hard t'miss the biggest man on the Patch, Miss Gussie, an' that was ol Jojo Tribbit. Stood tall as a tree, wide as a horse. Wasn't a soul on this island didn't know ol Jojo—or move out'a his way when he come walkin down the trail, him an' that great big ol hound that was always at his heels. That goes for whites and blacks, both. That was when I worked for Mr. Sam and Miss Maggie, over at Chaliboque. Most of the coloreds worked Chaliboque back then, 'fore the oyster factories come along."

Her silver head turned back to stove. Without looking, she dabbed upward to pluck miscellaneous leaves and petals from the hanging bundles. These were ground to powder in her finger pads and sprinkled into the pot.

Gussie asked, "Did you see how he died? Was it like they say?"

Again, the old woman was silent for a long moment, her lips working like a throbbing frog. At last she said, "How old is you, Miss Gussie?"

"Thirteen," Gussie answered. "Fourteen in November."

The old woman nodded. "Well, then, I wasn't even a full year older than you is now. Followed Miss Maggie when she went to have her little girl, was nurse to the poor thing after Miss Maggie passed. Then some bad things passed 'tween ol Jojo and Mr. Sam."

"Like what?"

Laylee sniffed over the pot, then stirred it with a long wooden spoon. "Miss Gus, you put two bulls in the same yard, one bound to get at the other. I said Jojo Tribbit was a big man? Well, the Patch never did take too well to a big colored man." She lifted the spoon out, frowned, then dropped it in again and kept stirring. "Always been that way," she continued. "You know, it was colored folks first come to this island after the Indians left it. Runaway slaves, they say, an' give this island its name 'cause it was a "sweet patch" of freedom. Come here 'cause it was safe an' so far away. An' maybe 'cause it was 'cross the water an' closest they could get to Africa. Even had themselves a king."

Laylee Colebriar gazed at the ceiling, seeing worlds and times beyond this cramped clapboard frame.

"Then the white folks come to settle, and they took 'em all back in as slaves, an' strung that king up. Strung up any other man tried to take his place, an' I guess it been the same ever since."

"What happened to him?" Gussie asked. "To Joker? What was the bad thing between him and Mr. Sam?"

"Money generally the thing starts trouble," she said. "*Root* of all *evil,* ain't that what they say?"

She looked at Gussie who nodded obediently.

"Well, I s'pose Chaliboque had itself a big money problem, Miss Gussie. Chali*broke,* folks started callin it. Seem like this land never had a decent crop after the war, and Chaliboque was all Mr. Sam had—that an' his baby girl. Miss Maggie, was a Sladeshaw from Statesboro, and Sladeshaws had more money'n the Rockefellers. When Miss Maggie died, Mr. Sam worried sick all that Sladeshaw money was gonna fly off."

"What was she like?" Gussie asked. "His wife—Miss Maggie."

"Oh, she was a homely little thing. Ain't that horrible to say? But Gawd bless, it's true. An' no sturdier'n a baby bird. But sweet as sugar, that poor woman. An' oh Lord, did she worship Mr. Sam? Handsome as the devil, that man, an' sweet hisself, when the mood struck."

Gussie caught a glimpse of Boo Taylor through the kitchen window. He was carrying a load of weeds with the gray dog shadowing. She realized he must have heard this story from her, too.

"So, it was money started it," Miss Laylee said. "Fear of it runnin off an' maybe some big Negro with his big ol dog an' south-isle witch claimin the land. Bulls actin like bulls, an' Sheba makin it all worse, which seemed to be her callin in life."

She swiveled around and faced Gussie. Her delicate face, soft as an old cotton shirt, had become something hard as stone. "Was it like they say, Miss Gus? Child, it was worse. Worse thing there ever was."

The old eyes drifted slowly toward the window and then glittered through a kaleidoscope of colors, replaying some ancient sight. Then the old woman turned to fidget with the flame. The fragrance of burnt oranges lifted into the room.

"Have you lived here your whole life?" Gussie asked.

"Oh no, Miss Gus," Miss Laylee answered. "Spent most my years other places. Mostly just 'round the South. Most places in the South look the same as they does on the Patch—only they do smell better. I took a bus all the way to Baltimore once."

The answer was somehow a disappointment. Gussie didn't want to think of Laylee Colebriar living anywhere else but this magical cottage. "But you were born on Sweetpatch Island?"

"Why, yes I was."

"And you came back."

"Yes'm."

"Why?"

"Why? Well, I guess I'm like an old bird, Miss Gussie. Fly off for a bit, an' always come back home to roost. Sooner or later, those old wings git too tired to fly off, an' it's time for the bird to stay put. After Mr. Sam and Miss Maggie passed, their little girl went off to Statesboro with Miss Maggie's sister, and I went along to nanny the poor thing."

"Were you ever married?"

"Gawd, you full of questions. Yes, I was married."

The old woman took a deep breath, and then she spoke as if addressing the distant woods where the ragged rooftop of Chaliboque glowed pink and orange.

"His name was Eugene Colebriar, and I guess he was a fine enough man, though he drank a bit too much. But Lord, ain't that the way with most men? We got married back in nineteen-thirty-four. Snuff drove a truck for the Highmont Canning company. Had ourselves a nice little place to live. 'Lot like this one, I guess."

"Where is he?"

"Died. Dead and buried. Ol Snuffy—that was the name most folks call him by: Snuffy, 'cause he been partial to *Honey Bee Snuff* since long 'fore I met him. Well ol Snuff had hisself a heart attack. That was back one day in forty-five while he was on the road between Macon an' Albany. Snuffy, he jes pull that ol truck over to the side of the road, turn off the engine, then sat back in his seat and he died."

As she spoke, orange fire welled in her eyes, though the pleasant grin remained.

"Did you have any children?"

Her grin widened. "Well now, how'd I know you was gonna ask that?" she asked and giggled. The giggle was a charming little-girl sound and tragic under those teary eyes. She sniffled. "Naw, Miss Gussie, me an' Snuff never did have us a child. We was both a bit long in the tooth for such business by time I met him. Though, Snuff had a family by some woman in Valdosta who took his children an' left him cold, an' he never heard much from her after. Sometimes, I believe that's what broke ol Snuffy Colebriar's heart." She dabbed a spangled wrist at her nose.

"And you moved back to Sweetpatch Island then?" Gussie asked.

The old woman nodded, and Gussie could read the silent heartbreak in her smile. "Miss Mishelle was growed up and didn't have much need for me. So I come back to Sweetpatch and bought this plot with some money Miss Maggie left me. Cleaned fish at the docks for a few years 'fore Doctor Taylor give me a job. By then, I been gone so long, was scarcely a soul alive t'remember me or figure out who some ol colored woman with a name like Colebriar might be. And I didn't see fit to remind folks anyway."

Gussie wondered over this, but before she could speak, the old woman was coming to her with the poison. It was black as engine grease, packed from the pot into a round tin the size of a stack of quarters. Miss Laylee spit once into the tin. She stuck her pinky finger inside and swirled it around. A dab of saliva dribbled down her chin.

Gussie winced. "Is that it?"

"That's it." Burnt-rubber pungence curdled through the kitchen. Laylee capped the tin and wiped her finger on her apron.

"How does it work? How do I . . ."

"Jes smear a bit 'round where he sleep." The saliva still hung from her chin, wobbling as she spoke; she looked like an old, gray wolf. "Don't got to touch his skin, but it ain't gonna hurt him none if it do. Make sure he sleep right through an' smell it good an' strong."

"You mean I don't mix it in his food or his beer—he doesn't *eat* it?"

"Gawd no!" she said, and the spit finally fell. "I ain't never tasted it, an' I got no intention to. But I s'pect it's mighty awful stuff. Get a taste, you liable to puke out a week's worth of breakfasts."

Gussie walked to the counter, and the old woman pressed the tin into her hand. It was hot. The heat felt potent in her fist.

"What if somebody else smells it?"

"Ain't gonna hurt nobody, Miss Gussie," the old sorceress told her, wrapping a weathered hand around the hand that held the tin. "Just gonna heal the one got the sickness."

..*eleven*

Gussie entered the garden. Shamus heard her, emerged from leaves and shadow, and trotted after her at a rumble to give her a fright. His nose bumblebee-tapped at her hip, sniffing out the lethal tin buried deep in her pocket.

She handed Boo Taylor a glass of wine.

"Thanks," he said, brushing sweaty hair out of his eyes and smearing garden dirt across his brow. His smile crinkled the white bar of tape across his nose. When he sipped at the glass, she noticed for the first time the brown whisker-fuzz on his jaw, recently shaved. And the swirl of downy hair on his chest that caught the magic of the early evening sun to cast his body in a golden shimmer. Murphy's chest was hairless—but Boo's was already a sleek animal's pelt, and she decided it would be nice to run her fingers there.

She followed Boo (and Shamus followed her) to a spigot at the back of the house. She watched while Boo Taylor splashed water and washed himself clean. When he pulled his shirt on, she let out a dry puff of breath.

The tin was burning a welt in her leg. She flapped her hands. "Big garden," she said.

He made a face. "Just try *weedin* it sometime."

"So, what does she do with all those vegetables? She can't eat that much. Does she sell them?"

"Mostly gives 'em away, I guess."

Sipping wine together, Boo Taylor gave her a quick tour down rows of cabbage and squash and lettuce and cucumber, along strung webs of peas and beans, through high jungle stalks of tomatoes and corn. And, last, into a separate small patch close to the house, thick with a stunning burst of colors and wrapped inside chicken-wire.

"The magical herb garden," Boo told her.

They strolled through it and Boo named the things he knew: blood root, mugwort, dragon's blood, deer's tongue. Glittery gold pollen and snowflake buds confettied her feet. "Why does it have a fence?" she asked. The rest of the garden was fair game to the surrounding fields and woods.

"Keeps out rabbits and deer and things. I guess so they don't get poisoned on the stuff."

"Or grow bat wings," she said, and they both laughed.

Gussie pointed to a collapsed wooden structure sprouting vines and weeds. "What's that?"

Boo frowned. "*Was* a chicken coupe," he told her. "Miss Laylee used to raise chickens, too."

"Not any more?"

"No."

She followed Boo as he walked to the oak and stepped back when he tromped into the wreckage. He lifted out a rotting section of plywood.

KILL ALL NIGERRS

Spray painted in dripping green letters, like a plant's blood.

"See...well, these boys used to come around," Boo explained to her, "and they'd shoot the chickens."

She read a familiar viciousness in the rough letters and felt suddenly hot and sick. "Boys?" she said. And wasn't that Petey's handwriting? Or Harley's? Or even Wade's?

"Sometimes they took shots at Shamus, too. Hit him once or twice, I guess. Miss Laylee, she got worried about him, so no more chickens."

"Did you ever see who it was?"

"No."

"Did Miss Laylee?" She was near panic when she asked this.

He shook his head—but in the awkward way he looked at his feet, she knew he was thinking the same thing. An unpleasant silence fell between them. Gussie, nervous, looked around and realized the big dog had disappeared some time during the tour.

Boo Taylor brightened. "Want to go for a swim? We could go down to South Beach." She pointed off to Chaliboque. "I'd rather go there; can you take me?"

"Probably shouldn't," he said, frowning.

"But I've never seen it before."

"I don't think Miss Laylee would like it. It's not safe." He shrugged and smiled. "South Beach is nice, though—and it's not far at all. Hardly any waves. Great for swimmin."

"No," she said, then hesitated, embarrassed. "I don't know how to swim"

He was dumbfounded. "You don't know how to swim?"

"No."

"But you live on an *island*."

"I never learned."

"You never learned?"

"No, Boo Taylor, I never learned how to swim. Okay?"

"I could teach you."

"Maybe I don't want to learn!"

He looked away, her words still ringing when Eulahlah Colebriar called out from the porch that their supper was ready.

"She wants to see the house."

Dinner was over. Boo Taylor was coming in from taking out the trash when he made his announcement, and Laylee Colebriar's stern glare shocked him into adding, quickly, "I didn't tell her anything."

There was a moment of tremendous struggle between the two of them. Laylee turned and looked at Gussie—her wood-grain face molded into a mask of worry.

Then shifted into thoughtful appraisal.

Then to sad acquiescence.

The old woman took a pot of leftovers from the counter and handed it to her. "Mr. Boo," she said, "I s'pect you got some things to explain to Miss Gussie 'fore you go."

twelve

A large crow circled, not visible but close enough to read the young girl's thoughts: *How did this thing get here? How could it have always been here?*

Gussie Dutton's first up-close glimpse of the Chaliboque Mansion came as she and Boo Taylor took the final bend on the southwest bluffs, where the setting sun stained the lush plant life an orange-scarlet. Pigg's Creek was swollen full with high tide, so Boo had paddled her across on a fatigued wooden skiff he kept hidden nearby while she carried the pot of leftover beans and fish on her lap. As he tucked the boat behind a stand of roots on the opposite bank she noticed two alligators lying like fat, well-satisfied logs not ten yards from the spot where they landed. She spent the rest of their journey scouting the ground for snakes and lizards—even when they reached the remnants of an ancient brick walk, she did not dare to look up from the threat of lurking swamp creatures. It wasn't until Boo Taylor touched her arm and pointed up that she realized they had come upon the house.

And the house was immense. It lounged along the bluff in a broad, ramshackle curve, three stories high and a block long. Pillars buckled like broken femurs under the weight of a collapsed portico, and the front door was lost in the rubble. The blind eyes of the windows cast shattered cataract reflections of the sunset to make a nearly perfect illusion that the place was on fire. Charcoal dust of a real fire dirtied the walls above several windows, and—real or not—a thin wisp of gray-white smoke drifted from one of the surviving chimneys. Stucco walls (once a gleaming white; if she squinted she could just imagine it) peeled a drab calico of greens and grays and browns. Everywhere, ivies and mosses and parasite plants festered along great walls. It was like a lost city in a fable, a forgotten temple, though it was unthinkable that a place so imposing could ever be lost or forgotten.

The crow leapt off a nearby branch, startling her. It flapped twice then glided ahead of them toward a gaping window. "People *live* there?" she asked, and Boo nodded.

She took Boo Taylor's hand and let him lead her across the forested yard, around a broad oak, and up to the great house. She picked her way carefully around the rubble, and when she looked up again, a bloody corpse, hung and gutted, dangled on a limb of the oak and blocked her way.

She screamed. Boo grunted.

From the darkness of a window, a woman's voice spoke, and the bones in her hand were crushed in Boo Taylor's grip.

"Why, you the doctor's boy, ain't you?"

"There's people living there," he told her as they crossed the half-weeded garden on their way to Pigg's Creek. Shamus followed only as far as sight of Laylee's cottage would allow, then he turned and abandoned them. Boo's voice was low and secretive although no one was around to hear. "There's this colored boy named Solomon. He's hiding out there 'cause...some people are after him."

"Solomon?" she asked, recognizing a name spit frequently from her brothers' tongues like a profanity. Solomon Goody who burned down the colored school.

"Solomon Goody and his brother, Royal. His brother's not in any trouble— I don't think, leastways. Just mostly stays to make sure Solomon's okay. Nobody knows they're down here, Gussie, and you can't tell anybody...Not even Wade. You gotta promise—"

"He lives out there? In that ol place?"

"Well...he's just hidin out for a bit. Like camping. I mean, you can't hardly live in a place like that. Police aren't after him or anything, but some white men are. Royal says it's Klan. They shot out his momma's windows."

She looked toward the Yamawichee where three pelicans swooped in a lazy arch overhead; one made a sharp downward turn and dove, piercing the water with its beak, the rest of its body following in a clumsy splash. A moment later, the bird bobbed to the surface. A silver tail wobbled from its beak. The pelican threw its head back, rainbow flashed, and the fish was gone.

Molecules swirled on moth wings in the shadows, surrounding the voice that had spoken, coalescing into the grainy flicker of a shape that emerged, at last, at a casual saunter. The pressure on Gussie's hand relaxed.

"Well, *is* you?" the girl asked.

The girl was grinning at them from a ground-floor window where a pile of bricks and logs had been stacked to make a rudimentary stairway. She was fifteen or sixteen, Gussie guessed, glamorously dark, with a long and wide sweep of raven hair framing an exotic face.

The girl stepped up to the sill, barefoot. She was spilling out of a flower-print dress held together by a few insignificant buttons.

Boo Taylor cleared his throat. "Yes."

Movement behind the girl, something alive that tugged at her skirt. A little girl came forth: sandy-blonde pigtails, also in a dress and shoeless. She climbed hesitantly to the sill and hugged the older girl's hip. She trembled in the skirt like a rabbit in a trap, timid eyes widening as she saw the two of them and then the freshly dead deer dangling from the oak.

"Where's Royal?" Boo asked.

"Oh, he around. Though it don't look like he need the old lady's supper tonight." She nodded at the deer. It's guts lay beneath it in a mushy, purple heap, drawing clouds of flies and midges. Somehow not at all like the kills Petey and Harley dragged home. In the shadow of this dark place it was a ritual murder for some whiskey-mad dark mass. Hadn't she heard about such things in South Patch?

They should leave. Now. She should take Boo Taylor by the arm and drag him back into the woods before the sun fell lower.

But Boo Taylor was staring at the dark girl's breasts.

The dark girl placed a hand on the little one's head and looked at her lovingly. "Miss Cass, ain't he a handsome boy?"

The little girl looked at Boo and nodded.

"An' ain't that a pretty red-hair witch?"

The girl nodded again.

"This here's my sister, Cassie Burne." The older girl looked up with sly, cat's eyes, awaiting surprise and perhaps a comment because the two girls looked nothing alike. "Cassie, tell this pretty girl what my name is."

"Crystal Burne," the girl blurted, hurling the name like a stone. Then, she quickly shuffled to the protection of the skirt.

Crystal Burne chuckled—too gleefully, holding a lid over the boiling cauldron of hilarity. "Little Cass see all that red hair, an' she think you a witch," she said to Gussie. "All witches got red hair—ain't that right, Cass?"

The little girl nodded and Crystal Burne stroked her head.

"So here you is at last," she said to Boo. "You the famous Boo Taylor. The *doctor's* boy."

"How did you know that?" he asked.

She chuckled again. "Oh, you right popular, I guess. They's lots a' folks 'round here take a shine to you, boy. . .Solomon, why I guess he think you a regular prince."

Boo brightened, his head bobbing as if to nod—or to take up-and-down measurement of the girl's length.

"Though, look to me like *somebody* don't think so. Look like you got socked in the nose *good*."

From behind her, an anxious voice suddenly grumbled, "Who you talkin to?"

Gussie flinched when, from the same shadows that produced the two girls, a colored boy now emerged. A long knife gleamed from his fist. Blood slicked his clothes, his hands, and all the way to his elbows. His hair stuck out in lunatic spikes. The boy saw her and frowned violently. "Who the hell is *she?*" he demanded.

The little blonde girl jumped at his voice. Gussie tugged on Boo Taylor's wrist.

"This here's Gussie Dutton," Boo said calmly. "Laylee said it was okay."

The boy growled. "Well *I* didn't say it was okay."

"Boo, let's go," Gussie whispered and stooped to set the pot of leftovers on the ground.

The boy was stepping through the window and climbing down the rubbish steps. *"Dutton?* You said, *Dutton?"*

The little girl made a mewling kitten sound; the dark girl only watched with a delighted grin and shifted her hips to expose more leg flesh.

"You ain't related to *Harley* Dutton?" the boy said. *"Wade* Dutton?"

She took a step backward. "Yes."

"They your brothers?"

"Yes."

The boy winced, brandishing the knife and nearly collapsing with rage. "Boo Taylor, you dumb-ass white boy. You know who her brothers are?"

"Laylee said it was okay."

"Laylee said. . .aw, *shit!"* He turned on Gussie who was watching the sunset glitter against the knife's bloody edge. "Peas in the pod, man. That's the way it works. Duttons and more Duttons. Rednecks. I bet you tag along when your brothers go out tossin rotten melons at the coon folks. That it?"

"Stop it, Royal," Boo said fiercely.

Gussie shook her head. "I don't know what you're talkin about."

The boy came forward, and Boo stepped to cut him off, fists bunched (and his back suddenly so broad!) "She brought you your dinner, you dumb coon. Can you put the knife down?"

The boy gaped at the knife as if seeing if for the first time. Then he glared at Boo. "What did you call me?"

"A stupid coon. With a knife."

Gussie looked behind her to plot escapes. The boy stared wide-eyed at Boo, then turned to Crystal Burne who had burst into caustic laughter. "He called me a coon."

The dark girl bubbled derisively, "Look like the doctor's boy don't like you bad-talkin his girlfriend." The little girl was nearly sobbing in her sister's skirt.

The boy shook his blood-spiked head. "I can't believe you actually called me a coon."

"You said it first." Boo said.

"I'm allowed to say *coon,* Boo Taylor. You're not."

"Is that the rule?"

"Hell *yes,* that's the rule!"

"Then you can't call me a dumb-ass white boy. And you can't call her a redneck."

"You think that's the *same?* And anyway, she *is* a redneck. Peas in the pod, boy. She's a *Dutton.*"

"Miss Laylee said it was okay."

"Hear that, Mr. Royal?" Crystal Burne called out, "the old woman said it was okay."

Royal sighed. He flicked her a dubious glare. Then he smiled. "I can't believe you called me a coon. Solomon heard that, he'd whip your backside. He'd kick you all the way back Up Island."

Boo Taylor lifted the pot. "You boys want your damn dinner or not?"

thirteen

She didn't want to go inside the house.

Because the sun was dipping very close to the fuzzy horizon across the Yama-wichee. And under the spell of night, in this place (with this blood-soaked boy, broken toddler, leering snake-eyed girl—even Boo Taylor, who became so damn *unreliable* in South Patch) it seemed any manner of swamp-ripened bizarreness was possible.

But she followed anyway because to stay outside alone was worse—and to leave Boo Taylor alone with that chuckling, half-naked girl was worse yet.

As they walked, a spongy floor sucked their feet and made squishing sounds. Dim orange patches of sunset wavered through broken windows and revealed heaps of ruined furniture, walls mossy and stripped to bare plaster—in some places decayed down to ribcage lathing. Animals scuttled at their approach, some fleeing, others con-verging. Light fixtures skewed lazily, worthlessly, and trailed bride's veils of cobwebs.

The heat and the marsh stink were awful; sweat dribbled through her hair, down her back, between her legs. Boo was ahead of her, whispering banalities with Royal.

"Didn't know you boys had a gun."

"Just a twenty-two."

"A deer with a twenty-two? You shoot it, or Solomon?"

"I did—clean through the neck. Solomon can't shoot worth a shit."

"Can't leave it out there. Gators'll come for it."

"Haul it back to Miss Laylee's then?"

"Sure—she'll butcher it for you. Salt some of it, smoke most the rest. She'll keep it stored, too; you can't store it out here."

Then, in a dark scuffle, it was Boo Taylor trailing, snared by Crystal Burne who taunted him in a low murmur, occasionally spitting her lurid chuckle. Gussie couldn't hear the girl's words but could hear Boo's curt, nervous responses:

"...thirteen...friends, mostly, I guess..."

"...I don't know what that is..."

"...I don't think I want to..."

"...no, never anything like that!"

They crept through places charred by a long-ago fire. Through places pungent with urine smells. Climbing a staircase with mottled green-and-brown risers; she straddled the steps Royal told her to avoid. They followed single file through the second floor, suddenly dry as an Egyptian crypt, more turns and twists around hallways. Turning a corner, Gussie looked up to the front windows and saw a man, a great big colored man, swaddled in rags, and something was wrong with his face. He was sitting on the windowsill, leaning sorrowfully forward. As she got closer, she saw his face was a torture of scars, his eyes blind—but then his eyes locked grimly onto Boo Taylor and he straightened into an errant block of window light, and his face smoothed over; there were no scars after all; it had only been shadowplay.

Would he speak?

No, he only stared at Boo Taylor, reaching with his sad eyes, although his hands never moved.

Gussie kept walking, wondering if she should say something to him—then decided against it because Royal had completely ignored the man whose gaze now passed from Boo to Crystal Burne. The dark girl grimaced back at him, flicked her hand dismissively.

They moved further down a corridor leaving the man behind. Gussie purposely slowed, let Royal Goody drift ahead while Boo Taylor came closer behind. He bumped into her. Gussie grabbed his hand and held it.

Behind, Crystal Burne seethed a chuckle.

Around another bend, bright light glowed from an open doorway. She watched Royal slip inside. Then, trailing Boo Taylor, she went in and saw a tall figure by the flickers of a dim fireplace flame and a simmering gas lantern. Sprawled back in a broken chair like a king on his throne.

The same man she just passed on the stairs?

A large book was spread open on the man's belly. He leaned forward (not a man, just a boy, she saw) and bobbed a great fuzzy halo. His glasses aimed twin circles of blind, white-orange light at her.

Then his voice boomed at her like a radio alarm set too loud: "Thought I heard a ruckus out there. Guess you must be the new cleaning lady!"

fourteen

(*And he's hiding?* she wondered. What could *he* possibly be afraid of?)

Same hostility as Royal's, only more expertly bridled.

He was smiling broadly, unsheathing white knives against dusky, unshaven skin. "Thank you for fetching Miss Eulahlah's meal, Boo. Surprised you brought along Miss Dutton, though."

"You know who she is? You know who her brothers are?"

"Of course I do, Royal. Can't very well live on Sweetpatch Island and not know the Duttons." He placed his big hands together on his chest as if in prayer—a graceful motion, calculated to be impressive—and regarded her with a look that was cold but not quite unkind. "They tend to leave their *mark*."

Burned down the colored school. Yes, she was convinced this one was capable of lighting fires.

She looked into the glass circles that shielded Solomon Goody's eyes and saw the star-scattered reflection of dashboard lights and the dim alley of headlights on dusty back roads, heard hillbilly music blare in time with mad-dog laughter from Harley and Wade and Petey all crammed around her. Like peas in the pod. *"Here comes one, keep it down. Hey Gus, turn down that box and hand me a melon, girl."*

The fire died in the big windows over the Yamawichee and rose in Gussie Dutton's cheeks.

"Place is gettin too damn crowded," Royal grumbled. Gussie realized he was regarding her and Crystal Burne with similar disdain. Then she looked around the room. It was filled with books—had this been a library once? Old, moldy books filled shelves, made random stacks on the floor. The walls themselves were covered with graffiti. And most of it profane. Over the mantel, in rough red brush strokes, she read:

On this spot, I did two daughters
Ate one up & licked the other

Gussie heard the echo of schoolgirl chants in the words and couldn't help but think of the "sisters" in the room. The little girl was a rag doll propped at the foot of an old chair, pretending to read by lantern light from a thick, crumbling text, mouthing made-up words as she went. Her older sister managed to lounge herself behind Boo Taylor on a sheet-draped sofa where she toyed with curls of his hair and offered him a spectacular view of her spilling breasts.

"You a fine lookin boy," she cooed at him.

Boo was perched on the last possible inch of cushion, caught between smile and terror. The girl's belly was squirming against his back. "Hope whoever socked you in the nose didn't flatten it too much. Solomon got hisself a great *big* flat nose, don't he?"

Gussie watched this performance from a legless chair. Solomon, his owl glasses dueling with Crystal Burne's cat eyes, was now posed heroically by his throne. Royal Goody, all crusted deer blood, slouched by the fire and grumped silently. So far, the man she had seen in the hallway hadn't joined them.

Gussie wondered when she could manhandle damn Boo Taylor by the shirt collar and just *leave*.

Crystal Burne's hand was tickling the back of Boo Taylor's neck. "Think *I* got a flat nose?"

Boo waggled his head away from her fingers, grinned sheepishly. "No."

"That's 'cause I'm mostly *white*."

She flicked a taunting glance all around. Gussie Dutton was quite sure she wanted to scratch the girl's eyes out.

Solomon sighed expansively. "Look at that, little bro. Only a week, and already my girl found herself a new beau."

Royal grunted.

"Miss Crystal got herself a taste for *Caucasian*. Story of my life. You watch out for that one, Boo Taylor. She'll eat you alive."

Crystal Burne bubbled a laugh. *"Alive!"* she said.

Gussie looked away, but the sights surrounding her were little improvement. Vandals had been in the room. Derelicts (like the man in the hall?) who over the years had gathered the least-damaged furniture into this high-and-dry, least-damaged of rooms. And, before leaving, left their mark upon the walls, scrawled from floor to head-height in pencil and pen, paint, coals, and smears of substances she didn't want to guess at:

Mudman dus DOGS

Lord God hates all cunts

I suc (lots!) 4 Free

Directly across from Gussie, in red marker, the crude drawing of a leg-splayed woman, decapitated, furious strokes showing blood gushing from the neck. Primitive depictions of body parts. And, above the fire, that nursery rhyme twisted apart and debauched—*ate one up & licked the other.* She couldn't help but think of Henry Ray.

"I don't even see it anymore," Solomon Goody told her, noticing where her eyes had gone.

"It's awful."

From the sofa, Crystal Burne said, "Just a couple big fat cocks an' fuck-yous. Ain't that what they call modern art?"

"Watch your trashmouth, girl." Solomon Goody said sharply, either angry or just mocking. "We got young children in this room."

"Oh, they ain't *that* young." She purred something into Boo's ear that turned him red and made him pull away.

Gussie watched the little girl pantomime through her book, oblivious to the cloud of mean hilarity floating just above her head. Occasionally, she darted peeks at Gussie's red hair.

"How long have you been stayin here?" she asked Solomon.

"Long enough," he answered. "Not the best of accommodations, are they? But it beats the alternative. Miss Crystal and her sister are recent arrivals. Uninvited."

The dark girl's eyebrows went up. "You ain't complainin, is you?"

"Absolutely not!" That broad smile again. "Got plenty of room here, don't we bro?"

Gussie asked, "What about that man we passed?"

"What man?"

"On the stairway." She looked at Boo. "That man standing there when we were coming up."

"Who was?"

"That *man*."

Boo looked at her vacuously, numbed stupid by whatever fleshpot spell that girl was sweating into his pores. "Where?"

"*Where?* By the window, of course. He was starin right *at* you."

"Just now?"

She could ring his neck. "*Yes*, just now."

He squeezed his eyes in thought.

"Boo Taylor, you walked right *past* him. If he was a snake, he'd a *bit* you."

Boo made a slow, baffled shake of his head. Couched behind him, Crystal Burne sighed, "Oh Lordy-mae, here we go again."

Solomon, grinning, announced, "She saw him."

"So did you," Gussie said to Royal.

Royal Goody scowled, leaned away from her. "I didn't see anybody."

"What'd he look like?" Solomon Goody's face glowed with interest.

"He was big," she said. "He had old, raggedy clothes."

Solomon nodded, urging her to continue.

He looked like you.

"He was...a colored man."

Crystal Burne laughed. "Colored, was he? What color—red or purple, maybe? Maybe a dab a'green thrown in?"

Gussie flushed. *You saw him, too, you witch; I saw you go right up to him; I thought you were going to say hello to him.* "He was just standin there. He didn't say anything."

Solomon clapped his hands. "Wouldn't think he said anything. Seems you got a look at Mr. Jakes. That's what little Miss Cassie calls him."

The little girl said softly, *"Mr. Jakes?"* She looked hopefully to the door.

Gussie followed her eyes expectantly, but the doorway was empty. "Who's Mr. Jakes?"

"Oh, he the local boogey-man," Crystal Burne said, bored. "Ain't you heard?"

"I've seen him a few times," Solomon said. "Royal saw him once, but he won't admit it, will you?"

Royal snorted.

"Little Cass here has regular conversations with him. I can't speak for Miss Crystal..."

She grinned at him maliciously. "Ain't nothin but backwood foolishness. Thought an educated nigger like you *knew* better. Specially thought an educated *white* girl knew better."

Solomon shook his head and made as if to whisper to Gussie confidentially: "Sometimes it's better when Miss Crystal doesn't speak. But to answer your question, I believe the man you saw was Joker Tribbit."

She listened closely because the old house was beginning to speak to her in soft gibberings: rat tails flickering in the walls, bats scuttling leather sails in the attic, wet things moaning painfully in the damp floors below. Outside, the fetid Yamawichee, which separated her from sane mainland, sent mocking garbage breaths through a dark window. Solomon Goody, not mocking, watched her with private amusement.

"You mean...*the* Joker Tribbit?" she asked.

Crystal Burne snorted.

"It all happened right here, you know," Solomon explained. "He was the Chaliboque overseer and came to own half the property. Not bad for a man born of slaves."

Gussie looked around at the decaying walls. *It all happened right here.* "And they killed him."

"*Lynched* him."

"Because..." She looked into Solomon Goody's fierce smile. *(Because he raped a white woman.)*

"Because he was a black man who walked too tall, talked too loud. That's the way it works on Sweetpatch Island, you see? That's the *formula*—always worked that way, always will. Old Joker went struttin his stuff too proud; charge gets fabricated and he's convicted and strung up. No courts needed. Guess that got the man a little *angry*. Ain't that right, Boo Taylor?"

Boo nodded obediently.

"So now he a ghost," Crystal Burne said with languid weariness. "He the *Beast*. Come back to get his revenge; eat up little white girls and boys." She curled a hand around Boo Taylor's thigh. "But only the rich, pretty ones—ain't that right, doctor's boy?"

Boo Taylor had turned the color of a strawberry.

"And you saw him," Solomon said to Gussie.

She nodded.

"*The* Joker Tribbit, the one and only."

"I saw *some*one."

"The house ghost. Guess that makes you one of *us* now." Solomon Goody stretched his smile, white knives glittered. The little girl was looking up from her book, nearly sobbing again. Royal was watching his brother strangely. Across the room, Crystal Burne was gnawing Boo Taylor's ear.

Quietly, still smiling, Solomon said, "You know, lots of bad things have been done on this island, Miss Dutton. Hell, Sweetpatch Island is *full* of ghosts and beasts. All *kinds*."

fifteen

They crossed Pigg's Creek in Boo Taylor's skiff, crammed in with the deer carcass. Gussie Dutton waggled the light across the brush, searching for alligators. "Their eyes glow like fireflies when the light hits 'em," Boo told her. "You'll know it if you see it." Royal was toting the .22 over his shoulder in case she *did* see one. But she already knew well enough how to jacklight gators—and deer and coons and otters. That had been her job, handed down from her brothers, when her daddy or one of the others went hunting along the back roads and trails near the docks.

When they reached the other side, they slid the boat among the roots. Boo and Royal wrestled with the deer while she led the way with the flashlight.

The woods broke, and a thin curl of moon cast weak silver across the fields, alighting the million-leafed vines and stalks of the distant garden. Two unmatched yellow squares marked the windows of the magical cottage where Gussie spent an afternoon a hundred years ago, and between here and there, fireflies sparkled like enchanted matchsticks. She pictured the old woman within, at this very moment hunched over her kitchen counter, filling mason jars with stewed tomatoes or simmering some brew tanged with sprigs from her herb garden.

Night sounds serenaded them as they crossed the field. Crickets and frogs scattering before their steps, chirping reedy whistles and deep squawks. Birds she couldn't see called from the far-off trees. The distant wind chimes at Laylee's house danced a faint, pleasant tune. And from the north, a low rumble of thunder. As the three of them touched the border of the garden, the rumbling grew sharply louder. Gussie had gone a few steps down a row of tomato stalks when she realized she could no longer hear crickets or birds or wind chimes. Royal whispered something to Boo. She stopped and was turning to question them, when the lights split the night apart.

"Get down!"

Lights raged down Old Sugar Dam Road. Two lights. Now four lights. Sounds of dirt savaged loose under tires. Now six lights. Roaring engines and the belligerent chime of empty beer cans clattering in pickup beds. Now eight lights. Now ten lights.

"Put that thing *out!*" She was tackled across the leaves. Royal was on top of her, reaching down her arm. He grabbed the flashlight out of her hand and smothered it in the dirt.

Car doors opened. Pinned to the ground, she made out the throaty grumble of men, the ill-tempered idle of engines. She craned her neck—headlights burned through lima bean plants, lettuce sprouts, stalks of corn.

A man's voice lifted over the coughing engines. "Hey old woman! Get your black ass the fuck out here!"

"Hurry it up!" Another man, his voice a high, rusty dagger. A babble of gruff muttering. "Now, goddammit!"

Royal's elbow dug into her spine. The blood smell on his clothes wrapped over her with his sweat, his fear. She felt his heart and her own rippling through her body and into the cool garden soil. Gussie pushed her arm free and shoved her own elbow at Royal Goody. He grunted. She hit him again. He slid off of her some, and the pain in her back finally went away.

"C'mon y'old cunt, 'fore somebody tears down this piece a' shit ol house!"

"Ain't a house. More like a outhouse!"

Hoots of laughter.

"Hear that? C'mon 'fore one a these boys gots to take a shit!"

The flashlight, still alight in Royal's hand and rammed into the dirt, glowed around its plastic edges. Gussie reached for it, struggled briefly with the boy, found the switch, and finally clicked off the light. She pushed up with her palms and dared a look between the high, leafy stalks.

Three pickup trucks and two old sedans squatted at lazy angles across the dirt lane before Laylee Colebriar's cottage. Their headlights glared through the swirling motes of churned dust and sand and wavered around milling blue-jeaned legs. More flashlights danced jittery arcs into the night. As the men flung their threats at the house, Boo Taylor crawled to her side, panting, breathing the dirt. Sweat glittered silver rivulets down his bruised face.

She looked back to the cottage where the yellow light behind the screen door faltered as a shadow passed. Then the door opened. A brown arm decorated with a dozen bracelets appeared. The rest of the old woman slowly emerged, gray-white and hunched, steel-wool hair unbundled, lighting sparks. She was holding...*something* in her hand.

From the men, more bellicose laughter.

"What the hell you gonna do with that?"

"Best put that knife away, ol gal. Somebody liable to shove it up your old black ass."

Cackled hoots from the circle of men.

Miss Laylee's voice rang out, strong and clear as a church bell: "I see you Dink Potter! I see you Stevie Carmany!"

The laughter withered.

"I see you Vince Scanlan! You boys best git now."

Those names... Vince Scanlan owned the Go-Rite Diner over on Polk; Dink Potter worked at Whitman's Texaco at the docks with her father—Dink Potter and her father were *friends;* he came to her *house.*

Flashlights were pointed at Laylee's eyes, pinning her to the cottage. Gussie could see the old woman's face clearly: squinting, lips sewn together with steel thread, challenging. But the men were just shadows, shoulders and legs, caps pulled over eyes. A few heads were shapeless masses, and it took her a moment to realize these men were actually wearing *sacks.*

Vince Scanlan? Dink Potter? Who else was in there?

Royal Goody, his leg still draped over her hip, whispered, "Those dirty, white-trash rednecks!"

Boo began to claw into the darkness ahead of her, dragging something she couldn't see. She grabbed him by the waistband. "Boo Taylor, you stay back here," she said quietly.

Because they wouldn't hurt her—she was just an old lady. They *couldn't* hurt her. It was...what those old boys did when they had too much beer in them and all the ball games were over—just a little *scare,* was all.

The high, rusty-dagger voice lashed out again. "Where you keepin that Goody boy, old lady?"

"We got business with the boy."

"Got us some things to discuss."

Royal turned and glared accusation at her. She glared back.

"Y'all jes *git!*" Laylee yelled out. "I see you Jimmy Earl!"

Jimmy Earl? Jimmy Earl *Deeg?* She closed her eyes and breathed the smells of garden dirt and bitter green leaves. *Oh God, please don't let her call it out; please God don't let her say it.* Boo Taylor moved at her side, fumbling with something in his hands, and she heard metallic clicks.

"Quit fuckin around, goddammit! Where the fuck you keepin that scumbag nigger?"

And then Boo Taylor pushed to his knees with Royal's .22 pressed to his cheek. He aimed at the pack. "Boo, no!" she breathed.

Royal whispered, "Shoot in the *air*."

"Fuck this, that nigger's in there."

"Lady, we're gonna tear this fuckin shack to the ground, and we're gonna roast that darkie's ass."

"You try and stick that knife in somebody, you wanna be sure you stick it good."

Three men broke from the others and lumbered to the porch steps. The gun barrel followed them over the tops of the tomato plants. Royal's face was angled up toward Boo, urging him to pull the trigger; Gussie was reaching to stop him, *stop* him because—

Madness erupted at the porch.

Gussie looked around to see bodies lurching through the headlights, flashlights whipping across the night. Men shouted, backed away. Miss Laylee was gone, and a massive gray shape had taken her place at the door.

Shamus! She remembered—again emerging from nowhere, now snarling savagely, taking up the whole porch. *He got so big!* Gussie thought, and in the next moment, as the men cowered away from the shock of the great animal, the rifle exploded in her ears.

Glass shattered. A windshield.

"Jesus, who the fuck! Where was that?"

"Fuckin niggers got guns out there!"

Boo made furious manipulations with the rifle. Panic now in the shouting voices. Men's bodies circled wildly, searching the darkness.

Boo Taylor fired again, and a man shrieked.

"My leg! My fuckin leg, goddammit! Fuckin nigger shot me!"

Someone (Miss Laylee?) wailed a sharp note into the air, and Shamus sprang from the porch. He ripped into the men with great, frenzied growls, tearing at arms and legs, rupturing the crowd into a wild scramble of dust and flashing lights and raw, hateful squalls. Boo stood up, the .22 still aimed at the pack. Gussie got to her knees and searched through the panic for Eulahlah Colebriar. Shamus charged, snapping at ankles and hands, and men clambered for their cars.

Another shot cracked from the rifle, and more screams erupted.

"Aim high, goddammit!" Royal yelled. "You're gonna *kill* somebody!"

Shamus was clamped to a pant leg, viciously shaking his head, and brought a man down. The man yelped, got one hand on a pickup's tailgate and tried to haul himself up while another man kicked at the dog until the pant leg tore free. Then both men scrambled into the back of the truck. Engines bellowed. Shamus leapt at the windows, jaws snapping at the pale faces behind the glass.

Laylee—finally there—was lurching old-woman steps down from the porch, clapping her hands frantically and wailing at the cars. Tires spun through dirt. A sedan backed off the road at a roar. A pickup lurched forward. Another pickup caught Miss Laylee in its headlights just as she was reaching the ground. She fell away as wood splintered and a porch rail was swiped away by a fender. Gussie bolted for the house. Behind her, Boo Taylor and Royal Goody argued for the rifle. Gussie pushed garden plants, stumbled over a pile of dead weeds, caught her balance, and then her foot rolled over something round and hard, and she fell, scraping her knees.

The truck that swiped the house fired a wide circle toward her, plowing through vine trellises and corn shoots. She was half standing again when the lights struck her, filled her eyes, and she froze.

The truck swung past her. In the afterglare, she read the familiar rusted tailgate patterns, and her heart sank.

She turned toward the house. With the headlights gone, the only light to see by was the weak glow from the door and the windows.

"Miss Laylee?" she called.

Red taillights fled north to Old Sugar Dam Road. Shamus chased, barking in the trail of flying dust and stones.

A ghost figure hunched toward her from the house.

"Miss Laylee?" she asked hopefully, miserably. "Miss Laylee, you okay?"

From behind her, Boo Taylor fired one last shot.

sixteen

From the *Patch Caller*, July 27:

TEEN CLEARED IN SCHOOL BURNING

Corrington County police today announced they have questioned and released a seventeen-year-old boy in connection with a fire last May that destroyed the Palmer Washington Schoolhouse on Old Picket Road.

Sheriff Parker Tillman said the teen, who had been a suspect in the burning for some months, volunteered himself to police earlier this week. "He's being released because there's no evidence against him. Absolutely none. We've got no reason to hold him or charge him."

The fire occurred in the early hours of the morning of May 17. To date, there have been no witnesses. Police did not release the boy's name due to his minor status…

Of course, everyone on Sweetpatch Island knew the boy's name. Rumor was, Pastor Leroy Hatchel had gotten the *boy* a fancy NAACP lawyer all the way from Columbia.

Part Four
Past & Present

Biologically speaking, if something bites you,
it is more likely to be female.
—*naturalist Desmond Morris*

oo Taylor ran through the early morning, squinting against the low sun as a string of fish crows sang a daybreak symphony of *"uh-oh"* calls from overhead. *"Uh-oh, uh-oh, uh-oh, uh-oh."* An entire theatre of crows on the power lines, jittering nervous black feathers and black heads and black beaks.

The crows' eagerness and the shadow of their presence rendered dark memories from a long-ago childhood that cast a familiar dreadfulness over the dawn, conjuring in him wounded thoughts of Gussie Ransome and a fear that something very bad was going to happen, or had already happened, or was happening even now.

This feeling came to him just before the fierce blonde face abruptly ballooned from the street and shoved him toward the dead animal.

Above, the crows burst into laughter.

Laughter roused her from her dream, but she squeezed her eyes closed, refusing to acknowledge the sun and the dull pain in her gut.
(not yet!)
Refusing to look at the man lying next to her.
(not yet, please!)
Not yet, because she was still clinging to the rapidly evaporating dream, was craving to seep back into that shadowland where a different boy-man's flesh and brawn had been pounding her into the mattress only moments before. Was still writhing under the rhythmic crush of his weight, was bruised by it, raw with it. Could still smell him lingering like a vapor over the bed. And if she lay silent enough, wished it hard enough, there was a chance he might fuck her like this forever.

Still wet and throbbing, she groaned as wings, beating at her window, began to draw the boy-man toward the sun and away from her. The rough weight pinning her body to the bed lightened, his flesh diminishing until spears of light shone through him in a pinwheeling spiral further and further into the dawn and toward the harsh, hysterical laughing.

He wheeled through the air (he had jumped clear of the onrushing truck; the crows had not moved from their high perch) until he slammed into solid concrete, jarring reverberations through his skull as his body slid through (stiff fur and sharp bones and slimy, putrefied flesh) the toby-shaped corpse in the gutter.

He was deafened by a shriek of rupturing glass and metal.

Something very bad, he thought as time decelerated to almost infinite slowness through this fall. *But not this,* he decided (he was calm despite the shock of the Mercedes' sleek hood slamming into the bakery truck mere inches from his hip, despite the pain, despite the dreadful shadow of the crows) and decided further that the bad thing that had happened (or would be happening soon) was something else and certainly far worse—and embedded in this was concern for what horrors Gussie Ransome might be facing at this moment.

The exploding machines shredded the air surrounding him. The pavement peeled away his flesh. The dead animal's entrails mixed with his blood.

He skidded to a stop.

Time clipped back to normal again.

The world was quiet again.

Except for the crows, who laughed raucously.

Fire seared through his legs and arms; a duller pain pounded through his skull. He fought nausea as he pushed to his knees.

—*Are you hurt? Are you hurt? Are you hurt?*

A man on a bicycle was squawking a radio-like noise from somewhere close by, and Boo answered him truthfully in his own echo:

—*Yes I am, dammit.*

Across the street, a bright blonde face, five feet high, smiled gleefully over a slice of white bread from the dented side of a truck. She stared at him. The smile was for him.

—*I want another bite,* the smile told him.

—*Do you need an ambulance?* The man on the bicycle had asked him this as if through a long tunnel as Boo Taylor shakily stood and flayed chunks of the animal's days-dead entrails dripped from his legs. A fog of putrification rose with him, wrapped around him, claimed him.

—*No,* Boo answered.

Then he leaned over and threw up.

The crows squawked hilarity.

The blonde grinned hungrily.

The man in bed with her grunted.

She opened her eyes, and the dream was lost.

Painful sunlight seared her flesh from the window. She breathed in stale morning air and felt familiar sheets trapping her in the bed. Beyond the bedroom door, cartoons jabbered on the television, like so many thousands and thousands of other mornings, so undistinguished, so anonymous—like this one, blanched barren by the sunlight and always, always an awakening from some vague hurt.

Her thoughts were on the dream boy-man, not this body reclined next to her.

Where would he be now, at this precise moment? This present. This gift. Time, which had somehow managed to double back on itself and disappear as if it never was.

(You are the same; we are the same.)

No time had passed at all.

(I am in a dream, Boo Taylor, no time has passed, and I am in a dream.)

(I am holding your hand, and your hand is still whole, and you caress my cheek, and my cheek is unmarked.)

(And what damage was done to us and the worse damage we have done to each other has never happened.)

(Where are you now?)

To seek him out would be a sin. To let him seek her, and not refuse him— would that be a lesser sin? And how could such things be measured against the sin of renouncing such a gift?

Could a thing be both wrong and right? This gift. This present. This moment in time.

(No time has passed.)

The hands of his watch were frozen behind a cracked plastic face. He turned his gaze from this off toward the dawn horizon, thinking of Gussie Ransome and expecting to find her there. Maybe burnt and reduced to ash.

(What are you thinking right now?)

(Are you looking at the same sun I am?)

The roadkill that was now slathered over his arms and legs, where it mingled with his blood, had once been either a rabbit or an opossum. Dead certainly for weeks, which meant it had been rotting in the rain and sun since before he returned to the island and well before Sandy Baker had left it. Flies had been eating it when he was hauling Lester Meggett through his haunted house of eyes and chasing little black ghosts through South Patch. It had been decaying in the gutter while he was hunkered safely in his mother's house last night, daring himself to call Wade Dutton so he could face his ghosts in daylight. And it had been here, all the time, baking in the heat and turning more and more foul all through his lunch yesterday with Gussie Ransome when he had faced a different kind of ghost.

It had been waiting here for him all that time.

Gussie was out there somewhere, under this same sun, and the pain of wanting her was more than he could endure. He thought this as he stood in the gutter, smeared top-to-bottom with the stench of death.

The Mercedes' front grill was tangled up with the bakery truck's rear bumper, and fluids were gathering in puddles in the shadows beneath them. A distant siren sounded.

The blonde grinned at the orange juice and coffee he had puked onto the street.

The crows, en masse, took wing as they laughed on.

They were having the time of their lives.

❖   ❖   ❖

Something fluttered at the window; she looked up, hoping to see someone else and caught only a faint ripple in the horizon, like heat on a blacktop.

Gauzy curtains cast wispy shadows across her husband's profile. In this moment, he was a stranger. He was an intrusion. She watched this stranger's lips; even as he slept they were curled into a confident grin. She blinked, and then remembered him again. This was the grin she'd woken up with all those thousands of mornings—and before that, back to the years when she was a little girl and had a crush on him. And it was a wretched certainty that he would never be unfaithful to her and that he would always be confident that was all she could ever need or want—because those were the rules of the game, and Murphy Ransome always played by the rules and always played the game better than anyone.

And because those were the rules, he was eternally confident she would simply love him back. And she did, as best she could; it was a safe and comfortable feeling, her love for Murphy Ransome, this teenage boy she once thought was dangerous was now her husband and the most secure and least dangerous thing in her life.

The dampness between her legs felt like betrayal.

She watched the sun alight her husband's handsome, slumbering face. And as she listened to the faint children noises beyond the bedroom door, and as she breathed the stale air of another morning on Sweetpatch Island, Gussie Ransome closed her eyes to ponder the sins of omission and sins of commission.

If she sought him?

If he sought her?

He would seek her, she was certain he would; he wasn't (had never been) through with her, and the book on them would never close. And when he found her, could she (bear the sin) refuse such a gift? She was certain she (craved him) couldn't. She was certain she (this life) was doomed.

When she could at last open her eyes again, she saw her husband's (stranger's) eyes were open now as well.

"What are you looking at?" he was asking her, sleepily, and so she reached from under the sheet to touch his face and answered him: she was looking at the most handsome man on Sweetpatch Island.

But then he was asking her, "Just the island?" Smiling.

Smiling in return, though inside she was rusted metal twisting and breaking apart, she thought: Why can't that be enough?

two

"You had a call or two while you was out," Bess Pope announced. She wrinkled her nose but was otherwise doing a credible job of ignoring the stink coming off of him.

Boo Taylor stood at the kitchen sink. He was dabbing a wet paper towel on his scraped skin, removing road grit.

"That pretty girlfriend of yours, Miss Sandy," the woman told him. "Says you needs t'call her back."

Boo waved the paper towel at her in acknowledgement.

"Called three, four times already."

"Okay," he said, but he barely heard her. He was still listening for the flutter of crows' wings in the air.

three

A dead animal was plastered to the street a few yards from Ben Shallcross' feet. He could tell it had once been a squirrel because of the tail, though the rest of the creature was flattened beyond anything recognizable.

He sat on a bus stop bench in Chamberlain on Sixth Street in front of Doleman's Cafe and the bus depot. Roy Doleman had been a ranger as well some years back, before he got burned in a fire out toward Goatswood Ridge in the late '80s, and he had been collecting disability from the park service ever since. Ben Shallcross had thought to stop in to say howdy and have a cup of coffee after he'd done his grocery shopping. But the slack-faced girl who met him at the counter told him Roy and Darla had gone to Knoxville for the day. So he sat by himself. He had his coffee and a pack of Cheese on Wheat Crackers and then wandered out to the bench with his groceries.

He watched as each car rolled past and pancaked the dead thing a little more, made it a little more a part of the road and less something that had once been alive.

From where he sat, he could still hear the juke in Doleman's. It was playing a Conway Twitty tune about a man in love with a "purty-eyed" girl, and Ben didn't much care for Conway Twitty.

Why, that's very good Mr. Shallcross. He was remembering the teller in the Eastern Tennessee Trust who had watched over him signing his pension check like he was a toddler making potty for the first time. His too-big fingers fumbled with the papers *(doin just fine, sir)* and scratched out his large, shaky letters and numbers on the forms. When he looked up at her, the girl was fixing him with that patient smile it seemed all young folks put on for doddering old cooters.

Don't you worry Mr. Shallcross; you can just fill out another one, okay? Just remember, your account number goes in the red boxes, not the blue.

Ben Shallcross coughed harshly into his fist.

Mr. Shallcross, sir, are y'all takin something for that cough?

A big Chevy pickup rolled to a stop, pinning the dead squirrel to the street. A watery red-gray fluid leaked toward the curb. Ben looked up and saw Elton Cooper getting out of the truck.

"Say old fella, you 'bout ready?"

They loaded Ben's groceries next to the sacks of feed in the back of Elton's truck. A frost had settled into Ben's old joints while he was on the bench, and cranking them back into motion was an effort.

"Roy wasn't in," Ben said.

"What's that?"

"Roy and Darla gone off to Knoxville for the day. Roy Doleman."

"Oh."

Elton walked him back to the passenger door. The dash and the seat were littered with empty Styrofoam cups and feed store receipts. Ben leaned in to brush them aside as Elton waited patiently behind him.

"Probably went to see his boy," Ben said.

"Who did?"

"Roy Doleman. His boy's with the State Police. Probably went to pay him a call."

"I suppose," Elton said and helped Ben climb into the seat.

They listened to the two o'clock news on KOLM. When the weathergirl came on, she confirmed what Ben already knew because the dogwoods were thick with berries and hornets were nesting close to the ground: it was going to be an early winter. The thought of it made Ben shiver a little in the truck's cab. *Time to bundle up out there, East Tennessee. Weatherwatch says the big chill is headin this way, and it ain't takin no prisoners...*

Elton snapped off the radio when the news was over, and they rode mostly in silence. Ben watched through the passenger window as the town thinned away on the steady slope into the hills on Route 411. He coughed harshly.

"What're you thinkin about?" Elton was asking him.

Ben glanced at him briefly. "What's that?"

"Look like somethin's on your mind."

"Nope. Just woolgatherin, I guess."

Elton nodded. He was fingering his beard. "So you never did fess up about where you been runnin off to lately."

"Did so."

"*Fishin,* you says." Elton snorted. "Fishin for *what,* I says."

"And I guess I told you clear enough."

"*Brownies,* you says. Hell, brownies been gone from these parts for *years.*"

Ben's eyes wandered to the rolling, fuzzy peaks set against the cloudy sky. It was hard to tell where mountain ended and sky began. With the smoky mist and the red-orange trees, the world looked like it was on fire. "Well, I never said I was havin any luck."

Dead squirrels. He was thinking about dead squirrels getting thumped over by cars and trucks and ground away into the street until there was nothing left of them. Even the stain got washed away.

"Sometimes, Russell, it feels like he's my own boy."

"Never had your own, Ben. It ain't the same."

"No...I suppose it isn't. Never had my own...Do you know why, Russ? Do you know why I never had my own family? And instead I went and spent my life hidden away like some hermit up in these hills? Do you know what I left behind? Cause if you do, I wish you'd tell me. I can't remember, Russ; I'm an old fool and I can't remember 'cause it's been lost to me for so long, and the paths are all grown over.

"But oh, sweet Jesus, I think it's comin back to me now.

"And I'm scared, Russ."

It had begun that lost day in the woods when a black, musty corner of his mind was shattered by a swarm of butterflies taking wing, and in their passage Ben Shallcross had discovered a forbidding trunk crammed full with lost snapshots of a forgotten life. The pictures, torn and splattered with mold, were now floating one by one before him. They came to him in restless, strange patterns, unbeckoned. Over the rising steam of a cup of coffee one morning, he watched a peregrine falcon drift into the distant trees, and the photograph of a splintery old shrimp boat had come to him, and with it the story from a long-ago summer in his youth—casting a skein into muddy bottomed waters and hauling it back in over and over until his hands bled and his back ached and the sun blistered his skin while a raggedy old salt laughed at him and praised him. An evening later, as he turned the rusted spigot on the pump out his back door, there came the picture of a sprawling white tent ablaze with the fire-and-brimstone oration of a red-faced man he suddenly recognized was his Uncle Ezra from Macon. "All SINS are SINS of the FLESH! The FLESH poisons the mind; the FLESH poisons the spirit; the FLESH will lead you straight into that flaming oven of HELL, and hear me people when I tell you that oven will surely ROAST your flesh, 'cause Satan keeps that oven at THREE THOUSAND DEGREES!"

The pictures came fleeting and taunting and were gone, leaving a ghostly wake. Leaving him puzzling over the fragments they revealed.

And now, as Elton Cooper's pickup passed the tumbled ruins of the Texaco filling station that Cal Porchal shut down in 1983, and as Ben Shallcross looked at its pitiful, fallen-in roof, again the pictures floated from deep within the black and into his mind's eye.

In high summer, a dusty lane cobbled with flecks of bleached shells.

The smell of honeysuckle and fresh-cut grass, beyond that a whiff of marsh and brine.

Yes...he remembered it.

Along either side of this lane, huge magnolia trees sagged over lattice-and-lace homes. As he walked the lane and watched the fancy houses, a hand swung before his face, the color of ashes from a campfire. He looked up and saw a colored woman next to him. They were walking together, he and this woman—and the woman was pulling along a cart filled with tomatoes and summer corn and squash. She was whistling. He watched the woman's cheeks bellow and throb like a heartbeat as the tune poured forth high and sharp, a finer song than any bird's. It was an old field hand's tune, Ben remembered, and he remembered eight-year-old Ben trying to whistle along. The colored lady's face turned to look down at him, and it broke into a smile so wide that Ben thought a whole ear of that corn could fit inside with room for another. The ash-colored hand reached up and petted his young head. "You gittin the knack, y'old jasper," she was telling him.

They walked on, along the shell-cobbled road of his memory. Slow-moving horses pondered by, hauling wagons as lazy faced men sat at the tethers. Three little black girls played jump rope by the side of the street, their movements and chatter an infectious cadence of slaps and chants and shuffling feet. Gulls circled a fiery

*sky. The Negro woman at his side was whistling mightily, and Ben was now hum-
ming along with her. After they'd gone a ways, a whitewashed brick building rose
before them. Painted all around a garage-door-sized opening were huge pictures of
fruit and fish and cuts of meat, and Ben suddenly remembered the street they were
on was called Fulton Street, and this was the Fulton Street Market. And it was Yula
Jean who was walking with him, Yula Jean Colebriar who worked for Miss Elisa Tull
who came to the island every August and stayed to October in her big house just over
on Carriage Avenue. Fruit and vegetable stands cluttered the way ahead. People
were milling in and out of the dirt aisles—ladies in high-collared dresses with wide
skirts and men in buttoned-up jackets, even though the heat was thick and wet.*

*(A girl stepped out of the crowd and peered at him. He knew her. Not much more
than a toddler, but already striking with her long blue-black hair, her dark eyes,
her pretty pink dress. She saw him and waved, a smile lighting her miniature face,
and he waved back.)*

*And then the colored woman was stopping and leaning over to speak quietly to
him. Ben saw the sweat glitter in drops along her delicate jawline and smelled the
salt on her skin. The voice, sad and gentle as a night breeze, whispered to him.*

*Ben's eight-year-old hands reached for the woman's frayed shirt sleeve and held
onto it.*

*"Gwon now, little man," the voice was urging him softly. He felt the big hand
pat him lightly on the rump and push him toward the crowd.*

Still, Ben held onto the sleeve.

*The mouth moved, and more words came. The hand rose, clattering bracelets,
to point toward the crowd, and Ben's eyes followed her finger. Among the shuffling
figures his eyes came to rest on a man—a bantam of gray-white hair, a thin strip
of mustache. He strutted about the others like a rooster among hens. Ben looked at
him, then back at Yula Jean, and suddenly Yula Jean seemed as black as night, and
he understood.*

His fingers slipped away from her sleeve.

*Again he felt the hand urge him toward the crowd, and again he heard the
gentle voice. "You gwon, Mr. Ben. You gwon n'make your daddy proud."*

Ben coughed roughly, flaying his throat. He brought his hands to his mouth to
catch the last of his spasms and looked over at Elton who was staring blankly ahead
at the road. *Go on, boy, say something. Tell me I'm soundin like a wheezy old bear
today. Go on.*

The truck pulled off Route 411 and rolled over a winding dirt road that jarred Ben
on the seat springs. He put his hands on the dashboard to keep from bouncing against
the door or into Elton. A few hundred yards into the trail, and fifty yards further down
from the last of the tin mobile homes by the highway, the truck came to Ben's small
cabin, tucked alongside a sheltered bend in Palmers Creek.

❖   ❖   ❖

Ten minutes after Elton pulled away, Ben slipped on his parka and was on the slim path off the north side of the cabin. A few hundred feet into the trail he realized he had forgotten to put the groceries away, but he decided not to turn back. A little farther on, he realized he'd forgotten his hat.

What's the worst you been afraid, Ben?

It was midafternoon and the sky was darkening toward a deep slate blue. It was a color he associated with winter. Crisp air from the peaks swept down to feather his cheeks. He pulled the parka tight around his neck. Around him, sugar maples were forty-foot flames of yellows and oranges and reds. He watched his feet as he kicked through the calico leaves and tall bluegrass that carpeted the trail. His shadow crept along at his right side, clinging to his steps like a long dark scarecrow. Next to that shadow, another appeared. He looked up and was not surprised to see the brown-and-white shape of his old mutt, Willie. The dog was plodding alongside him, in the same lazy saunter just as he had before he died eighteen years ago.

"Hey Willie, hey old boy," Ben said.

The dog wagged his tail and turned his head to the sound of Ben's voice.

Ben walked along with the dog, enjoying the sound of their feet kicking at the fall leaves. He was a young man, wearing the park ranger uniform and walking with legs that did not ache as he breathed the rare autumn air.

"See if you can't find us a rabbit. *Rabbit,* Willie! *Rabbit,* boy!"

At the sound of that familiar command, the dog was off, eagerly sniffing the trail. Ben watched him go. When Willie flicked out of sight on the open trail, Ben felt a sharp stab of loneliness.

He came to a naked rise of withering timothy where the wind had blown away the dead leaves. Warblers and preacher birds rode the breezes and thrummed their calls. He listened to them and to his own heavy breaths. He was hurrying now, though toward *what* he wasn't sure.

And again, from the shadows, the grainy pictures fluttered before him.

Where was she; where was she?

"Come join me, Ben."

Laughter and voices all around him, the pictures showed a crowded table within a wide, screened porch. The porch hung beside a sprawling lawn of pink and red and purple azaleas, and beyond that was the stark blue-green of the Atlantic. A light sea breeze wafted through the screen to swirl amid the light chatter and the gentle clinking of crystal and china. He saw his own strong hands before him and knew he was older than the boy he had been in the earlier pictures—nearly a man. And recognizing this, he felt this young-man-Ben nervously distracted by the nearness of the man at the head of the long table. That man was speaking amiably with the others, but the force of his presence pinned Ben to his chair, measuring every word he spoke, every gesture he made. And because of this, young-man-Ben's every word was stuttered, every gesture halting.

Yet more acute than his awareness of his father's nearness was the awareness of another's absence.

Where was she?

He heard himself answering someone that, yes, he thought his studies were going quite fine. A quick glance to the man at the head of the table. Then back to his hands. Someone else spoke, and there was laughter.

Where was she, where was she, where...?

Another question, and again he heard himself stutter an uncomfortable response. No, he didn't think all that football was interfering with his studies.

His father spoke then, and the attention of those present shifted to him as if the table had been tilted in that direction and it was gravity that drew them. Ben, in the grip of that gravity, turned with the others. He saw only the steady light of sharp, gray eyes. The words drifted down the table. It was not all that football that worried him, his father was saying—it was the boy's preoccupation with the ladies.

This drew more laughter, and the table seemed to right itself again. Young-man-Ben looked at the man next to his father—a man whose name old-man-Ben now remembered was Raymond Satterfield—and saw him laughing obliviously with the others. Heat rose to Ben's temples, and he cast his eyes down again.

Satterfield, yes...

So young, those hands he saw before him.

Where was she, where was she?

"Yes, Russell," old-man-Ben now thought as he watched the fluttering pictures swim before him, "there was a time before these hills." He thought this while his knees flared and his breaths churned in cold rasps against his wounded throat. "There was another life before the hills, Russ. A boy you never knew. I'm just remembering it all now. It began that awful day in the woods, the day I first saw her dancing in the water and the lid on that old trunk opened up and I began to see those terrible old pictures again. But maybe it really began long before that. Maybe it began that day you asked me that awful question."

What's the worst you ever been afraid?

"I wonder what your grandson would think if he knew I was an educated boy from the low country. I wonder what he would think—what you would think, Russ—if I was to tell you what lay dead and buried back there."

And he watched again as the young-man-Ben Shallcross in the pictures stepped through a screen door and down steep, wooden steps. The air was cool under the soft glow of this friendly Southern evening. Fireflies dotted the night, and the sweet scent of oceans and spring flowers filled his lungs. He walked cobbled streets, past tall houses, past great moss-laden trees, past the dim, peppery shouts of boys playing baseball far away. And then ahead, in a garden across a field, he saw a barefoot girl—still in her expensive church dress—kneeling in a row of beans, tugging at weeds, laughing with the small black woman who worked alongside her. He watched as they giggled to each other, as the fire of the sunset sparkled in the floating tufts of dandelions, and as, seeing him, her face lit into a smile at once so tragic and so happy that he felt his breath leave.

"Come on Ben," he heard her calling. "Come join us!"

Riding above that, from a distance behind him, his father's voice. Asking where he was going.

Pretending not to hear, he went to her...

She was there, in the water, as he knew she would be. Dancing as before in the sheltered pool and waiting for him.

So cold, so cold in there.

He had been back to the crest several times since the day he first saw her; he could not say how many times, exactly. But each of those times he had found her swimming elegantly beyond a mist in the dark waters, and each of those times he felt the crippling, cold aches in his old man's joints melt away. And each of those times she would sense him and turn to him and raise her arms to him. And he would feel her calling for him.

But he would turn away from her and hike back to his cabin. And move through the mundane, solitary chores that made up a hermit's day while he tried to ignore the horrible truth that a ghost was calling to him from the woods.

In the nights, her voice sang to him as he lay within the timbered walls of his cabin; born by the winds from the peaks, her voice seeped through the cracks and seams in the old planks to find him on the edge of dreams. In the light of day, her voice came like a wood sprite, taunting him from behind trees and rocks, beckoning him to lay down his axe or his staff and come to her. A voice that was round and sweet like some fruit on a branch that was daring him to resist. And though he could resist for a time, he found he could not *completely* resist. The thought of it, the *pull* of it was with him always. The temptation built up on him, layer upon layer, until the weight of it was more than he could bear.

And so again, he stood on the crest in this secret cove of wood and watched her. He watched, entranced by her soft, white beauty and the promise of youth in her face. And he felt the weight shedding from his tired old shoulders. He was there for some time before he realized he was making a dazed climb down the slope toward the water's edge. The earth slipped beneath him, and when the more rational part of his mind understood what he was doing, he thought, *too old for this, you fool.* But he climbed on. His fingers trembled as they clung for holds among the rocks and roots. When his boots touched the ravine's bottom, he took several slow, deliberate breaths. He looked into the water's mirror. A young man's face smiled back.

The ripples that shook his reflection began to still, and he looked up and into the mist. She had stopped swimming. She was lifting her arms from the waters to reach for him. His own arms reached for her.

She began to float toward him. Her shoulders rose from the water and her breasts bobbed delicately on the surface. Her eyes shone steadily on him as her body rose further, drops trickling down the white skin of her arms and legs. The mist followed her, and when at last she drifted before him on the shore, the mist wrapped them both. He felt for a moment that she would walk right through him, right *into* him and possess him completely, and he tensed for it. But she stopped only a few inches away. Her hands came to his face, longing but not daring to touch. Her lovely sad eyes hovered achingly close to his own. He watched her lips begin to move and then heard the words—so raw in their closeness—as she spoke them.

"Do you love me?"

He shut his eyes. Felt his skin rippling. Listened to the sigh of her breaths. He stood with her for a time he believed was forever, his eyes squeezed shut. He imagined being drawn by her into the pond, the black waters, cold, running over him, into his mouth, his nose...

At last, he heard the delicate rippling of her retreat, alone, back into the water. It was the sound of heartbreak—such an awful and terribly lonely and hopeless sound, drifting further and deeper, fading until the last faintest trickle into silence.

He waited, listening, thinking of dead animals in the street. And then he turned away.

four

Boo Taylor sat down opposite Wade Dutton in Barney's Ribs 'n Sports on Merganser Street. "Look," Wade started, "let's get this straight right from the get-go. Murph's like a brother to me. You got that? So don't you go askin me to get involved in anything."

Wade was attacking a basket of wings. He had arrived in his police cruiser wearing plain clothes; to Boo Taylor he looked boyish out of uniform: freckled face slathered with sauce, glistening red crew cut, wiry arms poking out of a baggy polo shirt. He belonged in a Norman Rockwell painting.

"I don't know what you're talking about," Boo told him.

"Like hell, you say."

"Wade, I honestly don't know what you're talking about."

Wade lowered a half-gnawed bone. "Gussie, goddammit! You think I don't know you two had lunch at Del Rey's yesterday? You think I don't know how it ended?"

"You were undercover, watching the whole time. I knew that waitress looked familiar."

"Funny guy. Real funny guy. No, I talked to Gus this morning, and she filled me in."

"How is she?"

Wade's cheeks flushed beneath the barbecue sauce. "You think I'm supposed to tell you? I shouldn't even be talkin to you about her. You got no right!"

"You brought it up."

"I brought it up? Okay sure, then you go askin me a hundred questions, and I'm supposed to be in cahoots with you or somethin. Well quit askin, all right?"

"Wade," Boo said reasonably, "I only asked how she is."

Wade was approaching apoplexy, but it was hard to take him seriously with grease smeared over his little-boy's face. "And you think I'm supposed to tell you? Murphy Ransome's like a brother to me; what are *you?* You run off, forget everybody, then come waltzin back twenty years later like you can pick right up where you left off. Well, I'm not gonna pass along any notes for you, or whatever else you got in mind. You got that? You got some nerve, boy."

Boo Taylor took a deep breath. He wiped his mouth with his napkin, hoping Wade would take the hint. "Wade," he said, "I don't want you talking about Gussie if you don't want to, and that's not why I asked you to lunch."

Wade was eyeing him cautiously.

"I know," Boo continued, "some folks resent me being here. Well, I could give a rat's ass what Murphy Ransome thinks about it. But I *do* care what you think."

Wade dropped his eyes. Boo glanced around and saw the other diners either looking in their direction or pretending not to look. It was like his lunch with Gussie all over again.

After a moment, still looking down, Wade said in a low voice, "She's miserable, Boo."

"I'm sorry."

"You got her all worked up."

"I didn't mean to."

Wade glanced up; the accusation remained on his face. "Everything was all fine, then *you* come along. Stir everything all up again."

Wade poked dismally through the basket of wings trying to find an uneaten one.

Boo watched him and wanted to tell him, *Everything was not fine, and it never was,* but realized nothing good would come of it. So he was silent for a moment.

"*You* was like a brother to me once, too," Wade said.

"I know. Wade, please wipe your mouth, you're making me sick."

Wade Dutton mopped a balled-up napkin across his face and seemed surprised by how much sauce came away.

"I didn't have any real brothers," Boo told him. "For a while there, Wade, you were it."

Wade Dutton considered this solemnly for a few seconds, then a small smile appeared. "You didn't have any real brothers," he said. "Well, I got stuck with *three*, and I can tell you, boy, you weren't missin too much."

"No, I guess not."

Wade scrubbed his mouth again. "Anyway, Boo. I guess you need to know I ain't all that happy about things. I don't like seein Gus cry like that. And I don't like seein Murph..." He smiled unhappily and shrugged.

"I know," Boo said. "Murphy's a saint and he's like your brother and I'm just some jackass from up North. I got it."

"So don't expect me t'start gettin in the middle—"

"Wade"—Boo stopped him—"that's not why I asked you to lunch."

"No? You said you was lookin for some kind'a favor."

"I am. I want you to take a ride with me down into South Patch."

Wade glanced at his watch, then looked up with suspicion. "What the hell for?"

"I'll tell you when we get there."

"You'll tell me now. I go on duty in a couple hours."

"Somebody stole my wallet," Boo told him, but before Wade could question him, Boo changed the subject. "Speaking of your brothers, what ever happened to Henry Ray?"

Wade Dutton scowled fiercely. "You think I care? In and out of prison, like that's any big surprise."

"What did he do?"

"Who cares what he did. Assault. Possession. Auto theft. I hear he got religion. Only not in a good way; he got all caught up in that black stuff. And this is important for what reason?"

"Where is he now?"

The flush was rising in Wade's cheeks again. "Am I supposed to know? I don't keep track of that piece a' shit."

"I saw him at the docks," Boo said. "The first day I was back on the island. He was working the nets on one of the boats, and he saw me looking at him."

Wade threw up his arms in a gesture of aggravation. "So you know all about it. So what are you asking *me* for?"

"Do you see him much?"

"Christ no! I just told you, I got no idea what that lousy fuck does with his life. He can go shoot himself in the head for all I care."

Thirty minutes later, Wade Dutton's Sweetpatch Island Police cruiser was rolling along the back roads into South Patch. Through the passenger window, Boo Taylor watched sullen faces gazing back, and it took him a moment to mark the quiet resentment in those faces and the reason for it: he was riding shotgun in a police car through a modern Sweetpatch Island's version of a slum.

The sky pressed down low; gray clouds forecasted rain. The inside of the car smelled like chicken wings, and that somehow reminded Boo of the dead thing smeared over the road that he had fallen into that morning.

They were entering a part of the island that few tourists ever saw, a decrepit sprawl of old mobile homes and tin-roofed shacks. A few more modern clusters of condominiums and houses peppered the area, but these were no less cheap and depressing.

"What happened there?" Boo asked as they passed a burned-out hull of a building. The area was swamped under water.

Wade looked at him sharply. "I guess you seen the paper today. You tell me."

Boo turned to him. "Actually, I didn't see it."

Wade was gazing back at the road and muttering. His face was twisted and sour. "Where the hell you think I was all night, Boo Taylor? You think I got time t'go chasin around South Patch for three little black girls who took forty-six dollars from your wallet?"

Ribbons of yellow tape were strung around the perimeter of the wrecked building. Boo now noticed a number of police and fire vehicles parked near the site and several men poking through the rubble. "Was it arson?"

"You don't read the papers? You don't know how incompetent the force is supposed to be? How we can't keep the island safe?" Wade snorted. The driver side window was beginning to fog.

"It wasn't the first one," Boo said. "Someone's been setting fires."

Wade gripped the steering wheel so hard his hands shook. "Churches," he said. "Third one in the last year. Four, if you count one over in Corrington."

Boo Taylor considered this. "Has anyone been hurt?"

"A boy *died* last night, Boo. Like that's supposed to mean anything to you. What do you care?"

Boo leaned back in his seat. "I'm sorry, Wade, I didn't know. Look, if you want to just call this off—"

"Oh hell, let's just get it over with."

Boo let Wade stew quietly for the rest of the ride. A short while later, when they approached the Westview Court mobile home park, Boo directed Wade to turn in.

"What the hell we doin here?"

"It's where my wallet got stolen."

"*Here?* What the hell were you doin here? This here's the cesspool of the whole island. It's the fuckin capital of domestic disturbance."

"Pull over there," Boo told him.

Wade leaned over to read the house number. "This is Lester Meggett's place."

Boo looked through the window. Lester Meggett's shabby little home looked even more dismal in daylight. He turned to the equally dismal place next to it with its empty screened porch. "You've been here before?" he asked.

"Lester the Molester? Sure I been here, are you crazy? Ain't a week goes by we don't get called out here on a drunk and disorderly or some other ruckus."

"You've actually been inside?"

"Sure, I been—" and then Wade stopped. "Oh. You mean all them pictures on the walls?"

Boo nodded.

Wade made an extravagant expression of disgust. "That there is one sick pup," he said. "Left too many brain cells in the bottle, you wanna ask me. What were *you* doin here, anyway?"

"I gave him ride home from Oakies. He was passed out, so I had to carry him inside."

Wade was shaking his head. "Bet *that* was an experience. You know, growin up, I never liked them boys you hung around with much. *This* boy," he jerked his thumb at the window, "was the worst."

Boo stepped out of the car and onto Lester Meggett's scrubby front yard. Wade stepped out from the driver's side. A few residents had drifted into the road, uncannily like the walking dead from any number of zombie movies.

"Anybody look familiar?" Wade asked.

"It was three little girls."

"So you already said. You see any of 'em?"

Boo quickly glanced at the dead faces and shook his head.

Wade sighed. "So what, then? You wanna drive around a bit, see if you recognize somebody?"

Boo was taking in the house next to Lester's. It was painted green, he could now see in daylight—in fact, it was several different shades of green, all slopped on indifferently. A number of windows were boarded over with plywood. In the screen porch, he could make out a dank, trash-cluttered concrete floor. A rocking chair lay dead on its side, rotting amid wet newspaper and other debris.

When he turned around, Wade was staring at him impatiently with his hands on his hips. "Let's see if Lester's in," Boo said.

Wade grimaced. "Christ, why the hell'd we want to do somethin like that?"

"I want to talk to him."

"Well *I* don't!"

Boo thought for a moment, undecided. Then he gestured to the empty space in the driveway ruts. "He's probably not home anyway; his car's gone."

Wade considered the yard. "Best I know, old Les don't have a car. Lost his license for good a few years back."

A few more walking corpses were now milling into the graveled lane to watch. Boo walked up to Lester Meggett's front door. He climbed the steps and banged on the screen. Sounds of small things scurrying in shadows came through the thin walls, and Boo pictured the sick accumulation of a thousand eyes staring silently over a deserted, garbage-strewn room.

spred your legs for me
pleas I stil love you!

"You gonna 'rest that man?"

Boo turned to the tiny, hoarse voice. A small black boy, straddling a bicycle, had broken from the crowd and wheeled into the yard to stare at them. His face was very serious.

"We're thinking about it," Boo told him.

"What he do?"

Boo glanced at Wade who was glaring back at him. Then he hunkered next to the boy. "He's a known fugitive wanted in several states. Are you one of his accomplices?"

"Am I *who?*"

"You ever commit any crimes, son?"

The boy took a step backward. "Mister, I got no idea what you talkin about."

Grumbling, Wade made his way into the yard and shot Boo Taylor a furious gaze. He reached the boy and hunched down, hands on knees. "We ain't gonna arrest nobody," he said gently to the boy. "Say, I don't suppose you know three girls that live around here? About your age?"

"Three?" the boy asked. "I got my sister. She eight."

Boo asked, "Do you know who lives next door?" He pointed at the porch on number nineteen. Wade raised a questioning eyebrow at him.

"There? Ain't nobody live in that place, man."

"Are you sure?"

"Sure I'm sure. That place is *empty.*"

"For how long?"

The boy shrugged.

Boo sighed. He pointed back to Lester's door. "How about this place?"

"This here place? Sure. A man live there. He kill somebody?"

"Nobody killed anybody," Wade said quickly.

"Do you know if he's home?" Boo asked.

The boy shrugged again.

Boo looked away from the boy and glanced at the windows of Lester Meggett's home. They were shaded against the light of day as if those were the eyes that looked outside on behalf of the eyes inside—only now those outside eyes were closed in death. The home was a tomb, encased in a tawdry aluminum package, and this place was a graveyard, and only the dead walked its rutted streets.

The boy turned his handlebars clumsily and worked his way back to the lane, happy to get away. Boo moved toward the squad car, and Wade joined him.

"What's all this about the place next door?" Wade asked.

"I thought I saw something there the other night."

Wade's perpetually creased brow furrowed even deeper. "Something," he repeated ominously. "Like what?"

Boo looked at the ghosts filling the street. Above them, woolen clouds gathered and threatened. The air was growing thicker.

"Someone was in there," Boo said.

"The place is abandoned."

"I don't think so."

Wade Dutton folded orange-furred forearms across his chest as Boo watched the hundred questions burning inside that flushed, freckled, and extremely annoyed face. After several moments, Wade asked finally, "What did you see?"

Boo met his gaze without flinching. "You could call in and find out who lives there. Can't you?"

Exasperated, Wade threw up his hands. "Fine! You want to know so bad?"

Wade stalked around the cruiser and reached through the driver's window for the handset of the car's radio. As he spoke into it, Boo once again considered the blank façade of number nineteen. The screen's surface made slight metallic ripples the longer he stared at it.

Don't look nothin' like his momma, do he?

Them bones you found ain't who you think they is.

Behind him, a few beeps and then burst of static from the radio. Boo couldn't decipher the words, but apparently Wade could.

Wade's face had gone suddenly incredulous.

"Repeat that?"

Another squawk.

"Janine, that's just bullshit. That can't be right. Check it again."

This time Boo made out the words "already checked twice." Wade looked at the handset like he wanted to smash it into the ground. After a moment, he dropped it back through the window.

He stared at Boo Taylor. Accusation and loathing poured from him in waves. Behind him, the undead were beginning to disperse in blind-man shuffles toward their cheap, tin tombs as if they knew a joke was coming but had already heard the punch line. The little boy on the bicycle was nowhere in sight.

"Just what the hell's goin on here, Boo? You wanna quit fuckin around and tell me?"

"What did they say?" Boo asked.

"What did they say? Like you don't know!"

Boo ground his teeth angrily. "No, Wade, I don't know."

"Great!" Wade barked. "Okay, fine! The place is owned by Satterfield Properties and is currently leased to a Henry Ray Dutton."

five

Wade was silent.

Wade refused to speak to him.

One more stop, Wade.

Boo felt the heat of the man's fury raising blisters on his arms. They drove out of Westview Court. Boo pointed out the turns to make on the route to their next stop; Wade Dutton grunted and made the turns but refused to talk. A low rumble filled the car; it was either coming from Wade's throat or from the storm clouds. The clouds were swollen so heavy with gray-green rain they seemed to touch the roof of the cruiser.

Under this fat and ominous wetness, there were no shadows—or rather, everything had become shadow. A shadow of gray and green. The shabby homes along Westview Avenue swam in a gray and green sea; the street beneath them, the scrubby weeds, all bore the same sickish hue.

One more stop, he had asked Wade. Wade hadn't answered, but he hadn't protested.

Boo Taylor's head throbbed in the spot where his skull had connected with asphalt. His skinned elbows and knees sang alto melodies of pain beneath harsh denim.

"Turn here," Boo said.

Wordlessly, angrily, Wade Dutton obeyed.

"Stop here."

Wade stopped.

After a moment, Wade looked at their surroundings. When he saw and recognized the spot, he hung his head and curled a defeated, humorless smile.

"Culpepper Street," he said. "I should'a figured as much."

"Why does that name sound familiar?"

Wade glanced up at him with his bitter smile. "You really don't know, do you?" He shook his head in disgust. "This is the house where we found the doc. And since you're sayin you didn't know that, maybe you can tell me why the hell we're here."

Boo was momentarily stunned.

Wade Dutton was waiting for him to speak. Wade, like the rest of the world, was gray-green.

"This is where I chased the little girls to," Boo said. "My wallet was lying on the walkway in front of this house." *And there was someone inside, calling to me.*

Wade nodded. He spoke with resignation. "I guess you wanna get out and take a look around."

When Boo said yes, Wade opened his door and stepped out. Boo followed him, and they stood before the house. It was a two-story structure, slouched on squat stilts, dull and unthreatening, a blank face revealing nothing but quiet stupidity.

"I suppose you don't know anything more about the person who lived here?" Boo asked. "The tenant?"

"No."

Unlike Carp Street, no zombies emerged from the nearby homes to ogle them. "What does this place remind you of?" Boo asked.

"A toilet. Can we go now?"

He looked at Wade. "Doesn't it remind you of Chaliboque somehow?"

"I never laid eyes on that fuckin place. Boo, I need t'get goin."

"I want to take a look inside first."

Wade sighed. "Door'd be locked."

"Maybe. How long have these places been here, anyway?"

"No more'n seven-eight years. Didn't take long for folks down this way to turn 'em to shit, did it?"

Boo climbed to the front door and grasped the knob, fully expecting it to turn in his mangled right hand. When it held firm, he frowned. He jiggled it, but it wouldn't budge.

"Locked," Wade said.

"Let's try the back door." Wade was about to protest until Boo said, "Humor me."

Wade followed him off the front steps and around the shallow, sandy yard until they came to the back of the house. The back door was up three narrow wooden steps, wide enough for only one person. Boo went up, tried the knob, and found it just as locked as the front door. He cupped his hands to the window and looked in on a kitchen. He saw a table slopped with cups and dishes.

"We about done here?" Wade asked behind him.

Boo gave another futile crank at the doorknob. "I suppose I could break one of these windows," he said, "and just reach in and unlock the thing."

Wade scratched a line above his eyebrow. "Well the thing is, Boo, they call that sort'a thing breaking and entering."

"It's not breaking and entering if you're the owner."

"No. But I guess, technically speaking, you ain't the owner. MaeEllen is."

Boo released the doorknob and looked again through the window. He recognized the insanity of the ideas dancing through his mind. "What did it say again?" he asked. "The writing on the mirror?"

The question seemed to make Wade uncomfortable. "I told you. Somethin about 'He comes and he goes.'"

"I think you said, 'He came and he went.'"

"Fine. Great. Once again, you know all about it. What the hell do you need me for?"

"And you don't know who was living here?"

"I just told you we don't."

Boo considered this, recalled the yellow light at the window as a shadow passed and demonic voices called to him. Such things were supposed to seem less possible in daylight, but right now the prospect of running across a ghost in this place seemed eminently reasonable.

He checked the sky again. The day's remaining glow was being sucked into the thick cotton of clouds.

"Look, Boo," Wade was saying, "you wanna break into the place, I ain't gonna shoot you or anything. I just want you to ask yourself if it's really what you want to do."

"I appreciate that, Wade," Boo said. He turned his back to the door, winced, and slammed his elbow through the lower right pane. The glass shattered inward. "You coming in?"

Wade scowled. "You," he said, dripping contempt, "are one prize asshole, you know that?" He stomped down the steps and toward the front yard, leaving Boo alone.

❖   ❖   ❖

The house smelled like sour fruit.

(Sickly sweet peaches and a hundred lesser odors wrapping him like a blanket.)

"Hello?"

His voice rebounded back.

He flicked a useless switch on the wall. The gray-green was now gathering purple and pooling into the deep corners of the apparently vacant house, filling it with a fog that was as dense as wet concrete. He held out his hands as he entered this dim and bruise-colored room. Beyond the cluttered kitchen, a vague doorframe hinted at rooms beyond. His feet shuffled across old linoleum on a path that led deeper into the purpling, peach-scented house.

(...garage-sale furniture...newspapers in tall stacks, boxes swollen with scavenged baubles... glass bottles everywhere, hundreds of them.)

Weaving through a maze of garbage, picking around heaped stands of furniture and stacked nonsense, always keeping his hands before him to avoid colliding into something unpleasant. Deeper into the place, farther from windows and doors, the house fell darker and darker toward purple-green-gray twilight. His hands touched dried, autumn leaves that became old magazines on a high shelf, ancient animal hides that became an old sweater on a hook, dangling spiderwebs that proved to be the real thing. An ugly face swam toward him from the murk until it became his own dusty reflection in a mirror.

He thought of the side by side aluminum tombs on Carp Street, now this place, and remembered Pastor Hatchel's warnings: the island had *not* changed; the old mysteries and those who howled and chanted depravities by their midnight camp-fires had simply sunk deeper into the shadows.

(You sweatin like a frog on a griddle, boy.)

He tripped against the first step of a narrow stairway. When he looked up, he found a steady line of carpeted steps disappearing into the violet fog.

(Here were his father's last moments on earth.)

He took the first step. His foot sank through cheap shag; beneath, the wood squealed like a wounded animal.

(Here his father climbed these very steps.)

He took the next step up. Then the next. Now both above and below were completely enveloped in darkness and he was alone in a shallow tunnel. The spoiled-fruit stench rose with him.

(Here the doctor saw at last what had been waiting for him at the top of the steps.)

(You don't look nothin like your momma.)

As he neared the top, a dim glow from the upstairs windows brightened the way by infinitesimal degrees. His feet reached a landing. The hallway split off into opposite directions.

(Here the doctor followed her, wept for her.)

His father had died in one of those rooms.

His face contorted by something awful.

Boo looked up one hallway. Then the other. He made his choice, walked slowly to the closest of the closed doors, put his fingers on it, and pushed it open. The door opened into a room that *sounded* small, *felt* small, but looked somehow much too big. A vast space loomed beyond. After a moment, he saw the reason for this: he had come upon the mirrored wall of a bathroom. The mirror had been defaced by some illegible, too-dark scrawl.

Behind him, the stairway squealed as someone rose to meet him.

(Here he grabbed his chest, fell.)

Boo Taylor pushed the door open further, trying to coax more light into the room so he could read the words on the mirror.

"This place stinks," said the voice behind him.

Boo read his name, but could not make out the rest. He looked for a window in the tiny bathroom and could find none. "Can you see what this says?" he asked.

Wade Dutton, still reeking of barbecue sauce, stepped beside him in the door-frame. "I brought a flashlight," he said. He clicked it on and aimed it at the mirror. A flash of brilliance blinded them both for a moment until Wade lowered the beam.

They read the words.

(Here his head struck the floor.)

"Very funny," Boo said.

Wade sighed deeply; his anger was rising again and it was still focused on the man at his side. "That's not what it said before. Somebody changed it. Somebody's been in here, dammit."

The letters were smeared across the mirror in something red and pasty, possibly lipstick.

"Very funny," Boo said again.

Wade swept the flashlight across the cluttered vanity. The two small doors beneath had been kicked in; one hung by a single hinge and the other was split down the middle. In the sink, the light glinted off something shiny.

Wade bent to get a better look.

(Here his heart stopped.)

"Oh, Jesus," Wade whimpered.

(The knife dripped peach nectar into her knuckles. "Ain't Jesus, Boo Taylor. Jes an old coon.")

Wade Dutton reached into the basin. He lifted a smallish jar filled with an amber fluid. He set it on the counter, pulling his hand away quickly and wiped his hand on his pants.

"What is that?" Boo asked, squinting. "What's in there?"

The sharp tang of formaldehyde struck his nose. Inside, two small objects dangled as twin half-moons, suspended in sepia-hued oceans.

(Well, boy? Does you get the joke?)

(Here she reached down to kiss him.)

"Coon paw," Boo said. He looked down at the ripped-away gap in his right hand. A phantom pain seared through him.

Wade was gazing at the bottle in awe. "Christ almighty, Boo," he said, swallowing, "you know what that *is?*"

One was slim and long, as if torn from the root. The other was stubby, as if broken off mid-joint. Both were shriveled and pale as dead fish and decades old.

Boo turned from the little room. He walked to the end of the hallway where a window looked over the darkening vista; his hand absently patted his shirt pocket, looking for a cigar that wasn't there. From this high point, he could see squalid houses perched about like fat, splintered-wood birds on their scrubby lots. Nearby to the north, beyond a tall stand of oaks and gum trees, marsh gas swelled from the mud, bubbling the decayed, microscopic remains of dead things over the woodlands until they settled like a wet woolen sheet over the rooftops on Culpepper Street. If he could close his eyes to only the homes, and see only the distant trees and this flat stretch of wasteland, it would be the same South Patch he had traveled as a boy.

The stretch of water just north, he now saw, was Soap Water creek. He traced the length of ground between here and there, calculated distances, and confirmed the spot where he was now standing hovered over the very plot where Mamie Stuvant's house once stood.

(Don't look nothin like your daddy, neither.)

(Here she laughed over his dead body.)

He flexed his hand. *My fingers*, he thought.

His head thudded; Wade was speaking, but Boo Taylor had carefully switched off the sound and so he heard nothing but the dim babble of the things whispering to him from the gathering darkness outside.

Does you hear...?
His head hurt.
...how we laugh?
His limbs hurt.
...how we scream?

His skeleton throbbed to the kettledrum cadence of his thudding heart; his whole body reverberated with the pain. He was closed up down deep inside a box, a bottle, a jar where it was too tight, too hot, too dark, where he suffocated, where the world thudded, where his whole being pulsated, shrinking and swelling, hammering, and all thoughts were reduced to the insane gibberings of the gathering night creatures asking *have you seen...*

the pretty thing we left?

He wanted to go home, wanted to be back north *(in the street?...in a jar?)* curled up in his own warm bed and sleeping, *(the present...in a doll?)* the covers pulled over his head *(does you get the joke?)* somewhere far away from this throbbing, shrinking, swelling, too-hot, too-small, suffocating little jar full of whispers and jokes.

But Wade Dutton was next to him, shaking his arm, insistent. Boo blinked at him. He spoke groggily, "Was he missing a shoelace?" and surprised himself with his voice.

Wade gawked at him.

THUD!

Did you hit something...with your truck?

"It was a rabbit," Boo said. "I fell into a dead rabbit."

The rabbit died, he thought. That was the great dread that had consumed him this morning on the road.

"Boo, what are you talkin about?"

Boo Taylor put his palms against his temples and squeezed. The sick pain was filling him up. Wade was a dark shape at his side. He said, "Quit yelling at me."

Wade's gray-purple-green face had become a demon's mask. "Boo, I'm not yelling at you."

"You've been yelling at me all day. Quit it."

Boo Taylor inhaled fermented peaches. (*This here's how I make my bread,* she laughed.) He wiped his eyes to try to clear the thudding, muddy, squeezing, murky, pulsing, lunatic voices/thoughts/images from his mind; it was like pulling great gobs of spiderwebs through his eye sockets. Wade was only inches away. "When do you go on duty?" Boo asked him.

After a moment of hesitation, Wade raised his watch close to his face and read it through the gloom. "Ten minutes ago. Jesus, Boo. I mean, *Jesus.*"

Unhappily, resentfully, Boo Taylor turned from the window. He was forced to think of a burlap doll, slit open to spill the remains of the things upon which it had feasted, including a particular newspaper article and a child-sized length of shoelace. "I need to show you something," he said.

six

The eyes were blind. Black. Fire had been rammed into them, searing the pulpy flesh there and leaving twin black smudges deep inside the gnarled folds. Boo Taylor reached for his glass and took a long drag of ice-cold vodka that sent a frigid blast of fire down his throat. With his other hand *(my fingers)* he reached to pick up the toby's wrinkled head and its flaccid, burlap flesh. The face, unburned but withered dry, was a torture of angry grooves and knots. The white skin was made brown, and maybe that was the source of the troll's fury—the indignity of being peeled naked by omnipotent hands and molded by a cruel blade. Then, stripped of its smooth dignity, left to darken. Left to ferment.

The eyes were blind, but they were looking at him. He set the troll back on the desk, but turned the eyes away.

He took another drink.

"Boo sugar, are you in there?"

MaeEllen Taylor suddenly filled the frame of the office door. "I didn't hear you come in," she said.

"I'm sorry."

She squinted. "What's wrong with you?"

"Nothing."

MaeEllen swept the office with her eyes. She focused momentarily on the shredded doll on the desk, then fixed on the bottle of Grey Goose. She smiled grimly. "That poor little girlfriend of yours keeps calling. I am sure Bess has told you this several times."

"We broke up," Boo told her. His voice was hoarse.

"I am not surprised in the least. Do you intend to call her back?"

"I'm thinking about it."

The grim little smile remained. He knew he looked shell-shocked and battered, but MaeEllen was suppressing her observations and her questions—and he knew that was taking some considerable effort on her part. Though mostly numb at the moment, Boo did register a flicker of gratitude for this.

"I'll say good night then," she said. She turned and left.

"Good night," he called after her.

And he was alone again with the troll.

A strip of rumpled newspaper spilled from its abdomen.

Historic Church Consumed by Flames

Sighing, he reached for the doctor's old rotary telephone. He dialed a memorized number. After a few dim clicks, the purr of connection and distant ringing.

"Hello?"

Boo braced himself with another sip of vodka. "Murphy, it's Boo Taylor. I'd like to speak with Gussie."

Quiet breathing for an extended moment. "Well I can pretty much guarantee she doesn't want to speak to you, asshole."

"Just put her on the phone."

"Why don't you go the fuck home, Boo?"

"Why don't you blow me, Murph?"

The phone clicked and went silent.

Old Bones & Bridges Crossed - August, 1971

It was August and the month of her name, but he was thinking about someone else.

two

In a first floor room in Chaliboque, Boo Taylor cupped a palm over his nose and stepped away from the old bucket when the stench of its stagnant water rudely thrust itself into his bruised nostrils—and when he realized what was curdling on the water's surface.

"Vampires," he said, turning away on spongy floorboards and resting his hands on his knees. Dewey Fitch and Ashford Marchant heard him and rushed in from the next room. Boo grimaced and pointed and then watched the two step cautiously to the wall and pull away the vines that had bunched in through a broken window.

Ash pinched his nose. "Brother, that stinks."

Dewey bent to the bucket. "Smells like the time the freezer in the garage got busted. Had about twenty catfish and most of a deer in the thing, and it all went to rot."

"Did y'all look inside?" Boo asked.

Now they both leaned forward.

Dewey yelled, "Aw, there's things *movin* in there!"

"Mosquitoes!" Ash said.

"Vampires!" said Dewey.

Ashford Marchant took three quick steps back. "Mosquito larvae. Must be hundreds of them. Boy, that's gross."

Boo and Ash drifted further away, but Dewey kept peering into the rusty pail, fascinated. "Can't just leave em there, boys, these things'll be out suckin the blood of the innocent in a few days." He looked up, grinning. "Don't want these bastards suckin *my* blood."

Dewey gave the pail a strong kick. Swampy water splashed over walls and floor. The stink burst throughout the room. A hundred tiny, translucent fetuses speckled the old floor like soda pop bubbles.

Boo and Ash laughed, then faltered when a whiff of smoke blew into the room. (Rot and campfire? *Ate one up and licked the other*.) Before they could spin around, she spoke from the opposite door:

"See you brung some more friends 'round, Mr. Boo."

Jean shorts ripped high on her thighs, trailing drabs of white thread. Blouse ripped free of its sleeves, unbuttoned, lazily knotted beneath her breasts. For a long moment, no one spoke as each boy considered this new species of vampire with his own particular openmouthed fascination. She accepted their gapes, gobbled each of them with her sly smirk.

("That her?" Ash whispered, and Boo nodded.)

Somewhere behind all that long flesh, the little blonde girl cowered.

"Oh my, an' they some *handsome* friends, *too*. You gonna tell your Crystal what their names is?"

Boo cleared his throat and went through the preposterous ritual of introductions.

"So, your name is Ashford," the dark girl said, and Ash Marchant grinned sheepishly and nodded.

"And your name is Dewey?"

Dewey Fitch, standing in the middle of the spreading water, shoved his hands in his pockets and shrugged.

"Doooooweeeee. . ." Crystal Burne cooed. "Do we got manners, Dewey? *Dooo weee?"*

Dewey's face went scarlet. "Do we *what?"*

"Asked if we got manners," she said sharply. "Or do we always go 'round kickin up a mess in somebody else's house?"

Dewey gawked at her, weighed any threat she might pose. He folded his arms. "You gotta be jokin, lady."

"No, I ain't *jokin,* Mr. Dewey. Does I look like I'm jokin to you?"

"It's not *your* house."

Boo quickly stepped between them. "Didn't know you were still here. I figured you moved out when Royal and Solomon left."

"This place is a fallin down piece of junk," Dewey was rumbling. "There's garbage everywhere; there's shit *growin* in here."

Crystal Burne eyed Dewey Fitch coolly, and then slid her fire-and-ice attention onto Boo Taylor who froze and melted, froze and melted a dozen times over in the space of a few seconds. This is what he came for, wasn't it, hoping she was still here? Then why was he afraid?

The little girl, clutching a tattered encyclopedia volume to her chest, shuffled to see around her sister's hip.

Faint, from outside, Lester Meggett's excited voice: "Hey there's a skeleton out here!" He was climbing up the rubble stairway to the window two rooms over. "Hey where'd y'all go?"

"In here!" Dewey shouted.

While Crystal Burne locked the rest in place with her gaze, Lester blundered down hallways and into their room. "Lookit what I found! It's a dog's skull. Bet it's from the *Beast!* Lookit, Ash, look how *big* that fella is!"

Curiosity dragged their eyes from Crystal Burne to the grimy stone Lester bore and now shoved into Ashford Marchant's hands. It was all angles and sharp points and teeth. Ashford hefted the thing to his glasses. "That's a dog, all right," he announced.

Lester smiled proudly; dirty blond hair fell over his eyes. "Maybe even a *wolf.*"

Dewey huddled with them. "Ain't no wolf around here. Where'd you find it?"

"Near that side what's all burned up. Whole skeleton's there, layin behind some bushes. Bet that wolf's been there a hundred years!"

"Ain't no wolf 'round here you retard."

"Then I bet it's the *Beast!*"

Dewey took the skull from Ashford and held it to the light at the nearest window. "There ain't no Beast neither."

Crystal Burne, who had been watching all with great amusement, spoke from across the room. "Why, sure there's a Beast."

Lester Meggett looked up sharply at the unexpected sound, at the shimmering dark presence now sauntering casually into the room. She reached Boo Taylor and planted a hand on his shoulder. The little girl followed closely.

("Holy crow," Lester uttered; "That's her," Ash whispered.)

Her eyes, just high enough to see over Boo's head, drank in Lester Meggett in a single gulp.

Boo Taylor's eyes dropped to the slick skin spilling out of her blouse. This close, her scent conquered the smells of the old house and spilled bucket—the scent of rough soap and burned skin, of tart animal wildness that was something like Miss Laylee but nothing at *all* like Miss Laylee: potent and harsh—deer flesh searing over a campfire—and he wanted to dig his teeth into it. When he was able to look up again, her gloating lips were just inches away. The wet muscle of her tongue poked from a corner of her mouth. She squeezed it in her teeth.

Her eyebrows came together in mock curiousness, and she whispered, "What's this boy's name, honey?"

"Lester Meggett," Boo answered.

"Lester," she whispered again and nodded.

Her fingers gave a little tug at Boo's shoulder, and then moved past him, brushing a ripe breast across his arm. As she passed, the little girl trailed, gazing a lost puppy dog pout at Boo.

Crystal Burne purred, "You like old bones, does you, Mr. Lester?"

"Yes ma'am."

"You does? Does the rest of you like old bones, too? How 'bout you, Mr. Ashford?"

Ashford managed to nod.

"How bout you, Mr. *Dooooweeee?*"

Dewey, still cradling the dog's skull, grinned at her uncertainly and said, "Sure."

She reached Lester Meggett, wrapped her arm around Lester Meggett's waist. "You're a pretty one," she said softly near Lester's ear as she turned back to face Boo Taylor.

August heat splashed across Boo's cheeks.

"Think your friend Mr. Boo like old bones, too, Mr. Lester?"

"I don't know. I guess he does."

Lester looked away from her and stared at Boo.

"Why, I'se so glad to hear that, Mr. Lester! I reckon you boys is gonna *love* this place. They's *lots* of old bones 'round here."

◈ ◈ ◈

It was the first time he'd seen Crystal Burne since the night he fired on those white men. "Maybe you scared her off with that rifle," Solomon Goody told him as they loaded camping gear, clothes, books, empty pots and pans out of Chaliboque and into a '56 Ford pickup. Solomon and Royal were going home.

"Home?" Boo asked.

"Fun's over. I miss my bed and my momma's cooking."

"But what about those men? Won't they...come after you?"

"Hey man, police cleared me, didn't they? It's in the papers, so it *has* to be true. And those boys...well maybe we knocked a few fangs loose. Think maybe you killed anybody, John Wayne?"

"Twenty-two wouldn't kill a crow from that distance."

"Well you be careful anyway. Redneck gets his ass shot by a nigger, he's gonna figure he's got to hurt somebody for it. Most likely the nigger that shot him, and that's *you*."

"I'm not a nigger."

Solomon howled laughter at this. "No, but you sure pick your targets like one!"

And that was that. Nothing more about the shooting, no swarming police cars, no stories in the paper. A dark night exploding for a few terrifying minutes, and then once again dark and silent. Had it even happened? No, he was convinced it never had, because even Miss Laylee had been a party to the silence: "Policeman ask who was doin all the shootin, I suppose I gots to tell him. Best if he don't get the chance to ask, though by God, I ought to whip your backside with a stick for shootin at a man. Lord, what was you thinkin, boy?"

I was thinking they would kill you!

Nothing would be said to his parents, either, who would *insist* on the police. "May the Lord forgive me," Laylee Colebriar lamented, "I know Miss MaeEllen Taylor won't."

Some mysterious bleakness uglied her pretty face when she talked about the police. Shared in silent, icy glowers with Royal and Solomon. *Not* shared with him.

"But the police..."

"Not on this island, boy."

Not shared with Gussie Dutton, either, who was huddled unspeaking and forgotten in a corner of Miss Laylee's kitchen. (Her face and clothes dirt-smeared, leaf scraps in her hair. "Is you hurt, child?" He had really *forgotten* about her? "No, Miss Laylee, I'm okay.")

And then he insulted her.

"Gussie, you can't say anything."

"I know."

"Not to anybody."

"I *know*."

"Not even—"

"Dammit, Boo Taylor, I *know!* Why does everybody think the first thing I'm gonna do is run out and *blab* all about this to everybody? You go to hell, Boo Taylor, you damn snob!"

He rode her home as far as the bridge over Soap Water Creek before she made him stop. There, she hopped off and went the rest of the way on her own. And he hadn't seen her since.

❖   ❖   ❖

Now she was taking his hand in the swamps and afternoon shadow behind Chaliboque, leading him toward the ruins of an old stable. "You thinkin 'bout that pretty red-hair girlfriend of yours, honey?"

Crystal Burne's naked shoulder pressed against his arm, and he felt his breath go thin. "She's not my girlfriend," he said.

"No, but you thinkin 'bout her anyway, ain't you?"

"No."

"Aw baby, you can't lie to your Crystal."

The others were spreading out through the shrub in search of artifacts and old bones. There were remains of slave cabins and a graveyard out there someplace, even an old paupers' graveyard, she told them.

"So nice you brung all them boys here to play," she said sweetly. "Why don't we come over here by ourselves for a bit. I gots things I want to talk about, Mr. Boo Taylor. Just you an' me."

She sat him on a low, tumbled brick wall where one corner of the stables had collapsed. The little girl settled in the grass in front of them, opening her book. Beyond, Lester and Dewey and Ash hunched through high weeds, past other tumbled walls, and picked with sticks at clusters of stone and brick.

Dewey popped up and shouted, "You sure there's a graveyard out here?"

"Out there someplace!" she shouted back. (Boo watched her flesh quiver when she yelled. She slid her leg against his and stroked his thigh.) "Just got to keep lookin!"

"But how do you know?"

"Oh, I knows, Mr. *Doooweee!*"

He wanted to move his leg away from her fingers but couldn't do it.

He looked at the grass.

He felt her breathing on him.

"So, that pretty red-hair witch ain't your girlfriend? I bet you want yourself a girlfriend, don't you?"

He swallowed. She made a low boiling sound that might have been a chuckle. Her fingernails drew swirly patterns in his leg hairs, coaxing the hardness now growing only inches away. He squirmed, worrying she could see the effect.

"Think Miss Cassie here done take a likin to you. Maybe she be your girlfriend. She got nice light skin like you."

The little girl peeked up from her book, a streak of sun glaring off her pale forehead.

"Ain't this boy handsome, Miss Cass?"

The girl smiled shyly. "Yes."

"You want to take him for your boyfriend?"

The girl nodded.

Crystal Burne laughed. "Well, you too late, girl. I think he startin to like somethin a little *darker*."

Her fingernails whirled, dipped inside his thigh.

"Hey, I found an old coffee mug!" Lester yelled from the swampy field. Boo looked up sharply, could barely see him through the distant veils of jungle growth where he was raising a dirt-caked cup like a man proposing a toast.

"That ain't nothin; I found an old pair of glasses!"

"I found part of a shoe!"

"Hey you boys!" Boo yelled. "You watch out for snakes!"

Crystal Burne's free hand went to the unbuttoned collar of her blouse. She flapped the cloth open and shut against the heat. The urge to bury his face in *there* overwhelmed him; he imagined it for one glorious moment and felt the hardness flex suddenly, torturing the fabric of his shorts.

"You ain't scared, is you Mr. Boo?" she cooed gently in his ear.

Yes I am!

He shook his head.

Tongue flicking out, dabbing his earlobe.

Thumb dragging slowly up his thigh, dragging until it brushed a plump vein between his legs and sent a shock of warmth through him. A thousand miles away, the fading calls of his friends...

Don't go! Stay close—safety in numbers, remember!

"Naw, you ain't scared."

She breathed into his ear, licked the curve of his jaw. Her thumb stroked him methodically.

"Let's you an' your Crystal gwon back in the house."

Her lips drew across his cheek, circled the bruised patch near his nose, and then her mouth covered his.

How much time passed?

So much wetness, drowning him, and distantly he thought, *I never kissed a girl before.* Then even that thought disappeared when her other hand—the one not doing that unbearable clutching at his pants—took hold of his wrist. He let her pull his hand to her, let her run his palm across damp cotton until the cotton parted and it was the throbbing, inhaling-exhaling weight of her raw skin slipping into his palm.

"You ain't scared baby," she whispered.

His fingers trembled around a nipple and squeezed.

"Naw, you ain't scared. You want to put your sweet pecker in me, don't you, baby?"

Her tongue furrowed against his lips, urging him to unclench his jaw. When he did, her tongue was a living animal plunging inside him, and he heard her make a soft, hungry groan; he *felt* the groan in a spasm of vibrations down his own throat. A bare foot slid along his shin; she was like a lizard, curling herself around him.

She snapped for his tongue, caught it, bit it.

She's tasting me.

Her mouth slipped away. She nibbled the flesh at his cheekbone. "If you scared, just pretend you with your pretty red-hair girlfriend."

He opened his eyes and saw the sharp glint of her smile dripping near his face. A gator's smile?

(What did Hoss Beaudry see in the moment before the first scream?)

You watch out for that one—Solomon's warning—*she'll eat you alive.*

"You have *teeth*," he said.

He pushed away from her. His hand came away from her breast.

He waited for her to turn angry, but the smile remained. "Oh, I gots teeth all right, Mr. Boo. Nice *sharp* ones, too."

He stood and slid several paces away from her.

"These teeth do jes fine to gobble up a little doctor's boy." She patted the stone seat next to her hip. Her right breast hung plainly from the open blouse. "Why don't you come on back here, an' I show you."

"I don't want to."

"Oh, yes you do. Think I felt somethin said so."

"No!"

At his shout, the little girl dropped her book. She looked up at Boo with frightened eyes, and he wondered if she was frightened *by* him or *for* him.

"Hey, you boys—come look at this!" Ashford shouting in the distance.

"What is it?"

"It's a watch. Found it by this here tree."

"Where? Let me see!"

Poking sticks under rocks, prodding for old bones. Far off, cicada rattling rose like waves and then slowly died. The sound made Boo Taylor think of rattlesnakes in a desert. Poisonous things waiting in the August heat, lurking under stones and hiding in tall grass, waiting for boys to come around with their poking, prodding, eagerness.

"Who are you?" Boo asked.

"Why don't you tell me who *you* is, doctor's boy? Does you even know?"

"*Tell* me!"

"Tell you?" she asked sweetly. "Why I *already* told you."

He glanced toward his friends, wondering what he had done to them. "You'll hurt them," he said.

She sighed expansively, indulgently. "Don't know what got into you all of a sudden, but ain't nobody gonna get hurt—not these boys, an' not you." Her eyes dipped into a half-lidded leer. "Honey child, that ain't what I want at all..."

In the distance again: "Hey, I found it! I found it!"

"Found what?"

"Where are you?"

"Here! Graveyard!"

Boo stepped away from Crystal Burne, into the grass, backing toward his friends because there *was* safety in numbers. "Hey, you boys!" he called to them, keeping himself between them and her. "Hey, y'all be careful; there's cottonheads and water-mocs all around here!"

He watched Crystal Burne tuck her breast back inside the folds of her blouse. "Why Mr. Boo, you is scared as a little white rabbit," she said, laughing. "Well you missin out on somethin *good,* Mr. Rabbit!"

He turned away from her, wondering what had just happened to him.

❖   ❖   ❖

He had seen Mamie Stuvant.

Three times since Hoss Beaudry was killed.

The first time:

Riding his bike down Polk Road with fishing rod and tackle box, on his way to fish off the Mermaids Head River docks. It was barely a week after Hoss's funeral, his first time out by himself since. Passing shops and empty lots, the road slipped off either side to stagnant ditches where garbage accumulated, where—as he passed on his bike—he saw movement on the opposite side. A deer or a dog, he first decided, see-ing nothing more than a flash of mud brown. And then she stood up from the ditch. She raised one thick, rubbery arm and waved to him, and he almost waved back even though he saw right away it was Mamie Stuvant who was supposed to be locked away in jail. She was wearing the same brown dress, the same white apron as the day he had been in her house. Only the apron was now streaked and filthy. *Peach juice*, he thought vaguely. A breeze lifted the coarse black snakes of her hair. He rode in a zigzag daze, losing himself in the same kaleidoscope confusion that fouled his senses when he was inside her house. She simply waved and smiled happily.

Somebody havin a laugh at you, boy; somebody makin a joke.

Then a car blasted its horn at him.

He jerked the handlebars and fell over. The skin of his knee peeled away on the pavement, and he yelled out. The car veered around him, and he got a brief glimpse of an angry face and a shaking fist.

He stood up with the bike, rubbing his knee, blood weeping down his shin. Mamie Stuvant was still there, now laughing her muddy-water gurgle at him. Miss Laylee's wongah was still around his neck, and he touched it.

He jumped on the bike and pedaled away as fast as he could.

The second time:

Murphy Ransome's screwball hit him in the face (not a fastball and not a curve-ball; it was a screwball and it veered directly into his face because it was supposed to hit him, and that was something only he and Murphy knew). Gussie Dutton was holding his hand and smothering him under his own T-shirt, now a bloody rag, as they banged along in the back of Richie Deeg's pickup. He was vaguely angry with Murphy Ransome, and his head was a bag of sand and broken shards of porcelain—but that was *Gussie's* hand wrapped around his, so he couldn't mind the rest of it too much.

They stopped at the light on Fustuhdey and Atlantic. Gussie took the rag away from his face.

He breathed and blinked, and Mamie Stuvant was sitting in the passenger seat of a rusted white sedan that was passing through the intersection. Just a moment, but it *was* her. He knew because she lifted her big arm out of the window and waved to him again. And again he had to catch himself before he waved back.

The third time he had seen her was just yesterday:

Three weeks had passed since the last sighting. Mamie Stuvant was dead, so they told him—by her own hand in some strange ritual in her jail cell. He felt safe enough now that he hadn't asked Miss Laylee to replace the disintegrating wongah. He hadn't even told Miss Laylee about the first two sightings, and maybe that was the best evidence of his doubts. He'd just been seeing things. Guilt about Hoss. And his brains had been scrambled a bit by Murphy Ransome's pitch. Of course he hadn't seen her.

But yesterday, there was no doubt he'd seen her because she had spoken to him.

❄   ❄   ❄

She said, "You found it!"

On dark feathers, she somehow reached his friends before he could and stood approvingly with wings on hips, watching their undertakings.

"It's a gravestone, all right," Ashford announced as Boo Taylor arrived flushed and slightly bewildered at the border of a small clearing in the swamp.

Ashford brushed his sneaker across the fallen-over stone. "Somebody tried to carve something in it."

Dewey and Lester crowded around him, and the three cast stubby shadows under the blistering sun. Boo approached them, keeping a wary eye on Crystal Burne. "Hey you boys, I think we should leave."

The stubby shadows didn't want to move.

"Can you read it?"

"What's it say?"

"How *old* is it?"

Ash Marchant got on his knees and yanked away a vine. "It's mostly faded. Whoever carved this didn't make the marks too deep. If I had some water to pour in the cracks, maybe that would make it easier to read."

"Spit on it," Dewey said.

Ashford looked up briefly, the sun shattering violently at the edge of his glasses.

"I think we should leave," Boo said.

Then Ashford bent over and spit.

Boo Taylor winced.

"Hey, it worked!" Ashford hooted. "I can make out some letters."

"What's it say?"

"There's an R. And this one is an O."

Ash spit again, rubbed it into stone with the heel of his fist. The saliva seeped into the shallow markings; the ancient scrawl lines darkened.

"Hey, you guys," Boo said. He tapped on Lester's shoulder. "I think we should leave. Now!"

"*Robert.* It says Robert."

He spit several more times.

Boo turned to the sound of Crystal Burne gliding across the clearing. Little Cassie was trotting along to keep up, the moldy encyclopedia volume still gripped like a life preserver to her chest. A sooty cloud drifted over them, veiled their faces in a fierce plague of gnats.

"Find a dead snake there, Mr. Rabbit?" Crystal Burne asked.

"It's a grave!" Lester said.

"Course it is, Mr. Lester."

"Mason!" Ash said. "Robert Mason—that's the guy's name."

Dewey whistled. "There's really some guy *buried* here."

"He's probably all *skeleton* by now."

"What else does it say?"

"Does it got a date or somethin?"

"*Something,* but I can't tell...I think it says Son."

"Sun?"

Dewey and Lester dropped to their knees, and the three of them crowded over the stone as if praying over a sacred object. Over their monstrously eager and hunched backs, Boo Taylor faced Crystal Burne. She smiled at him cheerfully.

Ashford read, "'*My* son,'"

"Is that what it says? *Who's* son?"

"Don't know; it doesn't say."

"There's no date?"

"There's *something,*" said Ashford who again spit into his fingers and then went back to scrubbing the stone.

Crystal Burne winked at Boo, slowly rolled her tongue at him.

"Says eighteen something. Eighteen *forty* something, I think. Can't make out that last number. Can you?"

Lester and Dewey craned in, all clustered together and breathing excitedly.

"It's a five I think. Or maybe a three."

"Is that *born* or *died?*"

"Died, I guess. See that other number on the left—chipped away. I can't make it out."

Ashford Marchant leaned back on his haunches and gazed up at Boo. Sweat beaded down his forehead, and his big glasses slid down his nose. "Hear *that?* This old boy's been buried here over a hundred years. Right here, underneath us!"

"I bet he's all skeleton," Lester said. "I bet there's *worms* eatin him."

Dewey spat a laugh. "Ain't no worms eatin him if he's already a skeleton, dipshit."

"Oh, yeah."

"Eighteen forty something," Ash said wondrously. "That's even before the War between the States."

Lester, on his knees, looked about the clearing. "There's gotta be old graves all over this place."

Crystal Burne dropped her eyes from Boo and stroked Lester Meggett's shoulder. "Oh, you gonna find old Mr. Mason here got hisself a *lot* of company. This here used to be a right popular slave cemetery, then potter's field. Was buryin poor folks here till jes a few years back. You know what they say about a place like this?"

Openmouthed, Lester shook his head.

"They say folks was just *dyin* to get in."

Lester grinned, and she croaked her throaty laugh. Boo Taylor watched the way her lips turned like a barbed hook at the edges. Then his eyes fell to the round, heavy flesh that filled her blouse. His hand had been there. He put it there, and he *liked* it.

She'll eat you alive.

His friends skittered around the clearing for more signs of the dead.

"Here's another one!"

"This one looks new."

"I bet there's dozens!"

"I bet ol Joker Tribbit hisself is buried around here!"

Boo Taylor only stood and watched Crystal Burne within her cloud of gnats as she melted back into the shadows.

❖   ❖   ❖

He couldn't see her in the shadows, but he could hear her. Hear what that boiling, swamp-mud, gleeful voice had to say to him.

Hear you got some new friends, doctor's boy.

On his bicycle to Haufmann's Market, an errand for his mother to pick up a four-pound cut of sirloin and two pounds of ground chuck. At the butcher's counter, he looked through the glass at slabs of muscle and guts bleeding in pans, the wrinkled coon-paw clusters of sausage groping overhead. The aura of fresh kill lingered around Mr. Haufmann's great white mustache and streaked down his great white smock. Boo recited the order quickly and had to walk away.

He wiped the sweat off his face and browsed the comic book rack.

When Mr. Haufmann called him back, he took the heavy sack and ducked the sausage fingers, then he paid at the counter after tossing in a handful of jerky and two packs of baseball cards.

He went outside, jingling the bell over the door, and didn't see the thing on the seat of his bicycle right away because he was already shuffling through the baseball cards. The bike was parked near the alley between Haufmann's and the Five & Dime. Juggling the bag, inventorying his cards, he nearly bumped into the bicycle before he looked up.

He gasped around a pink stick of gum.

A burlap doll with an apple face was perched on the seat. It looked like a deformed little hunchback trying to steal his bike. In a brief romantic lapse, he imagined Gussie Dutton put it there—a token of reconciliation; *Boo, I'm so sorry I acted mad, will you forgive me?* But then he remembered the troll doll he'd found on the pier.

He wondered what ugly secrets were stuffed inside *this* one.

Then Mamie Stuvant spoke from the alley.

"Hear you got some new friends, doctor's boy."

He dropped the cards, the bag of groceries.

"You maybe shy a friend or two these days, so you gonna be special good t'them new friends, ain't you boy? And them friends be special good t'you."

Cards fluttered like dead leaves, like snowflakes. Meat splatted and ripped the bag wide open. Boo looked into the alley. Deep shadow, humped jigsaw-puzzle brick floor all the way to blasting daylight at the other end and strewn with abandoned crates and cardboard boxes and scraps of trash.

Was that a leg in there? A wrinkle of loose nylon? The flutter of a brown skirt?

Then something big shifted, shadows flitting like crows wings, and it became an animal shape, something massive, something burning in there. Eyes, red hot, glowed from the dark.

"Good Gawd, Boo Taylor, look at that mess!"

Boo jerked around and saw Pastor Hatchel walking toward him from the door of the Five & Dime, his white shirt a glare against his brown face. On the sidewalk, scattered cards blew about and clumps of meat leaked pink stains into orange-paper wrappings. The jerky had rolled into the gutter.

"Miss MaeEllen ain't gonna be too pleased you spread her dinner all over the sidewalk, now is she?"

"No sir," Boo mumbled, bending down to the flayed bag of groceries. He shot a worried glance to the alley.

The reverend stooped to help him. "You gonna need a new bag," he said and handed a package of meat to Boo.

Boo offered his hand vacantly; the damp bundle filled it.

Pastor Hatchel squinted at him. "You okay, boy?" He pressed his hand against Boo's forehead. "You sick?"

The man's hand was the texture of old baseball gloves. "I guess I'm okay," he answered.

"Well, you look sick." The pastor plucked a strip of jerky from the gutter. "No wonder, this stuff you eat. Eulahlah ain't feedin you good enough, son?"

"She feeds me fine."

A broad white smile broke across the reverend's face. "Course she do," he said, and he stood up. "You go on and pick up the rest of that mess, and I'll go see Miss Anna in the market and get you a new bag."

Tell him! his brain shouted.

The pastor walked away, never looking into the alley.

Boo Taylor did look, but the alley was now empty.

He swiped the burlap creature off his bike. It rolled into the gutter next to his jerky. A car pulling to the curb crushed the apple skull into the pavement, and the doll became like a boneless dead animal in the street.

But these aren't dead animals, they're dead people.

"I wanna see a skeleton," said Dewey.

"So do I," said Lester.

They had discovered nine graves in all, and Crystal Burne had promised more. Lester and Dewey were looking at her for permission, their smiles broad and greedy and perverse. Ash Marchant looked between Lester and Dewey—and then urgently to Boo Taylor. *He's dying to see a skeleton, too,* Boo realized. The others might be looking to Crystal Burne for permission, but *Ashford* at least...

"That's grave robbin," Boo said.

"Aw, they do it all the time," Dewey retaliated. "On the TV news they're always diggin up some old graveyard or another."

"It's not the same thing."

"It is too! It's *exactly* the same thing. They dig up graveyards all over the place. I heard they dug up an old churchyard cemetery right over near Charleston, and those were *white* people. And *Protestants*. Ain't that right, Ash-boy?"

Ashford Marchant shrugged. "It would be like a scientific expedition," he offered lamely.

"That's right," said Lester. "Like on TV."

Boo scowled. "Except none of you boys is a scientist. These are *people*. These are folks who used to live right here on the island. They could still have relatives livin here, even. You don't just dig *people* up like that." He waved his hands, trying to grab rational thought from the air. "What if one of them was related to *you?*"

But he was thinking of Laylee Colebriar. Born and raised on Sweetpatch Island. He imagined one of these graves her distant aunt or a great grandfather.

"They're *slaves,*" Ash said.

Boo gathered his fists. Why weren't they listening to him? They *always* listened to him!

"What if it was *you,* Ashford? And a hundred years from now, a bunch of dumb kids comes along and decides to dig you up."

"Hell," Dewey said, "who cares once your dead?"

Ashford Marchant, at least, said nothing, and Boo sensed weakening.

"What if it was *Hoss?*" Boo asked.

Everything went silent. The name echoed across drooping oaks and cypress trees, off swamp-ruined piles of bricks.

Ashford looked at his feet; his shoulders slumped.

Dewey sighed, grumbled. "But it *ain't* Hoss. It's like Ash says, it's just slaves—"

"Shut up, Dewey!" Boo pointed his finger at him, and Dewey Fitch fell silent. He glared sulkily at Boo Taylor and then looked at Crystal Burne for support.

She started into the clearing. "Look like poor old Mr. Boo ain't much for science—"

"*You* shut up, *too!*" Boo yelled.

Her step faltered.

For a moment, whatever black mist she had rained on the clearing threatened to break apart and float away on the mild breeze that pushed in from the Atlantic. She blinked and looked at Boo Taylor, and for the first time he saw the steady self-satisfied craftiness slip from her face. What remained was blank and colorless.

She's afraid of me, Boo hoped distantly.

But it lasted only a moment—his hope and her fear—and in the next moment Crystal Burne's face melted like coffee ice cream left in the sun.

The others backed away even before she sprang. Boo was too stunned to move. She crossed the distance between them on lightning and cracked her open hand across his bruised face.

The sound, a rifle shot, ricocheted off the trees and ruins. Crystal Burne loomed over Boo Taylor with her arms cocked at her side like iron rails, her face gathered in a hateful knot. Boo Taylor gaped back as two thin lines of blood trickled down from his nostrils. The other boys were gray sculptures.

Cassie, in the shade of the trees, began to sob.

"You listen here, you *rich* little *white-meat doctor's boy!*" Crystal Burne raged. Her arm came up; Boo flinched, but she only shoved a finger at his chin. "You don't tell *me* to *shut up;* you don't *ever tell me to shut up! You HEAR ME, BOY?*"

His face throbbed; invisible hands were inside his head alternately pushing and pulling on the bone and cartilage of his nose.

You gonna be special good t'them new friends, ain't you boy?

She'll eat you alive, all right.

Suddenly, the little girl was at Crystal Burne's legs, tugging at the frayed threads of the bigger girl's shorts. She was weeping fearfully. Crystal Burne's shoulders wagged backward at the urging of those little hands, and Boo Taylor saw the dark girl's face melt again, this time softening to a coquettish pout. "Don't make your Crystal mad like that, baby," she said in a child's voice. "She don't like it when you make her mad."

No, Boo resolved; he would never make her mad again. *Never* again.

The little girl's crying quieted. Around him, Boo heard the anxious breathing of his friends; it was the only evidence they hadn't run for the woods.

"Poor Mr. Boo, did I hurt you bad?" She raised a hand to his cheek where the sting of her fingers still tingled. "Oh, your Crystal made you bleed," she said.

She cupped her hand around his neck and drew his face to hers. Her tongue slipped out. Then she licked the blood that ran from his nose to his lips.

Vampires, he thought as the slick muscle dragged slug-like across his face. When she was done, she gave him a full, sweltery kiss on the lips and finally let go of his neck. The pouty mask was gone, and the sly smile was back.

"That make you better, baby. That some *good* medicine for the doctor's boy. You feel better now?"

Backing away, he answered, "Yes, I'm better."

"You ain't gonna tell your Crystal to shut up again, is you?"

"No."

Her smile spread, showing neat rows of white teeth. "And you ain't gonna stop your friends from havin their good time, is you?"

"I have to go," he muttered, taking another step back. He looked around to the others. "You boys comin?"

"Oh, Mr. Boo, you doesn't got to go nowhere!"

Boo continued to back away, but no one was following.

"Mr. Dewey," the dark girl called, "you stayin here, ain't you?"

"Yeah, I figure I'll stay," Dewey said.

"Mr. Lester, you stayin?"

Lester looked blankly at Dewey for a moment. "Okay."

"Mr. Ash, you stayin, too. You stayin an' have your good time with Miss Crystal and your friends. Right?"

Ashford Marchant coughed. He gave Boo an entreating wince, and when Boo shook his head, Ashford dropped his gaze and sighed. "It's just old bones," he said.

Crystal Burne clapped. "And Mr. Boo, he don't got to go, neither, do he Mr. Ash? He can stay, too, can't he?"

Boo kept stepping backward through the clearing. They all watched, all falling further and further away.

"Boo, you can stay can't you?" Ashford asked, pleading.

"How we supposed to come down to South Patch if *you* ain't with us?" Lester asked, worried.

Boo backed, held his arms up. "No, I have to go."

Cassie, her arms wrapped around Crystal Burne's naked waist, sniffled.

"That's okay, Mr. Ash," Crystal Burne said. "Old Mr. Boo Taylor be back 'fore too long. 'Fore then, we gonna have lots of company 'round here. Mr. Lester, know what so nice about a place like this?"

Lester squeezed his eyes to think. "What is?" he asked.

"Why, you can always dig yourself up another friend!"

She laughed, and the last thing Boo Taylor saw before he turned and ran through the woods, leaving his friends behind, was the thick swell of Crystal Burne's breasts rippling under the muddy stream of her laughter.

Her voice trailed him through the trees: "You be back 'fore too long, won't you baby?"

three

Later that day, he sneaked his skiff off Pigg's Point and paddled it into the Yamawichee Sound. He looked up from worsening waters to thunderclouds colliding across the early evening sky. A belly rumble demanded answers. Boo Taylor only had questions.

Am I my brother's keeper?

Traveling north, racing the storm to the cove where Palaman Creek split the marsh. He tied the boat off there, far away from where Ash and Dewey and Lester could ever find it. *Now,* if they wanted to dig up old bones, they'd have to *swim* their spades across Pigg's Creek—or wait for low tide and try to cross the soupy pluff mud on foot. Because there were no bridges to Chaliboque.

❖ ❖ ❖

She watched. Listened.

Tottered and swayed in her wicker rocker. Slowly. Timelessly. Watching the angry storm clouds gather over her garden. To and fro. Listening in on Boo Taylor's thoughts. Back. Forth. Her liquid lips puckered in worry.

four

"Hey Gussie! Some boy here to see you!"

Her brother Petey was calling from the kitchen door. Gussie withdrew the paintbrush in mid-dab.

"Who—?"

In the next moment, the screen swung wide and Boo Taylor appeared. Gussie went hot with embarrassment. Her father and Dink Potter were sprawled in old lawn chairs with a tub of beers and a radio between them. They were listening to the Braves game instead of delivering the new air-conditioning unit to Braxton's Salvage like they were supposed to. Her father, with seven innings of beer sloshing in that hairy white belly, was now tilting back to get a look at Boo Taylor. Dink Potter was drooling tobacco juice down his chin.

And now Boo was picking his way across the denuded backyard, around a barrel lined with useless outboard motors, past the rusted chassis of Petey's ancient Buick, by the up-ended sofa the boys had tossed indifferently into the backyard. And he would see her stupid painting—a mural of flowers on the sagging shed, something to brighten up the place, but she was certain nothing so blatantly *white trash* would be found on Carriage Avenue, and the painting wasn't finished yet, and she *hated* it when anyone saw a painting that wasn't finished. And her clothes were ratty, and her hair was in a messy ball on top of her head, and she had paint on her hands, and she was sure she smelled. And what rude things did Petey say to him when he came to the door? And he had been through the *house,* that cramped, junk-cluttered house, and if he came through the kitchen he saw last night's dishes still in the sink, the two stuffed garbage bags no one bothered to toss into the cans outside.

She tabulated the legion of humiliations and was ready to damn Boo Taylor. Here he came, smiling at her as he sidestepped a broken lawnmower. She put down the paintbrush and uselessly rubbed her hands against the seat of her shorts.

"What are you doin here?"

Her shame nullified her anger, and when the question came out, she sounded almost pleasant—and she was startled by something completely unexpected and wonderful:

She was glad to see him.

A tern wept somewhere nearby, and her breath failed her.

"Just wanted to say hi," he said. He crammed his hands in his pockets. He toed the ground. "Laylee wanted to know why you haven't been around."

"Oh."

"She wants to know if you're okay and everything."

"I'm fine. Been babysittin a lot for the Stedman's."

"She was worried..." He looked up hopefully. "You know, that maybe you were mad at somebody."

"I'm not mad at anybody."

He smiled, and she felt herself smiling in return. *Damn him, that's just like him,* she thought, *he smiles like that and you can't be mad at him anymore.* The bandage was gone; the bruise was a ghostly yellow splotch. She noticed the string around his neck, the small pouch like a swollen wound over his heart.

"Hey, that's really good!" he said. He was looking past her shoulder at the shed. "Did you do that? By yourself?"

She flushed, tensed. "It's not done yet."

He walked around her and stood, hands on hips, before the mural. "Gussie, it's great."

She took a step back and examined the painting herself. The mural was her father's idea, not *hers,* and she was prepared to tell Boo Taylor that if he made any smart comments. "Thank you," she said cautiously.

Across the lawn, her father and Dink Potter watched, and she nervously wondered what those two rough, drunken men would be thinking right now if they knew it was Boo Taylor who had been taking shots at them from Laylee Colebriar's garden. And, even more nervously wondered what Boo Taylor would think if *he* knew. And then a new realization swept over her.

She quickly looked at the screen door.

If Boo Taylor came through the house, he must have seen Henry Ray.

The magic had worked. She had come to believe it might; anything seemed possible in the generous, mystical glitter of the old woman's eyes. The world was a fairy tale in Laylee Colebriar's patchwork cottage, where she felt like a lost princess who had found her way home, and so she had accepted the promise of that magic. But even so, she couldn't have believed it would work so *fast.*

It was almost midnight when she had finally reached her own front door, running all they way after abandoning Boo Taylor at the bridge over Soap Water Creek. The familiar worry: it was nighttime and Wade wasn't with her, and Henry Ray might be bobbing like that giant predator fish somewhere inside. Petey's truck was parked in the driveway, but her father's was not. No sign of the Henry Ray's tired old Plymouth. From the windows, television voices, flickers of underwater lights. Maybe Wade or Harley or Petey would still be up; or if Henry Ray *was* home, maybe he was passed out on the couch.

But Henry Ray wasn't there; just Wade and Harley watching an old movie.

She had gone to bed without the hope of sleep.

Instead, she listened to the noises of the house and the movements of her family. First Harley lumbering up the stairs and off to bed. Then an unmuffled car growling up to the house, idling there for almost ten minutes, and finally Petey's voice as a door slammed and the car lurched away too fast. For a while, it was Petey and Wade mumbling downstairs before the television snapped off and Petey and Wade made their way upstairs. Later (how much later?—an hour?—twice that?), her father's truck pulled up and she listened to his stumblings through the house—living room to kitchen, back to living room, and then upstairs to the bathroom where he urinated for what seemed like five minutes straight. Finally, he was off to bed. And the house was quiet.

Except for the creaks and groans of old beams that played havoc with her imagination.

When the luminous dials of the clock on her bureau pointed to two-thirty, she crawled out of bed. She crept through the upstairs hall...down the first few steps... knelt...peeked. She studied the living room by moonlight. It seemed empty, but she waited on the steps, still not trusting herself or the moonlight. Finally, she summoned the nerve to go the rest of the way downstairs.

Henry Ray had taken to spending his nights on the couch in the nook between living room and kitchen. That night, the couch was empty.

Gussie pried open Laylee Colebriar's tin. A puff of burnt rubber blasted her nostrils; she pulled her face away and something swam past her eyes in a dizzy swirl of sparkles. After a moment the smell faded away, and she poked her finger in it, a black pulp, wincing in expectation of the burn, but it was as cool as damp moss.

For the next five minutes, she dabbed the potion around the couch—under cushions, on the floor beneath it—while she listened for Henry Ray, imagining him watching her from some dark place, imagining at any moment his hand would snake out from the shadows and grab her wrist, or her throat or worse. She worked quickly and had no idea if she was doing it right—how much was enough? *Just smear a bit 'round where he sleep*, the old woman had told her. When she had gone through half of the tin's contents, she stopped. She'd save the other half in case he needed another dose later.

When the job was done, she crept upstairs and went to bed.

The next morning, she looked out her bedroom window and saw Henry Ray's car slouched in its usual place on the front lawn. She had slept through his homecoming. She went downstairs and there, in work shirt and underwear, Henry Ray's bloody corpse was heaped across the sofa.

It was like watching a zombie in a movie dig out of its grave and lumber up to an unsuspecting victim. Gussie watched in horror as her father righted himself out of the lawn chair and staggered across the dead lawn toward Boo Taylor.

"You Doc Taylor's boy, ain't you?"

Hank Dutton slapped a bear paw on Boo Taylor's shoulder, nearly rocking him off his feet.

"Yes sir," Boo answered.

Her father's hand remained on Boo's shoulder. He was grinning impishly. "There's a fine enough man, your daddy."

Boo looked at her briefly, awkwardly. "Thank you."

"Yes he is, by God. Say Gus—this here that boy ol' Murph beaned?"

She nodded. Embarrassment trembled through her legs.

"Where your manners at, girl? We got some lemonade inside, don't we?"

"No," she answered.

"Well, we got us some root beer and Coke, then. Whyn't you get this boy somethin cold to drink." He turned his glazed eyes back on Boo. "How old're you, boy?"

"Thirteen."

"Thirteen?" He looked Boo up and down, frowning. "Guess that's too young for a beer. Gus, take this boy inside and get him some lemonade."

"Daddy, we don't have any lemonade."

"Then get him a bottle'a Coke. We got Coke, I know that much."

She didn't like the thought of taking Boo Taylor into that filthy kitchen, but now Dink Potter was struggling out of his chair too, and she thought even less of having him join in this merry little conversation.

"Come on, Boo," she said. She grabbed his arm and pulled him out of her father's grasp.

Inside, the garbage-bag stink had magnified three-fold since her last trip through the kitchen, and two or three previously unnoticed flies buzzed figure-eights over the sink. There were no Coke bottles in the refrigerator. There were none in the cabinets. There were none in the pantry. While she searched, she imagined Boo Taylor's appraisal of the clutter and smells that were very different from the big, immaculate kitchen in his own house. She turned on him, preparing to respond to his snobbish smirks.

He smiled again and disarmed her.

"We could ride over to Haufmann's," he suggested, "maybe get a couple snow cones, if you want."

It sounded like a date. Pinpricks attacked her temples. "I'll have to change," she said.

She was happy for a moment.

A moment later, it was gone.

Shadows moved along the door to the living room. She looked up to see Henry Ray limping into the kitchen. His face, sullen and pale, considered Boo Taylor for a moment then dragged into a bloodless grin.

"This here fella your boyfriend?"

Outside, the voices of her father and Dink Potter groused over the radio's chatter. Henry Ray slid across the kitchen floor in his socks; his movements were a lopsided shuffle. Boo Taylor was staring at the knee Henry Ray favored, which was swathed in a sloppy cocoon of gauze. Blood had soaked through the wrappings to make blackish-red splotches. Gussie felt her contempt rising, surpassing her fear now that Henry Ray was no more a threat than a toothless alligator. She suppressed the urge—the same urge she had on and off for the last two weeks—to kick him in the knee.

❖   ❖   ❖

Her first thought:

The old woman lied to me! I killed him; I killed him!—because Henry Ray's face had been a wax sculpture, his open mouth cocked toward the ceiling as if silently screaming up to God for vengeance. And all that blood—on his hands and arms, on his underpants, and especially on his leg around that swaddle of ripped up sheets.

But then she heard the raggedy draw of his breaths and saw the uneasy rise of his chest and belly.

And she understood what had happened. Laylee Colebriar's magic had been to work even before she had smeared her potion around the sofa.

My knee! Fuckin nigger shot me!

As far as she knew, Henry Ray didn't leave the sofa that entire day. He was awake when she came home for dinner, and he grumpily accepted the plate of fried chicken and creamed corn Harley brought him, but she didn't believe he ate much of it. And when her father came in, he barely gave his oldest son a glance.

It had been the same for most of the last two weeks. Neither she nor Wade dared ask what had happened, so it had been up to Harley and Petey to approach him. (Petey was big enough not to fear Henry Ray so much anymore, though she believed Harley still kept a healthy distance from him.) Henry Ray, they reported, gave a garbled fairy tale about a hunting accident, though he could not provide some of the more important details. And he was refusing to go to the doctor. Harley and Petey had gotten a good look at the wound when Henry Ray changed the "bandages" in the kitchen one day.

"Bullet wound, sure enough."

"Caught him right in the fuckin knee cap."

"Told the boy he better get his sorry ass to a doctor. Thing's all purple and swelled up like a fuckin eggplant, and it's got puss runnin out of it. Idiot just smiled at me and poured a beer over it."

"Told me he was huntin over in Corrington on the mainland with Vin Scanlan when it happened. What's that boy doin out huntin with Vin Scanlan?"

"Told me he dug the bullet out with a knife."

"'So what were you boys huntin for, Henry Ray?' I ask. He says, 'Grizzly bear, what's it to you, fuckhead?' So I stop askin."

"Ought'a get his ass to a doctor, or that fucker's gonna kill him."

But she knew Henry Ray had already been treated by a doctor. The medicine had itself a nasty kick, the old woman had told her, and she was right. For a while, it seemed as if the wound *might* kill him. Though she still avoided him, it was impossible to avoid anyone *entirely* in that small house—and it was impossible not to see the fever that poured out of him when he was like a pallid, wet sponge being squeezed.

But the spell didn't kill him (after all, that had been part of the promise, too); he rode through the worst of the fever, and the waves of it that returned, pounding him on and off for the first week.

And now he was getting stronger.

The tin was still half full with the original batch of poison. In another night or two, she'd plant the second batch. And if she needed, she could always climb on the back of Boo Taylor's bike and go back for more.

⬦ ⬦ ⬦

She grabbed hold of his chest and decided it *was* a date as they glided alongside the Polk Road traffic. Not their first date, though—that would have been their trip down to visit Laylee Colebriar. *Our first date, and I didn't even know it!*

In three minutes flat, she had changed into a clean pair of jean shorts and a white blouse, washed her hands, scrubbed under her arms, combed out her hair, all the time worrying about the too-serious face she saw in the mirror, wondering about Boo Taylor who waited in the front yard—the safest place, considering her father and Dink Potter lazed like fat lions in the sun out back and Henry Ray prowled the shadows inside. He had entered a den of sharp-clawed beasts and emerged undiscovered.

And now that they were away from the stinks and threats of the place, freedom billowed over her in the extravagant wind of their flight. The muscles in Boo Taylor's back pulsed before her; her legs straddled around him where, with each stride, the rough fabric of his jeans chafed her thighs.

She shouted near his ear: "Boo Taylor, you tellin me this is all the faster this thing can go?"

His shoulders turned, and he favored her with a wicked grin. And then he bent forward, pumping madly, and the hot breeze streamed across her cheeks, whip-cracked her hair, caught the loose cloth of her blouse. Cars and trucks rumbled and snorted by, their metal hides swooping thrillingly close, and she found her fingers stretching out to brush them.

As they approached the busy intersection of Polk and Fulton, she waited for Boo to slow for the crossing traffic—but he roared a swashbuckler's laugh and leapt the bike to the sidewalk. She let out her own laugh that was half shriek and clutched his shirt as he barreled off the sidewalk again and jarred her against the seat.

He veered onto the herringbone brick of Fulton at a sprint, just missing a yellow van turning off Polk, and then swerved around a parked station wagon so abruptly the Schwinn threatened to spill them both. But Boo Taylor's back leaned recklessly against the fall and she leaned with him, and somehow they brought the bike to right.

"Boy, you're crazy!" she yelled cheerfully as they were safely cruising along the curb again.

"You scared?" he yelled back.

"Hell no, Boo Taylor, you don't scare me!"

"You want to get off?"

"Keep goin!" She shrieked again as he jerked the wheels around an elderly couple who had stepped into the street. "You just watch *where* you're goin!"

They bolted down the cobbled street. Boo Taylor jigged and darted around obstacles, now purposefully charging telephone poles and trashcans and moving cars and then banking away in the last instant to goad more squeals from her. She held him around the chest, her fingers coiling over the pouch at his heart—something Laylee Colebriar had given him, she was sure of that now. And as she wondered what its purpose might be and was overcome with the urge to lay her cheek against that broad boy's-back in front of her, she remembered the old woman's words:

Far as boys go, he's about as fine as they get...You can trust Mr. Boo.

And she did trust him as he carried her crazily in and out of the rushing, belligerent traffic, clinging to him, leaning with his turns, flexing and unflexing the long muscles of her legs in time to his wild-man pedaling. He veered across Fulton, dodging a Volkswagen Beetle that bugled its tinny horn at them, and she was close enough to see the driver's scowling face. They soared to the opposite curb, and once again Boo Taylor launched them to the sidewalk, jolting her spine and laughing as she laughed with him.

Then he slammed the bike to a stop, leaving a long black snake's tail burning on the concrete. She lurched into his back.

"We're here!" he announced, and broke into more laughter.

Not so soon!—but she looked up and saw, regretfully, the green and black sign above the door of Haufmann's Market. Giggling, pushing the hair out of her face, she said, "And in one piece! Did you see that man's face?"

"The old man in the VW?"

"And that lady back there—Lord, Boo Taylor, I think you gave that poor old lady a heart attack! You're crazy!"

"You were *scared!*"

"Was not!"

They were both still laughing as they went inside.

Cool shade, oiled barnwood floors and lofty ceilings, fans making lazy spirals overhead, rich market smells throughout. It was nice at first; a pleasant break from the heat outside. Then, everything turned sour. And she stopped laughing.

Gussie Dutton walked right alongside Boo Taylor, but she had become a dingy, red-haired ghost.

Mr. Haufmann standing behind the butcher's counter: "Well hey there, Boo Taylor. How's your momma and daddy doin?"

Just fine, Boo answered.

What about my daddy?

Mrs. Kressner, strolling down an aisle with a basket looped over her arm: "So nice to see you, Boo. Tell your folks I said howdy."

He would, Boo promised.

What about my family?

Mrs. Morehead and her boy, Colin, standing in line at the checkout counter: "Why Boo Taylor, I swear that nose is just as handsome as ever; your daddy did a fine job. You give him my regards, you hear?"

He heard, Boo said.

What about me?

What *about* her? She eyed Boo Taylor, suspicious of his smile. Was he smirking again?

One after the other, they spoke their fine pleasantries to the doctor's boy and ignored Hank Dutton's daughter. When they reached the counter, Boo had to nudge her to make her order. Then, when she reached for the dollar she'd crammed in her pocket, Boo Taylor tried to stop her, and...

Hurtling toward another obstacle. He leaned one way. She leaned the other. The *wrong* way, but she couldn't make herself stop.

"Let me pay," he said.

"I can pay for my own."

"But I want to pay," he said, smiling.

"No!"

"Gussie, it's no big deal."

"Boo Taylor, you damn snob, I am not *poor*!"

It's supposed to be a date; he's supposed to pay, the reasonable part of her mind tried to explain. But the unreasonable part wasn't listening.

His face blossomed scarlet. "I didn't say you were."

"No, but that's what you were thinkin!"

The clerk gave Boo a sympathetic shake of her head. Boo smiled grimly back and dropped a quarter on the counter to pay for his own. Then he walked silently past the magazine rack toward the door.

No, wait—we were having so much fun! We were laughing!

She paid for hers. When she went outside, she cupped a hand to her eyes against the shocking glare of sun. Boo Taylor was standing astride his bike. She was walking to him, thinking what apology she could offer and resenting the need to apologize, when someone spoke from the street.

"So, this is where you two were off to in such a hurry?"

"Murphy," she said, turning toward him.

Murphy Ransome was leaning against the door of his pickup and grinning at them. "Hey Gus," he said. "Hey Boo."

"Hey Murphy," Boo Taylor answered.

"How's that nose feelin, boy?"

"Better."

Murphy nodded. *"Looks* better." He turned back to Gussie and his smile lengthened. "Saw you down the street a ways back there. Nearly ran y'all over."

Her heart was slamming against her chest. "Just gettin a snow cone," she said and held the dripping handful out as explanation.

Murphy Ransome popped open the passenger door. "I was just headin over to see Harley," he said. "Gus, you want a lift home?"

She looked at the open door and Murphy's tall frame leaned casually beside it. "Okay," she said quickly, and then turned to Boo Taylor who was holding onto his paper cone and still straddling his bicycle. "You don't mind, do you, Boo?"

He made another grim smile and shook his head.

As she turned back to Murphy Ransome and started for his truck, Murphy called over her shoulder, "Naw, you don't mind, Boo. It's a whole lot safer than ridin backseat on that bike, ain't it?"

She climbed inside, letting Murphy close the door for her. Then Murphy came around to the driver's door and filled the cabin next to her. Through the windshield, she watched the heat shimmering up from Fulton Street Market, making the people waver like phantoms.

As Murphy Ransome flicked on the truck's radio, she turned to wave to Boo Taylor, but he didn't see her. He was staring at something in the gutter. The truck pulled away and she tried to see what Boo Taylor might be looking at, but she only saw a trampled slip of burlap.

six

The bleachers were empty again the following weekend.

"Last hurrah for Round Roscoe," Wade told him. "Got football two-a-days startin next Monday, you believe it?"

So he spent his days fishing, throwing rocks, shooting baskets. He rode his bike to the docks, watched the brawny men and their boats. He tended Miss Laylee's garden. He swam in the ocean. He read Doc Savage paperbacks. He dodged his friends.

He prowled like a thief through library shadows, exploring the great stacks, guided by skeletal Dalton Satterfield to select certain musty texts. These he studied intently. He began to make notations in a spiral notebook.

Families on isle pre-1910:

Beaudry – yes	*Duff – yes*	*Meggett – no, but Mom is a Sheppard*
Marchant – no	*LaValle – yes*	*Dutton – no, but Gus mom?*
Hawthorne – yes	*Fitch – yes*	*Burn – no (Burne? Bourn?) Stuvant a married name?*
Satterfield – yes	*Standish – no*	*Colebriar – no, What is maiden name?*
Smith & Jones - ?	*Taylor – yes*	*Goody – yes!*
Stuvant – no	*Hatchel – yes*	

Others I never heard of:

Hatley	*Shallcross*	*Shone? (owned hotel)*

He discovered crumbling newspapers with stories about rapes and lynchings and deadly roadside crashes. He scanned police reports and obituaries. At Dalton Satterfield's direction, he wrote to mainland churches for marriage and death records.

Duncan Lee Burnett, of Powtonville in Corrington County, died suddenly on the evening of Sep 17. He was 32 years of age. Mr. Burnett was formerly employed by the county. He was preceded in death by his wife, the former Miss Luella Sturvant, also of Powtonville.

A manila envelope arrived from the *Macon Herald*, addressed to Dalton Satterfield, c/o Sweetpatch Island Public Library. Boo opened the envelope and held up a seventeen-year-old clipping with a seventeen-year-old photograph, dim with age, a pretty young brunette smiling shyly, hair sculpted in a standard fifties bob.

Girl Missing

Macon police ask that anyone with knowledge of the whereabouts of Ellen Belle (Honey) Hawthorne, to contact them with information. Miss Hawthorne, the niece of Mrs. Lucille Hawthorne of Macon, has been missing since July, shortly after graduating with high honors from St. Alwyn's School for Girls, a private boarding school near the town of Beaufort…

"How's the project coming, Boo?"

Boo Taylor swept the clipping into his notebook. He tried to think how he should answer.

seven

He was mowing his lawn one evening when Ash Marchant rolled up on his bicycle. Ash, looking cautious, looking bled dry, looking *lessened*.

What was she doing to them?

"Naw, we haven't been digging—mostly because there's nothing to dig with, I guess. Though Dewey and Les are pretty stuck on the idea."

"What about…her?"

"Her? She just teases. God, she hardly wears anything; it about drives me crazy. But she's, you know, just lonely I figure and just likes the company. Two of them living alone in that ol place—boy that's creepy, isn't it?"

She (hardly wore anything) was just lonely. That wasn't so bad?

"But, nobody…nobody's been hurt?"

"No."

"She never hurt any of you boys?"

"Hurt? No. Hey, she's not like that, Boo. You know, she talks about you. She's all the time saying…"

But the old woman was eavesdropping from her wicker rocker.

The runners rolled forward. Rolled backward. Weathered ship planks riding a creaking porch sea, which, for the moment, was deceptively calm.

Back and forth.

A clock's pendulum, cranking off the steady, unrelenting cadence of time, of life-times kindled and snuffed, of tides come and gone, of waves crashing and receding a million times over and a million times over again.

To and fro.

She lifted her hands and splayed ten fingers to the breezes. Ten fingers burned and cracked on top, pale and fleshy underneath; ten fingernails eroded down to buffed marble chips. She flitted, danced, stroked the whorls of her ten two-tone fingers through the air and felt the boy's secret pulse.

Rocking. Creaking.

She cocked her head, thrust a withered ear to the same breezes to capture fragile tremors of the boy's voice in the leaf whispers and cicada purrings and beach grass rustlings.

...tick...creak...tock...squeal...

She leaned an old backbone forward, one piano key at a time, squinted her eyes until just the finest flecks of light needled through: more marble—brown and yellow, shot through with shattered crimson veins. And caught the dim flashes of color, of a brighter and infinitely younger light, of a stronger marble sundered from a different hued mountain.

...tock...rasp...

She eavesdropped on the boy *(boy-child, boy-man)*.

The first boy-child born in generations.

Born into generation after generation of misery.

She knew all about his crimes: crimes perpetrated, crimes contemplated. Crimes he brought with him into this world without knowing; they were tangled up in his blood, snagged up in his hair, tattooed to his skin. Crimes he chose to commit of his own free will. Crimes he was yet to wreak but surely would because it was his nature to do so. Crimes he was being seduced toward; the poison taken, threatening now to leak down his throat and work its acid through his veins and arteries, seeking the blackness in his heart. He had taken the poison into his mouth. It was his choice, now: swallow or spit.

(Hated one; liked the other.)

His choice.

He was too old and grown up and wide-shouldered for her to make his choices for him any longer. Too big for her brand of magic to work on him—other than a few shoestring tricks and sleights-of-hand and smoke-puff illusions that still managed a minor charm. He would have to save himself.

Or maybe...

Miss Gussie?

How do you go about fighting a witch? With another witch. A different magic, but just as potent, and it might just be enough. And with a little more lovage root in her wine; a little more shoop-dust in his tea; just a bit of a push was all those two children needed, just a tiniest spark to unstick the wariness that gummed up their eyes...

Maybe.

...tick...scratch...creak...

(At her feet, Shamus fast asleep but motoring his throat at something his keener dog senses radared out of the air, certain alien molecules and ungodly soundwaves contaminating his dream mind. His sleep-grumble rose, his lip rippled, his silver fur prickled to attention on his shoulders. Whatever foulness he sensed heard him and cowered back into the bubbling swamp.)

...thump...squeal...

Yes, she knew about crimes. All about them. Had certainly witnessed enough of them on this island. Was herself many, many decades into a lifetime sentence; she had been the boy's age when she took the poison into her own mouth, made her choice and swallowed it down. In those days, a sturdy brick-and-wood bridge spanned Pigg's Creek to Chaliboque. Buggies, mule carts, horse-drawn carriages, and all manner of folks and beasts crossed it freely.

The bridge was gone now. The old folktales said evil couldn't cross water without a bridge, which was the reason islands were known to be stuck full with all kinds of inbred nastiness. But she knew that wasn't true. Evil traveled anywhere it wanted.

It just favored some places more than others.

...thump...click...

Haggard boards squealed. Antique nails screeched.

She played a soft piano tune as she eased back into the rocker; finger flesh tapping the wind, ear catching butterfly weepings, fractured marble eyes flickering light. Captaining from the deck of a clapboard barge, surveying the rocking oceans and headlands, touching, sniffling, glimpsing the infinitesimal hints of a gathering storm.

eight

In her bedroom, high above the brawling man's world, door barricaded with a wastepaper basket, Gussie Dutton mixed her paints and went to work on a new canvas.

nine

Boo Taylor itched, thrashed, seeped hot ocean swells into his mattress. At last, he swam his way up from soaking sheet-and-pillow depths to breathe the clean air of wakefulness. She was just *lonely* down there, in that creepy old house. All by herself. Whispering his name. In the dark. He sat up. Brushed sweat off his brow. He went to the window and looked out, seeing the endless black emptiness that was sky and ocean. And seeing the pier that poked into the sea like a broken spine, like an incomplete bridge that spanned half onto solid land, half into all that infinite nothing.

He left the window and pulled on a pair of shorts. Then he grabbed a bat and left the house to walk the old planks.

With his first step on the pier, a ghost's hand rippled around his ankle in a papery gust.

He choked back a scream, ready to sprint inside.

Then, seeing the page, reached down to remove it. By the pale moonlight, he read the mimeographed message. Then he folded it up and stuffed it in his back pocket.

ten

Boo looked at the doctor across the cleared dinner table.

The older man poked a cigarette into his mouth and lit it.

"So," Boo said, "I guess they're electing a new school board."

MaeEllen was clattering dishes in the kitchen. The doctor smiled and spoke around the jittering cigarette and a cloud of white smoke. "Not the whole board. Just the positions that come up this year."

"Why not the whole board?"

"The terms are staggered. Keeps from turning over the whole board all at once.

The district has six board members, and two spots come up every year. This year, Mr. Dufette's spot is one of them."

Boo nodded. The doctor puffed. A cigarette cumulus gathered above their heads.

"So who are you voting for?" Boo asked.

"Why, I'll vote for Matt Dufette, of course."

"Not Reverend Hatchel?"

"What?"

"I said, you're not voting for Reverend Hatchel?"

The skinny mustache betrayed a curl at the edges. "No."

"Why? Because he's colored?"

"Of course not."

"Then why?"

"Boo—" The older man sighed and tapped the cigarette above his ashtray. "Well, for one thing, the good reverend doesn't have any experience. But now, your old buddy Matt, well he knows how the system works. At least he should, he's been at it for twelve years." He favored Boo with a broad smile. "Schools around here have been just fine so far, haven't they?"

Boo grunted noncommittally. Then he pulled the mimeographed page from his back pocket and handed it to his father.

The doctor unfolded it and looked at it uncertainly. The blue headline hammered its stark declaration at him, and he barked a laugh.

NO NIGGERS ON <u>OUR</u> SCHOOL BOARD
Attentions to all decent white citizens of Sweetpatch Island

It is a well-known fact that the good hard working WHITE citizen of Sweetpatch Island and Corrington County are the ones built up this island and the surrounding area and made it something to be proud of. THIS INCLUDES OUR SCHOOLS!!!

Our schols are fine as they are, arent they? Now the Federal Goverment is tell the good people of this island what it is allowed. Such is forcing us to put nigger kids in the same classroom as our own dear flesh and blood!!! Which we will have to do this fall year. And if that is not bad enouhf all ready now they say we have to let a NIGGER PREACHER run for OUR School Board!!!!!! The Constitution of the UNited Sates of America says there is seppration between Church and State. So how can this be???? But the jews that run our Federal Goverment say we has to anyway. Deos this make sence???

The KNIGHTS of the KU KLUX KLAN says THIS IS YOUR ISLAND and we dont have to listen to the Federal any more!! The Knights are here to help the fine white people of Sweetpatch Island DO WHAT MUST BE DONE!!! You are not alone were alway here to help!!

OUR ISLAND DONT NEED NIGGER ON SCHOOL BOARD
DONT VOTE NIGGER FOR SCHOOL BOARD!!!!!!!!!

His father read. Boo watched the black square that was the screen window over his father's shoulder, a hole in the lighted world where, on the border, white-winged insects pirouetted and gamboled and pinged metallic dance steps. Beyond that, crickets screeched, nighthawks called, the ocean made great salt-water exhalations. He had the sense that something out there wanted very badly to be let inside.

As his father was coming to the end, Boo studied the tiny quivers of reaction in his lips, hints of piqued amusement in the wrinkles at his eyes.

"Hmph," his father said as he finished. He handed back the page.

Boo waited for more.

The doctor shook his pack of cigarettes and plucked another one free. He lit it and then looked up to see his son studying him. "Well," he said, and coughed. "I imagine this integration thing has got some folks on edge."

Boo ruffled the flyer and glanced at the smudged blue letters. The page had been run off on a mimeograph machine and reminded him of test papers and bulletins at school. "Who do you think made this?" he asked.

"Oh, I don't know. Could have been anybody, I suppose. Somebody who needs a dictionary, anyway."

"Do you think Reverend Hatchel will win?"

His father laughed briefly, then attempted seriousness. "Well, there are almost twice as many coloreds on this island as there are white. Did you know that?"

Boo shook his head.

"Doesn't seem that way because the tourists are mostly white, and of course they don't vote. And you know *that's* got some folks worried. Though it really shouldn't— most of the coloreds aren't registered."

"Are *you* worried?"

The doctor glanced briefly at the burning tip of his cigarette, frowning. Then he smiled. "Of course not," he answered. "Not a thing to be worried about."

But something worried the doctor. And the longer Boo waited—fidgeting digits under the tablecloth, pretending to look away, gathering cobwebs in his chair—the more certain he became that the *something* would go unsaid.

When he stood up to leave the room, cobwebs broke, and the doctor asked suddenly, "Son, how's that nose of yours?"

"Fine," he answered.

His father beckoned him with a thin finger. Boo came and allowed his face to be held for an examination.

The doctor came at if from angles. "So, everything's all right with you?"

"Sure. It hardly hurts anymore."

"Sleeping okay?"

Boo nodded.

"You...haven't seen anything strange lately, have you?"

Boo breathed the cigarettes on his father's breath, the disinfectant soap beneath his fingernails, the musk of day-old aftershave. "Strange like what?"

"Oh, you know…" He smiled ruefully, jogged Boo's jaw from side to side to see past the shadows. "Like that trouble in June?"

"You mean like what happened to Hoss?"

The fingers clenched on his chin.

"Yes. Anything like that?"

That trouble in June. "No."

"You're sure?"

"Yes," Boo answered. "Everything's fine."

"So what are you getting up to with Peach Satterfield's boy?"

"You mean Dalton? He's just helping me out at the library." He saw the picture of a pretty brunette in a fifties bob.

"Helping you out," his father said and pinned Boo still, now looked straight in his stranger-son's eyes. Boo peered back blandly.

After a long moment, the doctor said, "Okay." He made a small nod and released Boo's jaw. Then he picked up his cigarette and took a puff. "Dalton called for you earlier. He wanted you to know he had a package for you. He thought you might want to see it right away."

Boo thanked him, then turned to leave the room.

"Summer's almost over."

The doctor had spoken, quietly—loud enough that Boo turned, soft enough that Boo wondered if he was speaking to himself.

Again, Boo waited for more. *Summer's almost over.* He said it as if the summer's end would solve everything.

"Almost," Boo said.

His father took a long drag and sighed streamers of hot white clouds through his nostrils. He smiled. "You keep a lot to yourself, don't you, son?"

Boo stared at his father. He was itching to leave the room. *So do you*, he thought.

Later, he showed the flyer to his mother. "Who are you voting for?" he asked.

She waved a hand dismissively. "Oh, I suppose one crook is just as good as the next."

"Mr. Dufette's a crook?"

"Sugar, that old rascal is just as crooked as your broken little nose."

⸱eleven

"So tell me, little man, how do you like being the middle of an Oreo cookie?" Sunglasses hid Solomon Goody's eyes and turned his big-toothed grin into the snarl of some blind wolf.

"You let the boy be," Laylee Colebriar scolded.

Solomon sat in the pew to his left, and Miss Laylee settled next to him on his right. Solomon showed the old woman his wolf's grin and patted Boo's knee indulgently. He turned to utter some hungry plot to Royal's ear. Boo picked out the word's *fire* and *arms* and *revolution*. The flyer Boo Taylor had found was tucked inside Solomon Goody's breast pocket.

Then Reverend Hatchel came to the pulpit in a flourish and began the service. Boo dozed, his thoughts punctuated by words of the sermon...

...something about Samson and Delilah?

...Sodom and Gomorra?

...the temptation of Christ?

He came awake again when Eulahlah Colebriar nudged his leg. The pastor was shifting gears.

"As many of y'all know, there's an eee-*LEC*-shun this September!"

Scattered agreement rifled from the crowd. Solomon yelled out, "You know it!" Laylee only smiled.

"Does *any* of y'all know that?" the pastor shouted

More agreement this time.

"Who all knows that? Let me see."

Hands and paddle fans flew into the air. Boo waited for Solomon and Laylee to raise their hands before he did the same.

"Well there is," said Pastor Hatchel. "September fifteenth. Anybody know what this here election's about?"

"School Board!" people shouted.

The reverend squinted incredulously, put a hand to his ear. "What's that? A *scoreboard?* You say we votin on a new scoreboard?"

"SCHOOL Board!" they yelled, and Boo joined them.

"Ain't that somethin? We get us enough votes, we gonna get us a new scoreboard this September fifteenth."

"SCHOOL BOARD!"—a roar that loosened sawdust from the rafters.

"School Board!" he agreed. "That's right. Now let me hear you—what *day* you say is this here school board election?"

"September fifteenth!"

"That's right! September *fif*teenth." He smiled at the crowd and tugged playfully at his collar. "Now, I ain't gonna tell y'all *who* to vote for in this election," he said. "I ain't even gonna tell you what handsome gentlemen is runnin for school board in this election."

His smile brightened and laughter rippled the congregation.

"Cause *I* know *you* know. Just like *I* know every *soul* in this church, every *single one* of you, is gonna show up on September fifteen and cast a vote. Ain't that right?"

"That's right!"

"No matter *who* you votin for, you *all* gonna be there on September fifteen and cast a vote!"

"That's right!"

"Praise Gawd, that's right. And you know how I know that? I know that 'cause every *soul* in this church, every *single one* of y'all, is registered to vote. Ain't that right, too?"

A smattering of zealous *that's rights* followed, but mostly a lot of embarrassed muttering that collectively sounded like a low groan.

The pastor considered the assembly incredulously again. "You mean to say y'all ain't even *registered* to vote?"

After more muttering and a few *no sirs,* Reverend Hatchel shook his head sadly.

"Can't elect who you want if you don't vote," he said. "And you can't vote 'less you get yourself registered, ain't that right?"

Again, he shook his head, profoundly sad.

"Well then, I guess it's by the grace of God we got us some special visitors here today. Some folks from the state come all the way down here from Columbia. Come all that way to help you folks get registered." He smiled indulgently at the first pew. "You boys want to stand up?"

Three white men, previously invisible, now stood and faced the congregation. Boo turned to Solomon and saw the patient wolf's smile light his darkly pleased face.

On the church steps, Boo Taylor pulled away from Laylee Colebriar. He found Reverend Hatchel holding the flyer; Solomon Goody was holding the reverend's right arm. The three white men and several young black men in sunglasses surrounded them.

The gray, hunched crowd gave this group uneasy glances as they hobbled into the parking lot.

"Somebody got a fire burnin over there," confided a mound of a woman who worked in the cafeteria at the white school. She was looking unhappily over her shoulder. "Them young men gonna get theyself burnt they don't keep careful. Maybe get some other folk burnt, too."

"Ain't no keepin young men from settin fires," another offered. "S'pose sometimes they *got* to be set. S'pose it's generally the young men that need to do the settin."

Beyond them, Boo read a hand-painted sign leaning against the front left corner of the church.

REGISTER so you can VOTE
Calliope St. Cavalry Baptist Church
Wed-Fri AUG 24, 25, 26, 31 SEP 1, 2,
Bring ID!! Driver Licence or Birth Cert
VOTE! VOTE! VOTE!

twelve

She asked him to walk her home.

When they arrived at her front porch, he wandered into the garden with Shamus while she went inside. A few minutes later she brought out two glasses of yauponberry wine and called his name. The wine was a cloudy, red-black soup, and it was bitter. *Like the sacrament,* she told him.

(She's out there, right now)

They sat on the porch where Boo studied the distant Chaliboque battlements and listened for his name. He felt his brain being probed by the old woman's fingers, trying to get to his thoughts.

"Got me a chicken from Dottie Mae's man yesterday," she said lightly. "Went t'see how the baby was makin out."

Boo grunted.

"I can't seem to remember—you like fried chicken?"

"Yes'm," he answered distantly.

Of course she was reading his mind. Sometimes, talking was just a game.

"You sure? Thought maybe you didn't."

"Sure I like it."

"Good, then you come 'round for some tonight. And bring along Miss Gussie."

"She can't," he said. "She's busy."

"*Busy?* What she got to be busy about?"

He briefly pictured her in the high school bleachers, cheering someone else. He took another sip of the wine. He grimaced at the bitterness and held the glass against the sky. The murky crimson liquid looked less like sacramental wine and more like the real thing.

"You ain't even ask her yet."

"I don't have to."

"You *afraid* to ask her?"

He grumbled. "No," he said and set the wine on the bench. "I'm not afraid of anything." He felt his heart fluttering and thought it might be beating a hundred times a second. A cloud passed over the sun, setting the tiny shack into shade. At Chaliboque, that distant point of South Patch, the ancient spires were still caught in the angry glare of the sun. Boo Taylor banished images of Mamie Stuvant, of the girl with the fifties bob, of Gussie Dutton making her goo-goo eyes over Murphy Ransome—and replaced them with a picture of Crystal Burne, out there right now, languoring upon the bluffs and offering the length of her brown sugar flesh to the flaming sky and marsh breezes.

"Good t'be afraid of some things, boy."

He felt Crystal Burne's flesh under his hand.

Shamus, who had been sitting quietly at the foot of the steps, perked his head up as a crow flew overhead. The dog followed its flight intensely.

Boo turned to the old woman. *How much do you know?* he wondered. And now it was his fingers prodding the labyrinthine mind of this desiccated, centuries-old and infinitely unknowable being. It was like plunging his hands into the husks of a thousand dead crickets.

Thirteen

On the last Friday afternoon of summer vacation, Gussie Dutton watched the gray clouds drifting northward. Earthbound, she bore southward, crossing Soap Water Creek her arms aching under the weight of a newspaper-swaddled package. She nodded to the friendly looking colored men who were fishing off the bridge and briefly noticed one man who stood apart from the others. As if he wanted nothing to do with them, and they wanted nothing to do with him. Watching her and not smiling. A tall man in rags.

She looked away.

Five miles or so altogether, she figured, from her house to Miss Laylee's. An hour to walk, maybe less—not so bad; she could *run* that far, *twice* that if she really needed. But she didn't count on the painting being so heavy. And maybe it wasn't so heavy, not at first. But after fifteen minutes, she could feel its weight burning the tendons in her elbows. After a half hour it was like a slab of concrete, and she was sure her arms had been stretched two inches longer.

She stepped off bridge planks.

Stepped onto road hardpan.

A mildewy threat of rain thickened in her lungs. Sweat greased her face, her arms, her legs as she hurried to keep ahead of the storm, as she glanced constantly skyward at the swirling, low mass of gray.

The painting was for Laylee Colebriar, a thank you for the potion that knocked Henry Ray flat on his back—though she secretly hoped Boo Taylor would be there when she brought the painting to the old woman. Boo Taylor probably hated her, and she couldn't blame him. She had gotten all mad at him, called him a *snob*, and for what? For trying to buy her a snow cone? God, she was stupid sometimes, let that redneck temper get the best of her—and then Murphy Ransome had to come along and ambush her with his pickup and his smile. "Hey Gus; want a ride home?" Long and handsome in those faded jeans. And just as redneck as her.

But the ride home was a disappointment in the afterglow of her breathless race on the streets with Boo Taylor—wrapped around his chest, his legs, laughing with him, shrieking her terror and exhilaration. She had managed to ruin all that and hadn't seen him since to apologize. Now, she'd have to wait until school started next week. Unless, of course...

Why Boo Taylor, I didn't know you'd be here!

Thunder growled, closer this time, angrier. She looked at the sky again, forecasting that the swamp-green bellies of those clouds couldn't hold off much longer.

❖   ❖   ❖

Boo Taylor tossed a ball into the air.

Whacked it.

Sent it sailing through the thick haze and plopping into a barren left field where it rolled several feet through sun-withered patches of grass.

He spun sharply. Expecting someone to be there and not sure *why* he expected it because he had neither heard nor seen anything.

And there was nothing to hear or see. Just swollen clouds drifting in from the ocean, from the splintered old bones of the Indian shell pile. The shell pile. Was something moving there? Did he expect ribs, femurs, vertebrae to assemble from the heap and rise in ovation?

Still, he waited a moment. He worked his fists around the shaft of the bat and sniffed the metallic taste of a storm.

"Hey!" he called.

Nothing but an echo.

He grabbed another ball and whacked it into center.

Then another, clearing the invisible wall in right.

He went through the rest of the balls. When the stack was depleted, he trotted out to collect the balls and start over again. He was crossing shortstop when he *did* hear someone coming and, with thudding heart, wished immediately he still had the bat in his hands.

Then wished it would be Gussie Dutton coming.

Then wished it might be Crystal Burne.

But it was only boys on bicycles. Boo counted them: three boys on two bicycles—*all still alive*—and made a silent prayer of thanks. They were heading south, not seeing him, not even *looking* for him. They were laughing and whooping, celebrating. Slung over their shoulders was a collection of spades and picks.

Boo left the balls where they lay in the field and trotted to his bike.

Someone was following her. Keeping hidden in the woods off to her left. She heard the shuffling of dead leaves—sometimes like footsteps, sometimes like the step of a large animal. And sometimes, nothing. She had never been this deep into South Patch all by herself, never realized how barren South Patch went in long stretches. How much farther to Miss Laylee's?

She quickened her stride, would run if not for the heavy painting weighing her down. The tendons in her arms were being pulled like hot taffy, *blazing* hot taffy ready to snap.

A leaf crash in the woods. Then, softly, another.

She dared a glance over her shoulder, caught a brief flap of shapelessness, darkness that might be feathers, might be fur, might be ragged clothes.

Then, a simmering low growl—by that tree. Or, *that* one, up in the mossy branches. Or maybe it was unfurling through the olive-gray clouds—just the storm.

She groaned. She shifted the painting on her hip.

The dirt road straightened. She heard laughter somewhere up ahead. Her heart, already racing, raced faster when she was sure for just a moment that was Boo Taylor blurring by, certain he was among those boys bent over their bicycles, speeding across Sugar Dam Road just ahead in a cluster.

Then they were gone.

She kept walking.

Keeping an eye on the clouds.

Listening for the rustling that shadowed her in the woods and was surely just her imagination.

Ten minutes later, she heard the promise of Miss Laylee's home carried on the wind: a thousand jangling wind chimes. Still hidden beyond another bend in the trail, but at last a certain, makeable goal.

Lightning flashed.

She saw the man just as the first fat drop smacked her forehead.

She imagined he spit on her—though he was standing well back in the trees. The cold water trickled between her eyes and down either side of her nose. Then another drop shocked her bare shoulder. It was the same man she had seen at the bridge. That was impossible. How could he have gotten in front of her? She hugged the painting against her breasts like a shield, and it was suddenly not heavy at all.

Rain drops, still occasional, rhythmless, pattered the road and erupted dust plumes like tiny meteors colliding with the earth. She walked south, watching the man as she came closer to him and as he looked back at her, making no movement to acknowledge her. Not moving, but alive and watching with heavy-browed contempt. His eyes were an iridescent otherworldly shimmer, like moons, fluttering, pivoting to meet her own.

Thunder, on top of her now, crackling through a web of electric arteries in the hovering, shifting, olive-gray ceiling.

She tried to get her lips to move. They did, finally, quiveringly. Another drop slapped her cheek and filled the deceptive grooves of her smile. When she came abreast of the man, and he was no more than ten feet away, she paused in the trail. She forced in a breath, forced an exhale.

"Hey there," she said casually.

The man blinked slowly, his eyelids a black veil that snuffed the glow beneath. This close, she could see the flies that flitted about his shoulders, his ears, the misshapen sponge of his hair. The way flies might alight upon a dead animal, she thought. And then the smell of him came to her.

His mouth wavered. He spoke a gibberish grumble that was the exact pitch of the thunder. *"Nottin foeyah en dishyuh play."* No other movement from him—just the rusted iron hinge of his jaw.

A gust of wind breathed the scent of oceans to her, and the call of Laylee's broken-glass shelter rose higher. She stretched her smile wider, straining. "Excuse me?"

"Leeb dishyuh play!"

Leave this place?

A teardrop splattered beneath one glittering eye. It rolled a slug's trail down a chiseled oaken cheek, around walnut lips, then lingered on a cypress-bark chin, waggling there, begging familiarity.

Had she seen him before? The light had been different then.

Mr. Jakes?

Oh, he the local ghost. Ain't you heard?

Two beads of water struck her own face, exploded there. Lightning flashed again and filled the space just between her and the man in the woods. In the light shock that followed, she saw him plunge forward.

She squeezed the package to her breast and ran.

The storm split wide open and spilled ice-cold torrents over her. She leaned into the sudden, opaque sheets of water, slapped puddles with her sneakers, sprayed mud up the back of her legs. Overhead, the fierce growl of thunder, a huge sound. She broke through the last turn of the trail; Laylee Colebriar's cottage was there, a bleary illusion of angles, chime-clatter muffled by thick rain swells. She had the sudden certain fear that the old woman wouldn't be home, that she would run to the porch, trip up those steps and grab the knob, and the door would be locked and the man would trap her there. And then what would she do?

"*Laylee!*"

Perhaps, by some miracle, Boo Taylor would rise up from the garden with his rifle. And as she thought this, there *was* movement by the house! Something, a silvery shape, emerging from beneath the porch steps. *Another ghost,* her brain whispered as she raced closer to it. The shape charged toward her and she realized it was a huge dog, barking and snarling furiously.

"*Shamus!*" she screamed.

As if struck across the snout, the big dog abruptly stopped. It looked at her curiously as she continued to hammer down the muddy trail toward the porch. Then she realized that if the dog wasn't charging after her anymore, it also wasn't charging the thing behind her. She skidded to a stop, almost toppling over with the package, and turned around.

The path behind her was empty.

The rain continued to fall. Thunder echoed hollowly, distantly.

Gussie Dutton hitched her breaths as she looked into a barren trail that was collecting storm water in puddles, leading back to an innocent stand of trees. The painting, still swaddled in its layers of newspaper, was heavy again—heavier now that the rain was soaking into the paper. Newsprint ran over her arms like weeping mascara. Mud slipped down her legs. Shamus trotted up to her and pressed his nose against her hip. Gussie scratched his broad head, watched his tail swing amiably.

Behind her, she heard the screen door of Laylee's shack swing open on its old hinges. Kitchen smells and the pleasant hum of gospel music followed. Gussie Dutton turned and saw the old woman behind the striped waterfall that spilled off the corrugated roof.

"Gawd a'mighty, if you ain't a mess Miss Gussie! Ain't you got the sense to keep out of the rain?"

The first fat drop smacked his face so hard and with such cold, unexpected wrath that he looked up and expected to see a brown-sugar hand on its follow-through. The drop sent a pond ripple through his sinuses.

He had gone to Palaman Creek where he loaded his ten-speed onto the skiff he had hidden there. Now he was paddling up Pigg's Creek. He judged the sky. Lightning flashed. Should he turn back?

Ahead, the sounds of boys splashing across the creek, laughing and moaning. The rain started falling heavily. He hunkered and paddled, blinded from all but the most immediate few feet of river beneath him. To the south, something dark and light flowed like satin through the thick branches, moving to rendezvous with the boys on the approaching bank. He steered the boat to a crop of roots and vines, out of sight, and reached for the baseball bat.

fourteen

"I saw a man back there!" Gussie called out from the tiny cell of a bathroom. "I thought he was tryin to chase me."

"You wasn't hurt, was you child?" Miss Laylee called back from the parlor. Two rooms away, but in this tiny house the old woman might be standing just outside the bathroom door.

"No, he just scared me a little."

Across the miniature house came the smells of stew on the stove and the sounds of the old woman moving to a window—rustle of apron and skirt, jangle of bracelets. "Ain't nobody out there now. Don't you worry, Miss Gussie. That jasper come 'round here, ol Shamus take care of him. Most dark men 'fraid of dogs, you know that?"

Dark men? Is that what he was?

Leeb dishyuh play!

Gussie soaped and toweled newsprint off her sore arms, wiped mud splatters off her shaking legs. In the medicine cabinet, she found a big plastic fork that might be some kind of comb, and she ran it through the damp ringlets of her hair. She made a snarl at herself in the mirror, then a smile. Then let the real expression settle over her features: disappointment. Boo Taylor wasn't here.

Above, thunder boomed monstrously and threatened to collapse the house. The old woman called, "I'd throw them clothes of yours in the dryer, scept'n I ain't never had one. And I don't think it do too good to put them out on the line jes yet. You sure you don't want to take a shower?"

Gussie regarded coffin-sized stall beside her. The rusty shower head came no higher than her shoulder blades. "No thank you, Miss Laylee."

"Oh, I got plenty of hot water if that's what you worryin 'bout."

"No, I guess I'm cleaned off enough now," she said although she still felt gritty all over. She came out of the bathroom, and it took no more than seven strides to cross the parlor and into the kitchen.

Miss Laylee was sitting at the kitchen table, the wrapped painting propped in her lap. "Course I can always give you a bar of soap an' you can gwon back outside to use the Lord's shower. Though, *He* don't appear to be partial to hot water."

"I'm not taking a shower outside!"

Laylee mocked great distress. "Oh, Miss Gussie! There ain't nothin like the smell of hair that been washed in the rain. Get to carry that storm 'round with you all day."

Gussie settled into the deep cushions next to the old woman. "Outside? You take showers in the rain?"

"Why *sure* I do!"

"Right out in the open? *God,* Miss Laylee."

"Right out in the open. Strip naked the way the Lord made me and hop in His shower. Can't be nothin more natural than that. Anyways, it ain't likely somebody gonna come pokin 'round down here to see."

Gussie tried to imagine it: this wrinkled prune of a woman, lathered up beneath the wide-open, storming heavens.

"Why, even Mr. Boo do it," she said. "Least he used to."

"Boo Taylor?" she asked, startled upright on the sofa. "Boo Taylor takes showers in the rain? He gets...naked?"

"Oh, he *used* to all the time, Miss Gussie," she answered, waving a bracelet-spangled wrist. "Couldn't hardly keep that boy in clothes 'round this place. Like a child raised in the jungle he was when he was little—Gawd didn't his momma raise a ruckus? Then, I guess he figure he git too big." She sighed wistfully. "Boy git a bit of fur 'round his jewels, all of a sudden he figure he got to keep 'em hid."

The picture suddenly changed—now it was Boo Taylor in the storm, running a bar of soap across the nude breadth of chest, suds glistering his skin, glistering into the fur *(his jewels!)* between his legs.

Miss Laylee was smiling at her, and Gussie flushed.

"Open your present," Gussie said.

"My present!' she exclaimed. "Now, what on earth...?"

The old woman stripped off the layers of wet newspaper, mouth open with pleasure as the painting emerged.

"Oh *my,* Miss Gussie! Oh *my!*"

It had started as a field of wildflowers; just sponged dapples across the paper, streaks of violet sky above. Then her brush had surprised her by flicking long, perpendicular stalks, and she realized she was adding trees to the scene. The flowers became a patchwork of leaves, crimsons and golds, climbing from the ground to the grip of limbs. Then a splash of more violet in opposition to the sky, becoming a brook tumbling over rocks. The scene emerged as a quiet moment in a forest, crisp with an autumn chill that was nothing at all like the swampy woodlands of Sweetpatch Island; it was someplace far away.

"My, if this ain't the prettiest picture. Just the prettiest!"

"Do you like it, really?"

"Child, it's just wonderful! Lord blessed you with *talent*, Miss Gussie. My, you just so pretty and so smart and so full of *talent*." Miss Laylee beamed at her. "Ain't no wonder Mr. Boo think so much of you."

"It's a thank you gift."

"Well my, it's just the *prettiest*."

While the storm raged, they hung the painting on the parlor wall across from the sofa. Gussie held the painting; Laylee hammered a nail into the flimsy wallboard, her frail old-lady hands managing the hammer with hilarious competence, and somehow Wade's homemade picture frame didn't bring the whole shack tumbling down.

"Looks like a window, Miss Gussie," the old woman said. "Like a window right in the middle of the wall going out to a forest someplace."

The wide molding of the frame did look like a window, Gussie agreed.

"Where is that place, you suppose?" Laylee asked.

"No place, really. A dream place, I guess."

"*Looks* like a dream place. Some place you might want to go to someday."

"*Yes,* Miss Laylee, that's just what it is!"

"Some place a long ways off."

"Where it snows."

"A *pretty* place, anyway. Gawd, you got a talent, child." She clapped her hands happily. "Miss Gussie, Mr. Boo dragged me up a whole bucketful of oysters yesterday. Got some in a stew on the fire if you got a taste for it?"

"Yes ma'am."

"Good. Then you gonna stay and dry up some and eat some supper. And then you gonna tell ol Laylee what she done to earn such a pretty thank you."

The old woman creaked into the kitchen with the flame-haired colt trailing— her voice a whisper-breath, sweet-talking the mongrel pains that had awakened in her joints, aroused there by rupturing clouds and lightning. That was always the way when it stormed, when the air got souped up with surf tang and voltage: old bones quaked, tendons throbbed, ball and sockets swelled, and every hinge screeched under a coat of rust. She spoke to these long-familiar pains, cooed to them, mothered them, stroked them—and then she recognized a completely disparate sensation invading her body. Pain, or just alarm? The slimmest spiderwebs of fire and ice skittering anxiously through her veins. She paused to diagnose it.

(The boy?)

Absently, she lifted a ladle from a rack, dipped and stirred the stew. Henry Ray, Miss Gussie was saying behind her. Her brother, she confessed. Her own brother was the one she had used the poison against, smearing it where he slept. And Boo Taylor shot him.

Of course, she knew all that.

"My brother and my daddy—they were both *here* that night, Miss Laylee, with those other men. Oh, that's so awful; I've been so sick about it! You must think I'm the worst person?"

The girl was sobbing a little now, so the old woman went to comfort her. "No use shamin over family, Miss Gussie. Mostly, you never fair 'bout it. And anyways, there ain't much we can do 'bout who they is."

(But, what was happening to the boy?) "Maybe not, but I'm movin out as soon as I'm old enough. I'm movin off this island as soon as I can."

"Oh, no you ain't, child. An' leave me and Mr. Boo?"

"I am!"

She stroked the girl's hair lovingly and then turned back to the stove, letting the young one tell the rest of her story (still unsettled by that undercurrent hot-and-cold), dragged the ladle obliviously through the pot (the boy, was he at the bridge?), sprinkled in a pinch of rosemary, a nip of dried buckthorn, crumbled in a sprig of cat lashes, a stick of bloodroot. Miss Gussie was talking about another brother now—that boy Wade who just might make something of himself—who had taken a beating or two, Miss Gussie explained, to protect her. Outside, the storm geared up another notch. A thunderclap, like a great tree ripped and tortured through the middle, brought another pulse of uncertainty. The roof exploded under upturned buckets of marbles and nails.

She looked up sharply.

Because someone was watching her. (She was watching someone.)

In the window, the frog, with its glass amphibian hide slickened by the rainwater that flecked through the screen, watched. Crystal eyes. Mirrors reflecting futures and pasts, strobing through generations, cascading ever downward into ocean depths, drowning, falling into other worlds.

Down and down.

Empty.

Not alive.

(But seeing...)

(...*from a gravestone,*
ate up one! licked the other!
boys circling a fire...)

(...the bridge approached, inside her skull, watching the instant of choice...)

(...*warming themselves in pagan ritual, circling the little one who reads to them, succumbed to the flame, to the novelty of a haunted house and medieval graves, to the creepiness of old bones, to the mystery of dark and morbid tales spun by firelight in a storm—she knows what draws a boy, what makes him turn his head from the things he knows are decent; those boys are already lost, lost somewhere deep in the bottomless crystal sockets...but, Mr. Boo was hiding deep in the woods, and she was seeing through his eyes as he weighed his own conscience against such spells...)*

Miss Gussie, behind her, was still speaking: "Then, this army buddy of Henry Ray's shows up last week. *Reepo's* his name, and..."

(And she still heard Miss Gussie, dimly, half-listened at least because her mind had split; she heard from two sets of ears now—one set old and gnarled, the other young and smooth. Saw from two sets of eyes—one set dim and moist, the other bright as a lamp. Snuffled the air with two noses—one brown with gristly old flesh, one bruised and broken. She lifted ten fingers, made spider gesticulations upon the breezes, let the flesh whorls decipher pictographs carved in relief by the flooding raindrops...)

(...*and the man-child was not yet lost! but drawn apart, urged by a smooth young hand on his wrist—not yet lost, though his friends are helpless and gone forever; not yet lost, NOT YET, the boy brought to the brink of the last bridge while the storm rages around him, still clutching his wooden club, still searching the eyes for a truth, doesn't see it yet because he's young and foolish, because she has her black talent for hiding the truth, because she knows what tempts and blinds a boy, boy-child, boy-man...)*

"... and this Reepo boy's so bad, he makes Henry Ray look like a regular prince, you know...?"

(she shutter-flapped her wrinkled eyelids,)

(...fill their ears with her venom, luring him with tart molasses seduction because he is the boy-child, next in line, needs him to keep the generations alive, perpetuate the misery, from generation to generation; otherwise, she would surely rip him to pieces right now, him and those others, his friends, those boys she uses...
"Come with me," she commands, whispers, pleads, aches, tugs; and he has come to the INSTANT of decision, take her or not NOW, swallow or spit NOW, cross over the last bridge or step back NOW, and he holds back, wavers at the brink... compromise?... because...because...he is thinking about, cannot give up...Miss Gussie?)

"...well, he's been stayin at the house, and they drink their beer and get to talkin about..."

(sniffled and scrunched her nostrils,)

(...he hesitates; she turns her eyes upon him, spies him in his dark hiding place, spears him with her gaze, grins the grin of lunatics...)

"...crazy things, I guess. At first it looked like it would be twice as bad as before. And Henry Ray, he's still limpin around, but that..."

(flickered, tapped, whirled her fingertips,)

(...he pulls back—because of Miss Gussie, yes, but also because he is afraid...
... in his fear, the slightest drop of poison leaks down his throat...
...burns there...
...waits there...
...patient...)

"...knee's a whole lot better. So I figure I might have to come down to see you. Get some more..."

(exhales through her knotted throat, because the instant is gone, because the storm—*this* storm—has broken.)

(...not today, but he'll be back, because he tasted the poison, because there will always be other storms...)

"...medicine."

She blinked her eyes clear and stared at the dripping crystal frog. Breathed. Looked down at the kettle and wondered if she threw in too much basil while she was split apart.

She turned to Miss Gussie and fixed her a bright smile.

"...but then two days ago," the girl was saying, "Henry Ray tells us he and Reepo have jobs waitin for them at a textile mill in Decatur, Alabama. Reepo's daddy owns the place, he says. So, he says they're leavin in a few days. *Alabama,* Miss Laylee. That's *hours* away! Miss Laylee, it worked; he's goin away; Henry Ray's leavin for good!"

fifteen

"Miss Gussie, that storm done flown on past, and it's too nice to sit inside, even if we got that pretty window to look out. How about you and me go sit on the porch an' watch the sunset. Sunset after a storm is always the best."

Miss Laylee switched on the radio, and tinny prayer songs crackled with lightning ghosts as they stepped out to the porch. Gussie felt light and giddy now that the story was purged. The clouds had drifted over the mainland where the lowering sun put on a spectacular fireworks show of sparks across the leafy wet garden rows and scattered puddles. Gussie looked out on this, savoring the leftover storm scents. *My hair could smell like that,* she thought, recalling Laylee's story of showering in the rain.

A shower in the rain?

She had another image of Boo Taylor's naked body.

She glanced at the old woman who was grinning at her.

"It was some kind of magic, wasn't it?" Gussie asked finally. "What you did to Henry Ray, I mean."

"What did I do to Henry Ray?"

"You know. *Was* it magic? Are you really a witch?"

Laylee Colebriar crinkled her forehead with a look of amusement. She reached for Gussie's arm. "Child, you s'pect you really want to know?"

"Yes ma'am, I want to know."

Laylee shook her head affectionately. "Honey, what you got to know is this: sometimes askin 'bout a thing can spoil it. That's mostly what magic is, you see? It's in what *ain't* said. It's in the *secret.*"

Sounds of movement beneath them, something big and alive; Shamus was crawling out from under the porch. He shook once, spraying flecks of rain and old leaves. Then he looked off expectantly toward the woods and wagged his tail.

"Mr. Boo's comin," Laylee announced.

Gussie looked up hopefully, saw nothing but the big gray dog loping several steps to the edge of the garden. The dog sat, shoulders and ears perked high, tail swishing through wet grass. A few moments later, Boo Taylor appeared, pushing his bike up a sheltered trail in the woods.

"S'pect he's gonna want some supper," Laylee said, and she stood from the rocker— and then abruptly stopped. She gazed fiercely toward the boy. She frowned.

Gussie watched the dim boy shape coming through the trees. Then she saw another form, somewhere behind Boo Taylor in the trees. Someone taller and darker. She saw a flutter of white. A dress, billowing, long dark hair. She watched as the figure raised its hand and waved, laughing a gleeful, muddy chuckle.

sixteen

The remnant storm crackled somewhere far across the western sky where only the faintest blooms of pinks and oranges and violets separated night from day. Gussie stalked north with arms folded at her chest, stalked slightly hunched under the weight of her temper and watched the darkening route unveil with her steps.

Damn Boo Taylor!

She had done it again. He had *made* her do it again. Oh, that boy could be so infuriating! Just when she was ready to like the boy, really *like* him...

"Oh, hey there Gussie, what are you doing here?"—just as sweet and innocent as could be, rolling his bike toward her, bat poking stiffly from the basket while that evil girl was laid back in the woods somewhere, *gloating.*

"Playin games back there with your friend, Boo Taylor? Didn't know they had a baseball field in those woods."

"I wasn't—oh no, I was playin by the shell pile earlier. Then I thought I'd go—you know, just see the place, and I got stuck there in the rain."

"Oh, how horrible for you. Just you and your smutty little friend, stuck out there all alone in that house."

She looked up and around to get her bearings. The road bent around to the left and toward the bridge over Soap Water Creek. A low scimitar moon pierced the clear eastern sky, glinting its silver blade across the wet leaves and scattered puddles, just enough of a glow to make out the road ahead.

"It wasn't like that, Gussie."

She could have left it at that. After all, nothing would have happened back at that house; he was just a *boy*.

(but didn't he seem older now…?)

And Crystal Burne was really too old to be interested in him anyway,

(like…Murphy?)

and what in God's name was she thinking? And why should she even *care* so much?

She could have just left it at that and sat there with him and enjoyed his company while he ate Miss Laylee's oyster stew. And when he so casually asked her if she wanted a ride home she could have said yes, and right now she could be holding onto his chest and looking in to his wide back and breathing in the smell of him on that rushing breeze.

"Wasn't like that? What was she like then? Did she keep you warm in the rain?"

Instead, she was out seething her redneck temper across the dark roads of South Patch. She was coming to the bridge over Soap Water Creek now, and on gut impulse she slowed.

Had it gotten quiet?

What happened to the crickets and frogs?

A mosquito lit on her cheek. She swatted it, grunted at herself and started forward again. She reached the bridge: a low span of wooden beams, no more than twenty yards across. The timbers, well worn and splintered under a million footfalls over the years. The grain had thoroughly absorbed the rainwater, and as she touched down on the first of them, the wood soaked up her sneaker like a sponge. The creek beneath was a sluggish drag of oil drifting on the receding tide toward the Yamawichee. Stalks of cordgrass and cattails overran the driftwood rails at either bank and where oxeye daisies bobbed and winked their irises under the fetid breath of a marsh wind.

Crossing an empty bridge. At nighttime.

She stopped. Listened. Then hurried.

The echo of *Billy Goat's Gruff* and a dozen other fairy tales from childhood butterflied in her stomach. Trolls lived beneath such bridges, didn't they? Trolls and other wraiths and demons burrowed in the exile of mud and shadow, foul-breathed zombies with mossy, idiot intelligence, listening, always listening, for the trip-trap presage of approaching innocence.

And hadn't she seen one of those trolls earlier today? Watching her from this very bridge before sneaking ahead of her somehow and lying in wait in the woods.

Leeb dishyuh play!

Now lying in wait in the waters below among the slimy creek things. He was peering at her through the slits between the sodden beams, and if she looked down she would see the phosphorescence of troll eyes staring back. Soon, two dripping arms would reach up from the banks, grab hold of the weak rails...

The creek's gurgle became his whisper.

Leave this place!

Not daring to look down, she quickened her stride, aimed for the moonshade on the other side, and finally stepped from waterlogged bridge to solid street.

The fluttering panic quieted.

Think of something *nice.* Something safe and real. Not home, where she was headed—a place she could never think of as safe again. Think of...school! School, with its sturdy brick walls and brightly lit hallways, open again when the new term began in just over a week. Just next week, so close now, and Boo Taylor would be there every day!

She was ten steps past the bridge when a piece of shadow split away from the woods ahead and charged her. She gaped, not believing it.

It made a slobbery, hungry grunt.

The troll! she thought and, in her brain, bellowed at the unfairness of it: *but it's not supposed to be in the woods—it's supposed be under the bridge!* It bounded at her on a wounded shuffle, like an ape. For another frozen moment, she was locked in horrible fascination.

Then, when she realized how fast it was coming, terror blasted through her, got her moving; she turned, lunged, blundered back toward the bridge.

Oh God, not back there, not back there, that's where he LIVES!

She raced onto the bridge and heard-felt the lopsided scurryings and ravenous mewlings close in on her. *Laylee's house!* she thought frantically—sanctuary, beacon in the south. But how far away this time? *Miles?*

She made it to the middle of the bridge before rough knuckles scraped her neck and swept her hair into a bunch. Fire ripped across her scalp. Her head snapped back and she screamed. She went tumbling to the deck of the bridge. The troll collapsed across her, all brute heaviness, hot and dank, reeking of sweat and fermented fruit. A fat hand clamped over her face, blinding her. She screamed again, wordless, mindless, and the hand slithered down to smother it.

Her eyes freed, she blinked at the leering mask hovering over her. She gasped.

He breathed on her. Pressed stale beer and cigarette spittle against her cheek. "Hey sweet little baby," he whispered. "Been waitin for you most the day. Oh I been waitin so long, so *long,* so *looooonng.*"

The crescent moon sat on Henry Ray's shoulder and mocked his grin. She screamed under his hand and it came out as a worthless muffle.

"Aw baby, don't yell, please don't yell," he moaned. "Just a little present 'fore I go away is all, baby doll, just a little thing's all."

She was pinned to the wet planks of the bridge, old rainwater soaking her blouse, old splinters gnawing her back. Her left arm was free, and she swung it around. The heel of her palm clapped into his ear. He grunted and rolled so his elbow was crammed into her breast.

All breath exploded from her lungs, into his hand.

"What's my sweet baby doll doin down here in niggerland anyway? They like to hurt my baby, those dirty fuckin niggers, oh baby, so sweet, so *sweeeeeeet.*"

Her rib cage was going to collapse any moment under all that piercing weight. His hand was moving now, away from her hair—pain suddenly released from her scalp; she had forgotten about it with the unbearable pressure on her lungs. The hand went around her shoulders, but his elbow still furrowed into her chest.

Oh God, please…make him…him get off; I can't…breathe!

Firefly winks crossed her vision, crossed Henry Ray's face; in the sky beyond, the moon doubled its size, tripled it brightness, smothering her brain in a phantasm of light. She flapped her hand at the air.

…can't…breathe…oh God…

And then he was on his knees, and the stabbing bulk came free from her chest. His hand came away from her mouth. She gulped oxygen. It swelled into her lungs, full and painful, but it wasn't enough, so she forced it out and dragged in another breath. Henry Ray picked her up, gathered her arms roughly at her back. He began to drag her backward, using one arm to pin her forearms together while the other was crooked around her throat.

"Ain't gonna hurt you, honey, no I ain't gonna hurt my little girl."

"Stop it," she choked.

The clamp on her throat tightened. "*Please,* baby. Just a little thing's all I want, oh please, just one little sweet thing, sweet baby, oh it's so *pretty.*"

Her left heel got caught between planks, and her sneaker pulled free. She looked at it helplessly, at the moonlit stretch of bridge and road beyond unwinding southward while she was tugged in the opposite direction.

"Let me *go!*"

His arm clenched sharply, choking off her air and forcing her chin to the sky where all she could see was the the idiot smile of the moon. Her feet struck the hardpan on the north side of the bridge. Suddenly the fear of what he was going to do to her—the *knowing* of it—blasted through her heart. She planted her right foot and kicked her bare heel back, only glancing his shin.

"Stop it, *stop* it!" he growled and jerked her off of her feet.

Pain rippled through her shoulders; the bones in her neck were strained to the brink of snapping. *He's going to break my neck!* she thought dumbly, *he thinks he's going to rape me, oh God, but my neck is going to break first!* She kicked wildly, both feet now, as another field of lights and colors misted over her eyes, mingling with the lost stars and moon. Her sneakered heel smacked into his wounded knee, and he howled.

"Ow, goddammit, you fuckin *bitch, STOP IT!"*

He swung her around, reared back his fist. Something hard—a rock, an oak log, an iron bar—crashed into her temple.

Floating.

Flung in the air, light as a dead leaf on a November breeze. She rode the sky, floating higher and higher. Carried on balloon strings.

So nice to float.

Stars, clearer now, closer now. She tried to reach for one. Her fingers (she saw them opening) reached out and came very close to the nearest of the stars. Coming closer as she floated higher. She reached. Even when the ground rushed up to slam against her skull, her back, her shoulders, she still reached. And now that loamy damp bed rose with her.

Almost there! Almost have it!

Then she frowned because the stars went black as some blocky presence eclipsed the night sky. Yellow-gray teeth took the place of the stars. An ink-stitched skull took the place of the moon.

She tasted blood.

Some animal was tugging greedily at her breasts. The smells were all stinks, all liquid putrescence—marsh water and sweat, flat beer and fresh blood. Now, the animal was tugging between her legs, urging them apart. Her thighs slid open across wet grass. A snout, lumped and calloused, shoved itself rudely up her skirt and nipped at the fabric of her panties. Stop it! Stop it, you! She tried to swat it away, but her rag-doll limbs failed her. And was that the animal's voice now? Growling. It sounded (...drifting...on the surface of rough seas...) like a dog. And there was Henry Ray's face, so close to hers, and he was shouting at the dog; his face was bunched up like a fist—almost like a dog itself with that droopy blond mustache framing all those wet, snarling, snapping, yellow teeth.

She moved her head and looked toward the (...hovering in place...gently flying ...) sounds of the growling dog. *There,* a blackness, an anti-light, a point where the other light was neither absorbed nor reflected. Huge. Shoulders bunched threateningly. Red eyes, like blood set aflame. Teeth, much sharper than Henry Ray's, sharper than any razor, bared in an expression of slavering madness.

Shamus! she thought, but it couldn't be Shamus. This animal was too dark, *much* too dark. And though Shamus was big, this thing was a giant! The size of a bull! And Shamus could never manage to look so utterly insane with fury.

And then it came to her on a dizzy, zigzagging tumble of insights: she was looking at the *Beast!* The Beast of the Patch! The fairy tales *were* true, and wasn't it amazing to discover that from his high, floating place. She wanted to tap Henry Ray on the shoulder and tell him her discovery: *Henry Ray, it's the Beast! The Beast!*

She lifted her arm. Her head ached with the effort, but the arm *was* moving, and as she focused harder it lifted higher. She reached up (oh, how her head ached!) and brushed her fingers on Henry Ray's neck.

He batted her hand away without taking his eyes from the Beast. He was still shouting at it, and now she could make out some of the words.

"*...right now, you little cocksucker, or I'll rip your fuckin head...*"

She twisted her head again—pure, spangled agony—back to the Beast. It wasn't the Beast at all; it was the ghost-man. The big black man with the glowing eyes, only now those eyes weren't glowing seashell whiteness, they had gone a fierce red. How could she have thought it was a dog when it was *this* great hulk of a man? He was standing in the middle of the road, snarling with all the same feral insanity as the Beast. Like the Beast, he was a patch of lightlessness, a hole in the night, a blank spot in the galaxy. And no wonder Henry Ray was screaming at the man. But he was a ghost, too, and Henry Ray didn't know that.

"*...don't you fuckin dare, boy, you little fuck, don't you even...*"

Her arm came up easier this time. Both arms. Her head throbbed mercilessly. She flailed her hands against Henry Ray's chest. And this time when he batted them away, she swung them back, harder. She clawed at the flesh of his cheek, fishhooking her thumb inside his mouth. Why was she doing this—why was she trying to hurt him? For Godsakes, Henry Ray was her *brother!*

You don't understand, it's the ghost-man, Henry Ray! He's coming to get us; he's coming to get us!

Struggling with Henry Ray, she craned her head again to look for the ghost-man on the street. He was there, flickering in and out of the whirling snaps and flashing pulses of her bruised vision—taller now, then blinking into something small and lighter and coiled like a new bedspring, like a copperhead ready to strike, then taller again and all smooth, patient blackness. Her head, oh God, she groaned at the anvil-pounding of her temple.

Something bright and shiny, silver and blue, twinkled and sighed and spun a purring glitter from its side. An abandoned, cold metal carcass on the soggy foot-beams of the bridge.

"Don't *want* a ride!" she cried, clutching and unclutching at Henry Ray's hands. "Get out of here; he'll *hurt* you!"

"Get *off* her; leave her *alone!*"

It was Boo Taylor's voice coming from that blackness. His face *(ain't he a handsome one?)* wavering in and out, darkness and lightness. Here was the man-thing's shadow, and now that handsome face again. The face, fading, then back; blue-green defiance streaked like Zorro's mask beneath his eyes.

"...that fuckin thing down, boy. Put that fucking thing DOWN!"

"You get *off* her!"

"I'll wrap that thing around your goddamn *head!*"

"Get *off!*"

The great darkman tottered forward, club twirling, trembling high over his head. So cautious, why would something so immense, so *formidable,* move with such caution? Surely, he had nothing to fear. Then, shadow and light seesawed again, and it was Boo Taylor—so small now—coming forward with his baseball bat.

Henry Ray's hot, sweating mass swagged off of her. "Gonna fuck you up *good,* boy!"

She rocked up to her knees, and an entire new string of lights burst through her brain. The dog was back—the air above her was suddenly a horrible, wet shattering of barks and growls and roars. An urgent heat tumbled through the ground around her, grunts, words spit like loose rocks, flesh smacked, clothes ripped. A shriek of pain.

She stood up. The lights fell away now like the waning glitters of fireworks. She saw Boo Taylor, crouched over his bicycle at the border of street and bridge, just the frailest deer-boned thing under Henry Ray's lion bulkiness. Boo was getting to his feet as Henry Ray pounced toward him and swung his right fist around like a wrecking ball. The fist hammered full-on into Boo Taylor's face, cartwheeling him over the bike.

Boo made a breathy gurgle when he landed. Gussie rushed forward, fell back to earth when her bare foot slipped on something round and smooth.

"You little *fuck!*" Henry Ray screamed. "You stupid little *fuck!*"

Boo Taylor, breathless now: "...you...get away..."

Gussie rifled through the grass and dirt for the baseball bat she'd just tripped over. She found it, wrapped her hands around it. She looked up to see Henry Ray's back as he was taking another step toward Boo Taylor. Boo teetered backward and onto the bridge, completely uncoiled now, his arms spread in loose-fisted wings, bracing against the bridge's rails. Blackness dripped around his mouth, as if he had slopped a chocolate malt over himself. A leg buckled under him, he collapsed to one knee.

"... get...away..."

"Fuck you, snot nose!"

"Get away!" Gussie roared.

She sprang forward with Boo Taylor's bat raised two-fisted over her head—limping from grass to dirt road to wooden planks. Henry Ray was turning toward her as she unleashed a wild hatchet swing.

She had a moment to see surprise inflame his eyes.

Then the bat cracked into his injured left knee.

He yowled.

He crumpled to the floor of the bridge, still turning, and lunged for her off of his good leg. She dodged. His fingers swiped emptily down her skirt and legs.

"Shit, shit, *shit! Aaahhwwl goddammit!*"

He tried to push up again. She chopped the bat down again. It thunked into a bone in his shoulder, and he roared.

"Just get away!" she screamed at him. Scream and effort brought black spots and flickers of light to her eyes. She could barely make out Henry Ray crawling toward her, his face twisted up at her, a contortion of anger and disbelief.

"You *hit* me! You hit my fuckin *leg!*"

"I'll *kill* you!" she warned, backing away dizzily. Cattail fingers reached up from the creek's bank and tickled her arms. Her spine touched the brittle barrier of the bridge's railing. She slid down the railing, deeper into the bridge and away from Henry Ray. Splinters snagged on her blouse. She looked up frantically for Boo Taylor and found him still wobbling on one knee at the end of the bridge.

Henry Ray let out a wounded howl and lunged again. She pitched away from him, the rail creaking dangerously with her weight. She flicked out the bat and cracked his elbow.

"*Ow,* goddammit!"

"Henry Ray, you go on now," she squeaked.

He was inching closer. "Don't you hit me with that fuckin bat again."

"Get away."

"Put it *down!*"

"No!" she shouted and wagged the bat threateningly in his face. He snatched for it and caught the end of it in his right hand. She tried pulling it back, but he quickly brought around his other hand, and his grip was solid. "Let *go* of it!" she yelled uselessly as her arms were yanked back and forth.

"*Give it!*"

"*Let go!*"

Henry Ray was getting to his feet again, jerking the bat, jolting her elbows, her shoulders. Her fingers began to slip.

Behind him, Boo Taylor sobbed and bull-rushed. He collided with Henry Ray and slammed him into the railing.

Henry Ray yelped, tried to right himself.

But the bat was back in her hands. She swung it around. Hard. Wailing. It whacked solidly into Henry Ray's forehead.

Sounds of rocks colliding, driftwood splitting, lungs gasping. The bat suddenly became two bats: one piece still in her fists, the other whipping end over end into the cattails.

Henry Ray's shoulders crashed through the brittle railing. The rest of his body followed, arched backward in the curled shape of the moon. Then, like a ghost, he disappeared soundlessly into the black waters of Soap Water Creek.

seventeen

Gussie staggered away from the gap in the railing. She looked dumbly at the broken stick in her hands. Then she looked toward the water where the splash had come and gone, and where now there was only a thick silence.

He'll drown in there, she thought with a vague dismay, but that quickly turned to relief.

"Are you okay?" Boo Taylor's voice reached her. She looked for him and found him sitting lazily on the bridge floor.

She dropped the bat handle. "Yes."

"I think I broke my nose again." He was trying to stand. Gussie went to him and hauled him up. "Am I bleeding?" he asked. He dabbed a forearm across his upper lip. Blood came away on his arm.

"A little."

"You're bleeding, too." He brought a finger up to her face. He touched the corner of her lips, and she hissed.

Then, below, the slow pulse of the creek began to churn roughly. The un-drowned troll was thrashing up for air.

"Come on!" she whispered. She tugged Boo Taylor's arm.

Splashes moving beneath. The clear bark of a cough. On the north bank, reeds and cattails broke apart in a violent rustling. Gussie hurried to the south—flop-step, flop-step, flop-stepping on her one sneaker, with Boo Taylor staggering along willingly. When they reached the end of the bridge, she hurled Boo around the rail and into the weeds of the southern bank. She huddled there next to him, wrapped within the stiff, sharp stalks, breathing the sulfur marsh smells and letting the murky water and creek mud squish around her bare toes and fill her single sneaker.

They listened to the sounds of a wild boar climbing to the far side of the bridge.

Mosquitoes and other things scrambled over Gussie's flesh. Her head pounded; her skull had shrunk and couldn't seem to hold all the pulsing mass of her brain. Her lip was puffed like a toad and tender. How much worse was Boo Taylor? She looked for him in the shadows beside her, but the darkness here was complete. She could only feel him, teetering on his haunches like a drunk.

A full minute passed.

Then another.

Then, jarringly, an engine roared to life. Gussie inched her swelling-shrinking head through the reeds to see. Headlights splashed out of the woods on the far side of the bridge, and Henry Ray's Plymouth snorted onto the road.

It aimed northward, and she relaxed.

Until the car screeched to a stop. Brake lights threw a red glow on the trees. Boo was rising next to her as the brighter reverse lights flicked on, and she yanked him back down by the shirt. "He's coming back."

The Plymouth backed swiftly toward the bridge. Hunkered in the weeds, her eyes raced around the bank and she saw how poorly they were hidden and how vulnerable. Maybe they should slip under the bridge, she thought, and then heard the back-and-forth grind of metal and the squeal of tires. Henry Ray was running over Boo Taylor's bicycle.

"Oh," Boo said nasally, dizzily.

The red glow winked out. Then, one final and longest squeal as the car tore to the north.

At last, the engine roar faded beyond the trees.

Silence again.

Then the crickets and frogs were back.

Gussie stood. Boo Taylor seemed unable to do so on his own, so she helped him. When she began the climb up the bank, she lost her other sneaker to a straw-sucking tug of the mud. Barefoot, she led Boo to the firm dirt of the road.

I can't go home, now, she realized. *He might be there, oh God, he might be waiting there. I can't even go home! Where am I supposed to go?*

"That was your brother," Boo said.

Anger and a familiar shame throbbed inside her head with all the other pulsing clutter. She dropped Boo's arm.

"I know," she said dully and sat down. She felt the places where Henry Ray's fingers had touched her; his flesh still lingered there on a vile slug's trail. Her breasts, his hands had been on her breasts; her bra was still clasped in place, but her blouse was untucked from the skirt; his hands had slid up her stomach, her ribs, and he had been kneading her breasts through her bra. And his hand had been between her *legs,* too, at the skin inside her thighs.

Boo was wiping the blood away from his face. "Gussie, why would your brother want...to hurt you?"

Nausea rose like seaweed in her throat. "Boo, shut up, okay?" Shame and sickness, it was suddenly too much.

"But why would he—"

"Don't *ask* that."

"Gussie, but—"

"Boo Taylor shut up!" She glared at him through the dark, brought her hands up to his bloodied chest, ready to push him away. Then pain and sickness rose up and wrapped over her in a swamp-soaked blanket. She *did* push away from him, crawling to the road's edge where a great fist grabbed her, squeezed her stomach. Her whole body clenched with a violent shudder, and she threw up.

She went to her hands and knees and threw up again.

When it was over, she hunched in the grass, shivering. Her head was pounding worse now, and her chest and throat were raw. But the sickness was gone.

Boo's hand made soothing circles on her back. "Gussie, I'm sorry," he said softly.

She spat a sour, oystery film. It hung in a rope from her lips, and she had to reach up and flick it away with her fingers.

"When you're ready," he said, "I'll...well, I guess I'll *walk* you home."

"No!" she barked at him.

"Gussie—"

She scrambled away from him. "Get away, get away from me." She was weeping now. "I don't *have* a home, so just get *away!"*

He floundered after her, grabbed her around the waist and brought her back to the ground in a bear hug. "Get away!" she screamed, flailing at him.

"Gussie, don't!"

"I *hate* you!"

"Gussie, you're hurt."

"Get away, Boo Taylor, I hate you!" She thrashed in his arms, smearing his blood all over herself as the full volcanic enormity of her redneck temper blasted through her and swallowed him. But he wouldn't let go.

At last, in futility and weariness, she surrendered and collapsed in his arms, sobbing. She clutched the pouch that dangled at his chest. A tingle went through her hand and down her arm.

It was like floating again.

Boo Taylor stroked her back, rocked her, whispered gently to her as if she were an infant. He said her name over and over. She moved her cheek over his bloodied chest. "Don't go back there," she said and heard it spoken as a sob. "Boo, please don't go back to that old house with that girl again."

His rocking faltered.

Then, he whispered, "I won't."

"It's...*bad* back there."

"I know."

"Promise me."

"I promise."

"Boo, Murphy's not...I'm not..." She fell back into his arms. "Just don't go back to that girl again."

He rocked her. Chanted.

"...*Gussie*..."

(...floating...)

"Will you take me back to Laylee's house?" she asked. She looked up to his eyes. "Do you think she'll let me stay there tonight?"

"Yes. Of course she will."

He smiled, and on any other night of her life, the blood ringing his mouth would make the smile gruesome.

(...floating...rising to meet...)

Tonight, she drifted up to his smile and kissed him.

Part Five

Indiscretions

Look, her hair, how lovely,
It spills like blood down that long, long neck.
How lovely she hates
And how her teeth glitter red
                                    —*Easterman*

The bell above the office door jingled alive. Boo Taylor stepped inside the air-conditioned Taylor Dufette Realty office where a plump woman with short, curly hair greeted him with a smile. The woman introduced herself as Debbie Giegerman and offered to find Gussie Ransome for him when he asked.

He stood alone in the waiting room for several minutes, glancing through a brochure of rental properties. He tried to guess locations by the photographs.

Then he saw her, flipping a red-gold waterfall casually away from her face. She was framed in the window of a door, and he caught the moment her eyes first caught him, when the brightness within blinked on like two green lights on a Christmas tree. She came through the door. Billowy white blouse, dark skirt with a wide belt, very professional. She was leveling her green lights upon him. She seemed anxious, but not surprised to see him.

"Wade told me what happened," she said, her voice hushed. "Your *fingers,* Boo. How could that be?"

He placed the brochure back on the table. It was hard to keep from staring at her. "I tried to call you," he said.

"So I hear. You didn't actually tell Murphy to blow you. Did you?"

"Yes. Why, does he want to take me up on it?"

"Very funny. Murphy was furious." She stepped forward, reaching a hand out for him. "Boo, are you okay? I can't believe what Wade told me."

Her hand was on his forearm.

"I don't want to bother you at work," he said.

"Don't worry about that."

"I'm sorry about lunch the other day. I didn't want—"

"Boo, stop." She took another step forward and looked around self-consciously. Debbie Giegerman had returned to her seat behind the reception desk and was pretending not to listen. Gently, Gussie steered him deeper into the waiting area.

"You don't have to apologize," she said in a low voice. "Anyway, not anymore than I do. Boo, how could your fingers...? Are you all right?"

"Wade didn't tell you the rest of it, did he?"

"What's the rest of it?"

"What was written on the mirror. He didn't tell you?"

"No. Boo, what are you talking about?"

He noticed the thin web of scars at her cheek, hidden in the shadow of her hair. "Look, Gussie, I don't want you thinking any of what happened when we were younger was your fault. That's really not what I meant the other day."

"It's not?"

He smiled. "No. Believe it or not."

For a while it seemed she wanted to say something but couldn't.

He spoke again: "Anyway, I'm sure my welcome's almost worn out. I'm leaving soon, and I want you to know how——"

In a sudden and graceful movement, she rose forward to kiss him, silencing him even as his lips formed the next word *(sorry)* of this practiced speech.

He breathed her in. Tasted her.

A moment later, her face pulled away. Wide, green eyes glittered into him.

how sorry I am

for what I've done (am about to do) to your life

He held her out at arms length. "Can you take a ride with me?" he asked.

two

They took his rented Buick to the house on Culpepper Street. She got out to follow him to the back stoop where he reached through a broken window and opened the door.

She trailed him upstairs, looking into his wide back as she went, feeling instinctively the need to be quiet. As they climbed, a gradually increasing weight pressed down on her shoulders, her legs. They reached the landing, and he led her to the bathroom against a heavy hand that was trying to push her backward. As they approached the door, the force working against her was so great she had to grab the doorframe to pull herself forward.

Still unspeaking, he stepped aside, letting her see.

In blotchy red lipstick, she read her assault on him from twenty years earlier.

Boo Taylor is a LYING SNOB BASTARD!

She saw her reflection through the words.

three

"Don't take me back to the office," she told him.

They were in the car, on Pofoksgo heading east. They came abreast of a billboard announcing *SOLOMON GOODY, DEMOCRAT FOR U.S. CONGRESS!* and he stopped and turned to her.

"Where do you want me to take you?"

She directed him to the entrance of the *Sing Satterfield Wildlife Refuge* where they parked in a sandy, mostly vacant lot. To the west, palmettos dripped toward an open swampy area. Egrets and herons waded in the muddy shallows, spearing tiny fish. A mother and two little boys were posing for a photograph by a sign that read, PLEASE! DO NOT ATTEMPT TO FEED THE ALLIGATORS!

"Wait here," she told him.

He stood by the car while she went inside the Welcome House. After what seemed like an inordinately long spell, she finally emerged again, swinging her purse over her shoulder and waving a trail map at him.

"Let's go for a walk."

"Will we need that?" He was pointing at the map. "This place practically used to be my backyard."

"You'll be surprised how much it's all changed," she told him. She kicked off her shoes and dropped them through the car window.

Barefoot, she took him to an opening in the woods where they entered the trail. Oak branches dangled Spanish moss just above their heads. Boo Taylor looked at the thick growth surrounding them; he judged the Yamawichee was maybe two hundred yards to their right. Pigg's Creek would be another half-mile ahead. Laylee Colebriar's house, had it survived, would have been just a hundred yards or so south of the Welcome House.

They passed a narrow path that split off to the left. A small wooden sign for *Daffodil Lane* was planted at the entrance. Boo looked down the trail and saw a small cottage.

"What's that?" he asked.

She brushed up against his shoulder. She was walking close enough to him that he wondered if he was supposed to hold her hand. "They rent cabins to tourists here," she told him. "Boo, who else knew about that?"

"Knew about what?"

"About what I—what I painted on the wall back at that college?"

"Everybody on the third floor at Brown House."

She smiled. "I mean, who did you *tell?*"

The woods began to thin, and he sensed a clearing not far ahead. "No one," he said. "Who did *you* tell?"

She blanched. "Are you kidding me? Who would I tell? That was probably the most humiliating day of my *life*."

"Did you tell Murphy about it?"

She walked quietly for a few paces. Then, slightly hostile, she said, "No, I most certainly did not tell Murphy Ransome what I spray painted on your dormitory wall."

"What about Wade?"

"No," she said. "I don't know. Maybe."

A squirrel darted past, then disappeared again beneath the undergrowth. They took a bend in the trail and came to a meadow overflowing with white blooms of myrtle so thick the place seemed covered in snow. He was reminded of Christmas again. He looked at Gussie and found her green, glittering eyes watching him.

"What I mean is, who could be doing this?" she asked.

"I don't know. Ghosts," he said. "Maybe Crystal Burne is still alive. What does Wade have to say about it?"

She rolled her eyes. "He's *crazy* about it. He's so upset, he doesn't know *what* to think, except maybe someone with an old grudge."

"An old grudge."

"Maybe Crystal Burne *is* still alive somewhere." She looked at him, then looked down, uncomfortable. "Or maybe..."

Boo was expecting this, and he finished for her. "Or maybe I did it myself," he said. "Right?"

Gussie didn't answer.

He shook his head.

Of course, he had been the one to find the burlap doll on the pier. And he had been at the same house on Culpepper, just a few nights earlier, chasing little girls no one else had seen, speaking to ghosts no one else had heard. The doll got on the pier because he put it there himself. Those words got on the mirror because he broke into the house and wrote them there.

Churches were burned. Children were killed.

Where had he been then?

They moved from shadow to light, through the mosaic perfumes of dung and forest and myrtle blooms and animal hides. At his side, Gussie was contemplative. Looking at her, he wondered, what did *she* think?

"I was with you," she said. "Back then, it happened to *both* of us. Wade doesn't understand because he wasn't there; he didn't *see*. I mean—I mean those *fingers,* Boo. How could that be possible?"

Instinctively, he glanced down at his right hand. "Haven't you heard? I cut them off myself," he said. "I've been keeping them in a pickle jar in the back of my refrigerator for the last twenty-five years."

He held out his hand. A moment later, Gussie took it in hers.

four

The mauled hand was beneath hers; she ran her thumb over ancient gnarls of pink scar, worn and hardened through the years, and this was proof that monsters really did lurk in the shadows.

It happened to both of us.

Things bled. Things died. Some things, though badly wounded, survived.

The sensation of his flesh against hers, real enough, coursed on an anxious current up through her wrist, her forearm, her elbow, spreading higher to her shoulder, and then into her breast.

"You believe in spooks, Miss Gussie?"

The old woman had asked that question twenty-some summers ago not far from this very spot. This was before the scars, the ruination of flesh, the deaths. She had answered, *"I don't know,"* because she hadn't yet learned better.

"You believe in the Lord? In the Bible?'

"Yes ma'am,"

"You believe in Jesus and his saints?"

"Yes."

"And the angels? And all them devils and demons pesterin folks in the Bible? 'Cause that's all spooks is, really. White spooks and black spooks, good and evil, believe or don't believe, there's things about that you can't see, touch, smell. Things that love you like their very own, or kill you jes the same."

A faint clatter whispered from somewhere nearby.

"It was a long time ago," Boo said.

Yes.

"Did we just imagine it?"

Her hand tightened around his. *No*, she thought. *We have the scars to prove it.*

The trail beneath her feet was cool. She walked, digging her toes in the cool, sandy dirt, tugging Boo Taylor deeper into the labyrinthine woods. The trees and the sky and the great mounds of white blossoms all seemed amplified now that she had his hand inside hers. The connection with his skin had ignited something inside her and was altering her perception.

"Do you remember that time it snowed?" he asked.

She looked at him. "Barely. Why?" For some reason, she had been thinking about snow, too.

"Did I ever tell you what Laylee had to say about snowflakes?"

She frowned, shook her head.

"She said snowflakes are angels. When it snows it's the angels coming down from heaven to visit the people on earth."

He squeezed her hand.

Angels.

Devils and demons.

He was reading her mind.

"That's a nice thought," she said.

"I haven't been able to walk through a snowstorm since without feeling like I was stepping into heaven."

She realized his eyes were the same color of the old jeans he was wearing. She said, "This is a little like heaven, isn't it?"

A lethargic breeze touched off another glass-rattle echo. They were coming to a sharp turn in the trail where ivory piles of myrtle accumulated into a high wintry drift. Ahead, just above the highest spread of oak greenery, she saw the first jagged shadow of mortar and block. She only saw it because she knew where to look. Then it was gone as the woods grew up around them again.

"This feels like a maze," he said. "We haven't seen anyone since we left the parking lot."

"Are you lost? I told you we'd need a map."

The smell of marsh was growing thicker, more noxious. After another turn, they came to a rickety wooden hump spanning a stretch of pluff mud and a wide, brackish stream.

Boo Taylor stopped walking, forcing her to stop, too. "This is Pigg's Creek," he said. She watched as he took in the surrounding cedars and oaks, the steep bank, the soupy flow of water that had grown two or three times wider since his youth. "We're at Pigg's Point, aren't we? I used to keep a boat here."

The footbridge was narrow, climbing precariously on knobby stilts and looking like something from a fairy tale.

"Who built that thing?" he asked. He was pointing at the bridge.

"I suppose Sing Satterfield did. I hear she wants to renovate Chaliboque and turn it into a museum."

A thick chain barricaded the entrance to the bridge.

DANGER! BRIDGE IS UNSAFE, CROSSING NOT PERMITTED

"*Renovate* it," he said. "They should burn it. Is it really still back there?"

She nodded and pulled him several paces eastward where another break in the trees offered a glimpse of the decaying battlements of the old mansion, now nearly lost in the wild growth of vines and trees.

Boo took the map from her. He unfolded it and scanned the trails. "Look at this," he said. "They've marked the old graveyard and the old stables. They've even set up *picnic* benches there." He turned to her. "Have you ever gone over there?"

"Never. Not since..."

He turned back to Chaliboque; his blue-jean eyes betrayed the lure of the place. He leaned toward it. "Should we try to cross?" he asked. "Take a look at it?"

"Don't be stupid."

"You don't want to see it?"

"No. Not even a little bit. And anyway, that bridge looks like it's gonna collapse any minute."

She had a fleeting memory of Boo Taylor and Laylee Colebriar walking side by side, leaving her alone, sending her north while the two of them traveled toward the hidden graveyard on some terrible errand. Then she remembered what was buried back there and why he was drawn to it.

She felt her hand rising to pick brambles off his shirt, felt the cloth yield beneath her fingers, felt his skin beneath. He turned his head. He looked down to watch her fingers move across his body, and she smelled the sourness of his sweat in the shirt. "You'll have to look for ticks when you get out of these," she told him softly.

One of her fingers rose to touch the deep crow's feet above his cheek. And then his breath became hers. She drew it deeply into her lungs and held it there as she relaxed into his mouth. It felt like a gentle summer storm, all warmth and wetness. She rocked against him, riding the ocean-swell rhythm that rose and fell between them, dimly aware that his hand was now clenching a fistful of hair at the base of her neck.

I would have walked through fire for you.

The rhythm stuttered. His grip slackened and her whole body began to quake fiercely. She was pulling away—to cry, she thought in dismay. But when she opened her eyes to look at him she started to laugh.

"Follow me," she said.

five

"What's this?"

The cabin was set back deep down a private trail marked *Hickory Lane*. Gussie reached into her purse and, smiling shyly, dangled the key she had picked up at the Welcome House.

Inside.

It went quickly now.

He laid her on the bed and began to undress her impatiently and completely while she watched and he kissed and nibbled every newly exposed inch of her. The blouse, a fleeting wave of white flag lost quickly to the floor. Then his arms reached up her skirt to pull away her panties, letting his rough hands—one crippled and one whole—linger down the length of her legs. When he lifted the bra away and her breasts spilled free, they bore the weight and sag of twenty years and three children, and she wondered briefly if he might be disappointed. But his mouth covered them at once. She grabbed the hair at the back of his head and watched him move from one to the other. Then his sandpaper chin dragged down her stomach. Her nipples, wet with his kisses, were cold and hard in the exposed air. His left hand slipped to the small of her back and lifted her while his right hand yanked down the zipper at her hip. She arched her back to help him pull away the skirt.

She felt like a feast spread before him.

"Come up here," she said, yanking at his hair.

But she couldn't budge him. His head, his shoulders pinned her into place, his whiskery face bore down on her, his powerful arms locked onto her legs and she was trapped. His head moved beneath her hand as she looked wildly about the room at her scattered clothes. Her hips bucked and bucked against his face, as she tugged at his hair, and then she squeezed her eyes shut as the world rushed upon her so quickly, so quickly, and she breathed his name over and over until everything, so quickly now, came rushing at her though the walls and shattered into a thousand broken-glass wind chimes.

After nearly a minute, still panting, she asked, "Did I hurt you?" She massaged his scalp.

He smiled. "A little. Gussie, is it me or did your breasts get bigger?"

"My breasts did not get bigger."

"You got implants, didn't you."

She grabbed a handful of his hair and tugged him again. "Come up here, dammit."

He climbed up to her, still fully clothed, and covered her naked body. She wrapped her legs around him.

"When did you start waxing?" he asked.

"Stop *talkin!*"

Smiling, he pushed away from her and up to his knees. When he pulled the shirt off it was like an eagle *(an angel?)* spreading its wings, and she saw just how thick his chest and shoulders and arms had become from a lifetime in the construction pits—much more formidable than the eighteen-year-old body she remembered. Fresh scrapes meshed with old scars; he looked like he'd been through a war.

The buckle came undone; the jeans slipped down his hips. She took hold of him and slipped him inside where they became one being, locked together.

Sweat ringed his neck and glistened in the hair of his chest; it seethed, quivered over her, and the animal scent they were making grew stronger. She found his mouth in time as the last shudder rippled through him. He roared, and it was as if he was breathing life into her.

six

Ben Shallcross awoke from a doze and shambled to a window.

Hoarfrost shimmered the glade around the cabin and coated crystal highlights over the old hand pump and the skeleton arms of the trees that reached out for him. The leaves were gone from the walnuts and elms. A few still clung stubbornly to the maples, but those left were all brown. From a distance, the hills were gray fuzz: cotton balls dusted with ashes. It was too early for all of this. Autumn had come and gone like a flash; he had slept through till winter.

He drifted to the woodstove and sat to warm his hands.

The morning had been spent refilling the crate of fuel logs and starting the fire in the stove. The chore was made worse by the cold. His gnarled joints screamed frigid agony as he made them work. He broke several matches for each one that lit, and several of those fluttered out in his palsied fingers before he could get the flame to catch. When the fire finally got roaring hot, he settled in front of the stove and scalded his hands on the cast iron to melt the blood back into his old flesh.

He coughed a great deal.

He remembered.

It was three years ago when he first felt the peculiar heaviness in his lungs, lying there like a lead fishing weight. It tickled and made him wheeze when he took in too deep a breath. When he coughed, that weight jiggled loose inside his chest. And maybe every now and again he would notice a drop or two of blood on his hanky. He hadn't seen a doctor in nearly twelve years. Hadn't felt the need for it, and still didn't. He knew well enough there was something wrong inside his body—more than gnarled fingers and achy joints and a leaky bladder—and didn't need a doctor to tell him as much.

He was, simply, old.

Time, that most precious of things, of which he had wasted so much, was growing short. He drew his fingers, now warm again, away from the stove and reached for his pocket watch. It was hammering forward toward midafternoon.

So late, already?

The watch had been his father's; the realization caught him like a shove from behind—he turned to see the source of that shove, in the shadows beyond grown-over trails where a dim beast's shape crept toward him. Broad and dark, flesh-jiggling, coin-jingling, the shape stalked toward him; with each step through the haze, the lines sharpened, features honed. The spark of two yellow-gray eyes pierced the haze. Ben's own eyes locked onto them, cowered beneath the curdling fury in them. Then, he was weighted by the shame of his own sin, a cancer spreading through his body and making him weak...

Wait up, Ben!

The shape, closer, skin-changed into a man, clear and cold before him. Under the glare of yellow-gray, his father shoved money into his son's hands. Then shoved his son away.

And the son had stumbled onto the trails, drifting aimlessly toward the sunsets, losing himself in the twisting climb into the hills, and after countless days, weeks, months, years came to a path that wound upward to a quiet place in the wild heavens were he might forget. The trail hit a dead end, and the yellow-gray moon set forever.

It was coming back to him now.

His sin, in the shape of a beast, had followed him. Would *not* let him forget. So he sat in his cabin, looking at a watch that ticked away time in his hand. His lungs, pained by the heaviness there, heaved in a long breath, and he stood up and went to his kitchen. He drew back a curtain and looked to the sky. It was dark with clouds. *Snow clouds,* he might have thought had it been later in the season.

What's the worst you ever been afraid, Ben?

Wolf shoulders hunched from the nothingness of the brush, padded to the trail that was now melted of the morning frost. It was Willy, circling, panting, his dog's face pointed toward the cabin, expecting him.

The trail beyond wound toward the mysteries of the woods and the ash-gray peaks. A voice there, forgotten and wanting to be remembered, called to him.

He went to his bedroom to find his boots.

He found her in the woods, waiting for him.
She touched his face. For a while, he was happy again.

seven

"Good morning," he said.

She came awake. Boo Taylor was sitting up in bed next to her.

She shot a panicked look at her watch and then slapped her palm to her forehead. She had been asleep for almost forty-five minutes.

"Was it okay to let you sleep?" he asked.

She pulled the quilt up to her shoulders. Her chin and cheeks were chafed from his unshaven face. The smell of him was all over her. "I thought you were asleep, too."

"I don't sleep much anymore."

She leaned into him, laid her cheek against his chest, slung a leg over his. She had been dreaming, she realized. Three sets of eyes, three sets of sharp, smiling teeth all glowing within deep shadow, flashing at the cottage window, and then flashing away.

"How did you know about this place?" he asked.

She glanced up. "This cabin? These places are notorious down here." She burrowed into him again, trying to keep dismal thoughts at bay.

"Notorious," he said. "So, you've been here before?"

"Of course not!"

"Then I'm your first?"

"Yes." She tightened her fingers around his bicep as a deep ache began to burn in her stomach. "Yes, you are that." She realized that the enormity of her guilt was too much to consider, and so she was refusing to consider it. *I don't want to go,* she was about to say, but Boo held out his hand to her and opened it. A fire flashed there for a moment.

"I found this," he said, "on the windowsill."

As she reached for him—for the tiny glass flame in his hand, a breeze gusted from the south and sent a legion of snowflake angels across the bedroom window. The flame—the impossibly alive flame—froze in her fingers to become the tiny glass sculpture of a frog.

That little frog is you, Mr. Boo.

Elfish giggles seeped from somewhere inside the walls of the cottage. His face, she now saw, was drawn in suspicion. "Gussie, did you put it there?"

eight

The ride back to her office was misery.

nine

Alone, Boo Taylor drove to the high school.

He found a vast complex of modern-looking structures that bore no resemblance to the simple building he once attended. He parked and followed the sound of whistles and grunts to the practice football field. He stood on the sidelines to watch. He took out a cigar, clipped it, and lit it.

His hands trembled.

Royal Goody, dressed in a yellow sweat suit, spotted him and waved.

It was getting dark by the time a final whistle blew, sending the players hustling off the field. Royal jogged over, smiling, his face glistened with sweat. "Put that thing out," he said, "you're setting a bad example. Hey, you get my message?"

Boo Taylor blew out stream of smoke. "You left me a message?"

"I tried to reach you earlier. You got some time?"

"Sure."

The players were shambling toward the locker room, looking their way. "Don't tell me," Boo said, "that running back is one of Wade's boys."

Royal had started for the school, and Boo followed him. "Actually, that one is Pete Dutton's youngest. Won't surprise you to know the boy's brains wouldn't fill a shot glass."

When they reached the building, Boo stomped out his cigar. Inside, they traveled through a series of confusing corridors, finally coming to a door with a smoked glass window. *Royal Goody, Vice Principal.* Royal ushered him in.

Boo took a chair across from the desk. Life was a humming, jittering tangle of high-tension wires, strobing one frame of his time with Gussie for every frame of the here and now, and he could barely sit still.

"Listen," Royal began, "I put in a call to a friend of mine who's a professor of African Studies at Georgia Southern. He helped me with some of the research on my book, and I wanted his thoughts on this doll business. I hope you don't think I'm intruding, Boo. He came up with some interesting ideas."

"This doll business," Boo said.

"Right. You want to hear?"

"Fine."

Royal leaned back in his chair, placing his hands behind his head. "Okay, so basically he confirmed a lot of what the reverend had to say. A fetish or a toby or whatever it's called is supposed to be made by a voodoo priest or priestess. There's generally some kind of ceremony involved in the process. A lot of spitting and chanting, I guess."

After a moment of silence, Boo realized Royal was waiting for him to comment. "What's it supposed to be for?"

"*Psychology,* basically. It's a psychological weapon. The idea is, the thing represents a person—and by making it, the priest or witch assumes some power over that person. You're supposed to plant the thing where the victim finds it and gets terrified. Then the witch reveals herself, demands money to kill the spell or whatever. It's a scam, and a pretty old one."

"No one's asking me for money."

Royal waved dismissively. "You get the drift. Somebody's after *something,* anyway."

Boo looked around the office. A collection of memos were taped to the wall behind Royal's head. A *Solomon Goody for Congress* sign leaned against a cabinet. "So it's voodoo," he said dully. He wondered where Gussie was, if she had gone home yet, what she was thinking. A sudden picture of her, legs spread wide before him, flashed through his mind, and he clenched his jaw.

"You hear the word, and you think of Haiti," Royal was saying. "Or New Orleans. What was practiced on the barrier islands—what Laylee and Mamie Stuvant practiced—would have had roots in the same old African religions. Different from the Caribbean variety, but similar. Like the Gullah dialect. The isolation made it so every island had its own distinct version, but it all has the same roots."

"I'm not sure how this is useful."

"That's obvious, isn't it? It helps establish a *modus operandi.* I've already discovered something I think is important."

Royal reached into a desk drawer, rummaged through it, and came out with a slim book. He flipped through the pages. "One of the common properties," he said and came to the page he wanted, "is the use of native plants and animals to make various cures and narcotics."

He pushed the open book to Boo Taylor. It showed an ancient pen-and-ink drawing of a stub of plant. The caption beneath read *High John the Conqueror Root.*

"I think," Royal Goody told him, "this explains one of the things happening to you."

Boo looked up from the drawing. "Royal, what are you talking about?"

"A narcotic, Boo," Royal said simply. "To induce your hallucinations."

Boo Taylor was thunderstruck.

After a moment of incredulity, he burst out laughing.

Royal reached over and took the book back from him. "Actually, it would explain a lot," he said quietly.

"Like what?"

"Like seeing and hearing things that aren't there, the sense of dread. All that is apparently pretty common and managed easily with the right ingredients. That night you say you saw Mamie Stuvant rocking on a porch—you came from a bar, right?"

"Oakies," Boo said. The laughter was receding.

"Maybe someone put something in your drink."

Boo nodded. "Lester Meggett slipped me a mickey at Oakies. So I would see ghosts. Is that it?"

Royal, looking injured, said, "I'm not saying it's that simple, Boo. I think the issue is, maybe you have some enemies. Who else was there that night?"

"Dewey Fitch for a while, but he disappeared." Boo's humor suddenly fell; his head filled with smoke and sour beer. "Murphy Ransome was there with Harley Dutton."

Enemies.

He saw Murphy Ransome, standing over the booth, tipping a vile into his beer mug. Saw Dewey Fitch leaving some poison behind before slinking away. Saw Sandy Baker threatening to shatter like a porcelain figurine. Saw a shriveled, burned-out old version of Henry Ray Dutton glaring at him from the docks. Wade Dutton holding a jar. Gussie holding a glass frog.

"Wade thinks it's all self-inflicted."

Now Royal raised an eyebrow. "He thinks that? Really?"

Boo shrugged. He felt suddenly exhausted. Gussie's scent was drifting up from his hands; he wanted to get back to MaeEllen's house where he could wait for her call. "I've been thinking," he said, "about something Mamie Stuvant once told me. That time when I was a kid and went to her house, I asked her if she was related to Joker Tribbit. She told me most of the blacks on the island claimed to be related to him."

This made Royal grin.

"What about you?" Boo asked him. "Should I put you on my list of enemies, too? I mean, you seem to know all about these potions and spells."

Royal scratched his chin. "So far as I know there's not a drop of Joker Tribbit's blood in the Goody line. Also, I think maybe I'm one of the few real friends you've *got* on this island."

Boo smiled. *Enemies?* he wondered and remembered punching a young Royal Goody at the shell pile, fighting him for the rifle at Laylee's house. "Royal, do you recall me telling you there are two kinds of people in this world?"

He watched Royal thinking, watched the memory come back to him. "Those who ask about your hand," Royal recited, twisting a grin, "and those who don't."

Boo leaned forward, put his chin on his scarred right fist and leveled his eyes at the man across the desk. "I notice you've never asked."

Royal met Boo's gaze and was quiet for a long moment. His eyes flickered at the ruined fist. "Boo, I know what happened to your hand."

No you don't. You think you know, but you don't have a damn clue.

Another long spell of silence followed. At last, Boo looked away and shook his head. "Hallucinations," he muttered. Then he slipped two photographs from his shirt pocket. He handed them to Royal. "The reason I stopped by was to see if you might recognize any of these people."

Royal Goody took a breath. Then he held up the smaller of the two pictures. "The doc?" he asked.

"The woman with him."

Royal puckered his lips, frowned, considering. "Sorry." Then he looked at the second picture. "This big old gent," he said, and tapped a finger at the image, "looks a lot like old Danborne Shallcross. Is that you standing with him?"

"Yes."

"How old were you?"

"Nine or ten, I think."

Royal's frown deepened. "Couldn't be him, then. He would have died a few years before we were born, but it looks like pictures I've seen of him."

Dead, Boo thought. *Just another ghost.* "Shallcross. I've heard that name before."

"Old island family. Danborne Shallcross was a lawyer, very prominent. He defended one of the Carlyles at a famous lynching trial back in the thirties. Dottie Mae Jackson worked for them, as I recall, when they had a place on Carriage Avenue."

"Maybe this is a relative, then."

"Maybe. Though I can't think of any Shallcross on the island for the last thirty, forty years." He pursed his lips again. "If you want, I could show them to the reverend. And maybe Dottie Mae, too; she's still alive, believe it or not."

Boo glanced at the pictures, reluctant to part with them. "Okay, but I'll need them back at some point," he said. He watched the photographs disappear into the top drawer of Royals' desk.

Royal asked, "You want to tell me what these pictures mean to you?"

Boo Taylor stood, wanting to get to the door, get home, get to Gussie. He felt like a caged wolf, padding restlessly around its cell. "That woman with the doc is my mother," he said.

"That's not Mae—" Royal stopped, blanched when he realized what Boo just told him.

Boo checked his watch. "And the old man...he was some friend of the doctor's. He took me to visit him once, somewhere in the mountains. Shallcross, you said?"

"Maybe."

"You think you can find out?"

"Boo, I'll do what I can."

ten

He pulled the car to a stop in the driveway and killed the engine, sending the night into an abrupt silence.

He sat while the engine cooled and ticked, finishing his cigar.

Gussie was a perpetual ache in his chest.

Through the windshield, the house was black; a yellow porch light, like a single flame, showed the glowing rectangle of the front door. MaeEllen was in there. Asleep, Boo hoped, because he had no desire to confront her tonight.

Sighing, he shoved the door open and swung into the night, grinding the stub of cigar under his shoe. He walked around the car and across the darkness of the front yard.

He was caught halfway between the car and the first of the porch steps when a shadow disconnected from the bushes and seemed to move purposefully, angrily, toward him. The shadow took the shape of a large man. Boo froze on the lawn as the thing approached, remembering a big man in the wind and rain of a dying hurricane along a northern roadside. He lifted his hands in a weak, defensive gesture to his chest and took one small step backward.

As the moon's silver and the porch light's yellow touched the man's twisted and furious face, Boo recognized him and understood the anger. Oddly, he felt relief and a sense of grim acceptance. He let his hands drop.

A fist looped out of the darkness and slammed into his nose.

Cartilage snapped along a familiar fault line as pain and blood erupted from the middle of his face. He stumbled backward and fell hard to the ground. *Forgot to duck,* he thought distantly.

The man hung over him, fists clenched at his side.

"You lousy *fuck!* You *bastard!* I'll *kill* you!"

Boo swabbed his knuckles across his upper lip to catch the blood. The figure above him was heaving deep breaths, was trembling, waiting for Boo to move or strike back.

Looking up, Boo said, "You don't get to make her choices for her, Murph. Any more than I do."

"What's that horseshit supposed to mean? She already *chose,* you lousy, rich-boy prick. She chose *me!*"

"No, she didn't. And you know it."

Murphy's features twitched. It was perhaps the first time Boo had seen anything other than a lazy smile on Murphy Ransome's face. "We have a *family,* goddammit," Murphy growled, and now hurt mixed with his anger. A glaze of emasculating tears filmed his eyes. He quickly rubbed them. "We're *married.* Doesn't that mean anything to you?"

Dew seeped through the elbows of Boo's shirt. The taste of blood and stale cigar smoke filled his mouth. Perhaps, he wondered, Gussie was huddled in a ball in the dark somewhere, at this moment, loathing him for what he had done to her life.

At last, Murphy's fists unclenched. His body straightened, and he ran a hand through his hair. "You know," he said, his voice calmer, "I never did like you much, Boo Taylor. As far as I'm concerned, you were never more than a third-rate junkballer who got by on his daddy's good name and bankroll. You leavin this island was about the best thing you ever did. For Gussie. For everybody else. I think maybe you should be on your way again."

Murphy Ransome hung there another moment longer, daring Boo to disagree with him.

Then he stalked away.

Boo blew out at long, weary sigh. He listened to sounds of a car down the street kick into life and lurch away. Then he picked himself up from the grass and made his way toward the porch steps.

Inside, he flicked on lights just as the phone rang in the kitchen. He picked up the handset.

"Hello, Boo?" A girl's voice, like a deer, timid and anxious.

"Your husband just broke my nose," he said.

"What are you talking about?"

He slumped. It was Sandy Baker. A tide of impotence welled around him, dragged him down toward a swirling, black drain.

"Where have you been? Didn't you get my messages?"

He grabbed a napkin, dabbed it to his nose, and it came away red. "It's been a little hectic around here," he said. "And Sandy, I really don't know that talking will accomplish anything. I'm sorry."

She didn't respond.

Boo looked at the phone. After another moment, he said, "I'm going to hang up now, Sandy."

"Boo, we have to talk."

"No, we don't."

"*Yes,* we really do." A staticky sob came through the line. "Whether you like it or not, we really do."

"Sandy—" but he closed his eyes, and his heart sank.

Enemies, he thought.

There, in the darkness behind his closed eyelids, he was lying next to Sandy Baker, slipping in and out of dreams, making careless love while telephones rang and a shadow scratched its long fingers across his bedroom window.

"You're not," he said. "You can't be."

Another sob.

It was a dead rabbit, he thought, and almost laughed. *I fell into a dead rabbit.*

"How could this happen?" he asked, and then immediately regretted it.

"What's *that* supposed to mean? You were there, too. Last time I checked, it still takes two people."

The rabbit died!

"Boo, what am I supposed to do?"

Sins of the Father ~ September, 1971

His nose hurt. In the first weeks of school, it often started to bleed spontaneously in class, and he made frequent trips to the nurse.

He walked Gussie Dutton home after school every day.

He walked her to her classes.

He carried her books.

She painted the view of the pier from his backyard, and he hung it in his room.

Neither of them had seen a single monster in weeks.

It was September, a return to structure and order, which, considering the consequences of a reckless summer, arrived with relief. A period of calm. But structure and order and even calm were illusions. September was a mask the summer wore in its last weeks, behind which it still beamed a merciless flame-tooth grin. For example: the heat was *expected* to diminish, bank off a few degrees, extend some relief to August-basted flesh, melted-liquorice roads. But it never happened. Noontime mercury rarely dripped below ninety; midnight screens scarcely caught a breeze.

And there were other things that hadn't change.

Like the constant headachy throb in his shattered nose.

Like his nightmares.

He dreamed constantly, and they came in all flavors of brutality and ghoulishness. He dreamed about saltwater drowning pools, about tattooed trolls, about molasses-flavored flesh, about a scarecrow holding a lit match to a fuse that would set fire to the whole world.

One dream was the most frightening:

He is watching pudgy Hoss Beaudry lurch down a slippery, dark cave, plodding blindly in terror. He (in a safe place) calls out to Hoss not to be afraid, that he's too *old* to be afraid, that the coast is clear. Hoss cannot see him but calls out Boo's name. At the sound of his name, the whole weight of the gator's skull snaps down on the plump and pale boy-shape and twists him under, the water boiling and every living thing fleeing from the thrashing violence...In the end, as the bottom mud settles, flecks of sawed-loose flesh (missing parts) float away in the current to make a meal for the murk-dwelling scavengers. And he realizes it is not Hoss Beaudry who he has just watched get ripped apart by the Beast. It is himself.

Always, at that point, he would wake up.

And wonder what it (he? she?) was doing to his friends. Because they were still being bled, and that was another thing that hadn't changed.

two

Ash Marchant was all tics and twitches, sitting next to Boo Taylor in a pew at the First United Methodist Church on Loggerhead Street. The rocking, the bouncing, the leg wagging, the fingernail picking all stirred the acid that bubbled in Boo's own stomach.

This is what that girl was doing to his friends, turned the smartest boy he knew, the most *rational* one, into this fever-swept, bled-dry, sweat-slicked wreck.

Boo, you have to go with me; I can't go there alone.

But I made a promise!

Ash leaned into Boo's shoulder and whined softly, "How much longer, do you think?"

"About fifteen, twenty minutes," Boo whispered back and tried to sound reassuring, but Ash only rolled his eyes miserably and groaned.

The block of granite that was Garson Halesworth Marchant's back twisted in the pew in front of them. A formidable glare was thrown down a strong, aquiline nose, down an iron-gray mustache, down a pure wool shoulder.

Boo reached up with both hands and felt the twin strips of white bandage that stitched the cartilage of his nose in place. The gesture looked like he was in prayer. The pulse in his sinuses was a ballpene hammer tapping a lead weight: dry church air, booming echoes, surging and receding blood. He wished he'd taken another aspirin before leaving the house and hoped he wouldn't start bleeding all over his Sunday clothes.

That his nose didn't open up during the riot two nights earlier was something of a miracle.

Was he healing?

He gently fingered flesh and bone. The puffiness was gone, at least. Most of the rainbow bruise was gone, too. Gone for good this time, he hoped—as Henry Ray Dutton seemed to be gone for good. With that thought, he did make a quick prayer.

Then Pastor Greesome called upon the congregation to stand and sing hymn number 274, "Revive Us Again," and Boo stood up with the hymnal. Ash mimicked him a beat later. Boo flipped to the correct page, and as the organ thrummed and with Ash avidly tilting a disarray of brown hair to read the lyrics, the church filled with the rich, many-voiced song:

"We praise Thee, O God!

For the Son of Thy love,

For Jesus Who died

And is now gone above

Hallelujah! Thine the glory, revive us again..."

Ash sang an enthusiastic monotone. Boo's own efforts sent nasally vibrations deep into his face. He thought about Gussie Dutton and the promise he made to her—that he would never go back to that house. Never go back to *her*.

It's that...grave we dug up, Boo. You have to help!

Why do I have to? (Am I my brother's keeper?)

As he sang with Ash Marchant on his left, facing that granite slab back, and surrounded by the rest of the congregation of the First United Methodist Church, a fragile capillary in Boo Taylor's nose silently ruptured. He didn't feel it. He did feel the run of fluid down his lips, and instinctively he sniffled.

Ash tapped his shoulder, and Boo looked down.

Splats of blood had fallen on the page before him like raindrops of red ink.

three

Two nights earlier, it had been Gussie Dutton on his left, the doctor on his right. Not the rainbow of stained glass burning his cheeks, but the stark spray of halogen lamps. And not church pews that splintered his rump, but the rickety skeleton bleachers of the high school.

When Gussie tapped his knee and pointed out Ashford Marchant sitting miserably with his father in the shadows, it was early in the fourth quarter, and the Sweetpatch High Yellowjackets were up three touchdowns on the Lake Moultrie Badgers. If they could hold the lead it would be the first time in five years Sweetpatch beat Lake Moultrie.

"What's bothering him?" Gussie asked, nodding at Ash. "Looks like that boy's got his own private black cloud hangin over his head."

"Couldn't say."

"Where's the rest of them? Where's Lester and Dewey—and those Standish boys?"

Boo shrugged.

Then Murphy Ransome was taking the snap from center, tucking the ball neatly into Red Prettyman's stomach on a sweep. Red sprinted for the sideline with Petey Dutton pulling like a brick cart from his guard position to lead the way. Petey bulldozed the Badger cornerback. Red cut, shot up field—until a Badger linebacker swept over and brought him down after a six-yard gain.

The crowd roared its approval. To Boo's right, the doctor clapped; to his left, Gussie whistled, stomped, shouted: *"Nice block, Petey, atta boy!"*

The boys huddled and broke. Murphy called the signals as Red came in motion. Then Murphy Ransome had the ball, faked another hand off to Red and slipped the ball to Harley Dutton who went colliding into the line, toppling bodies like bowling pins, and then fell himself four yards later with five Badgers clinging and clawing over him.

The crowd cheered again. The band blared the fight song.

"First down! Nice run, Harley!"

Throughout the night, the Dutton boys had been a clan of storming Neanderthals brutalizing a rival tribe, and Gussie cheered her brothers with raucous, unbridled pride. Red Prettyman was swift and steady, the Deeg brothers sharp, and of course Murphy Ransome was sleek and confident at quarterback, guiding the team up the field, drive after drive.

But none of these boys were the real spark behind Sweetpatch High School's historic rout—and they knew it; and everyone on the field and in the bleachers knew it, too.

Boo glanced back toward Ash Marchant. Ash wasn't cheering; he wasn't even watching the game. He sat with his hands in his pockets, his face aimed into the blackness beyond the lights—toward South Patch. Where *were* the others? Down there? At night? Not even Les and Dewey were stupid enough to go to that house at night.

He felt Gussie's leg brush against his and warmed with the touch. He turned back to the game.

The players broke from the huddle and came to the line. Murphy bellowed the signals across the brightly lit field, his voice dominating an expectant silence. Red ambled in motion left. The ball snapped. Murphy had the ball as the lines clashed. He faded into the backfield, scanned the riot of bodies before him...waited... waited... and rifled the ball downfield.

The throw went too high.

But the wide receiver sprung from the grass and snagged the ball one-handed out of the air. He touched the ground at a dead run across the middle of the field. The Lake Moultrie safety rushed up to gather him in, but the receiver faked left, juked right, and then sprinted left into open field. The move cost him a valuable split second, allowing two Badger linebackers to close on him. But he out-raced them to the sideline and then turned up field for another five yards before the linebackers' rushed in to force him out-of-bounds.

But in the last instant, before he touched the line, the receiver dug his cleats into the grass and zagged back toward the middle of the field. He greased between the two backers who managed only to push him off balance. As he backstepped and stumbled another few yards, the safety finally caught up to him, slammed into his chest, and dropped him hard.

A twenty-four-yard gain.

The doctor clapped; Boo and Gussie shouted. But the crowd around them offered only a reluctant smattering of applause. Further away, in the south end of the bleachers, a great, merry celebration of hoots and hollers erupted.

Solomon Goody shook off the safety and pushed up from the grass. He flipped the ball to the referee and trotted back to the huddle.

Boo listened to the grumbles from a few rows behind.

"Did you see that monkey jump?"

"Them spooks, they got this extra leg muscle, you know."

The markers moved downfield. The revelry at the south end of the stands continued. Gussie stuck her fingers in her mouth and made a loud whistle and then fixed Boo with a wide, playful grin. She had tried to teach Boo her finger-whistle earlier but gave up when all he could manage was to spit on himself.

The doctor leaned forward and said, "I believe I'll go on down and get another one of those overcooked wieners. May I get you anything—Boo, Augusta?"

"Nothing for me, sir, thank you," Gussie answered and smiled politely.

"Can I have a Dr. Pepper?" Boo asked.

"*May* I have a Dr. Pepper," his father corrected.

Boo scowled embarrassment and glanced at Gussie as his father crabwalked toward the steps. He apologized as he went, but the people who stood or swagged their knees to make room all nodded respectfully to the doctor and called him by name.

Four plays later, Sweetpatch High School scored when Solomon Goody took in another pass and dashed into the end zone. Solomon had picked up most of the yards all night; he was a water bug, skittering, dancing, gliding across a pond and impossible to grab. He'd taken the game's opening kickoff on a eighty-eight-yard romp for a touchdown. Later, he took a punt fifty-eight yards for another touchdown. In the third quarter, he scored again after hauling in a short pass from Murphy and pinballing through the Lake Moultrie defense.

Monroe Timmons, another colored boy, was ably plugging the center of the field from the middle linebacker spot. And the Johnston twins, each better than 230 pounds, were playing tackle both ways and manhandling the line of scrimmage.

Their families and the other representatives of South Patch had gravitated, as if by instinct, to the southern end of the home bleachers where they formed a small but wildly enthusiastic troupe. The sense that some exclusive party was going on down there grew as the game wore on and the sons of South Patch proved their mettle. Several times, the group broke into chants and song. At halftime, they had clapped and whistled for the marching band, and it took some time for the rest of the crowd to realize the celebration was acknowledgment for the six Negro band members.

For a good number of the Sweetpatch Island white folks, it was the first time they had seen so many coloreds massed together. With the integration, they had perhaps expected to find all those dark faces in the bleachers this year. But they had *not* expected all that sassy hilarity, which, by now, had become a sideshow to the game.

Boo Taylor had picked out Pastor Hatchel and Royal Goody in this crowd. The reverend was wearing his dark suit jacket despite the heat, and the sling that cradled his right arm and the patch of gauze taped to his forehead stood out like a white moon in a black sky. Rumors about his wounds flitted up and down the coast like squawking gulls. Boo had heard that three men wearing sacks on their heads had pulled Pastor Hatchel from his car as he was driving home from church and beat him with axe handles. This was two days after he won his spot on the school board.

The final score was 37 to 13.

For Up Islanders, clustering down the bleacher steps, the celebration was reserved. Farther south, the planks rattled like a jazz piano under bolt-loosening stomps and rail-wobbling whoops and hollers. The black players loped over to the fence and saluted the crowd with upraised helmets.

As he milled down the steps with Gussie, Boo looked around for Ash Marchant but couldn't find him.

Gussie jabbed him with her elbow. "Dare you to hop that fence."

Boo went gray for a moment. "Dare?"

"*Race* you."

"Gussie—"

"I want to run on the field and catch Wade and Petey and Harley." She grabbed his arm and tugged him through the crowd.

She raced him over the fence and won. Dragging him along, she picked through the players. She spotted Wade and let go of Boo's arm to wrap Wade in a hug. Wade blushed as Murphy Ransome and Red Prettyman watched and ridiculed nearby.

"Big football hero, hey boy?"

"Best tackle you made all night, Wade."

"Hell, Gus, his uniform ain't even dirty."

Boo scowled, drifted away, got purposely lost among the grass-streaked shoulder pads and sweaty faces. A few boys called out to him, and he called back, clapped their backs. He measured himself against the stampede, decided he was already as big as at least half of what he saw, tougher than most, faster than all but a few—and yearned in his blood to be a year older and prove it.

"Next year for you, huh Boo Taylor." It was Jimmy Earl Deeg who read the fierce spark in his eyes.

"Next year," Boo said.

"What is it for you, backfield or line?"

Quarterback, Boo thought, and then he heard someone else call his name. He turned and found Royal Goody dogging along next to his brother and probably brewing with similar notions. Solomon was swaggering up the field, swinging his helmet by the facemask, wolfish sunglasses already blinding his eyes and reflecting the night lights. The helmet padding had cut a checkerboard into his afro. Monroe Timmons and the Johnston brothers followed.

"You see that, Boo?" Royal asked.

"I saw. Great game, Solomon."

Solomon Goody was munificent. "Well hey, you know—we had us a good day. Showed some folks a thing or two. Hey, how's Miss Laylee doin?"

"Fine, I guess." he said. "Asks how you and Royal are gettin along in school."

He laughed. "Well, you tell her there ain't been any broken bones—*yet*. That's about as good as I can put it."

Boo knew all about the fights and ambushes. The colored kids at school had learned to travel in small herds.

"She says you boys should come over for dinner some time. She says bring your momma, too."

"Tell her we'll be there."

Boo fell into stride next to them. The clamorous Negro crowd paced their progress toward the locker room in the north end zone. In the parking lot, the Lake Moultrie players were already climbing into the white-and-blue buses that would carry them back over the causeway. Boo's attention was drawn to a group of four boys scrabbling under the northeast fence onto the field, giggling, carrying something that looked like a bucket. *Dare you to hop the fence.* He suddenly remembered that first June dare at the hotel construction site, slipping under that fence, seven of them—all alive and all together—and Dewey Fitch trembling across a tightrope plank of wood.

Hey Ash, dare you to walk the plank...

Just a joke. Ash didn't bite; Ash was too smart for that. But the others weren't, and he should have seen it coming. And as Boo walked at Solomon Goody's side and thought of that long-ago dare—the first of them, the one that sent him stumbling down a path of darkness—it wasn't Hoss Beaudry he saw but Ashford Marchant's ghostly pale face, ahead, in that darkness, in a sea of faces beyond the fence. He saw

Ash at perhaps the same moment Ash caught sight of him; Ash's eyes suddenly magnified with recognition beneath his glasses.

He looks so sick, Boo thought, *What's that girl doing to those boys?*

The crowd buffeted Ashford like a scrap flotsam on the surf. He made a strengthless effort toward Boo, but the prattling, many-legged riptide swept him in the opposite direction. Then, sharp movement from Boo's right. Coming on. Those boys rushing at him on their dare, a wave gathering even as the undertow drew Ashford Marchant out to drown in the sightless abyss. Suddenly, a dark wave reared up, curling over Boo Taylor's head. He turned toward the wave as Solomon Goody spoke at his side.

"Hear you got yourself a regular girlfriend, now, boy. Hear you smooch with her behind the cafeteria."

"Well," Boo answered, watching the wave with disbelief.

The wave crashed—not on Boo Taylor, but on the colored boy walking next to him.

"HEY JIG, TIME TO HIT THE SHOWERS!"

Black paint splashed over Solomon's face, his hair, his shoulderpads. Black paint filled his mouth, filled his helmet. Black paint splattered and stained the green turf, splattered and stained Boo Taylor.

The emptied bucket plunked against Solomon's skull.

Solomon went to his knees, and Boo leapt away from him.

The crowd turned to see.

Brays of laughter as the boys—no, these were *men*—scrambled away. Monroe Timmons wailed and charged. He brought down one of the men with a cross block.

Yet another black wave rose up. In a roar of outrage, it spilled over the fence and flooded the field.

Gussie Dutton never saw what started the riot; she only heard the shouts—at first just a scattered few: bitter and shocked, some even laughing. The shouts stacked, buzzed, rifled through the crowd like falling dominoes, circled her, each one louder and angrier than the one before, building and building, rising, gathering momentum, surrounding her until she *felt* the sliding, out-of-control, domino rush of bodies. The ground thumped and quaked, the sky shuddered with a maleficent roar, and she was suddenly at the center of a tornado. Wade grabbed her elbow and pulled her close as a great dark mass swarmed over the field.

Wade yelled, "What the hell?"

Harley grabbed her other elbow.

Arms and legs exploded in all directions. Fists of all colors arched through the violet, light-sprayed sky. Helmets were flung like plastic skulls. Girls screamed. Two players stumbled past, retreating toward the parking lot; two others filled their place, attacking in the opposite direction. Someone ran into Wade's back, and she and Harley almost went down with him.

"Let's get the hell outa here!" Wade shouted.

She was yanked from the storm by her elbows. "Dammit Wade, that hurts!" she yelled and couldn't hear her own voice. A yellow-and-black cheerleader's sweater smacked into her and this time she brought Wade down, skinning her knees in the dewy grass. She felt the tide collapse on her, drowning her until Harley hauled them both to their feet.

She yelled again, "But Boo Taylor's back there!"

❄️   ❄️   ❄️

A voice somewhere near his ear spoke calmly to him. Or maybe it was only in his mind—it must be, because it was Laylee Colebriar's voice:

"That's right, Mr. Boo, you and me, we gonna stay right here and ride this out."

The world had tipped sideways. The ground was a vertical line, and feet were defying gravity, running up and down this steep slope, sometimes only inches from his nose. His cheek was sticky and wet and hot. From the grass, he decided, because he knew he was pinned to the ground, although the grass smelled like tar and the tar felt like blood. A black blanket had been flung over him, and under its weight he had been dragged to the ground. Before that. . .

What happened before that?

He remembered. . .standing with his fists clenched, trying to find Solomon and then trying to find Gussie and then trying to decide who he was supposed to hit. A roly-poly white teenager shook a fist in his face and shouted something at him, so he hit the boy in the mouth. Then a colored man—a face from Baptist Church—grabbed his shirt collar and shoved him. He felt his collar rip free, found his balance, and kicked the man in the shin. The man punched him in the stomach. He kicked the man in the groin. From the corner of his eye, he caught the flash of football jersey and a fist that crashed into his cheek. *Murphy, what—?* And then this darkness. This hot, sticky, turned-on-its-side universe. And Laylee Colebriar's lullaby voice.

"Ain't no need for more punches, Mr. Boo. Gawd, ain't we done had us enough punches already?"

A spiked shoe clapped the ground a slim centimeter from his forehead. He blinked as sprigs of grass were kicked into the air and fluttered like green snowflakes into his eyebrows. Somewhere beyond in that tilted world of feet and grass he made out Solomon Goody flailing punches at some man he was sitting on. He knew it was Solomon, although the face he saw—twisted sideways—was a black-slopped, bare-knuckle fist of hatred. The man beneath wagged his arms in a useless effort to ward off the blows. Was it one of those boys? One of those giggling, ignorant, dangerous boys sneaking under the fence on their dare?

Dare you to walk the plank, hop the fence, go inside Mamie Stuvant's house. . .

I'll do it!

Solomon Goody's fury rained iron bolts upon that giggling ignorance. The rain cut through the night on a crazy, ninety-degree slant. The world had upended. The storm had hit shore.

"You and me, Mr. Boo," Laylee crooned from the cyclone—now, oddly, a man's voice, and at last he realized it was Reverend Hatchel who had him pinned and protected, *"We got to learn to forgive and stop all this brawlin."*

A dozen brown, cuffed trousers and black shoes swirled out of the lunatic, sideways maelstrom, swirled around Solomon Goody. And Boo Taylor knew the county police had arrived.

❖   ❖   ❖

She picked her way around the driftwood bodies cast helter-skelter across the wide beach of the football field. Her knees and her elbows sore, her mind numb and weary with worry. Here was a cheerleader's pom-pom flattened like a giant bumblebee and trailing the streamers of its guts. Here was a county policeman's hat turned up to the sky waiting for some benevolent soul to walk by and drop in a quarter or a few nickels.

A shout near the concession booth, three men snarling in a dog fight, snapping and shoving—just a dust eddy, swirling lazily and dying quickly.

By the goal post, Mr. Haufmann, the butcher, weighed a slab of sirloin that was his jaw, dripping red marinade into his hand. Cross-legged on the ground, Billy Cooper in his band uniform, rocking and sobbing like an old Indian praying to a campfire. Was her father in this mess somewhere? Surely, he could not have missed this opportunity to embarrass her in front of the island. Here was big Mrs. Johnston, wailing to the moon although her two big boys guarded her on both sides like twin hippos and patted her shoulders softly. Here was a colored boy she didn't know, wrestling his arms beneath the grasp of a big policeman.

Here was a face, glistening black and alien beneath the harsh lights, some kind of monster raised from swamp mud, but. . .

. . .chestnut tufts of hair sprouting through the black mud.

That was familiar, wasn't it?

A light switch flicked on as the head turned and became at least half of the face she was seeking. The two strips of bandage across his nose stitched the white and black halves together.

"Boo!" she yelled out, but he didn't hear her.

A hatless policeman slapped a bear paw on her chest and pushed her back. "Said everybody outa here—ain't that clear enough, missy?"

She backpedaled, craning around the brown uniform. "Boo Taylor!"

He was walking away from her. Pastor Hatchel was with him; his white sling was gone but the white patch still shone brightly from his scalp. And between them, a blind, hunchbacked creature that dripped tar and completed Boo Taylor's dark half.

"Hey, Boo Taylor, over here!"

Her back trampolined into a fence. The paw closed on her sore elbow as a gate opened and she was slid into a squirming, silent mass. A chain-link web clinked shut before her face. She slipped her fingers through it and climbed sideways, following Boo Taylor's progress. The pastor had his arm on the tar-creature's back who she now recognized was Solomon Goody. Half-tarred, piebald, Boo was gesticulating fervently to the older boy. "Solomon, Solomon are you all right?"

"Boo Taylor!" she called out, but he still didn't hear.

Solomon Goody gathered black slop from his face and flung it to the ground. He blinked bright eyes out of the black. He spit. He spit again. He brought a knuckle to his eyes, but the reverend swatted it away.

"Don't rub, son—you jes make it worse."

"Solomon, are you okay?"

As they rounded closer to the fence, she could see Solomon run his tongue through his mouth and spit a watery-black string to the ground. "Boy, will you just leave me the fuck alone!" he growled. He pushed Boo Taylor away and left a muddy handprint on his shirt.

four

Ash crackled with summer heat lightning. Boo Taylor felt the charge of it spidering on invisible rays through the starch of his pressed, white shirt as they stood sweating together among men in suits and ladies in dresses. A small crowd of such men and ladies congregated around the doctor and Garson Marchant below the church doors.

Angry talk about fires and integration, about the riot two nights before. Garson Marchant, somehow not sweating under all that wool, thrust a finger at the air. Mushroom faces nodded.

The doctor, true to his calling, calmed and soothed, mended, splinted their fractured honor, administered medicines to cool their fevered tempers. "Unfortunate," he said.

"Damn right!" said Garson Marchant.

The congregation murmured, and there were several side discussions about how fine a place Sweetpatch Island *used* to be.

"Oh, come now," the doctor said, "you can't throw out the baby with the bathwater. The island has certainly gotten much better in a number of ways."

"Name one," the granite slab challenged.

"Sewage," Doctor Taylor said, and they all looked at him. "Remember how really downright awful it got before the sewage system was installed in sixty-two? Rats nested in the roadsides by the score; don't you remember? Lord, in high summer, ladies covered their faces with hankies."

"Silas, what on earth has *that* got to do with anything?"

"I'm only saying that the twentieth century is finally catching up with us backward folk on Sweetpatch Island—maybe seventy years too late. Like it or not. Change is inevitable. And it's not *all* bad."

Garson Marchant snorted.

Below, Ashford dragged a finger through his collar to vent steam.

The murmuring quieted; the crowd parted to admit a plump, baldish man with a pink face. Automatically, the men in suits and ladies in dresses looked back and forth between the man and the two boys who stood among them.

"Hey Mr. Beaudry," Boo said.

The man put a hand on Boo Taylor's shoulder and pretended to smile.

Ash Marchant, who looked ready to throw up, whispered into Boo's ear, "Can we get going, now?"

Twenty minutes later, after changing into T-shirt and jeans (Ash didn't change; he didn't want to take the time), Boo Taylor was riding Ashford Marchant's handlebars, gripping white-knuckled to the cold metal as the wheels pitched and yawed along the rutted lanes toward South Patch.

five

"She wantin what been stole." Ash Marchant sweated.

"Bring it back, boy." He fought with the pedals.

"Belongs to Sheba." Fought harsh breaths into his lungs

"Fo' she come collectin." Crammed fire into his thighs.

Ahead, a slim foot away from his face, Boo Taylor's back—somehow big as a full-grown man's—hovered, a sturdy presence, secure in its solidity, its *real*ness.

What was real anymore; what wasn't? Ashford Marchant didn't know. Didn't know! And only by the barest fingernail grasp did he care. He had been so confused for so long and so scared. And so god-awful *exhausted*. When was the last time he slept? A week ago, maybe, not counting an hour's nap here and there. Last Thursday, Miss Jackson caught him napping in third period English and slapped a book so loud against his desk he woke up with a scream, not sure at all about the florescent world he opened his eyes to, all those laughing, gleeful faces, shrieking merriment at him. Was that real? Were *they* real? Or was there, perhaps, one face among the others that didn't quite belong: lips taut in a fierce rictus, eyes blazing white-hot anger, smoldering an ancient contempt.

"Dez you even know what you done, boy?"

First, that girl spinning her sweet dark cotton candy snares, blowing perfume bursts into his face, tickling licorice knuckles along his neck and rubbing her ripe breasts everywhere else.

Fetch, she said.

So they pummeled each other to fetch water, firewood.

Follow, she said.

So they raced to be first in line.

Dig, she said.

Because she said so; because if he didn't then one of the others would get there first—and then what would she do? "You the smart one, Mr. Ash-ford; bet you even smarter than ol Mr. Boo." So close...a tongue lap away from something luscious and nasty, bubbling brown sugar, daring him to lean in and taste, suddenly burning the tongue out of his mouth, the flesh away from his bones, wafting on candy-coated fingers into his bed every hot, breezeless night, goading him beneath the sheets toward heart-thudding explosion after explosion of sticky, guilty pleasure.

Just a taste. Just a chance at that delicious burn.

Day blurred into night and back to sunlight again. Real and unreal no longer mattered. Right became wrong; wrong became the best thing there ever was.

So he dug for her.

"Why you is a natural born ditch digger, ain't you, Mr. Ash-ford?" Hanging over him while he dug, dripping those plump tits from her flimsy dress like a gurgling water jug poised to the lips of a thirst-stricken man. "Try a little more over that ways a bit, see if you don't find what you lookin for."

She led him by the hand to a damp spot beneath weeping oaks and mangroves and circled by the crumbling brick wall of an old stable.

Where the temperature dropped ten degrees.

"Dig here," she commanded. There was no marker.

The low green-gray-brown limbs cast the site into perpetual nightshade, making it a cave. He smelled tired old animals in the dirt, heard whispers in the leaves, felt his skin go cool-moss slick. He understood he had stepped into a place of old times. Older than Chaliboque. Older than the Indian shell pile. Perhaps the very spot where the island first poked its infant finger from the sea, a place witness to a thousand desecrations, and for generations now swathed in swampy secrecy. Forbidden.

"Dig."

He pierced the thick mulch with his shovel, struck ground.

Something groaned. Himself, he realized.

In this darkness, Crystal Burne's face disappeared beneath the straggling curls of her hair, but he sensed her watching him intently as he lifted out the first shovel load of blood-red clay.

"Dig," she urged.

He dug and dug. She watched, clenched up tight. "Mr. Boo like you the best," she whispered, "maybe *I* like you the best, too. Won't that be nice!" The pit sunk further beneath him; the dirt piles rose higher around him.

And at last he came to rotted pine planks all caved in on themselves. Waiting all this time. "Found it!" he had yelled, jubilant—but already sickened.

She had leapt into the pit, and it was her body slithering like a wounded python around him, around *him!* Not Les or Dewey. Not Boo Taylor. This time, her mouth was spilling praise for him, was slipping over his own to offer him a scalding taste.

And then she reached into the soil and thrust that squat, screaming trophy into his hands.

It was so cold.

"Why this ol gal is lookin at you, Mr. Ash, an' she smilin. You see that smile? You the first thing that woman seen in a coon's age. I believe she like you. I believe you and her gonna be *good* friends."

She placed the skull on the mantel, in that room with all the books where she and the little girl lived and where it could watch them all.

Reality blurred. Unreality focused.

Somewhere in all of this, school started.

Somewhere in all of this, his father yelled at him. Often. Demanded to know what was *wrong* with him.

But wrong had become right, and he couldn't explain.

And couldn't explain the *ghosts*, appearing to him now that he unearthed those bones.

The man, first, who had shown himself weeks ago, sliding on a lizard's shadow from a crack in the wall. A vagabond, they all supposed, skulking in and out of cobwebbed corners in that big, ruined house. Smoke and whispers. Another one of Crystal Burne's tricks. Always mute in the beginning; except the little girl with her books claimed she talked to him; she sometimes talked to an empty wall and maybe, maybe, *maybe* there was someone there...

"Oh, don't you mind him, Mr. Ash-ford, an' he won't mind you."

"Who is he?" he asked, they asked.

"Not a *who,* but a *what.*"

"Then *what* is he?"

"Aw, you know, doesn't you Mr. Ash? After all, you *is* the smart one."

But he no longer felt smart, no longer understood anything—or what he *did* understand made no sense. The eyes in the mantel-top skull considered him from their hollow, black, endless, angry depths.

He started to suspect. And one day, when he was sent for firewood...

Would it have happened if it were Dewey or Les who went on this particular errand? Probably not. It hadn't been their muddy feet in that grave, kicking that loose clutter of bones; it hadn't been their hands holding that bald, muck-caked face.

She was there, blocking the stairway, gazing up with blood and flames in her eyes. *Mamie Stuvant is going to eat me!* Ashford thought in that panicked moment, and so he shrieked. He shrieked like a little baby thrown alive into a fire. He shrieked to wake the dead.

When he stumbled back up the steps and into the smut-encrusted room with the others, Crystal Burne was laughing as if she'd just heard the world's funniest joke. "Don't you fret, Mr. Ash," she said between the gales of her heartless laughter, "Ol Miss Sheba there, she jes lost her head!"

"Sheba? Sheba Tribbit?"

The little girl started crying. Crystal Burne kept laughing and laughing, while inside his mind, Ash screamed and screamed because the face on the mantel had become the face he'd seen on the stairs.

He escaped that day with Dewey and Lester and swore he would follow Boo Taylor's example and never come back.

He swore.

But the seduction of those sticky, sugar-scented dreams was so powerful. The world blurred. Chores went undone. Homework remained untouched in unopened text books. "What's wrong with you, boy!" his daddy raged, but for once there were worse things to fear than Garson Marchant.

When he didn't come back, the ghosts came for him. Ash saw them in the street—faces unnoticed in the crowds, brief, glaring, and then gone. Outside the schoolyard fence. On a neighbor's lawn. At night, peeking through the second floor window. A week ago, riding down Fulton Street Market, a big dog darted from the alley between Haufmann's and the Five & Dime; Ash jerked the handlebars to avoid the thing and went tumbling off the bike, skinning the palm of his right hand—and there was an old dark woman, broad as a bull, in the road where the dog should have been, oblivious to the traffic that was miraculously avoiding her, oblivious to everything, it seemed, except the boy with the blood on his hands who gaped back from the sidewalk. And, as supreme punishment, a new element haunted his dreams—just beyond the slope of her shoulder, the rise of her naked hip. Watching. At first just two red-hot coals in the murk. Then gradually, as her body undulated to an ever quickening pace over his, the woman gathered shape from the smoke and moved closer and closer, her face becoming more and more rabid and clear until her eyes became wolf's eyes, skull eyes, raging down upon him, pounding into him, and so when the final eruption came, it was a mindless scream of carnal terror as the woman chose this moment to find a voice and gurgle her furious demands:

"Bring back what been stole from me!"

So, he tried not to fall asleep. Ever.

And sought out the one person in the world he knew would believe him and would help.

Boo held on for life, wondering how Lester and Dewey could ride like this all the time. It was suicidal, a fool's errand, and he was riding tandem with the genuine article.

"We got to bury that skull back, Boo. It's Sheba Tribbit; I swear it is."

"That's crazy, Ash."

"It's what she wants, what Crystal Burne won't let me do!"

"It can't be Sheba Tribbit. She didn't even die on Sweetpatch Island; she died somewhere over on the mainland."

"But I've seen her ghost."

"It's not Sheba Tribbit."

"Then it's Mamie Stuvant!"

"Don't be stupid."

"Well, it's *somebody!*"

Storm clouds prowled through the south. They came to the bridge over Soap Water Creek and saw the rumpled bits of machinery that were all that was left of Boo Taylor's bike. The gap in the railing torn by Henry Ray Dutton's shoulders had been replaced by a length of two-by-four, probably nailed there by one of the silent fisherman. Its yellow was a bright contrast against the worn-out gray timber on either side. The bridge's deck was spotted with an oily substance—fish blood, Boo knew, but it was easy to imagine it was his own. Or Gussie's. Or some monster's.

And then they were off the bridge and barreling into South Patch; one boy in a suit pedaling madly, one boy in jeans hanging on desperately.

"Slow down!" Boo called out. "You want to kill me?"

"But it's gonna rain, soon. See those clouds? I want to get there before it starts."

"Won't make any difference if I'm dead!"

Thunder growled like a giant hound somewhere in the distance. Boo kept his eyes straight ahead as he and Ash rolled onward. He dared now to take one hand from the handlebars to touch the flannel pouch beneath his shirt.

They reached Pigg's Point at low tide. The creek was a flat, turbid trickle in the middle of a wide pan of smelly swamp mud. Boo Taylor's skiff was moored on the opposite bank.

"She uses your boat sometimes," Ash explained lamely.

Boo studied the mud. Then he studied the gathering clouds. "You feel like gettin your Sunday best all muddied up?"

Ashford gazed dismally at the marshy expanse. "Hell, I guess I'm muddied up enough already," he said, and he managed a miserable smile. "Tell the truth, Boo, suddenly I'm not in any all-fired hurry to go on." The smile cracked and fell away, and now he looked worried and sick. "Up to you, I guess."

Boo tried to sound confident. "Well, we're here. Best to get it over with."

They stripped off their shoes and socks and rolled their trouser legs up to their knees. Then they climbed down the bank and into the muck where they held their shoes high and balanced like tightrope walkers. Halfway across, their feet squished ankle-deep into the slippery goop, and creek water rose to mid-thigh, soaking their pants. Boo stayed alert for gators and let his toes reach out hesitantly for the rocky backs of terrapins and snappers, remembered Laylee Colebriar's warning that if a snapper got hold of a boy's foot it wouldn't let go till its mother died.

When they had almost cleared the water, Ash's feet slipped out from under him, and he fell into a puddle. One shoe went burrowing into the mud with his fist. "Christ on a fruitloop, my daddy's gonna kill me," he muttered and stood himself up again. His starched white shirt and the seat of his double-knit trousers came away slopping olive-gray soup. He shook mud out of the shoe. A sock flopped into the puddle. Ash grumbled again and continued without it.

They climbed the far bank and carried their shoes into the trail that wound closer to the sound and on toward Chaliboque.

At last, barefoot, they came around the final cobbled turn in the trail. It rose like a giant tomb toward the leaden sky. Boo Taylor thought of a spiderweb, a great confusion of strands all connected and strummed like a harp. "Okay, Ash, we're here. So what's the plan?"

Ash Marchant looked at him with blank dismay. He wagged a shoe at the air. "I figured you'd think of something."

Boo sighed and rolled his eyes back to the house. He wished now he had gone to see Miss Laylee first. Thunder bellowed from somewhere close.

"I told y'all not to do it, didn't I?" Boo said.

"I know."

"But you did anyway. Ash, *you* did."

"I know, I *know!*"

Ashford had gone a pathetic shade of gray. Boo sighed again. "So it's on the mantel?" he asked. "In that room upstairs?"

"I guess. I don't know. Maybe she moved it."

"Then, I guess we just go in," he said. "We go upstairs, and we look. If it's there, we take it out and you can stick it back in the grave, or whatever. If it's not there, I'm not gonna stick around to look for it. You want, you can do that yourself."

"I'm not looking around, either," Ash said quickly. "But what if *she's* there?"

Boo looked into Ash Marchant's anxious, despairing face. "Then I guess we just hurry," he said. Then he sat down and began to tug his socks and sneakers over his dirty feet.

The first drops of rain began to fall.

Boo went in first.

The clouds wicked much of the light from the sky; only a feeble glow seeped through the cracks and broken windows. The glow and the thick, wet air crept like fog over everything inside the place: mottled walls, slumped floors, heaps of rubbish, splintered furniture. They passed through the first rooms and on into the even darker hallways, the burned places, moving slowly, listening—hearing the stifled patter of rain against the house, hearing dwarfish feet scurrying within the walls, hearing Chaliboque itself moan and tremble under its sagging old age.

Ash kept Boo Taylor's square back close ahead of him. His left foot, sockless in the shoe, clumped ponderously along the floor. His wet pant legs chaffed his knees and his calves. He looked back frequently, always certain either a ghost-woman or a ghost-man had slipped out of some cobwebby corner and was sneaking up behind them.

They came to the bottom of the wide stairs, and Boo paused.

He sniffed at the air.

Cocked his head.

Far away, a mechanical recording: music? humming?

Around a corner, a spray of white-blond hair, thick nose-packed breathing. Sparks and dust motes whirled on the air, either at a great distance or very close, gathering substance, trying to become something, trying to pick a spot to do it in. A cold mist swept their damp legs.

Ashford shuddered. He laid his hand on Boo's shoulder. *"Boo?"*

Boo gasped, jumped around. "Goddamn, Ash!" he whispered furiously. "Don't *do* that!"

Ash drew his hand back as if burned, unnerved that Boo Taylor could be so jumpy. "Sorry," he said quietly. "You hear anything upstairs? Gosh, I thought I heard something."

Boo held still for a moment and listened. Only the rain and the odd prattle of the old house. "No," he said with irritation. "Let's get going."

But they both faltered at the bottom step, watching the other steps looming like a mountain slope before them, rising into deeper and murkier blue-grayness. Boo held stiff a moment longer. Then started up. Ash followed, close enough to smell Boo Taylor's sweat, darting quick glances over his shoulder and dodging the rotted planks.

They passed into complete darkness and had to feel along the banister.

And then felt along the wall as they came to the second-floor landing where the mildew and rot and ancient smoke was worse. Boo held his right hand out, waving it at the dark, while the fingernails of his left hand scraped up chalk flecks and brittle remnants of wallpaper and stringy insect-things. Thunder tremored above them, around them in a long, restless rumble of indigestion. The corridor bent back toward the front of the house, and the dim glow returned. Boo let out a breath and took his hand away from the wall. He wiped it on his trousers.

They reached the row of mostly broken windows along the front of the house where rain spangled off the shards and sputtered through to soak the floor. Then around the last turn, toward the open door of the room they sought, a yellow light was flickering.

Boo heard Ash clip-clopping along behind him, pant legs swishing, could hear him breathing now, too, although the weird echoes off the walls amplified the sound and made it seem to come from the room ahead.

The rancid smells of the house gamboled around him, mixing now with some sharp spice—also coming from the room. The doorway was a hole in the wall, drawing larger as he rode this cloud of frightened breaths and sharp tang closer, until he realized the sounds and the smells were not behind him at all, they were billowing out of the room like smoke, and they were laced with fine steel threads: a web, coiling itself around him and drawing him inside. He was helpless to the pull, surrendered to it now, as light and reason and Ashford Marchant all faded to insignificance behind.

He opened his eyes, and he was in the room.

"Well, I'll be tied to a post and *whipped*—if it ain't my sweet Mr. Boo! You come home to your Crystal at last! Looks like maybe you come at a bad time, doctor's boy."

The walls of the room, writhing with its obscenities, rising and falling, groaning goatishly, shrinking around him, trapping him, squeezing the breath from his lungs. Crystal Burne, lounging in a florescent white slip before the great windows, was a jarring contrast of dark and light.

She was the audience.

Before her, mostly hidden to Boo's eyes behind a collapsed velvet sofa, a sick pagan dance was being performed.

A grappling of naked skin and blonde hair.

The little girl's eyes, swimming with pouty misery.

Above that, Lester Meggett's vapid face, hair fallen over the dull slits of his eyes.

A flash of lightning filled the room with white light.

"Les, what the hell are you *doin?*" Boo Taylor blurted.

Lester's face changed, bloomed with shame. "Oh shit," he said.

The little girl began to cry. It was a baby's wail.

"God *dammit,* Les!"

Boo took another step into the room. The mass upon the sofa shifted again, and another form rose into view. It took Boo a moment to recognize it, stripped of everything.

"Dewey?"

"B-boo, what are you..."

Dewey Fitch fumbled away from the heap of flesh on the sofa, his eyes left Boo's for a moment, as Lester's did, and they both turned anxiously to Crystal Burne.

The little girl's wails rose up to fill the room. She scrabbled from beneath the pile and floundered on doe's legs to the older girl. Crystal Burne was up on her knees now and accepted the child into her embrace.

The wails jagged through Boo Taylor's brain. Lester had gotten to his knees as well; Dewey was standing behind him. Their faces were fallen and blanched like half-empty sacks of flour.

"Why Mr. Ash-ford! You come along t'see all your friends, too?" Crystal Burne croaked, her voice lost in the little girl's ululations. Boo looked briefly behind him and saw Ash Marchant half-in and half-out of the doorway.

"You knew about this?" Boo asked furiously.

Ashford dropped his eyes. "Not really. Not..."

Crystal Burne chuckled. "Sorry, your sweet old friend ain't exactly here at the moment, Mr. Ash. But she be around 'fore too long." She made long, indulgent strokes through the little girl's hair.

"The skull," Ashford whispered harshly.

The words passed through Boo as meaningless—there were just the girl's wet shrieks and Crystal Burne's toothy smirk. And Lester and Dewey, stripped and stunned. Crystal Burne was starting to rise, gently pushing the little girl away. "Lord, you two boys stink—you step in somethin? I do hope you wiped your feet 'fore you came in."

Panic now in Ashford's voice: "Boo, hurry—she said *she* was coming! Get the *skull!*"

Why was the skull so important? He had forgotten. Boo's sight swam loosely from the scene before him and off toward the fireplace. The skull's face was poised like a gargoyle on the mantel. *Ate one up and licked the other.* The black pits of its eyes hid the knowledge of some ancient hurt.

"Boo she's coming!"

Ash shoved him from behind. Boo looked around, saw Crystal Burne skulking around Lester and Dewey, her breasts swaying easily beneath the silk, her teeth glowing white menace before the bleak, storm-battered windows. The little girl's fingers were fishhooks caught in the fabric of the slip. She shrieked and trailed the dark girl into the middle of the room.

"She's *coming!* Get the *skull!*"

Nothing important about the skull. Was there? Then why did it suddenly feel so important to have it in his hands. He heard a snatch of Mamie Stuvant's nursery rhyme, playing back for him. Part of her grand and ancient joke:

Tailor's mother had a son;
and never had another one...

It was Crystal Burne, singing in a faint but painfully sharp scream inside his head where dots were connecting and ancient patterns were coming into focus. Where buried things were being unearthed. Skulls and apple-faced grins and old black-and-white photographs. "The skull," he said, looking at it, trying to calculate its age. "It's not Sheba Tribbit's skull is it?"

Crystal Burne smiled happily. "Why, that's good, Mr. Boo! You figure that out by yourself?"

"Who's is it?"

"Oh, I think you know."

"Tell me!"

She slinked another step closer to the mantel. "*Tell* you? Why don't you ask that skinny white boy at the library." She arched an eyebrow at his reaction. "Oh, you don't think your Crystal knows what you been up to?"

Boo blinked at Crystal Burne. Then blinked at the bone on the mantel. He saw the photograph in the newspaper article clipped from the *Macon Herald*. A pretty young girl in a fifties bob.

"Her name was Hawthorne," he said.

Crystal Burne took another step, detaching the little girl from her hip. "Name? Names don't mean nothin."

"Her name was Hawthorne, and there used to be a family of Hawthornes on the island, years and years ago. One of them used to own an oyster factory. They were friends with the LaValle's."

"Were they now? Seem like you and that skinny white boy been doin your homework, Mr. Boo."

"Hoss Beaudry's great-granddad was Wirth Buckler, and he owned a grocery back then. Timmy Duff's granddad was a shrimper. They must have been there when they lynched Joker Tribbit. And a Hawthorne must have been there, too. Is that it? And she was related to him." He lifted a finger toward the mantel. "She was buried over here somewhere in an unmarked grave. She drowned, and nobody knew who she was."

Crystal Burne's grin became sly. "Nobody?" she asked. "Why, I guess some folks must'a known. Ain't that right?"

"Miss Laylee?"

Who else? Who else knew?

Behind him, Ash was whimpering. "Boo, what are you talking about? Get the skull!"

The dark girl laughed at him and slid toward the mantel. Boo, seeing where she was moving, lurched forward to reach the skull before her and snatched it up.

Her hand snaked around his wrist.

"Put it back," she said dully.

Boo jerked away, but her hand held tight. The evil good humor had left her face; she was glaring at him, now. The same inhuman, melted, angry-knot glare from the day they found the old cemetery.

"No," he said.

For a moment, his vision warped and Crystal Burne seemed to expand like a bloated frog, growing wider, taller. Her voice fell several octaves. *"You in my house, boy,"* rumbled a voice suddenly much older. *"An' dat oagly ol toad ain't here!"* The meaty hand of something very large flashed around. Boo ducked, yanked hard, and came free. He stumbled away.

Suddenly small and young again, Crystal Burne howled with frustration.

Boo backed toward the door, holding the skull close to his chest.

Crystal Burne was regaining her composure. She smoothed the length of her slip with her hands. She grinned at him.

"Mr. Boo, you come on to your Crystal."

"No."

"You come on. 'Fore it be too late."

Boo took another step back, darted a glance at the others and rejected them at once—they were still glued in place by shame and shock. Only the little girl seemed to be on his side as she clawed at the big girl's hip, shrieking.

Crystal Burne unleashed a howl and sprang.

Boo stepped forward, arched the skull up and beneath her arms. He slugged the heavy bone into her stomach.

She exhaled violently.

Collapsed to her knees.

The little girl's wails cut off abruptly; their echo rang through the room, rang through his head along with the echo of Crystal Burne's last, horrible shriek.

Thunder rolled.

"Oh gosh," Ash whimpered.

The dark girl, holding her stomach and sucking air, tilted her head up and looked at him through the thick spill of her hair with a single, blood-rimmed eye. She growled, gathered her feet. As she was preparing to spring again, Boo Taylor swung the skull again and this time crashed it into her head, skull against skull, sending a bolt of fire through his wrist.

Crystal Burne made a wet bleat and fell back to the floor.

Boo Taylor stepped away from her. He turned back to the others.

Dewey snatched his pants from the floor and covered himself. His breath came rapidly and erratically, and he seemed ready to cry. "Boo, I never...this is the first..."

But Boo shut his eyes. Then looked down at the face in his hands. Dead, but bleeding. Red splatters and black, spiderweb strands marred the temple.

"Can we bury it now?" Ash asked. He had chanced a few steps further into the room.

The little girl gazed miserably at him. Tears muddied her face. Her lips bunched into a soaking pout.

"Boo?" Ashford asked.

Crystal Burne was moving, a slumped creature trying to find its feet, but its feet were slipping drunkenly across a threadbare carpet. Lightning flashed; thunder exploded; the world heaved a long and heavy gasp.

At last, Boo Taylor said, "Let's just get out of here."

six

He led them through the jungle, uprighted his boat, and paddled them over a rising Pigg's Creek in the rain.

"But what if *she* comes back?" Ashford protested.

The skull, unburied, occupied the space between Boo Taylor's feet at the bottom of the skiff. "She's comin back no matter what."

"But, Boo—"

"*No,* Ash."

Dewey and Lester watched the rain make meteor splashes on the water and wisely said nothing. Lester attempted to light a cigarette, and Boo swatted it out of his lips.

On the northern bank, Boo dragged the skiff into the woods and hid it behind a stand of myrtle. He carried the skull and escorted the others with their bikes as far as the fork in the trail that split north to Sugar Dam Road and east to Laylee Colebriar's house. He pointed north.

"You boys go on home," he said. "It's my fault; I should have never let you get started in all this—but all that's over with as of right now. No more *dares;* no more *diggin!* You boys got that?"

They nodded sullenly.

"And nobody ever goes back to that house, either. I find out any of y'all come down here, *ever,* and I will personally pound the livin tar out of you. Then I'll tell your daddies what you been up to. Then I'll pound y'all some more." He balled a fist. "Goddammit, Les, Dewey, I ought'a do it anyway!"

Lester started, "Boo, you can't—"

"Shut up, Les! Boy, I'll whip you silly right *here!*"

Dewey grabbed Lester Meggett's arm and pulled him away.

Ash whined, "But that *woman,* Boo—Mamie or Sheba. The *ghosts.* They'll just keep coming around unless you..."

Boo tucked the skull under his arm like a football. "I'll take care of it."

He watched them mope away. Then he lowered his head to the rainstorm and pushed off toward Miss Laylee's house.

As he neared the garden, Miss Laylee's voice twittered to him like a sparrow's call amid the clatter of chimes. Boo smeared the rain from his eyes to see her, expecting her to be waiting for him on the tiny porch. But it wasn't Laylee Colebriar waiting for him at all. It was a tall stalk of whiteness, bending lithely to the rhythms of the storm, laughing at the thunder, whipping a great golden-red mane into the wind.

He dropped to the shelter of bean chutes.

The skull, a fumbled football, rolled lopsided into the garden rows.

He heard Miss Laylee's voice again and dared a look through the leaves. She was mounted half-out of the kitchen window, laughing, almost falling. He made out the words "soap" and "cold," and the rest was lost in the rain. Shamus was there, too, sharing the rain shower and prancing through the mud like a puppy.

Turn away, his mind shouted.

Turn away?

He pulled apart wet leaves and watched. Gussie Dutton, bathing in a thunderstorm in the very spot where he once did the same, under Miss Laylee's very same watch and just as nude.

He let the rain soak him.

Lightning flashed, and she squealed merrily. A roll of thunder followed.

Shamus let out a string of barks, and Boo had the sudden, horrifying certainty that Shamus would sniff him out and come bounding into the garden.

Then Gussie was splashing toward the house, scampering up porch steps to where Miss Laylee had come around to meet her with a towel. The door welcomed her inside, and she was gone.

He waited a good fifteen minutes before going inside.

seven

Gussie Dutton was nestled in the parlor sofa where she was gnawing a drumstick and sipping iced tea. Boo Taylor entered, soaked; he looked uncomfortable and spoke only perfunctorily. Gussie smiled when Laylee made him strip out of his wet T-shirt and his sneakers and socks. The old woman pointed at his jeans, too, and then cackled madly when he shot her a furious glare. She wrung out the socks and shirt over her sink and placed them on the warm stove to dry.

Naked to the waist, Boo settled into a parlor chair. "I went to Chaliboque," he said, and Gussie felt her face darken. "I'm sorry, Gussie. I know I promised. But, there's something—"

"Yes, you *did* promise, didn't you?" she blasted at him.

Miss Laylee was considering him with concern. Boo was looking back at her strangely. "Boy, why would you wanna go snoopin 'round that evil place?"

Boo looked at his hands. "There was. . .trouble."

"Trouble," Gussie said. She glowered and crossed her arms.

"I *had* to go."

"Oh, you *had* to go?"

"Yes, I did. Ash and Les and Dewey were in trouble."

"*They* were there?"

"Yes."

"And I suppose *she* was there, too!" She wanted to wring his neck.

"Gussie," Boo said, leaning forward, "Crystal Burne is Mamie Stuvant's granddaughter."

"She's *what?* Boo Taylor, what are you talking about?" She looked wildly to Laylee Colebriar.

But the old woman only pursed her heavy lips and sadly rocked her head.

"You mean that's *true?*" Gussie fired. She faced Boo again. "And you *knew* that? You knew that and you went there anyway?"

"Of course I didn't know!" he said staunchly, then faltered. "I only...well, I only just figured it out." He sighed and turned to the window. Outside, the rain rose and fell in fits and starts. "When I was in Mamie Stuvant's house that day, she had some pictures in her kitchen. I asked about them, and she told me they were her grandchildren. Crystal Burne and that little girl, Cassie."

"You saw their pictures?"

"They were *old* pictures, Gussie. I didn't recognize them. Before that, I thought..."

He glanced up. Coughed.

Across the room, Miss Laylee was quiet.

"Before that, I don't know what I thought," he said. "I went to the library, and Dalton Satterfield helped me look up some old articles. I found out Mamie Stuvant had a daughter and two granddaughters. Her daughter died; I think her husband beat her to death or something. Then *he* died, and I think Mamie Stuvant must have poisoned him."

Gussie folded one leg over the other and leaned back in the sofa. "Boo Taylor, you're either an idiot or just plain crazy."

He regarded her for another moment and then stood. Without speaking, he left through the front door. After nearly a minute he returned, wet again. He was holding out a human skull.

Raindrop tears dripped from black, sightless depths. Stormy saliva drooled from ragged teeth. Orange clay was caked in the suture cracks, in the fold of sharp cheekbones, in the gaps between granite-pebble teeth, in the deep wedge of a nose. A slim leathery strip of scalp still sprouted a few longish hairs.

"Ash and the others dug this up," he told them. "Crystal Burne got them to do it."

Gussie looked queasily at the chicken bones in her lap.

"I wasn't with them when they did it," he said quickly.

The old woman was studying the ancient, nicotine-stained face. Her own face, even more ancient, was a sagging web of wrinkles. She reached out and patted, tapped, fondled, investigated the slick misery of the skull's brow.

"It's my mother, isn't it?" Boo asked her. "My *real* mother."

Gussie, who had also been staring at the skull, brought her eyes up to Boo's. "Boo Taylor, you're..." She turned to the old woman. "Miss Laylee, that's just..."

But Laylee Colebriar was withdrawing her hand, frowning, drooping two coffee bean sacks at her jowls. Boo placed the skull on the table. He reached into his back pocket and withdrew a wrinkled strip of newsprint. He handed this to Gussie.

GIRL MISSING

Gussie read the article, feeling shell-shocked. She looked at the blurry old photograph, then looked at the face on the table.

"It's my real mother," Boo continued. "She drowned and was buried over there when it was a county graveyard. A graveyard for paupers."

"Paupers?" Gussie asked.

"She washed up on the beach. Nobody knew who she was."

He shared another mysterious glance with Miss Laylee.

Gussie was shaking her head. "I don't understand, Boo. How can you be sure she's your real mother?"

Now the old woman spoke up. "Cause somebody tryin to tell him so, Miss Gus. Left you a message, didn't they boy?"

Boo nodded, eyeing her carefully. "That article was inside a little stuffed doll. I found it on the pier on my birthday."

"Your *thirteenth* birthday."

"Yes'm."

"Day you stopped bein a boy."

"The night I . . ." He wanted to say more, but he stopped. He glanced at Gussie nervously.

"You found it inside a doll?" Gussie asked.

"Mamie Stuvant put it there, I'm pretty sure. And it explains everything. Why I keep seeing Mamie Stuvant. Why Crystal Burne keeps tryin to get me over there." He reached again for the skull, touching it lightly. Then he squared around to the old woman. "In one of the articles I found it talks about the medical examiner's report. It says the drowned woman had just given birth. Nothing else—just that she'd had a baby. Nothing about what *happened* to it. That was *me*, wasn't it?"

A breeze swept through the yard and brought a harsh clatter from the chimes and the rusty iron taste of rain through minuscule screen holes.

"Yes, boy," she said. "That was you."

"And you're the guffer doctor," Boo said, accusing. "The midwife."

Gussie Dutton looked back and forth between the two, enduring the anguish that flowed between them. Boo was glaring at the Eulahlah Colebriar. Finally, she asked, "Miss Laylee, what's goin on? Were you there when it happened?"

The old woman picked up her cane and shuffled to a window. She looked out upon the garden. "What's goin on, Miss Gus? Why, same thing that always been goin on 'round this mean ol island. Lot of old hurt gettin dug up and poked at."

Boo grunted.

"Girl in trouble come to me, the way girls sometimes did in them days. White or black, they come see ol Laylee. More often than you might guess. Stayed here in this very place, round with child." She glanced at Boo. "Time comes, some keep the child and some don't."

Gussie looked at the clipping that was still in her hand. "You knew Boo's mother?"

"Yes."

"And when she died, you took the child to the doctor and Miss MaeEllen. You worked for him back then, didn't you?"

"Yes, Miss Gussie, that's just what I did."

"And they wanted you to keep it a secret."

The liquid lips pursed; the ancient woman gathered breath, considered the both of them sadly, cautiously. "Miss Gus, I suppose that's somethin for Mr. Boo to talk over with his daddy and Miss MaeEllen. Think old Miss Laylee said enough."

She took a step from the window when, outside, from the belly of the storm, a voice roared thunder, lightning, outrage, a thousand wounded animal shrieks.

"Come out old woman!"

❖   ❖   ❖

Gussie Dutton flashed to the night this same little shack was surrounded by headlights.

They're back—my daddy, Henry Ray, all those others!

Then she recognized the voice, and a jealous furor snapped loose. She met Boo Taylor's worried gaze.

"You hidin that boy in there, ain't you?"

The gray tufts of Laylee Colebriar's eyebrows pulled together to make her own private storm clouds. She crossed the room and slammed open the screen door. Boo followed her. Gussie lurched out of her seat and came behind him.

Crystal Burne stood in the middle of the garden, bean chutes wrapped to her waist, rainwater splattering the length of her white slip, making it transparent and ghostly.

"Why there you is," she croaked. "Gawd, you does move fast for such an old, old lady. An' there's my sweet little boy, too; so young. You been hidin from me, Mr. Boo? You run off to be with that pretty little red-hair pussy?"

This was the girl she was worried might seduce Boo Taylor? Under the steady drizzle of rain, she was a rain-slicked, wild-eyed maniac, hair a splash of frantic, blacksnake coils. A gray mist of midges swarmed her as if she were some dead, rotting thing. And there was a line of blood trickling from her scalp, splitting like a crimson lightning bolt above her left eye, trailing down her nose and her cheek.

Gussie glanced briefly at the muscle along Boo Taylor's back. Had he done that to her?

Laylee marched down the porch steps and stood with her hands on her hips. She bellowed, "You gwon, girl! Git your trashy hide off my property, right now!"

"You hush up, old hag. I does what I wants!"

"Don't you hush me, girl. You gwon an' *git!*"

"Me git? It's that boy up there keep comin 'round to see *me*, woman! He likes his Crystal, don't you, Mr. Boo?"

"That's not true," Boo whispered.

"Well he ain't comin 'round you no more, so you git, you hear me? You git for *good!*"

Gussie looked through the greenery for sign of the little girl.

"Oh, he git all right, but he be back. He got hisself a taste of somethin *good*, don't you doctor's boy? You tell your little witch 'bout me, sugar? You tell her 'bout the sweet time you and your Crystal have together?"

Boo roared, "We didn't do *anything* together!" He half-turned and said quietly,

"Gussie, we didn't!"

Crystal Burne spit out a long, throaty laugh. The fierce malevolence never left her face. "Aw, baby, how can you say that?"

"ENOUGH!"

It was an eagle's screech, erupting from Laylee Colebriar's throat. It sent brittle, icy tremors through the wind chimes and made Gussie take an involuntary step backward. She looked down at the old woman, scarcely believing such a sound could have come from her. She had never seen Laylee Colebriar angry before. She noticed for the first time the way the steel-wool pigtails curled like devil's horns.

She reached for Boo Taylor's hand and squeezed it.

Crystal Burne straightened from her crouch, wary now, made a slow look behind as if expecting someone in the trees would step forward and take up sides with her.

"You gwon or not, girly!" Laylee shouted, back in her normal, shrill bird's call. "Either way, I'm gonna see to it Sheriff Tillman comes out to that ol house and clears you out."

The dark girl glared guardedly from beneath a tangle of hair. "Ain't no white sheriff gonna give a listen to what a ugly ol nigger-lady got to say."

"He listen to this boy's *daddy* well enough."

Crystal Burne whipped the hair away from her face. "That tired old drone ain't no more his daddy than *you* is, old woman. An' there ain't nothin some fool sheriff can do to *me,* anyways." Sly contempt crept back to the girl's face. "Seems like you knows all about that!"

Laylee growled. "You stay right where you please, then, missy. Sheriff Tillman be out there 'fore nightfall an' take care of you. You an' the rest."

"Then, you see where *I* be come nightfall," Crystal Burne answered. "Me an' all the *rest.*"

A moment of silence.

A moment when nothing moved—not Laylee Colebriar or Crystal Burne, not the flying midges or the clouds or the distant waves of the Atlantic, not even the breeze.

Not the misting rain, not the drops that had gathered at the edge of the porch awning, swollen ripe and ready to fall and burst.

Not Gussie Dutton's heart.

And then, as everything else in the world remained absolutely . . . *still* . . . for a beat longer . . .

Laylee Colebriar flew stomping, raging, trampling across the sloppy dirt yard and into the garden. By the time she reached the first of the low squash plants, Shamus appeared out of nothingness, hackles raised, and followed her precise trail. The old woman plowed into the green stalks like a rickety, antique tractor running untended and out of control, mowed heedlessly through the plants; leaves and beans and cherry tomatoes were flung like green and yellow and red confetti in her wake.

Gussie lost sight of Crystal Burne as the old woman bore down on her, ready to run her down with the same disregard as she had the plants.

And then the runaway tractor came to a stop.

Gussie strained around Boo Taylor's shoulder to see as the old woman's momentum carried her a step further into an empty space in the garden where a burst of black feathers suddenly mushroomed into the sky.

Shamus stood poised at the old woman's skirt boiling a savage volley of barks.

"What happened?" Gussie asked, still looking around Boo Taylor. "Where...?"

In the garden, the gnarled old troll-lady wavered, her gray dress and her stained, white apron fluttering in the breeze as a dozen or more feathers swirled about her.

"Boo, what happened?" Gussie whispered.

Then the old woman turned back to the house. She looked up at Boo with an expression Gussie could not read. Gussie tugged his hand, forcing him to descend the steps with her as Laylee Colebriar slowly worked her way back to them. "Miss Laylee, what just happened?" she asked softly as Eulahlah Colebriar approached. The old woman was limping, Gussie saw, just an old, gray songbird, a frail, hunchbacked, colored housemaid in a ragged dress and secondhand saddle shoes. As she neared them, Gussie saw a single black feather had come to rest on her shoulder.

Her bracelets suddenly spangled lightning, a whipcord flash smacking across Boo Taylor's face.

"Ow!" Boo bellowed. He bent over, holding his face, then stood up with tears rolling from his eyes and blood dribbling from his nostrils. "Dammit! Will people please stop hittin my *nose!*"

Laylee, her face loosely bunched in anger, told him, "Mr. Boo, you got to tend to that nose an' keep it clear from where it don't belong. You made a promise to Miss Gussie, an' you didn't see fit to keep it."

Shamus was still barking wildly from the garden.

"Made *me* a promise, too, a while back," she continued. "Said you wasn't gonna go near that Mamie Stuvant."

Still holding his nose, he countered angrily, "It wasn't like that, and you know it!"

"Don't know nothin of the sort. A promise is a *promise*, boy."

"But I was trying to *help*. And don't twist this around. You *lied* to me about my parents. You *knew*."

She sighed. Her eyes went terribly sad. "I know," she whispered. "Mr. Boo, I got my own promises to keep."

She moved toward him and tried to brush his hand away so she could hold his face. After a moment's protest he let her. She tilted his head in her delicate fingers and examined his face, wiping the blood from his lip.

"You got to learn to keep a promise," she said quietly. "Lord don't like it when you break a promise."

She released his face and wiped her hands on her apron. Then she turned to the dog and clapped her hands. *"Hiye!"* she cried sharply, and Shamus stopped barking at once. He wagged his tail and trotted back to the house.

Rain hazed over them, a wet sheet growing thicker as the clouds regathered above. Gussie moved to Boo Taylor's side, held his arm. Amber fluid leaked from the pouch at his throat, trailing a single line over his chest, wobbling through the ripples of his ribs, sliding down the tautness of his belly, disappearing finally into the waistband of his jeans.

"Miss Laylee," she said evenly, and the old woman looked at her, "I want to know what's goin on."

.. eight

"It's all true, isn't it?"

Boo Taylor was in agony.

"My mother was a Hawthorne, and there was a Hawthorne at the lynching."

He was pacing at the foot of the steps.

"And Mamie Stuvant and Crystal Burne and Sheba—they're gettin back at the people who were there.

"They know magic. And they want to get me."

He held out a yellow skull.

"It's Sheba's curse."

They huddled on the porch where Laylee Colebriar accepted the skull into her hands and, now, having waited for Boo to say his piece, was ready to speak. Gussie Dutton stared into the soggy, time-worn eyes, rimmed pink, still glittering silver and gold firework bursts and decided she could believe in anything the old woman might tell her.

"Time we stitch a bit of our own magic; weave our own spell. Boy, you got them black spooks hangin over you, that's for sure. You stir things up with Mamie Stuvant, like I tell you not to, an' look where you be? You go crawlin 'round Chaliboque, like you promise you *wasn't,* an' look what happen?"

Boo stirred restlessly in his chair. "But Miss Laylee, I was only helpin my friends."

"Helpin 'em to their *graves.* Set that *witch* on 'em is what you done."

Gussie looked toward the woods. "Witch? Really?"

"Mamie Stuvant's granddaughter, Sheba Tribbit's heir," the old woman said, "what else would she be? Young, maybe, but she knows her poisons and potions and all manner of dark ways. Steal skins? Oh, she knows that trick well enough, too. You faced her at day, boy, and you come through in most of one piece. You face her at night, an' you ain't gonna be so lucky. But she *bleeds.* She bleeds, got bones that break, gets sick—cause she jes flesh an' blood like you an' me. An' she can't do no harm if she locked up in jail."

"Jail?"

"That's right, Miss Gus! Cause that's where we gonna send her!"

The old woman reached for the screen door.

"Miss Gussie," she said, "Mr. Boo's got a call to make. You welcome t'stay for a bit, then you got to go on home. After that"—she pulled open the door—"Mr. Boo and me got a chore to tend to 'fore nightfall." She smiled widely, compassionately, stretching the turtle-flesh wrinkles around her mouth. "Best if you don't come with us this time, honey."

nine

All it took was a phone call, and his daddy fixed it all.

They followed Laylee Colebriar nearly a mile to the High Spot on Church Street where Boo used the phone to call Dr. Taylor. One skinny, silver-bullet dime clinking though the slot of a beat-up old pay phone, and the wheels of the great white-man machines on Sweetpatch Island were plunged into quick proficiency.

One call. And there they were, filling South Patch with squawking radios and round-and-round, red-and-blue popcorn lights.

Of course, the police found no one.

They prowled the woods, disappeared over the creek, returned after an hour, pants muddied, shirts brambled, faces blotched red and white.

Seems somebody's been livin there, sure enough. But they cleared off. No tellin where they got to, is there?

But what if they came back?

When the day gave way to the night?

You face her at night, an' you ain't gonna be so lucky, boy.

What happened when the squawking radios gave way to the crickets and frogs and bubbling swamp-water tides? And the red-and-blue police lights gave way to the placid, silver glow of the moon?

ten

He rowed Miss Laylee across Pigg's Creek toward the Chaliboque side. It was just the two of them now with the thick lump of bone and a buckram gunnysack the old woman had stuffed full in the kitchen.

"Mr. Boo," she asked, now that Gussie was well on her way home, "you ever lay with that girl?"

"What do you mean?"

She scowled. "You know what I mean."

He flushed. "Crystal Burne? No!"

She nodded, dipped a finger in the creek water. She looked away. Then, in a soft voice, she asked, "What about the little one."

"Miss Laylee!" Surprise, then recalling the image of Lester Meggett, Dewey Fitch climbing over tiny, white limbs. "Of *course* not!"

A bolt of sunlight filtered through the trees and lit her age-weary face. She looked immensely troubled. "You got to be careful, boy," she told him, though it seemed she was talking more to herself. "*Temptation.* Temptation of the *flesh;* it's bound to be your ruination, you not careful. It's generally the ruination of us all."

Still stung, Boo was silent as he brought the skiff to the opposite shore. He tied the bow line to a root, then helped the old woman and her cargo to land.

They didn't speak. It seemed they had come to a place where they needed to be silent.

Laylee Colebriar led the way through the swamp thicket, thrusting her cane through fat green leaves and serpentine vines like a machete. Boo followed, carrying the skull and the old woman's sack of magic.

Then they moved into a low, oak-tree cave in the jungle, wrapped on the east by mangrove, on the west by the tumbled brick wall that was now eaten away by moss and pennywort. At last she stopped.

It was a shallow ditch surrounded by clay heaps.

The shovels were gone. Rainwater had collected in the grave, bathing a headless skeleton in a rusty pool.

Boo stared into the hole, at the pathetic collection of bones. "There's no marker," he said quietly.

Miss Laylee was somber. "She died a pauper. Left nothin behind in this world but you."

They stood quietly for several minutes. Then, as if coming back to life, the old woman said, "Mr. Boo, you go fetch some sticks. Oak sticks, mind you—that cypress ain't good for nothin. 'Bout an armload might do her. Make 'em the length of your anklebone to your knee bone. Don't matter how thick they is, but the straighter the better."

He went off to do her bidding while she rummaged through her duffel. Then she took several loose bricks from the ruined wall and placed these in the rough shape of a cross at the head of the grave. "Sweet Jesus forgive me, this ain't rightly a Christian burial, but it have to do. Mr. Boo, now you jab them sticks in the ground all the way 'round that grave. Keep 'em close together, an' make sure they stand good an' solid. Make like you puttin up a fence. Gonna keep her in safe, an' keep the bad spooks out."

He did as she instructed, kneeling in the clay. She stood in assessment over him, her mouth worrying an invisible root over her gums. Boo's eyes were level with the limp stockings gathered at her ankles, the mud-splattered shoes, the buckram sack of magic.

When he was done, he stood next to her.

"Put this to your lips. Take a long, long taste of it and hold it in your mouth a bit."

It was whiskey. From the bottle he had watched her buy at the High Spot just before making the call to his father. Old Fish Hook studied her gravely when she slid the three crumpled bills across the counter to him, as if he knew exactly what old Eulahlah Colebriar was up to and was afraid for her.

Or afraid *of* her.

"Now, you spit it out. Every drop of it. Spit it right into that grave."

It was a mouthful of gasoline and cider. He spit it out, but his tongue was already burned, and despite what she commanded, a drop slid like a hot coal down his throat. He wiped his mouth and spit out strings of foul-tasting lava as he watched Miss Laylee do the same. Then she upended the bottle and let whatever was left splash over the bones.

"What's this for?"

"Why, this keep her happy for a bit, so she likely to forget how much she miss you."

She reached back into the sack. Then reached for the skull.

"Take this now, Mr. Boo," she said, reverently handing the skull to him. "You put it where the head suppose to go. Then you turn it 'round, so she lookin straight down."

"Downward?"

She nodded. "It's so's the black spooks won't recognize her."

Delicately, he stepped over the stick wall he'd built. He crawled into the pit, straddling the muddy bones as best he could.

He laid the skull into place.

Above, Miss Laylee was speaking to him, telling him that next he was supposed to sprinkle cornbread and molasses and coffee grounds around the head *so's she can sup on her long walk to heaven,* but he was distracted by a locket, strung from a thin chain around the corpse's neck.

He touched it.

Not a locket, but a watch.

He scratched his thumb over its surface, scraping away the muddy clay until a stray flicker of sunlight glinted off the old silver. He read the engraved initials.

eleven

Come nightfall, Eulahlah Colebriar kept watch on her porch.

She was weeping.

Over secrets and lies and promises broken. Over spilt blood and fractured bones. Over a past brimming with misery; over a future doomed to more of the same.

She had told the boy he wasn't a man yet. True. But he was close to it, closer than even he knew. And that was what they *(he/she/it)* wanted: him, a man, so they could take from him, have yet another generation to haunt, bleed, break, keep the misery breathing and themselves fat with it.

She had learned a thing in her many long, bitter years: all hatred was self-hatred.

They hated the boy, because they hated themselves. They haunted him and became haunted. They bled him and ripped open their own flesh. Their fires were acts of self-immolation.

It was all about punishment for long-ago sins.

They punished. They punished themselves.

For the sins of the father.

The boy becoming a man. It would be coming soon.

She sat, watched, waited.

twelve

Come nightfall, an abandoned house on Rue Duck Lane was burned to the ground.

No one claimed responsibility.

A few thought they saw an old woman in the area before it happened. Or a tall, frightening man. Or several boys on a prank.

thirteen

Come nightfall, Gussie Dutton raced on foot across Sweetpatch Island; the distance between the white trash hell of Shell Pot Lane and the grand old homes of Carriage Avenue had never seemed so far. Marsh smells, grease smells, garbage smells followed her like a swarm of gnats.

Boo Taylor's house was less than two miles from her own. But it might have been on a completely separate island for all the difference of their worlds.

"Boys, this here's our island—always has been, and by God it always will. I say we got to put it back to right."

Headlights struck her, splashed over her, swept on to the pavement as a car slowed and passed. Her sneakered feet flapped the blacktop like a rough hand smacking flesh. Her hands, balled into fists, pumped stagnant night air.

"This is bad business, Lou Bob, what you boys is sayin."

"Bad business you say? Hell, Hank, what happen at the high school—you sayin that ain't bad business, too? Nicky Haufmann gets hisself thirteen stitches in his cheek, and for what? A little tar? Boy, that's bad business. That spook preacher gettin all the coloreds to gang up and vote for him—hell, I say that's cheatin, Hank. I say that's bad business. Now that Mamie Stuvant got kin runnin 'round the island, an' somebody somewhere is puttin 'em up? We supposed t'stand for that?"

Bad business. Promised to be a night for bad business; her own little errand, this desperate, sick run to Boo Taylor and the supreme respectability of his well-bred family—this was the very *worst* of business.

Running.

Running away from a dismal, fetid house that bred ignorance and meanness just as capably as it bred lice and bedbugs. Running away from stale beer and stale cigarettes and loud, late-night cursing and the grumble of savage dogs and pickup trucks at two o'clock in the morning.

After this, could she ever go back there?

I'll go live with Miss Laylee, she thought, and that was suddenly a wonderfully romantic notion that seemed almost possible. Living in that little cottage of spice-perfumes and bird songs, wrapped in the ripe, mysterious greenness of the garden. Old Miss Laylee by her bed at night, singing her to sleep; Boo Taylor at her window each morning, calling her awake. After all, didn't she just say she took in girls who were in trouble?

But that dream was dashed by the fear that Laylee Colebriar might not want her, that Boo Taylor wouldn't want her either. What if she arrived breathless and panicked at their door, and they smelled the Shell Pot rot on her and sent her back into the night? What if they told her to go back to her own family?

Not my family.

Not my father.

Not my...

❖   ❖   ❖

She'd arrived at the house on Shell Pot Lane after the long walk from Miss Laylee's. Henry Ray's Plymouth was parked in the front yard, but no one was home.

Inside, the house was silent and still. She switched on every downstairs light and waited in the kitchen. She thought about making the boys dinner, but she never moved from the table, never made a sound, didn't breathe. She sat, watched, waited—because that car meant Henry Ray was back.

Finally, the throaty roar of engines descended from all directions, stuttering to a halt amid the clamorous bark of boys. She rushed to the front window expecting Wade and Harley and Petey and maybe Murphy or Red or the Deegs—all damp from their showers and hauling their gym bags and muttering about practice or homework.

But it was men's faces, not boys'. Her father's was there. Vince Scanlon. Lou Bob Osterman. Slip Callahan. Others. Snaking amid them—half in shadow, half in headlight glare—was that a troll's face?

She raced to the back door, slipped into the gloom. She leaned on the door, listened as the harsh babble spread into the kitchen. "…upstairs?" someone asked; "… don't know," someone else (her father?) answered. "Take this out back where it's private," said another, and she felt the heavy bootfalls approach the door. She bolted into the yard, feeling exposed. Then she saw the mural of flowers she had painted and darted there, slipping inside the shed just as the men emerged from the kitchen door.

"We got to stick together, boys. We don't, and 'fore you know it, the nigs, why they just gonna take over this ol island. Look what they done to that school already. Let 'em in, and by God, right off, look at the trouble!"

The stale air inside the shed clung like hot, wet leaves to her skin. A seam in the corrugated wall, a gap of light striping her leg. She bent to it, pressed her eye to it. The men were murmuring in low, murderous tones, gathering themselves toward a boil. There was her father, face slouched with the weight of too much drink.

"Why, when I was a boy, them jigaboos knew their place well enough. They spoke polite as could be to a white man. Cause they knowed we was the ones built this place up while they was all just pickin cotton and gettin drunk on their cheap wine and singin their fool songs and collectin their government checks. Us boys, by God, we're the ones made this island what it is. Our taxes and our hard work. You think them jiggies been payin taxes down there?"

Who was that talking? Was it Lou Bob Osterman? She bent her head around all sides of the gap, saw a blur of arms and thick backs and rolled up sleeves. A skull tattoo on a fat, muscled shoulder. And her own father's droopy red eyes staring back at her.

"Them spooks, they're just gonna come on up to the white Baptist on Polk. Same's when the old school burnt."

"Ain't same's when the school burnt. For one thing, there ain't no federal government says we gotta take no niggers in our church. 'Sides, nigger tries to step foot in my woman's church—my momma's church, church where I was baptized—well, I guess he's gonna find my steel-toe boot up his backside."

"Or a load of buck."

"Or the blade of my ol Jim Bowie."

She was afraid to move, certain that if she did she'd wind up tripping over a rake or the lawn mower and raise a rusty clang into the night. Her thighs cramped where she knelt. Something brushed her knee, and she stifled a gasp—just the sweat dripping from her chin? Or a spider? Or a mouse? Or a lizard?

Burning? Did one of them say burning?

"It's what they got comin,"—this time, it really was Henry Ray's voice. His limp, unshaven face poised so close to his father's that their cheeks almost touched. It was Siamese twins she spied through the crack in the wall: one old, one young, dripping identical peasant brutishness. That was her face, too, wasn't it? Something in the eyes that marked a Dutton? Or the set of the jaw? Or some complicated tangle of features and postures and gaits that made it impossible to conceal the truth of her heritage?

"I don't know, you boys...It's breakin the law, you know?"

"Hank, it's breakin the law only if the law gives a flyin fuck about it. I happen to know that ain't necessarily so. Anyway, them burnin down the old school like that, that's breakin the law, too. Didn't see nobody get locked up for that, did y'all?"

"No."

"No. That's right. I say them nigs started it, right? I say, things was fine on this island till that darky preacher decided to go upendin the kettle."

"And them black panthers."

"And them white, suck-dick, fag instigators gettin 'em all registered."

"I say we put things back to right."

"Oh boys...this is bad business. How many we talkin about? Is Terry Lee gonna be there?"

"Twenty, twenty-five I figure, if all y'all boys is in. And I ain't tellin you who all the names is, so don't you start askin."

"Just like the old days. Like a great big party!"

"Who's bringin the wieners? Who's bringin the beer?"

Laughter now, roiling across the small lawn and through the slim fissure, filling up her shed-cave until the cobwebs quivered and flecks of rust rained down upon her and became lost in her rust-hued hair. Dutton hair, of course—the same hair on the Siamese twins out there gargling their mean laughter.

"Put it back to right," they said. "Tonight," they said.

Tonight, then.

Her knees strained in this crouch, fire rippled up from her ankles and cramped through the long muscles of her thighs. She blinked through the slim gap in the wall that allowed her to see Henry Ray and her father in the dying light. Beyond that, the house she had lived in all her life.

"What if they got guns again?"

"What if they start shootin again?"

"Oh, they don't wanna go and do that, Hank. I guaran-damn-tee you, that's the last thing them fuckin spookies wanna do, boy."

She blinked again and imagined it all—the faces, the house—gone forever.

"Oh Lord...oh shit. Well all right Vin, y'all can count me in. Me and my boy."

❖   ❖   ❖

How long had she waited in that little tin oven? Long after the men had left and she was sure none had lay behind in wait for her—because surely she had made some sound in there that echoed like a toy drum across the yard. Long enough that her legs turned from fire to ice, back to fire, then to ice again and then turned completely numb, so when she finally tried to stand, she had to press her hands against the mildewy floor for balance, and a million sharp teeth needled her thighs.

By now, she had run the needles out of her legs on the dark streets of Sweetpatch Island. Running, drinking down great gulps of tainted air. She was coming to Polk Road, almost halfway to Boo Taylor's house, and she wondered if she would ever get there.

From behind, headlights again. They slowed and held onto her. Gussie stopped, turned to see the car, and heaved for breath. She took a few backward steps like a hitchhiker as the car inched closer and as she squinted through the glare to make out its shape.

She stopped. Ice again—this time slamming through her heart.

It was Henry Ray's car.

From the driver's window: "Hey Gus, that you?"

She turned to run again as her brain exploded with terror and revulsion. The voice, at her side now, called her name again. She recoiled from it.

"Gussie, it's *me* dammit. Where the Sam Hill you goin?"

"Wade?" she called, breathless, turning again but still backing cautiously from the car. "Wade, good Lord you creep, what are you doin in that car? You scared me half to *death!*"

It *was* Wade's voice—and his shoulder and arm leaning through the window. "Gussie, don't you dare tell. Henry Ray sold his car to Petey, and he came 'round today to drop it off."

"So what are *you* doin in it?"

"Petey don't know! And don't you tell him, neither. He's up to the Burger Pen with Murph and Red, and he'd like to bust me up if he knew I was drivin his car."

"*I'd* like to bust you up," she said."

"Oh hell, so what? Harley was drivin Zack Steedman's pickup when he was twelve."

"And he wrapped it around an oak out on Green Way Road, remember?"

"...oh yeah."

Gussie walked to the car, breath and heartbeat cantering back to normal. She rested her hands on the roof.

Wade was looking up at her hopefully. "You gonna tell?"

The lowland stink still breezed from the western marshes. It rose from the car, too; it was in the vinyl seats and the cracked dashboard and the gray, chugging exhaust. *Yes, Wade, I'm gonna tell; that's exactly what I'm gonna do.*

"Wade, you have to give me a ride. And we have to hurry."

She padded around the car and opened the passenger door with a rusty squeal. When she slammed it closed, it was like banging an old carpet—layers of cigarette and beer stench puffed into the air.

"Where are we goin?" Wade asked her.

"We're goin to Boo Taylor's. We have to go to see his daddy."

"Gussie, you ain't hurt or anything? Dammit, Henry Ray, he didn't. . .?"

"No. Wade, just drive, will you?"

Eyeing her with suspicion and concern, he slid the gear lever into drive, moving awkwardly, released the brake and the car jerked forward. He grabbed the wheel with both hands and looked at his feet as he started them rolling down the street.

Gussie leaned her sweaty back against the old vinyl, hating the feel of it, hating the old smells of decay and corruption that filled her lungs.

Those smells, she thought, *they're coming from me.*

fourteen

They found Boo Taylor sitting beneath the overhang of the wide front porch at the doctor's house.

"I was worried maybe you weren't home yet," Gussie told him.

Then she exhaled her story. Boo was leaned forward on the dead-still glider, gripping the wicker armrest. He seemed barely interested.

"Boo, didn't you hear what I said? They're gonna go burn down the colored church. Maybe hurt somebody. Maybe even Miss Laylee, like last time."

Wade, off by himself on the top step, picked at his fingernails. Occasionally, he looked back at them, his face yellow in the porch light and screwed tightly in on itself as if pondering a complicated riddle. Boo looked up, awareness finally seeping into his features. "Burn down the church?"

"I was hidin in the damn shed! I was scared. But that's what it sounded like to me."

"And they have guns?"

"Oh hell, I'm not sure of that either. It *sounded* like it. Your daddy can do something to stop it, can't he?"

Boo's face darkened; it was like watching the moon disappear behind clouds.

"Can't he, Boo?"

"He's not here," he said brusquely.

"When will he be back?"

Boo shrugged.

"Well, can you *call* him?"

"Gussie, I don't know where he *is*." He glared at her with bloodshot eyes.

Her eyebrows collapsed with exasperation. "What about your mother?"

"In bed with a migraine."

"Can't you wake her up?"

"MaeEllen Taylor? In the throes of a migraine? Not hardly, Gussie."

She wagged her arms, frantic. "Boo, what are we supposed to do?"

He got up, and she and Wade followed him inside to the kitchen. Boo dialed Matthew Dufette's office phone number and got no answer. Then he tried Matthew Dufette's home. Gussie stood anxiously at his side, knitting her fingers together. Wade wandered in behind them and stood in the dining room, looking lost and out of place and not at all happy.

Sarah Rose Dufette answered. No, her husband and the doctor weren't there. Perhaps they were at Mr. Dufette's office. No? Well then, Mr. Dufette had mentioned something about some beach-front property on Atlantic Avenue. No, she wasn't sure exactly *where* on Atlantic Avenue. One of the old hotels, perhaps.

Boo hung up and let his face answer Gussie's questions.

"Let me try something," he said.

He searched the directory again and frowned. No number listed for the Baptist Church. He flipped through the pages for Pastor Hatchel's name, found it, and dialed again. An elderly woman answered, said she was the reverend's aunt. "I'm afraid he's not in," she told him. "Expect he's still down to the church—been there most nights, lately."

He laid the receiver on the hook and faced Gussie. She ran a hand through her damp hair and grabbed a fistful. "Damn it all! Maybe we could go to Atlantic Avenue. Maybe we can find your daddy there somewhere."

"No, we should go to the church. Before...those men get there. While we still have time."

"But we couldn't stop anything."

"Gussie, I don't see what else we can do. At least we could warn the reverend."

Boo Taylor's bruised face shimmered under the kitchen fluorescents. His face seemed different, she now noticed. He looked like he had aged ten years since she left him and Miss Laylee, when they were off to do their "chore" at the graveyard.

She turned and grabbed Wade's hand. "C'mon, Wade, you're drivin us into South Patch."

Wade looked up, shocked. "Oh, like hell I am. No way, Gussie; I ain't part of this. I don't even have a license!"

She stopped, planted her hands on her hips. "Wade Dutton, you big coward, I'm not askin you! Now you get movin or I'll drive myself!"

fifteen

Behind her, Boo Taylor called out another turn.

Beside her, Wade jerked the steering wheel.

She only half-heard, half-saw. She was thinking about her father and trying to recollect a better side of his nature. Surely, he had one; there were tender smiles she could recall, and tender strokes of those rough hands as they wiped away tears and bandaged skinned knees, and tender words in that hoarse voice. *"Why, just look at that picture. Where'd you learn to draw so good? I believe you got a real talent there, girlie."*

Petey had told her the serious drinking hadn't started until after their mother died. Oh, Hank Dutton would never have been confused with a saint even before that, Petey told her. He hit. He yelled. He disappeared for a night every now and again. But it had gotten worse after Clara died and after the months of silent mourning on the back porch where he seemed like a dead man himself—like a hanged man, swaying back and forth in an old rocker and gazing with a dead man's eyes into the backyard.

"Make this right."

Boo Taylor in the backseat, ordering Wade.

The car slowed, jerked and pitched them all forward, went ahead again. Wade spun the wheel, turned them down another dark road. This one hadn't been paved in decades.

"How much farther?" she asked.

"Only a little bit ahead and then another right, and then it's back down that road a bit."

Gussie tried to swallow. Only a little bit ahead. Where were her father and Henry Ray at this moment? Huddled around a tribal campfire with the rest of them, throwing back shots while engines revved and torches kindled and rifle chambers were oiled and locked into place. *Put it back to right,* they said. She thought of Laylee Colebriar's cinnamon face, framed in a vine halo of morning glory and evening primrose and a mystical swirl of herbs and wind chimes and gospel music and stove-scents. Would her father, would Henry Ray, would *any* of them talk their mean talk and throw their fists and fire their guns if they spent just one afternoon with Laylee Colebriar?

Well, maybe they would.

Probably would.

There had to be *somebody* to blame.

"No use shamin over family, Miss Gussie. Mostly, you never fair 'bout it. And anyways, there ain't much we can do 'bout who they is."

Boo Taylor called out, "Here's the turn, Wade."

The car made a too-fast swerve to the right, rocking her almost into Wade's lap. Then they straightened onto a dirt trail. Ahead, beyond a screen of towering magnolias, headlights crisscrossed the night.

Caught in the beams was a rickety, tinderbox church.

Beetles, fireflies in the shape of men danced around it.

"Oh my God, look, they're already here!" she cried as Wade killed his own headlights and slammed the car to a stop.

sixteen

Hunched low to the ground, Boo Taylor took the lead across the sandy field toward the trees, toward the still-intact church beyond, toward the merry man-roars that rose and fell in rhythm to the nearby waves on Sadfellers Beach.

Wade whispered, "What the hell are we supposed to do when we get there, tell me that!"

Gussie hushed him.

"I say we find a phone and call the police."

Gussie swatted his shoulder and hushed him again. "Wade, there's no time!"

Boo hushed them both.

When he reached the first tree, he rose to a crouch and brushed dirt and sand from his shirt. Gussie and Wade huddled with him; Gussie's body melted like hot wax onto his and the urge to slink away with her and maybe make their way alone to

Sadfellers Beach was so strong he was willing to forget the church and Reverend Hatchel and these men. But Gussie, always tugging, tugged him deeper into the shadows. He followed at first, then jerked her arm back so he could resume the lead.

Ahead, the torches, the voices:

"Get your ass over here, you lousy jig!"

"God you stink, boy. Anybody tell you spookies got a funny stink to 'em?"

The church doors were opened to the north where the sprawling, dirt-packed parking lot was now cluttered with a dozen or more cars and pickups that blazed a crazy, all-angle spray of headlamps. Boo brought Wade and Gussie up from the southeast corner where the woods bunched close to the church wall. They snuck through the growth toward the front of the old building until the men and their cars and their torches came into full view.

Arms and shoulders and rifle barrels, all lit amber and blue and harsh yellow-white—but not a single face among them, he saw, and felt Gussie squeeze his hand as she saw it, too. Just dull and lifeless masses above the shoulders, ghost faces, illuminated and hued by the same spectral lights, with black and depthless cut-out eyes. Some had ears set high on their heads like wolf's ears, tied off in twine; others had only round and featureless burlap skulls. No mouths at all on those flat, expressionless faces. Not on any of them. And yet the hard and sanguine threat they bawled was unmistakable.

"Quit rasslin, you nappy-headed freak, or I'll bust you!"

"Aw, just whack him already."

"I will; I'll do it!"

Ping-ponging between them, wrists bound at his spine, kicking and head-slamming into them, raging obscenities, was Solomon Goody. His face, so unlike the dull masks, was naked and raw without his glasses.

He bellowed, "Fuck you, you lowlife motherfuckin hayseeds!"

An axe handle clapped into his jaw. He staggered.

A raucous chorus of cheers.

Solomon righted himself and bulled into the closest man. The man went down, and Solomon tumbled over him. As he got to his knees, a rifle butt chopped his scalp. He fell to the ground again, twisted to his back and kicked out. One of the faceless ghosts—a great lumberjack shape in a red flannel shirt and cuffed dungarees—stepped forward and pinned Solomon to the ground beneath his boot.

Another rise of cheers.

"*Gentlemen, PLEASE!* There just ain't no *need* for this!"

At that shrill, familiar plea, a dark blanket was thrown over Boo's shoulders and the world tipped sideways. He searched the loose stampede of ghosts as the ground trembled around him, as Gussie Dutton's arms shuddered around his arms and the trees shook above him with the threat of riot, and then, at last, he found the reverend knelt in prayer before his church. His hands clasped and bound before him, a rifle aimed lazily at his head. Two others—a black man and a white man, also bound—crouched at his sides. Another white man, groaning and spread-eagled on the ground, clutched at a blond-haired scalp that had gone red.

A slim, girl-sized specter in a yellow T-shirt flitted out from the others and kicked this man in his side.

Another, in a short-sleeve shirt and tie, flitted out and kicked the reverend.

"Gentlemen! Gentlemen!" the pastor shouted.

"Gentlemen! Gentlemen!" someone mocked.

"Who the fuck d'you suppose that nigger's talkin' to?"

"Sure as shit ain't talkin' to *you*, boy!"

Laughter from the chorus.

"Gentlemen, I *implore* you! Gawd a'mighty, gentlemen, don't you see there just ain't no *need* for all this!"

"Fuck you, spook!" Another wraith, in greasy coveralls, darted out, kicked the reverend hard between the shoulder blades and sent him face-first into the dust.

A great, merry roar of approval.

"Oh, we got a *need*, all right! We got us a real *big* need!"

A ghost in a plaid shirt had yelled that out, and Boo knew it was Terry Lee Hardsdale. Terry Lee used to be the stock boy at the Five & Dime before he got hired on at Kressner's Drugs, and Boo knew it was him because of that shirt and that screechy high voice.

And that was Lou Bob Osterman who kicked Reverend Hatchel in the back.

And that was Marty Kressner himself, lay-speaker at the United Methodist Church, who kicked the reverend in the arm.

I know these men, he thought. *I know all of them.* He could pick each out by the clothes beneath his mask; could name every one by his voice. He knew them, had known them all his life, had been to their homes, inside their shops, on their boats. He had ridden in the back of their trucks with his face in the wind. He had waved to them from the street, had shaken their hands. He knew them all.

"Set her a'fire, boys! Set her a'fire!" That was Hank Dutton's voice, Hank Dutton's white T-shirt and frayed, oil-smeared brown pants.

Gussie moaned in his ear. Somewhere behind him, Wade breathed a high, painful whine.

The reverend, powdered white, pushed back to his knees, spitting and blinking away dust and dead grass. *"Gentlemen—"* the reverend coughed; the wind was gone from his voice—"ain't we had enough of this ugliness between us? Please, ain't there been enough? Gentlemen, gentlemen, now *please!"*

From the ground, struggling beneath the heavy boot, Solomon rumbled, "Don't you go sugar-talkin these animals!"

The boot (belonged to Slip Callahan—*I know you!*) stomped on his chest. Solomon howled pain and anger and writhed in the dirt like a snake.

"Fuck YOU, redneck, white-bread slimy *cock licker! Fuck you!"*

"Gentlemen, *please!* Gawd a'mighty, please, please don't hurt the boy!"

"Shoulda thought of that before you rigged the *vote,* preacher!"

"Before y'all burnt down that old school!"

"Shoulda thought of that 'fore y'all brung these fagotty long-hairs on down here to our island! *Our* island! Maybe you just shoulda thought of all that 'fore you and them boys went and stirred up the *pot!*"

A shriek then: triumph, fury, agony, self-immolation—*something* horrible, anyway. And from this, a brilliantly orange meteor was flung into the sky.

Tumbling end over end.

Trailing napalm sparklers.

Descending, a comet.

Clattering at last on the church steps.

Others followed, a biblical hailstorm of fire cascading from a moon-empty night as a dog-pack snarl erupted and all those hooded, faceless-but-familiar bodies surged toward the church. A rattle of broken glass lifted wind chime notes above the snarls and glad shrieks and the new and growing sounds of a single flame built from many that now raced as gleefully and anonymously as the mouthless skulls.

An ancient ritual between tribes, these war-masked conquerors and their prisoners bound and bent before the annihilating flames. How many times this cruel dance must have raged to the amusement of angels and devils and the great killer beasts of this world. On this very island, how many times, Boo Taylor wondered, and recalled the tragedy of Joker Tribbit with his curse-weaving wife; this must have been the very last thing he ever saw—these same men, not far from this very spot. Gussie was in his arms, sobbing against his cheek. All about them, shadows leapt crazily, and voices as ancient as the fires and as anguished as the eaten-alive church walls chanted and wailed from the trees. Mamie Stuvant's grimace flashed on the trunk of a mammoth magnolia and then flashed away. A man's face, dark and brooding, becoming a skull's face skimming in and out of a stand of palmetto, the miserable leaves of dying bayberry and sumac. Crystal Burne must be in here too, he thought, laughing her ugly creek's gurgle at this collection of romping boys performing for her.

Lightning cracked with the splitting of the church roof.

"Damn, that sumbitch ain't nothin but balsa wood!"

"Burn that fucker!"

"Look at her go! Look at her go, boys!"

Brassy voice, green Texaco coveralls. *(I know you.)*

Horse-laugh, khaki slacks, and red golf shirt. *(I know you, too.)*

Ripped sleeves and black skull tattoo. *(Oh God yes, yes, I know that one!)*

The fire clawed its way higher, filling the thin walls and spitting its way through shattered windows and clapboard seams. A great spire now rose, lapping orange, crimson, golden toward a smoke-dirty sky; sparks broke loose, shattered rubies flittering, coiling, sweeping up and then disappearing into powdery gray plumes.

Men now fell back. Men he knew. Slim shoulders, seersucker jacket *(you!)*; gray stack of woolen granite *(oh! you, too!)*; the yellow T-shirt, girl-sized, firelight glinting the lenses beneath *(you?)* He rubbed his eyes, looked again—*(not you!)*.

He reeled back, looking, not wanting to look.

And yet, still looking, seeing…*(no!)* recognizing…long black slacks, loafers, gold watchband.

Behind him, Wade was complaining, "Boo, I think there's somebody in here," but for the moment Boo Taylor was seeing, not hearing, recognizing, not listening. Wade's complaint went unheeded. His stomach twisted abruptly, threatened to spill his dinner into the toadflax blossoms at his feet. Gussie was draped over him like a damp blanket, and now he only wanted to shove her away. The night was suddenly too muggy-hot with all those headlights and that great flame and the soggy, forest loam and Gussie's slick skin.

His stomach lurched again.

"Boo, Wade's right," Gussie whispered. "Someone's *in* here." This time he did shrug her away and charged into the fire.

"Boo Taylor, come back here!"

Gussie stumbled after him.

Then halted on the border of shadow and light. She looked backward for the figure in the woods and was startled when Wade's chalky white face loomed up from the shadows.

"Gussie, dammit, you stay put!" Wade ordered and seized her around the waist.

She turned, watched Boo Taylor sweep into the ranks of the men who were all transfixed by the tall flame. No one saw him. It was as if he were invisible to everyone but her, same as the thing in the woods whose face had been so clear for a moment and who must still be somewhere behind her.

Wade whispered, "Gussie, I want to get out of here. Right *now!*"

Then someone shouted, *"Boo!"*—the little one in the yellow shirt who was stepping forward with skinny arms held forth.

Another said, "Holy Crow, that's the doc's boy!"

Boo rushed the small one, swung out a fist that landed squarely between the hood's eye holes.

A boy shrieked; men were stepping forward now, swinging around guns and clubs, fencing in Boo Taylor and hiding him from her.

"My glasses, my glasses!"

"Christ, what did you do to my *boy!*"

"My glasses, I can't see!"

"Hey, let go there—that's the doctor's boy! That's Boo Taylor!"

Time jagged—it was the riot on the football field replaying itself; those men and that bright, hot light, Wade's hand clasping her elbow. And Boo Taylor lost beyond a tangle of bodies. "Boo!" she shouted.

"Shut up, Gussie!" Wade growled, whined.

"I can't *see;* he hit me in my *glasses!*"

"Aw Jesus Christ, look at that blood; you blinded him, you little fuck."

"No, no! Keep his hood on."

"Shit, it ain't like he don't know who it is."

"Oh my God, what did you do to my boy?"

"Here, here, I said—you let him go right *now!* For God's sake, that's *Boo Taylor.*"

"Well, look what the little fucker did!"

Gussie turned to Wade; the look of fleeing was bright and round and orange in his eyes. Beyond his shoulder, a shadow grinned and capered and was quickly gone.

Gussie pushed hard, escaped her brother, and ran into the clearing.

"Boo!" she shouted.

The hooded men pivoted, parted for her, and a hundred dead, black eyes looked down on her.

"Hank, ain't that your little girl?"

"Well, just shit on a toadstool, if this ain't grand!"

Burlap mouths fell mute.

The only sounds now were the airy crackling of the church fire and the strangled, steamy breaths from unseen nostrils. Boo Taylor was propped up by the shoulders like a scarecrow in the hands of two larger scarecrows. A few feet away, a weeping and unmasked boy was made as unrecognizable as the others by the blood covering his face; yet she recognized Ashford Marchant anyway. He was on his back, head cradled in a lap of granite.

"What the hell *you* doin here?"

The question was thrown at her from one of the men holding Boo Taylor. The sleeves had been ripped from the man's shirt exposing balloon muscles and a grinning black skull. She could feel his smile beneath the sack.

She sniffled, wiped at her tears. The greasy smells of smoke and men crowded her. "Let him go," she said, trembling.

"I say we throw his ass in the fire."

"Stop that now, dammit. That's Doc Taylor's boy."

Boo Taylor was rattled like a stuffed doll.

She yelled, "Let him go, Henry Ray."

Her brother barked a sharp laugh, grabbed the top of his hood and yanked it free. Wispy red-blond hair stood on end. He glared at her with his real eyes now. "*Caught* me! Well, you was always the smart one in the family—guess that means you win the booby prize, don't it, sis?"

"Just let him go."

"Or *what?* You gonna call the cops, Gus? You wanna sic the cops on your poor ol bro and his buddies?"

A few dozen feet shifted nervously through the dust.

Her chin quivered, threatened to collapse. Boo Taylor, still hanging limply in those big hands, was gazing off at some point beyond her. Maybe back in the trees where Wade still hid and an angry ghost sat, waited, watched.

"Maybe," she said unsteadily. "Maybe I will."

Henry Ray laughed again, spit through his mustache. "Tell you what, sis, I'll save you the dime. Hell, we must got us a couple peace officers 'round here someplace." He made an elaborate show of searching the hooded faces. "Ain't that right, Waldo? Where'd you get to, boy?"

From the crowd, someone shouted, "Shut up, you ignorant asshole."

"That's the doctor's boy, Henry Ray. You let loose'a him."

"I ought'a break his fuckin neck, is what I ought'a do."

The old church's roof pitched in, making a sudden explosion, freeing new flames through the volcano vent. Sparks rained over them like the trail of spent fireworks.

Through the muddle of bodies she glimpsed Pastor Hatchel, now standing and covered completely with gray dust as if risen from the ashes. Beyond him, Solomon Goody was on one knee, catching his breath. His right eye and cheek were split and bloated. A masked executioner held Solomon's shirt-collar like a noose.

Half of her body was stinging hot from the flames. The other half went cold and dark.

She hitched her breath and yelled over the fire's roar: "You tried to *rape* me, Henry Ray! He tried to *rape* me! You hear that? His own *sister!* Is that what kind of men y'all are?"

She sobbed and let one stream of tears scald her cheek while the other froze.

Henry Ray's eyes thinned to slits. He shook Boo Taylor's shoulder violently. "Dammit, that's a *lie!*" he raged.

"You did!"

"That's a fuckin LIE!"

The sobs cramped her belly and bent her in half. "His own *sister!*"

"You *shut up!*—you *bitch!*"

Another man stepped forward, and she knew who it was even without seeing the grease-stained pants and sagging gut and the knobby, thick hands that now held a shotgun but which had once wiped her tears and bandaged her skinned knees and steadied her as she rode his shoulders. "Goddammit, boy," her father said slowly, "just let him go."

Henry Ray gaped at the mute, mouthless creature.

The barrel of the shotgun lifted a fraction of an inch.

Daddy!

Grunting, Henry Ray threw his mask aside. Then he pushed Boo Taylor, who only swung around like the gate, still in the grasp of the other scarecrow. The scarecrow jogged his burlap chin downward, saw what was in his hands, and then let go.

Boo's shirt sprouted rumples from his shoulders where the hands had clutched him. She watched as he glared around at the masks, recognizing all the sweating faces beneath and marking them so he could name them to the doctor later. And they all seemed to know this because several of the men stepped back and looked away. Was it shame or fear that made them look away, she wondered? Fear, she supposed. Fear of Boo Taylor; fear of what vengeance his daddy might wreak upon them for this outrage.

On even her own daddy.

"Boo, you hit me," Ashford Marchant whined.

Garson Marchant, showing neither shame nor fear, held his son's head in his knees and shook his fist. "What did you do to my boy? You *blinded* him!"

"It *hurts,* Daddy!"

Boo glanced at the boy and briefly considered his bloodied face. Then dismissed him and looked back at the others. The ice-cold, dispassionate expression was too much like the blank masks that surrounded him, and it scared her. He pushed one of the tall ghost-men aside as if searching for someone. Amid the snap and whoosh of flames, she heard footsteps approach on broken sticks from the woods behind her. And then violently shuddering hands reached for her elbows. "It's true," Wade told the crowd. "What she said—it's true."

Henry Ray was grinning again. "Well hey there, little bro, ain't you just a little late for the party? Was you back there shittin your pants?"

"Fuck you," Wade said in a voice with no strength at all.

"Fuck *me?* Hell boy, I know you—this here's *your* kind'a sport too, ain't it? I'da saved you a beer and a nigger if I'da knowed you was comin."

Gussie, still cramped and bent at the waist, cried, *"Henry Ray, just STOP IT!"*

In the echo of this, from the crowd: "Somebody shut that asshole up."

Her father's mask came away in his fist. Doughy, unshaven cheeks, florid and burning. The shotgun barrel wavered in the slim place between his belly and Henry Ray's chest.

"Boy..." said her father.

Shoot him, she thought wildly, tiredly, her stomach aching. Only Wade's grip was holding her up now. *Just go on and shoot him, Daddy*.

Henry Ray leaned forward and sneered back at him.

None of the men moved now—except where Boo Taylor pushed through them, still marking faces.

Shoot him!

"Stop this nonsense," Pastor Hatchel said calmly.

The men turned to the sound of his voice.

The reverend reached out both dirt-gnarled hands, still bound together, and touched Boo Taylor's arm. "You go on now, Mr. Boo. You take Miss Dutton and Mr. Wade away from this place. This ain't your business, here."

Boo Taylor stood before the reverend, looking up at him. Again, it was the aftermath of the riot and Boo's face was painted half black by the night and half white by the fire.

"Das right, dere, Mr. Boo, suh!" Solomon Goody blurted happily. "Dis ain' no place fo' a fine, upstandin white boy sech as yo'seff." A sick, toothy smile fanned across his face.

"Shut up, jig," the executioner muttered.

Solomon got to his feet and shook off the executioner's hand. He wobbled but held his smile.

"Ah s'pects dese fine ge'muns gwanna be leavin shortly, anyhows, Mr. Boo, suh. Ain' dat right, Rev?" He shuffled to Reverend Hatchel's side. "Lessen a'course y'all ge'muns see fit ta lynch we here coonfolk fust, dat is."

The reverend shook his head sadly. Dust and flecks of dead grass sprinkled from his hair. "You just go on now, Mr. Boo. We'll be fine." He rocked Boo gently as if to push-start him along.

"I'm not going anyplace." The words came from Boo Taylor's mouth, but she couldn't recognize that lifeless and frightening voice. He wheeled back to the others, searching them.

And stalked up to a tall, slender man in black pants and white shirt with a flour-sack hood sagging over his head.

The man lifted his hands, took one backward step.

Then stopped.

Boo Taylor reached into his pocket. He took something out and shoved it into the man's hands. By the firelight, it looked to Gussie Dutton like a pocket watch.

"You," Boo said. "Your initials."

He reached up and snatched the man's hood away.

The northern wall of the church collapsed. And in the roar and burning that followed, Sweetpatch Island itself collapsed. Gussie swooned in the violence and awoke in a new place an instant later. Wade was calling her name, but it was Solomon Goody's braying laughter she heard.

"Hey, hey looky dere, if dat jes don't beat all! Great Gawd a'mighty, what's up, Doc?"

He laughed and laughed, and she was suddenly sure it was the same merry, bruised face she had seen cloaked in the trees.

Part Six
Masks & Murders

October 30

The man in 18C was cooling his forehead against the thick glass, watching the Atlantic coast slowly unfurl thirty-five thousand feet below. He was traveling alone; that was one thing. And he was single; she had seen his ring finger the last time she passed as he held a grimy pocket watch in his left hand—*cradled* it to be more precise, as if it held some great value—and that finger was bare. Also, an aura of mystery hung over him. Something a little desperate. A little dangerous. It showed in the way his jaw throbbed. In the way he immersed himself into the white-noise hum of the jet engines to tune out the world. And, most incriminating, in the furtive glances at the oncoming drink cart, the involuntary swallow as if he were already tasting the drink. Scotch, she predicted. He would stop her when she reached for the Dewars and ask for the Chivas.

She rolled the cart, sneaking glimpses of him through the slow progress down the aisle, seeking eye contact but not yet successful.

When she pulled to his row she cleared her throat, smiled. He looked up. She leaned forward fully, looming, inducing dominance.

Would he like something to drink?

She arched an eyebrow.

Vodka, he said, and turned back to the window.

Well she was wrong on that count. But he did stop her when she picked up the Smirnoff and requested the Absolut.

As she poured, she asked where he was heading?

Home.

Was he glad to get back to his family?

Sure.

Not very forthcoming, this one. She tried a different tack, asking what had happened to his nose? He looked like he might be a boxer—was it some kind of fight, maybe?

She turned, holding out a napkin and the overflowing drink. He was looking back with an expression she couldn't read. Then a badly scarred hand, lumpish and minus some number of fingers, rose to take the plastic cup. The hand was grotesque; its effect profound. Her grin collapsed.

Jealous husband, he told her. He removed a ten dollar bill from a thick wallet and handed it to her, and she accepted, trying to avoid contact with that awful hand.

He told her to keep the change.

Recovering, she offered him another smile and moved quickly on.

❖   ❖   ❖

You're a man now, or so you think.

Then let me ask you this: what do you do when you meet the great love of your life…and you're already spoken for? Or, for that matter, she's already spoken for? I'm talking about that person who, upon connection, elevates your soul beyond anything you considered possible. Magnifies awareness. Makes you see someone else in the mirror. Becomes your single purpose for existence—not in a needy, obsessive way; rather, because the combined being you produce when you come together is the divine thing you were made to accomplish with your life. How many people do you think get blessed with such a thing—even know such a thing is possible?

Except that one of you is already married. What then?

You think this is easy.

The truth is, what it comes down to is, the cruel nature of it all is this: it's all about timing. You do the right thing one day, and years later, when it's all too late, you find it was the wrong thing—because the rules changed. Now she's there. You never knew; you didn't have a crystal ball. What then?

Pay attention, because this is the story of your life. I took her. I took her because of love. I took her because I couldn't do anything else. You think there's a choice involved? Grow up. You do what you have to—what you were meant to. And if that means you go to hell, so be it.

I took her. So, fine, now go ahead and judge me.

The doctor wept.

From thirty-five thousand feet, Boo Taylor watched the coast below through the thick, curved glass. The coast was not, as the maps showed, a single line that made a convenient separation between land and sea. Instead, it broke apart and stuttered its way along as if uncertain of itself. The land crumbled where it met the ocean, and the sea split apart where it met the land, traveling hesitantly through runnels and channels deep into alien territory. The coast was a miles-wide compromise that was neither land nor ocean but its own, distinct domain. It was a world of misdirection; it toyed with the senses, and the people of such a place knew not to trust what they saw or smelled or felt or heard because they came from a soggy realm that constantly shifted between two massive forces. And in such a place, it was impossible to know what was real.

You're a man now. You want to know?

The doctor was weeping—and at the same time defiant. The defiance was a surprise. Outwardly, the man had never been anything but the consummate Southern gentleman. Courtly, almost. Now here was this defiance—something else the doctor must have hidden beneath that burlap mask.

Easy for you to point fingers. Just wait. When you've lived through what I've lived through, seen what I've seen, then come tell me.

Tell me what you would do.

Modernized words—no longer courtly or gentlemanly or even Southern. The doctor complained of the unfair trick time played; the same time abused Boo's memory, the words transmuted over the years. This was not the language of the doctor, but it had been what he said.

He picked out familiar shapes along the unraveling coast, that land of shadows and shifting sand, and she was down there, at this moment, alive and breathing. Perhaps was even looking up at the passing jet but, more likely, moved about through her day unaware that she was being looked upon.

So, I'll tell you, and then you can decide. The doctor was weeping. He was shattered. *But in the end, you need to understand two things:*

I took her because of love.

And sin is more often than not in the timing.

two

Three hours later, Boo Taylor was in the Tahoe pulling onto London Park Road where he passed through the intermittent pastures and heavy woods of the White Clay Creek Preserve. He first stopped at the Passarellas' across the street to gather his mail. Ray Passarella invited him to stay for a beer and a cigar. Boo thought of Gussie, wanted to get home where he could call her, then tried in vain to imagine anything good coming from it. One beer became three, and it was near dusk when he was finally pulling up the driveway to his house.

The driveway snaked through a low canopy of overgrown pines and maples until reaching a stone ranch surrounded by four acres of woodlands. He parked, gathered his suitcase, and stepped into the vague stink of marsh gas and air that was suddenly ten degrees cooler. Leaves crunched under his shoes. The place was under a heavy blanket of crimsons and yellows and browns; the house seemed to have fallen quickly to neglect. He might have been gone for months.

He crossed the driveway crushing pine needles and leaves beneath his shoes, jangling his key ring until the house key swung into his fingers. At his approach, the garage floodlights snapped on automatically, and he was alone and exposed. He looked off toward the trees and a dim rustle of leaves. A titter, a giggle, some soft voice out there. Continuing, he rounded the garage wall and the front floodlights snapped on; the irritating stink became more pronounced. He stopped. Sniffed the air. Then moved on again, more slowly now, unsure of that smell that was so like the marsh rot from the western banks of Sweetpatch Island, six hundred miles south. The stone wall rolled past his left shoulder; toward the right, in the vague blackness, a dry rustle echoed his footfalls. He reached the front stoop amid the gathering strength of something foul and there found the Mischief Night prank, waiting for him. The stench rose up to draw blood from his battered nose.

WELCOME HOME!

Finger-painted in gore across his front door in great, sloppy letters. Beneath that, on his welcome mat, the ripped-apart carcass of some unidentifiable animal.

A toby, he thought.

Bits of fur and bone, strips of gristle. Flattened skull of some roadkill. Something like the dead thing he'd fallen into days ago. It occurred to him that he had been expecting something like this.

Sighing, less upset than he figured he should be, he tiptoed around the mess to reach his door. He had the key in the lock when the phone inside began to ring. Hurrying, dodging innards and bone, he pushed through the door and sprinted for the phone on the kitchen wall.

"Hello?"

Gussie Ransome's voice.

"I wanted to make sure you got in all right."

The sweet sound of her voice was soured by the stench breezing in from the door. He flicked on an overhead light. "Where are you calling from?"

"The office, of course. I'm either working late or in hiding, I haven't decided yet. How was your flight?"

He tossed the keys on the counter, swung the suitcase to the floor. "You don't really want to talk about my flight, do you?"

A spell of silence. He waited for Gussie to speak again. Her tone would tell him everything.

"He told me you didn't fight back," she said. "He called you a coward."

At least she said this without accusation or disapproval. Boo pushed his hand through his hair. "Gussie, I just slept with the man's wife. I suppose he was allowed a free shot."

"That doesn't mean you should let yourself get beat up."

"Great. I have your permission to put him in the hospital next time. Why are we even having this conversation?"

They fell silent again. *Pregnant pause,* he thought, and then caught his own pun. He glanced at the key chain on the counter and remembered Gussie wagging the key to the little cabin on Hickory Lane under his chin. He remembered her clothes falling to the floor. He remembered her dozing on his chest as if they were an old married couple. At last, she said, "How did MaeEllen take the news?"

"How do you think? She's thrilled to find out she'll be a grandmother. She's already knitting booties."

"Don't be smart. I mean how did she take you having to leave so suddenly?"

He was going to launch into more sarcasm until remembering that the woman had just lost her husband of more than forty years. Somehow, he had forgotten about that. Amidst her grief, MaeEllen Taylor had to deal with her son's whirlwind home-coming—and now its aftermath. He was gone now, and she was left all alone in the house on Carriage Avenue. He tried to imagine her shuffling through those vacant rooms. It was almost too painful to bear.

His voice softened. "Not quite the usual theatrics, at least. She was sad."

"You've never forgiven her, have you? Her or your father."

"I haven't thought about it."

"Oh, baloney. How can you not think about it?"

"I don't think about it. I got very good at not thinking about things. I'm an expert. I went twenty years without thinking about my parents. Unfortunately, I couldn't *stop* thinking about you."

"That's sweet."

"Is it? I didn't mean for it to be."

A staticky chuckle came through the line. "So, you've never forgiven me, either."

"No." He sighed. This wasn't going where he wanted. "I never forgave you, Gussie. Forgiveness takes too much effort; it's a lot easier to stay pissed off."

"I was thinking I might drop in on MaeEllen. See how she's doing."

"Thanks; that's very thoughtful."

"Don't thank me. I think I'm just looking for excuses to avoid Murphy."

Yet another silence fell. Boo hooked his foot around a nearby stool and pulled it close so he could sit. He felt every mile between them weighing him down like a load of bricks. "I wish I was there with you, Gussie," he said. "I'm sorry I had to leave."

No response to that.

Finally, she asked, "What are you going to do?"

"About Sandy?"

"Of course about her."

He sighed. He had no answer for her. He hadn't slept in almost forty hours, and he wanted to lie down.

"Leave him, Gus," he said. "Leave him and marry me."

"I'm already married." She sounded distraught.

"Then *leave* him."

"It's not that simple."

"Sure it is; people do it all the time."

"Boo, it's just not that simple."

"Don't you want to marry me?"

Now even more distraught, she said, "What I *want* doesn't really matter. He'll never let me go, Boo, at least…I don't know, give it some time, maybe he'll change his mind."

Give it some time. How was he supposed to do that?

"So that's it," he said.

"Yes."

"Just wait around until Murphy decides enough is enough."

"Boo, it *has* to be his choice! You're not married, you don't have children, you don't know." The exasperation, the *despair* was pouring through the phone. "Jeremiah isn't even six yet. Savannah just turned thirteen. How could I take them away from him, even supposing he'd let me? How could I do that to *them?* Besides, he's always been good to me, Boo; he doesn't deserve this."

"I know. Murphy's a gem. Murphy's a prince." He looked off toward his liquor cabinet, judging distances, and decided the phone cord wouldn't stretch that far. The stink from the front door was getting worse.

Gussie scolded. "Quit sulking. He *is* a good father."

"He's a jerk, Gussie, and he always was. He got you pregnant so you'd have to marry him."

"Boo Taylor! That is the stupidest thing I ever heard come out of your mouth."

This reaction was what he expected, and he had to smile. "Well it's true, isn't it?"

"No, it most definitely is *not*. I think maybe you're confusing Murphy with that little girlfriend of yours."

She's not my girlfriend, he thought. "I'm not marrying Sandy Baker."

"You may change your mind."

"I most definitely will not."

"You may decide you want a child."

"Never. Not with her, anyway."

"Never say never, Boo. Children change things; you have no idea."

"I guess I have *some* idea," he said. "Anyway I'm not talking about Sandy Baker— I'm talking about you and me. I'm talking about you marrying me."

"Boo, be serious."

"I'm very serious. Tell me what to do, Gus, and I'll do it. I'd walk through fire for you."

"So you keep saying. But your feet don't look burnt to me."

"My feet?" He glanced at his fingerless hand. "My feet are just fine. Not a mark. Look, can I ask you something?"

Cautiously, she answered, "Go ahead."

"You really didn't put that glass frog in the window?"

"Boo, I told you I didn't."

"Then how did it get there?"

"You tell me!"

He glanced at his suitcase; the figurine was packed away inside there, wrapped in a T-shirt. Before two days ago, the last time he had seen the thing was when Laylee Colebriar was tucking it into the breast pocket of her dress, maybe a few days before her place burned to the ground.

He really needed a drink.

"Going to that little cottage was your idea," he said.

"Boo Taylor, is that what this is about? Are you accusing me of something?"

"You *lured* me there, Gussie," he said. "You seduced me, and then you took advantage of me."

"Ha! You better be joking."

"You're saying you didn't take advantage of me?"

"I didn't hear you complaining. You *are* joking, right?"

"Of course I'm joking," he said, the smile on his face feeling very good, having her on the phone with him felt even better. "Look Gussie, I'll do the right thing, I promise. The right thing for everyone. Once I figure out what that is."

He hung his head.

Hoping that what he just told her was the truth.

"It's just," he said, "I don't think I can live another twenty years without you."

Her response was the last thing in the world he wanted to hear. "Boo, you may have to."

❧ ❧ ❧

He carried the dead thing into the woods, using the welcome mat as a sling. When he reached the corner of his property, he flung the carcass and mat over the split-rail fence into the adjoining crop of parkland. He then gathered a bucket and brush to scrub the words off the door. The stink was an infection that seeped into his pores. He tried not to think about what the letters were written in.

With that done, he went inside to shower and punish his flesh under scalding water and a violent scouring until a new body emerged, one square-inch patch at a time, pink and raw like a fetus.

He snapped off the shower knobs. As the steam rolled and frolicked around his new flesh, he kept his eyes closed and pressed his skull against the wet tile.

Welcome home!

"Leave me alone," he said out loud, echoing through the stall. He pushed wet hair out of his face and grabbed an oversized towel from the rack. He dried himself, stepped onto the cold tile of the bathroom floor and went to the sink to brush his teeth. A cold draft wafted through the bathroom door, prickling him with gooseflesh.

He looked in the mirror. Thick and scarred shoulders, hair splayed on end, splotchy red and blue skin around his nose, blood rimmed eyes. Jaw shaded with a day's coarse, red-brown growth, sparkling heavily with a silver that could not have been there a month ago.

The right thing, he thought.

He was reaching for his toothbrush when he heard echoed footfalls from somewhere inside the house. The sounds came from the foyer. *Click...clip...click.* Light, like a bird's foot. Stealthy, like the toenails of a wolf's paw. He pulled the towel around his waist. A faint whiff of gore and decay lingered through the open bathroom door with the approaching steps. *Click.* Closer. In the kitchen.

The light bird-wolf steps were lost on the carpet now—in the hallway, whispering toward the bedroom. Then a voice, high and tentative, also like a bird. *"Boo?"*

His muscles sagged; a dull pain pulsed through his temples.

"Are you here?"

More whispers, now across the bedroom carpet until Sandy Baker reached the bathroom door. She was wearing jeans, a navy blue blouse and a short leather jacket. And brown, ankle-high boots that had just click-clacked through his house. "I knocked and rang the bell, but you didn't answer. What's that smell—did your toilet back up?"

Boo grabbed a second towel from the rack and rifled it through his hair.

"I guess you were in the shower."

"I guess so," he said.

She leaned carefully against the doorframe and watched him. She was looking very pretty—and only slightly fractured, like an eggshell tapped gently against the rim of a skillet. "Welcome home," she said.

Boo pulled the towel away from his scalp and looked at her cautiously. "What's that supposed to mean?"

Another crack appeared—across her brow. "It means 'welcome home.' Why are you biting my head off?"

"I thought the door was locked."

"I do have a key, you know." She dangled it before him. He saw Gussie Ransome making the same gesture, then forced that image away. "If you're in a mood, maybe I should just leave you alone," she said, although she gave no indication of moving.

Boo dropped the towel across his shoulders. He squared around to face her.

Sandy Baker managed to look brittle and fierce at the same time. A whole series of new cracks split across her delicate, tanned forehead. "You blame me, don't you?" Tears began to well through the cracks.

He was trapped. If he walked to the door to get some clothes from the bedroom, she'd think he was coming to comfort her.

Her knuckle came to her nose, and she sniffled into it, turning away.

"I don't blame you. It's my fault." His words came out devoid of inflection, like a robot.

She shook her head, not looking at him.

"I'm sorry," he said.

He waited for her, but she was content to lean in the doorway, looking away and hitching tiny, wounded sobs. He wondered how long this little scene would last, when all he wanted to do was crawl into bed and get some sleep. She was hoping he would crumble, avoid conflict, relent, give her what she wanted. She expected to stay the night, more than likely had an overnight bag out in the car.

He stared at her a few moments longer. Then he went to the sink and began to brush his teeth.

Her wounded, baby's-voice choked across the tile. "Allen said you'd be like this."

He spit toothpaste into the basin. "Allen said that, did he?"

"He said you didn't care about anyone but yourself. He said you were selfish. He said you were irresponsible."

"This is Allen Noble, my attorney, right? Did he say all this *before* or *after* he introduced us?" He straightened up and took a step toward her. Sandy cowered back, eyes suddenly fearful, and he stopped.

Did she think he was going to *hit* her?

He opened his palms to show he meant no harm.

After a moment, the fear left her eyes, but not completely. He realized that the fear never really left Sandy Baker's eyes. Perhaps that had been part of the attraction, early on—those big, frightened doe eyes.

"Well?" she asked.

"Well what?"

She clenched her fists at her hips, stomped her heel. "God, you *are* a monster." She made a whiney, disgusted grunt.

"Sandy, what do you want me to say?" He was about to take another step forward— then held back so as not to frighten her.

"I want you to tell me what you *want*."

"I don't think it really matters, does it?"

"What does *that* mean? Of *course* it does."

He sighed, leaned on the sink. He wiped his hand across the raw, newborn flesh of his chin. "I'll support whatever decision you make," he said, a robot again. "Whether you want to keep it or not."

She glared at him, horrified. "Is *that* what you want?"

"I told you," he said, as the doe eyes ripened full and bleary, and the entire tanned, delicate shell shattered to pieces, "what I want doesn't matter."

❧　❧　❧

11:20 p.m.

Lights off, lying on his back, eyes closed, he allowed an old memory to seep from his living room speakers and immerse him in the quiet fog of lost summers. The sound carried him back, the sofa now a litter being born into a mid-seventies evening on the beach, an era when he and Gussie were together, were inseparable, when all good things seemed not just possible but *certain*. She was lying next to him, her young flesh pressed so tight to his he couldn't tell where he stopped and she began, the moon peering down on them with what must have been jealousy as the 8-track speakers from his old Vega offered this same tune where it was parked just over the dunes. *Houses of the Holy*. Nothing at all romantic about the music, except its absolute inseparability from that moment, one that defined the brief bit of complete happiness he had known, he and Gussie addicted to an all-consuming, breathless, sweaty, and raw teenage lust: making love every place they could sneak off to in every moment they could steal in as many ways as they could imagine. Like it was a crime. Like it was something they invented.

He felt himself smiling, despite the ache of loss.

He was there, and she was connected to him as he held this chilled glass of vodka to his chest in one hand while the other manipulated the catch of his father's pocket watch, flipping it open and shut, open and shut. Content to be settled here, in this place, until somewhere from deep within the decades-old memory, an alien sound emerged. An irritation. It took him a moment to mark it.

Something was scratching at the living room window.

"Go away," he said, annoyed.

A moment later, he opened his eyes. A white, ghastly face was pressed to the window, staring in at him. Then, quickly, it was gone. Sandy Baker, he thought automatically, although it was certainly not her face.

He realized his heart was thumping madly.

The watch, ticking, was clenched inside his fist.

He considered getting up. Then decided he was too drunk to move, too happy to just lie where he was and see if he could sink back into that pleasant nostalgia—let the demons caper outside; he was safe in this warm, dark place.

His fist unclenched. He closed his eyes again.

Sandy Baker, thankfully, was gone—although she had required a solid hour of apologies and pampering as she lay curled on his bed like a baby, crying and pushing him away, alternately attacking and pleading, and God help him he had started to get an erection tussling with her on the bed like that in only his towel. When he went to get dressed, sending the firm signal that spending the night was not on the agenda, she at last got up to leave, and it was a broken eggshell he thought of again. Every piece of her was fractured. It had been like watching someone get up after falling from a skyscraper and then tottering away. She refused to look at him. She refused to speak to him. *I couldn't have done all that*, he thought and wondered what secret torments a little girl might have suffered within the Baker's happy, picket-fenced, Midwestern home.

I want the child, Boo.

She wanted the child. Of course she did.

He wondered what the doctor would think of that. Had he lived another few short weeks, perhaps the man would have seen his defiance rewarded: his son, the pot, had called the kettle black. That had to be worth a laugh.

I took her.

And sin is in the timing.

It happened like this.

He placed his father's pocket watch on the low coffee table, let the music seep over him, take him deeper into alcoholic numbness.

To begin with, you should understand that her fate was the same as her own mother's. And maybe it went back farther than that: to her mother's father, maybe— you understand? And on to her mother's father's mother and so on. I don't know, but you get the point. It may even be your fate, too. So pay attention.

It happened like this:

The first time I saw her she was standing near the banks of the Yamawichee, looking off toward the mainland. I was driving back to my office from a house call in South Patch, and she was just there. Just suddenly there. It was not far from the bridge over Soap Water Creek.

I asked if there was any trouble, was she all right? She turned to me, and that was all it took. I was finished. You want me to explain it? Well, I can't. You might think that maybe someone drugged me, cast a spell, some local witch (we have a few, don't we?) and I suppose that's possible, but at the same time it's not possible. It was something different, something greater, certainly, and nothing you could truly comprehend unless it happened to you. I was lost from that first moment; everything in my life up to that instant was a mistake that needed to be undone. Except some things can't be undone—which is, of course, the nature of tragedy.

She told me she had been watching a woman out in the sound. A white woman, who seemed to have drifted up from the water and was swirling about, as if dancing. She wanted to know if I could see the woman, too. Of course, I saw nothing.

She told me the woman was her mother.

I was shaken.

I offered her a lift, because it was getting toward dark and this was near South Patch and she was a white woman, but more because I couldn't imagine letting her go; already I was recognizing the empty place that would leave in me. I had to be near her. She said yes, and then surprised me by having me turn around and drive south. And then she surprised me more when she directed me up Eulahlah Colebriar's little lane.

She was staying there, she said, which was a preposterous thing. She was lovely and cultivated and a white girl—and that poor, run-down shack in South Patch was the last place in the world you would expect to find such a creature.

But I found her. Was meant to find her. You see that, don't you?

Then she told me her name, and I realized that it actually made perfect sense. Perfect sense that she, now grown, had come to seek Eulahlah of all people.

You see, the woman in the water really had been her mother.

She waved and went through that screened door and passed out of sight. And I had to sit and bear that. Had to somehow drive away.

I see what you're thinking, but you're wrong. She was very pretty. Not beautiful, but certainly pretty, and what she looked like had nothing to do with it. You don't believe that? Yes, it was what I saw, but it wasn't how she looked. It was more like...recognition.

You can't imagine what it was like for me after that, driving home to MaeEllen. MaeEllen still hadn't reconciled herself to life on the island; I suspect she never will, not entirely. We had been married for more than five years by then. She wanted children, then she didn't want children, then she thought maybe she wanted to leave me; there was an attorney in Beaufort, an old beau, a lost love. She wanted us to move back to Charleston together, or perhaps on to Savannah or Atlanta, and I think she even once mentioned a desire to settle in Manhattan.

I was never handed a crystal ball. Who is? We were married, and I thought I had done the right thing.

Live long enough and you find that a great many people are happy to tell you what the right thing is. Funny that two people can be so secure in their convictions when those convictions are in opposition. If only one way is right, then someone's conviction must be wrong. Does that make sense?

But the truth is something else. What's right is the thing you do. You don't choose it. Your right may be someone else's wrong—in fact, it will almost surely be. That is the great paradox and calamity of mankind. That we have differing notions of wrong or right, notions that are sincere and valid on their own merits but which cannot be reconciled, cannot coexist. Look at these men I stood with tonight, those men and their fire—and look at the men I stood against. I have obligations. You can believe the right thing is easy all you want, but it isn't. Read the paper, you see it every day. You want proof of God? There it is. Only God knows what's right and wrong because only God knows what's in our hearts—and sets within those hearts our separate notions of what's right and wrong.

God is my judge, boy. Not you.

So I went back to see her. Often. Of course I knew when Eulahlah would be there and when she wouldn't. And of course Eulahlah probably knew all about these visits anyway, and I had no need to worry she would be anything but discreet.

Imagine my joy when your mother, that lovely blessing, came to feel the same for me as I for her. Imagine that! Imagine your most fervent desire coming true. Imagine bliss! Imagine heaven on earth!

She came to be with Eulahlah, which I told you before made perfect sense. She had no money, no job, so I took care of her as Eulahlah also did. I bought her an old Willys Jeepster from the junk yard so she could at least have something to get around in. And I spent as much time with her as I could, which was not nearly enough. She wasn't there to be with me, but with Eulahlah, though that was what brought her to me, and I will always believe it was designed to be that way.

You say you're a man now, so you need to think like one.

A day came when your mother told me she was with child. She told me that Eulahlah had confirmed it for her.

You think you understand the concept of paradox? Of conflict? It was the best and worst thing at the same time. She was ecstatic, she was miserable, she was afraid, she was full of hope. She worried what I would have to go through—the decisions she knew I was confronted with— MaeEllen, my standing in the community—and blamed herself for it. Scandal is a bitter word. You'll find that folks feast on it. Here was a great feast; if folks north of the Soap Water got wind of it, they would be plump with it for years. I didn't care. She could terminate the pregnancy (Eulahlah knew a dozen or more ways to accomplish this; and, of course, I was a doctor) or run away and have the child elsewhere or stay with me; it was my choice, she said. Except for one thing: she would not give the child away. If it was to be born, she would keep it. With me or without me.

Giving the baby up for adoption, you see, was worse than having an abortion— to her. That was her wrong and right.

Of course I wanted the child. It was her child. Our child.

Maybe you already know this (you've certainly been through more and are further along than I ever was at your age), but you'll find that sometimes you just need to set yourself down a path on faith alone. Trusting only that you've done the right thing, not knowing how you'll get to where you're going or what will happen along the way. Those are details, and the big things can't be burdened with details. Otherwise, you find you're making excuses to justify taking the easy way. Details will keep you from the right thing—which more often than not (don't ask me why; ask God) is the hard thing.

You can call it reckless if you want, but you weren't there. We knew that somehow this would work. We would have the child. We were decided.

In this case, the main detail of concern was MaeEllen. A woman who was doing the best she could. A woman who had (what I came to understand only too late because I wasn't given a crystal ball) a very different notion of wrong and right from mine on many things. A woman who nevertheless didn't deserve suffering and humiliation and the infidelity of her husband. She took the news poorly, of course she did. Was for months either hysterical or comatose, and I didn't blame her. The fault was all mine, all of it—you see, I'm declaring my absolute guilt in this, and I always have.

Among other things, MaeEllen demanded that I let Eulahlah go (neither the first nor last time she made this demand of me, by the way) because she blamed Eulahlah for the whole thing—or, at the very least found her complicit. But perhaps it had more to do with the embarrassment over the situation: the Negro housekeeper knew her shame.

Which is why, in the end, no one else got wind of that brewing scandal—at least, no one north of the Soap Water. MaeEllen wanted it kept quiet, for as long as possible at least, which was more of a non-response than response: by not confronting it (and I didn't blame her) then it hadn't happened.

And while I was willing to give MaeEllen anything and everything else she asked for (she deserved no less, didn't she?) the one thing I would not do was punish Eulahlah Colebriar.

There, you have another example of my sense of wrong and right.

Eulahlah handled this well—which is to say she suffered quietly. Suffered MaeEllen's wrath, certainly, but also shouldered much of my pain and your mother's pain. That's something else I take responsibility for.

I can't say I recall exactly what resolution we arrived at about...arrangements. Would MaeEllen and I stay together? Would your mother stay with Eulahlah? Would I divorce, would I set your mother up somewhere on the mainland, would your mother go off on her own? Would MaeEllen maybe rekindle a romance with that pompous little twit in Beaufort? At some point or another all of these and a dozen more options were discussed. But I don't recall what was decided, or if a decision was ever made—these were just details.

The big thing was the baby. The big thing, it turns out, was you.

Then again, there was another detail. Go back to the beginning. Remember, I found your mother when she was watching a ghost in the Yamawichee. Her own mother, whom she had come to believe had died there years before. This is part of what drove her to the island, you understand. To Eulahlah, the guffer doctor. And, by extrapolation, it's what brought her to me.

I drove down to see her one evening. It was twilight. Eulahlah, I knew, was out tending to an ill woman near Bluff Beach that night. Your mother would have been six or seven months pregnant at the time, and I didn't like the thought of her alone at night in her condition. And since MaeEllen was in one of her comatose phases, I thought it okay—which is to say I believed it was right—to check in on your mother.

You may remember a large oak that used to tower over Eulahlah's cabin. It's gone now; I believe it finally fell when you were three or so. It had a tire swing on one of the branches, and when you were little, you played on it often.

When I drove down Eulahlah's lane that night, that was where I discovered your mother. I couldn't find her at first. I called, and she didn't answer. I searched the house, searched the yard, the garden, and then I saw her: sitting on the tire swing, deep in the shadows where it was dark as midnight. And she wasn't alone.

Three little girls were huddled around her. Three little colored girls. One, the smallest, was practically cradled in her lap and was suckling at your mother's breast.

I was stunned. It was like being inside a nightmare. Yes, it was dark, but I know what I saw. Three eager little girls, one making sloppy, wet noises, face buried in your mother's blouse. All the time, your mother rocked quietly on the swing, holding the child with one arm while the other braced on the rope. I couldn't see her expression, but she hadn't answered me, had she? I had been calling for her, but she never answered. It was madness. Or, as it turned out, something worse.

When I was able to collect myself a bit, I ran forward and yelled. All at once, the little girls flew off her, like bats flapping away, shrieking and then laughing until they disappeared off into the woods.

When I reached your mother, she was in a daze. I shook her, and she started to weep. She started clutching for me, and I remember an immense relief that she had come around from whatever trance she'd been under—for that was what it seemed to be.

I carried her inside Eulahlah's house and made her some tea. She confessed it all to me. The girls had been visiting her. Coming at night, calling to her from outside the window. They were so sad, she said. So lonely. They couldn't find their mother. They were scared. Timid, at first—like birds, keeping back to the shadows, fluttering away when she showed herself. Then, gradually, they let themselves be seen. Let her come out to sit with them. Let her hold them.

Eventually, she drifted off to sleep. I watched over her, furious, determined to go searching the nearby shanty villages as soon as Eulahlah got home, determined to find wherever these girls came from. Have the authorities get involved.

When Eulahlah arrived, I confronted her. After some time, I supposed she managed to calm me down.

Yes, she knew about the girls. Yes, your mother asked her not to say anything to me so as not to make me worry. No, she said, I would not find the girls in any shanty village nearby or anywhere else on the island.

The girls (whose names she never knew), she said, had drowned more than thirty years earlier. They had lost their mother in the panic when the old ferry caught fire and sank and had been searching for someone—some kind, nurturing soul— to take care of them ever since. Spooks, she said, who would never allow her (Eulahlah) close enough because they knew the guffer doctor would "send them on their way to fellun city" forever, without a mother. Had, in fact, latched on to your mother's mother when she herself was pulled down into the same waters (it was a story I'd heard before, and I suspect you have as well—do you see where this is going?) and had now been led to someone alive and strong who would surely never leave them.

Now, you need to understand that such talk was not unexpected from Eulahlah Colebriar. She was the guffer doctor, witchdoctor, local perpetrator of all kinds of hoodoo and keeper of ancient secrets of the life beyond. I knew this when I hired her and was well used to her sage suggestions for applying root cures in place of medicine and the general value of chants and spells in the art of healing. Some might find this annoying. But I love the woman.

(I see your expression; I know what you're thinking. Can I love her and still burn down a colored church, set those colored men, those instigators, right? One has nothing to do with the other. I have a place in this community. I know what my responsibilities are. You don't have to like it, but there it is.)

Yes, I love Eulahlah Colebriar, as I know you do. Always have and always will, and even in my most staunch doubts, I respected the undeniable thread of truth— and even practicality—of her methods.

Nonetheless, I was not going to be deterred from finding those little girls in the flesh. I raised hell. Got the local constable to conduct raids, and…well you can imagine. And, as you have surely already guessed, I turned up nothing.

My recourse was to watch over your mother whenever I could—and make sure Eulahlah did so whenever she could. This was not as easy as you may think. As a physician I am called upon at all hours of the day and night to tend to one emergency or another. It's a burden that comes with being the lone doctor on an isolated island. That, and then there was that troublesome detail of MaeEllen—who certainly deserved my time and attention, a sometimes very intense need as you can imagine, given her state of mind.

It may surprise you to know that Eulahlah carried a similar burden. As the guffer doctor, her healing services may have been in even greater demand than mine by the local coloreds and ignorant whites—which is to say ninety percent of the island's population. Scarcely a night would pass without one or another poor soul calling on her to rid a family member of some plight, real or imagined, or to otherwise provide counsel to those in need.

That's another lesson you need to learn: if you're living anything close to a worthwhile life, you're going to find people have more demands of you than you have to give. So you parcel yourself out the best you can, feeling guilty that it won't be enough for someone who deserves it, knowing you're disappointing and maybe even hurting someone. No matter what you do, someone's going to get hurt. Get that now, and save yourself some grief later.

Which is a long way of explaining that some nights your mother was left alone. What went on those nights? I never knew, could only guess and worry. I know those little vampires were fixed on your mother, and I had some sense of the reason for it. I imagined horrible things, and this may be one case where reality could have actually been worse than imagination. Some days she looked fine after a night alone; others she looked dreadful. Like she'd been bled. I feared for her health—I feared for your health. It never occurred to me until much later that I was probably misguided in not considering what might be happening to her in daylight. Who's to say what such creatures are capable of, day or night?

I kept watch when I could, which was not more than one or two nights a week—and even then not always as late as I would have liked.

The sounds you hear at night. Whispers. Shrieks. Laughter. Grunting. Animal sounds. Things on wings, on four legs, swooping and circling, taunting. Hungry things. Desperate and lonely things. Are they always there? Or only when you listen *for them. I heard them; they meant to be heard; it was like some terrible chess match played through the long dark hours by opponents who, though unseen, knew of each other's presence. I helped your mother to sleep through these nights so she wouldn't suffer them as I was made to—in the beginning, I administered mild doses of a sedative until I relented and used some potion Eulahlah brewed up that she claimed was safer for the baby.*

The nights were endless, sitting on Eulahlah's broken sofa, more often than not your mother's head quietly at rest in my lap. Excruciating, those relentless assaults of horrifying, otherworldly sobs and moans—sometimes silent for long stretches, luring you toward peace, toward sleep, only to erupt suddenly in an explosive roar or fit of maniacal laughter, slamming you back to wakefulness and panic.

They wanted your mother. They wanted you. Perhaps, (and as I see it now, I'm more convinced of it) they wanted you more than her. And since I'm being honest, let me tell you this: I couldn't have cared less about you. I was there to protect your mother. Not you. I didn't know you; I loved your mother. You were promise; she was reality. And it became more fixed in my mind that you were the cause of it. That if you were gone—which is to say (and let's go ahead and be blunt) if she had a miscarriage I think I would have been happy. Because, maybe that would make it stop.

Is that something else you want to judge?

A night came when I was pushed beyond my limits. Eulahlah was off delivering Florita Johnston's baby (which would have been young Tobias Johnston, who you know) and I had been up to my ears in patients at the office and MaeEllen was going through a frighteningly suicidal spell and I likely hadn't slept more than an hour in three days. A particular groan came seeping through Eulahlah's parlor window— long and despairing, like the dying howl of a great hound. I got up, tore through the front door to the porch. Something scampered around the side of the shack, and I followed—caught a glimpse of a shadowy figure disappearing toward the woods and raced after it. Not a little girl this time, but a full-grown woman—long, dark hair. Was it the woman your mother had seen in the Yamawichee? I didn't think so; this one, though it was dark and I had only the fleetest glimpse, was surely colored and dressed like a poor colored woman. I felt a brief moment of triumph—perhaps this was the person behind your mother's torment. A living being I could confront.

As I reached the tree line into which the figure disappeared, something massive lurched up from the brush. Something huge. With red eyes. Just a shape; it couldn't be seen well in the shadow. I was stopped in my tracks, almost falling, waiting for it to come forth, to come take me now that I was so foolishly lured into the open.

I waited.

It watched me. I sensed evil. I sensed madness. I sensed a centuries-old hatred.

Then it spoke. It growled, and then it spoke, and it said, "Doctor man" in a voice that was like something vomited from hell. I wanted to scream—but I couldn't. And then it spoke again, the same voice but so very different, now whining and tortured and heartbroken, saying, "Gib me what mine; gib me mine oh mine, pllleeeeaaaasssssseee, oh please, mistuh doctor man."

You've never heard such torment. Please God, you never will.

My shriek became a wail, a sob, and a scream at the same time because I was just as gut-wrenched by that voice as I was terrified. And as my wail spiraled into the night, that thing wailed with me, and that almost splintered my mind into pieces right there—that horrible thing yowling along with me in its ancient, lunatic misery, like it wanted to reach out and embrace me and kiss me and devour me. I was nearly driven insane—surely, from a purely clinical perspective, I actually was insane, at least briefly.

How long did this last?

I don't recall how, but at some point I realized I was backing away, was also sane enough to piece together the understanding that the thing was waiting for my answer.

That horrible thing. That horrible, pitiful thing.

The red eyes blinked, and I turned and ran—ran because I was certain it was going to pounce. Behind me, trees crashed, branches were ripped free. I pulled myself around the front of the shack, stumbled toward the porch steps with earth-thudding steps close behind. Shrieking, I snagged the front door and threw myself inside, slamming the door closed behind me—in the very moment I realized that mammoth beast could shatter this scrawny little hut with one swipe of its claw.

But the world was suddenly silent.

More than just silent—a stillness so complete it was as if there had never been anything out there at all.

Had I dreamed it?

I got to my feet. Your mother was still sleeping peacefully on the sofa, one arm curled beneath her head, a slim curl of her hair across her cheek. I was slick with sweat; my breath was ragged.

No dream.

It would be an immeasurable relief, would restore my faith in this world, if a dream was all it had been, but it wasn't.

Listen. You need to understand that, boy. It wasn't a dream. You need to pay attention because this is the thing you're dealing with.

So.

What happened then? You're going to be disappointed, because what happened then was that your mother died. I waited up with her through the night, Eulahlah came home near dawn that morning, and then I drove home, and the next morning I got word that your mother was dead. I had spent that day with patients and a fragile MaeEllen, and then literally collapsed at my desk until nine o'clock the next morning, when my nurse at the time, Juney Saunders, came in to work and woke me up.

Sometime later that day, Darnell Bean, who was sheriff before Parker Tillman, phoned to ask me if I was available to sign a death certificate. Some white girl found drowned after her car, an old Willys, went off the causeway.

I'm sure Eulahlah has told you what she knows about what happened next.

Which isn't much. Sometime during the night, your mother must have gotten into the car and driven off and...well, like I said, I'm sure Eulahlah has told you.

Where was she going? Eulahlah never knew, and neither did I. I like to think maybe she was trying to protect us—Eulahlah and me—from whatever curse was haunting her. From that tortured monster in the woods or that sad woman in the water. I like to hope she did it as something planned and wasn't chased off; I like to hope it wasn't because I was safe and asleep at my desk, leaving her all alone to that thing. Did she drive off the bridge on purpose? Did something force her off? I don't know. And I don't know which would be worse.

A curl of blonde hair across her cheek, her head cradled in the crook of an elbow. That's the last I saw of her, alive.

But then...then, I had you.

Thank God for you.

And that's the end of it. You wanted to know? Now you know. Was I wrong to keep it from you? MaeEllen insisted on it, but I won't lay that on her. And you may want to consider how heroic she was, boy, taking you in and loving you despite what you maybe represent to her. Maybe you want to think about that next time you're angry with her. If anybody's a hero in this, it's her.

Maybe I would have told you in my own time, but probably not. Out of respect for MaeEllen, perhaps, but also because I think it would have been easier on me to keep finding reasons for putting it off. Maybe you just didn't need to know. What good will come from it?

So think what you will. Judge me. Judge me for this and whatever other crimes you think I've done; my right and your right aren't always the same, and you tell me when you find someone in this world who's always right when you are. Tell me when that happens. I come from where I come from, and I stand for what I stand for. You don't have to like it.

I loved her because I had no choice in the matter.

Sin, more often than not, is in the timing.

Fine. Go ahead and judge.

The doorbell rang. He lay still. The ring pounded through his chest and electric-shocked his heart.

A moment later, it rang again. Then a knock.

Boo glanced at the clock and frowned. Sandy, of course, ringing and knocking—specifically *not* using her key to make some kind of point. But if he didn't answer, she *would* use her key.

He sighed, trying to summon the energy for another scene, thinking it would be a simple thing to have the locks changed. He swung his feet around and stood. The movement sent a nauseous wobble through his temples. He placed his glass on the coffee table next to the pocket watch. Robert Plant was still cooing "No Quarter" from the living room stereo as he padded through the house. When he approached the foyer, the wraith of a decayed animal bloomed stronger, and he decided he would have to open the windows to air the place out.

He pulled open the door.

Nothing.

Just the lit porch beyond the storm door, and an invisible, depthless black behind that. Then he saw the burning fetus on the stoop floor, and he yelled.

He whipped open the door and saw it was another toby, set ablaze and left to torment him. *Burn it! Kill it!* Was that what they had planned for him? Was that how this was all going to end? In his sudden anger, he let out another yell and stomped on the thing.

His shoe smashed through it—not a toby at all, just a paper bag—and made a squishy explosion. A brownish sludge splashed over the stoop and covered his foot. Amid the blackened, glowing ashes rose the unmistakable aroma of excrement.

Happy Mischief Night!

Welcome home, Mr. Boo.

Somewhere nearby in the night lilted the merry laughter of children.

four

October 31

All Hallow's Eve.

Daylight, which had emerged normally that morning, collapsed rapidly that afternoon when an unpredicted cold front and its accompanying clouds overwhelmed the east cost of the North Atlantic continent.

Bodies were sent scurrying for cover.

Royal Goody was sitting in front of his old Tandy 486 computer, rubbing his hands as the CPU beeped and buzzed to life—rubbing his hands because he was just off the practice field where it had dropped to something like forty-two degrees. He sipped at the cup of hot tea Martha had waiting for him when he got home. Forty-two degrees was unheard of for October on the island. Rare even for January.

Not bothering to remove his jacket, he punched a slightly numb finger on the keyboard. Beyond the closed door came the doorbell's muffled sing-song. He heard Martha answer this to an off-key chorus of *trick or treat!* An icy breeze streamed under the door, whirled at his feet.

The program manager popped onto the monitor. He clicked on *Ami Pro*. Then, clicked FILE, OPEN.

Then DIRECTORY, BOOK.

Then FILE, sect_two.chap_3.sam.

The system paused. Purred. And the file appeared on the screen.

After a moment, he picked up a pentaflex folder and shuffled through it. Then he pulled out the pages he had scribbled on earlier in the day when he was in the Records and Archives Room in the basement of the old town hall building on Fulton Street.

He placed these notes next to the monitor and looked at them, looked through them, not seeing them, but seeing the desk beneath them, and then the carpet beneath that. And then the cool gray dirt packed under the foundation of his house. He looked all the way to the bottom of the island.

Blood crept back into the capillaries of his fingers. Absently he wondered, *Is this what people deal with up north? All the time?* He looked at the screen again and then, with sore fingers, reached for the phone.

Tidewaters peeled away from the sand. Cowering. Seafoam was lifted to the air and batted somewhere deep across the vast, pulsating flesh of the frigid Atlantic. In the west, the sun touched the distant horizon, signaling the fall of night.
The ghost opened its eyes and screamed.

The near-dead man in the mountains stirred, swam up from the depths of unconsciousness hearing the scream as the song of wolves outside his door.

A fierce pain shrieked through MaeEllen Taylor's skull; the pain so sudden and blinding an almost-full glass of bourbon slipped from her hand. Glass shattered; whiskey splashed across the kitchen floor; the sharp tang of alcohol exploded through the room.
Before she could grab her head, the pain was gone.

Gussie Ransome faced an onrush of unnaturally cold air, shuddered, caught the faintest cry within the breeze, as if a small child was weeping somewhere in the night.

"So then, you weren't adopted after all." Elgin Highsmith was turning a pocket watch over in his hand.
Boo Taylor swatted at an invisible insect whine.
"You're not paying attention. When my real mother died, Laylee Colebriar took me to my father. As far as anyone else knew, he wasn't my real father."
"What about his wife—your other mother? She must have known. She must have known everything. Right?"

No answer.
Royal hung up. For a long while, he sat quietly as the echo of the failed rings from the handset faded in his ear. His need to talk to Boo Taylor immediately was enormous. Standing abruptly, almost knocking over the chair, he grabbed the folder and a cassette tape from the desk. He started for the door, buttoning up his jacket as he went.

five

Gussie Ransome swatted the little boy's finger away from the doorbell. "That's enough; I think she heard you the first two times."
"Then why didn't she come?"
"Just hold your horses." Gussie licked her fingers and wiped at the boy's hair. The boy flinched, slapped at her hand. His stick and pouch swung around and almost clunked her head. "Okay then," she said, standing up and hugging her jacket close, "I guess you'll just be a very sloppy hobo."

She was at the top of a stage, sensing an audience behind the many windows up and down Carriage Avenue, judging her. It was a feeling she carried with her wherever she went now, wondering if she might as well have a bright red "A" carved into her forehead.

The door opened, and the boy shouted, "Trick or treat!"

MaeEllen Taylor smiled grandly and invited them inside. Her smile to Gussie was meaningful and, to Gussie's tremendous relief, empty of judgment. "Whoever heard of such weather in October. And look at you, Jeremiah Ransome, if you're not the spittin image of your daddy!"

"I'm a *bum,*" the boy declared happily.

Gussie followed them inside where it was suddenly too warm. She said, "He remembers Bess Polk's candy apples from last year. He's been talking about them all the way over."

"Have you?" MaeEllen was leading the boy toward the dining room. For a moment, it was like seeing the woman with a six-year-old Boo Taylor. "Well, Miss Bess made those apples again this year, and she made *two extras* just for *you!* Augusta, for heavens sake, take that coat off and visit for a bit. We can sit in the parlor."

Gussie shook off her jacket. From a distance, MaeEllen Taylor was still surprisingly pretty and youthful. It was only when she came closer that Gussie saw the razor-thin pain lines that mapped her face.

"I think we're in for an awful night," MaeEllen said, rubbing her hands as she came back to the foyer. Jeremiah was wandering toward the parlor, already smearing the candy apple into his charcoal beard.

Behind them, someone knocked at the front door.

Far away, an axe was splitting wood to a relentless, urgent rhythm. Ben Shallcross was lying on his side watching the blue-lit shape of a wolf panting at him from a few feet away. The shape eventually sharpened into a table and chair. He listened to the sound of splintering timber, imagining a twenty-foot wolf crashing against the cabin, and tried to remember his dream. Something about a young boy playing checkers on his front porch and a canoe tipping into Sugar Dam Creek behind his cabin. No, that was Palmers Creek behind his cabin, wasn't it? And what was that boy doing up here, anyway? He tried to remember, but the pounding axe kept interrupting his thoughts. *Little PIG, little PIG, let—me—IN!* His skull was being shattered to pieces with each blow. Then he realized the angry voice he was hearing between the pounding was summoning him by name.

"Coming, Papa," he whispered just as he recalled a letter he had received long ago telling him his father had died.

"Ben, for Godsakes" he heard. It was Russell Cooper's voice, and Russell was long dead, too. He sighed, wondering that the dead had suddenly become so impatient. He swung his legs around and settled stocking feet on the cold, rough-hewn floorboards. Shadows of little Negro girls scuttled out of sight. He stood up. A massive, liquid weight

shifted in his chest, and purple and scarlet spots pattered across his vision until, for a moment, he was almost completely blind.

When his sight returned, he began a slow shuffle toward the banging front door. A splinter snagged his left sock. He remembered picking a splinter out of a girl's foot once. She had brought him a lemonade on his daddy's porch and got a splinter in her heel. The feel of her skin in his hands had made him weak and short of breath. And when he had dared to look up, her face had been as red and frightened as his. But she had not turned away.

Do you forgive me?

Then he was looking out a window and watching a miracle of silvery-blue snow blanketing the wood stack on his back porch. He wondered if he had slept through autumn and right into the middle of winter.

"Ben, dammit, open up!"

"Comin, Russ," he whispered. Russell would give him a ride home in his red pickup if it could make it that far. Sweetpatch Island was a long way off, and that snow would make for a tricky ride down the winding mountain roads. Ben reached the door, and as he fumbled with the lock the banging stopped. He pulled the door open, worrying it might be the wolves out there and the voice had been just a trick.

The cold struck his face like a fist.

A head crammed into his doorway, topped by a furry, plaid hat with ear flaps. "Jesus, Ben, you scared the hell outa—" And then the face faltered, went flat. "Ben, you look horrible."

Ben Shallcross reached up to scratch at the grizzle of five-days' growth. "Oh, I got a bugger of a flu, I guess. What day is it, Russ?"

"It's Elton, Ben. You don't know what day it is?" The face was a calico of red and blue splotches.

"Shouldn't be snowin yet. Must be December already. I guess you folks must be gettin ready for Christmas."

The boy moved as if to come in; Ben shifted his bulk into the cold space between them to block the way. "C'mon Ben, let me in."

"Not by the hair of my chinny-chin-chin. Say, you ain't seen a big wolf out there, have you, boy?"

Elton Cooper blinked.

"Big one. 'Bout as big as your truck. Maybe you seen his tracks."

The boy made another move, and Ben stopped him again. "Quit foolin, Ben."

"I got things t'do right now, Elty. How 'bout stoppin back tomorrow? Play us some stud, if you're up to it."

Then the old man bent his head to his fist and coughed violently, and it felt like all the molasses in the world had gotten into his lungs. When he was able to look up again, Elton Cooper was studying him warily. Ben's legs were very tired, his cheeks seared with heat. He seemed to recall waking up at some point (was it today?) to go to the bathroom and surprised himself by throwing up an endless rush of red.

"Ben, I talked to Pete Greenly this morning. Says he was out patrolling the hills last night, and he come across some old fool wandering around out there with no coat, no hat, and his fly undone. Sound familiar?"

Ben tried to smile. The effort made his cheeks crack open.

Elton growled and reached for the door again, but Ben took the young man's wrist in his big hand and held it as firmly as he could, aware that his fingers were trembling horribly. He fixed Elton with a steady, solemn glare. "Elty, please. I'm tired. Just let me sleep."

Ben watched the boy hesitate, and he clenched the wrist tighter. "Let me sleep tonight," Ben said quietly. He peeled his hand away from Elton Cooper's wrist and reached up to rest it on the boy's shoulder. The boy was not coming inside, not tonight, no matter how much he might want to—Ben Shallcross tried to confirm this message with the weight of his hand.-

"Okay, old man, you win," Elton breathed, and Ben relaxed. "Eva's gonna whup me, you know. She's gonna whup my hide but *good*."

Ben smiled at him.

When the boy's truck disappeared down the trail toward the big road, Ben Shallcross took his bright orange parka from the hook next to the door. It was almost too heavy to lift. When he checked through the window again, the wolves had already stepped forward from a stand of naked maples.

They were calling for him.

Asking him:

What's the worst you've ever been afraid, Ben?

❖   ❖   ❖

Elgin Highsmith asked, "How did she die—your mother?"

"Her car went off the causeway," Boo told him. "The bridge that connects the island to the mainland. She drowned."

Boo Taylor sat in a fog of cigar smoke. His hand cupped a double vodka on the rocks. Next to this was an empty tumbler that was making a round water stain on the table. A plastic clown's mask was pressed to the top of his head like a hat.

"Were you with her when it happened?"

"Elgin," Boo said, pinning the man with his eyes, "I was still *inside* her when it happened. Boy, aren't you listening? They got her up to the beach and...she died, and I didn't."

He reached across the booth, and Elgin placed the pocket watch back in his hand.

SBT

Somewhere beneath all of these facts, somewhere under the *forensic evidence* of his birth, was supposed to be a love story. Somehow, the doctor had met the love of his life, who had somehow come to the island to find Eulahlah Colebriar, who had somehow known the girl's mother long ago. And the doctor, who was already married to a refined-if-frivolous beauty from Beaufort, knew this girl's family, and he was smitten despite all of his best intentions. And the girl was grateful, and Miss MaeEllen was oblivious until the girl wound up pregnant.

"No wonder," Elgin Highsmith said, after whistling through his teeth, "you're so fucked up. By the way, do you know you call me 'boy' all the time?"

"I call everybody 'boy,'" Boo Taylor groused, "I'm from the South. I call my mother, 'boy.'"

The waitress passed, costumed as a fairy princess. Boo flagged her, got her attention, and made a circular gesture with his hand, signaling for another round. Half of the faces at the bar were hidden behind Halloween masks.

"But do you know how much I hate it when you call me *'boy'?*"

"Do you know you call me 'man' all the time? What's your point, Elgin?"

Elgin Highsmith raised both hands in a gesture of surrender.

"Can we please change the subject?" Boo asked.

"I'm all for *that.*"

"Look." Boo leaned forward, deep in a grand and self-absorbed drunk. "What I wanted to ask was, what would you think about taking over?"

Elgin waited, expecting another sentence or two. When none came, he asked, "Taking over what?"

"The *company*. Taylor Builders."

"I'd have to change the name," Elgin deadpanned. "I mean, it couldn't stay *Taylor* Builders, could it?"

"Fine. Change the name."

"I'd have to name it after myself."

"Great. Eight Ball Builders has a nice ring to it."

"You're not serious."

"Hell yes, I'm serious. 'Eight Ball' works nicely."

"Boo, I can't take you serious with that stupid mask on your head."

The lights flickered. Boo glanced up, recalling the night of the hurricane. He swept the mask off his head and placed it on the table next to his empty drink. "I know Stoney figures some day he'll get it," he said, "but Stoney's got less sense than you. Also, he never showers. I can't turn things over to someone who smells that bad, can I?"

Elgin laughed as the waitress arrived. She placed a fresh beer in front of him and a fresh vodka in front of Boo Taylor.

"How many is *that?*" Elgin asked, pointing at the glass.

"Are you keeping score now?"

"I should give you a ride home."

"Don't be stupid, I'm fine. Anyway, do you want it or not?"

"What are we talking about here—selling the company? You going somewhere?"

Boo Taylor pursed his lips and studied the watch in his hand. When he looked up again, the room was a smoky blur. Vague shapes hovered beyond Elgin Highsmith's shoulders. The night the lights had gone out was the night his father died. The night his truck might have clipped a dog, or a man, or an ancient black ghost with a bone to pick. It seemed that night must have been years ago. "I'm thinking of making some changes, Elgin," he said. "Maybe move back South." He blinked. "You think I'm just running away from Sandy, don't you?"

Elgin raised his hands in innocence again.

"It's got nothing to do with her."

"If you say so."

"And no, I'm not talking about selling anything. I want to *give* it to you. And yes, I'm serious."

"Give it to me? Now I *know* you're drunk."

Boo swirled ice in his glass. "Elgin, after twenty-five years I find my long lost fingers floating in a pickle jar in some South Patch bathroom. My father died. My ex-girlfriend is pregnant and thinks getting married will fix everything. I'm hanging on by a thread."

"You're not driving, Boo. Come on, I'll give you a ride."

"Besides, what is there to sell? A few trucks, a few tractors, some equipment and a stack of bills. You'll be doing me a favor." Boo set down his glass. Someone had scrawled graffiti into the top of the table, scratching it with a knife blade. Some innocuous profanity that, for no good reason, made an obscure connection in his mind to the message left for him on the mirror in the house where his father died. Or the words slopped on his front door. *Welcome Home.* "You may have to look for a new law firm, too," he said. "I've got the feeling Allen Noble doesn't like me anymore."

Royal Goody, crestfallen to learn Boo Taylor had flown home, stepped into MaeEllen Taylor's parlor. At MaeEllen's insistence, he took a seat while she tried to reach Boo by the kitchen phone.

"He has one of those awful answering machines," she said, returning to the room. "I left him a message. I asked him to call back right away. Royal, dear, you look ill—are you all right?"

After a moment of thought, Royal Goody showed MaeEllen and Gussie what he had brought. It was a copy of his story, *The Haunted Ferryboat*, printed double-spaced on 8x11 sheets.

"I've read this before," Gussie told him. "This is in your book, isn't it? About the first Mrs. Satterfield who died when the ferry caught on fire."

"Would you mind reading it again?" he asked. "Right now. I'd like to know if you see the same things I see. I want to make sure I'm not just making this up in my mind."

Gussie settled Jeremiah in front of MaeEllen Taylor's television in the den. Then she and MaeEllen read the story, Gussie going first and handing the finished pages to older woman as she went. Royal stood over them while they read. He had been standing since she came back to the parlor, and Gussie could feel the nervous electricity radiate from him in jolts and twitches. He was between her and MaeEllen, and both were now studying MaeEllen closely while she read the last page.

MaeEllen laid down the page and looked at Royal. She mimicked Royal's worry now; she had made whatever connection Royal had made but which Gussie still failed to see.

"Okay," he said, "so somebody tell me what this means."

MaeEllen let her gaze dip quietly to her hands, so he looked straight at Gussie for help.

"It has something to do with Boo, doesn't it," she said and felt stupid.

"What makes you say that?" Royal asked.

She noticed he didn't disagree. "Well, there's that witch-girl that Dottie Mae Jackson describes. That sounds a lot like Crystal Burne, doesn't it?"

Royal shook his head at her impatiently. "*If* there even was such a girl, it certainly wasn't Crystal Burne. But I'm pretty sure I know who it would have been. I thought you would, too."

She glanced at the pages again. That had surely been a description of Crystal Burne rampaging through Laylee Colebriar's garden and screaming for Boo Taylor. She had imagined so the instant she first read "half-dressed girl."

She said suddenly, "It's Mamie Stuvant, isn't it? In nineteen-thirty-six. She would have been just a girl, then, wouldn't she?"

"She would have been in her twenties, is my guess," Royal told her. "But 'girl' is probably an apt description—coming from Dottie Mae, who's almost ninety."

"What does Dottie Mae say about that? Does she think it was Mamie Stuvant?"

"No, she thinks it was Bathsheba Tribbit's ghost, remember?"

"What about your aunt?"

Royal scowled; scratched his chin. "My aunt was never there for any of it. She picked up the story the way most other folks did—talk over the woodstove or the clothesline. I'm sure that story stewed in the pot a bit before Aunt Nattie got a chance to add her own salt and pepper to it."

Royal paced to the window and looked out absently. Then he turned and leaned on the sill.

MaeEllen still hadn't said anything.

"Anyway," Royal began again, "I've been at it for years, but I still haven't been able to confirm where Mamie Stuvant was at the time. And nobody I've talked to can remember her being on Sweetpatch Island before the fifties. Story goes that she was raised by Bathsheba Tribbit on the mainland in Kowe, and Bathsheba was supposed to be her grandmother. We know Bathsheba wound up in Kowe after Joker was lynched—she even started a church there."

Gussie said, "But no mention of Mamie Stuvant."

"No, *but*..." Royal paged through his folder. When he found what he was looking for he said, "Church records are a great place to look for these kinds of things. And several years back I came across this entry in the marriage records of the Progress Baptist Church in Barleysville—that's the town next to Kowe. The entry says a Cecilia-Mae *Tibbit* married a Felix X. *Stuvant* in 1938. I found another record that Felix Sturvant died in 1943, but nothing more about his wife."

"Cecilia-Mae," said Gussie. "That was her real name?"

Royal Goody sighed heavily. He rubbed his eyes. "Who knows? And who knows if there really was such a girl on that boat to begin with. But you know, when I first heard the story from Aunt Nattie it's what struck me. Particularly when you consider we're talking about the Sladeshaws and the Satterfields."

Gussie was momentarily lost. She turned to MaeEllen Taylor who still had not looked up since finishing the story.

Royal explained, "Reliance Satterfield was Raymond Satterfield's father. And not a very pleasant man—according to any number of people, including Margaritte Sladeshaw LaValle, who mentions him several times in her journal."

"Margaritte LaValle," Gussie said. "You mean Samuel LaValle's wife."

Nodding, Royal said, "Reliance and Samuel were friends. Between the two of them, they owned most of the island."

Gussie considered this for a moment. "Mamie Stuvant," she said. "So you think Reliance Satterfield had something to do with Joker Tribbit's lynching. Right?"

Royal Goody made an unhappy smile. "Samuel LaValle didn't lynch Joker Tribbit by himself. Reliance Satterfield was one of his few friends. Do the math."

Gussie remembered Boo Taylor, long ago, telling her that his own mother was a Hawthorne, and there had been a Hawthorne at the lynching. She picked up the pages of the story, scanning them, realizing that her hands were trembling. "Sheba's curse—Mamie Stuvant was after Reliance Satterfield's heirs. The same way she was after the Hawthornes. And the Duffs and the Beaudrys. Royal, why on earth didn't you put any of this in your book?"

"Look," he said, gazing down. He glanced at MaeEllen and seemed at once uncomfortable. "Look," he said, more softly, "it's all just speculation."

"So why bring it up now? What's so urgent about it all of a sudden?"

He was about to answer when MaeEllen Taylor finally, wearily, looked up. She glanced at Royal, then squared around to Gussie. "Because he found out Ray Satterfield lied to him," she said.

A breath of wind moaned woefully through the high Victorian eaves. Royal stepped away from the window. "Boo showed me some pictures," he said, holding out two photographs, "and I showed them to Dottie Mae Jackson yesterday."

Gussie took the pictures. She looked at the images as Royal's hand disappeared again into the thick folder. He shuffled through his papers, then the hand reappeared holding a cassette.

"Miss MaeEllen," he said gently, "do you have a tape player?"

The tall trees all along London Park clumped so tightly together it was completely black inside them once the sun went down. The white lights from the sparse homes could not penetrate more than a few feet. The ghost, liking dark places, waited comfortably there. It was like crouching in the middle of a primordial forest—or perhaps being wrapped within the dank bark of one great and ancient tree, peering through knot holes while all of the tiny little creatures with so many skittering legs had their taste and tried to feed—or perhaps hiding inside an abandoned shell of a house where the little creatures also liked to skitter. And, here in this dark place, it smelled something like the abandoned old house. The years and layers of rotting maple leaves and oak leaves and dwarfish cadavers brewing with the sharp pine needles so far from home—that was almost the same as the rotting plaster and furniture and carpet and floorboards: the smell of dead things, cast-aside things, cramped into a lightless and overlooked place.

The ghost who crouched in this dead and lightless place watched the front door of a particular stone house. Few children had been through this secluded street after sundown (and the ghost had not arrived until well after sundown). Even fewer dared the long walk up that driveway. But three of those children were up there now, and the ghost watched as the biggest among them pressed the doorbell. A tall, broad-shouldered man came to the door, swaying, and the children shouted at him. The tall, broad-shouldered man was wearing a mask, too. A big, white clown's face. The ghost had seen this before. That was the man's joke. He was playing the same game as the children. He had even placed lighted jack-o-lanterns along the long walk and hung a cardboard skeleton on the front door.

The tall, broad-shouldered man laughed like a barroom drunk as he spoke to the children, but the ghost was too far away to hear the words.

The ghost checked for the heavy sack at its feet. It felt inside. Yes, everything was still there. The little creatures with so many skittering legs had not skittered away with anything.

The tall, broad-shouldered man was waving good-bye to the children, stumbling, tottering. The ghost watched as he closed the door again.

The ghost hid and waited among the tightly clumped trees that were so much like a forest or a single, massive and ancient tree or the ruined old shell of a once-grand house.

Soon, the children would stop coming.

As Ben Shallcross crossed a high meadow in the hills, the snow was already inches deep. It was filling the brim of his old Stetson. The wind had died, and a crisp, blue tranquility had settled over the night. He stopped for a moment. Listened. The only sound was the dry rattle of snowfall as it sprinkled into the beech trees and yellow birch and the tall slips of oat grass. The woods had gone silent. Even the wolves were still. They had been trailing him since he left the cabin. *Escorting* him, he decided. Yes, that was what they were doing, gliding in and out of the trees like the lost wind itself, appearing on one side of him, and a moment later on the other side, and a moment after that in front of him.

Now they stopped with him.

The snow pattered like hourglass sand. Patient.

A bluish glow was seeping up from the white clouds at his feet, turning the world upside down. *I'm in heaven,* he thought and remembered a wrinkled cinnamon face once telling him that snowflakes were really angels visiting the earth. The trail had become one long and shallow blue-gray shadow in an endless blue-gray heaven. *I see you. I see you out there among the angels.*

A wolf's howl split the night in two. Ben watched the wolf as it stepped into the clearing and its snow-colored throat warbled mournfully against the lightless sky. The howl ended abruptly as the wolf snapped its head down to mark him again.

"I'm coming," Ben whispered to the wolf and to all of the others still in the trees. He tugged the old Stetson to his brow and then spoiled the silence with grunts and sloppy footfalls and the dig of his staff into the snowy trail. The gray lump of his heart pulsed heavily in his chest. He turned his face to the steady stream of angels.

He coughed again, and Russell Cooper appeared at his side.

So Ben, you never did fess up. Why don't you tell me now.

Tell you what?

You know what, Ben. What's the worst you ever been afraid?

The big old man poked his staff into the mystery of the snow. When had it ever snowed so early in the season?

Her name...He remembered that now. He remembered the touch of her fingers on his face, like snowflakes tapping lightly upon his skin. He remembered traded glances across dinner tables and the secret, accidental brush of a skirt against his leg and stolen afternoons to whisper about music and books: jewels he collected and later marveled and wept over when he was alone. He remembered her trapped, quiet beauty and the secret hate he held in his heart for the man who was her husband.

He remembered the trail he wore between his father's house and her husband's porch and the unsettled peace this had brought for a time. But only for a time.

He remembered one day.

One day, when at long last they made another trail over the water and deep into a warm place away from the sea, where a bed of wildflowers and a low-country brook and a compassionate blue-heaven sky were the only witnesses to their sin. In that perfect light, the agonized beauty she showed him was nearly unbearable. The world beyond the meadow—his father, her husband—became nothing. Nothing. Nothing but this simple, uncompromising joy that had lasted forever and only a moment, and later, he broke down in laughter and in tears and clung to her. And toward evening, as the sky flared orange, he lay in the flowers and watched while she danced gracefully in the stream. Her smile offered everything he desired. *"Come in. Come join me."*

"But you look so beautiful from here."

"And you look so beautiful when you hold me. Come join me, Ben."

He remembered her. Could he explain all that to Russell Cooper? Could his rough, mountain-man words—the only words he knew anymore—could they possibly describe that lost life back in the lowlands, far beyond a snag of trails so long and twisted and grown-over with generations of scrub.

"The worst I ever been afraid? I was a lucky man, Russell...but Lord forgive me, I was a weak man, too."

He was in the trees on the steep downward slope when the staff slipped across the face of a hidden bulge of sandstone. He went down. There was a glaring snap in his left hip as he hit the wet trail and tumbled down the slope. The staff fell away from his hand. His face slapped against the snow, and the Stetson was gone. Still falling, his coat rode up to the pits of his arms, then his flannel shirt, and the wet ground dragged under his thin long johns. He stuck out his hands to slow the tumble. His left glove came away. Then his right wrist snagged against something sharp, and he screamed. The world rolled blue-and-white, blue-and-white. He tried to dig his left hand in the dirt to catch a hold, tried to dig in his boots. Then all wind left him when the glossy, thick trunk of a birch slammed into his stomach and he finally stopped falling.

He lay at the base of the birch, gazing toward a snarl of branches lifting like claws toward the night sky. Snowflakes fell in his eyes, and he tried to blink them away. Then he realized he had stopped breathing; the tree had stolen his breath. *Am I dead?* It seemed to be death. There was so much pain—his hip, his wrist, the fingernails of his left hand, his back—everything, everything was pain, and so it must be death. He couldn't move, and so it must be death.

But the muscles of his stomach spasmed suddenly and forced a violent inhale.

The breaths came back to him now in harsh, heavy draws. The gray lump throbbed madly. He moved his head. He flexed his fingers and sent a jolt of pain down to his right elbow. His left hip was bluish-white fire.

"No Lord," he whispered. The snow began to fill the creases of his face. He muttered bitterly, and the snow fell into his mouth.

After a time, his lips twitched soundlessly. The clamor of the gray lump quieted, and the frost seeped through his clothes and took root in his limbs. Somewhere beyond the swirl of pain and despair, a ring of yellow-eyed faces looked down at him. The yellow eyes reflected vapid gluttony.

No. Not here, not now...

Deep in the woods, lost far away from the unsympathetic faces above him, a voice called. *"Ben, don't turn away!"*

He listened and remembered

her voice.

Carrying down from the high wooden porch, and along a warm ocean breeze, and from her lips just an inch away from his ear. Singing love songs in whispers. And then his own voice, answering in vows, which, now remembered, ripped through his sobbing old man's heart like ice sickles.

"Do you love me, Ben?"

"You know I do. I'll take care of you, Mishelle. Always."

"And you'll always be with me?"

"Yes," he breathed into the wet ground, and the wolves broke away. "Yes, I'm coming."

He propped his head against the birch. That small movement brought excruciating pain. "Yes," he breathed again. The snow buried his hands. He clenched them again, felt the weak pulse urge blood back into his fingers. He braced his left hand against the tree and tried to press up from the snow. The effort ripped lightening through his left hip, and he groaned.

Ben, don't turn away.

"Yes, I hear you," he wept. He pressed again. The pain was blinding.

After a lifetime of struggle, Ben Shallcross climbed to his feet. He tottered. Snow slipped from his clothes in wet lumps. A thin line of blood dripped from the corner of his mouth. His throat was a bloody mush from screaming. His hands were frozen porcelain figurines that were heavy but no longer significant. He was a corpse risen from a snow-white grave to answer an ancient promise.

The wolves watched from their hidden places as the dead man faced the storm.

The ghost slipped out from the trees. Some length of time had passed since the last of the children had been to the door.

The heavy sack swung at the ghost's side as it hurried to the driveway. It passed the first of the candle-lit pumpkins and paused there a moment to watch the bright orange mouth fluttering an evil grin across a bright orange face.

The ghost answered the jack-o-lantern's grin with its own grin.

The candle flame wavered in terror.

On up the driveway, now. Its feet made small explosions in the leaf litter. A chill seeped through the barrier of harsh lights, pooling around the ghost, comforting it.

It passed another grinning pumpkin. The ghost let the cool breeze carry it along now with the dry leaves and the scent of burning wood from a nearby chimney. It passed the stone wall. Another jack-o-lantern, and the ghost stopped here and reached into the sack.

Then it bent to the jack-o-lantern's grin for a moment. Kissed it briefly.

Floating now; the breeze had become a strong wind, and the ghost was lifted momentarily into the air where it was cold and black and empty and every sweet thing the ghost craved most, and when it compelled the wind to return it to the ground, the ghost was standing before a door. Its right hand went behind its back; its left hand reached for the doorbell.

Stillness.

Footsteps.

The doorknob jiggled.

The door opened, and the tall, broad-shouldered man was there in his drunken, smiling mask. A different mask, now. "My God, you must be a ghost," he said.

The tall, broad-shouldered man sniffed the air. He smelled the ghost now. His eyes went bright.

"BOOOOO!"—the ghost shrieked and took its right hand from behind its back, and dashed the flame at the man's feet. Glass shattered, and fire vaulted from the floor to the man's belt. The tall, broad-shouldered man in his mask bellowed and swung his strong arms for the ghost, but the ghost put its hand on the man's chest and heaved him away. The man fell backward—still bellowing—and toppled over a table as the ghost took an open jug from the sack, stepped through the door.

"No!" the tall, broad-shouldered man screamed from the floor, his legs already ablaze. So much fear in that scream, and the ghost delighted.

It pitched the jar at the man. Gasoline spilled, splashing across the man's hair and broad shoulders and down his thick chest. These places immediately burst into flames, and the masked face disappeared.

"Booooooo!"—the ghost yelled again.

The table and the wall behind the man were on fire now. Trails of smaller flames spilled out in all directions. A frame filled with wildflowers crashed off the wall. The man—a sprawling, kicking thing of solid fire now, no longer a tall, broad-shouldered man—wailed tortured animal sounds that were no longer like words. The ghost took a third and fourth open jar from the sack. It threw one of these into the living room. It threw the other into the dining room.

Somehow, the tall fire-thing had risen to its feet, still making its horrible animal noises. It staggered into the living room, howling, and now setting that room on fire. The man disappeared somewhere deeper into the house.

"Boo," the ghost said after him.

The ghost backed through the raging furnace of the foyer, and as it touched the cool night's breeze, the world became a roar of lights and screams and pain and shattering wind chimes.

MaeEllen Taylor had an old console stereo with a cassette player in the dining room. There, Royal Goody fiddled with the tape player's controls—fast-forwarding through the cassette and sending an occasional burst of an old woman's voice through the speakers. Jeremiah was asleep in front of the television in the den. Gussie had called Murphy to tell him where they were and that they would be home late. "You do what you want," was all he had to say to her. Her stomach felt dry and achy. Some atrocity was storming about her, something tragic she could not see but could sense in the preternatural winter wind that was attacking the house in gales. The wind was wrong. The cold was wrong. Everything about the night was wrong. Royal pressed another button and stepped away from the stereo. Gussie sat on the edge of a moss green armchair, wishing she could call Boo Taylor. A stack of old LPs leaned inside the cabinet; the album facing her was a Duke Ellington. Royal's cluttered folder lay across the top of the cabinet.

Royal turned, showing the same electricity jittering through his body, and spoke: "Boo gave me two photographs. He said one was his birth mother."

MaeEllen Taylor was sitting upright in an ornate, antique dining chair.

"The other he said was somebody the doctor knew. Anyway, I showed them to Dottie Mae Jackson. I generally record my interviews when I'm researching for a book. In this case, I recorded what Dottie Mae had to say. And..." He flapped his hands. "Well, just listen." He turned back to the stereo and pressed the play button. Dottie Mae Jackson's ripe, slightly quavery baritone rolled across the parlor. Gussie tried to forget the wind outside and focus on the voice. She leaned toward the speakers.

"It's coming up..." Royal said over the old woman. He held his finger up like a man hailing a cab. "Coming...Okay, *now*."

Through the speakers: papers shuffling, Royal clearing his throat. Royal's voice: *"What about this one?"*

Dottie Mae: *"Why, that's little Boo Taylor. That boy had hisself a nose for trouble, Gawd didn't he though?"*

"What about the man next to him?"

"Don't know. Looks a bit like Davey Morse."

"Dottie Mae, Davey Morse isn't even sixty yet, and this man was old when Boo Taylor was a boy, thirty years ago. It's not Davey Morse. Does he look familiar to you?"

After a considerable pause: *"Oh my word, I believe that's Mr. Dan's boy."*

"Danborne Shallcross? The family you worked for?"

"Lord I ain't set eyes on that boy since Methuselah was a cryin baby. Mr. Benjamin, that's who that is. Gawd, look how old he got. Used t'be such a good lookin boy. Was he polite? My word, he was nothin like his daddy, I can tell you that much."

"Benjamin. He was Danborne Shallcross' son? You knew him?"

"Did till his daddy sent him off, leastways—after he got mixed up with Ray Satterfield's wife. Never noticed how much he look like Davey Morse. That Davey Morse married one of them Vickery girls, don't recall which one but she was an ugly thing. Had about twenty childrens, did you know that? Oldest was Sarah, I believe. Look nothin like her momma, thank the Lord. And hips, Gawd, they went on as wide as my boy Elrod's old Buick. You know, that was a fine runnin car. Now, what d'you suppose that boy went and done with that old car?"

"I couldn't say. What happened to Benjamin Shallcross? I never heard of him."

"Give it to Willy Parker, maybe. Though I swear to Jesus I saw Hank Dutton drivin 'round in that thing once. Big ol shiny black thing. I s'pect my Elrod may be 'bout the first colored man on the Patch to own a car."

"Dottie Mae—"

"Took me for a ride all the way to Savannah, Georgia in that car. Whole bunch of us fit in that big ol monster. Alma Johnston come, and her man, Elmo. And old Lila Sue Henry. And...oh, I don't know who all."

Traffic noises in the distant background.

"Dottie Mae, we were talking about Benjamin Shallcross?"

"Catholics, I reckon. With all them childrens."

"Yes. Did you say Danborne Shallcross sent his boy off? Something about Raymond Satterfield's wife?"

"First Mrs. Satterfield, anyways. Miss Mishelle. Can't recall the name of his second wife."

"What about Miss Mishelle?"

"Gawd, boy, ain't you been listenin to me? That baby she was carryin was no more Ray Satterfield's than it was Teddy Roosevelt's. Seem like everybody on the Patch knew as much. Leastways, all the white folks on North Beach and their colored help knew it—boy would'a walk straight through fire for that girl. Seem like mean old Mr. Ray, he the last to figure it out. I guess nobody 'round like that old skinflint well enough to tell him the truth. Sept'n maybe Mr. Dan. But nobody liked Mr. Dan much, neither."

The complex crags and ravines of MaeEllen Taylor's face rearranged themselves into a knit of wariness. Gussie looked at her worriedly. *Boy would'a walk straight through fire for that girl.* Royal drummed sparks from his fingers on the top of the cabinet.

"You're saying the child Mrs. Satterfield was carrying when she died wasn't her husband's?"

"Boy, ain't you been listenin?"

"Yes ma'am—"

"Eulahlah Colebriar was with her to take her to Mr. Ray's sister, Miss Lucille, in Charleston so she could have her baby. Miss Lucille was always fond of that girl, no matter what wrong she done her brother. Birthed a lot of babies before she died, old Eulahlah. She done most them Morse childrens. Twenty childrens, at least. Martha— ain't that it?"

"Martha, what?"

"Second Mrs. Satterfield. Martha or Antha. Antha Satterfield—that sound right to you?"

"Dottie Mae, you said—"

"That first girl Mr. Ray marry, though, she was a pretty young thing; oh my, was she ever. Miss Michelle, she had hair like a Indian or one of them Chinee ladies. You ever seen them, boy? Jest like that—so black it almost look blue. Jest the prettiest thing, and was she sweet? Too sweet a peach for a sour apple like Ray Satterfield, I reckon. But I guess them rich white families, they do their marryin like two banker men shakin hands. Lord, it done my heart pain knowin that sweet little dove got caught payin the tab on her husband's cussedness. Though, I guess with that child not being Mr. Ray's, Miss Michelle, she got her own carpet to beat."

Gussie eased back into her chair. She looked away from the spinning reels of the tape first to MaeEllen, who looked away from her—and then to Royal, who closed his eyes and made an almost imperceptible nod.

"Who was the real father, Dottie Mae? Did you know?"

"Why, Mr. Dan's boy, a' course. Royal Goody, ain't you been listenin to me?"

"Yes ma'am, but—"

"What I been sayin is, nobody blame that girl too much for what she and Mr. Dan's boy done. You understand that?"

"Yes ma'am."

On the tape, Royal cleared his throat again. A truck horn sounded.

"Then some birdie come along and whisper the truth to Mr. Ray, and he kicked his wife out the house. That poor girl, she must 'bout been ready to burst, else I guess she'd a done track down Mr. Benjamin—either that, or get herself on back to her people in Atlanta or Macon or whatever place it was they come from. I guess it been a while by then since her people come regular to the island, you see. They was nice folks, too. Had a house on Rain Guild Road, and Mr. Larry Dufette moved in after they moved out. Had cats."

"Who did?"

"Mr. Larry. Gawd boy, you don't listen too good, does you? Good thing you got that machine takin this down."

"Yes ma'am."

"Never thought much of a man who like so many cats. Guess Miss Sarah, she put up with it well enough after she married him."

"And Mr. Dan's boy, Benjamin, was he——"

"Oh Gawd, Mr. Dan done throw him out, too. Without so much as a penny or a prayer. He done gone off to the mainland to find work and near died of grief when word come 'bout Miss Mishelle passin. Hear he wound up fightin in the Pacific durin the war, though since after Mr. Dan died I can't say as I ever heard another lick about him. Boy's been out'a my mind till you shown me that picture——"

Royal snapped off the recording. In the sudden quiet within the room, the sound of the cold wind outside reared again and became like howling wolves. Although the house was warm, Gussie wrapped her arms around her knees to ward off a chill. She felt as if some important message was in the picture before her, but she was failing to recognize it and bring it into focus.

She tapped her lip, frowned at Royal. "The child didn't die," she said. "That's what Raymond Satterfield lied about, isn't it?"

Gussie turned to MaeEllen Taylor who was gripping the arms of her chair as if she were about to stand.

Royal said, "It's all just speculation. You see that, right? That, and the memory of a ninety-year-old woman. But, yes, I think the child lived. I'm convinced of it, actually. And it was a girl."

"And since it wasn't his child," Gussie continued, "Raymond Satterfield didn't want anything to do with it."

Royal, reluctant, nodded.

"So he lied about it. And Laylee Colebriar was there—Royal, could that really be *true?*"

Sighing heavily, Royal began to pick at one of his fingernails. Gussie realized he was extremely uncomfortable and wondered why, wondered if it had something to do with her. She risked another glance at MaeEllen Taylor, who seemed to have locked herself within some self-imposed prison. "According to Dottie Mae, at least," Royal was saying, "Eulahlah Colebriar was more than just *there*. She would have actually delivered that little girl, maybe even the same night as the fire on the ferry. And then she took it to Raymond Satterfield's sister in Charleston. His sister *Lucille*."

He said this name meaningfully, but it meant nothing to Gussie. Then Royal turned to MaeEllen Taylor, more uncomfortable than ever.

The old woman gave him a shooing gesture with her hand. "Why Royal Goody, there is absolutely no need to be melodramatic. You found out Lucille Satterfield's married name was Hawthorne."

Royal bowed his head. "I did some checking today," he said. "Yes, his sister was Lucille Hawthorne."

Gussie stuck her fingernails between her teeth and bit them. She glanced at Royal Goody who was watching her expectantly. Then she glanced at the photograph Boo had given to Royal—a young-boy Boo standing beside a giant old man whose name was Benjamin Shallcross and who apparently had an illicit affair with Raymond Satterfield's wife and was sent off to purgatory for it.

Then it struck her like a thunderbolt.

"Oh, God!" she said. "*Lucille.* Lucille *Hawthorne.* She must have been Belle Hawthorne's aunt, wasn't she? The child was Boo's birth mother!"

MaeEllen sighed. She stood up and primly bounced her gray hair in her hand. "Well yes, dear, of course she was. Shall I get you folks some tea? Or would you prefer coffee?"

Neither answered. The wind rattled the windows. After a moment, MaeEllen Taylor started for the door.

Gussie, still thunderstruck, watched MaeEllen Taylor drift out of the room, trying to summon some fractured air of dignity. A slight smile was propped on the woman's lips. A mask. She seemed almost not there at all, as if the floral print of the wallpaper showed through her as a dim, half-seen blur.

Gussie turned back to Royal Goody. Royal, stoic, was also watching MaeEllen Taylor's graceful exit.

Gussie waited for him to speak.

When he didn't, and didn't even look at her, she said, "There's more, isn't there?"

The smell of burning filled the inside of Sandy Baker's BMW. Even before she pointed the headlights off of London Park and toward the fire.

Oh, God. What has he done!

The heat whipped across her face the instant she left the car. She was sprinting to the house, the heat building upon her in sheets and blankets the closer she came. She watched a flame twist twenty feet into the night through a hole in the roof. Other flames, nearly as high, rolled like upside-down lava flows from the windows. She pulled her way tree-by-tree toward the front door. The heat was enormous; it was shoving her away like an ocean wave. She bent her head to it. Grabbed a pine trunk that melted and stuck to her fingers. She lifted her eyes, and the heat scalded them.

Through the dining room window—a reeling, fleeting shape.

"Boo, get *out* of there!"

The entire front landing was a blinding whiteness. A nearby pine cracked like a rifle shot, new flames were suddenly eating it whole.

She turned away—sudden coolness on her face—and weaved through the pines. Her foot mashed into the teeth of a pumpkin, and she kicked it away. She reached the garage door, bent to grab the handle, and yanked. Smoke avalanched over her. A new heat exploded behind it, and she staggered backward. Then the smoke and the heat were lifting, and she could make out a gray rectangle deep in the corner and an orange square inside that. She was looking at the door that led to the back hallway. Shrieks and a volley of gunshots followed her as she dashed inside.

The garage was a brick oven; smoke burned through her nostrils. She gulped a breath, and hot oil leaked into her lungs. She coughed harshly, covered her mouth with her hands and breathed again. Her knee crashed into Boo's mountain bike, and she stumbled the last several feet to the door through a blistering black cloud.

She tried to peek through the window, but her eyes stung and watered, and all she could make out were white flashes amid a roiling grayness. A frightening roar rolled from the other side of the door. When she put her hand on the knob, the metal scorched her flesh, and she yelled out, taking in another scalding lungful of oily smoke. More screams echoed somewhere behind her. Her stomach churned horribly. She dropped to her knees on the warm concrete floor, and coughed and coughed until her throat was raw. She was unable to stop crying. Her hands patted into the rag-carpet doormat. Sobbing, she brought her hands back to cover her nose and mouth, took a deep breath that was like inhaling an ashtray, and held it, fighting the urge to cough again. She grabbed the mat and wrapped it around the doorknob.

She pushed open the door, and fell inside an incinerator. Smoke draped over her like a shaggy bear rug. She screamed, *"BOO, THIS WAY! THIS WAY!"*

The roar of the fire deafened her to her own words. Through the great, fat billows, she saw the kitchen. She took two more steps toward it, tried to yell out again, but when she brought in a breath it was nothing but liquid fire that crisped her nostrils and her mouth and her lungs. She fell over.

The smoke thinned near the floor, but her palms blistered on the ceramic tile, and there was no way Boo Taylor could be alive in this furnace. She bent into herself and coughed so hard and so long her throat was flayed to shreds and her stomach squeezed into a rock. A monstrous crash thundered from somewhere far away. She could not stop coughing; her eyes were blinking through hot grease. Her stomach shuddered with sickness, and she threw up on her legs. She scrabbled back for the door, scalding her arms and legs wherever she reached. The door had moved. She had gotten lost, turned around. Had she kicked the door shut?

Another crash, nearby, as if a freight train slammed into the house.

She wretched and sobbed and felt herself being boiled alive. She groped, unseeing now because her eyes were swollen shut.

When the last bit of air was wrung out of her lungs, she collapsed.

Sudden movement around her. Through the roar, sounds of retching. A dark heap on four legs, snarling insanely, loomed over her and slicked a hot tongue across her cheek and down to her throat.

Hands came under her arms. She was sliding across the blistering hot tile...

...and then over a bed of razor blades...

...and then into an ice-cold pool of water...

...and then into...

...she woke up in a cool place, the side of her face pressed into the damp loam. She curled her knees up to her chest and coughed out slick strings of grease. Bits of her lungs and throat were being drawn out of her by a sharp claw. She coughed until her back and stomach muscles clamped shut like a vice. Somewhere in the process of coughing, she managed to vomit over the yellow blanket that had somehow been wrapped around her legs.

The roar was in the distance now. She heard more gunshots. A strong hand was clapping against her back. If she could speak, she would tell whoever was doing it to stop because it hurt.

Then at last, real air slipping inside her and filling her up.

"Are you all right, honey? Can you breathe? Ray, do you think she can breathe?"

She blinked. Her eyelids felt strange; somehow lightweight while the rest of her was so heavy. She ached everywhere. The palms of both hands stung, and her throat had knives slicing through it. Her face was swollen like a balloon.

"Ray, do you think she can hear me?"

She blinked again. An old woman's face, wrinkled with deep concern, flickered gold and shadow above her. It was a familiar face, and it took her a moment to recognize Bonnie Passarella, Boo Taylor's across-the-street neighbor. Standing behind her was a tall, angry looking black man she had never seen before. The man had been burned in a fire. Beyond him, a crowd of about a dozen men and women had gathered. Half of them were watching her while the other half gazed worriedly at the flames.

"Sandy, sweetheart, can you hear me?"

"Yyyyeeessss," she croaked, and started another fit of coughs that was agony to her throat. When she could open her eyes again, the black man knelt to her side. He was holding her hand, and oh, how he had been burned by the fire, too—and now she did recognize him, and it wasn't a black man at all. It was just the soot making a disguise.

A wail of sirens sang out in the distance in tune to the snap and roar of the fire and the steady, loud pop and sizzle of pine trees. The smell of smoke was smeared over her hair and clothes like tar.

"Boo?" she asked.

Boo Taylor's neighbor, Ray Passarella, was looking down at her. His eyebrows were burned away. Two white lines trailed from his bloodshot eyes to his mouth where the curls of his handlebar mustache corkscrewed at opposing angles. He looked at her without smiling, and then he turned away.

A cramp suddenly seized her abdomen. She cried out. A giant white fist was squeezing her, grinding her organs together and forcing them out of her. The first spot of blood appeared on the blanket. Shuddering with pain, she wept, "No, oh God please, not *that!*"

Through the agony—beyond the others who were now all looking the other way—she saw something dark and mindless shambling away through the trees.

Gussie Ransome, still grabbing at random thoughts, half-formed concepts, something about Eulahlah Colebriar giving birth to twenty Morse babies, taking Mrs. Satterfield's baby to Lucille Hawthorne's home in Charleston, incoherent connections, vague strings of logic, said to Royal Goody, "So this man was Boo Taylor's grandfather." She tapped the photograph of Benjamin Shallcross.

Royal, looking exhausted, nodded.

"Do you think she knew—Belle Hawthorne—do you think she knew about her parents? Her real mother, and what happened to her?"

He shrugged. From over his shoulder, sounds of MaeEllen Taylor clattering china in the kitchen.

"I don't know," Royal said. "But she came looking for Laylee Colebriar didn't she? And it appears,"—he nodded toward the kitchen—"MaeEllen Taylor knew about it all, too."

And Mamie Stuvant, thought Gussie. *Cecilia-Mae Sturvant*, descendent of Joker and Bathsheba Tribbit and keeper of their curse.

Did Boo know any of this, too?

The question struck Gussie. Boo had given the photograph of the old man to Royal; he must have known something. Then she remembered Wade's warnings about Boo, that something was always just plain wrong with Boo Taylor, that none of this made sense—the toby on the pier, the stolen wallet, the writing on the mirror, the fingers—unless Boo was behind it.

Which, of course, couldn't be true.

She saw his face, earnest and passionate over her, carved with an unfathomable pain above his naked shoulders and boxed in by the four shabby walls of a tiny bungalow. Boo Taylor was a part of her; he was incapable of deceit, not with her, she would see it, would *feel* it. And he should be here right now.

She glanced at the phone.

MaeEllen Taylor was coming in, burdened by a silver tea set. Gussie got up to help her clear a space on the table.

"He was certainly never going to abandon me." MaeEllen spoke to Gussie in confiding tone. "Even after that poor little thing became with child, it never once crossed his mind."

Royal fidgeted. Gussie took MaeEllen Taylor's hand as the older woman settled into one of the dining room chairs.

"I really didn't bat an eye when he told me," MaeEllen was saying to Gussie, leaning toward her, "but I was *horrified*. Can you imagine? Can you imagine how *embarrassing* that was?"

A slightly hysterical glint flashed in MaeEllen's smile. Royal didn't see it. He asked, "Miss MaeEllen, did Dr. Taylor know Benjamin Shallcross?"

MaeEllen Taylor didn't appear to hear the question. Instead, she stared toward Gussie. Her eyes were focused just off center from Gussie's eyes, as if the woman were seeing something in the distance. The disturbing smile remained.

Gussie let go of her hand and reached for a cup of tea. She passed this to Royal, then took another for herself.

"Of course, Silas knew him," MaeEllen said suddenly, softly, speaking again to Gussie. "Silas had lived on Sweetpatch Island since he was a little boy, and he knew most of the families. He would have been several years younger than Dan's boy, Benjamin. Benjamin was long gone by the time I came, though of course I heard stories about him from Aretha Satterfield. You see, I didn't really spend much time on the island until Silas and I were married."

Gussie nodded, indulgent, took a sip of the tea that burned her tongue.

"You know," MaeEllen said, "Eulahlah always had my Silas in the palm of her hand. I was always convinced she put things in his food. Does that sound foolish?" A tear slowly rimmed her left eye. "Oh, I *know* she did."

Royal brooded into his cup.

MaeEllen Taylor's eyes became distant again. Gussie wondered if something inside the woman had been broken tonight—and that notion wrought forth the bleak uneasiness that had been lurking in her belly throughout her time in this house. *Boo Taylor should be here,* she thought. *This is all about him.* With him absent, it felt as though they were speaking about the dead.

"Miss MaeEllen?" Gussie spoke in a gentle, hoarse whisper. MaeEllen blinked and found her as if looking through a crowd. Gussie held up her cup and saucer. "Thank you; the tea is wonderful."

MaeEllen smiled gratefully. "Why thank you, Augusta. May I get you a scone?"

"No thank you, ma'am."

"Are you sure? Royal?"

Royal coughed and shook his head.

MaeEllen said, "Well, I think I might like one myself, if you don't mind."

She stood and moved on fragile deer legs into the kitchen. Gussie and Royal sat quietly in the dining room and listened to the sound of a cabinet opening, bottles rattling, a drink being poured. At last, Royal looked at Gussie and said, "I want to show you something."

He picked up his folder from the cabinet and drew a page free from the others. It was a typewritten chart; he handed it to Gussie.

"This is all still speculation, you know," he said.

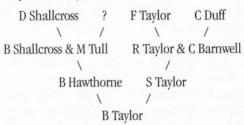

Royal half-sat on the stereo cabinet. He rubbed his fingers over the pebbly width of his forehead. "It looks like Boo might have at least three relatives that would have been on the island at the time of the lynching." He pointed to the names at the top of the page.

"Duff?" Gussie asked. "The same family as that boy who got killed when we were little?"

"Timothy Piedmont Duff," Royal said, nodding. "The doctor's maternal grandfather was Clement Duff, from Savannah. Family was into shipping. He was one of the men who bought up the land near Shell Pot where they used to have a hunting preserve."

Boo is related to the Duffs, she wondered. What else didn't they know? "And all three of those men were involved in the lynching?"

"I don't know. I don't think anyone alive *could* know."

Gussie glanced at the chart again. "But it would explain a few things."

"Maybe. But don't get too carried away; this is all still a guess. I put a call in to my friend at Georgia Southern today. I want to get another look at Margaritte LaValle's journals. It might say more about these people."

Gussie realized the wind was no longer howling around the house. There was no sound at all now. And somehow, that was worse than the wind—it meant that whatever had happened was done now and couldn't be taken back. "Sheba's curse," she said, mostly to herself.

"Maybe more like a feud," said Royal. He was moving toward the phone. "I think I should try Boo again."

Before he reached it, the phone suddenly rang, surprising them both.

MaeEllen called from the kitchen: "Augusta darling, will you be a peach and get that for me? I'm up to my elbows in soapsuds."

Gussie glanced at Royal nervously. She went for the phone.

After the third ring, she lifted the receiver.

"Mrs. Taylor?"

The voice on the phone was an old woman's, and it was shaken.

"Um," Gussie answered. She checked her watch and saw it had somehow gotten to be nearly ten o'clock.

"Oh, I'm so sorry, Mrs. Taylor. This is Bonnie Passarella, and I'm Boo's neighbor. Boo—your son?"

"Yes?" she said.

"Mrs. Taylor? The police are with me."

Inside the telephone, faraway voices shouted. A staccato note blared from a mechanical trumpet. Engines snorted. She knew those sounds, didn't she? *The police?* Her stomach was suddenly filled with old rags. She took the handset away from her ear as if it were on fire and stared at it.

Distantly: "Mrs. Taylor, are you there?"

Am I Mrs. Taylor?

"Mrs. Taylor?"

Gussie spoke into the phone, "Just a moment, please."

She held the phone out to MaeEllen who was approaching and drying her hands on a tea towel. As soon as the phone was out of her hands, Gussie backed into the wall.

"Hello, this is MaeEllen Taylor."

Gussie slid another step down the wall. Her thigh bumped against a chair. Behind her, the dead wind rose up so abruptly and so violently that the dining room window burst open in a great explosion of glass, and the floor buckled and rocked her off balance. She backed away from the phone, away from MaeEllen Taylor's frozen face, and got her legs tangled in Royal's legs. She was falling. The smell of burning rushed into her lungs as she fell. In slow motion, she grabbed for Royal's shoulders. Her hand clawed his neck. Caught the collar of his shirt. One of his arms lumbered up and caught her around the waist as MaeEllen Taylor started to wail.

Gussie turned, still caught in Royal's arm. Royal's tea had spilled down the front of his sweatshirt. She was shrieking; behind her, MaeEllen was shrieking.

"My *son!* My little *boy!*"

Gussie's spine ached within Royal's grip. She pushed at his shoulder, and he released her. She was trying to run from the room, run from the phone, running to find her son. That was the most important thing; she must find Jeremiah. But a crazed, wild-haired woman blocked her way.

"My *son!*" the woman wailed at her.

No, no—he's just asleep in the other room, Gussie thought, trying not to consider what horrors might be visiting Boo Taylor six-hundred miles away.

MaeEllen Taylor pulled a spray of hair until it stood from her skull like a gray flame. Gussie tried to push away, but MaeEllen fell into her arms. Gussie collapsed under the weight, sitting hard on the floor.-

Behind her, Royal Goody moaned.

The night capered outside the window; the big house on Carriage Avenue with the high spires and the tall porch—the doctor's house—became an insignificant island of light lost deep in a sea of absolute darkness. Gussie cradled a gray head in her lap; her boy was safe, but she knew Boo Taylor was lost. He was out there, somewhere far away from her. And he was alone.

six

She was waiting for him at the water's edge, holding out her arms, and Ben Shallcross limped dizzily for her across snow-slicked rock. In the faint, blue-silver shimmer of the mist, her eyes were ghastly.

"You left me alone," she said.

He brought his useless hands to his face and wept into them. A wolf's howl spiraled upward to meet the cascading snowflakes. Then another. Then others, and the night was filled with their voices. In his misery, he felt her cold fingers slip around his wrist. "Look at me."

"I can't," he sobbed.

"Ben." She drew his hands away and touched them to her cheeks. "Don't turn away from me now."

He breathed the sour breath of graveyards she offered him. Trembling, he looked up into her lost, forever lovely face. The wolves were a pleasant, faraway song, a carnival's calliope, loaded on a train and chugging away...leaving this place...forever... He gripped her hands, and she smiled. The smile was harsh.

Turning at last from the long, cold trail that led him to her, he said, "I love you," and he followed her into the waters.

It was the worst he'd ever been afraid.

Smoke & Whispers ~ October, 1971

Did you hear?

The voice whispered—from inside her own heart or amid the clatter of the school cafeteria; it was the same ugly voice regardless of its source. The same ugly voice that had been whispering to her since sunrise; the same spiteful, evil, sniggling, whimpering, insane, lying voice.

Gussie, did you hear? In the fire...

Her lungs burned.

In the fire...

Her skull, swelled with smoke and poisonous fumes, cracked apart. *Don't say it! Don't tell me that!*

...they found...

Stop it!

...oh, what they found...

Did you hear?

Gussie, where is Boo Taylor?

❖   ❖   ❖

Sunrise, October 31

"...who?"

Word spread as fast as the flames, and so they rushed from all across Up Island to see for themselves. But all that awaited them was the blackened skeleton of a beached whale. Too late. The flames, gone. The damage, done. The beast, dead. Someone killed it.

The whispering began.

"...but, who could have?"

The remnant steeple was a drunken dwarf leaning for balance against the buckling southern wall. Wide concrete steps climbed to a hollow, brick shell. Nothing to find through the false front doors but a soaked, smoldering pile of rubble that leaked ash-colored tears and could not be real, must be someone's joke. A Halloween prank.

"...who could have done such a thing?"

Cast over the crowd like a fisherman's net, pinching them together, an oily murk wafted across the warm, damp air and veiled the morning sun. *Thunderclouds,* they whispered among themselves and glanced accusingly at the Atlantic—not knowing the sky everywhere else above the Carolina coast was as yet a perfect, lovely blue, and that when the storm did come later that night, it would hit not from the ocean but out of the mainland.

KEEP BACK! SWEETPATCH ISLAND VOL. FIRE CO. stenciled in red on barriers that sentried Loggerhead Street. Two behemoth fire trucks filled both lanes. Flattened canvas hose crisscrossed the church lawn and dozens of oily rivulets, still trickling from the church, fed the black river that had formed in the gutter near the crowd's feet.

Cushioned in a bright green pile of azaleas, undamaged, a glass-framed sign announced the smoking ruins:

The First United Methodist Church
of Sweetpatch Island
WISE MEN STILL SEEK HIM
SERVICES SUN. NOV. 3 - 10:30

"There was a fire last night, Gussie.

"Somebody burned down the Methodist Church. The white church.

"Somebody with a bone to pick, all right.

"Gussie, where's Boo Taylor?"

They whispered, and their anger grew. Lost weddings and funerals and baptisms. Bake sales and charity fund drives. The Easter egg hunt sponsored every year by The Daughters of the Confederacy took place right there on the church grounds. Last year's Christmas pageant, all three Kressner girls singing carols as Marty Kressner played the organ and eight-year-old Nate Lewis stood up and recited the story of the nativity all by himself.

They scrambled behind the barriers for the best views, admiring the important men permitted on the other side. "That's Reggie Sheppard in there," someone whispered and pointed at the fire chief who was tromping inside a brick shell that had been peeled back like wet cardboard on its north and east sides. They identified his volunteers, knee-deep in the still-hot ashes and coals. "Hey, that's Vinny Scanlon, and that's Dink Potter." "There's Carol Basset." "That one's Buddy Olson, I think." Soot-covered, they were nearly invisible in the smoldering refuse. "There's Parker Tillman and his deputy, Waldo Lewis. And that newspaper man, Franklin," said someone who pointed at three men standing by a fire truck. "Anybody see Pastor Vic?" "Over there with Doc Taylor." Reverend Victor Greesome and Dr. Silas Taylor were speaking solemnly with the policemen. The policemen's gray uniforms were black. The pastor's black suit was gray. A greasy fingerprint streaked down the pastor's cheek like an exclamation point.

Among all of these men, only the doctor was spotless.

They whispered:

"Look how tired..."

"Look how sad..."

"Look how worried..."

"...what kind of animal would burn down a church?"

Silas Taylor rubbed his eyes—tired, sad, and worried—and gazed hopefully into the crowd that gazed hopefully back at him. Every face on the island was out there, except the one he needed to see. There was the Fitch boy and the Meggett boy crammed up front. Were they looking at him? The Standish boys and their father. What were they saying to each other? Further back, that glitter of red flame: Augusta

Dutton standing with two of her brothers. What dreadful things was she thinking at this very moment?

Whispering. Watching him and whispering about him—of course they were. Whispering and blaming, he was certain.

But he didn't see that all eyes were turned southward.

"Oh hell, that weren't no accident. Y'all know as well as me who set that fire. Anybody with half a fuckin brain knows it."

"It's the niggers done it."

"To get back for that shitty little Baptist church gettin burnt."

"Niggers, all right. And y'all know which nigger, too."

"Only one jig that fuckin stupid, all right. Same's burnt down the colored school."

Then, a shriek. Like a bucket of ice water ripping down from the sky. And, for just a moment, the whispers went silent. Shoulders, elbows, hips fought at the barriers. Was that a scream? Someone fell. Someone got burned. Someone fainted. Someone...

...called for the doctor, and there he went, trotting along with his black bag, Parker Tillman holding his arm and that newspaper man, Franklin, following them as all three men dodged the fallen bricks, as all three men were disappearing...

" ...who?"

"...who could have?"

A hand clawing up from the ash, camouflaged in the exact gray-mottled tones as the rest of the world. A doll's hand.

The men lifted a board, and the dead church belched a cloud of ash as a cadaver in the morgue might belch the sweet rot of its death. The doctor's white shirt and tan pants turned gray. His face turned gray. His vision wavered in and out of gray and black and bright white—all sense of color left him. The screams of dead timber being strained away deafened him. His chest clamped under the weight of an entire building. An arm, blistered and blackened and as dead as a brick, reached up for him.

A boy's arm.

"...who?"

"...but, who could have?"

"...oh great, good God almighty, give a hand with that—you boys, grab that beam and give her a heave. Doc, you all right? Doc?"

The crowd watched and whispered as the doctor called for a blanket and as he and Dink Potter and Parker Tillman and Pastor Vic raised a shrouded mummy from the hellish depths of the First United Methodist Church and ushered it, like pall-bearers, into the back of an ambulance.

"Look how tired..."

"Look how sad..."

"Look how worried..."

The doctor climbed into the ambulance to be with the dead thing. The ambulance pulled away from the collapsed church and the whispering crowd; it left without running its lights or its sirens, and inside the doctor was tired and sad and worried.

And so much more.

Because his son hadn't come home last night...

Gussie, did you hear...
...who they found?

two

October, month of pagan rites. Blood sacrifices were demanded, were eagerly offered. Shadows grew bold. Thermometers cowered. Trees shed chlorophyll flesh to weep as stark and angry skeletons; the sun, wounded by Father Time, was rendered less significant, a pumpkin shell brooding through shortened daylight journeys. Ancient curses (promises?) like seedlings sown and buried seasons ago, day after day after day patiently tended, fed, stormed upon and long silent until now, fully ripe and dripping, fully potent acid, came the grim moment of reaping.

October, when the ghosts opened their eyes, rose from earth and ash, and called the night their own.

❖   ❖   ❖

Sunset

"Wade, let me out here."

"You're nuts, Gussie. We're smack-dab in the middle of nigger country, and it's gonna be dark soon."

She glared at him with red, swollen eyes. "It's not that dark."

"Gussie—"

"Dammit, Wade, you stop the car and let me out before I have to bust you one."

The Plymouth slid off the street where Sugar Dam Road bent eastward and where a slim dirt trail snaked off to the south through cedars and oaks and palmettos on its way toward Laylee Colebriar's house. "How long you gonna be?" Wade asked. His eyes patrolled the darkening roadside.

Gussie opened the door and got out. "I don't know. Maybe I'll spend the night."

"You ain't spendin the night down here again. You know how much I hate that?"

"It's all right."

"I'll wait here."

"No."

"Okay, then I'm comin with you."

"No, Wade, you just go on."

"Gussie, it's gonna be *dark* soon!"

She closed the door and then shoved herself halfway into the window. "Wade, thanks for the ride. I'll be all right. Now, just get goin, will you?" Then she was off down the trail at a sprint.

Wade watched her arms and legs pump around the last visible bend of the trail. He swore to himself and threw the car into gear.

❖   ❖   ❖

Gussie heard the car spraying dirt and sand behind her. She didn't slow down. She was aware of the thick stand of woods around her. She didn't look into them. If something lurked in there and wanted her, it would just have to chase her. Things worse than shadows and shadow-men frightened her now. She had spent an entire morning and most of the afternoon wondering if the charred thing they pulled out of the Methodist Church was Boo Taylor, and there couldn't be much worse than that.

She cleared the trees, and there was Laylee Colebriar's shack jutting up from the field like a broken, cast-aside bottle. The westering sun sent a prairie fire across the garden and the wild expanse of autumn grass.

"Shamus, hey boy!" she yelled out in warning. "It's just me! Hey boy!"

The world had gone golden down here. Laylee's parlor windows sprayed huge, blinding gold flames, and wind chimes danced and sprayed smaller flames. From beneath the house, a lazy, golden figure lolled into view and wagged its tail.

"Hey, good boy!" she yelled.

The dog trotted to intercept her, but she ran past him—putting her hand out just to whisk his head—and then pounded up the porch steps. She banged on the screen door. "Boo, are you here! Miss Laylee?"

No answer. Shamus padded to the foot of the porch and watched her.

Gussie banged again. It was a hollow sound. Flakes of blue paint fluttered away with her fist like fingernail clippings. "Miss *Laylee?*" She bent to listen and to catch her breath. "Boo Taylor, dammit," she called, "where *are* you?"

A gull laughed from a distance.

She stepped away from the door. She leaned over the porch railing and pressed her face to the parlor window, cupping her hands around her eyes. She tapped the window. Inside, the only movement was a slow ballet of golden dust motes and the shadow parody of her body striped across the red carpet and yellow-green sofa. She came away from the window, walked down the steps, stared out across the garden. *"Boo Taylor!"* she yelled. The name rang in the sky for a moment before getting swallowed up by the great openness. Only the soft tinkle of wind chimes answered.

With Shamus following, she prowled to the north side of the house, prowled behind the house, to the shade of the tall oaks where the moon, neatly sliced in half, was already risen to the high tree branches. She tromped to the south, under the kitchen window, before the fenced, magic-herb patch. From a caved-in chicken coop, she saw the words KILL ALL NIGERRS. In the letters, she saw Wade's face (nigger country) and Harley's and her father's and any number of the fat, unshaven brutes who littered Shell Pot Lane.

And, on Carriage Avenue, the slim, handsome face of the doctor.

He's a liar, Gussie. He lied to all of us.

Boo, he's your daddy.

And he thinks I'm not supposed to judge him? Pay attention, he says. You saw him, Gussie, same as me—wearin that mask like the rest of those cowards.

Boo...what are you going to do?

She returned to the front of the house, up the steps. She opened the screen door and went inside to an empty parlor, an empty kitchen, an empty bedroom. She knocked on the bathroom door and it swung open to more emptiness. Back in the parlor she found her painting dangling mute lavenders and pinks and greens over the sofa.

Smack-dab in the middle of nigger country.

She stepped back onto the porch. She sat on the bench across from Miss Laylee's rocker. The golden world was deepening to a less pleasant orange one. Clouds that looked like hunks of broken coral were drifting in from the west. A single line of gray soared up from the trees and broke apart in the breeze like a swarm of mosquitoes.

Watching. Waiting. Fearing the worst.

The same now as this afternoon when she had sneaked like a dirty thief onto Carriage Avenue and spied on Boo Taylor's house. That house was dead, too, although people came and went regularly. Sheriff Tillman had been there. Mayor Crowley. Mr. Dufette. Old Mr. Beaudry (oh, that was almost too much to watch). Miss Annie Brighton from the school. Mr. and Mrs. Atkins from next door. MaeEllen Taylor, forlorn on the high porch, taking hands, on the verge of swoon—while a crippled, docile Eulahlah Colebriar served as gatekeeper. They all looked dead to Gussie.

Dental records, someone had whispered.

Verifications were being made. The news, good news, *best* news of all was telephoned in, and the house came alive again.

But...

But the whispers never died.

Then who was that poor, dead...?

Where is he; where did he...?

Oh, what did he do, our boy, our son...?

It grew darker. Shamus, tired of waiting for her to do something, vanished beneath the shack.

And emerged some uncounted minutes later.

Gussie watched the big dog lumber to the front of the house, alert and rigid, his attention bolted to the trail toward Sugar Dam Road. All at once, his shoulders relaxed, and his tail wagged. Gussie stood up and brimmed her eyes with her hand. She saw nothing. "Is it Boo?" she asked the dog. A moment later, a wounded gray form, propped up by a cane, wandered into view. From this distance, it was a much older and sadder version of the woman Gussie knew. Head down. Shouldering a lead-weight hump. The same docile, bone-dry woman Gussie had watched at the Taylor's front door.

Gussie was about to call out to announce her presence when Shamus tensed again and began to growl.

Headlights. A dirty white sedan lurched onto the trail. Laylee Colebriar backed away, stumbling as the car stopped and three white men got out. Gussie recognized Terry Lee Hardsdale and Slip Callahan. The driver, who she didn't recognize, said something to the old woman who then raised her cane and shouted a high-pitched warning. Shamus, his throat idling, eased ahead several steps.

The trio advanced; Terry Lee reached for the old woman's arm. She batted his wrist with her cane.

Shamus slithered forward.

Gussie shouted, "Hey there! Hey, Miss Laylee!"

Immediately, the men looked around. They saw Gussie on the porch, saw a dog that had now approached almost twenty yards up the trail. Terry Lee Hardsdale let go of Eulahlah Colebriar's sleeve, muttered something at her, and then all three men quickly disappeared into the car.

The wounded old woman dropped her head, shambled down the trail without watching the car leave. Shamus went to greet her and then shadowed her back to the house. Gussie came down the porch steps. "What did those men want?" she asked, although she already knew the answer.

The old face drooped desiccated leather pouches.

"Miss Laylee—"

Tartly, without looking up: "You best gwon home now, girl."

"Miss Laylee?"

"Go!"

Gussie Dutton was stunned as if slapped. She backed a pace and watched the dried-out husk of gray waddle step-by-step up the porch and disappear into the house. The door swung shut.

Gussie reached for the porch railing, hurt blossoming as a black rose through her breast. Her throat collapsed. Thorns jabbed her stomach. She wilted into the bottom step and let the tears come. With each sob, the thorns cut deeper and the pain unfurled another dark, choking petal.

Shamus settled into the dirt a few feet away. He rested his chin on his forepaws and watched her.

Doesn't she love him?

A dim echo of crows, far off, taunted. The leeward wind grew stronger as the sky darkened, as the storm clouds in the west gathered. She glanced at the trail north. Go on home? To *what?* She sobbed. How could she go home?

Behind her, a timid creak. Gently now, guilty now: "Miss Gussie?"

The sound of Eulahlah Colebriar's dry voice only made her cry harder.

"Miss Gussie, please. Oh, I been in agony, child, forgive me. Miss Gussie, you come on up here and sit with me."

Old shoes shuffling on the porch floor. Old flesh settling into the rocker with a weary breath.

"I...I thought," Gussie started, her constricted throat chopping the words to fragments, "...thought maybe...he was...was *here!*"

She smeared tears from her eyes, made a sloppy sniffle. She turned and faced Laylee Colebriar who was sitting in the wicker rocker without rocking.

Gussie sniffled again. "They were...those men, they were looking for Solomon Goody, weren't they?"

Laylee Colebriar stared at the porch floorboards and made billowing motions with her mouth. Her knobby, stick fingers twitched along the hook of her cane. "Gawd, it been an evil day," she mumbled. "Ankles been all swolled up. And my hip been painin me, Miss Gussie—oh, somethin awful." She sighed a long, parched, desert-wind exhalation.

Gussie wiped her nose with her fingers. She stood, quietly walked up the steps and sat on the bench. "They say Solomon's the one who set fire to the Methodist church. To get back for the colored church."

Laylee lifted her droopy eyes. "That's what they say, is it?"

"Miss Laylee, it *was* Solomon Goody who started that fire," she said, and her chin began to quiver. "Wasn't it?"

Ancient torments pricked and quivered in the old woman's face. She sighed again, bitterly. "Well, that boy surely is a fire starter, Miss Gussie. I s'pect he apt to light a few more fires in his day. Leastways, if he can keep hisself alive long enough."

She rocked now, gingerly.

"Oh, Mr. Solomon Goody, he sure enough is a fire starter," she said. "Only, he don't use a match, child. That boy, he do all his fire lightin with his *mouth*."

"But—"

"He been gone up to the state capitol building in Columbia last two days. Maybe he been startin his fires up there, but he didn't have nothin to do with that Methodist church. Parker Tillman already knows that." She cocked her cane toward Sugar Dam Road and scowled. "I s'pect word didn't get 'round to them ol boys, yet."

Gussie glanced toward the empty lane. "Miss Laylee, if Solomon Goody didn't do it, then who did?"

No response.

Her stomach felt sick. "Miss Laylee," she said quietly, almost a whisper, "where's Boo Taylor?"

But Eulahlah Colebriar had drifted somewhere else, drifted as the chair rocked, her eyes seeing far off in the distance. Tears scrolled freely down the weathered grain of her driftwood face. Black rivulets gathering into a dark river. "Thought I lost that boy today," she muttered. "Gawd, it been about the evilest day."

Gussie looked away. The sun had dipped out of sight.

Where did all Sweetpatch Island fugitives go to hide?

She noticed the smoky gray pillar rising from the swamp, from that old, old mansion beyond the trees.

"Lord knows, he's lost to his daddy, now," Laylee Colebriar was saying.

The pillar's crown shattered and floated off like a swarm of mosquitoes. "You know where he is," Gussie said. "You knew all the time."

"Such an evil, evil day," said the old woman, whose unfocussed gaze was off in the same direction. Watery eyes blinked toward the fading sunlight. Her face melted into her gray dress. "Mr. Boo stopped bein a child, Miss Gus. He turnin into somethin *different*. And she'll be comin for him tonight."

Gussie leaned away, repulsed, horrified. She had an urge to run, but the ancient being above her rocked forward and clamped one mummified hand over her wrist.

She?

Gussie tried to pull free. Boney fingers curled into her flesh. "We have to go get him," Gussie cried, panicked. "We can't *leave* him out there."

Laylee Colebriar's eyes had gone crimson. She spoke sadly. "Fool I was to think I could keep that boy from her. Best you go on home, Miss Gussie." And then the old woman released her, settled back on the rocker and into whatever miseries were consuming her. Gussie Dutton rubbed her wrist and stared at the mute and suddenly unfamiliar figure, mind ablaze with a thousand confusions. She wanted to speak. She wanted to scream.

After several moments, unable to do either, she turned and ran.

three

She went alone into the dark. The clouds—which had gone deep violet—had not yet swamped the half moon in the east, and so she had at least that frail bit of light to see by. Moss-laden branches whispered and grabbed her clothes. Unseen frogs and birds gathered to her in multitudes and filled the night with one relentless, cacophonous screech. She slapped and obliterated mosquitoes and midges. She kept her eyes on the crooked footpath, slim as a deer trail, and reached Pigg's Point. Boo Taylor's skiff was gone. The tide was down but starting to rise. She kicked off her sneakers and held them high as she grabbed handholds in the bare roots and climbed down the bank.

Into pluff mud.

Sulfur fumes sputtered from a million tiny air bubbles. The mud slid halfway to her knees, and she had to grunt with each step to pull her feet loose. She couldn't help feeling she was walking across a field of excrement. Every shadow, every log, every silver ripple in the stream was an alligator or something worse, coming for her, sensing her helplessness. When she reached the midpoint, a sludgy, piss-warm water soaked her thighs. Her right foot came down on something sharp and jagged, and it split open her big toe. She yelled and snatched her foot away, certain she had stepped into a gator's jaws, propped open like a bear trap. She stumbled and sloshed across the water, somehow clearing the stream without falling.

She pressed on.

Every step brought an ice-pick jab all the way from her toe to her ankle—and the certainty that her foot would come down on the *next* set of jaws. When she reached the opposite bank, she tossed her sneakers and grabbed a clammy finger she prayed was just a root. She pulled. Swung herself up. And there was Boo Taylor's skiff, rammed between two cypress trunks, belly-up, like a dead porpoise.

She sat on the bank and gathered her breath, rippling her nose at the smell around her, on her. She tried to examine her throbbing toe, but the meager light and the black mud that covered her feet made it impossible.

Still carrying her sneakers, she limped onto the trail ahead, imagining the blood squishing from her toe with each step. The animal chirps and screeches followed. The trail spiraled in circles, forked indiscriminately, became not a trail and then a trail again. Something bigger than she wanted to consider crashed heavily through the brush at her left and then made a large splash in some body of water she didn't know was there. Her toe grew twice its normal size and palpitated like a frog's throat. Sweat dribbled down from her hair to her eyebrows, welled there, then tickled her cheeks and stung her eyes. At last, the trees on her right fell away as she reached the western bank of the island. The light and the air improved. A faint, purplish glow still hovered over the mainland and glittered emeralds and rubies on the Yamawichee. The breeze had strengthened during her time in the woods and now it cooled the sweat on her face. Her feet came down on a cool, slippery ridge of brick, and she knew she had reached the cobble walk that led to the old house. She paused briefly to pull her sneakers over her muddy, battered feet.

Miss Gussie, I thought I lost that boy today.

Her disappointment in Eulahlah Colebriar left her hollow and dusty inside. She had imagined the old woman taking charge. She had imagined sage instructions and comforting words and maybe a magic pouch. She had imagined that root-fingered hand holding her own hand on this dark trail, transmitting in their mingled sweat the old witch's warmth and courage and explanations for everything.

Moving forward, the blackness before her exploded into a dozen cackling fish crows. In their departure, the night was suddenly very quiet. The water trembled. She caught a whiff of burning, a whiff of rot. A whiff of rain.

The clouds reached the moon and plunged the night into invisibility.

(An almost soundless inhale…)

In the dark, she sensed a gargantuan presence looming nearby, something utterly massive and bloated with evil.

(…exhale…)

A separate universe umbilicaled to the familiar, dwarfing the familiar, threatening to swallow the familiar in one, snaggle-toothed chomp.

(…inhale…)

She saw galaxies twirling firework sorcery and bright lights of every color.

(…exhale…)

She saw endless, mindless black.

(…a child's laugh.)

Boo Taylor is inside there.

Oh, Boo, what did you do last night?

She groped around an ancient oak and saw Chaliboque.

Did you hear?

Whispers.

Stepping into that gaping, black grin…

Laying her hands on those moldering walls…

Inching sneakered toe by toe over sodden floors…

Blind. A blurry gray snow and garbled static—like the dead signal on a television set. A fog of spoiled oysters. Swamp smells and bathroom smells. *(…inhale… exhale…)* Footsteps and creaking walls. Birds flapped leather wings and became bats.

Vines and cobwebs erupted into flies. Mice and lizards squealed and sniffed at her ankles and ripened into rats.

She's here...do you see her, trembling?

Lightlessness. Gibbering whispers.

Can you smell the fear...in her flesh?

Time crumbled like moldy flakes of wallpaper, like moth wings, breaking apart, disintegrating, fluttering away from her fingers.

*Can we...*the walls breathed upon her, exhaled...*can we, pleeeeeese...let us see it.*

Something as light as an eyelash scampered over her chin.

A leaden, drenching heat, like rags dipped in fish guts, clogged her nose, her mouth, her lungs, her belly. Stale cigarette smells. Stale beer smells. Her hair was snagged by an iron talon; she ripped it free.

Let us touch it.

Slick, needy hands shivered over her neck, her ribs, her soaked thighs...her breasts, inside the waistband of her jeans and welling between her legs.

Pleeeeeeese, little girl...

Suffocating.

...let us...

Climbing.

...we just want...

Twirling sightlessly, aimlessly around and around—into wide, echoing plazas where she was a toddler, an insect, a speck of dust...and then into cramped shafts where she was buried alive.

...let us taste it...

Her fear was a great whale that had swallowed her whole, choked to death on her and now drifted rotting on the waves somewhere deep in the middle of a great black ocean.

On and on and on.

(...inhale...exhale...)

Sightless. Endless. Mindless. Suffering into that gaping black grin. Fleeing slow-motion into that rumbling, cancerous black throat and black stomach and black bowel. Climbing and searching...and searching...and searching *(please God)...* and searching *(how much further?)...*and searching *(oh God I'm so scared I'm so scared)...*and searching...

...let us have it!

...and searching...

...and found at last...light, blinding.

 four

It was not Boo Taylor.

He turnin into somethin different.

"You scared me," he said, although he did not move and might be nothing more than a gargoyle carved of granite. Naked, except for white boxers, sitting in the big chair (*Solomon's throne,* she remembered) before the fireplace, twinkling in and out of reality.

"Then we're even," she said, and her voice was impossibly casual and sane. She crossed toward the fire on her wounded foot. The flames, which a moment before had been blindingly bright now receded and became the dimmest, wavering glimmer. The words and images on the walls were only dark, unreadable squiggles—all except the savage scrawl over the mantel. *Ate one up and licked the other.* She passed a sagging couch and saw a pyramid of neatly folded clothes on its cushions.

She knelt quietly in front of the flames, grimacing at the sharp jab in her toe. A jumble of sticks and logs were piled at the hearth. The charred and chewed bones of a small animal littered the embers not far from her knees. The person who was no longer Boo Taylor did not get up from his throne. He did not seem embarrassed by his nakedness. He did not seem to be feeling anything at all.

"So, you plannin on staying here a while?" she asked.

He breathed. Inhale, exhale. "I really wasn't plannin anything."

"I guess that includes not tellin anybody where you were."

He didn't respond. Books were stacked on either arm of the chair making a brick wall that sealed him within a chamber within a room within a house within an island. One very thick book lay open at his bare feet, but she couldn't make out the title.

"They pulled a boy out of that fire this morning," she told him.

No response. The firelight sparkled in his eyes, and it seemed he might be crying, but his chest rose and fell evenly, steadily. Inhale, exhale.

"I watched it," she said. "I thought it was you. It about killed me."

"I'm sorry."

"It about killed your daddy, too."

Finally, a reaction. The sparkle disappeared as he closed his eyes. When he opened them again, he was glaring at her. "Gussie, that man is not my daddy. I don't care what he says."

She growled. "Boo, he *is too* your daddy, and so what?"

The anger died quickly. When he spoke again, it was in a dismissive tone that she found, under the circumstances, almost intolerable. "He's been lyin to me my whole life. About my mother. About everything. And you were there that night at the Baptist church, Gussie. You saw it, too."

Gussie felt her fear and exhaustion rising to a boil. In that moment, she wanted to slam one of those brick-shaped books down on his head. "Your daddy was there that night? Well my daddy was wearin his stupid hood alongside him. Right along*side* him, Boo." She clenched her fists. "But you don't see me settin fire to some white-folk's church to make up for it."

His glittering eyes rose to meet hers. He frowned. "Is that what you think? Gussie, I didn't set that fire last night."

She faltered. "You...what...?"

"Ash Marchant did it. I tried to stop him."

She sat, stupefied for a moment. And then relief surged over her. She forgot her anguish, and she launched herself into Boo Taylor's lap. "Boo—all this time, I thought...I thought you were *dead*; then I thought you were a *murderer*." She slipped her arms around his back, laid her cheek against his chest.

Then she bolted upright and gaped at him.

"That was *Ashford's* body they found!"

He looked into the fire and said nothing.

"How do you know Ash did it? Tell me what happened."

He reached for her arms and pried them off his back. He gently but forcefully pushed her away. She settled back on the floor, waiting for him to speak. But he only gazed into the fire.

"Boo Taylor, you tell me what happened."

His head swiveled slowly. He looked her up and down as if seeing her tonight for the first time. "You hurt yourself," he said, nodding at her sneaker.

She glanced down; the white canvas had bloomed crimson all the way to the laces. "Oh hell, I stepped on something."

Then his eyes went to the muddy stains on her blue jeans. He turned briefly to the dark window that overlooked the Yamawichee Sound. "Oh, Gussie, I'm sorry," he said dismally. He leaned off the throne and raised her foot to his knees. He slipped off her sneaker. Her big toe puffed out like a black toad.

Tenderly, his fingers prodded her toes, sent a tingle through the arch of her foot. The tingle reappeared in her stomach.

"It's still bleedin some," he said. "Gussie, you need to clean this out."

"With what? This whole side of the island is nothin but filth."

"Hold on." He placed her foot in the chair and went to the sofa. She watched his muscles flex and relax in the dim light as he returned carrying a plastic jug.

"What's that?" she asked.

"Just water."

"Water? I suppose you figured you'd be here a while." She was angry again. He'd run off without telling her anything. "I suppose you stocked up on food, too."

He looked at her briefly. "No, just water." When he sat down again, he straddled her leg. He uncapped the jug and poured water over her foot.

She drew a sharp breath at the sting.

"Okay?" he asked.

"Just be careful."

He poured again, letting water splatter on his legs and over the floor. He worked his fingers gently through her toes, washing away the green-gray muck and dried blood. "Ash wanted me to make sure the coast was clear," he said.

Cool water was running down her thigh. "But why would he—"

"He was makin up for the night at the colored church. He kept apologizing. He kept tellin me what his daddy was like. Not that his daddy *made* him go there that night—but, at the same time he *did* make him."

Boo's eyes had gone back to the fire, his fingers still prodding, massaging.

"What does that mean? Did his daddy make him go there or not?"

She watched him think about this for a moment. Then he said, "It's hard to explain. But I think he was just...*honored* that his daddy wanted him to go along. He was always scared of the man. Him gettin to come along with the rest of those men, I guess, made him feel important. At least important to his daddy, which is somethin he almost never felt."

"He told you that?"

"No. But it's what he meant."

Boo set down the jug. Fingers, thumbs, palms kneaded the sensitive nerve endings of her foot. "But afterward," he continued, "I believe he went half crazy with guilt. And I guess I'm mostly to blame for that."

"You? Boo, that's just stupid."

He looked at her sharply. "Gussie, you know I wouldn't talk with him after that night I socked him. And you saw what that was doin to him."

And of course she had seen it. Bound up in that frightening anger Boo Taylor had been nurturing since the night at the colored church—anger at the doctor, certainly, and anger at so many other things. Including Ash Marchant, who pathetically trailed Boo Taylor around school and anywhere else, eager to explain, make amends, regain favor. But for Boo, everything had become betrayal. No one could be trusted. She alone seemed to be spared this anger—though she wondered at even that, certain there were times she caught him watching her and imagining plots and treachery.

"I guess," Boo was saying, "burnin down a white church was a way to set things even. I don't know, Gussie. But I think mostly he was doin it for me. To impress me. I wouldn't talk to him, and I guess he figured it would make us friends again."

Her body rocked with the pressure of his hands.

"He set a fire to *impress* you?" she asked. "Boo, that *is* crazy."

Boo Taylor's eyes came away from the flames, stared at her, purposefully. "Gussie, maybe he had a good reason to think that."

Through the touch of his fingers, she felt his body stiffening. Preparing. A feather of dread brushed across her heart.

She asked, "And what does that mean?"

He considered her quietly. He seemed intensely nervous. At last, he said, "Gussie, I was the one who burned down the old colored school last May."

She pulled her foot away from him. "Boo *Tay*lor!"

He looked at his empty hands.

Then he reached over and tossed two small logs into the fire. Bright red fireworks spit and sizzled and twirled up the chimney. He leaned back in the throne. When he put his hands behind his head, she saw the defiance had returned. "It was the right thing to do," he said.

Nothing was making sense to her. "Burnin down a school was the right thing?"

"You know it was. Think about it."

"Boo, I can't...who put you up to it?"

"Nobody put me up to anything," he answered testily. "Tell me, when you first heard about the school, what'd you think?"

She blinked, tried to remember. Awful shouts up and down Shell Pot Lane. Outrage. Outrage because...

"I thought what everyone else thought," she said. "That some Negro did it to get at the school board. Make them integrate the coloreds into the white school."

"Is that a bad thing?"

"No, I guess not," she answered, knowing her thoughts on the matter had evolved considerably since the incident. "But Boo, a *fire!*"

"Did you ever go inside that place, Gussie? Did you ever see how bad it was in that school?"

"Boo, that's not the point."

"Then what *is* the point, Gussie?"

"The *point,*"—she felt her hands becoming fists again—"is why *you?* And you never told *me.* You told Ashford Marchant, but you didn't tell me. Who else did you tell?"

"I didn't tell Ash anything; he figured it out for himself. I guess Miss Laylee figured it out, too, but she never said anything to me. Ash, he just came out and said what he thought, and I didn't lie. The only person I ever told straight out was Solomon Goody."

"You told Solomon Goody? Boo Taylor, why in God's name would you go and do somethin like that?"

He sighed and leaned forward. He looked exhausted. She wondered when he'd slept last. "Folks were talkin about stringin up Solomon for it," he said. "They already convicted him. So, I told him what I did and said I'd go to Parker Tillman if he wanted."

"What did he do? Was he mad?"

"He told me not to bother with the police. Then he asked if I liked to stay up late and watch old movies on television."

"He asked *what?*"

"He asked if I ever saw a movie called *The Man Who Shot Liberty Valance.* I said no, and he said I should and then maybe I'd understand. Look, Gussie, everybody in South Patch talked about burnin down that school. They all wanted it burned, more than you know. Even Pastor Hatchel talked about it. But a colored person couldn't do it. You see that, don't you? Look what almost happened to Solomon Goody, and he didn't even *do* anything."

A spell of silence followed, and it took her a moment to realize he was expecting her to comment. But she could think of nothing to say. Instead, her eyes went to the dark side of the room. Her mind was a confused jumble of thoughts. She was out in deep water where her feet couldn't touch. It was about the evilest day and Boo Taylor was turning into something different and Laylee Colebriar was a spent and worthless old sorceress. Obsolete. No help at all. Boo was just grieving, she decided. He was mad at the world, distrustful of everyone, but mostly he had come here to grieve.

She looked at him, at the broad, flame-lit outline of his shoulders.

Finally, she plopped her foot back into his lap. "Can you rub my foot some more? That felt good."

After a moment, his hand came around her foot again. He doused it with more water and began swabbing the grit from her toes.

"What about Ash?" she asked.

Boo kneaded her foot. She closed her eyes at the touch.

"Ash came by the house yesterday. He told me what he wanted to do, and he wanted me to help. Make sure the coast was clear. I told him I wouldn't. I still wasn't talkin to him; I was so *mad* at him, Gussie! He told me he'd do it anyway, but I didn't believe him. He told me he'd do it to show he wasn't really like his daddy."

Inhale. Exhale.

"Then last night I had another argument with the doctor. I forget about what. Mostly, I was just mad at *him,* I guess. So, I came down to stay on Miss Laylee's couch again. She didn't like me comin, but I didn't care; I wasn't goin back home. And then..."

His body tensed again. His fingers stopped.

Inhale.

"I guess I woke up and...I think I must have had a dream or something— maybe about Hoss because I realized I couldn't just let Ash do it. Like I let Hoss go up to Mamie Stuvant's house. So I got up and started runnin, even though I knew I wouldn't make it there in time. The church would be on fire, I figured, and Ash Marchant would be in jail or something bad like that."

Exhale.

"When I got to Loggerhead, I saw the church. It was still there. And I'd just run I don't know how many miles in the middle of the night..."

He closed his eyes. He sighed. A knot popped in the fireplace and hissed like a deflating tire. The blood was rushing down the veins of her propped-up leg. Her toes, even in his warm hands, were turning cold.

"Then I heard a scream."

He stopped speaking for several seconds again.

Gussie wiggled her toes in an unconscious gesture to urge him on.

"I could see it, then," he continued, "the flames lightin up the stained glass windows. I ran again and reached the doors, but they were locked. He must have gotten in through a window or something, but I didn't figure that out until later. So I kept on pullin at the doors. Like an idiot. They were getting so *hot.* I could hear him screamin inside. He must have gotten mixed up in the smoke. I think I was screamin, too; I'm not sure. And then I heard..."

Silence.

"...I heard..."

The silence went on forever. Clocks wound down, stopped.

"...he screamed my name."

He leaned back into the chair, like bones collapsing. His hands slipped away from her foot.

"And then the screamin stopped."

His chin dropped to his chest.

"It was just like Hoss, all over again. My name—he screamed my name, Gussie, and I couldn't do anything. And then it stopped. . .and I ran."

Gussie pushed up from the floor. Boo Taylor looked like a stripped and wounded king on that throne, a warrior king: the king of Sweetpatch Island. She touched him. Climbed onto him; curled into his lap. She pressed her face against his. He wasn't crying, but she stroked his cheeks as if to wipe away tears.

Beyond, fingernails softly tapped at the big window, and that was where the tears were—falling about the both of them, falling about this house; the storm had snuck up on them while they were distracted. Boo Taylor's strong arms came around her shoulders and pulled her even closer; his strong hands took hold of her hair. She put her own hand on his neck, reached for something, realized she was reaching for Laylee Colebriar's pouch, realized it was gone.

"Boo, let's leave the island." She whispered into his throat. "Tonight. Let's go someplace where there's mountains and it snows all the time."

His breath on her cheek.

"How will we get there?"

She smiled, stroked his hair. "We'll swim. Right now—we'll go out and swim across the Yamawichee and then on up the river all the way till the first snowflake hits us. Then we'll build us a cabin right there on the spot. You'll hunt bears or somethin, and I'll keep a garden."

"Won't work."

"Sure it will."

He pulled her head up by her hair to look at her eyes. "You can't swim, remember? And I told you, I'm never leavin the island."

"I'll learn to swim for you, if you leave the island for me. Boo, you think I'm kiddin, but I'm not. We could leave right now."

"And never come back?"

"Never."

He kissed her. She kissed back. Then she fell into him, breathing his breath, tasting his flesh.

Inhale. Exhale.

His mouth came away too quickly, and he studied her closely, the pain squinting his eyes. "You would do that? Go away with me?"

She bent her forehead to his lips. She swept her cheek across his, circling his mouth, "Yes," she said.

His arms tightened. He was trembling. He was growing hard beneath her legs. "I don't know what I am, now," he said. "He lied to me. The doctor lied to me."

"I won't lie to you," she said.

He grabbed a fistful of her blouse. He was changing, becoming something like the fire and something like the storm. "Never?" he asked.

She shook her head.

Growing. So full of heat. "Do you love me?" he asked.

"Yes."

The house shifted and moaned, inhaled and exhaled; the wind found a thousand shattered and decayed fissures, stealing its way inside, carrying the storm's wet, electric scent with it piggyback. She brought her legs around on the throne and straddled him. He unclasped the thick, confining canvas at her waist. A firestorm raged at her from his eyes.

"Are you as scared as I am?" he asked as he peeled the swamp-drenched fabric from her hips.

Her hand fell to Boo Taylor's chest, and she dug her fingers into his flesh and muscle, wanting to touch his heart.

The old woman was right. Boo Taylor was changing into something different. It was happening right inside her.

five

Waking. Dreaming.

He had left her. He was settled in King Solomon's throne again, and he was something different—tall and strong and hard and dark—and he had made that pleasant ache in her nipples, between her legs. The King of Sweetpatch Island.

No, that was not him on the throne—he was right here with her, on the sofa, his skin wrapped around hers, and so he was like a second skin now, and he was still filling her up even if he was asleep.

Someone else on the chair.

Someone who'd been burned in the flames, although the flames in the fireplace had become small and harmless as the storm had grown wilder, and maybe he was not burned after all, and this man, blonde hair she could see now hanging in his once-handsome but now-ruined face, was speaking.

"I took her," the king was saying, "because of love."

The king wept. The king was bloody and defiant.

"You think this is easy. You think it's as simple as black and white. You're wrong."

...inhaling...

"You want to judge me?"

...exhaling...

"Go ahead."

She blinked, and she knew she was coming awake. The throne was empty now, and the storm was ripping the great house apart. This was the present; the king had been the past. The storm was the present. Boo Taylor's naked body wrapped over hers was the present.

Movement by the fire drew her attention and she saw the girls there. Three of them, huddled together like kittens in the rain, cold and hungry, staring at her raptly. They were like a photograph, devoid of movement and texture, although their presence was startlingly real. Three haunted little figurines staring at her, daring to reveal themselves from the deepest shadow.

(She wondered —I am awake, aren't I?)

The girls were ravenous.

"We so scared," one of them squeaked.

"She mean to us," said another.

The body in her arms shifted. She glanced down at Boo Taylor's arms, his hip, his legs to be reassured of his existence. When she looked up again, the girls had somehow advanced. Not kittens, but dolls—abandoned, something disposed of in a junk pile. Their eyes were wide and desperate; their cheeks hollow; their limbs sticks; their clothes rags. Wet, black snakes of hair dripped over boney shoulders. Starvation hung over their doll-bodies like a low, black cloud, soiling their plastic flesh. They were leaning forward, trembling to pounce, to devour, were being held in place by only the slimmest thread of uncertainty.

"She gwon take your skin," wailed the third, smallest, saddest of the doll-girls.

The girls, without moving, now somehow loomed over the sofa. Their hunger was so great they were nearly drooling. Somewhere behind her, at the opposite side of the room, a door squealed on rusted hinges. The girls' eyes went wider—their rapt attention broken from the meal of entwined flesh on the sofa. Doll mouths contracted into tight, frightened little circles.

One of the girls moaned.

A rumble filled the room, gathering strength, an idling engine accelerating until it became a sharp, world-splitting crack of thunder that seemed to engulf all of Chaliboque. A wild flailing of crow wings erupted from the fireplace, whipped through the room like a great black cape—and sent the frail dolls diminishing toward some faint corner. They became small and transparent, kittens again, sobbing in either fear or frustration at the dark thing that had banished them, wisps of gauze fluttering into the distance. Fireplace soot, roused from the sudden wings, swirled through the air.

"We so scared."

"She so mean."

Voices dwindling, kitten shapes evaporating into soot-laced air...they retreated... deep into the murk...wailing...pleading...fading...until they became...

nothing.

She shook Boo Taylor's shoulder.

"Boo," she whispered.

Slow footsteps from the direction of the door. The body in her arms refused to stir.

"Boo!"

The door again, creaking, clicking softly closed as the footsteps of whatever just entered the room now advanced toward the sofa. She pinched Boo Taylor's arm. "Boo get up!" she hissed, but he only made a small grunt.

She chanted —"this-is-a-dream-this-is-a-dream-this-is..."

From behind the sofa, hidden, trudging up from the now-silent, now-closed door, progressed a certain presence. Gussie Dutton heard its breathing, shallow and labored, heard this clearly over the onslaught of the raging storm, and so it must be something alive, and this didn't feel like a dream, but it must be a dream. It came on slowly. It came on at its own pace, taking its own sweet time. It came on with all the patience in the world. Boo Taylor's slumbering weight had her pinned to the sofa, but she couldn't have moved anyway because the thing was coming closer and she was paralyzed. In a dream, you're paralyzed when the thing is coming for you.

It made a sniffle. Gussie craned her neck to see over the arm of the sofa as the thing shuddered into view.

A humped, smallish shape.

Something old.

Something, very, very, very old.

Slowly, patiently, the very-old thing settled into King Solomon's throne. Settled with a dusty sigh.

"Miss Laylee?" Gussie chanced.

The shape was still.

Inhale. Exhale.

She felt Boo Taylor's bones trembling through her.

The dim glow of the dying fire illuminated a faint orange-tinged silhouette. Steel wool hair. Stumpy pigtails. Round, burnt-umber curve of cheek. Delicate nose. Butterscotch jowls. Familiar, but not familiar. Like Eulahlah Colebriar, but not like her at all. Someone else.

Then it came to her in an inspiration of clarity. It was so simple. "You're Bathsheba Tribbit," Gussie told the thing—this dream thing that was real even though this was surely a dream, must be a dream.

The dream thing showed no indication of hearing this revelation, and yet Gussie sensed acknowledgement coming from it. Wafting like an odor. Something stale. Something left out in the sun for generations, obvious but ignored.

Then, riding the coattails of one startling realization, another came. She could see it now, gazing upon the dream-creature seated upon the mighty throne. The resemblance, the inescapable similarities of family.

"Eulahlah Colebriar," Gussie said, "was your daughter."

The words were barely out of her mouth before the ramifications buzzed through her mind like a swarm of angry hornets.

The dream-woman, Bathsheba-thing twisted a rusty bit of sinew in its neck; it's head inching about as if blind and honing in on the sound of Gussie Dutton's voice. Orange firelight glinted off a slim nose, a leathery strip of jawline, the craggy wrinkles at the eye. The eye itself was black and lightless.

"You tinkin you knows sump'n."

It took Gussie a moment to realize the shape had spoken. The voice was a deep, garbled sound. Trapped fumes bubbling up from a swamp. Dusty air belched forth from worlds and time beyond. It seemed disconnected from the body that had issued it, as if coming from a speaker hidden somewhere off in the shadows.

"Dat one you speakin 'bout be callin e-seff Eulah," the voice continued, "her mehbe come frem outa my hole, but her ain' nebber bein no chile t'me."

Gussie recognized the cadence, the lilt of vowel, the simplification of consonant; it was the old tongue of the Gullahs. The language of the island a hundred years ago.

The face had taken on an expression of distaste. "Mo' sump'n like a toad, mehbe," it said. "Come out wigglin, bawn wit tail n'all, dat one, like a tadpole. Oagly lee'l ting, dat. Growed up, her b'comin dat oagly ol toad."

. Eulahlah Colebriar, ugly toad. Bathsheba Tribbit was her mother. Joker Tribbit was her father. Did Boo Taylor know about this? Ugly little tadpole, calling itself Eulahlah, grew up into an ugly old toad. And that child, no child to me, had grown up to give birth to its own daughter, hadn't it? Its own daughter, not a toad, because it was raised somewhere far off, raised not by its mother at all.

Leaning forward, snapping brittle bones, the dimly illuminated, leather-bound skull came closer.

"You be tinkin yuh knows sump'n, gal, but trute be, yuh doan knows shit."

The Sheba-thing's dry, swamp-laced breath dribbled over Gussie's face.

(Just a dream, Gussie thought.)

She was still unable to move; Boo Taylor was still a slumbering sack of flesh and bone.

(She's come for him. It's like Miss Laylee said it would be.)

Gussie tried to move her mouth, wondering if the rules of this dream would still allow her to speak. When the words came, she surprised herself with them. "You stole her daughter from her."

Tendons pulled a grin across the Sheba-thing's face. Mirthless, black-pit eyes glittered. "Stole? Ha! Dat one, her mo' like t'be chasin' lee'l white babies den seein affra her own kine, gal. Dishyuh boy, fuh one. Dishyuh boy an' all'a dem uhdder white babies, sho."

The taut, smiling tendons threatened to snap. The shape wavered—solid, then translucent, then a wisp of smoke, then solid again. (Just a dream!)

"Only take dat what mine, gal. Dat what b'long t'me! Lissen! You lissen good, gal, an' mehbe you be yearin de trute."

The animated wisps of smoke pranced about the steel-wool scalp, moth-like, with human faces that had sewn-shut lips and sewn-shut eyes. They were grinning with the Sheba-thing, and the Sheba-thing was gazing its blank, depthless, pitiless black eyes upon the two naked bodies with mean satisfaction.

"Dem dat be comin fo my man," it croaked, "dey come in daahkness, dem. Comes take 'im frem him'own house, frem him'own' 'ooman. Takes 'im frem dat lee'l toad, too, an' de toad's black baby, dat. Takes 'im, dem. Cuts 'im troat.

"Cuts 'im troat, gal!

"Bleeds 'im, dey. Bleeds 'im like swayne; dreen 'e blood. Den drags 'im wit de rowup. Be draggin 'im tru wood, tru bresh, all 'cross de island. Takes 'im skin, dey, clean offen 'im bone. Bleeds 'im dry.

"Dem mens.

"Dem white mens."

On the Sheba-thing's cheeks, tears dripped like candle wax.

"Bleedin end. Bleedin end, an' all'a dem mens sets dey beast-es on 'im. Him still be drawin breht, gal, an' dem beast-es be suppin on my man. Dems all laffin, all'a time 'im be callin t'me, an' all'a time dem beast-es be suppin.

"I spies mistuh Sam, 'im be laffin right 'long wit odduhress'a dem white mens. I screams, 'Plee mistuh Sam! Plee mistuh Sam! Do sump'n mistuh Sam! Das Sheba's man, das Big Jo dems got. Stop dis mistuh Sam, plee!'

"Mistah Sam, you tink 'im stoppin dis?

"I s'pec 'im dids, gal. I s'pec 'im rightly dids.

"Mistah Sam, 'im take 'im gun out. An' den 'im shoot Big Jo in de haid. Shoot 'im good, 'im. Him be sayin, 'Looky dat, 'ooman. I'se jes shoot me-own bredduh.' Das what 'im be sayin. Den 'im gwine an' crack dat gun well 'cross my own face."

Hate and sadness mixed in equal measures. The Sheba-thing dripped its hottar tears down its leathery flesh, spilled its swampy breath and moaned its ancient, sad hatred into the room.

Gussie Dutton felt her own tears. Fear and sadness in equal measures. Laylee Colebriar was this thing's daughter.

"You tinkin yuh knows, gal? Well, git knowen dis: dems put dey beast onnuh 'im. Sheba put she own beast onnuh dem. Dems be comin in daahkness; Sheba comin in daahkness, fuh true. Mistuh Sam be lawnin sech soon-nuff, sway-gawd, 'im do. Be lawnin damn good, 'im.

"But 'im jes de fuhst."

Just the first, Gussie thought, being drawn deeper into this smoky dream. How many more came after? Her eyes stung. Sniffling, unable to stop herself, she asked, "What happened to Miss Laylee and her baby?"

The Sheba-thing spat contempt. "Dat oagly ting! Ha! Eulah, dat weepin toad, her mo' 'freed fo dat white baby mistuh Sam done gots den wit her own lee'l black chile. Dat crookety bukruh-man be layin daid, an' her weepin fo' t'fellun light. Bery man shootin her own farrah, an' her weepin on 'im.

"'Sheba plee, doan huht de baby!' she be weepin.

"Mistuh Sam daid, Miss Maggie daid, an' her be weepin on sech! Doan care fo shit 'bout her own black baby, sho true.

"So Sheba taken dat chile her own seff. Baby b'longen t'Sheba, not dat wiggly toad 'ooman. Oagly toad-ting. Dat baby, an' all'a dem babies come affwer, dems b'longen t'me, dey black skins b'longen t'me! Tuh me, gal! Damn true."

Ash fell about them like snowflakes. The Sheba-creature, still leaning just inches away, was getting lost in a thickening smoke.

"You took her child," Gussie said. "So she followed the white baby. To protect it."

The thing leaned closer. Gussie looked through its wavering, grainy, in-and-out flesh to see the last flames of the fire. "Tuhk her chile? Tuhk her black skin, sho'. Dat black baby b'longen t'Sheba. Dat white baby b'long t' de beast."

Its bony hand snaked out and grabbed her wrist. The grip was like ice.

"Beast come fo dat white baby, due time. Due time, de beast come fo all'a dem white babies."

Gussie struggled to pull away. The ice was burning her.

"Fo dishyuh boy, it comin," it said. "An' dat beast, 'im gitt'n hongry."

The ice was searing through her flesh. The thing attached to her wrist began to chuckle, and Gussie screamed.

six

She snapped her eyes open to darkness and smoke and confusion. The throne was empty. Her wrist stung. The nude body stirring in her arms was Boo Taylor, and they were in Chaliboque, and something was on fire.

"You yelled," Boo said sleepily from her breasts.

Rain was pounding against the big window, flooding into every shaft and crevice of the house. She could hear it inside the walls, could hear it dribbling from the ceiling. She looked around through the dark for signs of Bathsheba Tribbit but saw only a thick fog. The pain in her wrist was like rope burn.

She shook Boo Taylor. "Boo, get up!"

"What's wrong?"

I saw Bathsheba Tribbit.

"I had a dream," she whispered, urgent, rubbing her wrist. "Boo, I think something's in here. Can you hear it?"

"I hear thunder. Gussie, what's burnin?"

They looked toward the fireplace: red, smoldering shrapnel from some explosion was strewn across the rug, sending tendrils of smoke up from the floor. Boo grunted and uncurled from her, getting to his feet. Instinctively, she crossed her legs and covered her breasts with an arm. The room was quickly filling with smoke. Boo approached the fireplace, a smooth shadow against shimmering heat, kneeling to tamp the embers with a book.

"It wasn't just thunder," she whispered after him.

A growl rose from the shadows, and Boo froze.

"Something's in here," he said flatly.

"I *told* you!" she said, scrambling off the sofa and rushing to him.

"Some kind of *animal*."

No, it's Bathsheba Tribbit!

Boo's hand swooped into the woodpile and came up with a woefully brittle-looking stick. She crouched beside him and held him by the shoulders. "I can smell it," he said.

Gussie searched for movement, but the murk was getting thicker as more and more smoke feathered up from the rug. Her clothes were vague yellowish splashes on the floor. The odd scraps of furniture were indistinct heaps without color. The walls beyond were invisible.

The growl again, a boiling wet sound that surrounded them, bleeding from the shadows, from everywhere, from no single source. Boo stood up, and she stood with him, clinging to his back as he circled and as the sound circled them. Boo was trembling. She was trembling. Her wounded toe came down on a hot coal, and she stifled a cry.

At last, the growl slipped back into the gloom. Only the sound of rain. And the house breathing.

Boo mumbled something.

Breathing. Exhale.

She could smell it now, too—animal pungence beneath the smoke.

"Boo," she hissed, looking for her clothes again, "we have to get out of here—"

He hushed her. His body, rigid and cold as marble, neck tendons creaking as his head shifted from side to side.

"We have to get out of here *now*," she said.

A howl burst out from the smoke. Gussie yelled out, but her voice was lost in that bellowing wail. Boo's shoulders quaked. He thrust the stick out with one hand while the other snagged the small of her back and pressed her close. "Boo!" she croaked as the wail spiraled around them like a rope, like a whirlpool, like a dragon, now fading...

...now spilling over into an entirely different sound—bubbling, muddy, brimming with savage hilarity.

From this, a startling voice:

"Gawd a'mighty, if it ain't the doctor's boy!"

This time Boo Taylor yelled out. The voice came from the direction of the window, although Gussie saw nothing but a black glob that interrupted the silver spattering at the glass.

Boo whirled Gussie about to shield her.

"Look at you, boy. Jes as raw-naked as a little frog."

"Who's there?" he called out.

"More like a bullfrog. My, if that ain't a fine length'a hog gut for a boy your age."

Laughter. Laughter becoming the growl. Gussie darted her head about because the sound was behind her. Then it was off to the left, near the door. Then, inside the fire. She crept with Boo further into the room, still pressed to his back, her fingernails digging into his marble-hard, marble-cold shoulder. The growl followed them, rebounding off walls and sofa and brick-stacked books, seeping from the floor, clambering from the chimney flue, billowing and billowing, rising higher and higher, a truck engine with gas pedal floored, brake pedal floored, whining and screaming and smoking, racing higher and louder and fiercer, ready to explode.

And stopped abruptly, as if hacked by an axe.

Just the breathing.

Gussie stopped breathing. Something cold splashed on her shoulder. She yelped, then realized it was rain dripping from the ceiling. She looked back to the window, but the silhouette was gone. The smell of soaked pelts and sour breath swirled through the smoke. Her eyes stung and started to water.

"Get away!" Boo yelled out.

"Get away?" The voice boomed. "Get away? Why, you in my house, boy."

Boo slid Gussie around again, shifting about, still trying to shield her. The shape was coming forward again, behind the throne now, and it was huge—as huge as that voice. It floated forward, gathering into itself molecules from the fire's glow, becoming whole, becoming tangible, becoming enormous.

"Jes invited yourself on in, didn't you? What you figure on sellin me this time? You bring a magazine with you, boy? You got a sack of pumpkin seeds?"

Boo Taylor was backing in the direction of the door. Gussie backed with him. A drip splatted on Boo's scalp and made a teardrop that slowly trickled to his jaw.

"Got another little white boy for me to gobble up? Pretty soon we gonna run out'a little white boys."

Through smoke and shadow, eyes burned like fireplace coals in the midst of that indistinct, gathering shape. The hint of a grin, black tar crammed between sharp teeth. Something regarding them hungrily, something wanting to eat them one little piece at a time.

She steals your skin.

"It's a trick," Gussie whispered in Boo's ear. "That's really Sheba Tribbit."

The glowing eyes slashed toward Gussie, ripping her open right down the middle. "Who that you brung with you, doctor's boy? Some white trash you been slidin your fat pig-sticker in?"

Boo backed another step, waggling the stick like a small spear.

Gussie called over his shoulder, "I know who you are."

Taunting, smiling. "Does you? You tinkin you knows sump'n, gal?" The voice had made an abrupt change in pitch; someone else was now speaking.

"Get away from us," Boo said evenly.

The shape drifted forward in the haze. Gussie's eyes were bleary with tears. She wiped at them, but she was nearly blind.

"Lawd boy, ef dat gal ain' a pale-uhn. She be pale as a feesh onnuh beach."

Coming closer.

"Pale as an ol bwone, dat. Pale as snow. You ebber seein snow, boy?"

"Just get away!" Boo shouted.

"My Crystal, she meat too dahk fo' dat fine white cock, boy? Dat it?"

Now a child's giggle. Smoke rose, fell, clotted to a hazy curtain, the shape fading, drifting, disappearing back into shadow. Gussie rubbed her eyes, tears flowing freely now. The giggle broke apart, went north, east, west, then rolled into dead silence.

Gone.

The rainfall. Smoke.

"Boo," Gussie whispered in his ear, sniffling. Her heart pounded. She was aware of the door behind them, couldn't guess how far away, was too afraid to turn and see.

Well off in the distance, from some black and furry remoteness, came another hint of a child's laugh.

Then, much closer, a whisper: "Ol toad ain' tellen you de trute, boy."

Storm waters flowed. Smoke shifted. All around the room, raindrops pattered the carpet. The dying fire crept closer to permanent death. Smoke and rain dripped through an hourglass, measuring the on and on and on and forever stillness; hundred-year-old roof beams creaked and clock-ticked toward another century. Out of this eternity, Gussie Dutton faintly, hopefully, light-as-clouds, breathed:

"Is she gone?"

Boo Taylor was rock-still and silent.

"What about that animal?"

Followed by more silence.

And more.

Teeth pinching her lip, Gussie gently nudged Boo Taylor's shoulders backward toward the unseen door.

They took a single step.

A roar, slavering, snapped at her exposed buttocks. She *shrieked,* shoved herself violently into Boo as a ferocious volley of barks followed at her hip, flecks of saliva splattering her skin. Boo pivoted, threw the stick, and it vanished end over end into the smoke.

"Run for the door," he shouted.

He shoved her in the back, and she fell. Something was rising from the shadows, bared teeth, hooked fingers. Hot coals burned her back, her legs. She pushed to her knees and scrambled toward the door, searching for Boo Taylor's back, but he was gone.

"Boo!"

The smoke had consumed him. She kept lurching on hands and knees for the door, peering back over her shoulder. Flashes of movement back there. Something grunting, making pig noises. Boo called out in pain.

"Boo!" she screamed.

The tall rectangle of the door finally appeared in front of her. She got to her feet, reached for the doorknob. She pushed the door open and turned again, hoping to see Boo Taylor. Nothing but the sounds of a battle and vague bursts of movement in the smoke. Boo called out again. Then a loud thud as something—the sofa?—toppled.

A body suddenly burst into view. Eyes wide and shocked. "Come on!" Boo shouted at her. Smoke swirled around him. His forehead was scratched open and bleeding.

Gussie blinked at him, waiting for her heart to start beating. Somewhere behind Boo Taylor, a great mountain of flesh was surging forward. Boo grabbed her by the shoulders and hurled her through the door. "Close it!" he screamed at her.

She managed to grab the edge of the door. She slammed it shut. A moment later, Boo, grunting, flung an old bookcase across the frame.

"What *was* that?" she asked.

Boo was hurling odd pieces of furniture at the door, barricading it. Something massive crashed into the opposite side. She stood dumbly. The door was being beaten into splinters. The heap of furniture was moving.

Boo finished heaving a small table onto the pile. He stretched his hand to her. "Gussie, just come on!"

seven

They ran, blind and naked. Boo Taylor somehow seemed to know where he was going, so she let him drag her along, lurching around one turn and then the next, rushing, fleeing. She could see nothing but grainy, gray snowflakes that flew into her eyes. She clung to Boo Taylor's arm, her legs sometimes skimming against his. He banged into furniture and heaps of garbage, tripping and swearing. Breathless. Panicked. Her breasts throbbed; she was vaguely aware of the pain in her toe and knew it must be bleeding again. They splashed through water she had not remembered. Down a long, twisting stairway now, her weight driving down the risers as if they were set on springs. When they finally reached the bottom, Boo stumbled silently on a broken last step and went crashing completely through a wall.

He yanked her down with him. Ancient plaster and lathing avalanched over them.

She lost his arm and went into free fall where the grainy snowflakes pinwheeled crazily. She stabbed her arms into the directionless void, calling his name, grabbing, and then he was calling back, yelling at her to let go, *screaming* at her to let go, because she had fallen on top of him and had an iron grip on his scrotum. She slapped her hands around, found his forearm, and pulled him back to his feet.

They raced on.

She heard Boo Taylor wheezing as he plowed through vines and spiderwebs, wondered how bad the fall hurt him, listened for the beast's roars, listened for it to slip out of this endless darkness and sink its teeth into her thigh or her naked rear end. A slimy finger grazed her ear. She yelled and lowered her head. She ran hunched over.

When does it end? When is it ever light again?

Her flesh recoiled at everything she touched except Boo Taylor's skin. The stench of the place poured in and out of her lungs, and she imagined a hundred different diseases taking root inside her.

"Boo, what did you *see?*" she asked as he jerked her around another blind turn.

"*What?* See what?"

"What *was* that in there?"

Above them, lost somewhere in the dark corridors, a wounded-animal yowl rose and fell and twisted like a snake. Boo stopped. The world stopped. He leaned onto her, breathing harshly, smearing her with grit and his sweat.

"I don't know," he said, panting. "Crystal Burne, maybe. I'm not sure."

"You're not *sure?*"

"Gussie,"—bent over, gasping for air—"you saw what I saw!"

She held onto him and kept him from tottering over. Above, the wailing went on, *far away, she thought, it won't come for us,* she hoped, and at last, when it was just the sound of rain and Boo Taylor's ragged breaths, her hope became the hope that this was just a dream and she and Boo were still curled together on the sofa. The fire had gone out. The darkness around her was only her closed eyes. Boo Taylor's gasps were only his passion.

Above, fingernails were clawing over wood. *Squirrels on the roof. Rats in the attic. Nothing dangerous.* But it was an urgent noise. And it was moving toward them.

"It's comin," Boo moaned—just his passion, and so she was convinced it was only a dream.

Until she tumbled into a sudden squall and was drenched.

Tumbled down a craggy, junk-pile hillside, scraping skin off her shin and her elbow. She had fallen on top of Boo, who was now on his back, kicking in the mud. "Gussie, get up!" Grunting, he struggled out from beneath her. He grabbed her wrist, dragged her off the junk pile, and they were running again, across Chaliboque's ruined front lawn and toward the trail she had come through earlier. The storm made the world a runny, dark mess, but after the house they'd just escaped it was like stepping into sunshine. She could see Boo Taylor's broad, reassuring back again, the muscles throbbing as he ran; she could see the shape of trees and a wide open space where she knew the Yamawichee would be.

When they reached the woods, Boo slipped on the mossy cobbles, yanking her arm as he fought for balance, yanking her so her own feet slipped straight out from beneath her. She fell. Her back landed squarely on a gnarled crook of root.

Every bit of air mushroomed out of her lungs.

Rain pattered through tree limbs and struck her eyes.

She couldn't move, couldn't breathe.

Boo's arms came around her waist. He lifted her up. "You okay?" he asked breathlessly. His face was a wet blur.

Unable to speak, she nodded.

He kept one hand around her waist and made her move forward again. Her feet skimmed across the slick rock. Wet beards of Spanish moss flapped in her face. The flat shimmer of the Yamawichee appeared on her left.

At last, her breath was coming back in small puffs.

"I think I hear it," he yelled, although she could hear nothing but the leaves thrashing under the downpour.

"Will it——" she managed to stutter, a fist still buried deep into her back, "will it come after us?" For some reason, she imagined rain destroying the beast, purifying waters striking it, obliterating fur and flesh in a dazzling performance of lights. Would anything really follow them into this storm?

Boo didn't answer.

They were off the cobbles. Mud and leaf mold squished through her toes. Her body ached and bled in a dozen places, but she could move on her own now. "Where are we goin?"

"The creek!" he yelled.

And then she heard the Beast. A guttural bawling somewhere behind them, free of the house and loose in the storm. Boo made a small yelping noise; she screeched and batted his arm away so she could run faster. The trail narrowed and darkened and twisted to the right, away from the Yamawichee. Boo fell in behind her. She thought about the creek ahead of them. All that mud—that would slow them down, wouldn't it? They'd get stuck in it, like quicksand, and that thing would catch them there and rip them to pieces. Maybe they should climb a tree. Hounds couldn't climb trees; did such rules apply? She and Boo could climb up one of these old oaks, go up high and out of reach. And then...

And then she comes.

And then what?

Her foot slipped through a puddle, but she kept her feet. She ducked a branch. A howl reared out of the trees and sent cold needles through her heart. Too close! How could it get so close so fast? She stole a glance over her shoulder, and there was Boo Taylor, fallen several yards behind, clutching his side and looking over his shoulder, too. He turned back sharply, and even in the sloppy darkness she could make out the bright, round circles of his eyes. He had seen it.

"HURRY!" he screamed.

Gussie turned forward just as the trail made an abrupt jag to the left. She slid into a tree, pushed off the trunk, and kept moving. The trail was opening up again as they neared Pigg's Creek.·

And then what?

And then the mud. Stuck. Trapped.

From behind her, a crashing of branches and leaves. She spun around, pushing hair out of her eyes again, and saw Boo on his hands and knees, scrabbling at the mud and trying to stand. The guttural baying of the Beast was coming from just beyond the last bend of the trail behind him, almost on top of him.

She darted back, snatched a wet clump of Boo Taylor's hair and yanked. He came with her, slipping and stumbling, pushing her along at the small of her back. At last, they rounded the last of the trees.

And slid to a stop at the creek bank.

"Oh Boo, no!" she cried.

The tide was in.

The shallow trickle of creek she had walked through only hours ago was now a river, and the growls were rushing up behind them, building to a roar.

"Your boat!" Gussie yelled, her eyes firing madly through the trees, and then spotted the squat shape.

"No time!" he yelled back. He grabbed her elbow and jerked her to the creek's edge.

"But I *can't*—"

And then her shoulder was unhinging from its socket.

She was flying.

She was falling.

The world went black again.

Back into the belly of a whale. Muscle and viscera undulated around her, drawing her deeper. She tried to claw her way out, but an arm pinned her shoulders. She tried to breathe, but another arm was wrapped around her throat, and her insides seized up. Suddenly, she was spit back into the sky. She came up on her back, gagging warm salt water, trying to breathe again, but the water was filling her throat.

"Stop kickin me!"

Boo Taylor's voice, only inches away. He was beneath her in the creek. His arm was crooked around her ribs, a hand clamped firmly on her left breast. She tried to spin and grab him around the chest.

"Gussie, stop kickin!"

She was getting only half-breaths into her lungs. A tangle of seaweed had gotten caught on her face. She flailed her hand up, tried to slap it away, and realized it was her own hair. Brackish creek water was splashing into her nose, filling her mouth. Her ears were covered under the plaster of her hair, but she could still hear the angry baying of the Beast somewhere close. *"Where is it?"* she gasped, and choked down more seawater.

"Gussie, you have to stop *kickin* me!"

"Do you—" coughing, gagging "—do you see it?"

"No, but I hear it."

Her head went under water. She clawed at Boo's shoulders, felt the both of them falling deeper. A current was carrying them toward the sound. She thrashed at the water, and then Boo's arm twisted around her neck and jerked her hard and back into the air. Water poured out of her nose.

"*Stop it,* dammit Gussie," Boo yelled, coughing now, too. "Get on your back and lie still!"

A wet spasm rippled through her chest. She gagged harshly, sputtering out streams of salt and slime.

"Gussie, lie still!"

And she tried to, but she was sure she would sink like a lead weight. Boo had a hold of her breast again. She felt his legs scissoring beneath her. She looked for the bank, but rain and creek water kept splashing into her eyes. She was a rag doll being dragged through a puddle.

The Beast? Animal sounds—still there, but further back. Stopped by the water after all? Unable to cross? Boo's grip was slipping loose. She clutched for his arm, slipped below the water again and thrashed, filling her nose and mouth with more of the warm water. She swallowed and gagged, blinded under the surface. Her feet got caught up in something thick and mushy. She punched at it, and her fist sank to the wrist. Mud. She had hit the bottom of the creek.

She got her knees under her and flopped up for air. Spitting, coughing, she saw Boo Taylor curling his arms over the shallow rim of the creek only a few feet ahead.

She tried to stand in the mud.

Just past Boo's shoulder, a dark and massive shape lifted to life.

Gussie choked out a shriek. She beat at the water, but her limbs were getting limp with fatigue. The shape heaved off the bank and splashed into the creek, ignoring Boo Taylor and coming for her as she blundered backward into the current.

She slipped under.

Drifted toward blackness.

Saved *(trapped?)* by a strong hand seizing her biceps, drawing her back up. A voice was bellowing nonsense from the surface. She came out, swung her arm around, and it clapped across Boo Taylor's nose.

"It's just a *gator,* Gussie!" he screamed into her face. *"Quit it!* We just spooked a gator! It's okay; it swam away!"

He jerked her back to the bank and released her again in the mud while she spit and coughed and tried to find room for oxygen in her saturated lungs. Boo took hold of a root, reached back for her hand, and hauled her to his side. He put her hands on a cypress knee. "Hold this," he shouted. She obeyed. Groaning, Boo climbed over the bank. A moment later, he had her by the forearms and dragged her out of the water.

She flopped to his side.

There was no sign of the Beast anywhere.

..*eight*

She brought her knees to her chest; her whole body clenched as rigid as stone for several painful seconds. And then she silently wretched. Ropes of warm goo spluttered from her throat and hung from her lips.

Boo was smacking her back. "Can you breathe?" he asked.

"Stop it," she croaked and swiped at his hand. "That hurts."

"Sorry."

Clenched again, the pain even worse, two giant hands wringing her like a washcloth, squeezing, squeezing, rupturing, creek water straining from her nose and her eyes, from her scalp, from the tips of her fingers.

And then, the release, and a great ocean waterfall came gushing from her throat.

She flicked the streamers from her mouth. Boo rubbed her back in small, gentle circles.

Breathing again, spitting at the ground, spitting: "Dammit, Boo Taylor, I *told* you I couldn't swim."

"You did okay," he said. When she was able to look up, she found him squinting across the creek.

"Is it comin?" she asked.

He wiped his eyes. He curled around and got to his knees, and she glanced involuntarily at his dangling penis, which was now level with her head. "I don't know," he answered at last. "I heard splashin up stream a ways, but. . ."

"Splashing?"

"Yes, but I didn't *see* anything. Don't hear it anymore, either, do you?"

She only heard the rain in the trees. "No," she breathed. She circled her tongue through her mouth, spit, ran her wrist over her lips. Was that silver light coming from the moon? Was the storm breaking apart? A hazy euphoria settled into her exhausted muscles. She couldn't keep her eyes from peeking between Boo Taylor' legs. She smiled.

"Maybe we're safe, then," he said.

"Do you think that. . .*thing* can swim?" she asked, staring at his penis, and felt unbeckoned laughter tickling inside her. *Exactly which "thing" are you referring to?*

Boo looked down at her and seemed suddenly conscious his nakedness, suddenly awkward, suddenly dropping a forearm across his waist. "Gussie," he said seriously, "who the hell knows what that thing can do."

The laughter sprung loose. It was like vomiting again; it just seized her body and demanded to be released. She collapsed in the mud, laughing uncontrollably despite the shrieks of protest from every sore muscle, every square inch of gashed, bruised, flayed-raw skin. "Oh, I guess I have a pretty good idea," she said between gasps. She saw Boo Taylor's confusion and laughed harder. She rolled into a ball. The laughter burned her stomach, crushed her ribs, but was beyond stopping.

Boo scrunched back on his haunches and crossed both forearms over his lap. He sat and watched her and looked pathetically miserable. He tentatively reached one hand out to touch her arm. "Gussie?"

It came in torrents, like the rain.

"Gussie, are you okay?"

The ragged edge of hysteria cut into the laughter now. The smile was locked taut across her face. She pleaded with Boo Taylor through her eyes, trying to explain that she was unable to stop. Boo was starting to stand, and she threw out a hand to hold him in place. She clutched his thigh, pressed her face to it. "I'm sorry," she managed to choke out. His hand came back, stroking her tangled hair. The laughter gurgled through her throat and came out bubbling against his skin. "I'm sorry," she said again, as finally the hysteria unhooked itself. She sighed, stuttering through it with chuckles. She kissed his thigh and resisted the urge to reach over and tweak his penis.

"Better now?" he asked.

She nodded and released his leg. She shivered with cold. The rain, she noticed, was thinning. The storm really was passing.

Boo straightened up, and she climbed to her knees next to him, a few vagrant giggles still shuddering through her. Then she pictured that crazed, half-melted shape in the smoke, and that killed the last of the laughter. "Really Boo, you don't think it made it across, do you?"

"I don't know. I told you I heard splashing."

"How do you...how do you know it can even swim?" *"It?" she thought. Should I be saying, "she?"*

His muddy hand came around her waist. "I don't."

"Did you see it?"

"I *heard* it. I saw..."

"What?"

He gazed into the mist. "I don't know. Something."

She sniffled. She followed his gaze across the creek where the emptiness beyond the haze was absolute. It was like a woodcut print she once saw in a schoolbook depicting a clipper ship sailing over the edge of a flattened globe. That was why the thing *(she?)* could no longer be heard: the Beast and Chaliboque were gone; the opposing bank of Pigg's Creek had fallen off the misty rim of the world where dragons lived and swallowed ships whole. *We survived that!* she thought wondrously.

Then she saw the blood forking down Boo's forehead. She had mistaken it for mud earlier, but there was a gash at his hairline and another above the brow. His right cheek jutted up to blind his eye as if the bone beneath had grown a bud. A series of deep cuts crisscrossed his left shoulder. She remembered his crash through a wall inside Chaliboque, seeing it now where before it was only vibrations and concussions in the dark. She wondered about her own wounds, saw Boo Taylor's assessing, quietly guilty expression and decided she must look just as bad.

"Guess we better make our way to Miss Laylee's," he said.

Another laugh bucked from her lungs. "She's in for one big surprise when she gets a look at the two of us!"

Boo frowned. He stroked her hip. "Somehow I doubt it."

He stood with old-man grunts and stiffness. She took hold of his hands, and she came up beside him, yellowjackets stinging her knees and elbows.

"Think you can walk?" he asked.

"I can walk. I'll run, if I have to, Boo Taylor. Just don't throw me in the damn water again."

The outgoing tide had swept them downcreek toward the Yamawichee, far down-woods from any trail Boo recognized. So he hacked one out with his hands.

She followed.

Followed by sound, brushing invisible ivies and mosses aside, ducking a branch when Boo warned, moaning when she had to bend the wreck of her body. They paralleled the creek bank. Crickets and frogs and all the night animals were silent. A slim silver-blueness from the half-moon slicked in and out through the thick trees and glistened in the surrounding leaves, making the feeblest light for navigating. She listened to the whispers from the creek, smooth, unsplattered trickles, offering hope that the storm had withered and had maybe even drifted away entirely. Roots, fronds, pebbles, sticks stung the soles of her bare feet; her toe pulsed sharp heart-beat throbbings. In her back, a small knot, like a dwarf's fist, knuckled and tightened. Her nipples were raw, cherry-swollen, and she went suddenly warm remembering Boo Taylor's teeth.

What would Miss Laylee possibly think when the two of them arrived like a mud-pie Adam and Eve at her front door? Surprise maybe, shock, disappointment, hilarity, furiousness. Fully expectant. She didn't care; she only wanted the hot showers and soft pillows. Warm blankets and a roof. A guffer doctor's ministrations, wounds swabbed and dressed and the promise of explanations by breakfast sunlight. She inhaled, anticipating it, yearning for it and trying to breathe it closer to her . . .

Nearby, a heavy splash. She jerked to a stop, hissed a breath.

"Just another gator," Boo said, but he whispered it.

They stood quietly. Listening. Gussie inched through the dark, bumped into Boo's back, and slid both hands down his arm until she was holding his elbow. She heard the creek rippling. She heard raindrops in the leaves.

The frogs and crickets were still unnervingly silent.

"How much farther?" she asked softly.

Boo waved a hand to silence her.

Off to the left, deep in the woods, a small, spongy sigh. A footstep?

The familiar dread rose through her gut. *Not again, please. I can run if I have to, but, please God, I can't be that afraid again.* Her fingers tightened on Boo's arm, gauging his pulse. She waited, he waited, for the next sound.

When none came, Boo whispered, "I think Pigg's Point is just ahead."

She released his arm as he crept forward again. She followed closely, mimicking his half-crouch.

They reached a flat, open area where the creek sounds sharpened and a wide patch of sky offered a momentary wine-hued flush. Pigg's Point; familiar ground at last. Boo stopped abruptly. He cocked his head, listening to the woods.

He held still. She listened with him. Another breathy tamp—ahead of them now. A branch settling under the rain's burden? A possum scratching leaves?

Another footfall?

"Nothing," Boo said at last.

And they were turning back into the woods, following a real trail now, like a dripping tunnel. Somewhere at the other end was Laylee Colebriar's house. Walls and a roof, again. And clean water and a mattress. She could hear the jingle of wind chimes already—although from this distance the chimes were more like a voice, humming and giggling a faint, discordant hymn.

She watched the vague hulk of Boo Taylor's shoulders dipping and rising before her. She thought about his naked body and wondered if he was thinking about hers. She wanted a steaming hot cup of Laylee's spiced tea. She wanted soft cushions and electric light. She wanted Boo Taylor to turn around and make love to her right here on the wet forest ground, his tongue and his teeth on her nipples again, his body over hers, inside hers. She wanted to see his face again by firelight, the way it shuddered— she had done that to him; she had caused that exquisite expression of agony, and she had never felt more powerful. She could reach out now and touch his hand. She could tug him down beside her, feel his skin draping over hers. They were Adam and Eve, and this swampy forest was the best Eden the island could offer.

The wind chimes, closer now, were more and more like a voice calling to them. Perhaps Miss Laylee was on her porch, right now, rocking in her chair and waiting for them. And inside a kettle was already whistling, and clean towels were stacked on the sofa. As she thought this she realized she had gotten her directions confused because the humming was off to the right where Pigg's Creek should be. The creek sounds themselves were lost.

They followed the trail. A wisp of ocean breeze stroked the trees and brought the first unspoiled scent she had breathed since she had left Miss Laylee's house earlier that evening. The tunnel was bending again, promising an opening. She sensed open sky blooming not far ahead. And the wind-chime song was only around the next turn.

Boo's hand came clamping down on her shoulder. "Do you hear that?" he whispered.

"What?"

"Listen!"

The breeze and the jingle of chimes separated from the voice that had become a distinct, dissonant babble inside the trees to their right. It was a sound she half-remembered from earlier tonight but couldn't recall when. An innocent sound— *should* be an innocent sound: a child's voice, alone in the woods. Her heart sunk inside her ribcage like a rock.

"She's here," Boo said dully. He took his hand from her shoulder, found her hand, and squeezed her fingers until they hurt. They eased down the narrow path as if gliding on thin ice. Watching the woods. One blue-gray tree trunk slid past her eyes.

Another.

Another.

The child's voice was in there, but she could see nothing but a confusing tangle of branches.

Another trunk.

Then moonlight, as sudden as a lamp.

The little girl was not twenty yards away. She was seated on the carcass of an oak. A book was open in her lap, and her lips moved ceaselessly as she read aloud in a voice that was mostly whisper. She might be reading to herself or to someone close by.

Gussie stepped away, made an infinitesimal crackling of pine needles.

The girl's head snapped up at the sound. Moonlight shuddered over her face through broken pieces of cloud. She spoke aloud, her baby voice quavering with worry.

She said, "You should go."

The moon clicked off.

Again the girl's voice—now, somewhere in the dark: "She's coming for your skin now."

Gussie tried to take another step back, but the moonglow seeped back into the woods a moment later and with it rose the steady rumble of thunder. Behind the girl, a dark heap—it had been there all the time—now lifted to its haunches.

Boo squeezed her hand so hard she thought it would break. He whispered, *"Run!"*

Nine

She ran.

Sweetpatch Island, beneath her, pounded up through her bones, her aching thigh muscles. The air rushed around her, sluicing ice-water winds through her hair, escaping, fleeing in all directions. Boo Taylor sprinted behind her, trying to keep up and in some dim corner of her mind she tallied with satisfaction that she could outrun him. Behind him, she could hear the grumbling and thunderous sound of something big.

Ahead, across an impossibly wide expanse of field and garden, flashing in and out of clouds, rose Laylee Colebriar's tiny shack. Gussie Dutton flung her body toward it, bounding, leaping, reaching, stretching through the here-then-gone clouds.

Someone is gonna die tonight.

The thought was as crisp and real as the pain in her spine.

Ahead, a picket fence of tomato stalks marked the border of the garden. She yelled, breathless, "Laylee!"

If they made the garden, they might make the porch.

If they made the porch, they might make it inside the house.

If they made the house, the old woman might be awake, might be armed, might have a spell for slaying beasts.

"LAAAAYLEEEEEEE!"

The night wind burned her lungs. Broomsedge whipped her ankles. She listened for the runaway-truck snorts and roars that chased and wondered how close now, how big, how fierce, how *real*. And then, because she couldn't help it, she turned her head to see it.

In the brief, earthquake view of the world behind her, she saw only Boo Taylor's wildly thrashing arms and legs and the black rise of trees and night behind him. Again, it seemed as if they had escaped from the misty edge of the world—only this time, one of the dragons had clawed over to follow. She could hear it, even if she couldn't see it.

She turned forward again. The garden was closer, and for the first time, she believed they might actually make it to safety. A frail, sepia glow now colored the parlor window—a light somewhere in the back, probably the bedroom.

"LAYLEE!" she called, "HELP, IT'S US!"

But her foot was suddenly snagged by a stray root, and she went sprawling into wet grass.

She cried out. Boo Taylor was a whitish blur flashing past to the finish line. *He's leaving me!* She rocked to her knees, cursing whatever she had tripped on, as a locomotive rumble bore down on her. *He left me.* She floundered to regain her feet, but her ankle collapsed with a white flare of pain. An instant later, an enormous weight slammed into her back.

Her breath was gone.

Her sight rolled to wide plains of black and red.

Her heart closed up like a turtle.

You win, she said silently to the Beast or to Boo Taylor, and understood how foolish it had been to ever believe she might actually have escaped this thing.

In the little house, two mummified hands laid ten desiccated pads of fingerflesh on window glass, and the steel-wool skull lowered and focused its two muddy, sad, infinitely troubled sockets on the glass, through the glass.

Light.

Then dark.

The moon was playing tricks, making shadows. Something there, silvered upon the fields; then something gone, blackened behind a cumulous blink.

Hated one, liked the other, she thought.

And then she heard it: her name, screamed.

She sighed.

A child, her child, her cherished and deepest loved one gone astray, abandoned, poisoned by the black spooks and her own sin—her child would die tonight. The old lizard muscle in her breast swelled, summoned electricity, bubbled, bubbled, churned out sparks, spat strange oils and exotic spice. She breathed ancient scents from the bat-dangled garden, sniffing out the ancient, nearly lost secrets gathered from the continents.

And tried to conjure one last, cruelest spell.

Alive... she thought.

Steam blasts scalding her cheek; spikes blunting, jabbing, digging her scalp.

She thought... *eaten alive.*

Thoughts swirling, swimming in a faraway place. A woman in the water. Not alone. She saw the woman, watched helplessly, horrified, as she was attacked by a frenzied shark, the image flickering black and white from a television screen (a year ago, maybe?), and that gruesome notion had occurred to her all the way back then: *why, she's being eaten alive—I wonder what that must feel like?* Now she had become the woman, and she knew the answer. It was disappointingly simple and obvious.

What does it feel like to be eaten alive?

The worst thing you can imagine.

While these thoughts swirled, stroked, swam tranquilly in a place as far away and insignificant as the half-moon, a wet roar was being snorted directly into her brain through her ears, and this more immediate place was utterly insane.

The Beast.

It was made of iron bars and hornet nests and sopping-wet shag carpet; it reeked of garbage pails and low tides; it burned like shards of dry ice.

And it had her pinned to the mud.

Claws flayed her back and shoulders. A snout dug at her skull, dug for her neck. She jerked back her arm. Jaws snapped, and a patch of skin near her elbow got pinched and ripped open. She screamed into the mud. She tried to turn over, punch at the thing, but the teeth stabbed at her neck again.

The worst thing.

She worked a hand under its neck and pushed. The jaws came away to snap at her fingers, and she was able to flop over, blinded by mud, by the clouds momentarily swamping the moon. She caught a flash of red that might be rubies, might be blood, might be coals from a fire. A wild, girlish face. A flash of pale teeth. A black-gummed mouth lunged, aiming for her throat. She deflected it, twisted her head, and the teeth sank into her cheek, close to her ear. Her face burst into flames.

Oh, the very worst thing there is.

The teeth pulled apart the strings of her flesh. The teeth were not sharp like knives; they were blunt and relentless. They did not cut; they ripped. The teeth picked up her scalp and shook it violently. Her hair whipped across her eyes. The Beast's drool burned her like acid and mingled with her own blood. She felt her veins absorbing it. She felt her pulse catching it, her heart pumping it throughout her body and spreading the burn everywhere. She no longer heard the Beast's snarls—it was making pig noises now, and it was a vulgar, sloppy sound.

The worst there is, the worst there is . . .

Somewhere beyond was a high-pitched cry. All at once, the great weight was pitched off her body.

The cool night air crashed over her like a wave, and she gasped it down. She lifted her fingers to her cheek and felt a blast of pain there. She had the startling realization that only a few seconds had elapsed since she had been on her feet and running.

A ferocious battle was churning through the mud close by. She reeled to her knees, blinked mud; clouds parted briefly, closed up again, and she saw, *might* have seen a two headed beast at war with itself. One dark head, the other white. One a monster. The other . . .

"*Boo!*" she cried.

Those were his arms and legs wrapped around something that was at least twice his size and must be a bear or a panther.

She screamed his name again.

In blackness, then flickers of silver, she heard, tried to see the bucking and thrashing, Boo Taylor riding the thing, jaws gnashing with the sound of windows slamming shut. Boo grunted and whimpered. In another flash of moon-silver his eyes met hers and sent some panicked message she couldn't read. Was it, *run away!* or was it *help me!* He gargled something desperate. Then darkness, a flail of legs, the earthquake slamming of bodies in the mud.

She searched the ground for a weapon: shadowy heaps of broomsedge, snarls of mud, the long, flattened streak where she had fallen. The garden was just a few feet away—and she saw the stakes roped to the tomato plants.

She pushed to her feet, and a bolt of pain blasted through her right ankle.

She collapsed to her knees, struggling, limping to the garden, falling again when she reached it. She seized the closest stalk, tore both plant and the stake from the ground and spun back around just as Boo Taylor shrieked.

Ripples of light.

Boo Taylor was being shaken like a bit of loose rag. Pounding fists against a head that was buried into the meat of his thigh.

His screams cut off. *He's dead,* she thought miserably, and the world wound back to the lifetimes-ago whispers of this morning.

Did you hear?

Did you hear, it was a boy's body they pulled out . . . ?

Gussie, where is Boo Taylor?

A weak, yellow porch light winked on.

"Laylee!" she screamed—sending pain roaring across her jaw and into her scalp. *"Here,* Laylee! We're *here!"*

She pulled the stake free from the twine and tomato stalk. The stake was no more than a half-inch thick, but it was sharp on one end, and maybe...

"Laylee!" she called again, "Laylee are you there?"

Roars in the darkness; the Beast charged.

She pushed backward deeper into the cover of leaves and shoots. Plants burst apart as the Beast exploded into the garden. Gussie remembered the stake and thrust it forward, but the stake was nothing, was less than nothing against that great mass. The thing, all heat and stink, was on her again. She shoved and kicked blindly at a muck-splattered belly. She punched at a face—and glimpsed two faces again; one the pitchest black and the other the palest white; one a demon's and the other Boo Taylor's who had somehow come alive and had leapt onto the thing's back again. Boo and the Beast rolled off of her. The garden was being shredded all around them.

(Far off, but rushing closer, came another growl of thunder. *The storm?* she wondered. But the storm had passed...)

Dark shoulders whipped about. Boo Taylor rammed out his fist, and a demon mouth gobbled it. The thing's head shook, flinging its long hair about, and Boo Taylor screamed as if his lungs were made of glass and the glass had shattered. She heard the shatter—like wind chimes in a gale, or twigs snapping on a forest trail.

(and heard the other storm charging, thundering, thrashing closer)

The thing's head shook again, and Boo Taylor was tossed clear.

But his fingers ripped free, were still poking like a pale tongue from the Beast's jaws.

(thunder racing in quickly from the faraway half-moon world; she waited for the flash of the thunderbolt)

The Beast swallowed.

The worst thing you can imagine.

The storm struck; silver lightning erupted. A large gray hound, barreling through tomato stalks, slammed head-on into the beast-shape.

Leaves and dirt and blood spewed across the sky.

Gussie lifted her head. Out in the darkness, a frenzy of shrieks and yowls and gnashing jaws spiraled upward, fell to the mud, tangled through the shredded plants, rose again. Somewhere apart from that noise came the distinct warble of Boo Taylor's groans. She crawled to him through the ripped bits of plants, grabbed his arm and shook it. She called his name, and the effort shot streaks of acid through her cheek. Translucent, amoeba-like blobs clouded through her brain and bleared into her eyes. Boo wobbled his head and made a murky questioning sound.

The battle deafened her.

She screamed at Boo Taylor that they *HAD* to get inside *NOW.*

He swung his arm around. The gore-splattered pulp at the end of his wrist flapped into her lap.

She screamed at him that oh my God oh my God they *HAD* to *HURRY.*

He swayed to a sitting position.

While she staggered on her good leg and wrestled with Boo Taylor's slack limbs, another shrill yelp erupted over the tops of the tomato stems. Gray and black tumbled and thrashed; the Beast's jaws were clamped into the gray hound's snout. The hound whined and yanked madly; blood sputtered from its nose; it circled and bellowed, circled for leverage, circled as the Beast circled with it, gray and black.

Boo Taylor tried to lean on her and nearly knocked her over. She had *BROKEN* her *ANKLE*, she yelled in his ear, and did he *UNDERSTAND?*

He nodded dizzily; the amoebas gurgled across the air between them, then shot away as the air was filled with a tortured shriek—the gray dog's nose ripped free, and a great gout of blood looped skyward and cascaded into the mud.

The opposing shapes, opposing colors rammed together again, pistoning up on hind legs, muzzles whiplashing back and forth, flicking spit and blood, seeking advantage, snagging a black ear, gnashing a silver neck. Boo Taylor, who teetered in a strong wind that did not exist, flung his ruined hand over her shoulder. A blackberry goo bubbled from the punctures in his thigh and streaked down his naked leg to his foot. She stumbled and yawed through the garden with him, hopping on one leg while he kicked through lima bean plants and squash vines. They made a zigzag track to Laylee Colebriar's front porch.

Behind them now, the war raged on.

ten

They collapsed inside an empty house.

Sometime later, all went quiet.

eleven

Church Road, in the deepest and stillest moment of night. Breezeless. Sea grasses hung limp at the roadside. Waves steadily, softly, continuously feather-stroked the night beaches; clouds shifted and rolled between land and stars, sea and moon.

Empty. Quiet.

Until a distant puttering interrupted.

Unseen, small creatures scuttled for the gullies.

Coming on now, the headlights of a rickety '62 Buick cast two exhausted shafts of light down the middle of Church Road, glinting mud puddles and setting moths alight. Inside, Solomon Goody wrinkled his nose at the sulfurous smell that rushed through the window. It was the same smell that had hit him in the face when he stepped off the bus back on Sandpiper Boulevard twenty minutes earlier. The smell was always worse after a day or two free of it.

At the wheel beside him, his uncle Nate watched the road like a zombie. Solomon fidgeted with the radio button, seeking the jazz station out of Charleston, the one that only really came in well on clear nights. This wasn't a clear night. A storm had been through. The worst of it might have passed, but clouds and electric disturbance still hovered over the coast. All he could manage from the dashboard speaker was a steady stream of static.

Uncle Nate spoke softly.

"Jehosophat."

Solomon looked up. Saw a tired surprise lift the sags of his uncle's face. He turned to look through the windshield.

Staggering along the roadside, past the dance of moths, was a ghost.

Uncle Nate spoke again.

"Great jumpin Jehosophat."

The Buick slowed.

Solomon watched the headlights steadily brighten the unsteady, stumbling-forward swathes of whiteness.

Closer, and he saw the whiteness was sheets stained with black paint.

Closer, and the black was revealed as blood.

Closer, and he recognized the boy in the bloody sheets. And the boy (yes, very much a ghost), looking over, recognized him.

"Help me," said the ghost.

The Buick stopped. Solomon got out, and the ghost collapsed in his arms.

twelve

The water in the glass bowl looked like pink lemonade. It wouldn't *taste* like pink lemonade, but that's what it looked like, and the thought of real pink lemonade made Gussie thirsty. Maybe there was something cold to drink in the little round Hot Point refrigerator in the kitchen. A bottle of yauponberry wine, perhaps—or dandelion wine, or a pitcher of spiced tea, or a bottle of Coke. Or lemonade. The more she thought about it, the thirstier she became. Her tongue turned thick and pasty in her mouth.

She wasn't going to get up and go into the kitchen, though. The bleeding had mostly stopped, but if she jostled the head in her lap, the blood might start flowing again. For a while there, it had been gushing so furiously that she had thought...she had feared...*the worst.*

The worst? Time to change her notions about what *the worst* might actually be. Time to change her notions about good and bad, dark and light, life and death. Time to re-think everything she had learned. The planet had slipped off its axis; all things were thrown out of balance. Reason tottered on a mean slant, and the chasm beneath it was as bottomless as the misty edge of the world where the dragons ruled and swallowed clipper ships whole. The old rules no longer fit. It was...*the very worst*...like looking at the world through a glass bowl filled with pink lemonade. Everything was distorted. Everything was tainted with blood.

Yes, a beast had been run off. But a million others had been unleashed.

She lifted a pink washcloth from the bowl. She pressed pink lemonade against her cheek. The poison was still in her veins; its burning was like needled threads swimming down her arms and legs, around her breasts, swirling in her stomach, clawing into her back, stitching a horrible macramé pattern in her right ankle. But it was still *the worst* in her face. *How bad will the scar be?* Pink water dribbled down her jaw and her neck. It was absorbed into the white sheet that was wrapped around her like a shroud from her chest to her feet. Just another stain on the sheet. The sheet was covered with stains; blatant scarlet-black ones, not this timid pink. Some of the blood was hers, but most of it was not.

The head in her lap joggled restlessly and drew in a raggedy breath.

"Okay?" Gussie asked. Acid darted across her ear.

The eyes above the shredded flesh blinked at her lovingly. "Okay as can be, I reckon." The bird-song voice had gone nasally flat; the nose was a mangled horror. "Does your face hurt, child?"

She smiled. "A little."

"Well, it's killin me." The old woman's laughter was a happy witch's cackle.

Boo Taylor had gone for the telephone because he was in the best shape of the three of them. *That* was impossible in the world she had formerly known—his thigh was bloated like a watermelon and bled from a wide crescent of puncture wounds; two fingers had been ripped clear off of his right hand *(oh God, they really were and that was just too final and too grotesque to be possible)* and a third was stripped to the bone. One eye was swollen shut beneath a deep gash. Egg-sized knots contorted the curve of his scalp. And every bit of his skin had been flayed to bloody strips with scrapes and gashes. In the world she had formerly known, *he* would be sprawled out on the sofa. In the world she had formerly known—where boys prayed in churches and were not burned alive in them, where hounds only chased down rabbits and squirrels, where Reason smiled and sat smugly on its purple-cushioned throne—in that world, Boo Taylor would be in a hospital bed.

Or a coffin.

But at least he could walk.

"Mr. Boo, you get along to Mose Johnston's and call your daddy. Mose'll answer, you bang on his door loud enough. You be sure you yell out who you is, or he liable to wag that ol shotgun at you—the one he keeps on his pantry shelf. High Spot's closer, though you have to break a window with a rock to get in. You make your own mind up when you get there."

Boo Taylor had gone into the night wrapped in a white sheet. Like a phantom. A phantom with a fat, bloody towel turban-wrapped over his right hand. Before he left, the old lady with the shredded face shoved dried leaves into his mouth. *"Chew on this, boy—you goin into shock, and this keep it back for a bit."* Gussie had propped herself up on the porch railing to watch him go and had not been surprised at all when he limped straight through Laylee Colebriar's garden instead of turning right to head for Sugar Dam Road. Because he had to see. He had to go into the garden and see it for himself.

In the world she had formerly known, Boo Taylor would be curled up on this sofa with her right now. She would be holding his hand, and his hand would be whole, and Eulahlah Colebriar would be peacefully asleep in her bedroom—and a big, gray dog would be peacefully asleep under the house. And in that world, she would wake up from this dream and would shake Boo awake to tell him about it. And maybe he would smile.

But that world had cracked apart like a cheap movie set built of paper and kindling. And someone had put a match to it.

"How long do you think he's been?" she asked.

The old, silver-haired witch moved the towel from her nose and favored her with another smile. Surely, it was torture for that face to smile. "Oh, not more than ten minutes, I s'pect," Laylee Colebriar answered.

In the world she had formerly known, it seemed like two or three hours had passed. In this new world, even time was distorted.

A lacerated, cinnamon-colored hand patted her own lacerated, pale white one. "Mr. Boo be jes fine out there, child. Don't you worry." The head in her lap closed its eyes, but the ruined smile remained.

Outside, in the field just beyond Laylee Colebriar's garden, a girl should be lying with her head in a lap of mud and broomsedge. Her eyes should be closed. She would not be smiling. Her throat should be ripped open—as if by a big, gray dog that had somehow broken apart like gray snowflakes and was swept far away from Sweetpatch Island in an autumn night's breeze. Of course, the girl was not there, had also magically broken apart—only like crow feathers instead of snowflakes. Gussie had not needed to see this to confirm it, as Boo Taylor *had* needed to, because in this new world, she knew without seeing.

The old woman had started bleeding again. Gussie dabbed the pink washcloth against the delicate wrinkles. The water made dark tears that fell across the old face, catching the wrinkles, riding them, unraveling, and spilling away. Spilling into Gussie's lap. The wrinkled face still smiled, and it was still filled with magic even though the nose had been torn apart by a black hound that never existed. The rise and fall of the bony chest was peaceful and easy and steady and eternal. It was a pendulum, marking the time Boo Taylor had been gone, marking years, decades, marking the triumphs and tragedies of a century.

...rise...fall...inhale...exhale...

The old woman looked as if she were asleep. Gussie Dutton had never known exhaustion so utterly consuming, but she could not sleep. Because Boo Taylor was out there, somewhere far away from her. And he was alone. And it was dark.

Interludes
In the Season of Heaven & Hell

In the deepest heart of winter, something that should have been dead stepped through heavy snow and up the steps leading to Elton Cooper's front porch. It knocked, wanting to be let inside.

two

They were looking for the next King.

The search had been going on for thirty years, and there had been a great many applicants. A great many fine resumes. A great many shouters and fist pounders and Bible squeezers and cajolers and comedians and warriors and criminals. "Listen to me!" they all cried, but the interviews were never convincing. Madmen, Preachers, and Republicans. "Next applicant, please,"—and on it went. The ad was never pulled. The resumes kept coming in the mail. But the position remained vacant. For thirty years.

Thirty years ago, he had taken the King's hand in his own. The high-tension voltage of the King's regency buzzed and crackled into his own hand and up his arm and into his heart, and in that moment an electric brilliance filled the room and made the others in that dusty schoolhouse invisible as he and the King stood alone on the misty mountain top and saw, through that great and horrific light, the fabled promised land.

The kingdom.

Can you see it, boy?

Holding hands. Only an instant. A flash of lightening. Perhaps the King had felt it; if so, his eyes never wavered from their steady and humorless brown. It was just an instant. And it was thirty years ago.

Why is she crying?

(She knows. She knows the planes are coming.)

Some fires were started by sparks: matchsticks struck, flints rasped, metal and stone cracked together. Other fires were started by lightening when, for that fleetest of moments, heaven and earth touched.

Look, boy, and see it. See the kingdom. See the people in need of a king. It will always take a king, you see. It will always take one man to stand above the others, to accept that touch from heaven and say, "Yes, I shall serve my God and lead my people." One man, a normal man made glorious because he did not fear to bathe in that dazzling fire. One man to lean his spear toward the enemy and say, "No, this belongs to my people. And we shall have what God has willed."

On that day, thirty years ago, lightening struck. And at last he had understood his birthright.

In the deepest part of night, when everyone else in the city was asleep, a famous murder took place. Carl Denham looked at the police officer and spoke the truth of it. "No. It wasn't the planes..."

❖   ❖   ❖

April 23
9:40 a.m.
Nathan Booker, a tall and completely bald young black man in Brooks Brothers tweed, pushed his head through the office door in the basement of the Cannon Building in Washington DC. "He's here."

"He's twenty minutes late," the reply came a beat later.

Booker ignored this. He waited for the man with the skinny brown arms that poked out of rolled-up, white sleeves to finish reading and signing the letter on his desk. Paisley red-and-yellow suspenders looped over wiry shoulders. The suspenders matched the bow tie. The man insisted on wearing bow ties.

When Solomon Goody laid down the pen and looked up, the slimmest of wry grins shaded his face. Sunlight glinted from his rimless spectacles. "You feel like sitting in?"

"You need the bad boy's protection? Sure."

Solomon Goody barked a laugh. "Yeah, I'm gonna need some protecting all right. What time's my flight again?"

"Eleven ten. Percy has the car ready—whenever you're ready."

Solomon checked his watch. "We have to make this quick, then. Go ahead and send him in."

The morning sun slanted in yellow bars from the boxy windows near the ceiling and picked up the scuff marks on the walls. On clear days—like today—the morning light was so harsh and the air was so stagnant that it gave Solomon Goody headaches. It was like working inside a lightbulb. The place needed better air-conditioning. It needed a fresh coat of paint. It needed something a little grander than the sparse, cherrywood and leather furniture that did not go well with the moss-green carpet. All things considered, it was an ugly and inconvenient office, but freshmen took what they could get. So far, Congress was a giant step down from the ACLU in regards to comfort. Even his first job out of George Washington, in the Department of Health and Human Services, offered plusher accommodations. Maybe next term (he was already thinking about next term) he'd luck out in the lottery and move to one of the nicer offices in the upper floors of the Rayburn Building.

Since those frantic first weeks of January there had been little time for decorating. A few potted plants that weren't handling the lifeless air any better than he was. Two giant prints of exotic birds, purchased from a catalogue. A dried flower spray on the coffee table. Covering one wall, photographs of Rosa Parks, Bill Clinton, Thurgood

Marshall, Jackie Robinson, Muhammad Ali, Louis Armstrong, and Lyndon Johnson. A photograph of his wife and his four girls on the desk. Behind his chair, the oath of office in a cherrywood frame and a photograph of two black boys watching a younger white boy shaking hands with Martin Luther King.

Solomon Goody bent back to his desk, slid over another document, and was reading when he heard the subtle change in the air and sound waves and knew that someone was standing at the open door. After several seconds, during which he did not look up from the document (he did not know what he was reading), the man at the door at last cleared his throat and said, "Congressman Goody?"

Solomon held up his hand—a gesture for silence—and still pretended to read. He picked up his pen and circled four words at random, jotted a nonsense phrase in the margin. Then he stretched an immense, well-practiced grin. "Zach Beasley! Come on in," he said happily. He did not stand up.

"Bill Markey sends his regrets," the man said, now entering the office. He carried a briefcase the size of a small suitcase. He was also a tall, young black man in an expensive suit, but he walked as if a broom handle was shoved up his ass, and he wore an afro that was two inches long and twelve years out of style. There was not a single notion of threat in Zach Beasley's aspect (unless you were worried he might drop that big briefcase on your foot). He held out his hand as he crossed the office floor. Solomon—still not standing—accepted it with a firm, well-practiced shake. "A constituent group came through last minute and he couldn't get out of it. He was hoping you and I might be able to...well, you know, hack away some of the brush."

"Did he now? Some of that nasty ol brush, eh? Zach Beasley, you know my aide, Nathan Booker?" He motioned with his hand. The two men shook and settled into the leather chairs directly opposite Solomon's desk. Solomon pressed his slender fingers together and brought them to his lips. "So tell me, Zach, what sort of brush we boys gonna be *hacking at* today?"

Very serious now. "Well, among other things, Representative Markey wanted to impart his enthusiasm for your appropriations proposal—with a few modifications."

Solomon, still smiling broadly, shared a look with Nathan Booker.

"And he wanted to hear your thoughts on the labor bill."

Solomon Goody nodded gravely at this. The language inside the beltway was still English, but it shucked and jived to an altered cadence, and that alteration was about as subtle as a drunk on Sunday morning. "Few modifications" equaled "rip apart." "Hear your thoughts" meant "twist your arm."

He leaned into the high-backed leather chair.

So Bill Markey was sending his man Friday—this smiling robot in black face— to reason with the wild nigger from Coonsville, South Carolina. *You boys can work it out. Throw him a bone or two and let him gnaw on it a while.*

"Well Zach, it's very gratifying to know I have the congressman's enthusiasm for my appropriations proposal. *With* modifications. I didn't know he was even aware of it. Since he's not on Ways and Means."

"Oh yes, Representative Roberts briefed him."

"No doubt. And the modifications?"

While Zach Beasley snapped open his briefcase and flipped through it, Solomon Goody shared another look with Nathan Booker who was doing a fine job of making himself a quiet and graceful bookend. Booker was a poli-sci grad from Florida A&M who'd made it through school on a work-study program and a partial basketball scholarship. In Solomon Goody's opinion, one street-hungry, streetwise nigger like Nathan Booker on his staff was worth a dozen Yaley MBA drones like Zach Beasley. The drone was droning about the proposal, snapping shut the big alligator mouth of his briefcase, which had just gagged up a stolen document. *Four-hundred-and-sixty million over four years for road and other infrastructure development in your district?* Why did so many of these boys feel the need to have their skin bleached? How did they get so good at forgetting? Solomon Goody was eminently certain that Zach Beasley had never once in his life so much as held a basketball.

Beasley looked at him, his face wracked with milquetoast concern. "Roberts and Markey are both worried it won't make it through committee without revisions. It's clear the proposal is a bit too...aggressive."

"Too aggressive."

"It's the Republicans, of course. You know how stiff they're being."

"Of course." Solomon sighed and checked his watch. He felt suddenly tired. "And I'm sure the congressman understands the reason it's so aggressive?"

Beasley smiled sympathetically.

"Zach, do you know how much federal money has been spent in my district in the last sixteen years?"

"Not precisely, no."

"No? Well, Mr. Booker does." He reached into the middle desk drawer and withdrew a thick report. "Mr. Booker drafted this for me a few weeks back. I had planned on presenting it to Ways and Means myself. But now that your boss has taken such an interest in my cause..."

He tossed the document across the desk. Beasley picked it up and glanced through it. When he got to the last page, he frowned.

"A little pathetic, don't you agree, Zach? I believe that's one of the reasons why Mr. Calloway is no longer serving in Congress."

He let Beasley read some more. When he looked up again, Beasley said, "We were thinking the Republicans might go for something in the order of eighty million. Enough for the sewage program in Brighton County, and that new causeway to your island— providing, of course, you can secure matching funds from the local governments."

See if he'll go for eighty million... So that was how much bones were going for these days.

"You can't have a causeway without access roads."

"There's always state money."

Solomon slowly peeled off his glasses and looked at them. Then he scratched a spot above his left eyebrow that did not itch. "Zach, how much federal money do you figure was spent in Representative Markey's district in the last sixteen years?"

Beasley's eyes shifted briefly to Nathan Booker. "I don't suppose you have a document on that, too."

"I appreciate Bill Markey's concern for my business, Zach." Solomon spread his arms expansively. "I'm a freshman, I need all the help I can get. Of course, I want to look out for *him,* too. Right?" He replaced the glasses. "We're the minority party, and us minorities, why we just have to look out for each other. I'm sure that's why he sent *you,* Zach—when he couldn't come himself."

Zach Beasley said nothing. Nathan Booker stared straight ahead but was obviously on the verge of laughing out loud.

"So he wants my thoughts on the labor bill?"

"Yes. Well, he was hoping to have your support on that one. *And* to share your ideas on it, of course."

"Oh, of course." He mused, rubbed his chin, "The labor bill...Mr. Booker, that wouldn't be the time machine bill, would it?"

"Why, I believe it is, sir," Nathan Booker deadpanned.

Beasley looked back and forth between Solomon and his bookend. "I'm not sure what you mean."

"Explain it to him, Mr. Booker."

"The *time machine* bill. That's where we all hop inside a time machine and go back to the good old days thirty or forty years ago."

Beasley's eyes were turning to paste. "What specific provisions were you concerned about, Mr. Goody?"

Solomon glanced at the photograph of Ruth and the girls, and his mind split. He was half hearing and answering this Pillsbury Dough Boy, and he was half thinking of Ruth, who had become more business partner than wife in the last five or six years.

"Oh, only the really juicy provisions."

They had shared a passion for a while. And then her passion died while his flared off in another direction (or returned to its original direction). Now he had all this, and she had the girls.

"The provisions that do away with affirmative action programs."

She would stand by him, stay his running mate, despite the other women. She knew all about them.

"The provisions that limit rights to sue for discrimination."

If he wasn't sure about her knowledge, he had become so the night four years ago when he came back from a rally in San Francisco—she was already in bed, and when he got in next to her, she was sobbing gently. Quietly. Loud enough for him to hear. Not loud enough to protest. Not loud enough for him to ask what was wrong—but he knew.

You're flying back to the island?

Yes.

Are we coming with you?

It's business. I'll only be two days.

It was business, and it would only be two days. There was no girl waiting—this time. But of course, she wouldn't know that.

"The provisions that set us back thirty or forty years."

He had all this, and she had the girls. She would stand by him because she was the kind of woman who knew how to cry quietly. She even seemed happy in DC.

"The time machine provisions."

"That's a bit of an exaggeration, isn't it?" Beasley was saying to him.

"Is it?" that other half of him answered Beasley. "That's what Mr. Calloway would have said, too. But of course, he's no longer here." He meant for this to sound biting, but thinking of Ruth had softened his animosity toward Zach Beasley. Beasley was a product of the same, fucked up history that had produced those dim-faced, kowtow Negroes he had grown up with on Sweetpatch Island. The same history that produced Nathan Booker and Solomon Goody. The same history, it seemed, just spit out different kinds of creatures. All Beasley needed—all any of them needed—was the next good King. "Tell me, Zach—why does an old-time liberal like Bill Markey want this piece of shit to pass?" Nathan Booker was tapping his watch. Solomon nodded to him.

Beasley was sighing. He spent several seconds thinking. At last he said, "Accommodations."

"Favors."

"Whatever you want to call it."

"Let's call it a spade, then." Solomon grinned unhappily. "He wants the new stealth contract to go into his own backyard. He's doing Lansdale and Roberts a favor. Lansdale has a lock on defense."

"The committee heads call the shots, you know that. Look it's very difficult with the Republicans in majority."

Solomon raised both hands in a gesture of sympathy. "I understand, I understand. Got to bend over a little to get a little." He pointed to his watch and sighed. "Sorry Zach, but I have to give you the bum's rush. I have a plane to catch."

Nathan Booker stood and backed to the office door. Zach Beasley gathered papers into the jaws of his great briefcase.

"I hope we made some progress today," Solomon said.

Something that couldn't quite pass for a smile writhed on Zach Beasley's face. "I hope so."

"Hacked away some of that brush."

"Yes sir."

Beasley reached across the desk. Solomon Goody took his hand and held it for a moment. It was like holding a lump of cold pasta. "You'll be seeing Bill Markey later today?"

"Yes sir, I expect so. Is there anything you want me to pass along?"

"Yes." Solomon released the limp hand. "You can tell him that the nigger in the basement wants his four-hundred-and-sixty million dollars."

❖ ❖ ❖

Don't cry, don't cry, Ruthie honey. Don't cry in my bed. I can't sleep when you cry. Where are you going?

Nowhere. (Nowhere?) Not far. (Home.) Watch some television. I can't sleep.

Can I come with you?

(Don't cry in my bed!) I'll be back. I can't sleep.

He was a God in his world...

The showman extolled this to the impeccably dressed Manhattan crowd and to a robed Solomon Goody.

...but we brought him here in chains, and now he serves only for your amusement...

Black-and-white curtains lifted and there was the King—and Lord bless us he was every white man's nightmare: a nigger, sixty feet tall...bellowing rage and defiance, and worst of all, he wanted himself a pretty white girl. Could those chains possibly hold him?

...made of chrome steel, Denham promised...

He was roaring. He was magnificent. He was the Eighth Wonder of the World, with a mug straight off an old Jim Crow poster: slope head...heavy brow...fat, stupid lips... and huge white teeth and bright, seashell eyes that glowed from that negroid face.

And then they shot him dead.

Lansdale wanted his time machine bill to pass, and Roberts wanted his defense contract, and they were happy to pay the radical African (by way of Sweetpatch Island, South Carolina) to jump on board and keep the liberal press bloodhounds off their snowy white asses. Get those dogs sniffing down the wrong trail while King Solomon stood at the fork with his eighty million dollars and explained why the approach was sensible, why the moderation was healthy, why the dialogue was so encouraging. "By signing this bill, we are declaring that African Americans stand on equal ground with whites; that exceptions should not be made..."

Accommodations and Favors—that was what ran the machine.

The life span of a King was a short one. King Kongs or Doctor Kings or Joker Kings. Or King Solomons. They climbed while the others (they were all such patient men, the others) while the others waited because sooner or later the King climbed too high and made too tempting a target.

And they had planes.

He was a God in his world. The tribes prayed to him, honored him, sacrificed to him, feared him, loved him. Until the white men came in their ship and hauled him away in their chains of chrome steel. To an island, far from his home.

...for your amusement...

Chains couldn't hold him. He rampaged—of course he did. What did they expect? What would any of those fine tuxedoed gentlemen do if it were them, instead?

Solomon, honey, are you coming to bed?

(Who's bed?) Did she at last stop crying? He couldn't sleep when she cried, and the movie was almost over now. The planes had taken flight. The rifles had been loaded. The beast was raging.

He made only two mistakes. He climbed too high on that island. And he went for the girl.

The flying machines got him.

No, it wasn't the planes…

❖　　❖　　❖

3:30 p.m.

The white woman coming out of Royal Goody's office was very pretty and very pregnant. And she had obviously been crying. Mrs. Poole, the office secretary, seemed distressed when the woman passed.

"All right if I go in, now?" Solomon asked.

Mrs. Poole smiled at him and nodded. Solomon found his grouse-faced brother on the phone. Royal raised a hand—a gesture for silence—and continued speaking while Solomon leaned on the door and waited and grinned at being put off. *Royal Goody, Vice Principal,* the plaque on the door read. The vice principal was in a foul mood, that much was obvious.

The air was alive with the cluttered and nostalgic redolence of school. Paste, construction paper, blackboard chalk, industrial cleaner, science projects. And bruised knuckles and bloody lips and spoiled melons—the bittersweet smells of those first schoolyard victories. And slithering beneath the surface—constant—the silent rot of swamp and marsh. The smells evoked an amazing tangle of contradictory emotions and stirred the lousy in-flight meal that laid like swamp mud in his gut. He supposed he might have breathed the air of a hundred schools throughout South Carolina in the past year. Perhaps the inner-city schools were tainted by cheap perfumes and diesel exhaust. And the backwoods schools were flavored by peach blossom and cow manure. Only the Sweetpatch Island schools had this smell of spoiled meat.

When Royal was done speaking, he gestured at the chair in front of the desk. The vinyl was warm when Solomon sat in it, and he thought of the hundreds of delinquent rear ends that must have warmed this seat before the wrath of Vice Principal Royal A. Goody. Then he remembered the pretty white woman who left crying.

"So, tell me, little bro—what did you do to that pretty thing back there? You break the news that you're married?" He flicked his head toward the doorway.

It took a moment for Royal to understand what he meant. When he did, his gloomy face screwed with disdain. "That's more your department, isn't it? You know, I still have a good reputation around here." He got up from the desk to close the door. "I'd hate to think I'm gonna loose it because of my brother the congressman whose dick is too big to keep in his pants."

Solomon laughed, but the guilt switch had been tripped. "So that ain't your cookie in the oven?"

"No, that ain't my cookie, you asshole," Royal said, sitting down again. "If you really want to know, that particular cookie belongs to an old friend of yours."

Solomon waited.

"You remember Boo Taylor?"

"Oh," Solomon said. He looked at the door. "Oh, man." He now understood the glum demeanor.

"So where's the entourage?"

Solomon was still looking at the door. "What?—oh, no man, I'm solo this trip."

"Business or pleasure?"

"Hey, it's always a pleasure seeing my baby brother." He managed a smile, and Royal scowled. "Business," he said. "Just a quick overnighter. Meeting on the island later today. Then a luncheon with the Meatpacker's Local in Corrington tomorrow—I hear they're serving a vegetarian plate. You want me to save you a seat?"

At last, a smile. "I suppose you've already made arrangements—you know, you can always stay with us, Sol. If Martha knew you were coming, she'd insist on it."

"Martha likes to keep an eye on me."

"She and Ruthie talk."

"I think Ruthie pays her. As a matter of fact, I'm already booked into the Hampton—and don't worry, my man, because your tax dollars are paying for it." Solomon grinned; Royal was shaking his head. "Maybe next month, when I deliver my exceptionally brilliant commencement address for your sorry-ass school."

"Bring Ruthie and the girls."

"I'm sure Ruthie will insist on it. By the way, how's the rev?"

"Rev's fine. He asks about you."

"And you don't tell him the *truth,* do you?"

"I tell him to read the papers." Royal leaned back in the chair and clasped his hands behind his head. "You haven't seen him in a while have you? You should think about getting over to see him."

Solomon shrugged. "I should." Little brother was having a good old time tripping that guilt switch.

"I suppose you can't make it over for dinner tonight."

"I have a date." Royal began to scowl again; Solomon waved his hand dismissively. "My *meeting*—with the famous Sing Satterfield, and I don't know how late that's supposed to go. If she serves dinner, I'll bring Martha and the kids a doggy bag."

"I didn't know you knew Sing Satterfield."

"I never met the old girl. Have you?"

"No. Nobody I know has, either, even though she owns half the damn island. So, I take it she's a sweet old Dixiecrat?"

"A sweet old Dixiecrat with a very generous purse. I've been summoned."

Royal pursed his lips. The disgusted expression returned to his face. "Summoned for what?"

Keep flicking that switch, bro. "The payoff," Solomon answered testily. "Some string needs pulling, I don't know. Shit, you know those old widows, Royal—maybe she just wants the congressman's big dick."

A silence hung in the redolence of paste and construction paper and blackboard chalk. And swamp rot. The in-flight meal was making itself known again.

"You *are* gonna ruin my reputation, aren't you," Royal said, but he was smiling.

"Fuck your reputation. You're not running for anything."

"I may surprise you some day."

Solomon snorted a chuckle. He removed his glasses and wiped his eyes. "Why don't you just stick to high school babysitter. At least until I need your ass when I run for senate." He noticed the series of photographs lined across the desk. He replaced his glasses and picked up the picture of Martha. Was she the kind who cried quietly in bed at night? No, not that one. She had those don't-fuck-with-me eyes that only certain black women possessed. Martha was the kind who'd take a rolling pin to Royal's head if he ever gave her cause. Royal was not the kind to give her cause. Royal kept it together. Glue-Boy. Always. *I may surprise you some day*. Not like that, though, not his brother the Glue-Boy—Jesus, not like that. Not because of the ladies.

"How's the new book coming?" Solomon asked.

"Slow. End of the school year gets busy. And," he added vaguely, "I've had some other distractions."

Solomon thought of the pregnant girl who had been sitting in the same chair. Pretty thing. And Boo Taylor was the father...The last time he had seen Boo Taylor had been Royal's junior year in high school. Boo Taylor, who was maybe just a sophomore then, was throwing a two-hit shutout for the conference championship. Boo Taylor, with that stubby, three-fingered hand of his.

Solomon placed the frame back on the desk. He checked his watch. "Damn, boy. I have to go."

❖   ❖   ❖

"Send the airplanes after him," they said.

"I had a dream," he answered.

But sleep would no longer come because she was crying, and the dream was fading, and the black-and-white flicker was taking its place. Accommodations and Favors. A spade is no longer a spade, and the flying machines were on their way.

Thirty years without a King.

The planes. They were looking for the next King. The planes and their guns.

"It wasn't the planes..." Denham told the police officer—the press was listening closely. What would the King have said to him: behold Prince Solomon? (His dick was too big for his pants—Glue-Boy said so.) But the King had held his hand thirty-five years ago, and the brilliance had filled the room with the strike of lightening, and the kingdom was spread beneath him like the lights of Manhattan from atop the Empire State Building. The chains were broken, and for thirty-five years he had climbed so high.

But the girl in his hand was crying.

Solomon, honey, are you coming to bed?

No. (Whose bed?) Not this trip.

"...it was beauty killed the beast."

❖   ❖   ❖

4:35 p.m.

Sing Satterfield's estate dominated the southeast point of Sweetpatch Island where Southern Bluff Beach and Sadfellers Beach rounded together and the Atlantic and Yamawichee blended into an indistinguishable body. The roads leading to the estate were lush with live oaks and impeccably landscaped lawns that complemented the nearly hidden cedar homes and tiny coves of expensive gift shops. The estate proper was packaged within a tall fence of rough-grain cedar, stained creamy beige and capped by white lattice panels. Palmettos stood sentry along the fence at even, ten-foot intervals along with billows of azaleas that had already lost their spring color and must have been a glorious explosion of corals and fuscias and lavenders only a month earlier. House and gardens poked over the fence, offering a teasing glimpse of a grandeur Solomon Goody found impossible to reconcile with the South Patch poverty of his youth. A ramshackle sprawl of Negro shanties once laid claim to this property. His own Aunt Nattie lived in a three-room hut right on the point. Her privy never worked. When he and Royal visited, they either ran into the ocean to do their business or knocked on Miss Pansy's door three houses down.

He swung the rented Buick Park Avenue into the red-and-gray cobble driveway. A sign planted at the corner showed the silhouette of an alligator and the playful announcement that *TRESSPASSERS WILL BE EATEN*. The outer gate, festooned with bougainvillea, had been left open for him. He drove in. The drive circled around a landscaped island and was bordered by palmettos and white-blossomed dogwoods and violet-blossomed rhododendrons. The house beyond sprawled in a crescent that mimicked the bend of the island. It was all glass blocks and tiled roof and creamy stucco. As he pulled the car around the circle, he saw the edge of a many-tiered deck that wrapped around the back of the house. An old black Mercedes was the only other car in the drive. It looked like a hearse.

He parked behind the Mercedes and stepped out of the air-conditioned car to a hot land-breeze and the fuzzy crash of waves. The splendid house and plantings still seemed unreal to him. This could not be South Patch. This could not be the place were raggedy old clothes fluttered on clotheslines. Where gray-faced men slouched in the shade with brown bags molded in the shape of wine bottles. Where chickens and stray dogs and naked toddlers prowled freely from house to house. Perhaps a dozen families had once been crammed into this place where now only one rich old widow lived.

He checked his watch and saw he was seven minutes late to meet the old widow herself. The old widow who had either directly or through her many companies provided the *Goody for U.S. Congress* committee with sums that totaled over six hundred thousand dollars. Accommodations and Favors. *Time for the payoff,* he had told Glue-Boy Royal. *Strings needed pulling.* He worried what kind of strings they might be. Puppet strings, perhaps?

Mrs. Satterfield would like very much to arrange an intimate conference...

To reach the front door he had to cross a small Japanese-style bridge that spanned a white-pebble beach and a Koi pond. Splotched fish, whose scales seemed to be rotting off their backs, kissed at sickly green patches. He climbed the three short steps of the front stoop. Two man-sized evergreens, sculpted like poodles, bracketed the door. He rang the doorbell. Somewhere inside, an animal went crazy. Frenetic barking, first distant, grew louder and closer, reminding him of a boulder running out of control down a hill, until something big thunked heavily against the door. Whatever it was, it was clawing and chewing its way through the wood to get to him. Without being conscious of it, Solomon took a step back. He looked around the well-tailored grounds to see if another dog might be charging from the flanks.

The doorknob rattled, and the barking stopped immediately. An elderly black gentleman in a blue sport coat and a red tie appeared at the door. Cool air rushed out from behind him. "Congressman Goody?" the man asked with an affable smile.

"Yes." Solomon tried to see through the man's legs for the dog.

"Very good. Please come in, won't you?"

He stepped in hesitantly, looked around. He was standing in a marble-tiled foyer and looking at himself and the elderly black gentleman in a pewter-framed mirror. A rounded, white-pine stairway circled off toward a second floor. Either side of the foyer opened to luminous, beige-and-white furnished rooms. Except for a faint sour-breath aroma, there was no sign of a dog.

The elderly black gentleman introduced himself as Patterson and led him through a series of bright corridors to a glassed-in patio. Patterson informed him that Mrs. Satterfield would be with him shortly. He offered a drink—which Solomon declined—nodded stiffly, and then whisked silently away. The afternoon was becoming a gothic romance. *The lady will see you shortly, sir. Please help yourself to a brandy and feel free to browse the library. You'll find several rare and interesting selections, I'm sure...* Only the cheeriness of the furnishings and the bright, sunlit exposure saved the moment from parody.

Solomon wandered through the room and eventually settled into an overstuffed chair that offered a view over the deck he had seen earlier. The deck proceeded down the slope of the bluffs, terminating in a long gazebo on the beach. White wicker chairs and tables occupied various points of the descent. Beyond was the uninterrupted southern scape of granite-blue water. Whitecaps dazzled in the sun. To the east, the olive-drab splotch of mainland and various vagrant islets. To the west, the water stretched endlessly.

Not endlessly. Another continent lay out beyond the line of sight. The home of kings. Stolen from their jungle temples and palaces, stolen from their tribes, bound in chains, and brought to this place. Brought to this machine.

Accommodations. Favors.

He waited for the famous, never-seen Sing Satterfield who owned half of Sweetpatch Island, wondering what she looked like, wondering if he had been bought for eighty million dollars or a mere six hundred thousand.

From somewhere above came the scratch of a dog's toenails on hardwood floor. Clouds passed over the sun briefly, and the ocean went dark. The sun reappeared. It was suddenly too hot in this glassed cage over the sea. The toenails became the click of a woman's shoes. Not an old woman, by the buoyant pace. He thought of Ruthie and wondered if it might have been better to bring her on this trip after all. He thought of the pretty girl who was crying because she was carrying Boo Taylor's child.

The click step of the not-old woman was coming down the round, white-pine staircase.

Boo Taylor had ripped that burlap hood off his own father's head one night, somewhere less than a mile from this spot. Had used the same hand that pitched a two-hit shutout a few years later, a few fingers fewer. It had occurred to Solomon Goody often in the years since the Cavalry Baptist Church was arsoned by those pigs that maybe Boo Taylor had saved his life that night. He had never thanked him. He had never liked the idea of being indebted to that strange white boy.

The steps were in the hallway now. The sour dog's-breath smell preceded them.

He had never liked the idea of being indebted to anyone. Sooner or later, accommodations were requested. Favors were collected.

He looked out upon the place where the Yamawichee and the Atlantic met and became one. Pelicans appeared, riding the air on their crooked wings like old-time biplanes. The sun on the water hurt his eyes. He heard the subtle change in the air and sound waves and knew that someone was now standing at the open door. After several seconds, during which he did not look away from sea (he did not know what he was looking at), the not-old woman at the door chuckled and called for her lover—called him by name.

three

Henri! Où allez,-vous?

A bolt of sunlight pierced the cabin window, moved steadily across the dark places inside on the steady path of the sun, disturbed only by the steady rocking of the hull, moved through stale air, moved through dust, moved until the bolt stabbed Henry Ray Dutton's eyelids. Behind the eyelids, his dream suddenly blossomed red. He muttered, still asleep, still dreaming, and swatted at the beam. The red wouldn't go away.

Henri! Me suivre.

The red was the glow of the sun.

The red is his dream on fire...

He is coming awake in an alley, deep in the night, coming to and finding blood dripping from a gash above his eye. The floor of the alley is a mossy brick, wet from a recent rain. The red comes from a neon light, the only light in the alley. The red glints in the puddles like rubies. Garbage cans overflow around him, and the harsh red light is burning his eyes, and he wants to throw up. He can't remember how his eye got cut, can barely remember Kelso and Dinky Pete bugging out on him after that slant with the birthmark on her chin wrapped a thigh around his lap. Her thigh was like a snake. "You got long cock." The birthmark was shaped like a mushroom. He didn't like looking at it. Easier to look at that boa constrictor squeezing his lap. "My pussy all wet. You buy me drink?" He can't remember what happened after that; Dinky Pete and Kelso were gone. It was Kelso's Gunnie who told them about the place; said you could watch some slant whore go down on an actual donkey; the Gunnie had seen it himself, so he said. The Con Tho Chân Bar—something about a rabbit—and the place is a fucking armpit. Back deep in the east crags, lost in a neon fog, and the MPs steer clear of it. Hot as a fucking oven and the drinks suck and the music is some lousy, brassy European crap with a lot of horns. No donkey either, at least that he can remember. The slant with the mushroom birthmark must have slipped something in his watered-down mash, and then the lights go out, and then his eye gets cut and somebody dumps him in the alley with all these fish bones and piss and cat shit. He feels his pockets. In his red dream, he feels his pockets and his wallet is gone. In his red dream, his hands are still patting his shirt, still looking for the wallet that smelly whore lifted from him when the spook first speaks to him. Big fucking jig in a black suit, silver afro. The spook is filling up the alley beneath a red swirl of neon that spells something over his head in neon gook gibberish. The big spook smiles at him, and he has a gold tooth.

"Henri. What are you doing down there?"

Speaks with a slippery French accent. Smiling like he has some secret joke.

In his red dream, Henry Ray pulls his knees under his waist and wipes at the blood above his eye, tells the spook to fuck off, but there's something else in the red shadow; something scuttling like a dog-sized crab at the spook's feet, and whatever it is makes the need to puke even worse. The spook keeps smiling at him—like maybe he's some fag looking to suck cock, though he doesn't seem at all like a fag. The spook's shirt is bright white—now glowing bright red—and a large tiepin flashes from it. A well-dressed fag slumming the back streets of Saigon and looking to suck some fat GI cock while that crab-thing picks at the fish bones at his feet. So he tells the jig to fuck off again, but the jig doesn't move. Doesn't stop smiling. The big jig just stands there burning under that red neon like a silver-headed statue caught on fire. "Henri, nous avons quelque chose montrer." The voice is smooth as silk. "Quelque chose geler le sang dans des vos veinses." He's seen the jig before, hasn't he? Maybe in one of the food stands on Rue St. Claire, maybe not in Nam at all, but maybe back in the world, maybe even back on that smelly shit hole of an island. The crab thing has blonde hair, and it lifts its red eyes up to look at them. "Henri, such manners! You must follow me now. I have something important to show you."

He snorted awake, muttering at the dream as sunlight pounded his eyes. He looked around, saw where he was and grumbled into his beard. His head was throbbing from the heat. The cabin was hot, and the bolt of sunlight spearing his eyes was making it hotter. He stood and pushed open the hatch. More sunlight poured over him. Grunting, he pulled himself up to the deck and the smell of marsh. The boat was anchored in the Yamawichee, two hundred yards off shore near Trapper Hammock. A number of other craft, mostly tourist, peppered the flat water, lines cast and bottom fishing. You could tell they were tourists by the flaming bright colors they always wore, by the sunglasses and the fat bellies. Tourists were always fat and they wore colors so bright they made you sick. Henry Ray walked to the starboard bow, unzipped his fly, and urinated over the side. The arch flashed gold sunlight and plummeted into the soupy green water, disappearing down where all those fishing lines went. Off the bow, a tourist couple watched him from the deck of a thirty foot Bayliner. The woman had her hands on her hips, scowling. The man just looked embarrassed. "Fuck's your problem?" he growled at them. The man ducked his head and took the woman by the arm, trying to pull her away. The man was fat and wore a yellow shirt and blue pants and bright white socks and sneakers. The woman was fat with pasty legs under bright red shorts. She wore oversized sunglasses that made her face look like a bug. Henry Ray waggled his dick at her and grinned.

The big spook looks at what he's holding in his hand and keeps smiling. "Henri. C'est impressionante, ton épée."

How do you know my name?

The big coon with the gold tooth never moves when Henry Ray takes out the long blade in that red-glowing alleyway. Never flinches. He just keeps smiling. "Follow me, Henri. I have something you will want to see. Une beauté terrible."

The pasty white, fat tourist woman opened her mouth, showing disgust and finally allowed herself to get hauled behind the mast by her fat tourist husband.

"Put that thing away, and follow me."

He tucked his dick back into his pants and zipped up.

The knife isn't going to bother the jig in the least. The jig is waiting for him. The jig isn't scared at all. The jig wants him to follow, has something to show him. So he gets up from the wet, mossy brick and follows the spook into the deep red mist of the alley, steps carefully around the crab thing with blonde hair crouched at the man's feet. "How the fuck you know my name?"

"I know many things, Henri. I have many things to show you. You are a man of unique tastes, I can see this is so."

The man is tall. The man looms six inches over him as they walk, side by side, deep into these pungent back trenches of East Saigon. The man puts his arm around Henry Ray's shoulder, and Henry Ray surprises himself by letting the man do it. Whatever the girl with the mushroom birthmark had given him must not have worn off yet because the man's hand is on him, and the man is a coon, and he smells like a girl, and his arm is around his shoulder like they were grand fucking buddies, and doesn't he know this jig from somewhere? "There is someone special I want you to meet. She will like you very much, I am certain." The hand squeezes his shoulder. The eyes wink. The gold tooth winks.

The inboard on the Bayliner revved into life. The man and his bug-eyed wife were beating a retreat. The name *Star Brite* was painted in swirling black letters above the inboard. *Havre de Grace, Maryland.* Fucking tourists. Fucking tourists thought they owned the place anymore. Henry Ray went to pull up the anchor. He thought he might follow the *Star Brite* for a while, see where she went.

Fucking tourists *did* own the place.

"I got no money, mister. Slant bitch micked me."

He remembers Dinky Pete telling him about the time his patrol came across the trunk of a woman's body. No head, no arms. A white girl in the jungle, torn apart and just this much of her left. Two days later, same patrol but a good twenty clicks south, they find a missing arm. Three weeks after that, they find her head—what they think is her head; after more than three weeks it's tough to tell. Same platoon coming across parts of the same woman, weeks and miles apart. "What are the odds of that?" he asks Dinky Pete.

Henry Ray cranked the engine. The Bayliner was bearing south at a slow crawl. After another crank the twins caught, sputtering diesel fumes. A few tourists on the other boats were watching him now, seeing what was making that sloppy noise. He spun the wheel about and pointed it into the Bayliner's wake.

He was twelve years old when his father took him to the graveyard. It was a hot and flat and dry place. He expected trees. And rain. On television, it always rained at graveyards. This was a dry, flat place with gray slabs of stone. The grass was brown. His mother had been dead for two weeks, had been buried for nine days. It was his first time ever to a graveyard. "You wanna see her so much? There she is; so you can just quit your blubberin now, can't you?" He expected a marker for her, but there was nothing. Just some upturned dirt. That's how he knew where to look. His father's hand bit into his shoulder where he was holding him and pointing him in the direction of the brown grass disturbed by fresh dirt. His shoulder hurt. He knew he was supposed to stand there and watch, so he did.

It wasn't like he missed her. It wasn't that. She was skinny and weak. She wasn't even pretty. He didn't like her. It was mostly that whenever she was around; *she* was the one his father...

Now he was oldest.

He had a black eye where his father punched him when he dropped a jar of nails and it broke and the nails and broken glass went everywhere.

The fingers left his shoulders, but his shoulders still hurt. He knew his father was walking back to the truck where he could get out of the sun and where he'd left the bottle. He knew he was supposed to stand here and look at the upturned earth. He stood that way for a long time. Not far off, he could hear little nigger girls laughing and playing jump rope.

Queenie, queenie had two daughters
Hated one and like the other
One was milk and silk and spice,
The other not so very nice.
One got married, one got sad,
One got killed, and one got glad.

He suddenly felt jealous of those little nigger girls. They were playing together. They were singing and having fun. He wanted to be with them, playing with their jump rope and singing. He looked around. His father was back in the truck, leaned into the shade behind the wheel—not looking and probably asleep, and so he stole away from the graveside and followed the direction of the little girls. They were across the road, in the shade of an old shack that might once have been a run-in shed for horses. Two girls were holding the rope, looping it high, while the third jumped it in the middle. Three little nigger girls in little dresses, pigtails, skin so dark it was black. He stood on the opposite side of the road and watched them, jealous of them, hating them, wanting to be with them.

He watched them for a very long time.

❖ ❖ ❖

"Money?" The big spook laughs, flashing all those big white teeth and the one gold one. "Henri, we have no use for your money. There are other things than money, are there not?" He lets the big spook lead him down dark passageways, someplace deep into ancient times, penetrating the black depths of an endless maze. He can't remember how long they travel, but it seems like hours. The brick beneath his feet becomes rock, becomes dirt. The buildings become more decrepit with age and neglect. Clotheslines crisscross over his head, flapping dead, empty scarecrows. Cats scurry away at their approach. A bit of moon peers over the rooftops to glint on wet puddles.

"Where the fuck are we?" he asks the big jig.

"Where? As the poet might say, 'we are in Rat's Alley.'"

"Poet? What poet?"

This makes the big jig bark a hearty laugh. The gold sparkles. "You are not familiar with the works of T. S. Eliot? Brilliantly twisted mind, Henri. The Waste Land? Délicieux!" He laughs again. "But to answer your question, my new friend, we are now precisely where we are, and we are on our way to see someone. She believes you may be of value someday. You see, she is always in search of men of talent. Always recruiting."

"She wants to see me?"

"Of course!"

"Who is she?"

"Who?" The jig pats his shoulder. "Patience, Henri. We will be with her soon enough."

On and on they walk until they turn to pass beneath a low arch and into an even narrower sliver of a passageway behind a squat, three-story tenement. Almost completely dark back here. Rows of black windows. A single lightbulb over a single door at a single concrete step. A sign is taped to the door in black tape.

Le Trou de Lapin

"We have reached the rabbit's hole, Henri. Inside."

He (stood on the road, wanting to cross but not able to) *doesn't want to go in, but the jig's powerful arm* (the girl jumping stopped, looked at him, asked him if he wanted to play) *urges him forward, makes him go forward, and then* (he picked up a rock) *knows that as long as he has the knife he'll be okay. He walks to the door* (crossed the road) *and opens it. Somewhere inside, somewhere deep behind a series of hallways, a blue light is glowing. "Inside, Henri. She is inside. She is waiting for you."*

He goes in. He touches the blade in his belt and shivers, and he goes in. He feels the way with his hands, touches the walls, finds the twists and turns as the blue grows brighter. The place smells like spice and ashes. The walls are made of stone, and they are slick with cold sweat. Water drips from the low ceiling. The big spook, he realizes, has not followed him. He is alone. He is alone with the blue light.

"Venez être avec nous!"

"Meurtrier!"

He quickens his pace. There is a voice in the blue light ahead. Her voice, he realizes. She is waiting for him. She is someone special.

"Venez à moi, Henri!"

He finds her, painted blue in a painted blue stone cell. Nothing in the room except her and a wooden slab bed and a blue light hanging from the low, dripping wet ceiling. She wears a black mask. Her hair is spread out around her in a bright red flame with blue highlights. A black strip of leather around her neck. A black strip of leather at her ankles and her wrists, strapping her to the wooden slab bed. Her legs are pulled wide. She may have been there for days, strapped down like that and waiting for him. She is sobbing. A frightened rabbit.

This is the rabbit hole.

He hangs in the doorway to the little room, watching the sobbing girl with the red hair that is painted blue. Blue light glistens on the damp, shadowy hair between her legs. The leather crackles where it cinches her flesh. He can smell her—she smells like a frightened animal. Then he steps forward, and as soon as he enters the dim little room, the walls come alive around him, bodies leaking out of the stone: little girls in dresses, little girls with pigtails, then something else, more bodies—not little girls at all, but women in masks—skeletal old bodies, round fat bodies, breasts sagging, boney hips, gelatinous mounds of flesh, thick swathes of pubic hair, all pained blue. Hungry fingers reach for him, tug on his clothes and draw him deeper into the room, deeper toward the wooden slab bed. He lets himself be led until something bites into his shoulder. He cries out. He can now see the eyes inside the masks—blue eyes, fierce. Teeth flash, sharp as a tiger's. The teeth rip into his shoulder again. Then he remembers and pulls the long, stiff blade from his pants as he is carried closer to the wooden bed and as the teeth tear at his shoulder. He feels a leathery explosion engulf him—wings, he realizes, black wings painted blue. He sticks out the blade. The room is a chaos of wings and masked women and little girls and teeth and blue light. Somewhere behind him, the great jig with the gold tooth is laughing. Somewhere in front of him, the girl on the bed is sobbing. He is dragged another step forward, thrusting the blade as the mass of black wings and blue flesh rise up to smother him.

A Coast Guard patrol boat drifted into view from the Sugar Dam inlet. Henry Ray caught the movement from the corner of his eye and dropped the twins back. The boat slowed. The hull settled in the water as the waves around him flattened. A uniformed man appeared on the deck of the patrol boat. He waved at Henry Ray. Henry Ray jabbed his middle finger at the man in return. Ahead, the *Star Brite* was storming south and growing small.

❧   ❧   ❧

He was twelve years old when he found his father passed out across the bench seat of his pickup in the cemetery parking lot. He knew better than to try to wake his father up when he'd been drinking. So he sat on the running board and tried not to make any noise. The sun was finally starting to go down, and the heat wasn't as bad. He sat and waited for his father to wake up. Somewhere off in the distance was the sound of a child sobbing. While he sat and waited, he saw movement on the other side of the parking lot. A tall man was standing there, looking at him. It was a big spook. A big spook who knew better than to say something, here in a parking lot at a graveyard on Sweetpatch Island. This was north of the Soap Water, and the big spook knew well enough to stay where he was. He watched the spook until the sun went down and his father finally came awake.

❧   ❧   ❧

He snorts awake. He is lying in an alley, half-in and half-out a doorway. The sun is up. Around him, garbage spills over the rims of metal trashcans, and the morning sun glints gold hues in puddles on the brick floor. Blood is running into his eyes. His hands are covered in blood. His clothes are torn apart and covered in blood. He brings his legs around and looks at the blood in his hands. Dinky Pete had brought him to this place. Dinky Pete and Kelso. Someplace called rabbit something. He remembers a python leg worming into his lap. Remembers blue wings. Remembers the torso of a woman with pieces missing. Remembers little hands clawing over him, stealing his wallet. Remembers his knife. Remembers watered-down whiskey and running his fingers through a rope of intestines, pulling these out of a warm body like they were sausage links. He remembers the sign on a door beneath a single lightbulb. "Ke giet ngu'oi!" He is preparing to stand when he looks down and finds his wallet splayed open on the wet brick. The money is gone, but his military ID and everything else is still there.

Ke giet ngu'oi!

His shoulder hurts. He is covered in blood, and his shoulder hurts. He remembers something bit him there.

"Henri!"

He looks up at the voice that called his name and finds a tall jig in a black suit is standing in the alley. At his feet, a small blonde haired girl crouches and whimpers. She looks like a crab scuttling through the trash. This part of town is no place for a little white girl.

How the hell does that spook know his name?

Henry Ray cranes his neck to look at his throbbing shoulder, remembering teeth digging into his flesh. The tattoo of a black skull screams back at him. He puts his hand on his arm, pulling the skin of his shoulder as he tries to get a better look and as the little blonde girl sobs. His fingers slop blood across the skull. A fucking tattoo? How drunk had he been?

"Bienvenue, Henri," the spook calls to him. He smiles and glints gold between his lips. He lifts his hand, showing a mirror of the skull in his palm. The spook seems like the happiest man in the world. "I think you are one of us, now."

four

May 14

"Say, you're a darky fella."

The old man's face folded wrinkle upon wrinkle, studying Royal Goody through heavy, black-framed glasses as if he were considering a jigsaw puzzle or a strange species of bug.

"That's right," Royal answered.

This answer seemed to confound the man even more. "Didn't say you was gonna be a darky fella."

Royal was seated sideways in a plastic chair. His elbow rested casually on a table top that was cluttered with the items he had brought with him: a folio, three spiral notebooks, several pencils, a Styrofoam cup of coffee, an apple, and a portable tape recorder. The old man was in a wheelchair, and he was holding a rolled-up copy of *Blood on the Beach*.

"Didn't you see my picture?"

"What's *that?*"

A flesh-toned hearing aid plugged the old man's right ear. "Did—you—see— my—*picture?*" Royal repeated. He tapped the book in the man's hands.

The old man jerked his head with surprise when he saw the book. Royal had sent a copy to help convince the deputy administrator of his credibility. Thick, fleshy hands unrolled the slim book. The hands were a translucent, bluish-white in the places where they weren't mottled with liver spots.

"On the back," Royal enunciated clearly.

The hands worked slowly, methodically. The book was turned over. Then it was brought up close to the face. The ancient nose scrunched, circled over the photograph, as if the man were sniffing it. A flesh-toned Band-Aid secured a hinge in the glasses. Watery, red sores cut deeply into either side of the man's nose where the glasses were perched. He was slouched so deeply in his wheelchair that his scrawny shoulders were almost higher than his head.

"Sure I saw the picture," the man said. He spoke in quick, loud bursts. "Thought it got smudged, maybe."

"No."

"What's *that?*"

"*No.* It's not *smudged.*" Despite the noise they were making, the other residents milled quietly about the recreation room without paying them attention.

The man sniffed the photograph again. The eyebrows and the spray of hair that circled the man's ears were the finest, purest white. He was dressed in a pale yellow polyester shirt and pale lavender slacks. So pale he was nearly invisible. He looked up at Royal with magnified, rheumy eyes, and now the expression of puzzlement was replaced by a painful scowl—as if the man had just bitten into a wedge of lemon.

"Didn't know you was a darky fella."

"Well, I am," Royal said. "Is that going to be a problem?"

The book came back to the man's lap. "Shit, no!" he said. The wrinkles fell. It was a curtain dropping loose with the tug of a chord. Teeth that were gray and brown pearls appeared along an impish grin. "Hell, I rooted for OJ."

Royal laughed, and the old man followed suit with a laugh that sounded like the husk being pulled from an ear of corn.

The old man's name was Judson Meriwether Tull. He was ninety-one years old. According to Sandra Washburn, Deputy Administrator of the Smith-Todd Nursing Home in Cordele, Georgia, Mr. Tull was a retired pharmacist, shopkeeper, and school teacher. He had been a resident of the home for eight years. He had previously lived in Bolinbroke, a small town Royal was eventually able to locate on the map. His wife had died fifteen years earlier. They had no children. On the registration form Mr. Tull had completed when he entered Smith-Todd, in the box labeled "Next of Kin," he had scrawled a series of names of several deceased siblings, including: *Mishelle Satterfield—Sister*. The same name as the woman he suspected might be Boo Taylor's maternal grandmother, the woman who died on the ferry to Stono Point and who once loved a man named Ben Shallcross.

"Do you mind if I record our conversation?" Royal asked. He gestured toward the tape recorder.

The old man made his sour-face expression again. He looked at the machine. "Oh, hell no. You go right ahead. You bring that apple for me?"

"I don't know—can you eat one?" Royal had forgotten about the apple. It was supposed to be his lunch.

Judson Tull looked furtively around the room. The soiled pearls returned. "Can if you cut it up for me," he said happily.

Royal slipped a pocket knife from his trousers and went to work peeling the apple and cutting it into small squares. He handed the first piece to Mr. Tull who immediately stuck it in his mouth and sucked on it. Royal pressed the record button, positioning the microphone between himself and the old man, and continued cutting.

He slid him another chunk of apple, and Mr. Tull sucked it down like a trained seal who had just performed a trick. Royal Goody had been inside a number of nursing homes since taking up his avocation as casual historian and folklorist. The Smith-Todd home was not the best of them, but it was better than most. It was a five-story brick building set too close to noisy Highway 280 but on otherwise pleasant wooded surroundings. The rec room suffered from a generic shabbiness and dreariness—the walls were barren, the furnishings beaten and worn, corridors too dim, the air too rank with antiseptic and dead skin. At least the place was clean. And the white-frocked staff, who wore the same vapid, utterly bored expression as their charges, had so far been polite and pleasant when Royal had spoken with them. There was very little sound. The cinder-block walls and drop-tiled ceiling and carpeted floor absorbed noise the way Judson Tull sucked down bits of apple. It was the great tragedy of such places, Royal had found—that lack of sound. There were remarkable tales and operas and great epic verses that might forever be lost in here, treasures that should be spoken out loud and put to song and performed day and night throughout the lighted, young world. But these old voices...they were buried beneath so much block wall and drop-tiled ceiling and carpet. And then, buried beneath so much gray, disregarded flesh. Muted. Silenced. A way station to the real burial.

Once upon a time, Royal Goody had decided to track his roots. Perhaps, as Alex Haley had, to discover his own Mandingo warrior ascendant swinging on a vine through the jungles of Gambia. He had dreamed he might find himself a distant son of Absalom Jones or Frederick Douglass or Henry Box Brown or Peter Salem or Booker T. Washington or Jack Johnson or even the fierce Joker Tribbit. The trail, however, had spiraled like a withered vine through a tedious and complicated and eventually impenetrable morass with tendrils that snaked into Alabama, Florida, Mississippi, Georgia, and Virginia. Too many voices had been buried, and their treasures had been buried with them. But along the way, he had scavenged some nuggets he had not expected to find. Witches and hoodoo men. Ghosts. Murders. Secrets. Skeletons. He had started collecting these in his notebooks and on his tape recorder. He had been unable to find his own family's treasure, but maybe he had scraped together a worthy booty after all.

Royal piled the remaining apple slices on a napkin and pushed them over to the old man. "Mr. Tull, would you like to get started?"

"What's that?" He poked another square of apple into his mouth. His entire face waggled liquidly as he worked on it.

Royal tapped the recorder. "Do you want to get started?"

"Thought we was already." He frowned.

"Okay." Royal adjusted the microphone again. "Mr. Tull, the first thing I want to ask about is—"

"You wanna know about the spook," the old man said casually. He popped another bit of apple.

"The *what?*" Royal straightened. "You've seen a ghost?"

"Well that's what you're here about, ain't ya? You're a *spook*-writer." He waved the book in his lap.

True enough, Royal thought and smiled. *I'm a spook, and I'm a writer.* "Tell me about the spook, then."

"Grew up with him. He lived in the attic, you know. Big fella, I'd say by the sounds of him." When the old man spoke in his quick bursts, it was as if he were winding up, summoning air into his lungs, and then pitching a baseball. Wind up—speak—wind up—speak.

"What did he do?"

"What he do? Well, he made an awful racket, I guess. Threw things around. Had the foulest temper, he did. I never saw him, myself."

"You never saw him?"

"What's *that?*"

"I said, you never *saw* him?"

Another apple chunk. The flesh waggled. "Made an awful racket. Mean old rascal, I guess. Maybe I saw him once. Had a fire in the barn, and I saw this big fella out standin in the corn. By the wagons. Just watchin that fire—that's all. I figure maybe he set it. Then Missy grabs me by the arm, and she says, 'Looky over there, Cal! That's our spook.'"

Missy—Royal seized the name and felt a tingle of excitement. Perhaps "Missy" was "Mishelle Satterfield—Sister." "You say *Missy* saw him?"

"You hear what I just said?"

"I'm sorry, what—"

"Said he was *out standin in his field!*" Judson Tull sputtered his dry laugh. Royal offered an indulgent smile in return.

"And Missy saw him?" he asked.

"Oh hell, she saw him all the time. Course, that was just a man standin in the corn. Wasn't a spook. Leastwise, I don't think he was—but Missy thought so. Said he chased her in the barn 'fore it caught fire. Maybe he did."

"And that was the only time you saw him?"

The old man picked at the napkin, but the apple was gone. His lower lip unrolled in a wet pout. He glowered at Royal with accusation. "Heard him all the time—up in the attic. Kickin things around. I guess we all did. Missy, she was the only one who saw him regular, though. Only one who *said* so, leastwise. I guess Eulah Jane did, too, but she never let on as such."

Royal bolted upright in the chair. "Eulah Jane?"

"What's *that?*"

"Eulah Jane, you said."

"What about her?"

"Was her name, Eulahlah Jane Colebriar? Was *Colebriar* her last name?"

"Well I suppose maybe it was. After she married our man Snuf, anyways."

"What was her last name before that? Was it Tribbit?"

"Tribbit? What the hell's that?"

Royal blew out a breath. "Mr. Tull, how old were you when all this was happening?"

"Oh, most the time I was a boy, I guess. Up till I went to clerk at my Uncle Furman's. Maybe I was fifteen, sixteen."

Royal leaned back and breathed heavily. He glanced at one of the cell-block windows. The bright square of sunlight beyond seemed completely separate from anything inside this thick, life-sucking tomb of a building. It was late springtime out there. Inside, it was some endless, sterile season.

Eulah Jane.

He asked, "Eulah Jane, she worked for your family?"

"Worked? Took care of us—me and Sarah and Missy and Tom. Raised us, fed us, washed us. Lovely woman. *Darky*, you know—just like you. I guess I loved her a lot. Say, I don't suppose you got another apple."

Royal shrugged apologetically. Judson Tull scowled at him.

Royal stared at the rolling tape recorder. He had forgotten his questions; he had forgotten why he was here. When he looked up at Judson Tull again, the scowl was gone; the old man was making a quizzical expression with his mouth open wide and his tongue out. *Eulahlah Colebriar helped raise Boo Taylor's grandmother.*

And then his mother.

And then Boo.

How far did this go back?

"Eulah Jane," Royal said, "you say she saw the ghost?"

"Maybe she did; she never said so. She was a witch, you know," he added confidentially. "Always figured she and that ghost sat by the fire at night and had regular conversations."

I'll bet they did. "So what else did he do—this ghost?"

"Well, I told you, didn't I? Made a racket up there in the attic is what he did. Knocked over an old sideboard once, spilled Aunt Audra's china plates. Then he went around and stomped on 'em. Broke every single damn one. Not a piece bigger than your pinky fingernail when he was done all that stompin." He raised his shaky old hand and poked out a finger that was bent in three places, all in the wrong directions. "Oh, he had a foul temper."

"And you were there at the time," Royal said. "You heard it."

"Heard it? Hell, boy, I guess I did. Sarah and me hid in the closet most of an hour that night. Nobody had the guts to go up there to look till next morning. Not even Papa would. He was a scary bastard, that old spook."

"What did he look like?—that time you saw him."

"Big fella, I guess. I don't know; it was night."

"What about Eulah Jane or Missy—did they ever say?"

"What's *that?*"

Loudly: "I said, did *Missy* ever *tell you*—"

"Oh shit, I don't know," the old man interrupted, waving at Royal with irritation. "Maybe she did. Big fella, that's all I know. And I know another thing, too," he said, and his face darkened.

"What's that?"

For several seconds, Judson Tull did not answer. At last, he said, "I was scared shitless of that old spook."

Royal watched the old man carefully. The wrinkles folded dourly over his eyes. "Do you know where he came from? Did he have a name?"

The old man brooded silently. When he didn't answer, Royal asked, "Mr. Tull, was there ever a big dog that you saw around the house."

"*Dog?*" He looked at Royal incredulously. "Chrissakes, boy, we had a *farm*; there was dogs *everywhere*."

Royal nodded. He scratched his chin. "The ghost—did Missy say if he was a black man?"

"What's *that?*"

"I said, was he—was that spook a *darky fella?*"

"Oh hell, I hope not!" the old man answered, and suddenly spit a merry laugh through his sick, pearly teeth.

Royal saw a whitish blur from the corner of his eye. An attendant—a stocky, fortyish woman with a severe red haircut and an anemic complexion—was approaching them, smiling, from a row of chairs. There was menace in her carriage.

"Well now, Mr. Tull, how are we makin out?" she asked. Her accent was pure Southern twang. Royal had noticed her earlier, checking on the other residents in the rec room with considerably less animation in her pallid face. She placed her hand on Judson Tull's sleeve, and he slapped at it with *Blood on the Beach*. "Everythin all right here?" she asked, still dripping honey.

"Everything's fine," the old man grumped.

The woman fussed with the collar around the old man's nonexistent neck. The tag over her nonexistent breast read a cheerful: *Hello! I'm Rochelle Gurinskas*. Royal glanced at the rolling cassette. When Rochelle Gurinskas was finished with Judson Tull, she turned her ghastly smile on him. "And you are...?" She placed her hands on the old man's shoulders and stood behind the wheelchair.

"Royal Goody," he answered. It said so on the rather large Visitor tag that was clipped to his shirt.

"Mr. Royal, perhaps Mr. Tull would like t'git some rest, now," she suggested pleasantly in her infinite drawl. The smile was a red smear on a slab of white marble.

"I don't need to rest," Mr. Tull snorted.

"We'll be done shortly, I think," Mr. Royal told her—and then added, "if that's all right."

"I really think it might be better if y'all were done, now." Ice crystals flashed in her slit eyes. It was not just paranoia. He had seen the expression before, behind all sorts of masks. This here, he realized, was pure-bread, Southern-fried loathing from a pillar of Dixie womanhood.

"We ain't finished!" the old man said gruffly and tried to shake off the woman's hands.

She patted his head protectively. "Well *(whale)*." She sighed through her smile, summoning extraordinary patience. "I suppose y'all can talk a little while longer then *(thi-yen)*. However, Mr. Royal, perhaps I need to explain to you that our residents are served a scientifically balanced diet that provides them with all the nutrition they need. Many older people cannot handle...variation? They have *extremely* delicate systems."

The apple—she was talking about the apple. Royal closed his eyes briefly, and then offered Rochelle Gurinskas a guilty shrug. "Yes, of course," he said.

The woman sighed patiently. "*Hope*fully, Mr. Tull will suffer no ill effects." Mr. Tull had sagged deeper into his chair and sulked. His lips twittered silent remonstrations. "Also, Mr. Royal, I'd like to ask you to please refrain from using cuss words with our residents."

She offered one last jab of her smile and then turned abruptly to leave as he tried to think of what *cuss word* he might possibly have used. He watched the stocky white frock march toward a row of chairs along the wall where three elderly ladies were whispering together. He was angry; but somehow he knew he would be angrier if the woman wasn't so god-awful ugly. He was tempted to shout after her that Judson Tull was his grandfather.

A single word bubbled out of Judson Tull lips. Royal decided it was *bitch*.

The recorder was still rolling, hissing, taking everything in, absorbing the sounds like all of these walls. *That'll be a hoot on playback,* Royal thought.

"Mr. Tull," he said.

For a moment, the old man did not respond. Then he jerked as if suddenly awakened. "What's *that?*"

"I'm sorry about that," he nodded in the direction after Rochelle Gurinskas. *Why am I apologizing?* "Would you like to continue?"

"Oh, hell yes." He shuffled himself up in the chair a bit. "Fire away. Hey, that was a damn good apple." He grinned like a schoolboy.

Royal smiled back and tried to collect his thoughts. What were they talking about? Laylee Colebriar and a ghost. And a sister, Mishelle, who might be Boo Taylor's grandmother. He was walking the bizarre trail of Boo Taylor's heritage. More like leapfrogging than walking. He had been able to track his own line back five generations and discovered an unintelligible accumulation. No patterns; no sense of destiny—other than a plodding, piecemeal awakening to freedom. So far, he had traveled just two generations into Boo Taylor's ancestry and he had uncovered a trail of orphans and fiery deaths and spooks and broken old men. Too many patterns on that brief, leapfrog trail. Too much tragedy. And apparently, Eulahlah Colebriar's trail had shadowed it. *Sheba's curse,* Gussie Ransome had suggested a long time ago. He had disagreed at the time. Perhaps he was wrong.

The tape was rolling. "Mr. Tull, can we talk about your sister, Missy?"

The rheumy eyes blinked at him. "What about her?"

"Was her real name, Mishelle?"

"She was three years younger'n me, you know," the old man said. "Mishelle? Everybody called her Missy. I believe Eulah Jane started it, and the rest of us went along with it. Everybody but Papa. She wasn't really my sister, though—she was my cousin."

"Your *cousin?*"

"Awful, how she died." The wrinkles folded up on themselves again. "Died on a boat, ain't that just awful, Mr. Goody?"

Of course she died on a boat. "And she was your cousin, Mr. Tull?"

"Come to live with us when she was a baby. Pretty thing. Just the prettiest there was." The watery eyes went wistful and distant. "Had a Saturday picture show down on Baylor Street. Used to take her with me. Back then, was more buggies than cars on the road. Used to hitch up one of the horses and go to town for the day. Sometimes, Tommy'd come along. Never Sarah, though—she was too old. Then we'd sit by the Okmulgee with a lemonade. Always some of the boys there played guitar and did a dance."

"Mr. Tull, how did she come to live with your family when she was a baby?"

"What's *that?*"

"Mishelle. How did she come to live you?"

"Parents died," the old man answered.

Another orphan, Royal noted.

"Came from that island in all your stories," the man continued. "We used to go there fairly regular when I was a boy, you know. Always too damn hot there."

A nervous excitement was building in Royal's stomach. The whitish blur was infesting the corner of his eye again, but he tried to ignore it. "Do you remember what happened to her parents?"

"No. Died, is all."

A stocky, intolerant mass had drifted to his shoulder. He sensed a fat, white finger looming over the recorder, threatening to hammer down on the STOP button, the interview is over, *Mr. Tull needs his rest,* and so he held out his hand over the machine, palm down, as a shield. He had time to ask his next question but he already knew the answer.

five

May 23

MaeEllen Taylor was on her knees, hands deep in manure and vermiculite, when Bess Pope called to her from the back door. She looked up from her bougainvillea. Royal Goody, Bess told her, was on the phone and it was urgent.

Royal Goody.

She imagined awful news.

She stripped off the gloves and went inside. The phone's handset was abandoned on the kitchen counter. "Why Royal, how are you today?"

"I found him."

A kettle of peaches bubbled on the stove, and a steamy, sour film covered everything in the kitchen. Bess was making peach cobbler. MaeEllen Taylor ran a hand through her hair. She was suddenly aware of how badly she smelled of bourbon and sweat.

"Are you there?" Royal asked.

She cleared her throat. Her vocal chords didn't want to work. "Yes," she gargled. "Alive?"

"Yes, of course. I spoke with a man named Elton Cooper this morning who's been renting him that cabin. There's no phone out there, which explains a lot."

"And you're sure it's him—did you *talk* to him?"

"There's no phone; I *couldn't* talk to him." A pause. "So I think we should drive up tomorrow. I think we need to convince him to come back to the island with us. Don't you?"

MaeEllen Taylor listened to the sound of peaches bubbling away. Tennessee? What in God's name was he doing living in some cabin in Tennessee, anyway? "Yes. Yes, Royal, of course we should."

six

May 24

Steam rose from countless green leaves gathering at the peaks and then rolled away with the hills on all sides—forever, it seemed, as if, as they drove, they were really rolling across the great unmade bed of mother earth. And Elton Cooper supposed maybe they were—these were the most ancient mountains on the continent, after all, and they were showing their age: cracked and weathered granite croppings, beaten and exhausted slopes rounded by eons of rain and wind. Even the trees, which had found root in every slim crevice of rock, were gnarled antediluvian relics of myth and fairy tale. Elton had believed that whatever enchantment this view of the hills might once have held for him had long since died. But today it was reborn. Today he saw wizards in those trees, lifting green-laden limbs skyward. Today a vestigial pagan magic mingled with the steam. Not hard to imagine that at all. Today he was seeing it new through the eyes of his passenger.

Some bad trouble here, Elton thought. He tried to concentrate on the gray, two-lane snake that twisted before him. *Some terrible bad trouble.*

"Is it always like this?" she asked him, "so hazy?" She was leaning toward the dash to get a view of the peaks, giving him a better view of her.

"Pretty much," he told her, smiling. "That's why they call 'em the Smokies."

She smiled back and, despite his worry that an ancient trouble was being convoked from the land, his heart broke for this beautiful girl sitting next to him with her tragic smile and her hugely swollen belly. In ten minutes of driving he supposed he had fallen a little bit in love with her. Hell, he had fallen in love with her before that—the first time she had stepped out of the car with those other two back at the ranch and took his hand and thanked him for his help. Such an odd group they were: this pregnant girl and the black fellow and that regal woman. Each clouded by identical, gray dolor as weary as the mountains, and nothing good could come from such a look. But the girl…When she had said, "I'll ride with Mr. Cooper," why, his heart had fluttered like a schoolboy's, and every protective instinct in his young-man's breast had been unleashed. Then she had taken his hand again as he helped her into the truck. "Please watch your step, miss," he had told her, brimming with gallantry, and he must have been grinning like an idiot because Eva made a grumping noise from the porch. When he was able to look Eva's way again, she was fixing him with that wiseacre smirk of hers that said, *Now Elton Cooper, don't you go makin a fool of yourself,* and he felt himself go all-over red.

"It's very pretty up here," she was saying.

He grinned, could think of nothing to say, and was sure he looked like a jackass. He was eminently aware of the smell of axle grease inside the cab and the crumpled receipts and McDonald's wrappers littering the floor and the dash.

"Is it much further?" she asked.

"Not much. Maybe five minutes."

He flicked a glance at the rearview mirror. The black fellow and the regal woman were following in the maroon Taurus. Such an odd group, these three, and there was bad trouble hanging over them all—he had seen the look before, and he supposed he could recognize it for what it was.

Rounding a bend, they came upon a long red smear in the road terminating in a spilled sack of gore and bone and fur—unrecognizable, even to a man who lived in the mountains his whole life and was acquainted with every species of roadkill there was. Dog, perhaps, or a big coon or even a wild boar—he managed to guess all this in the time before a big semi coming the other way forced him to hug the shoulder, and so he could not avoid running over the carcass. A tortured yelp sounded from beneath the truck when the tires joggled. Whatever he had hit was still alive. Nausea clutched his stomach. He looked at the girl, and it was not obvious if she had heard it too.

"Not much further at all," he said because it was something to say.

Then, before he could help it, his eyes flitted to the rise of the girl's belly. She saw this, batted her eyes with slow self-consciousness, and looked toward the window.

He stared at the road ahead and the steam that rose from the hills.

The steam, which might be the brew of a great, underground cauldron, and all of them—this strange threesome and himself and the one they sought—were being stirred in the pot. He tried to concentrate on the road, but his attention remained on the girl, and he had the strangest thought that the yelp had not come from beneath the tires but had come from her.

She let time go off on its own for a spell while she froze into one moment of solid green.

She no longer sensed the road passing beneath. She did not acknowledge the blur of the leaves as motion—it was only the painter's brush running together jade and emerald and olive and moss and sage. The window, cool against her cheek, was a flat, glass pane of a picture frame. Perhaps it would stay this way forever—this moment of anticipation—wondering but never seeing what was so long hidden behind so much leaf and limb.

The perfect place to hide. Because, here, time really did stop.

"We're here." When the man spoke, the world snapped back into motion.

She automatically touched both hands to her belly. We're here, she whispered.

The truck turned off the highway and onto a rutted, unmarked road, bending behind the trees, and suddenly it was a dismal chaos of tin shacks and mobile homes.

We're here.

The road and the homes got worse the deeper they traveled. The truck slowed to a crawl, circling around the worst of the gullies and rifts but bouncing like a balloon anyway. She imagined the others, just behind, watching this as she was and drawing their own conclusions. Breedless beasts that might be dogs barking and straining at their chains. Mountains of old tires and rusty appliances and spools of wire fencing. Clotheslines knitting odd angles, drooping with the limp, dead weight of scarecrow families. And rising like high-tech shrubs from the midst of so much neglect and rubbish, in almost every yard, the incongruent sight of the satellite dish. Besides the dogs, the single evidence of animal life was a toothless woman of indeterminate age who sat motionless in a plastic chair beneath the overhang shade of a porch. Not even the rustic, Appalachia poverty of movies. This was a slum.

We're here, she thought, and she braced for the truck to stop, wincing at the notion that a man from a rich Sweetpatch Island family could possibly wind up in such a place.

"It's past all this," he told her, reading her thoughts—or, perhaps, her expression.

The homes rolled past. Snapshots of misery. Eventually, the trees crowded in again as the road twisted and worsened, becoming not a road at all but two runnels in the dirt. She held her belly protectively as the trail shocked through the truck. She imagined the car behind making this same journey. The trail wound on and on, and she had the sense of time stopping again, locking onto the moment of anticipation, preventing that last, most awaited click of the second hand from ever tripping forward with the pronouncement, at last: we're here.

Empty.

Not empty. They found pieces of him.

But he was not there, and time must stop again, holding back that last precious tick. "He likes to go for long walks in the woods," Mr. Cooper told her, and so they would wait for that last tick while trespassing among his private pieces. She gathered a handful—red, yellow, orange leaves, curled and abandoned from another season—and wandered into his bed of stargrass and blood root and rhododendrons and black-berries and trout lilies. An axe blade sank into a flat, hickory stump; its handle was a flagpole waving red and black checkers. A kingfisher glided between distant trees. A woodpecker rattled invisibly. Cottontails rustled the ferns. The others, still inside, fol-lowed her nonetheless with their worry; she felt it like hands on her back or cupping her elbows as she walked. She followed a trail, beckoned by the wind-chime clatter of brook water, and held the red, yellow, orange pages to her belly so her child might read them. A warbler called. Again, she thought how perfect a hiding place he had chosen. The trail spun through silverbells and sweetgum and dogwoods. Sweat bubbled to her temples because it was hot, even up here, and each stride was child-burdened. She reached the brook's edge. Mayflies cavorted along the bank. She cupped a hand over her eyes and followed the water against current, seeing it turn from silver ribbons to a bored black-purple, rolling backward over moss-painted rocks and rising to the green sag of trees, fading steadily upward as it was lost in the forest and she saw him com-ing down the trail. An old man. Moving ponderously on a wooden staff—like Moses down from the mountain, down from the burning bush. Mumbling to himself—or to something not there. He looked too thin. He did not see her yet. As he came on, she read from the pages in her hand.

They fall
> *one at a time*
> *ten at a time*
hallowed, silver-haloed, falling
>> *hundred at a time*
>> *thousand at a time*
falling about me by ten thousands
>> *at a time.*
It is the angels' season. And they are
blanketing my dead blue flesh
that I might rise above the seas and fires.
And take my place. They take my
blue, unfeeling fingers, and they
call to me:
> *Come be with us,*
> *And sing your story to the dead.*
I rise on borrowed wings with them
and settle, looking down to find the bridge
has burned behind me. Nowhere to go
but climb.
Away from her.
And take my place. They take my
nights away from me, and they
promise me:
> *Come be with us,*
come be with us,
come be with us,
> *You belong here with the dead.*

Dear God, had it been as bad as all that? She dropped the page to her hip and now, closer, he saw the movement. He looked in her direction to find a deer or a fox, half lost behind the dappled green, and she watched the slow emergence of recognition as he saw her face and the slow emergence of understanding as he saw the swell of her stomach. It was the moment at last, the second-hand dropping the final tick, and in that moment, along with his recognition and understanding, she would witness the emergence of either his salvation or damnation.

"Gussie?"

She waited.

A frog blatted from the brook. A bumblebee whined by her ear. She placed a hand on her belly. The clock ticked again. In the same instant he smiled and wept, and she knew he was saved.

seven

Wade Dutton, head lolling on black vinyl, flickered open his eyes and sucked in a line of drool. He had a horrible moment of disorientation; nothing of his surroundings was at all recognizable. Then, blinking awake, he made out the front door of the hardware store, and it came back to him. He was here for the hardware store. For the man in the baseball cap and shabby, olive clothes who had gone inside. The store was beyond the windshield, beyond a tangle of oaks and moss, and he had somehow dozed off.

He had been dreaming of the old woman.

You got steel inside you, Mr. Wade.

A bar of sunlight was slanting through the windshield, filling the cruiser with the dull, afternoon heat. He was parked in the sandy lot of the Sing Satterfield Wildlife Refuge. Parked where he could get a good look at the store on the other side of the tree line and where the patrons going in and out weren't likely to see him.

Got to keep an eye on them two.

The heat in the car was making him ill. He pushed open the door and set his black shoes on ashes and dead cigarette butts. The slightly cooler air outside bathed his head, filled his lungs. He wondered if the man in the baseball cap was now long gone—and wondered what the old woman would think of him if she knew he'd been sleeping on the job.

Late spring on Sweetpatch Island. Here, inland, it was nothing but green. Deep shadows and dangling moss. A line of azaleas bordered the lot, the blossoms burnt and shriveled. The old woman's shack had not been far from this place, somewhere back behind the Welcome House and into those green trails. When the old woman's shack had finally burned down, killing the old woman inside, he had been crushed. He hadn't known her very well, had only been in her company two or three times, but in a very real way, she'd had a profound impact on his life, and the news of her death had cut through him like a knife.

You a special one.

She told him he had *steel* inside. That he was special. He didn't feel so special right now, but he had when she told him this; he had been sure of it.

Got to keep a watch over them two. Mr. Boo, he got a fire lit inside him, and Miss Gus, why she standin too close. They gonna need lookin after. You gonna know when the time comes. That's when you gotta be strong, Mr. Wade. That's when you gotta remember that steel you got inside.

As if she knew she was about to die.

She was dead. Why did she keep coming back to him in his dreams?

He grabbed a pack of Marlboros from the console, shook one out, and lit it. Then he turned back to the hardware store where an elderly man in a red and white striped shirt, two little boys trailing, was stepping inside. A teenage girl in a blue miniskirt was coming out. He watched the girl and reached for the dash to turn on the radio. Static and squawk fizzed out of the speakers. Bart Monroe had desk; he was pissing and moaning to someone. A restaurant on North Beach made a 911 call on a loiterer, a nuisance call, and nobody wanted to respond. Bart Monroe was an asshole, and whoever he was jawing with—sounded like Freddy Taggart—wasn't putting up with his shit today.

Wade listened to the banter and wiped saliva from his jaw.

He never knew who set the fire that killed Eulahlah Colebriar all those years ago. No one did. He had always blamed that uppity jig, Solomon Goody. Maybe Solomon Goody didn't set that *particular* fire, but he sure as shit started it all when he burned down that old colored school. After that, it seemed like there'd been about a fire a week. Schools and churches and people's homes. Throw in the occasional riot and a few wild animal attacks. Somehow, Solomon Goody had been behind it all; he just knew it. And now, that nappy head was in Congress, rubbing elbows with all the rich folks and politicians up there in Washington DC, which just went to prove how fucked up this country had become.

At least that last fire seemed to bring the end of it. The old woman was dead. Her bones collected from the ashes and laid to rest in the cemetery off Pofoksgo. He had even gone to the funeral, holding up Gussie who was in a cast and all taped up with bandages, inconsolable in her grief. He had never been to a Negro funeral before. It was great theatre: fat colored women wailing and collapsing, jazzy hand-clapping hymns, more cardboard fans waving at more dark faces than he had ever seen at one time. And that spook preacher bawling up to the heavens as if he expected the brown hand of God to come reaching down and scoop them all away.

Her bones in that simple box, but she still came to him anyway, reminding him of his promises.

He remembered something Yogi Berra once said. *Always go to other people's funerals. Otherwise, they won't go to yours.*

Somewhere around the same time as that carnival funeral, the town fathers got together and decided to create their own police department. Parker Tillman and the rest of the county got their pink slips, and Jan Hibbits was appointed the island's first police chief. Whether or not any of that had anything to do with the relative peace and quiet that followed was purely a matter for speculation. At the end of the day, it didn't much matter. The violence had stopped. The fires were put out.

For a while, anyway.

He took a drag off his cigarette and blew smoke at the sun. At the Island Wares & Goods, a steady stream of tourists was entering and exiting. The store sold bait and ammunition alongside the typical hardware fare and, for the tourists, beach umbrellas, beach towels, and all manner of junk souvenirs.

Last fall, the Feds had found an empty gas can in the ruins of a church in Wilbursville, Georgia. The can was burnt all to shit, same as the church, but the forensic team discovered the scorched remnants of a price sticker affixed to it. It took some doing, but eventually they were able to read most of the letters and numbers on that sticker. The can had been sold sometime last September at Island Wares & Goods located at 1012 Old Sugar Dam Road, Sweetpatch Island, South Carolina. The can they found a week later at the Baptist church fire on Polk—the fire that killed a boy—didn't have any sticker, but it was the same brand as the one from Wilbursville. There weren't any stickers on the mason jars they found at Boo Taylor's house, either—although, lo and behold, Island Wares & Goods stocked mason jars, too.

An FBI task force descended on the island.

"Dutton, where the hell you at?"

Fucking Bart Monroe. Wade picked up the handset and thumbed the mike button. "Cruisin Fellers Point," he answered, "what's it to you?"

"No, you're not. You're stakin that damn tourist shop again; Packer saw your car. That's the Feds' job—you know that."

Wade flicked the spent cigarette to the ground and stomped it. Whatever the Feds where doing, they were keeping it to themselves.

"You there, Dutton?"

"No, I'm drinkin champagne in Paris with your wife sittin in my lap. You want somethin, Bart, or you just bustin my balls?"

"I want you to keep your radio on, is what I want. And get the fuck out of there and let the Feds do their job. You got two hours left on your shift; hit the Point like you're supposed to."

Fellers Point was where all the new mansions had gone up. The rich folks there wanted to see a nice clean squad car rolling past every twenty minutes. Wade was about to respond to Bart Monroe when he saw the man in the baseball cap and drab olives stepping outside of Island Wares & Goods.

"You hearin me, Dutton?"

"Yes, I hear you." *Fuckhead.* He clicked off the mike and slid the set back in its plastic nest.

He had been the one to drive the old woman home from the hospital in Corrington. Gussie had been released with her ankle in a cast and a dozen or so stitches in her cheek, but she wasn't leaving Boo Taylor's side. Boo was still in a pretty bad way. Half of his hand had been ripped off, his femoral artery had been nicked, and he'd lost enough blood to fill a fucking keg. He couldn't get Gussie to leave his hospital room. He supposed that was about the time he realized Boo and Gussie had something special, something that ninety-nine percent of the population would never have. Something he never had.

The man in the baseball cap was coming down the front step, toting a paper sack.

The FBI had run its list of suspects against the store's credit card records and didn't come up with much. When Wade started poking around on his own, he was surprised to find a full third of the store's transactions were in cash. And although it catered mostly to tourists, a fair number of locals shopped there as well.

Wade had come up with his own list of suspects. He figured his list was a lot shorter than the Feds'.

You got steel in you, Mr. Wade.

The old woman's voice muffled and nasally under all of those bandages. The eyes above those bandages boring into him, powerful, making him a little boy again.

Her hand over his, sending some kind of electric shock through him. Her hands had looked like old roots.

Miss MaeEllen and the doctor, who mostly blamed the old gal for what happened to their boy, didn't seem all that interested in ferrying her back to the scene of the crime. So it had been Wade Dutton to drive the old woman home.

Looking back, it seemed she had planned it that way.

They gonna need lookin after.

Her face wrapped up like a mummy.

And less than a week later, she was dead. Some final sacrifice to end whatever madness had infected the island that year: Solomon Goody, Henry Ray, Mamie Stuvant, and the return of the fabled Beast. She was gone, and she had left it to him to look after Boo and Gussie, and every now and then she popped up in his dreams to remind him of this little pact.

But he had been going through basic when Boo left for Duke, leaving Gussie alone back on Sweetpatch Island and effectively sinking whatever chance those two might have had for a life together. He could have told them what would happen. His hot-headed sister certainly couldn't sit still for four long years, not without blowing the works well and good. Not even for one year, as it turned out. Even if he hadn't been stuck on Parris Island with the rest of the new meat, had been back home, could he have prevented it?

He wondered if the old woman blamed him.

Boring her little brown eyes into him. Clamping her little brown-root hand over his.

You gonna know when the time comes.

Wade Dutton closed the cruiser's door and turned the ignition. The man in the baseball cap was moving up the lane, moving against a tide of brightly dressed tourists. In his drab olives, he was like a ghost amid all that garish color, invisible.

Wade slid the cruiser into gear, wondering if maybe his time was coming.

eight

In his nightmares, Elgin Highsmith is coming for him. In his nightmares, he is lying in bed and unable to move as Elgin Highsmith, unseen but surely a moldering corpse in a Halloween mask, is shuffling through hallways beyond the bedroom door. He can hear the sounds the corpse makes as it bangs blindly off walls, working its way closer. He can smell the burnt flesh. The Elgin-thing makes whiney, impatient sounds as it comes on. He tries to move, to get up and get away somehow, but he is paralyzed in his bed—paralyzed and as useless as a drunk passed out on the kitchen floor. He hears the Elgin-thing calling to him, "You're too drunk to drive." Calling to him, "Let me take you home." Calling to him, "Let me answer your door." In his nightmares, wolves are howling outside his window as the ruined body gets closer and closer. The wolves are messengers. There are words in their howls, words distorted and unrecognizable, spoken in some ancient Gullah-wolf tongue, and so he cannot decipher them. But he senses their meaning. He is being punished. The Elgin-thing is coming for him because it knows he is useless. In his nightmares, that's what the wolves are telling him: Elgin Highsmith died because he is drunk and so useless he can't even drive himself home, can't even answer his own door.

The old man's words, now silenced by Royal Goody's finger, echoed across wooded lawn.

Boo Taylor had only been half listening. His attention had been on the golden dust motes swirling across the air, riding the breeze until they were expelled over Gussie Ransome's sweating body. The slope of her belly was a perfectly descending arc, gathering momentum as it canted down the flowered print of her dress and over-lapped her groin. She was achingly beautiful.

"Boo?" Royal's finger was still on the tape recorder. Boo Taylor looked up and realized Royal and MaeEllen were studying him as he had been studying Gussie. Royal Goody was clearly irritated.

He turned back to Gussie. *He has something important to show you,* she'd told him.

"Am I to take it by your reaction," Royal was saying, "that none of this comes as news to you?"

Boo didn't answer, and Royal sighed heavily.

"You're saying you already knew that you're a direct descendent of Samuel and Margaritte LaValle?"

It was hard keeping his eyes off of Gussie. She was imperious in Ben Shallcross' beat-up recliner. Her hair palpitated under the breeze. Perspiration gathered and glistened in her eyebrows. Earlier, she'd told him that Royal had discovered some-thing important. Something they needed to show him. It was the reason they'd come for him.

The only reason?

No, of course, not. We want you to come home.

We?

"Yes," he said, speaking to Gussie. "I already knew."

Royal was leaning against the picnic table. The tape recorder and several folders and folios were spread over the rough planks of the table top. "Eulahlah Colebriar told you."

"No," he told Gussie, then turned to Royal Goody. "I hate to break the news to you, Royal, but you're not the only one who knows how to use a library. Did you really think I wouldn't look into this on my own?"

"You found out?" Gussie asked. Her brow wrinkled. The pink, ragged edge of a scar poked from beneath her hair and ruined the perfect, now slightly distended curve of her jaw.

"Yes."

"And you never told me?"

"No, I never told you."

"Why?"

"Because,"—he took her hand, held it, looked at her closely—"you went and married one of the great assholes of the world. We went about twenty years without telling each other things."

She scowled at him, but he wasn't concerned about her anger. He felt the steady warmth passing like seminal fluid between his hand and hers. His child was pulsing within her flesh. He put his hand over her belly. Beneath his hand, something rumbled. He imagined a little finger reaching to touch him.

Royal asked him, "You knew about Benjamin Shallcross?"

"I figured it out, yes. You helped when I showed you that picture of him."

"And you had contact with him before he died?"

"Only that time when I was a boy, the time the doc brought me up here. That was it." He glanced at MaeEllen who looked away.

In another nightmare, it's Sandy Baker looking up at him from a hospital gurney. In this nightmare her belly is swollen, contorting as something within writhes to get out. Her face, grimed with soot, is twisted in pain. She is screaming. Screaming his name, over and over. The thing inside her is being burned alive. The thing inside her is his child. The child is in a frenzy, and Sandy's screams are ripping through him. Her hand snakes out and takes his wrist, her flesh scalding his. She keeps screaming his name, and the trapped thing inside her is nearly bursting through her belly. The flesh on his wrist where she holds him begins to melt. In this nightmare, Sandy's eyes are locked onto his. They are open wide and completely insane.

When he looked around, he saw again that everyone was staring at him. The day was beginning to feel like a staged event. An *intervention*. They had all come to save him. To save him from *himself*. He realized he was clutching the vertical rails of the chair he was straddling as if they were prison bars. He let go, ruffled a hand through his hair.

Judson Meriwether Tull's recorded voice had explained that his mother was a Sladeshaw. His aunt had been Margaritte Sladeshaw LaValle, married to Samuel LaValle. Margaritte died in childbirth, and Samuel followed her in death a short while later after Joker Tribbit's famous lynching. The LaValle's daughter, Mishelle, survived and came with her nanny, Eulahlah Jane Colebriar, to live with the Tulls.

Gussie squeezed his hand.

You didn't have to hide.

I'm not hiding.

No one knew where this place was, Boo.

No one needed to know.

"Mishelle Tull Satterfield was your grandmother," Royal said. "That makes Samuel and Margaritte LaValle your great-grandparents. But of course you already know this."

Boo, looking at Gussie's belly, nodded.

Sighing again, Royal Goody withdrew a page and placed it on the picnic table.

Boo Taylor leaned over to read it.

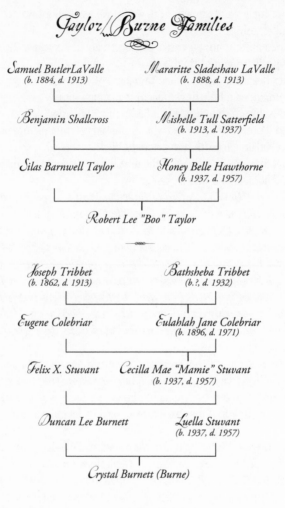

Taylor/Burne Families

Samuel ButlerLaValle
(b. 1884, d. 1913)

Mararitte Sladeshaw LaValle
(b. 1888, d. 1913)

Benjamin Shallcross

Mishelle Tull Satterfield
(b. 1913, d. 1937)

Silas Barnwell Taylor

Honey Belle Hawthorne
(b. 1937, d. 1957)

Robert Lee "Boo" Taylor

Joseph Tribbet
(b. 1862, d. 1913)

Bathsheba Tribbet
(b. ?, d. 1932)

Eugene Colebriar

Eulahlah Jane Colebriar
(b. 1896, d. 1971)

Felix X. Stuvant

Cecilla Mae "Mamie" Stuvant
(b. 1937, d. 1957)

Duncan Lee Burnett

Luella Stuvant
(b. 1937, d. 1957)

Crystal Burnett (Burne)

"It's one great big mishmash of last names," Gussie said. "How can you even keep this straight?"

"Orphans," said Royal.

Boo, studying the document, said, "It's something Mamie Stuvant tried to tell me. That day I went to her house, she told me a poem. She tried to get me to memorize it. Something about the tailor's mother having a son but her grandchildren having different last names." After a moment, he added, "It's *supposed* to be confusing."

A cloud passed overhead. Boo bent closer to the page.

"You see something?" Royal asked.

Boo placed a finger on the page over Luella Sturvant's name. "Mamie's daughter was born in nineteen-thirty-five. You can find it in the records of the First Methodist Church in Powtonville." He looked up. "Felix Sturvant was a Methodist, not a Baptist."

Royal Goody raised his eyebrows. "You don't happen to know what ever happened to her, do you? There's no record of her death."

"According to Mamie, she died. I got the impression her husband beat her to death."

"But there's no record."

Gussie sat up. "You think she's still alive?"

"I think it's highly suspicious," said Royal. "Boo, what else do you see?"

Boo Taylor pointed to another spot on the chart. "Snuffy Colebriar could not have been Mamie's father. Mamie would have been born somewhere in the early to mid teens, and Laylee didn't meet Snuffy until the early thirties."

"I asked her once if she had children," said Gussie, "and she told me she didn't."

"Well, she didn't with Snuffy, anyway."

"Does that mean she was married before him?"

Boo shrugged as Royal folded his arms. "Anything else?" Royal asked him.

Boo glanced again at MaeEllen who had remained mostly silent after giving him a reluctant hug when they greeted. She clearly didn't want to be here. He remembered his father, strangely defiant, telling him: *If anyone's a hero in this, it's her.*

"Just the obvious," Boo said, recognizing how irritated Royal was with him. Royal Goody was tapping his foot, waiting. "You're making the assumption this only goes as far back as the LaValles and Joker and Sheba."

And yet another nightmare. Perhaps the worst of them. Sandy again, hunched over a crib. Beautiful Sandy with her straight blonde hair, tan face. In this nightmare her face is pure joy as she dangles a stuffed animal over the crib, cooing to the child inside. The animal is a bunny with a scarlet ribbon tied about its neck in a bow. He comes closer as Sandy looks up and tells him, "It's a girl, Boo. A beautiful baby girl. What should we name her?" Beautiful Sandy, with her slim hips and delicate features. In this nightmare, he approaches until he can now see inside the crib. "Look, Boo. Isn't she beautiful?" But in this nightmare there is no child inside the crib at all. Sandy is dangling the bunny with its red ribbon over a smoldering black lump. When he looks up from the lump in the crib, it's no longer Sandy Baker standing there. It's Hoss Beaudry, torn and bloodied. Then it's Ash Marchant, a gray statue. Then it's Laylee Colebriar, a pitifully charred mess. She is holding out her blistered arms. "Ain't it beautiful, Mr. Boo?" she asks.

Royal was lifting the page from the table. "I'm not making any such assumptions. Samuel LaValle's grandfather was Permanence LaValle, a second generation planter whose family emigrated from France in the early eighteen hundreds. The family history is well documented in the historic record. Margaritte Sladeshaw's grandfather was the secretary of state under Andrew Jackson, and the library at Georgia Southern University has practically an entire room dedicated to the man. Bathsheba Tribbit supposedly came from somewhere in the Caribbean. And who knows about Joker Tribbit's ancestors. The point is, this could go back generations and generations further—not that we'll ever know."

He looked to Boo Taylor for confirmation.

"Can I get you a beer?" Boo asked him.

"What?"

"You look like you could use a beer."

Royal glared at him. Boo stood and excused himself. MaeEllen followed him inside to Ben Shallcross' tiny kitchen where the cabin walls were filled with Ben Shallcross' bric-a-brac: a topographical map of the surrounding hills, prints of mallards and Labrador retrievers, a rack of antlers laden with hats and wool scarves, ancient photographs. In all, the place was like a minor variant of the doctor's office.

Boo removed two bottles of beer from the refrigerator, and his mother filled a glass with water from the tap. "That girl should not have made this trip, you know," his mother scolded.

"Yes, I know."

"Do you have any idea how bad the roads are up here? What an awful thing to put a woman through when she's that far along."

"I'm sure it is."

"*Especially* at her age."

"Mother, I'm pretty sure they can hear us in here."

"You had no business leaving her alone like that."

The air inside the kitchen was still and heavy. Summer weather. He wondered how much hotter it would be in the low country today, and then wondered if that meant he was already decided about returning to the island with them. "I didn't leave her alone. She has a husband back there who doesn't seem to mind that she got knocked up by her old boyfriend."

MaeEllen mocked horror and swatted him. "You know what I mean."

"You shouldn't have let her come if you were so concerned."

"And you believe for a minute I could have stopped her?" She barked a sarcastic laugh.

Light canted through the small kitchen window. Outside, it seemed so serene. Birds flitting about a tall maple. The brook beyond, rippling shards of sunlight. As if nothing dreadful had ever happened or ever could happen. Like something from a storybook—probably the very thing that had lured Ben Shallcross to the place so many years ago. Bad things could not happen here. As good a place as any when there was nowhere else to go. As good a place as any to hunker down. He was going to miss the place. He would miss the place, but not the nightmares. Those, he decided, would probably follow him. "I'm not sure what I'm supposed to be coming back to," he said.

MaeEllen said nothing. She dropped ice cubes into the glass.

"He won't let her go," Boo said. "He's holding her children over her head. If she leaves him, he'll take the kids."

"I know."

"He's doing it out of spite."

"He'll get tired of that, Boo," MaeEllen told him. She placed her hand over his. "Eventually."

He leaned against the counter, looking at his mother as he sipped from his beer.

It was the doctor's words again, those defiant words, he remembered. *You may want to consider how heroic she was, boy, taking you in and loving you despite what you maybe represent to her.*

MaeEllen left him and went back outside. Boo watched through the window as his mother handed Gussie the glass of water. A smile dimpled Gussie's cheek and wrinkled the scar. A glean of sweat stood on her forehead, and he tried to imagine her nude and waiting for him beneath a quilt as he had often imagined her in the last months, remembering the one hour of his adult life in which he was completely, uncompromisingly happy.

He comes to the pond, and there is something waiting for him beneath the water, and he thinks he sees it, something shiny beneath the surface, something catching the sun, flashing, and he thinks maybe it's a glass frog—that's you, Mr. Boo—but when he reaches in and closes his mangled right hand around it and draws it away from the melted waters, he finds something he has not expected. A silver pocket watch. Something an old man might carry. Frozen in the moment of death because it has spent a season in heaven under the ice. Something old that has not changed although time continues and seasons revolve, and everything in this world—and every other world—changes, and then a blue hand reaches up from the water and grabs his wrist. He is being dragged under water. He tries to get away, but the pull is too strong. And it's the worst he's ever been afraid.

He took a long swallow of his beer. He was sweating heavily. Outside, the others were speaking in hushed tones, making hesitant glances in his direction. He wondered if they could hear the wolves howling on the mountain trail.

Nine

A reminiscence of cigar smoke lifted from him. He looked like he must have lost twenty pounds since she'd last seen him. And aged about twenty years. She noticed how much he had gotten to look like the doctor: those lines crisscrossing his face, like driftwood left to blanch and wither on the sand. She liked looking at him as he drove; she liked studying his profile while his presence filled up the small cabin. His hand shifted on the wheel, and the faded-denim eyes flicked over to her and were filled with reflections of the sun.

She remembered, but she said nothing.

So it would've been better if it had been you and not your friend Elgin who died in that fire?

She hadn't liked the answer she had seen in those blue eyes. She knew she was looking at a man who had been pushed all the way to the crumbling brink of despair. It had not helped that he was in love with her and that she was most of the reason for his anguish.

A wave of indigestion burned through her stomach. The bucket seat in the Tahoe was becoming hot and uncomfortable against her back.

A primal theism Royal Goody had told them.

"Something the pastor was trying to tell us that day, Boo. About the old island

ways still being practiced. Gone underground maybe, but still around: the root cures and mojos. You while away enough hours in old folk's kitchens like I do and you see plenty of it. They still burn old shoes to keep germs away. They still spit grain liquor in stove fires so flies won't bother the food. You drive down Pofoksgo and every other front door is painted blue to keep out the ghosts. It's always been there. It was there when we were growing up. It was there in the thirties when Mishelle Satterfield was having her baby. At the turn of the century when Joker Tribbit was lynched, and long before that. Underneath the changing face, that part of the island—that primal theism—has never changed. It's still an active part of the culture. Only now it just sort of slinks somewhere in the shadows behind the putting greens and tennis courts."

A belch slipped through her throat before she could stop it. Embarrassed, she put her hand to her mouth and grinned ruefully.

"You okay?" Boo asked her.

She placed her hands on her belly, hefting that liquid mass and trying to find a comfortable position. It felt as if an iron rod had been riveted to her spine. "I think we need to stop at the next place with a decent bathroom."

"I'm sorry, I should have asked earlier."

"Don't be sorry, just find me a bathroom."

They had passed Asheville, North Carolina about fifteen minutes earlier and were now southeast on Interstate 26 toward Spartanburg. Royal Goody and MaeEllen Taylor were somewhere far ahead. She and Boo had detoured to Elton Cooper's ranch before starting back. Now, the sun was starting to drop behind them, the shadows reaching toward the still-distant ocean.

Boo was staring at her, and his smoky eyes were filled with guilt and concern. "Watch where you're driving," she told him.

Laylee Colebriar's glass frog squatted on the dashboard, its nose pointing eastward, navigating the descent from the hills. A worn old pocket watch wobbled from the rearview mirror on a length of rawhide. She had watched Boo hang it there.

"When did you start writing poetry?" she asked him.

He snorted, and she waited for his answer. When it never came, she asked, "What did you do all day at that place? It didn't even have a TV."

"I went for walks," he said. "I read books. I tried not to get anyone killed."

"Don't be so melodramatic."

"Fine. But if you haven't noticed, people have a habit of getting killed around me, and I was kind of hoping you wouldn't become one of them. Can I ask you something?"

"Of course."

He glanced at her briefly, then back to the road. "When Royal was talking about *patterns*. About psychological terrorism. I was wondering…"

"Have I been terrorized?"

He nodded.

Not since the night of the fire, she thought. Not since that terrible phone call. "No," she said.

"Nothing's tried to hurt you?"

"No."

"No dreams? No voices?"

Dreams? Voices? She wondered about all that time he'd been alone, no phone, no company, not even a television. "Jeremiah says he's seen a big dog in the yard from his window."

This brought another worried glance from him that irritated her. "I'm sure it's nothing, Boo."

You're a target, Royal had told him.

It was what the police up north had called him, too. A target. According to Royal, he was a target because someone knew he was LaValle's great-grandson and elements of that primal theism had been busy executing Sheba's curse. Most likely it was Crystal Burne—possibly Luella Sturvant, who seemed to be the only other unaccounted for descendent of Sheba Tribbit.

"The curse was an invention by a people who had no other recourse. You have to remember these were the days after Reconstruction collapsed and Jim Crow laws nearly restored the antebellum status quo. The blacks on Sweetpatch Island only knew the white man's whip and a bit of sharecropping. Then, this important black man emerges, a man of property and influence. Certainly, he was a symbol of hope. When he was murdered, the blacks on the island would have been outraged. So how did they respond? The way they were culturally conditioned: they invented a curse. That primal theism was the only power they had. In all other ways, they were dominated by whites. But they had their black magic and spirits and tobies. That's how they struck back. That's what they invoked. But it was people who carried it out. People in the shadows never changing, never forgiving. What we're really looking for are elements of that primal theism. The people behind the psychological terrorism and the acts of violence. Someone following the pattern."

The pattern?

"The child, Boo. The next in line."

But there was another part of the pattern, too. Eulahlah Colebriar. Certainly she was steeped in that primal theism. A servant in the LaValle household—in Chaliboque—when she was a girl. She would have been a teenager around the time Margaritte LaValle had her baby, had even accompanied her off island as a sort of apprenticed midwife, hadn't she? And after Margaritte LaValle died, Eulahlah Colebriar took care of their child even as Sheba Tribbit stole away her own baby. *Protected* their child. And that's what she had done the rest of her life.

Only now she was gone. Who was supposed to help them now? Who was supposed to protect *this* child? And then she had a sudden insight. Royal Goody himself was stepping in to fill Laylee Colebriar's place. The performance today had been his interview for the position. Protector and guardian, keeping the pattern inviolate. Toting his rational magic in manila folders instead of a burlap sack.

"Next exit," Boo said. He was nodding to a sign showing a number of gas stations and fast-food restaurants just ahead.

She laid a hand on his thigh. "Try not to be so miserable," she said. "We're having a baby together; that's a good thing, isn't it?"

"And I'm supposed to do what? Hang around at MaeEllen's house, twiddle my thumbs, get a peak at the baby over your backyard fence every now and then?"

"It won't be like that, Boo, and you know it. It'll work itself out. Anyway, it's a damn sight better than you hidin away up in the mountains."

"Is it?"

"Yes. I want you near me. I want to be close to you." She squeezed his leg. "I want us to be together. What do you want?"

"I want to put my fist down Murphy Ransome's throat."

"He wants to do the same thing to you."

"I'm sure he does. I'm sure he wants to do worse. Gussie, I wasn't hiding, I was trying to keep you safe the best way I knew."

"By staying away?"

"*Yes,* by staying away. You want me close, and that's fine. I want to be close to you, too. More than you know, probably; more than *anything*, Gussie. But I just don't think me being on the island—or anywhere *near* you, for that matter—is a good idea. And no, I don't give a shit what Murphy thinks, but I do care about what happens to you." He stopped to breathe. "Gussie, I'm not joking about people around me getting killed."

He slipped the Tahoe into the exit lane. Gussie Ransome took her hand back and placed it over the distended curve of her belly. The pavement rumbled beneath them; she had the sensation of rushing down hill out of control. *The next in line,* she thought. "I know you're not joking."

By the dashboard clock it was 4:52.

It was near dark when he let Gussie off in front of the house she shared with Murphy Ransome. She did not kiss him. He watched from the cab as she lumbered up the stone walkway. She opened the door and then disappeared inside without looking back or waving.

He started the engine and drove toward his mother's house on Carriage Avenue. He pulled a Maduro from the case in the glove compartment, snipped the end, and lit it. The roads and sidewalks were bustling with tourist traffic. Horns sounded frequently. People were shouting happily. He felt as if he had awoken from a long sleep, that the island had been awake all that time. He made a detour to stop in Oakies long enough to finish his cigar and have a beer. The bar was packed, and a country band was playing very loudly. Mean, grinning faces, whooping and laughing like donkeys, pressed around him in impossible numbers. He looked for Lester Meggett or Dewey Fitch but did not see a single person he knew. The music and the faces were making him ill. When he left, his ears were ringing. He lit up another cigar to kill the dueling smells of the saltwater and marsh. Driving along Sandpiper Boulevard, he imagined he saw Mamie Stuvant. She was alone and laughing—at first an old woman in a brown dress, and then a young girl. He almost stopped to see if it was really her but then thought if it was he might possibly go insane, and so he kept driving. Cigar smoke burned in his lungs. He was sweating. The island knew he was home.

ten

Allen Noble woke up. He thought he'd heard the phone ringing. And there had been a dream...something about the ocean?

In darkness, he sensed the cool emptiness in the bed next to him.

"Sandy?"

He found her: a vague, gray shade near the window, nearly lost among the other gray shades of clutter in the room. He swung out of bed and walked to her side. He placed a hand at the small of her back. "Sweetie, are you all right?" he asked gently.

She turned from the window. Her round, baby-doll eyes were glowing with fear. "Allen, someone's out there," she said. "He was looking in."

eleven

June 6

Two weeks later, as commencement exercises were underway in the Sweetpatch High School football stadium, Solomon Goody sensed (as had Boo Taylor) a dim, reptilian consciousness within the island becoming aware of his homecoming. Had Solomon heard Royal's theory about a primal theism, he would have disagreed. He suspected the evil was actually steeped within Sweetpatch Island itself, something alive and interwoven on a molecular level with the grains of sand and drams of mud and swamp water and detritus and the moss dripping from the oaks. It even hung in the air. He might have told Royal (who was sitting three chairs away on the makeshift plywood stage) that he had been closer to the mark with the name of his little book of folklore: *Blood on the Beach*. Sweetpatch Island had soaked up too much blood in its history, and the blood had become the perfect, festering medium for the lunatic and the malevolent. Not even the twice-a-day scrubbing of salt tides could wash it away.

Like a disease, once exposed you were infected. Like a disease, it lay in wait in your body until a trigger released it.

(Is you comin to bed, sweet sugar honey?)

Like Boo Taylor two weeks earlier, Solomon Goody recognized a face in the crowd. He lost the face moments after seeing it.

Boo Taylor paid the fifty dollars in cash and puttered the launch through the green-wood pilings and walkways of the circus marina, through the alien faces too clean and too white to be of this rough place. Other faces, bored, watched him from behind polarized glass in fine establishments, places where the gulls and pelicans should be roosting and making chalky mounds of guano. He churned up speed now, feeling all those blank eyes watching as he approached the mouth of Mermaids Head Creek. He twisted the throttle steadily, enjoying the forgotten, angry whine of outboards, the vibrations jittering up his arm, the rocking planks beneath. Soda cans and scraps of plastic and paper rippled at the banks. He pushed through the last of the confining marsh boundaries and stranded hammocks and, in that moment of breaking free of the blood-soaked shores, acknowledged the release of his fear. The circus and its calliope complexity were melting in the heat behind him, and it was just the straight glass of the Yamawichee and the molten white sky and trees far enough away not to matter and the climbing whine of the motor.

Though his instincts beg he steer the craft northward and go on and on, embracing the mainland shore for as far as his fuel and the tides might carry him, he listened instead to the relentless voices of the dead. Wearily, he cut a slow, southerly bend in the waters.

Flags hung limply in the breezeless air. The early evening sun blistered behind a stringy haze. On the field, surrounding the stage, a yellow cap-and-gown ripple thrummed with heat and nervous expectancy. The stands brimmed with a slightly less disciplined crowd of parents and aunts and uncles. Occasional pops of lightening flashed. The valedictorian was at the podium expounding to her classmates that they were the future of America, that with freedom came responsibility, that they were going off in different directions like the branches of a tree but would always have their roots right here in Sweetpatch High. She spoke into the microphone at the podium, and her voice boomed from the speakers after a second's lag with an occasional screech of feedback that shot through his brain like a stiletto. She was a mouse of a white girl with a nose ring and green hair. The green clashed so harshly with the yellow cap that it hurt to look at her. She had already used the word "shit" at least three times in her speech.

(I'm out here, sugar baby.)

Searching for the face again, Solomon found Ruthie and the girls instead. Next to them, Martha and her children. Bored, all of them, but faking it well. They made a good photograph. On the stage, he was wearing his own ceremonial yellow gown, and he believed that with his hands folded neatly where the gown gathered in his lap that he looked composed.

(Does you see me? Does you remember how I taste?)

The perspiration dripping down Solomon Goody's face from beneath the ceremonial yellow cap was only from the heat. He was sure he didn't look at all afraid. He was sure he would make it through his speech, and then he would make excuses to Royal and Martha and he would load Ruthie and the girls in the rented Lincoln and drive away from the island as quickly as possible.

Boo Taylor followed the sub-tropical spits of oak and cypress and palmetto, cutting the engine because he was in no hurry to see what he had been drawn to see again, and in no hurry to return to port once this too-brief voyage was complete. The poisoned fingers of the wind ruffled through his hair and pressed the sunglasses against his face, wormed the taste of sulfur into his mouth. He spit into the water. Twenty yards off starboard a dolphin's spine emerged, a sleek, silver crescent rising, keeping pace, slipping easily in and out of view, free in all that space to go wherever it chose. Did dolphins hear the voices calling to them from haunted shores? Was that what drew them suicidally to the sand, where they might rot and let their blood spill and mingle with all the others'?

(Does you see me out here?)

He cut the engine again, slowing, sensing an arrival around the next fuzzy elbow of green or the next after that. The silver crescent moon fell and disappeared.

When applause erupted around him Solomon Goody realized the valedictorian had at last finished. A sudden cramp of nausea seized him as Royal took the podium and made a short speech introducing the congressman, an island native and the first African American to graduate from Sweetpatch High School. Solomon found himself standing to applause from the stands and the field. Several hundred plastic eyes pointed at him like gun barrels, shooting his picture and siphoning his image onto videotape. More lightening popped. He walked across the stage on legs he couldn't feel. Royal's hand was out. He shook it automatically, and Royal looked at him oddly when he felt the cold, shaky, sopping wet thing Solomon's hand had become.

Solomon grasped the podium. He felt every friendly and unfriendly face staring at him. He looked for Ruthie and Martha and the children but could no longer find them.

When he spoke, his own voice came roaring down on him a second later.

"Thank you, my friends." It was another's voice, disconnected from him. "I am so very proud to be standing before you, today. So very proud. Like many of you, I grew up on Sweetpatch Island. And I can tell you, I have seen a great many things transpire upon its shores. Certainly many fine and noble things. But just as certainly, many troubling things. I have seen prosperity touch lives and pass others by. I have seen men being beaten and men being healed. I have seen churches being burned and churches being built. I was fourteen...

...*years old when the motherfuckers shot the King in 1968. That it was the King who was killed was an outrage. That I had seen the King in person and had spoken with him and held his hand on this very island had made the outrage personal. I was fourteen and I wanted to take a gun and shoot the first bohunk white asshole I saw. Someone important. Someone I knew so the response would be personal, too. You shoot our King, then we shoot your King—sound fair enough?*

(Does you see me out here?)

The stadium jagged out of proportion around him, rising too high, stretching too wide, canting at illogical angles. The dull, stupid faces with their plastic gun barrels warped in and out of the rows, impossibly close and impossibly far away. He touched his palm to his forehead, mopping away the sweat. He was standing within the fetid and dank jaws of a beast or a carnivore plant creaking on strained tendons in the moment before snapping shut. He talked on, but he was an automaton, and it was instinct that allowed the words to continue. His mother had always told him he was born

(on this rottin' island, boy, and the rot's in your blood)

talking, and that he had never stopped. His words droned on, squealing on knife blades from the speakers. He kept speaking in this detached way, searching through the mass of blurred and warped faces. After fifteen minutes he knew the speech was certainly not one of his better performances, but he was beyond caring about that. It would be over soon and he could get away from the island.

"...the question all young people ask when they reach this special moment of achievement: 'What comes next?' Some of you are eager to go on and make a life for yourselves. Some of you are eager to go on and make a statement with your lives. Some of you, like me..."

"*...in my outrage, I was both impotent and omnipotent. I did not go out and shoot a white man, but I knew I could. I knew I could kill any one of the mother-fuckers right in that moment and they couldn't stop me. And so, in that moment I understood that I could surely do anything. For the first time, I realized I had all the power in the world right there in my finger. My trigger finger. I could do anything. They could not stop me. They were incapable of taking away my power to do anything I wanted at any time I wanted.*"

"...what excuse will you use to keep you from achieving your dreams? There are a whole lot of excuses out there to choose from. I'm too poor; I'm too weak; I'm too fat; I'm too ugly; I'm too black. The cops pick on me. The government picks on me. My

(dick too big for them pants)

boss picks on me. So easy to blame others when we despair. When we hurt, we point fingers. We seek enemies. We *manufacture* enemies. And, more often than not, that finger of blame lands upon whoever looks different from us..."

"*If they knew I had learned about my power, they would have been very afraid of me.*"

(climbin too high, an' forgettin where you come from)

He found the face again, cool and filled with merry hatred, clustered among so many others near the top of the stands. Over her shoulder was an angry black face that registered his moment of recognition.

" ...and so I challenge you to look your enemy in the eye..."

"*I have all the power.*"

(The King is dead, boy.)

A gun barrel lifted.

"...and tell him, 'I know your fear, because I suffer too,'"

"*All of you have this power, too.*"

(Long live the King.)

"...and that makes us brothers.'"

Someone behind him screamed. Shots rang out.

(Does this mean you ain't comin to bed, sugar?)

❖   ❖   ❖

Boo cut the engine and let the launch drift. The house stood on the site it might have occupied for a thousand centuries, jutting gray and broken from the rusty banks like a bone. A skull, many-eyed, peering out timelessly at a fierce sun—empty of reason, empty of sanity, empty of conscience or morality, empty of life. But not dead.

(You was born on this rottin' island, boy, and the rot's in your blood.)

"I'm here," he said out loud, and it was the only sound upon the water.

(dick is too big for them pants)

He spit, ridding himself of the poison.

(climbin too high, an' forgettin where you come from)

"I never forgot. You never let me."

He watched the many eyes, and the many eyes watched back. He looked for the changes. The further encroachment of vines and scrub. The remnants of the glass windows exterminated; some of the eyes closed behind plywood eyelids, eyes winking at him lasciviously. Another chimney fallen. The broken spine of the roof caving inward. The whole gray face peeling, falling away in the inevitable corruption while the crows and grackles and nighthawks flapped heedlessly in and out of the hollows. The sway of the tide caressed the boat, lulling it to sleep while he searched for some answer in the empty dark eyes, feeling himself being lulled to sleep while snatching vaguely through the ripe marsh, the smell of home, the call homeward...

...and realized the tide was drawing him into shore. He yanked on the outboard, heart flaring wildly, and when the engine caught, he jagged the craft away, heading for the open sea, escaping while a voice from the island, one voice out of many, happily laughed and called after him:

(The King is dead!)

Within ten minutes, the screams and stampeding ignited by the first shockwaves had receded. The crowd had shifted to the north end zone and the surrounding parking lots where graduates huddled together in clusters and parents attempted to reunite with them in the confusion. The stands were empty except for the two dozen or so people who had been hurt in the panic and those who had returned to tend to them. The wails of several police sirens were closing in from different directions. An ambulance had already pulled onto the field.

On the stage, Solomon Goody's dead body was surrounded by several people, including his wife and two policemen. One of the policemen was Wade Dutton. From a distance, it looked like vultures picking over a carcass. Also from a distance, Solomon's blood painted an abstract design of the stage floor. The blood found the seams in the plywood flooring and fell drop by drop into the island's soil.

Next to the steps, at the front of the stage, Dr. Theodore Sampson (who had taken over Dr. Silas Barnwell Taylor's practice twelve years earlier and was in the stands to watch his nephew graduate) and a paramedic tended to Royal Goody's wounds. Martha Goody stood above them, crying, with her hands clutched together at her chin. Royal, who had jumped forward as the first shots were fired, had been hit twice:

once in the shoulder and once in the leg. He was still conscious, but there was a great deal of blood.

By the refreshment stand near the north end zone, Gussie Ransome was hugging her daughter, Georgia, who was also in the graduating class. Georgia's boyfriend stood dumbly next to them—and next to him, in one big huddle, were Jeremiah, Shannon Leigh, Murphy, and Murphy's parents.

The gunman was caught without a struggle.

Empty Gardens ~ November, 1971

He realized why it was so quiet. The sound of wind chimes was gone.

Boo Taylor was kneeling in the ash and looking out upon the abandoned garden. November, he decided, was the very worst of months. Things died. Others clawed into the dirt to sleep. Yet others flew away, leaving behind only the promise (or threat) of a return in some distant, yet undreamed-of age. In this cool November season of death, the weeds had wasted no time in securing a foothold among the limp bean stalks and tomato plants and vines of squash and cucumber. Obviously, some things thrived in this season.

Gussie, in her cast, propped up on a pair of crutches, stood behind him in the shade of an oak. Further behind them, up the trail toward Sugar Dam Road, Wade was waiting in the car, motor running.

Boo was wearing a navy blue jacket with the right sleeve hanging limp and empty. His right hand, pressed to his waist, was wrapped so heavily with bandages that it looked like a white boxing glove. His shirt had been slit open from underarm to cuff, allowing him to fit it over the hand. A series of seven safety pins now clinched the sleeve together. The pins were just one more element of discomfort to accompany a grand accumulation of discomforts: the throbbing and itching beneath the bandages, the ache in his stomach from the rabies shots, the stitch inside his thigh muscle where a crescent of pink studs made a constellation in the shape of the moon. The hand was the worst, hiding beneath all those layers of gauze where it kept its secrets, where it slept, where it would someday come awake again like some cocooned creature and emerge and show what mutated new shape it had decided to take. The process of healing was anything but pleasant. His hand was a horror. At times it felt as if a swarm of beetles were feeding at it.

He had been through the ashes of the old shack, and it was like walking through a corpse. No matter how beautiful it had been in life, in death it was just a pile of dust. He supposed he had seen a good bit of death over the last months of his life and was becoming something of an expert in it. They found what was left of her in roughly the place where the bedroom would have been. A collection of old bones, folded in a fetal pile. Maybe she had even been asleep when it happened. He kept seeing the bandages on her face, mocking the strips of tape he had worn all summer over his broken nose.

"Who is that?" Gussie was calling behind him.

He was about to turn to ask what she meant when he saw movement in the distance. People were coming toward them from the direction of the woods and Pigg's Creek. Boo lifted his good hand to shield the glare from his eyes. Three people. One tall, and two smallish.

As they came closer, Boo recognized the tall one as Lester Meggett. He was trailed by two young boys, one on either side.

"What the heck's he doin out there?" Gussie asked.

Boo felt his good hand curling into a fist.

Lester was loping forward, arms swinging happily as the two small boys chattered with excitement. One of the boys was Kenny Hibbits. The other looked like one of Red Prettyman's little brothers.

Lester waved. "Hey there, Boo!"

Boo stomped forward, kicking ash and then dust to meet Lester Meggett at the border of the garden.

"Lester, just what the hell are you doin here?" he growled. "What are you doin out *there?*"

Lester looked honestly perplexed.

The boys stopped their chatter. They considered Boo Taylor with apprehension.

"Doin?" Lester asked. "Why, we wasn't doin nothin, Boo. Just takin a look is all."

One of the boy's chimed, "There's a witch lives out there. An' I *seen* her!"

"Aw, you didn't see nothin," chimed the other.

"Did too! It was a ugly old *witch!*"

Lester was smiling at the boys.

Boo took another step forward. He wanted to throttle Lester Meggett. "Les, are you really that stupid? After everything...and you still go over there? You take these *boys* there?"

Lester was about to answer. Then he recognized Boo's fury and hung his head. He kicked absently at the dust. "Police been out there, Boo; you know that," he said glumly. "Ain't nothin there to hurt nobody no more. Told these boys there was a witch use'ta be livin out there, but...well, they just wanted to *see.*"

Boo turned to the boys. They were now staring at the lumpy bandage consuming his right hand. Boo Taylor's anger was making him dizzy.

"You boys are trespassing," he said evenly. It sounded lame even as it came out of his mouth. "You got no business here. Or out *there,* especially. Ever."

He looked up at Lester who now cowered like a kicked dog.

"Les, I'm only gonna say this to you one more time. Don't you ever come down here again. You got that?"

Lester nodded slowly.

"Ever!"

His shout echoed over the open field. In the woods, birds took flight.

Gussie had limped forward on her crutches. Boo felt her hand on his shoulder, and he realized he was trembling with rage.

"Okay," Lester said softly.

And then Lester was walking up the trail toward Sugar Dam Road, passing Wade in the old Plymouth. The two boys followed him, sneaking occasional glimpses back at Boo and whispering to each other.

Gussie took Boo's left hand. Together, they walked back to the ruins of the old shack, when Gussie let out a small gasp. He looked at her. Then looked in the direction of her stare.

A shoebox.

Left at the foot of the gate to the old magic herb garden. Somehow not damaged when fire had taken the tiny shack and scorched the herbs into a field of black husks. Boo Taylor's name was scrawled on the box in childish letters.

Boo left her side.

The box was full of dirt. Laylee had put it there, because she had been expecting this. As he stared at the pile of dirt and as his anger with Lester Meggett melted away, he decided that maybe the old woman had set the fire herself. Maybe because she was too old and all used up. She had left the hospital in Corrington as an old woman, no longer using the cane as a prop, but hobbling on it. The steel-wool hair had gone a fine, cottony white. The crystal bright eyes had gone dull and yellow and watery. "Aw, don't you fret, Mr. Boo,"—the bandage robbed the sing-song lilt from her voice— "Mr. Wade can take me home. Where I belong now anyways. You come see me soon's you can, boy, an' we gonna have us a long chat.

"Think I'll just keep this next to my heart,"—and then the glass frog went into the pocket of her dress. And then she left the room on Wade Dutton's arm. And then she went away.

Where did the dead go?

"I know where they go," he said to the pile of dirt, and he knew because he had become an expert. He knew because he had kept company with the dead. He looked across the abandoned garden and the meadow beyond and the woods beyond that. And stared at a distant rooftop.

Final Part

Spooks

July 13
9:40 p.m.

The thousands of cycles—unstoppable, each unique and slave to its own innate chronology and yet intertwined in a complex symbiotic reliance that was the very essence of Sweetpatch Island—crept forward, steadily, relentlessly, on their invisible, time-out-of-mind ambition: tides and winds, sun and moon, storms, seasons, planets, stars, life and death, birth and decay. It was five weeks since the assassination on the school grounds, and as Boo Taylor sat high on the porch on Carriage Avenue, a dark woman who knew him well stood eight miles south on the crumbling ridge where Southern Bluff Beach and Sadfellers Beach lapped together. She watched the same violet shadowing of the sky, watched the same tide beat against the same blood-infected shores. The same expectancy for the things riding toward them, even now, from across the ocean. Before her, wide as a prehistoric reptile, an osprey flung itself talons-first at the water. Giant, shell-less snails pulsated in the shallows to feed on decaying matter. A fruit bat jagged clumsily, expertly, to catch a sulfur moth in its teeth. The woman—who knew all about stealing skins and things infinitely more horrible—began to hum a song she had learned long ago as a child. A song she had learned from her grandmother. Like her grandmother, she had a beautiful singing voice, had earned her nickname from it, had earned her last name from the weak little rich man with his deviant appetites, who had a passion for her voice, who was obsessive and carnal—but she had always preferred humming to singing. Humming was a more subdued sound. A more patient and secret sound. Humming traveled like smoke, seeping through screen windows and the cracks of walls, into ears and nostrils, curling around lungs and hearts and brainstems, squeezing and bringing death and madness. A sound that sunk beneath layers of blood-soaked dirt, long undisturbed, where it charmed the inert and decayed with an invitation to dance again in the moonlight. A sound that tormented the instinctive but stupid minds of dogs until they either broke free of their chains to join her or strangled themselves. A sound that coaxed men to pull triggers or set fires or throw rocks. (She'd always had a fondness for rock throwers.) Even now, her humming was lifted into the cooling air and was scattered smoke-like to a billion places, near and far, mingling with the churning of a thousand wheels. She stood on the bluff, patiently waiting until the sun was securely settled behind the mainland and the full sable trap of darkness was secured like a net over Sweetpatch Island—when the things of night arose from their slumber to play.

❖   ❖   ❖

Boo Taylor sat high on the porch on Carriage Avenue. A glass of ice was fitted into his mauled hand. A heavy ceramic ashtray, filled with three squashed cigar butts and a good bit of ash, sat between his hip and a half-empty bottle of Absolut. At his mother's request, the light was off so the neighbors wouldn't see him out on the porch every night smoking and getting drunk. He was not drunk, he had told her—just painlessly buzzed—his tolerance for alcohol had increased measurably over the past year. And he was not smoking now, only sitting and sipping melted ice and watching the street. He found he was less afraid at night when he was outside—as long as he was close to a door. Being inside filled his brain with claustrophobic inventions of horrors stalking toward the house. Outside, he decided, you could see what was coming. If the logic was faulty, he didn't care. Being outside was *better,* and that was enough.

He reached for the bottle and tipped a fresh inch into the glass. He remembered sitting across from Elgin Highsmith in the darkness of Buckley's Tavern a lifetime ago, drinking vodka, and a few hours later Elgin's charred remains were being lifted from the charred remains of his house. Charred remains that were supposed to be him and that were so much like Ash Marchant. He took another sip. Nothing had moved on the street for more than an hour. Not even a car had passed. An occasional, distant echo of a dog barking. The steady throb of the surf. Birds he could not identify flapping somewhere high in the silvery darkness. The alcohol was pleasantly numbing his brain, and all sounds were becoming fuzzy and far away, like the faint signal of an old radio. Or an animal purring in the night. Or a woman humming.

Awake in bed, Gussie Ransome heard the droning purr of an animal thrumming through the closed window. She would not look at the window. Bright moonglow sent watery shapes across the bed and the carpeted floor. Like clouds in the sky, she watched the shapes forming and reforming in the images of beasts and human faces in exqui-site detail. The animal sound rose and fell in a woman's voice—an old woman's song, but a young woman's voice.

She was alone in the bed. Murphy was asleep two rooms over, on the sofa in his office.

She stroked her belly, feeling for the heartbeat within.

The humming made her uneasy.

When she could stand it no longer, she slipped laboriously out of bed and, for the fourth time that night, went to check on the children in their rooms.

Henry Ray Dutton snapped open his eyes when he realized the low, mournful crooning he had been hearing was not in a dream. A crooked shape in the shadows at the corner of the room—clothes draped over a rack, he thought at first, but the shape was moving and the song was coming from that place in velvety waves. He let his eyes accept the darkness, and in time the lines of the shape, trembling in that lonely corner, sharpened into the ruined vision of his dead mother. She was slouched against the wall, wounded, bandaged and blind, hands held out in a feeble gesture of imploring.

Do you see me?

"You ain't there," he said.

Oh, I am. I need you, darling. I'm so lonely.

Her voice was a wind of sighs and despairs, smoke slipping through the cracks in his mind and rending his heart to pieces. "You're dead."

The sheets stirred around him. That stringy bar hag; she'd picked him up at that dive on Calhoun. The hag pressed a warm hand on his shoulder. "You havin a bad dream, baby?" she asked in a sleepy voice.

Henry Ray swatted the hag's hand and watched the shape of his dead mother, waiting for the spell to burst apart. Instead, the ghost sang to him.

Royal Goody drifted fuzzily from a fitful, nightmarish sleep to the sound of the humming. He blinked at the bedroom window, which was where the sound was coming from and where he now noticed a shape silhouetted against the curtains. *Solomon*, he though dreamily, and he rolled to his stomach as a dull bolt of pain bored into his thigh. It took him a moment to remember that Solomon was dead and that the pain in his thigh was from a bullet that struck him weeks earlier.

The silhouette moved, and he was about to call out to Martha to ask what she was doing up in the middle of the night—then he remembered Martha wasn't home, was on night shift at the Emergency Center this week.

He cleared his eyes with his fingers. The shape was no longer there.

Damn Percocet, he thought, dizzy.

It didn't take long for the Percocet to seep back into his blood, luring him toward a slumber where he heard his name being whispered from a musical fog.

Aiden Ballantine, who lived four blocks north of Royal Goody, saw a man he recognized at his window. Mr. Ballantine was unknown to Royal Goody and was therefore never interviewed by him. And yet he had lived on Sweetpatch Island for most of his ninety-eight years and certainly knew more dark secrets about the island than Royal Goody would ever discover in his books and computers and his interviews with those other old-timers. He was the oldest man alive on the island. Eight years earlier a series of strokes twisted and paralyzed his right arm and right leg. His right eye was pasty and unseeing. The right half of his mouth sagged and drooled. But he could still speak well enough for people to understand if they listened carefully. And his mind was still essentially reliable, although he sometimes confused names and the order of events. He had known dozens of hurricanes and a handful of snowfalls; he had known fires and mobs and many more catastrophes of man and nature, and he accepted them as part of the comings and goings of a century. Of course he had been a patient of Doc Taylor's and knew his elegant wife and their adopted son who was always getting into trouble. Thirty years earlier, when he was still driving, it was Hank Dutton who regularly serviced his Chevrolet Impala, and Mr. Ballantine could still recognize those pug-ugly boys and that pretty, fire-haired daughter. He had been a neighbor of Dan Shallcross and had known his boy, Benjamin, had even taught the boy how to shoot a rifle when the woodlands south of Mermaids Head and north of the Sugar Dam had been a hunting preserve. He knew Raymond Osgood Satterfield, too, though he never much liked the man. Had known Satterfield's young wife, had known exactly who she was, who the father of her child was, and knew all about the tragedy that took her life. He had been to Chaliboque as a boy when the mansion was a sturdy, bustling place, buzzing like a hornet's nest with colored hands and the fields surrounding it filled with October snow when the Sea Island cotton came to season. Samuel and Margaritte LaValle had been guests in his father's house. He had seen Joker Tribbit often when that largest and most powerful of black men was still alive—and like most boys of the time had been scared silly of him. He had seen Bathsheba Tribbit slightly less often but had been even more afraid of her, although he realized later in his life that he lusted for her, too.

When he was eleven years old, Aiden Ballantine had been with his father and Samuel LaValle and several other white men as Joker Tribbit was forced at gunpoint from his little cabin in South Patch. A big seaman named Cope Bullock hit him over the head with a coal shovel, and the others moved in to tie his hands and legs. They dragged him to the giant oak off Southern Bluff Beach where a skinned-alive Joker Tribbit had roared at them all—and maybe that was what brought that fierce, beautiful devil running. He remembered her screaming when her husband was cut down and thrown into fire, still screaming when the charred lump was dragged out by Cope Bullock and two other men and fed to the animals. He remembered every word that witch yelled, knew damn well it was a curse, and he had seen that curse come to pass time and time again—like the storms, unpredictable but inevitable.

It was from his bed where now, with his good eye, he saw the man he had helped kill those long years ago. He was there, accusatory, and then gone. On to some other errand—leaving a smoldery trail of mist and the faint, lovely hint of a song, which might be a woman humming. Aiden Ballantine, who had seen Joker Tribbit many times since his murder, this time felt a very gentle pop somewhere deep inside his skull and then a flood of warmth. His left eye closed. His right eye continued to stare. The last thing in this world he knew was the sweet, lonely humming that traveled through his window like smoke.

Winston "Fish Hook" Johnson, who once owned the High Spot not far from Eulahlah Colebriar's house and who had been interviewed by Royal Goody several times, was awake and sitting in a La-Z-Boy recliner watching a pornographic movie on cable television in the back room of his niece's place on Culpepper Road. The television was turned low so his niece and her husband—a lazy half-Mexican he despised—couldn't hear the grunts and groans. He jerked around when he thought someone was at the window, looking in. Maybe one of the many children who ran this ugly street and the neighboring trailer park at night like rats. He saw no one. He snapped down the chair and went to the window. Still no one. But he was sure somebody had been there. Because he had heard a girl humming.

So did Marcie Stone, four miles away at the toll booth at the foot of Dedmen's Causeway; Marcie Stone who used to be Marcie Glandon and who had recognized Boo Taylor several months ago when she had accepted his seventy-five cents the day he returned to the island in a big Buick rental, a pretty blonde at his side. She had once nursed a powerful high school crush on that same Boo Taylor, but at the toll booth, she was suddenly too stunned by a girlish embarrassment to say a word to him, and so she had melted in silence when he drove away, and—though she did not know why—she thought of him again when she heard the woman humming that song. A radio, perhaps—Pat Filemeno in the next booth must have left it on. It was such a pretty but lonely sound, she decided.

So did the Reverend Leroy Gibson Hatchel who was at the kitchen table in his house on the western bluffs where he was working on the speech he would give at an upcoming vigil in remembrance of Solomon Goody.

So did Archie Finkle, who had once hopped a fence at the old high school with friends he no longer remembered so they could dump a bucket of tar on some jig football player.

So did Sylvia Whitney, retired school teacher, now listening to the soft, sad music from her bed, retired now but who's first job forty years ago had been waiting tables where she briefly shared a shift with a strange and beautiful girl named Honey Belle Hawthorne.

So did Dewey Fitch, listening through the window of his Toyota Corolla, now parked in the Circle K convenient store on Pofoksgo where his ex-wife had sent him to get milk so the kids (some of whom were his, some of whom weren't) could have some for their cereal in the morning.

So did Jimmy Hibbits and a handful of his derelict acquaintances who were sitting in old lawn chairs behind Hanneman's Garage on North Polk Avenue and passing around a joint and a bottle of Thundercloud; Jimmy Hibbits, who had long ago been a friend of Henry Ray Dutton's, had once personally kicked-in and spray painted the roof of a chicken coop that belonged to an old nigger-lady somewhere in South Patch.

So did several patrons who were leaving Oakies after last call.

So did hundreds of others from every point on the island.

Six hundred miles away, Allen Noble sat on the side of his bed, hunched over, head cradled in his arms. Since leaving his wife, he was renting an apartment in Claymont near the Delaware River. He was rocking lightly. The space next to him in the bed was empty.

Deep in the vast Atlantic, tropical depression Constance swirled into hurricane strength and was just hours away from battering the Caribbean island of St. Maarten on a path that would inevitably lead it to the eastern cost of the Unites States. Meteorologists were applying their models, calculating scenarios, evaluating trajectories, making projections. They were forecasting a category two hurricane at minimum, likely bound for the Carolinas and certain to make landfall within the week.

Sweetpatch Island slept.

two

Royal Goody lifted the receiver.

"Mr. Goody?"

"Yes."

"Mr. *Royal* Goody?"

"Yes, can I help you?"

"This is Nathan Booker. I was an assistant to your brother. Solomon."

"Yes?"

"You're busy. I'm sorry, I didn't realize how late...Should I call back tomorrow?"

Royal dragged his body to the edge of the bed, grunting as his bandaged thigh shifted on the mattress. He cleared his eyes with his thumb. "It's okay, I'm up now."

"You're sure?"

"Yes. Who is this again?"

"Nathan Booker. We spoke once before. Shortly after your brother was, um— after he was killed."

Your brother was killed. The idea of it could still shock, could still paralyze. Royal's heart pounded sharply.

"Are you there, Mr. Goody?"

"Yes. I'm sorry. I'm just..."

"You were sleeping. Yes, I'm sorry to bother you—and it may be nothing important at all. You sure I can't call back another time...?"

"No, it's all right. Please."

"Well, as I said, it may not be important at all. I've been going through Congressman Goody's things at the office, and this evening I came across an entry on his personal calendar that's not on the calendar I kept for him. I thought I'd call in case...well, in case he didn't get the chance to tell you."

"Yes?"

"Yes, well apparently you and he had a luncheon meeting at the Sing Satterfield residence scheduled for twelve o'clock on July sixteenth. This coming Friday. Did you know about it?"

"No, I didn't."

"Well, good—then I didn't waste a call. Below the entry he wrote: *Royal needs to know!* He underlined it several times."

"And that's it?" Clarity was returning to his brain.

"Yes, I'm sorry I didn't get to you sooner. Our calendars usually matched, and I just noticed the discrepancy this evening."

"I'm sure if Solomon had a lunch meeting planned, it's been cancelled."

"That's what I thought, too. So I called to verify, and Mrs. Satterfield says she hopes you'll still be joining her."

"You actually spoke with her?"

"Of course."

"What does she expect to meet about?"

"I really couldn't say. As I said, I expected the congressman would have discussed it with you."

Grunting again, reaching to flip on the light on the nightstand. He took a pen from the drawer. "All right, fine, Mr. Booker. Do you have Mrs. Satterfield's number?"

He took down the number and cut short Nathan Booker's offer of condolences. After hanging up, he tried the number for Sing Satterfield. There was no answer.

Boo Taylor had last seen the inside of a jail when he was eighteen years old and was arrested for assaulting a security guard. His recollections of the experience were vague, indistinctly colored by humiliation and depression, a bit of fear, but mostly a great simmering anger. He had been too lost within himself at the time to really assess his situation or his surroundings. He was sure the place must have been murky and run-down, stagnant with the dead air of a thousand lost souls. In contrast, the Corrington County Correctional Facility seemed almost cheerful. The complex of buildings was clearly of recent construction. Dewey Fitch followed a half-step behind as he strode on a prim stone path toward the lobby of the administration building: elegant, beige stucco with a red tiled roof, a lawn of palmettos and myrtles and young pines, precise lines of cedar mulch, an automatic sprinkler system. When they pushed through the glass doors to wait in line at the security gate, an air-conditioned breeze scented of fresh wood and new paint frosted the sweat on his face, made him glad to be indoors. He might be stepping into a shopping mall.

They had some trouble at the security desk when it was discovered that Dewey wasn't listed among scheduled visitors. When asked, Dewey was unable to produce any ID and upon further questioning grew nervous and suggested he was just as happy to wait in the car until Boo returned.

Alone then, Boo Taylor shuffled along in a long column of mostly quiet, mostly fat women, mostly black or Hispanic, mostly wearing spandex pants and open-toed sandals, a few carrying small children and several with visible tattoos. They came to intermittent, stop-and-go gates where he held up his Delaware driver's license and the visitor tag that dangled from his neck and signed his name. After one such stop, a small, wiry officer in grays, who reminded him of Wade Dutton, took him by the bicep and led him down a separate corridor away from the rest of the crowd. They went up a flight of steps and entered another corridor and stopped at a door with a tiny, caged-glass window. The guard produced an impressive collection of keys and unlocked the door, then instructed Boo to step inside and have a seat. They were the first words the man had spoken. Boo did as instructed, and the heavy door closed and the key rattled in the lock behind him. There was no knob on the inside of the door.

The room was windowless except for the little square in the door and another in a second door. Boo sat in one of six vinyl-and-metal chairs that surrounded a heavy wooden table. The table was deeply scarred with scratches and engraved profanity and cigarette burns. The building might be new, but it was obvious the furnishings were holdovers from some previous incarnation of the Corrington County penal system.

He sat and waited.

His fear, which had become a constant thing, was worse in this place. He was learning to function despite the fear, but it was not always easy. He steadied himself as best he could with deep breaths, listening to hard-soled shoes clatter across the tiled floor in the corridor. Tedium, he recalled, was one of the sensations from jail in North Carolina. It had carved deep, glum, permanent grooves into every face he had encountered: civilian, non-civilian, and inmate. Tedium was its own prison. Sitting in silence, dull routine, like now—without a clock in this room it was just as possible that five hours had passed as five minutes. Occasionally, the decapitated head of a guard or corrections official (always bored) hovered past the small window. He drummed his fingers on the tabletop near a bit of etched graffiti that said *Praise the SONS of SETH*. He wished Dewey Fitch was with him. As much as he disliked Dewey's company, it would be better than waiting in this room alone.

A sudden noise announced the abrupt opening of the second door to the room. He straightened in his chair as the same wiry prison guard entered the room. A moment later, Lester Meggett—tall, insipid—was ushered in by another, burlier guard. Lester was wearing bright orange coveralls. His head was completely shaved; his mouth was hidden beneath a scrappy mop of mustache and beard. His hands were cuffed to his waist in a heavy contraption of chains.

He smiled happily. "Hey there, Boo!"

"Hey Les," Boo answered quietly.

A deep and obviously fresh cut was carved across the bridge of Lester Meggett's nose, and the middle of his face was slightly bruised. The burly guard was removing the chain contraption while the wiry one held the door open. Lester stood patiently while this went on. When the chains were removed, the burly guard gave Lester a shove into the room. "Fifteen minutes," the wiry guard said, looking at Boo. He had a strong hillbilly accent, and he looked as tough and uncompromising as a steel beam. "You want out earlier, you just give a knock at the door. I'll be in the hallway." Boo nodded. The guard coolly considered him for a moment, sizing him up, Boo decided, determining the best place to deliver a crippling blow with that stick strapped to his waist. Then the door closed, and Boo was alone with Lester Meggett.

The room suddenly seemed hotter.

Lester Meggett was rubbing his wrists and smiling his banal smile. He sat in a chair across the table from Boo. "You shaved your head," Boo said.

Lester patted his bald scalp. Three or four angry nicks stood out in the stubbly shadow. "They got bugs in here that get in your hair," Lester said. "Boy, I don't know if I could stand that. Hey, how you doin, Boo? You're gonna ask me why I done it, ain't you?"

"I wasn't planning on asking you anything, Les. You wanted to see *me*, remember?"

Lester answered by grinning and showing his teeth through his mustache. The smile chilled Boo. Lester Meggett was suddenly like this room—misleadingly innocuous. His eyes were half-lidded narcotic dreaminess. A smell of cigarettes and urine emanated from him. He reminded Boo of a taller, softer version of that long-ago monster, Henry Ray Dutton.

"Say, I don't suppose you got a cigarette on you?"

"Sorry."

The smile went sour. Lester leaned forward, resting his forearms on the table. His demeanor was now one of suspicion. "My lawyer told me not to talk to you, you know. He's a nice enough young fella. Don't figure he's been at it too long. Don't figure he likes me much—just *pretends* to. You know?" He made a hopeful expression. "You like me, though, don't you Boo?"

"I think you're a prince, Les."

"We're still buddies and all, ain't we?"

Boo felt himself losing his grip on reality. Lester Meggett was sitting across from him and he wanted to still be buddies. "Sure, Les," he said. "What's a little thing like murder between old friends?"

Lester dropped his head and pouted. One of his nicotine-stained fingers flicked at an itch on his damaged nose. "Heck, Boo," he said, "you killed folks before."

"That's not true," Boo said quickly and felt anger and uncertainty. He glared at Lester Meggett, overwhelmed with an urge to flee the room.

Lester squinted, amiably ignorant. "You're mad at me."

"Shouldn't I be?"

"You been by my place lately?"

"Your place? You mean your cell?"

"My *place*. You never came back around after that first time. Had somethin there I wanted t'show you."

His eyes sparkled.

"You mean your artwork?"

Lester smiled greedily. "My *eyes*. Eyes of my soul, Boo. Every one's a way in. Every one's a way out. Fixed her up some since you was there last."

"Sounds like I really missed out, Les."

"But I guess maybe you was mad at me. My daddy used to get mad at me. He used to . . ." The light in Lester's eyes flickered. Then, without warning, he slammed a fist against the table. *"I don't have to talk to you!"* he yelled, suddenly miserable and enraged, *"I don't have to!"* He stood abruptly.

Boo, heart racing and too stunned to move, glanced at the door where the guard's face had now appeared at the window. After several seconds, when the guard saw only Boo Taylor sitting and Lester Meggett pacing, the face disappeared again.

Lester was staring at the block wall, heaving deep breaths. Boo could almost see infection oozing from the man's pores. The air in the room was being poisoned. "You figure I was a good ball player, Boo?" Lester asked in a small voice.

Boo answered, watching him closely, "You weren't half bad."

"I wasn't." Lester was still staring at the wall. "I had a good glove."

"Good speed, too," Boo said, his heart gradually slowing to normal. "As I recall, you did a lot of stupid shit on base, and you couldn't hit the junk worth a damn. But I couldn't get a fastball by you."

"Never as good as you, though. Wasn't never in your league."

Boo said nothing.

"Goddamn, Boo Taylor, you was just about the best there was. Even with your hand all fucked up." Lester closed his eyes and laid his forehead against the concrete. His skull was covered in a thin sheen of sweat. Boo imagined a future of prison cells papered with nipples and cunts and red-rimmed eyes. "Never meant to hit that boy Royal," Lester said quietly, and Boo took a deep breath. "He's gonna be all right, ain't he? Solomon was a punk jig. He was a talker. But Royal, he was always a good enough boy."

"He'll be fine," Boo said. "Why did you want to see me, Les?"

"Why?" Lester turned from the wall. His head rocked back and forth; he smiled faintly and mysteriously. Boo waited. Lester's head rocked like a metronome. He gazed ahead as if he had found something interesting on the opposite wall.

When Lester would say nothing further, Boo rubbed his hand across his jaw and was surprised to see it come away with a fair amount of sweat even though the little room was just as frosty as the lobby had been. He watched as Lester kept at his steady rocking. This was not the simple, dimwitted boy he'd grown up with; this was something else. A complexity of disease and wickedness danced behind those once-simple eyes. It was not Lester Meggett. Someone had stolen his skin. Lester's flesh was a discarded hand puppet; he would need someone else's hand to slip inside that emptiness to animate him. The extent of Lester Meggett's originality was a pornographic collage taped to the cheap panel walls of a trailer.

Lester's eyes slowly came around to look at him. "They're listenin, you know," he said.

Boo looked around the room for a microphone. "Who is? They can't do that, Les, it's illegal."

Lester was staring at him dully. For a moment, Boo saw a younger Lester Meggett, hair spilling over the dull slits of his eyes and a simpering, miserable little girl beneath him. Beyond him, watching that spectacle, something dark and female and filled with malevolent good cheer. It was not the guards who were listening.

"I hear you confessed to setting some church fires, Les," Boo said. "Did you set fire to my house while you were at it?"

But Lester Meggett was drifting off again, becoming lost in some other place. That empty, discarded puppet. "Les?" Boo urged quietly.

Nothing. His head rocking again.

"Lester?"

Rocking, gently rocking.

"Les, did you set fire to my house? Did you try to kill me?"

"Kill you?" Lester said dreamily. "You can't kill a dead man, Boo; you know that." He closed his eyes. The slick bald skin above his brow wrinkled, curling in upon itself, and Boo realized Lester Meggett was on the verge of crying. "You know what she told me, once?" He ran a wrist across his lip and blinked several times. "Told me blood ain't really red. Said blood runs in two colors: black and white. Said they don't mix, and tryin to's like mixin oil and water. You try mixin em in the same person, that person bound t'be crazy. You ever here tell of such a thing?"

Boo Taylor blew air through his lips. "Jeez, I really couldn't say, Les."

"Said that person bound to show two sides, one side hatin the other. Said best thing t'do t'such a person is shoot it dead." He chuckled, wiped his nose again, and turned his back to Boo to face the cinderblock corner. "She promised me things, Boo."

"Who did?"

A high, wounded sound.

Boo leaned closer. "Lester, *who* promised you things?"

"You know who. She sings to me . . . I can hear her at night, clear across the sound. She sings. She sings so pretty."

"Tell me who, Les." He waited. "Les, is it Mamie Stuvant?"

Another long, wet sniffling breath. Lester Meggett's back shuddered. A darker orange triangle of sweat was appearing in the middle of his coveralls. *"Yes."*

Boo went cold. "But she's dead."

Lester turned again and leaned on the wall. His eyes were bleary and red. "Aw, she's dead then—so what? Okay, it ain't her."

"Quit fucking around, Les."

"Okay, then it *is* her."

Boo Taylor dabbed a knuckle at the sweat on his upper lip. "It's Luella Stuvant then, isn't it. Or Crystal Burne."

"She never left, Boo," Lester said and was grinning again. "That's the joke—do you get it? She never left. She was always around, gettin older an' older, never dyin . . . *promisin* things."

"Promising things," Boo said.

Lester pivoted his head on the wall and looked at him, puzzled. "Hey, I didn't set fire to your place, Boo. You and me, we're buddies."

"Then who did?"

"Others did, I guess."

"Others? What others, Les?"

No answer.

"Les, you lived next door to Henry Ray Dutton, didn't you?"

Lester Meggett took a sudden step forward. His eyes became fierce, and Boo Taylor flinched, lurched backward involuntarily. "Let me tell you somethin, Boo!" The voice had dropped an octave, took on a growl. Lester was looming over him. "Royal thinks maybe it started before Joker Tribbit. Well he's *wrong!* He's wrong, and he's *right,* too!"

Stunned, Boo said, "How do you know anything Royal Goody said?"

"Shut up! You listen, Boo. He's right 'cause they got the mark on 'em, all that brown skin, can't you see it?" The growl was unearthly. "He killed his brother, and then God sent him away and give 'em all that mark, like it says in the Bible. It's *us* against *them;* it's always been that way. *That's* how far back it goes. Oil and water. *That's* what she wants you to know, and she's gonna rip the flesh *right off your bones,* and there ain't *nothin you can do about it!"*

"Who?" Boo was grappling to keep calm. "Who wants me to know?"

The light in Lester's eyes blinked out. His face sagged. His expression went muddy. "Who?" Boo demanded.

But Lester was turning away again, slowly, like a bloom wilting. For the next several minutes, Lester Meggett said nothing. He leaned, slightly hunched into the cinderblock corner looking like a wayward child in a schoolroom and might have been humming lightly or may just have been breathing. Nothing Boo Taylor said to him had any effect. It was like talking to a stone.

Then Boo was shaken by a sudden voice from the opposite side of the room. "Your fifteen are up." He jerked around and saw the wiry little guard glaring at him from the door.

three

On the drive back to the island the newscast on the radio was all about the approaching storm. Constance. Might strike the barrier islands head-on, might veer north. Still too early to confirm but not too early to consider precautions, particularly in the low-lying coastal areas. The newscaster cautioned against over-reaction and suggested tourists sit back and enjoy the sun until further updates could be provided. This was an old drill on Sweetpatch Island, after all, and there was no need for concern.

Boo Taylor let the breeze pour over him through the open window, sniffing for any scent of the coming storm.

Thump.

What did I hit?

The wind was scrubbing his skin of Lester Meggett's pollution. Beneath him, the Yamawichee was tranquil. If a hurricane was coming, the sea showed no sign of it. He thought he might go for a swim before the day was over; the water seemed particularly inviting today, something old and cool and forgiving. He crested the causeway and Sweetpatch Island and the Atlantic beyond sprawled out before him. He thought, as he often did, of the misleading nature of the coast, a region caught between land and sea, neither one nor the other. It sometimes took a storm, when whole coastlines might shift overnight, to make that distinction obvious.

The news went on to announce yet another candlelight vigil in memory of Solomon Goody. This was being greeted with growing consternation from elements of the tourist industry who'd prefer the whole matter simply go away.

"Think we'll get hit?" Boo asked.

Dewey Fitch was sitting in the passenger seat with his hands in his lap. "That hurricane? I guess we're about due. Last real good one was Hugo and that was in eighty-nine. Tore the place up somethin awful."

Thud!

Something streaking through the storm. Something big.

Boo felt himself breathing easier. After Lester Meggett, spending time with Dewey was like a vacation. Dewey had been an ignorant and obnoxious boy, and it was hard to think of him otherwise. But he seemed to be on good behavior today, and

Boo wondered if this was requiring much effort on his part or if he had, against all odds, actually evolved some. He had given Dewey a sanitized version of his visit with Lester Meggett. Throughout the telling Dewey shook his head and whistled in disbelief. "Never realized how far gone the boy got," Dewey had told him. "Once I got married I guess I mostly lost track of ol Les. He was holdin down a job at least. Which for *him* is sayin somethin."

"He worked construction, right?"

"Last eight years. Handled a backhoe and some other big equipment for Satterfield."

"Do you know how he spent his spare time? Who he hung out with?"

"Got drunk mostly," Dewey told him. "Don't know as he had any friends to speak of."

"What about women?"

Dewey laughed meanly. "Les? He used to brag about some girl, but I never saw her. You think any woman would go into that awful place he keeps?"

No, Boo guessed that was unlikely.

Dewey Fitch's neighborhood was on the marsh side, a clutter of low ranch houses bound tightly together on sandy roads. When Boo pulled the Tahoe down Dewey's street he found the place only slightly less depressing than the trailer park where Lester lived. Dewey's house was a flaking red structure choked by runaway sumac and scrub evergreen. A battered Toyota Corolla took up the driveway. Two rusty bicycles lay dead on the lawn. As Boo pulled his truck behind the Toyota, a pudgy little girl, naked except for a diaper, trundled by on a plastic tricycle and shrieked in a tone too piercing to be human. A ragged dog circled her, barking incessantly.

"Say, how 'bout comin in for a beer? I'd sure like you t'meet Cloretta."

Boo sputtered; an excuse for declining didn't come to him fast enough, and so he reluctantly climbed out of the Tahoe and followed Dewey across the driveway to the backyard. It would be worth something at least to get a look at the woman who had actually married racist, piggish Dewey Fitch.

Out back, they found Cloretta Fitch seated in a lawn chair before an inflatable pool that was spilling over with small children of various colors.

"Daddy!"

A skinny dark child sprung out of the pool. He ran on deer legs toward Dewey who caught the child and swung him up to his waist.

"Wesley," Dewey told Boo. "He's second youngest. That other is DeeDee; she's second oldest, and them other kids is the neighbor's. Honey, where's the rest? This here's Boo Taylor I been tellin you about."

Cloretta Fitch was a heavy-set black woman with a pleasant smile. She extended her hand to Boo Taylor. Boo accepted it, looked at Dewey Fitch and the dark little boy in his arms, and had his first good laugh in months.

four

An hour later, Boo Taylor carried two pizzas and a six-pack to Royal Goody's front door. Martha Goody scowled at the beer but led him to the study where Boo found Royal spread out on the sofa under several books and errant piles of pages. Reverend Hatchel was perched like a bird at the edge of one of the few chairs not covered under paper. Royal was scribbling in a spiral notebook with a pencil. A second pencil was clamped in his teeth.

"You studying for a test?" Boo asked.

"Something like that," Royal gestured toward an armchair. Boo had to move a stack of books from the seat before he could sit. He placed the beer and pizza on the coffee table. Royal was wearing a T-shirt and faded red gym shorts; his heavily bandaged left leg was propped across the sofa on two pillows. Royal remained bent over the notebook. Boo shared a glance with the reverend and an uncomfortable spell of silence drew out. The smell of pizza was distracting, and Boo's stomach rumbled. It came to him that he hadn't eaten in nearly twenty-four hours.

Finally, still not looking at him, Royal said, "So."

"So," Boo answered.

"You're back."

"I'm back. Dewey Fitch is married to a black woman."

The pencil stopped moving; Royal glanced up. "You didn't know that?"

Boo shrugged. He reached for one of the pizza boxes. "How's the leg? Can I have some pizza?"

"The leg's better. Are you gonna tell me if you learned anything?"

"Besides Dewey Fitch marrying a black woman?"

"Yes, besides that."

"Can I have some pizza first?"

"I thought you brought that for me and the rev."

"You can have some too." Boo swung open the lid. He offered a slice to the reverend who accepted it and another to Royal who waved him away.

"I get the impression you're pissed off at me for some reason," Boo said.

"I'm not pissed off at you."

"Seeing him wasn't my idea, Royal. He asked for me."

"Did I say it was your idea?"

"If it makes you feel any better, it was an awful experience."

"That makes me feel just great. Did you learn anything or didn't you?"

Boo sighed. He looked at the pizza in his hand. Then he set it back in the box. "He's crazy," Boo said, then he reached for a beer.

Reverend Hatchel looked unhappy. "So you didn't learn anything."

"He mostly wanted to pass me along some messages from the great beyond." Boo told him. "He barely mentioned Solomon. He asked if Royal was okay."

Royal rolled his eyes. "What can I say, I'm honored. Did you happen to have a chance to speak with the DA?"

Boo settled back into the chair. Yes, he told them, he had briefed the District Attorney although nothing he had to say had seemed very useful. Lester had ranted; Lester was sick. "Who are the Sons of Seth?"

"I have no idea," Royal answered. "Seth who?"

"Just *Seth*."

"Seth was one of Adam's sons," the reverend told them. "Cain killed Abel, and then Adam and Eve had another son named Seth."

Boo Taylor considered this. "He was one of the ones who lived to be something like seven hundred years old. Right?"

"Why, I suppose he was."

"And if he was Adam's son, then that means we're *all* supposed to be the sons of Seth."

"Maybe. Although Cain went on to have his own children. Boo Taylor, don't you know your Bible?"

Royal brought his bad leg around, wincing as he set it on the floor. Several pages floated to the carpet. "Is that what Lester told you? About somebody named Seth?" He was suddenly eager.

"Not exactly," Boo said. "Look, I could try to tell you what Lester said, but it wouldn't make any sense. I don't think he acted on his own, if that's what you want to know."

"Lester Meggett could barely tie his own shoes," Royal said, disgusted. "Of course someone put him up to it. The question is *who?*"

Royal was staring at him purposefully. His expression seemed oddly mistrustful.

Boo grunted and spread his arms in a gesture toward the accumulation of books and folders and notepads. "Royal, just what exactly are you trying to accomplish here?" He grabbed one of the books on the coffee table; speckles of mold blemished the cover. *Sea Island Folk Customs and Rituals* by Dr. Donald T. Oeser. The copyright date inside the cover was June, 1924. "What's *this?*" he said, brandishing the book. "What good is any of this?"

Royal looked injured. "I thought I was trying to help us both."

"You think what happened to Solomon is related to me," Boo said. "Well, your brother made plenty of enemies on his own. He didn't need me for that."

"To my knowledge, he didn't have any enemies." Royal placed his beer on the table. He clasped his hands together lightly. "Your house was burned down, Boo," he said patiently. "And Lester set those church fires. I'm just doing the math. Which, by the way, is the same math the police have been doing."

Boo looked at the pizza in front of him. It was now making him queasy. "Lester didn't burn down my house," he said. "Lester and me, we're old buddies. He said so."

"But maybe," said the reverend, "whoever did burn down your house is the same person who was sitting on Solomon's grassy knoll."

"Reverend, you're still assuming it's a *person*."

"A person?" Royal asked, scowling. "You mean, as opposed to a ghost?"

Boo Taylor smiled grimly. "Somebody turned up with my *fingers,* Royal. What kind of *person* can do that?"

Knuckles rapped at the study door, and a moment later Martha Goody stepped in carrying a glass of water. Boo Taylor looked at her, feeling guilty and not sure why. She handed Royal the glass along with two pills. As Royal swallowed the pills, Boo turned his attention to the book he'd grabbed earlier. The book smelled of musty old basements. He thumbed through the pages, registering chapter headings: *The Role of Animals in Healing, Several Related Blood Rituals, Perspectives on Death and Dying.* He set this down and then gathered a wad of xeroxed pages that had fallen to the floor. He recognized the words as passages from one of Margaritte LaValle's journals. Royal's friend at Georgia Southern had personally copied the seven volumes in the university's care, page by page, and gave these to Royal. Having spent some considerable time himself poring over the documents, Boo had come to admire Royal Goody's genius for discerning anything like a coherent narrative from so many pages of monotonous and mostly irrelevant scribbles. Royal's current mission was to find evidence to support the theory that Eulahlah Colebriar, as a servant in Chaliboque, might have been a confidante of Mrs. LaValle's. The difficulty was that Margaritte LaValle's narrative was hopelessly sloppy and disjointed. Her handwriting was so excessively ornate as to be hieroglyphic; she bounded from one eccentric topic to another without transition, and she generally referenced others only by initials. In short, it was the diary of a turn-of-the-century woman who never intended her words to be deciphered many years later by a couple of nosy men.

Boo flipped to a passage that Royal had marked in yellow highlighter.

> *Informed Mrs. L and EK I have decided on Mishelle Elise for a girl. For a boy, to spite SV, Marque William and <u>not</u> that horrid Victor Aubrey. CV will no doubt be displeased as well...*

And another highlight, two pages later:

> *...had the pleasure of being reacquainted with the estimable Dr. F. over breakfast, who by all accounts is a worthy physician. He is not nearly the social bungler I recall from our earlier meeting in Savannah. On the contrary, he evinced much charm and compassion over the course of our meal, and I believe I detected a wink of subtle disdain for the insipid CV who nevertheless gushed shamelessly over the poor doctor's every syllable.*
>
> *It appears I am to avail myself of Dr. F. this afternoon for an examination, and already I sense his concern for the state of my health. Well, he is competent enough. Still, I might prefer to have Mrs. L attend me instead as she will be tending to YT who is fairly bursting herself. Shall I shock the good doctor and <u>demand</u> Mrs. L be present?*

When Martha Goody left the room, Boo looked up from the page. "This stuff reads like a Victorian romance. MaeEllen would eat up."

"I know you think I'm wasting my time," Royal said. "But it's actually quite fascinating. Finding something meaningful is like coming across a golden needle in a haystack."

"Who's *YT*? Could that be Laylee? Yulahlah Tribbit?"

"It's possible. In that passage, she's 'fairly bursting,' and the time coincides with when Mamie would have been born. Here, read these." Royal handed him a page with a highlighted section.

Boo read:

> *I may assume I am merely the luggage on this voyage. My fetal cargo is the legitimate treasure Mdsl V and her cousin truly cherish. Or rather, it is daddy's purse they covet and endeavor to secure by the rather old fashioned methods employed by the late kings of Europe for more political ends. SV's island barony requires a wealthy prince or princess lest it sink around him on its cottony foundations. Pity he overestimates the depths of such fortunes and underestimates the depths beneath him.*

Boo looked up as Royal picked out a new page for him. "Here's another Laylee reference."

> *On our way to the seaside, we intended to visit the stables where EK desired I see Candy Apple's newborn foal. However, SV was there with his negroe partner already examining the animal. They are an intrigue, those two men. Polar opposites: one so dark, gruff, and noble; the other so pale, refined, and ignoble. It was their laughter we heard as we approached, big J's fairly conquering my husband's, and I commented to EK it was a healthy reversal from the typical bout of shouting one is more likely to pose of those two. I then saw Big J's lovely child was nearby, no doubt spying on my husband with adolescent notions of romance. She is quickly becoming the image of her exotic mother, and I wondered if she were not the reason for such conspicuous civility. EK and I spoke with her briefly and, having no wish to spoil the morning over an unnecessary encounter with SV, we then...*

"SV is Samuel LaValle," Boo said.

Royal nodded.

"Not exactly a loving marriage." *My great-grandparents,* he thought.

"Don't draw any conclusions from a few passages. In other places, she raves about him in terms that are almost poetic. She wasn't much more than a girl when she died, and she was obviously in love with him. Or *infatuated,* at least. *He,* on the other hand, seems to have been...apathetic, at best."

"He had affairs," Boo said.

"Constantly. If you believe what she had to write, anyway."

Boo handed the documents back to Royal Goody. "What do you believe about Samuel LaValle?"

Royal sneered. "What's the correct thing to say these days? 'He was a man of his times.'"

"He was a murderer," said the reverend.

A man of his times.

"It was a different era," Royal continued. "Different standards. Jefferson had slaves; half the founding fathers did. Isn't that what folks like to point out? In the context of his times, what kind of man *was* Samuel LaValle? Or Joker Tribbit, for that matter?"

Royal was gazing at him intently.

Boo leaned over and set the beer down. The beer was tasting like water, and he wanted something stronger. The want was so powerful it scared him.

He was a man of his times, Boo thought. *Like me.*

five

Wispy bands of cotton streaked the blue sky. Gussie watched these through her dark glasses on the drive home from the obstetrician's office. Dr. Jossick was concerned her weight was too low; he was concerned about her back pains; he wanted her to stop working. *When it gets worse, give it a break, will you? You may look it, but you really are not twenty anymore. You have three weeks, maybe four to go. Your child has requested through me that you get your blood pressure down and your weight up.*

The specimen tests had been clear; the heart rate was fine; the culture for Strep B was negative. The baby was in position and even dropped a little, according to Dr. Jossick, although she was still nearly four weeks away—but that had also been the case with her first three. Her blood pressure was running a little high, but not danger-ously so. Also, her weight was off—she'd been nearly fifteen pounds heavier at this point with Georgia and Jeremiah and twenty-five with Shannon Leigh. She didn't *feel* exceptionally light, however. In fact, she felt very much like a stuffed sausage.

She wondered if she would see Boo Taylor today and wondered if it was just her raging hormones that made it hurt so much not knowing where he was every moment of the day.

A wave of heartburn caught deep in her chest. She reached for a pack of Tums that was jammed in the ashtray. She popped two, chewed them quickly, and swallowed them down.

She stopped at Wade's house to pick up Jeremiah. Wade was on duty. Gussie spoke for a few minutes with Becky Jo, used the bathroom, and drove the rest of the way home. Murphy's truck was not in the driveway when she pulled up to the house. In-side, Shannon Leigh and a friend were watching television. Gussie went upstairs and changed. She called the Taylor house. Bess Pope answered again, and Boo was still not home. From the bedroom window she saw Murphy's truck pull into the driveway. She went downstairs and met him as he came through the kitchen. His collar was unbuttoned and his tie was loosened. Without speaking or looking at her, he went to the refrigerator and took out a beer. "I'm grillin some burgers for the kids," she said. "Should I make you one?"

"We're out of charcoal." He said this to his beer can.

"I picked up a bag yesterday. It's in the shed."

"Fine, then. Do whatever you want."

Murphy disappeared upstairs to change. Feeling heavy and hot and exhausted, Gussie sat down in the living room, accepted a kiss from Shannon Leigh, and pretended to watch television. She heard Murphy head out back with Jeremiah and a moment afterward heard the shed doors being opened. Twenty minutes later, she opened her eyes and realized she had fallen asleep. She got up to use the bathroom again. She thought about calling Boo Taylor but walked out back instead. Jeremiah was throwing a ball at his pitch-and-catch net while a younger boy from the neighborhood watched. Murphy stood with his arms folded, watching the hot coals and radiating his steady aura of fractured dignity. Eight hamburgers were sizzling on the grill. Gussie went to stand beside him. The heat from the grill made her dizzy. After a minute of silence, Murphy asked, "What did Jossick have to say?"

"He says everything's fine."

"He didn't tell you you're too light?"

"Well, he *did* say that."

He made a grumping noise. She waited through more silence. A mosquito landed on Murphy's lip and he killed it by scraping his teeth over it. She wondered, as she often did, if he hoped she'd have a miscarriage.

After several more minutes of silence, Murphy muttered something about a "refill" and went into the kitchen. She followed him to get out of the heat. She put a baked bean casserole in the oven and made a tossed salad. She looked at the phone in the kitchen several times, knowing that Boo Taylor would not call her at home. When she was done in the kitchen, she went to the living room to sit down again.

Gussie was half-watching the news when Georgia came home from work. She thought about getting up to see her, but her back was so sore she decided not to move. Amazingly, she felt the need to urinate again. Eventually, Georgia came into the room. Wordlessly, she sat on the arm of Gussie's chair, and the two of them pretended to watch television. Gussie let her thoughts drift, lazing in the still bright sky, thinking of Christmases and snow and other things that were far away, and sometime during this drifting, Georgia's hand had begun gently stroking her hair. It was the exact gesture of comfort and acceptance she needed the most in that moment, and she wondered if she had decided so just before or just after she felt her daughter's fingers. Tears stung her eyes. She fought them away before they could spoil the moment.

She conjured vague, surviving images of her own mother and wondered if that almost-forgotten woman had ever experienced some similar conflict. And if so, did that conflict feed the cancer that had sent her to her early grave? Would it do the same to her?

Murphy, who was at least a hundred times the man her father had been, took his dinner to his second floor office and ate at his computer. Gussie and the children ate in the dining room. All through dinner, she could not keep from glancing at the phone on the wall and wondering about the man who might or might not be at one of the millions of other ends of the wire. She ate a little bit of salad and beans and could only manage four or five bites of her hamburger. She sensed the sun gaining speed on its plummet over the mainland. Remembering Dr. Jossick's benign concern, and spurred by her own maternal impulses, she forced herself to eat more. The hamburger increasingly tasted like a wad of putrefying flesh. She looked out the window and worried that it would be dark soon.

At 9:20, she told Murphy she was tired and was going to bed. He nodded indifferently, not taking his eyes from the baseball game. Shannon Leigh was sprawled on the carpet at his feet, watching the game with the same intensity. Georgia had left over an hour ago on a date.

She went upstairs, checked in on Jeremiah who was asleep in his room, and she changed into a billowy T-shirt. She sat up in bed with the lights on, listening to the nighttime sounds of the house. Beneath the closed bedroom door came the muffled chatter of the television and the barest hints of Murphy's and Shannon Leigh's voices. Alone now, thoughts of Boo Taylor burned through her ravenously. She stared at the telephone on the nightstand, working her fingers together in complicated knots. She felt the blackness at the window. Grunting, she swung her bulk around and very carefully picked up the handset. She dialed the Taylor house while she watched the bedroom door.

Boo Taylor answered.

"Thank God," she whispered, "where have you been all day?"

"I went to visit Lester Meggett. You remember."

"All day?"

"No. After that I flew to France. It's very nice there this time of year."

His voice was heroin seeping into her blood. She closed her eyes. "How did it go?"

"The flight was a little bumpy, but the food was great."

"I mean with *Lester*."

He breathed heavily through the line. "Goddamn spooky," he said. "How about you—what did the doctor say?"

Was that a creak at the steps? She held the phone to her chest. "Everything's fine. Boo, I can't really talk now. I want to see you."

"...I know."

"Tomorrow."

"Okay. I'll come by the office."

"No, I haven't been alone with you for over a week."

"Come by the house, then," he said. "Bess Pope is driving MaeEllen to Charleston to do some shopping. Lingerie, I think—I heard one of them mention something about Victoria's Secret."

"Is ten o'clock too early?"

"Ten is fine. I love you, Gussie."

She hung up quietly. She turned off the light and sank into the bed. Heartburn flared in her chest, and so she grabbed the last two Tums in a pack on the nightstand. She ignored the pangs of guilt and the sudden craving for cold hamburgers that went through her in waves, and she drifted into sleep.

She woke up when Murphy walked past the bedroom door. He was on his way to the sofa in his office, where he now spent his nights. Still disoriented from sleep, she imagined he was crying.

At 3:48 a.m., on the fifteenth of July, the National Weather Service officially upgraded Constance to a category three hurricane and predicted it would strike the coast somewhere between Brunswick, Georgia and Myrtle Beach, South Carolina within forty-eight hours.

six

The following morning, Boo Taylor moved MaeEllen's patio furniture into the garage and secured the shutters on the seaward side of the house. He was bringing down the rear window awnings when the doorbell rang. He worked his way to the front of the house. Gussie Ransome smiled at him through the screen.

"Yes, can I help you?" he asked.

"Quit foolin, it's too hot out here."

He held the door open for her, and she stepped inside.

"I'm playing hooky," she said, and then handed him a large envelope. "Here, you have a FedEx. It was on your doorstep."

Boo took the envelop and tucked it under his arm.

"You're not going to open it?"

"It's probably from my lawyer. He's been trying to call me, and I've been trying to avoid him."

She nodded. Then she leaned against the foyer wall, watching him closely. She seemed off balance and a little frightened. He was about to ask her what was wrong when she came forward, wrapped an arm around his neck, and kissed him deeply. When her face came away, she said, "I hear you have the house to yourself for a few hours. I was wondering if you'd like to make love to a fat woman."

He held her at arms length. "Is it...?"

"Is it *safe?* Of course it is."

He flicked a glance at the door, tried to dismiss rogue images of Murphy Ransome. "Are you sure you want to?"

"Yes, dammit. I drove over here, didn't I?"

"I mean, are you really—"

"Oh, shut up, and help me up the stairs."

All flesh, all roundness and damp. He was, more than ever, intensely aware of the texture of her skin against the tips of his fingers. Taut. Smooth. Wonderfully quivering—alive and throbbing at his touch.

Look at you.

He spent a great deal of time paying attention to her face, watching her smile, watching her wince as if in pain. Watching her mouth open wide to call out:

Oh, that's it. Right there. Oh, God.
Move me a little this way.
It's okay—you can go harder.
I want to see you.
Let me touch...oh God, yessss, oh I can't...I can't stand it.
A glass frog watched from the bureau.

❖   ❖   ❖

A fan in the window blew hot air across the bed. Gussie lay on her side, her head resting against his chest. Her belly, hidden beneath the sheet, was curled tight to his side. Boo and the frog were staring at each other across the room.

"I'm afraid," Gussie said.

"Me too."

"And I can't live like this."

Her hair was spread in damp ringlets over his shoulder where he absently stroked it. "I should have closed the door on you and sent you home."

She smacked his stomach, and then rolled to her back, groaning, smiling. "Like you ever had a chance."

Sunlight was banking through the open window. Construction sounds echoed up and down the shore as shutters and plywood were nailed over windows. Gussie absently reached for the Federal Express envelope on the nightstand. "What does your lawyer want?"

Boo took the envelope from her. "I have no idea, but he keeps calling. Maybe its another paternity suit." When he glanced at the return address he saw that it was not, as he had supposed, Allen Noble, Esq. of Flickinger, Kipp, and Diamond. Instead, it was a local island address.

Gussie scowled at him. "Don't tell me your gonna read your mail now."

Boo smiled back at her. He put the envelope back and rolled to his side, drawing the sheet down to her thighs. He stroked her huge belly. Gussie's fingers went to his neck. "Does he move around much?" he asked.

"Not so much anymore. He's running out of elbow room."

Boo let his palm run in circles over her flesh. The fan whirred steadily behind him, sending ripples across the bed sheets. Outside, between the occasional burst of hammers, cicadas shook the white-hot day like a thousand rattlesnakes. Gussie was trembling. Boo pressed his face to her hip and breathed in the smell of her. He looked to her eyes.

"Yes," she said. "We have time."

seven

Walking her down the porch steps, he was already suffering her departure as a hollow ache in his chest. "Storm's coming," he said.

They stopped at her car, and Boo opened the driver's door. Gussie took his hand. "I heard it might swing north."

"Just the same, I hope you have plans for getting off the island."

He helped her to the seat. She settled in with a sigh. "Murphy's aunt in Lake Moultrie is putting us up, if it comes to that. What about you?"

"MaeEllen wants to ride it out."

"That's not very smart, Boo."

"Then *you* talk to her. She says the house has survived two hundred years of hurricanes, it can survive a few more."

Gussie slid on a pair of sunglasses. She looked improbably domestic and cute stuffed behind the driver's wheel in her pretty floral maternity dress. She started the engine and rolled down the window. "Call me tomorrow," she said, very serious, and she drove away.

Boo went back inside and up to his room. He looked at the return address again on the Federal Express envelope. Then he stripped it open.

Dear Mr. Taylor,

Or shall I call you Boo? My late husband spoke so well of you, I feel we must be old acquaintances.

As I am sure you are aware, I have in my possession on this island a certain property of no insignificant historic value. One with which, I'm led to believe, you have your own unique familiarity. Unfortunately, the property in question is in a state of extreme disrepair. It is, in fact, a ruin. While there are many who'd prefer this magnificent relic be destroyed completely, I remain a staunch advocate of preserving "tresors historiques." Religiously so, I've been told. We cannot allow the past to simply die, Mr. Taylor, can we? It is a passion I shared with Solomon Goody, who was gracious enough to secure funding for my pet "adventure." A magnificent soul, the congressman, whose tragic passing we shall long mourn.

I understand you are a craftsman of some experience and talent—capable, certainly, of bringing my beautiful artifact back to life. I also understand, through the consequence of recent events, the prospect of a new venture might be of interest? I am committed to the home's complete resurrection, and it would greatly please me to entrust the labor of so intimate an endeavor to the hands of one of this island's most celebrated sons.

I propose we arrange to become "re-acquainted" for the purpose of exploring the possibilities of such a thrilling proposition. I have a residence at #1 Queen Avenue on the southern shore of the island. Shall we say noon on the 16th of July? I can promise you a wonderful meal and enlightening discourse.

No need to *RSVP*. I'll be expecting you, rain or shine.

—Mrs. Dalton James "Sing" Satterfield

He read the letter a second time. Then he went for the phone to call Royal Goody.

It was just past one in the afternoon when he made another call, this time to Wade Dutton to tell him he wanted to see Lester Meggett's trailer.

"What the hell you wanna go pickin around that dung heap for? Police and Feds already been through it."

"I know," Boo told him. "I just want to give it a look. It's something he said to me."

Wade's deep sigh came through the phone. "Well, Boo, I don't see's you got a legal right to enter that place."

"It's not a crime scene, is it?"

"No. But this time it ain't your property—*or* MaeEllen's."

"Who's is it, then?"

Wade was growing impatient. "Why, I guess it's that Satterfield company. It's a rental; all them places are."

"Good. I'll tell them I'm interested in renting and I want a look around. I'll meet you there at three. I'll buy you dinner afterward."

"I don't want your damn dinner. And what the hell you need me for anyway?"

"Witness, bodyguard—I don't know, Wade. Maybe they won't let me in. Flash your badge and look official."

"I ain't showin my fuckin badge."

"Fine. But make sure you bring your gun."

eight

Wade Dutton did not have to flash his badge. The resident manager of the Westview Court mobile home park—an emaciated, genetically deficient woman of indeterminate age—returned Boo Taylor's smile with a sallow, gap-toothed grin and handed him the key to number seventeen Carp Street. "Just drop 'em off when you boys is through," she said happily.

The key was attached to a white, plastic diamond upon which the number seventeen had been squiggled in magic marker. "Did you know the previous tenant?" Boo asked the woman.

"Naw, he was a quiet fella. Don't think nobody ever saw too much of him."

"No one's come in to clear the place out, have they?"

"No sir, that unit come fully furnished. Two-fifty a month plus utilities."

"No, I mean to *clean* it. To pack up the junk from the last tenant."

Her grin evaporated. "We ain't got no maid service," she said dully.

The woman disappeared back inside the office. Wade was leaning on his Oldsmobile, arms folded, and Boo wagged the key at him.

"What are you expectin to find in there, anyway?" Wade asked. "Not more fingers, I hope."

"No. Did you bring your gun?"

"I always bring it. It's locked up in the glove box, and that's where it's stayin."

"It won't do us any good there."

"We ain't gonna need my gun, goddammit." Wade circled around his car and opened the door. "Now, let's just get this fool's errand done with so I can go home and get some sleep. I got to start a twenty-four-hour shift soon as that friggin storm hits."

"I thought it was swinging north."

"It ain't swingin north. It's gonna bust us right in the teeth. And if you listened to your damn radio you'd know they just ordered a mandatory evacuation. So, if you don't mind, let's get this damn thing over with."

Wade followed Boo Taylor's Tahoe on the short ride to Carp Street. They pulled in front of Lester Meggett's home: a tin box broiling in the sun, olive-drab and forlorn. The windows were drawn and dark, expressing nothing, like eyes hidden behind sunglasses.

Boo got out of his truck, and Wade Dutton joined him on the yard. "And I don't know what the hell I'm doing helpin *you* for anyway," Wade said, continuing the conversation.

"You're not helping me," Boo told him. "You're helping Gussie."

"You're damn right I am. And that's the only reason I'm here."

Wade looked up and down the road, seeing only a few nondescript residents milling through the late morning heat. The rusted-out Monarch had been impounded, but its cinderblock roost still occupied the driveway. The next unit down, number nineteen *(Henry Ray lived there)* was deserted and effusing a breath of mildew. Boo swung open Lester's creaking screen door and held it ajar with his hip. He slipped the key into the lock. A low rumble poured forth from behind the door, and Boo Taylor immediately recoiled from the doorknob. He backed away, and the screen door slammed shut. The sound from inside dissolved and blew away.

"Did you hear that?"

"I heard something," Wade said, suddenly cautious. "What was it?"

"Sounded like a dog to me."

"I don't know what it was."

"It was a dog."

"It didn't sound like a dog. It sounded like...somebody laughing."

(Or humming?)

Wade searched the street again, found nothing out of the ordinary. Then he glanced at the bland windows of Lester's trailer. Had the drapes moved? A black, vertical gap now appeared down the middle window on the left—it had been pulled shut before.

"Get your gun," Boo said.

Wade glared at him. "Shit on that," he said and turned to gape dumbly at the doorknob where the plastic seventeen was still swinging. He stepped to the screen door and gave it a brisk rap.

They listened for the sound of laughter or humming or a dog attacking, but the house was mute.

"Hello!" Wade shouted at the door. He knocked again. "Anyone in there?"

Boo moved next to him. Wade pounded several more times.

"Police officer; open up in there!" Wade yelled, and in self-disgust muttered "shit" under his breath.

They stood by the door listening. When there was nothing, Wade walked to his car. He leaned in through the passenger side, flipped open the glove compartment, and retrieved a black leather bundle. Discreetly checking up and down Carp Street, he moved back to the door of the mobile home. "Okay," he ordered, shouldering Boo Taylor aside, "you hold that fuckin storm door open and keep the hell out'a my way."

Boo gripped the handle of the screen door and opened it, standing in the yard well away. Wade fixed his gaze on the door; his jaw was clenched and throbbing. He unholstered the handgun and pointed it at the ground.

"Police," Wade shouted, "coming in!"

He let the holster fall to the ground. He reached for the key, turned it, and threw open the door.

The stench struck them both immediately. It came rolling out in a sour cloud, hot and thick, like smoke pouring from an open oven. Wade grunted and took a step inside, bunching his nose in revulsion. Flies were buzzing in great numbers. As he made a quick sweep of the front room, Boo Taylor followed him inside.

"Nobody here," Wade announced, still grimacing.

"You're sure?"

"Hell yes, I'm sure. I don't know what that noise was, but there's nothin in here but a lot of fuckin garbage." He bent to retrieve the holster, dusted it off, and tucked the gun back in it.

Inside again, he stepped with Boo Taylor deeper into the room. The stink had not diminished since the first blast.

"Maybe we should skip dinner," Boo said.

Wade ignored this.

The smell—part garbage pail, part sewer, part cigarette—wafted over them. Ahead, a sofa was piled with clothes and newspapers and empty beer cans. The smell seemed to be coming from everywhere but most strongly from the kitchenette where the buzz of flies was like a small chainsaw. Wade picked his way carefully over the junk on the floor: more clothes and beer cans, reams of newspapers, raw splashed-open pages of pornographic magazines, dried pizza crusts, empty bags of chips. *We ain't got no maid service.* Well that was true enough. When he felt he could handle it, he looked up at the walls.

The eyes had spread.

"Crazier'n a bedbug," Wade said and gazed around at the multitude of staring, lunatic eyes.

The last time he'd been inside Lester Meggett's place this bit of artwork covered a swath of about four feet wide, starting about a foot above the sofa. Now, the eyes covered every inch of the living room paneling. They had even crept onto the ceiling— by several feet in some places. He imagined a fungus growing out of control, feeding on stale chips and beer.

Boo Taylor said, "Reminds me of a room in Chaliboque. Upstairs. The walls were covered in graffiti. It was pretty sick stuff."

"*This* is pretty sick stuff."

Christ eyes, Elvis eyes, beer-model eyes. Nipples, staring. Cunts, winking. Eyes from the *TV Guide,* from sports pages, from cereal boxes, from the Sunday funnies and centerfolds and magazine covers and catalogues. Several sets of hand-drawn eyes, distorted and child-like. *How much further would he have taken it,* Wade wondered, and then realized Lester Meggett had taken it as far as it could have gone. Madness and murder. He now noticed the newspapers and magazines on the floor had been cut apart. The eyes must have been Lester's singular obsession over the last year or so.

No, that wasn't quite right, was it? He'd been up to other things, as well.

...quiet fella. Don't think nobody ever saw too much of him.

From the corner of his vision, Wade saw Boo Taylor weaving through piles of junk closer to the wall. Instinctively, he shadowed him. While Boo studied the collage, Wade leaned over to poke through a stack of trash that hid a coffee table. More cans and empty pizza boxes. An envelope with a vaguely familiar name scrawled over it.

Sandy Baker, Sand Meggett, Mrs. Cassandra Bakr-Meggett

When he looked up he saw that, incredibly, Boo Taylor was reaching that scarred right hand toward one of those eyes, was actually going to touch that thing. "Don't—" Wade started, but it was too late.

Boo peeled a small photograph from the wall. He held it close to his face and stared at it.

"What is it?" Wade asked.

A moment later, Boo looked up. He was frowning. He held out the picture, and Wade took it from him.

"That's me," Wade said. He was in a softball uniform, mugging for the camera. The picture was at least six years old and should have been in a photo album back at his house. "How the hell'd Lester Meggett get this?"

"Good question. Was this here when you searched the place before?"

"I didn't search it—that would'a been the Feds. And maybe a few guys from our detective unit."

"Sweetpatch Island has a detective unit?"

Wade stared at the picture, dumfounded. "Becky Jo took this." He held the thing at arm's length. He felt sick. His picture was in Lester Meggett's home. Was stuck in the middle of that *monstrosity*.

"Look at this one," Boo said. He had stripped off another picture and was holding it up.

"Solomon Goody?"

A young man, glowering, wide afro.

"It's from the high school yearbook," Boo told him.

"Who the hell else is in there?"

"I don't know. I'll keep looking. Why don't you check around some of the other rooms?"

Wade glanced again at his photograph. He slipped it into his shirt pocket. "What am I supposed to be lookin for?"

Boo Taylor was pressed even closer to the wall now, squinting and running his finger over various bits of human anatomy. "Shrunken heads. Maybe a bubbling cauldron."

Sighing, Wade jammed the holstered .38 into his waistband. He watched Boo Taylor's back, watched the big muscles bunching at his shoulders as Boo leaned further into Lester Meggett's nightmare. He wanted to haul the man off by the shirttail and get the hell out of this creepshow.

You got steel in you, Mr. Wade.

A nasally voice under a mummy's wrapping. Root fingers holding his hand. He had promised...

"Fine," Wade grumbled and tiptoed around mounds of Lester-debris toward a door that turned out to lead to a small bathroom. The bathroom was, as expected, filthy. A handful of flies pinged at the window. Magazines were clustered by the toilet. A single, yellowing towel looped over a broken railing on the shower stall. When he opened the medicine cabinet he found it much like his own: green bottle of Excedrin, Band-Aid tin, striped can of Barbasol, razor. Collecting dust, a single prescription bottle, which he picked up and rattled. Compazine suppositories, prescribed in 1988 by a doctor whose name Wade didn't recognize.

On to the bedroom and an old mattress with bedcovers he couldn't bring himself to touch. He made a cursory sweep of the room, found nothing of interest, and then backed out.

Boo Taylor was still studying the walls.

"Find anything else?"

"This one"—Boo held up a picture—"looks like Garson Marchant, probably back in his twenties, in an army uniform. Also, there's a picture here of my old girlfriend."

"Your *who?*"

"The one I brought to the funeral, which I think is where this picture must have been taken. Les had a crush on her. Did you check the kitchen?"

Wade glanced toward the filthy kitchenette. Flies were ricocheting madly around an overflowing trashcan—electrons whirling about an atom. "I guess that's next," he mumbled. He inched forward, and as he entered the kitchen area, the flies fizzed apart, rising and circling him. He swatted a clear space in front of his face. Around him, the sink and countertop were slopped with dishes of rotten food, Styrofoam cups, assorted beer cans. He opened cabinet doors, finding nothing exceptional. Wincing, he grabbed the handle of the refrigerator. He tugged it open. Lightless. Only a pungent sourness. A single jar, filled with some moldy fluid, sat on the middle of a rack. Wade was reaching for it when, just inches from his nose, a tail switched, a set of yellow eyes blinked. "*Jesus!*" he yelled and banged backward.

The thing scurried away.

Boo, from the living room: "What? What is it?"

Wade bent over, hands on knees, on the verge of vomiting. "Just a rat."

"A what?"

"A *rat*. It scared me."

Wade took several deep breaths and stood straight again. He looked to see where the rat might have disappeared, wondering if there were more. Of course there were more. He felt a depression settling over him; the place was depressing; the place was filled with germs and who knew what other species of sickness. He wanted to grab

Boo Taylor and get out now, but when he looked over, Boo was engrossed with Lester Meggett's collection of eyes.

"Boo," he called out.

But Boo Taylor was reaching again into Lester Meggett's masterwork.

♭nine

"Is this you?" the boy asked the old witch, when the smell of peaches filled the kitchen because the man stepped on a peach and it gave a little wine. Dried-root bats and mummified coon paws dangled above his head while poisoned ice cubes swam in jelly jars and rats gnawed away inside kitchen walls. It was the last day of his innocence.

"My little girl," the witch crooned to the boy, "my only little girl," laughing her awful laugh. "Girls always been what we do best in my family.

"Strong little girls."

"Who's that supposed to be?" Wade had moved up beside Boo Taylor and was looking over his shoulder.

"Luella Stuvant," Boo told him. His own voice seemed distant. "Mamie Stuvant's family. This picture used to be on Mamie Stuvant's refrigerator."

A dark young woman sitting, holding a fair-haired infant while a black-haired toddler smirked at her side.

Hated one and liked the other.

A flick of the old woman's knife, a snap of the young woman's teeth. Two fingers, drifting, pickling in a sea of formaldehyde. *Coon paw.* The missing parts, curling in a dismembered sign of peace, signifying the magic number.

"Boys ain't nothin but a curse."

"Two daughters," Boo said.

"What?"

"She had two daughters. Mamie Stuvant had two *grand*daughters." The photograph was badly faded, held to the wall by two strips of duct tape. A circle, dark red marker scribbled heavily, over and over, made the picture a bull's eye in the middle of the room's southern wall. *Ate one up and licked the other,* Lester had scrawled above the picture. "Royal was right—we're not looking for ghosts. We're looking for Mamie Stuvant's granddaughters. *Both* of them."

An hour later, Boo Taylor was staring at an uneaten plate of ribs.

"You know what I was thinkin about?" Wade was saying, "About that time you whooped my ass on the playground. You remember that?"

Boo pushed the plate away. "You made me eat grass."

"I don't remember *that.* I don't even remember what got you so riled."

"You broke the news to me that I was adopted."

"Oh." Boo watched the memory come back to him. Wade suddenly became sheepish. "Oh, right. Now, who'd figure that'd be a thing to get somebody so mad."

"I don't know, but as I recall that seemed to be the purpose."

"I guess. Dumb kids." Wade wiped a napkin across his mouth and dumped it on his plate. "Poor fuckin Les. I used to pick on him, too."

"Don't start feeling guilty, Wade. You pretty much picked on everybody." Boo took a long gulp of his iced tea, emptying it. Wade was looking glumly at his plate. Boo watched him, thinking about that long-ago day on the playground. The taste of grass leaking down his throat. The anger that felt like a hot ball lodged in his chest.

You're a liar!

Sighing, Boo reached into the rear pocket of his jeans and withdrew the letter from Sing Satterfield. He handed it over the table to Wade.

"What's this?"

"It came today," Boo said. He watched while Wade Dutton read. When he was finished, Boo asked, "Do you know her?"

"No. *Nobody* knows her. The sixteenth, she says. That's tomorrow."

"I know."

"There's only a fuckin hurricane on the way." Wade handed the page back. "That's some strange fuckin letter. Who the hell talks like that?"

Nobody, Boo thought.

Nobody knows her.

"I spoke to Royal this afternoon," Boo said. "Did you know he and Solomon were supposed to have lunch with her tomorrow, too?"

"How would I know somethin like that?"

"And Lester worked for Satterfield Properties. And rented that place from Satterfield, too. Kinda makes you wonder, doesn't it?" Boo folded the letter and stuffed it back into his pocket. Wade was eyeing him cautiously.

"You're not thinkin of goin there," Wade said. "To her house?"

"Royal Goody thinks it's a good idea. The reverend, too."

"It's *not*. It's a *bad* idea. Among other things, in case you're wonderin, there's this little thing called a mandatory evacuation."

"She says 'rain or shine.'"

"I don't care what she says."

"You don't think there's something strange about that letter?"

"I just said there was, didn't I?"

"Royal thinks she might be Crystal Burne."

Wade was silent. He leaned back in his seat and folded his arms. "In that case, Royal's as flat-out stupid as you."

The waitress came by, and Boo asked for the check. Wade was still staring at him, unhappy.

"What are you thinkin of doin, Boo?" Wade asked quietly.

Boo Taylor fished for his wallet. The tables around them were empty. It finally registered to him that the restaurant was about a third filled. The exodus from the island had begun.

He looked up and met Wade's gaze. "Whatever I have to," he said.

He paid the bill. They left their mostly uneaten dinner and walked toward the parking lot. A strong wind was gusting through the marina, jostling boats where they were bound to their moors. Bits of trash danced along the boardwalk. A vinyl banner over a book store snapped and kicked viciously. Up and down the Harbor District, shop windows were being boarded over.

"Start my shift soon," Wade said. "Got to make sure all the lemmings exit in an orderly fashion. I suppose that ain't gonna include you, is it?"

Boo shook his head. "I have a lunch meeting with the famous Sing Satterfield, remember? Besides, MaeEllen wants to ride it out."

"That's damn foolish."

"You sound like your sister."

As they turned off the boardwalk into the parking lot, Boo was able to make out the words on the whipping banner. GO AWAY CONSTANCE!

"It's always the damn locals," Wade groused. "Tourists at least got the brains to clear out, but you just go ahead and try gettin the island folk to show any fuckin sense. We'll be fishin 'em out of their homes for days, and they'll all be hollerin about why we took so damn long."

They had come to Wade's Oldsmobile. Wade unlocked the door and climbed in. When he reached for the glove compartment, Boo realized what he was up to. "Wade, I can't take that," he said.

Wade shoved the holstered pistol into his hands. "Sure you can." He was looking furtively around the parking lot.

"But it's your gun."

"It ain't my duty gun, it's my *own*. Smith and Wesson thirty-eight. You know how to handle it?"

Boo hefted the thing, and it was deceptively heavy. He wondered if he could even hold it with the three remaining fingers in his right hand. "Is it loaded?" he asked.

Wade barked a laugh. "Hell, if you can't figure that out, you better give it back right now."

Above, gulls bounced across the sky, cried sharp complaint. In the distant east, a flat spiral of white cotton, hovering over the ocean, turned like a slow-moving merry-go-round on its way to landfall. Boo Taylor stood and stared at the heavy lump in his hand like a backwoods rube. He felt as if he had just taken a step forward, committing to something he wanted no part of. Wade Dutton was fixing him with a gaze that was an amalgam of worry, reverence, and resolve.

"Murph's family," Wade said. "You're my friend, okay?"

"Okay."

"I don't know what's goin on here," Wade continued. "But I'm scared for Gussie." He raised a stringy, orange-tufted arm, pointing a finger under Boo's chin. "Boo Taylor, I'm tellin you, you better look after Gussie and see she don't get hurt."

"I will," Boo told him.

Boo went back again to the day on the playground. The big fist that had slammed like a cannonball into his cheek and sent him into the clouds. *Liar! You're a big fat liar!* No, Wade Dutton, at least, had not lied to him. He was one of the few who had told the truth.

Boo Taylor, you're a bastard!

Wade got into his car and pulled away.

Squinting to keep the flying sand from his eyes, Boo made his way to the Tahoe. He climbed inside and hid Wade Dutton's .38 under the driver's seat.

The three-mile drive to MaeEllen's house took him nearly forty minutes as Boo fought cross-purpose against the stop-and-go traffic that was migrating en masse toward the causeway. When he reached home, the night was prematurely dark and the wind had increased markedly. MaeEllen was in bed early, and Bess Pope was in the kitchen inventorying provisions.

It was quarter past nine when Bess Pope called him to the phone. It was Gussie, calling from home.

"When are you leaving the island?" he asked her.

"Tomorrow, sometime early afternoon."

"That's cutting it close, Gussie. Landfall's supposed to be at four."

"I have some things to mop up at the office in the morning. Besides, Wade says it's still enough ahead of the storm, and most of the traffic should be gone by then. He says you can't even walk across the causeway right now, it's so packed."

"How long will you be away?"

"I guess that depends on the damage back here."

He didn't have a phone number for her. He wouldn't be able to reach her. She wouldn't be able to reach him.

"You're still going to Sing Satterfield's with Royal?" she asked.

"Royal and the rev. The rev insisted on coming."

"Boo, how do you know she'll even be there? Have you tried calling?"

"About a dozen times."

"And?"

"And, no answer."

"Well, there you go. She's long gone, like anybody else who has any sense. You know, the power's likely to go out, and who knows for how long? Are you stocked up? Do you have enough drinking water? You really should leave the island, you know."

"I know."

"I have a bad feeling."

So do I. "I'm sure it's just your hormones acting up," he said. "Gussie, I'll be fine; I'm not the one who's almost nine months pregnant. Get off the island as early as possible tomorrow, okay?"

"I will. Boo, I need to go now."

She was whispering. He imagined her looking over her shoulder, and he hated himself. "Fine. Give Murphy my best," he said, and he hung up.

He wandered out to the front porch and sat on the wicker bench.

Wind was blowing firmly from the Atlantic. From the beach, the surf thudded over and over, unrelenting. Monsters swam beneath the waves. Boo Taylor breathed in the brine and electricity of the coming storm.

The letter from Sing Satterfield was still in his pocket. He took it out and read it again. He had read it over a dozen times now, and with every reading could hear Crystal Burne's gloating voice ringing more clearly between the lines.

I feel we must be old acquaintances.

Royal's reaction to the letter had been almost violent. Royal had wanted to go barging down there immediately with the police.

"And tell them what, exactly?"

"Boo, if there's any chance she's really Crystal Burne...If she had anything to do with Solomon's death...Boo, she's taunting us, can't you hear that?"

Yes, he could hear it. He wondered what he would be driving to tomorrow morning. And wondered if it would be better to go alone.

After a half an hour of sitting and mostly staring at the street, he stood up. Nothing had happened, other than the wind becoming infinitesimally stronger. Quietly, he went inside, returned minutes later with a bottle of vodka and a handful of cigars.

A little more than a mile away, at the island's single point of egress, all four lanes of Dedmen's Causeway were clogged with out-bound traffic. At 7:00 p.m., access onto Sweetpatch Island had been officially discontinued to all but emergency vehicles, which now had to take the ferry over from Corrington Landing. Soon, the waters of the Yamawichee Sound would be too rough for even that traffic. Wade Dutton, on duty at the Moses Hammock Lookout, sat in his police cruiser watching the endless crawl of brake lights as bits of jetsam strained across a darkening sky. The view reminded him of a movie he had once seen about the end of the world.

On the southeast corner of the island, where the Satterfield Estate kept vigil over an angering Atlantic Ocean, two sisters *(daughters)* celebrated a dark reunion. They sat on the back deck in wicker chairs, high above the rocky sea wall, letting the hot winds of approaching Constance toss their hair.

"Tomorrow," one *(hated one)* said.

"I'm afraid," the other *(liked the other)* said.

From a lighted window behind them, another watched.

ten

July 16

He woke up on the porch, not sure where he was at first, thinking he was perhaps back in his home in Delaware before it had been burned to the ground, killing one of the few men he could honestly call friend and putting an end to what had once been his life. Back home in his bed, everything that had happened since was just one long bad dream—or a series of bad dreams all strung together. Then the wind was rippling his shirt, and he lifted his head from the pillow on the wicker bench, and it all came slamming back to him. This was not a dream, and this was not his bed, and this was never his home. The rough wicker had cut grooves into his skin. The empty bottle of vodka was on its side. The ashes from the cigars had been blown to the far corners of the world.

He pushed up from the bench until he was sitting.

It might be seven o'clock in the morning, he judged, though the sky was unnaturally dark and it could be much later. Somewhere behind him in the east, the rising sun was buried behind a colossal pinwheel of cloud and electric fury. There would be no sunrise today.

He thought of Gussie.

He wondered if she had risen yet. He ran a hand over his face, feeling the rough edge of whiskers and was thankful his metabolism and vodka made for a good partnership; he never got a vodka hangover and, although it would have been close to four in the morning before he polished off the last of the bottle, he was perfectly sober.

Stiffly, he rose to his feet and stretched. He went inside where the absence of wind made the world remarkably quiet and where the clock in the kitchen showed it was nearly eight o'clock. Bess Pope had made coffee. He poured himself a cup and drank it black. It was a ritual of sorts. Bess Pope, who would always be a pathetically inadequate version of Laylee Colebriar, would have coffee waiting for him whenever he came in from his nights on the porch. She would not acknowledge him in any other way than to make the coffee that neither she nor MaeEllen (bred a morning tea drinker from her girlhood days in Charleston) would touch, would radiate a non-too-subtle disdain for his presence. He no longer bothered to thank her for the coffee because her lack of response made it clear she held no regard for his expressions of gratitude.

He took the coffee upstairs to his room where he showered and shaved. He changed into jeans and a denim shirt. The glass frog was squatting on his bureau. After a moment's consideration, he dropped it into his breast pocket.

MaeEllen was waiting for him in the kitchen when he came back down. MaeEllen was bubbling with excitement over the hurricane. "It's going to be a great show." She asked him to drill a few holes in the parlor shutters so she and Bess Pope could get a good look at the ocean when the storm hit. After he did this, he told her he needed to get over to Royal Goody's house. Royal still couldn't get around well, and he needed help shuttering his own windows. MaeEllen didn't believe this bit of fiction, but she didn't question him either, and for once he was grateful for his mother's finely nurtured ability to ignore unpleasant truths.

It was just after eleven o'clock in the morning when he left to pick up Royal Goody and Reverend Hatchel.

❖   ❖   ❖

"I see you dressed for the occasion," Boo said.

Royal Goody was crammed into the back seat of the Tahoe; he was wearing khaki slacks and a sport coat. "It's supposed to be a luncheon, isn't it?"

"Is that what it is?"

They had talked about going to the police again and then rejected the idea. Not only would their *theory* about Sing Satterfield sound preposterous, it was certain the police had more immediate things on their minds with the approaching hurricane.

"What did Wade say?" Royal asked Boo.

He hadn't told Royal about the gun. "He says you're as stupid as me."

"He knows where we're going?"

"I think he's made the conscious decision to not think about it."

Now, driving south, Boo Taylor felt his brain slipping into overdrive; sounds were amplified; colors were bolder. He tried to calm himself by counting the few cars they encountered, all heading in the opposite direction toward Dedmen's Causeway. Streets were eerily deserted. Palm fronds and newspaper and other debris swirled in wind eddies around curbs and store fronts. Homes were boarded and silent. The high-rise condominiums along Atlantic Avenue were completely dark; the palms decorating their grounds bobbed leeward like drunken sailors. White foam blasted up from the dunes, and the driver's side of the Tahoe was getting greased with salt spray.

They came to the reverend's house near Mermaids Head. The reverend trotted out to the car, bent to the wind. Boo watched the old man and felt a lump rise in his throat—a mixture of sadness and nostalgia and generational guilt the old man made worse when he poked his head through the door and smiled broadly at him. "We all set?" He was eager. His brown face and his gray afro glistened.

In the backseat, Royal cleared his throat. "Before we get started, I have something for everyone. And don't you dare laugh."

Boo watched from the rearview mirror. Royal Goody reached into his jacket pocket and withdrew two small pouches strung on strips of rawhide.

"Wongahs?" Boo asked. "You made wongahs?"

Royal looked sheepish. "Found the recipe in a book I was researching. Had to cheat a bit on some of the ingredients, as I guess you can imagine. Maybe they're not up to Miss Laylee's standards, but I suppose they'll do."

He handed the two the flannel pouches to the reverend where they dangled in the old man's hands. The reverend's smile had gotten wider. A bit of gold blinked between his lips. "Didn't think you believed in this stuff," he said.

Boo took one of the wongahs from the reverend. He draped the rawhide strip over his head, and the pouch settled on his chest, next to the glass frog in his breast pocket. "Where's yours?" he called to the backseat.

Royal lifted a string of rawhide from his collar, and Boo laughed.

❖   ❖   ❖

Gussie Ransome felt a sharp pain run up her back as she dumped a box of catalogues on the hand truck. She uttered a soft cry and straightened, putting a hand to her hip. Pulled a muscle, she thought—her back had been bothering her for days, now. Too much extra weight and too much work.

Grunting, she tilted back the hand truck and backstepped through the Taylor Dufette Realty lobby. She fought the wind to open the door. As soon as she cracked it a few inches, the wind tore the door out of her hand. *"Bastard!"* she mouthed, startled. She kicked down the jamb and wheeled the truck onto the sidewalk.

Shops were closed and boarded all along Fulton Street Market. A light still shone in the Steamers & Grinds coffee shop on the corner, but she hadn't seen more than three or four people go in this morning. A van in front of Periwinkle's Gifts was idling. She counted five cars parked on the road including her own, saw no pedestrians, no traffic coming through—this, on a street usually crammed with hundreds of tourists.

Where is he now?

Her thoughts had been with Boo Taylor all morning. The work had been an exercise in dreadful monotony, allowing her apprehension to blossom like a deadly flower. Boo Taylor was on the island, would be riding out the storm, would be driving to Sing Satterfield's house. It all seemed terribly wrong. *Just your hormones*, he had told her.

She would smack him for that, if he were here.

If he were here.

Where is he? Where is he right now?

She looked down at her stomach. Her *(his)* child. Her burden. Red hair whipped across her eyes. With pain throbbing like fire and ice across her back, she began to lift the heavy boxes into the trunk of her car.

The ride to the Satterfield Estate was uneventful. Cars passed them in sporadic groupings, all burdened under heavily laden roofs and all moving north for the cause-way. Royal Goody brooded quietly with his injured leg propped across the backseat. The pastor fiddled with the radio to find the latest on the hurricane. Constance was still a category three and still expected to hit land sometime late in the afternoon.

As they approached the southern Atlantic corner of the island, tall oaks and palms loomed impressively over stately lanes. The houses were magnificent, Boo observed—the new wealth of Sweetpatch Island had decided to settle in a place where poverty had once ruled. Spanish moss splayed out on tree branches, flying off in clumps like wads of hair ripped out by the roots. Royal called out the turns, and Boo followed his directions through the elegant lanes. Finally, they came to a stretch of road bordered by a tall, cream-toned fence and evenly spaced palmettos. "This is it," Royal announced.

"All this?" Boo asked. The fence ran on the full length of a long block, dominat-ing the southeast bluffs of the island. He slowed as they came abreast of an opening in the fence. Tall, wrought-iron gates opened inward. A sign, red letters on white background, stood near the gate. The sign was in the shape of an alligator.

TRESSPASSERS WILL BE EATEN

Royal grabbed the front seat to pull himself forward. "What are we doing here?" His face was grave.

"I was invited," Boo answered.

"We both were. But I suddenly don't know if this is a good idea."

Boo looked at him. This was the same Royal Goody who wanted to charge the place like the cavalry last night. "Then don't go," Boo told him, sounding more harsh than he intended. He cleared his throat. His nerves, he realized, were suddenly raw. "I'll go in. You two should stay in the car."

He rolled the Tahoe through the gates and along a long driveway of red and gray brick. Wind strewn sticks and branches crunched under the tires and cluttered what was an otherwise immaculate lawn. They could see the house now, a modern affair with angles of stucco and glass blocks. The house was sprawled in a vague semi-circle, like an open mouth, and they were driving into it. Beyond the house—just the abyss. Ocean and sky meeting violently.

Boo stopped the car in front of the house. The driveway was otherwise empty. "Okay," he said. Through the windshield he could make out a tiny Japanese-style bridge crossing a man-made pond. The front door was hidden in a shaded alcove beyond that. All across the prim lawn, crepe myrtles and hibiscus were doubled over by the wind.

"I'll go up and check it out," Boo said and had to clear his throat again. "You two wait here, and I'll be right back." He reached for the door, but the reverend put a hand out to stop him.

"We're *all* going," the reverend said hoarsely. The lines of his face were set firmly.

From the backseat, Royal said, "It seems deserted doesn't it?"

It's not deserted, Boo thought, and he breathed heavily. He looked again at the little bridge, wondering why it looked familiar. Bits of moss and grass clippings blew onto the truck's windows and clung there. For no particular reason it occurred to him that he hadn't seen a single bird all day. He looked toward the reverend again who was staring back at him. "Then let's go," Boo said, and he pushed open the door.

Salt wind blasted his face.

The reverend helped Royal out of the back, and the three of them started toward the still-hidden front door. Boo was watching the small bridge as they approached it, wondering what it reminded him of. Dedmen's Causeway? A fat drop of rain splatted across his chin. Another one struck his ear. He looked up at the swirling mass of gray edging toward them.

Limping beside him, Royal said, "Look at that." He was pointing down at the pond where the surface was clogged with dead koi fish. Moldering orange-and-white bellies were aimed skyward, and a viscous substance clung to them like a caul. Boo got a whiff of decay before the wind hurried it away. When they crossed the bridge, a sense of finality came over him. The door was visible now—a heavy oaken thing with thick brass hinges. Two evergreen plants sculpted as poodles stood sentry on either side. A small, lead-glass window over each poodle's head were the only two windows not boarded up as far as Boo could tell. The windows were dark.

Hurrying as more heavy drops struck them, they reached the protective overhang. A note was taped to the door. A wind eddy was tossing it playfully.

Royal tore off the note. As he read, his face registered a mixture of relief and disappointment. "Wild goose chase after all," he said.

R—

Door unlocked, come in. Sorry, unable to greet you. Help yourself to something to eat. Leftover turkey in fridge—you still like dark meat?

Miss C left samples in Mstr Bdrm. Hated beige, liked the taupe. Hang ASAP & b <u>sure</u> to lock up when done. Police say looters posble.

—S

Royal handed the page to Boo.

"What is it?" the reverend asked.

"Note to a handyman or a decorator or something."

Boo read the note. The handwriting was the same flowery swirl as the letter he had received in the Federal Express envelope. "I don't think so. It's Crystal Burne, and it's for me."

Queenie, Queenie had two daughters,
Hated one and liked the other.

Royal leaned over his shoulder to read it again. "For you? I don't see it, Boo."

"Of course it is. She's playing with us." Boo glanced up to Royal and then reached over to press the doorbell. The wind was howling so loudly through the porch that he couldn't hear if there was a ring. He pressed the bell again, and then knocked. Raindrops were now steadily pinging off the Tahoe. From somewhere, he heard a ceaseless clattering of broken glass.

No movement from inside.

"Try the lock," the reverend said.

Boo put his right hand on the oversized knob, sensing Royal tensing at his side. He turned the knob, expecting stiff resistance, but the knob rolled over with smooth, mechanical ticks. *Lock up when done.* A sense of unreality washed over him; the hand doing the turning was disconnected from his body, the knob was an overly bright bronze, the wood grain on the door too deep, the sound around him too harsh. He looked at Royal and read the apprehension in his face. Carefully, he eased open the door just as the wind rose to a baleful moan and the stench of rotten flesh came pouring through the doorway. Wisps of smoke, in various semi-human shapes, cluttered the darkness within.

A moment later the wind settled; the smell blew away and there was no movement at all.

From inside, nothing except a soft music.

Royal reached out and touched his arm. "We're not going in there," he said.

"I am."

"But it would be breaking and entering. We may have just set off an alarm, did you think of that?"

"The power's probably out."

"Then where's that music coming from?"

Boo sighed. "Royal, I'm going in. It's what we're supposed to do, and that note confirms it. You don't want to, you can go wait in the truck."

"But there's no one *here*, Boo."

"I don't think it matters."

Royal's distress was mounting. "There's a garage around the side—I saw it on the way in. We should check to see if there's a car or something."

"What good will that do?" Boo asked. Beyond Royal Goody's head, the music was speaking to him like soft gibberish. The words were just beyond comprehension, but they were urging, cajoling; they were whispering to him, calling him to enter. Boo looked into this empty dark space and ground his teeth. The need to go in there was suddenly strong.

The reverend squeezed his arm.

"Okay," Boo said, breaking his gaze from the void. "I'll check for cars and be right back. You two stay here."

And then he was trotting down a windswept path of stone, squinting against flying debris. He hugged the front of the house until he made the corner. An arbor, straining under an enormous growth of wisteria, made an arch through which another path led to the western side of the house. Boo followed this and found three large garage doors, each with a pair of clam-shaped windows. He went to the nearest and cupped his hands to the glass to peer inside. The bay in front of him was empty. In the next a red, convertible BMW. And next to that a long black Mercedes.

Proof of nothing, he decided.

He was about to turn away when he noticed a large sign propped against the rear wall of the first bay.

Historic Chaliboque Restoration Project.

Funded by Satterfield Properties.

He turned from the garage and started back toward the front door. After a moment's hesitation, he veered toward the truck and opened the passenger door of the Tahoe and removed Wade Dutton's .38 revolver from the glove box.

Royal and Pastor Hatchel were waiting for him at the entryway.

"What's that?" Royal asked.

"What does it look like?" He jammed the gun into his belt at the small of his back. "There are two cars in the garage. Have you heard anything from inside?"

Royal and the reverend were still staring at him. "Just that music," said the pastor.

"Fine," Boo said, gripping the doorknob again. "Then I guess it's time to go in."

The Cannon was humming through the last of the brochures when the phone rang. Gussie assumed it was Murphy but hoped it was Boo Taylor. She had not expected a woman's voice.

"Yes, I'm looking for a Mr. Robert Taylor?"

"Do you mean *Boo* Taylor?"

"The name I have is Robert. Is he there?"

Gussie looked around the vacant office. A hard rain was steadily smacking against the lobby windows. "I'm sorry, you'll need to try his home. He doesn't work here."

"I thought this was the Taylor Dufette company?"

"It is, but he doesn't work here."

"Oh, my." The woman said nothing for several seconds. Gussie leaned forward on the counter and massaged her lower back with her free hand. "Oh pardon me, this is Mavis Bledsoe—with the Sweetpatch Island Historical Society? I have a document for Mr. Taylor. I think it's—well I'm *certain* it's rather important." The woman sounded distressed.

"Well, I can give you his number at home—"

"Oh no, oh dear. I've tried that number, I'm afraid, but the phones must be out from the storm. There's no answer at Mr. Goody's home, either, and he gave me this number to reach Mr. Taylor in an emergency."

Emergency? "In that case, I don't—"

"Oh, I just don't know what I should do!"

The woman was panicked. And she was with the historical society. Gussie's worry piqued—what horrible new secret had this woman come across?

"Mr. Goody said it was urgent that he see this document as soon as it came in. He was quite emphatic. Quite *upset*. But now my husband is picking me up in fifteen minutes and I don't dare leave it here. We're leaving the island for Greenville, and I don't know *when* we'll be back—"

Gussie cut in, "You don't have a car?"

"—and Mr. Goody was so *eager*."

Gussie checked her watch. Five past noon. "Where did you say you're located?"

After asking twice more, the woman finally gave an address on Cupid Street. That was just off Polk Road and only five minutes away—less, with no traffic. If she hurried she could drive there and back and still have the last brochures packed before Murphy would start worrying.

"Okay ma'am, please calm down. I'll be there in just a few minutes, so you just stay put. *Please* don't leave." And then she winced as another painful spasm went pulsing through her back—a much deeper and sustained one this time, almost like a labor pain.

❖   ❖   ❖

(You in my house now, doctor's boy.)

Royal was crowding into him at the door, and he really didn't want to go in there because now he was certain this was Crystal Burne's house. If he wasn't convinced by the letter, by the note, by the intuition that had fastened itself onto him as if with safety pins, he was more than certain now. He was certain because he sensed things moving around in there; things that were no more human than the hurricane bearing down on the island. And because his blood had gone cold.

The music was coming from every part of the house, seeping from the walls, luring them inside *(door unlocked, come inside)*. Boo Taylor took two steps into a dark, exquisitely appointed foyer, feeling like a thief, and *(trespassers will be eaten)* the music surrounded him, an elegant and hypnotic sound—light piano strokes beneath a rich, throaty humming. "Hello!" he called out, booming, his own voice a discordant insult. The only response was a melodic thrumming that vibrated through the marble-tiled foyer and up his legs. The gun pressed against his spine. On his right, he found a series of light switches and flicked them all up with a sweep of his hand. A verdigris chandelier and some number of lamps threw off their light as the shadow-things scampered into hiding places. He felt small. He felt the shadow-things turning about in their various hiding holes to watch. He took a third step inside, and on the opposite wall found his twin: bruise-eyed and haggard, rawhide cord at his neck, a thick-chested man stuffed into an old work shirt that was out of place in these plush surroundings. "It's just a stereo," he said quietly, now gazing around the entry hall and the long stairway that circled up toward the darkness of a second floor. He called out again, "Hello!"

His voice echoed.

Royal crept behind him. "We're in*trud*ing," he said. He was whispering. Royal, who had gone from Rambo to Bambi, was now whispering.

"Funny, but I don't see a cop."

"A stereo," the pastor said quietly. "The music, it sounds..."

Familiar, the old man was about to say, and Boo had been thinking the same thing. The music was seawater seeping into his ears. Royal and the reverend were both looking at him cautiously. The foyer spread into three directions in addition to the stairs—a hallway straight ahead and impeccably furnished drawing rooms on either side. The air was electric with humidity and the constant sound of the storm and the guttural music. All about them, eyes were peering down.

Royal limped to Boo Taylor's side. "Awful hot in here," he said.

"Smells funny, too" said the reverend. He was wrinkling his nose. "What's it smell like to you?"

"Spoiled fruit," Boo whispered back. It was faint. It was a lesser-version of the smell in Lester Meggett's house.

"It's absolutely suffocating in here," said Royal. "Did they lose their air-conditioner?" He ran a finger under his collar. Sweat stains were beginning to show at the armpits of his blazer.

Boo Taylor took a deep breath and looked at the others. "I'm going in and have a look around."

Reverend Hatchel gave him a nod. "Yes. I believe you're right, Boo. I believe that's what we're supposed to do."

They turned to Royal Goody, waiting for his protest. But Royal, glancing nervously around the high walls, seemed resigned. The reverend drew the door closed behind them as Boo assessed their three ground-floor options—left drawing room, right drawing room, and stairway straight ahead. *Three directions, and three of us,* he mused, and then Royal spoke the words he was thinking: "If we're doing this, I think we should stick together."

❖   ❖   ❖

They made a quick sweep of the ground floor, finding little except elegant furnishings covered in dust. "Maid's day off," the reverend said after wiping his finger through a deep layer of dust on a mantle. Boo Taylor continued to feel the presence of others, watching, following, scampering just ahead. Lester Meggett's eyes in the walls, hidden under paint and fine wallpapering and damasks and gilded frames, spying at them through the unnaturally soupy atmosphere—and all the while slipping surreptitiously beneath: the relentless, throaty humming. And deeper beneath that: whispers, the rustling rat tails, the faint and lunatic giggling. *(Jes invited yourself on in, didn't you, boy?)* Decay and worm-eaten timbers *(Chaliboque)* masked under layers of fresh plaster and drywall. *(Does you get it, boy? Does you get the joke?)* All the finery was like the dust, just a filmy covering, an illusion; the real world of mold and corruption would slip into view at any moment.

They passed through rooms of startling luxuriousness, overflowing with antiques and artifacts from around the world, plush leather furniture, broad canvases and tapestries. They turned on lights wherever they went, but the lights seemed insignificant. The thick, slightly ripe air pressed down on them, swallowed lights whole, and seemed to slow them down. It was like walking through deep mud. Royal began hobbling badly and had to grip Boo Taylor's arm for support.

They had nearly circled back to the front of the house when they finally found the stereo: a top-of-the-line Bose that appeared to be connected to an extensive speaker system. Boo pressed the eject button on the CD player. The music abruptly ceased— and seconds later, so did the mad whispers. He held the disc up to read: *Old Fashioned Indiscretion* by Murielle Davis, a name he didn't know.

Royal eased himself into a chair, the pain on his face obvious. Sweat was coursing down his face. "I want to go home."

"Have you boys noticed?" the pastor said, his rough whisper stark and grating. "No family pictures, anywhere. No personal items. Feels like a model home, like nobody really lives here."

"Doesn't feel like that at all," said Royal. "Feels more like a swamp dressed up for a masquerade ball. And frankly, I don't want to be here when the mask comes off." He glared at Boo. "I'd like to leave."

The reverend was mopping his brow. "I can't barely breathe."

Boo was standing at the door into the foyer. The foyer seemed to have changed somehow since they first entered the house. Furniture slightly moved. The lights had gotten dimmer—some of the lights, in fact, were off. Hadn't he switched all of them on when they came in? He took another step and noticed markings in the dust on the hardwood floor.

"Come look at this," he said.

Pastor Hatchel came to stand next to him. "Are those tracks?"

In the dust, twists and swirls, the marks of small bare feet clustered at the foot of the stairway then climbing in a curving sweep up the steps.

"We didn't make them," said the reverend.

Boo shook his head.

"Were they here when we came in?"

"I don't think so," Boo said. He squinted up to the second floor.

Miss C left samples in Mstr Bdrm.

Royal had now risen to join them. He peered over Boo Taylor's shoulder and frowned at the series of little smudges capering up the stairs. A landing at the top of the stairs branched toward corridors that appeared to lead into either wing of the house. A large, round window, now sealed against the storm, dominated the point at the direct peak of the stairway. Boo struck another switch, and lights came on in the landing.

"Looks like I'm staying down here," Royal said. He bent over to hold his thigh. "Unless you feel like carrying me."

Boo gave the pastor a worried glance. "Why don't you stay with him?"

The old man grunted. "If you're goin up, I'm goin up."

"I'll be fine," Royal told them. "It's empty down here, remember?"

Is it? Boo glanced again around the tall walls, catching subtle and clever movements from the corner of his eye. He took Wade's revolver out of his belt. "Take this," he said, pushing it into Royal's hands.

"I don't want it."

"Take it anyway."

"Boo, I don't think—"

"I'm not giving you a choice, Royal."

Reluctantly, Royal accepted the weapon. He held it mistrustfully, at arms length, like it was poison.

"Oh, knock it off," Boo told him, "you've handled guns all your life."

"Rifles, maybe. Not a pistol, and not in somebody's *house,* Boo. Is it loaded?"

Boo sighed. He looked over to the pastor who was looking back, smiling grimly. From the front door *(bang ASAP)* came the roars of the storm's escalation. From inside, a startling contrast of the mute and placid. Putting his right hand over his heart, he felt Laylee's glass frog. Splitting up frightened him. He stared up the stairway again.

"We'll be quick," Boo said, and he started up. The pastor, his old legs trembling, slowly followed.

Yes, I have been here before, Boo thought, again recalling Chaliboque with its rotting stairway that led to the second floor—and the house on Culpepper, climbing to the place where his father had died. The air grew thicker with each step, seeming to suppress light as hazy circles formed around the chandelier and the several blazing lamps. He realized he could only see a few yards in any direction. It was like walking through a dense fog. Near the top, he turned, and Royal Goody was fading into the murk. "Be careful," Boo called down in a whisper. Royal's vague shape was transferring the gun to his belt; he hadn't heard him. Boo glanced at the reverend who was watching him closely.

"Getting thick," the reverend said quietly. "You notice?"

Boo nodded.

"Ain't natural. Whole *place* ain't natural."

"Stay close to me," Boo told him.

They reached the second-floor landing and faced the circular window with its ornate wooden curls in the pattern of a rose. Planking now covered the glass on the outside. "This way?" the reverend asked softly. He was nodding to the left and a hallway jagging at odd angles. Doors, open and inviting, widely spaced, the corridor beyond disappearing into the same thick fog. Boo nodded. He found another light switch, flipped it, and floral sconces down the corridor came on in a feeble yellow glow. Boo and the reverend started along the banister and lost all sight of Royal Goody.

The first door led to a model-home bedroom. Bureaus and closets were empty. "Dead up here, too," the reverend whispered. "No photographs. No magazines or books. Never been used, has it?"

"Doesn't look like it."

Boo drifted ahead of the pastor toward the next room down, finding more of the same, although this one had a door connecting to its own bath. While the old man searched the bathroom, Boo made a cursory look at the bland surroundings and then turned around one of the jags in the hall to another door.

Samples in Mstr Bdrm.

Hated beige, liked the taupe.

The master bedroom, he saw at once: wide and opulent, with wide windows that were now shuttered against the Atlantic. The walls were knurled walnut panels. At the head of the room, a king-sized bed was draped with a lacey spread—like a white spiderweb. He took a step further into the room. The bedspread, he now noticed, had been turned down. Something was spread across the pillow. He stepped forward again and saw the object was a nightgown, pale yellow, made of some sheer fabric.

A faint giggle. The lights wavered.

Boo came forward as the house around him shuddered and the reverend's voice, nervous, called out from the next room. He reached out to touch the gown. He rubbed the rough, gauzy fabric through his fingers.

"Boo Taylor?" The reverend was anxious.

"Here," Boo called back.

In the room, a smoky voice called his name in the very moment the lights blinked out.

Seventy-nine Cupid Street was a one-story brick building crammed between taller clapboard structures. Soot stains rising up from the two windows left of the front door were evidence of a recent fire. It was an improbable location for the Sweetpatch Island Historical Society, and no sign marked it as such, but the numbers affixed to the metal door matched the ones the woman had given over the phone. Gussie laid on the horn—the second time—and waited.

She was scared now. The cramps rippling through her lower back could very well going on before that? She hadn't been paying attention—all morning, it seemed, and she hadn't been paying attention because she'd been sure it was just a pulled muscle. With her first three children, she carried the labor up front, the pains scorching through her lower abdomen. But she knew women who'd carried it in their backs, instead. Something about the position of the baby.

But it's too early!

Too much activity, too much worry. She had been spending too much time at work, throwing around boxes, bending and lifting and now maybe had brought on labor two or three weeks too soon. Maybe. It could still be only a crampy muscle...

No one appeared from within the building. Groaning, she pushed open the car door and stepped into the fierce wind and cutting rain. She waddled uncomfortably to the door and, not bothering to knock, pulled it open to the smell of ashes and stale sweat. The front room, dark, was filled with cardboard boxes and tied-up stacks of newspapers. Some of the boxes were splitting at the seams, and multi-colored papers poked through.

"Hello?" she called out.

A voice—the woman's voice—tiny, from a room far in the back: "Oh, you're here, thank goodness! I'll be right out."

Gussie stepped further into the front room, picking her way through the mounds of clutter. Olive drab walls, empty of hangings. Rough indoor-outdoor carpeting. A single lightbulb dangling naked from a water-stained ceiling. Not at all what she expected of an historical society office. Perhaps this was just a storage site—a place to keep old documents, and maybe whatever sorting and cataloguing they did was conducted in one of the back rooms. And perhaps they were packing up to move. The fire, which must have been in another room, was forcing them to relocate she decided, and then felt a brusque tug between her legs.

Warmth and wetness streamed down her thighs.

"Oh God."

Sharp panic spiked through her.

Moaning, she shuffled toward the door to the back rooms. "Hello!" she called out. "I need to use your phone right away!"

She turned through the door, finding another room almost identical to the first. In a moment, the woman appeared from behind a stack of boxes. Her first thought was that this woman was too young for the voice she had heard, that the voice had been a disguise. Her second thought was that she knew the woman (girl)—and with that thought came utter confusion.

"But what are—?"

(two daughters Boo said two daughters and oh my God oh my God my child)

And then the smell of smoke came whispering around her from behind as two strong, cold hands took hold of her.

❖   ❖   ❖

A cold hand fell on Royal Goody's shoulder. He screamed and lurched away, his spine barking hard into a marble-topped table. He looked furiously around the darkness. A meager glow from the two small windows near the door—the only light—was broken by a black, straggle-haired silhouette.

"It's over now, bro."

Royal's heart cramped; his breath left him.

Just moments ago, every light they had carefully and methodically switched on had snapped off all at once. Now, total darkness. Above, he heard Boo Taylor cry out.

"King climbed to high, and the flying machines are in the air."

The straggle-haired silhouette made a lurching, broken step toward him. Familiar slim shoulders. Familiar curve of jaw. "You're dead," he whispered, crawling to the steps.

"Locked and loaded, bro. That's how it works."

The hand had been real. He had felt it—cold and solid. That voice was real, too, and it was Solomon's voice. Solomon was standing in front of him; Solomon was speaking to him. *Some kind of trick,* he thought numbly but every window was boarded over, every light was gone, and it had felt so *real*. It had *touched* him. And it *was* Solomon. An immense stink of decomposition wafted off that horribly familiar shape, enveloping him as the thing moved forward and as he tried to back away.

From upstairs, the sounds of struggle, and he turned to look up there, seeing only blackness and a thin seam of light from the window at the top of the steps. Boo yelling. Now the reverend yelling, too—some indecipherable plea.

"It's over for that white boy. Boy never had a chance. Boy was never meant to have a chance."

The shape shambled forward another step, a pathetic, broken shadow, arms out and beseeching. It was going to touch him again, and the thought of that threatened to split his mind apart.

"You're not real."

"Come on, bro. Time to put an end to it…"

The smell was gagging him.

"Planes are circling; guns are cocked. King's got to fall. Ain't no stopping it."

Upstairs, another shout from Boo Taylor. Royal Goody whined. "You can't be real." The thing took another step, and Royal lunged up the stairs, crashing on his bad leg. That hand had been real. That hand had touched him, and it had real weight and it was freezing cold. He dug at his belt, found the gun, ripped it free.

"Royal? Bro?"

Royal pointed the gun at the shape. "I know you're not real."

Another step. Royal cowered back. The thing was *leaning* toward him. It was going to touch him again; that cold, lifeless mass of flesh and bone was going make contact with his own flesh again. He tugged on the trigger. Nothing. He tugged again, desperate, "It's *not* you, because you're *dead!*" still pulling on the trigger until he realized there must be a safety. His fingers scrabbled across the handle, clicked a metal tab; he pulled again and the world exploded.

A bright flash—in that instant, the image of his brother, Solomon, masked in bloody gauze, eyes just two empty black pits, hair spiked like burnt straw, tattered and rain-soaked suit, arms held out for him, reaching for him, wanting him, wanting to touch...

Then blackness again.

The shadow hung in place, not moving, not falling. Only watching him. Shoulders sagging, regarding him with absolute heartbreak. A pitifully tiny and disbelieving lament: "Royal...why?"

Boo's shout again from above. "Boo Taylor," Royal breathed, and he turned from the shape of his dead brother and began to crawl up the steps.

Reverend Leroy Hatchel fell; his foot caught something in the dark *(something alive, dead?)* and his left thigh slapped into something wet. He shrieked surprise, landing on the carpet as lightening seared through his hip and a table spilled over him. He tried to stand, could not, and instead began to crawl blindly across the floor. He was lost in the room; the darkness was complete.

"Boo Taylor!" he yelled out—but he had heard Boo's cry seconds before, just as the lights had been snuffed, and knew Boo was in trouble, too.

Whispers in the dark, gibberish, sense of movement, a leathery weight stroked across his hand and he recoiled, hissing. Icy fingers went trembling down his back. Somewhere—over in the same room as Boo Taylor, he guessed—was the simmering growl of an approaching beast. He pushed up to his right knee and reached out desperately, unable to see even his own hands. It was as if he had been dragged to the bottom of the ocean. And the smell—pungent and vile, like sweat, like the pelt of a large *(dead?)* animal, and how could he not have noticed that before? Only after the lights had gone out...

We here, old man.

Does you see us?

We so scared.

(He smelled his daddy but couldn't see him because it was the hour before dawn and they were rowing through dark so complete that the darkness itself had substance to it; like a woolen blanket. "Where we goin, daddy?" he asked, but his daddy was quiet. His daddy was the smell of old sweat and grease and the movement of arms and a back and the sound of soft grunts as they rowed through the invisible black morning up the equally invisible black creek. He was scared, because he heard a girl giggling up ahead in all that woolen blackness. A little girl who was drowned in the creek, they all said, brought back by a black witch, and so his daddy, the preacher, had to go send the little girl back to God. The little girl's family had paid the witch with three chickens to bring back their drowned baby girl. "Daddy, I'm scared," he said, but his daddy was still quiet, and the sounds of girl were getting closer and closer until he was sure the boat would run over her. All at once, his daddy stopped rowing and their boat just drifted on the creek. The early morning had gone silent. And then the water beneath them rumbled, and a cold hand snaked out of the water and grabbed hold of his wrist.)

A finger slicked over his cheek. He swatted at it, hit nothing. The stink was awful. The sounds of the storm outside were hollow and ocean-like, waves coming one after the other. Something tugged on his shirt and giggled. He lurched away from it, fearing what he might bump into, and the movement sent another blast of fire through his hip. From a distance that seemed impossibly far away, he heard Boo Taylor yell. The direction of the hallway, he hoped, and he groped for that even though it was the same direction of that awful growling sound.

Does you see us, old man?

Old, old, old man.

He could see nothing, sensed only the movement around him and the rustling and the gleeful voices. Another burst of that foul odor, another snatch at his shirt. "Be gone!" he yelled, stumbling in the direction of Boo Taylor's voice. Who was he shouting at?

He fell into something immense and soft—recoiled again. And then realized it was only the bedspread he had somehow pulled from the mattress. He put his hands on the mattress and pushed up to his right leg. Then he felt his way around the bed, working his way in the direction of Boo Taylor's voice and that steady growl. From below he heard another shout—was that Royal Goody? A cold mass brushed against him, and he clutched the bedspread to his chest like a shield.

Where you goin old man?

Old, old, very old man.

We so scared.

Don't leave us.

"Be *gone!*" he yelled again.

An explosion from downstairs. Royal Goody—he had the gun, and the reverend was suddenly horrified by what Royal might be shooting at down there. He stumbled across the room, each step bringing fresh agony to his hip, and banged into a wall. Boo Taylor's voice was closer now and suddenly (somewhere?) there was a crashing sound, something (window, mirror?) shattering. Dragging his bedspread shield, the reverend slid down the bedroom wall. He toppled another small table, sent invisible museum pieces scattering and fell through the open door just as Boo Taylor's voice came screaming into his face only inches away.

—*I'm here.*

He was falling down a deep well. The gauzy nightgown slipped out of his fingers, flapped somewhere above him as he fell deeper into blackness.

He called out again.

—*I'm here!*

Cold stone walls raced past as he continued to fall, continued to spiral deeper and deeper, the air around him growing cooler and thicker and wetter as years flew past now, became decades, all streaming by as he fell and fell and fell until at last...

He was a little white boy.

And he climbed into the old black woman's lap as if she were his very own

*grandmother. Or great-grandmother, or even great-great-grandmother, for this
ancient creature was certainly old enough.*

"Mr. Boo!"

*He looked up at her with his little boy's eyes, and he knew her. She was exotically
beautiful. Exuded exotic spices and Gullah mysteries. Her body was spangled with
all manner of exotic ornaments.*

"I ever tell you about this here frog I come across once?"

("You married Dalton Satterfield," he told her.)

His voice surprised him in this deep, dark place.

"Princess kissed that ol frog."

("Then you killed him.")

"Frog turned into a slug."

("You killed Elgin Highsmith, too.")

He was shouting. He didn't know why he was shouting at her.

"Princess turned into a Beast."

("You killed Hoss and all the ones who came before that.")

"Beast killed that slimy ol slug. Ate him up!"

("You killed Laylee Colebriar.")

"That little slug is you, boy."

*Her face was obscured in this deep murk, but he could see she was beautiful.
Could see a ripe bosom spilling out of her dress like exotic fruit. Could smell her
exotic fragrances. Red eyes raged out of her dark beauty. She was stroking his little
boy's hair with her fingers.*

"You always been jes a slug. Slug thinkin he's a prince. Ain't that a good joke!"

("You set fire to her house, and you killed her.")

*She laughed, and the sweet pickaninny voice suddenly dropped several octaves.
"Kill dat ol toad 'ooman? Dat oagly ol toad?" The laughter was like muddy water
running down a drain, and his little white boy's heart was suddenly afraid. "Mehbe
dat what she wahnt, but trute be dem bones ain't who you tinkin dey is.*

"Dems you own bone, boy.

"Dems you murrah bone."

My mother's bones?

His hip checked into a bureau. He blinked the murk from his eyes. Somewhere
close the reverend was crying out in pain. Somewhere closer the mass that was in
the shape of an exotic woman shifted, and a deep animal's growl shifted with it. He
brought his hands to his face, rubbed it, cleared his eyes. "What do you want?" he
asked. It was pitch black, but he knew he had backed into a bureau. His hands came
around a lamp. "I'm here now, so what do you want?"

The shape in the room was sparkles. The shape was a constellation of stars. It was
moving steadily closer to him.

*"Always pokin dat fine white nose out an' get it busted up. Always pokin dat
hand in an' get it bit off. Das you, Mr. Boo!"*

He yanked at the lamp, pulling it from the socket. The reverend was calling
out again.

"Always pokin dat fine white cock where it doan b'long, an' look what happen! Tuhk what doan b'long to you!"

He edged in the direction of the door. The reverend was out there somewhere, shouting and in pain. *("No," he told her, and he realized a part of him was still in that deep, dark place with her, still in her lap—brought there by some glamour, some poison she breathed into the atmosphere. "I took her for love. I took her because I had do." He was speaking his father's words, his grandfather's words, his great-grandfather's words.)*

"Tuhk my-own sweet baby 'way from me."

She was getting closer.

"Tuhk my chile!"

The sparkling shape was getting closer. The growl seeping from the shape was growing louder and louder. He swung the lamp; the cord bullwhipped about and snapped at nothingness.

"Tuhk my man, too. Strung im up. Cut im troat, sho!"

("Sin is in the timing," he explained to her. "Don't you see that?")

The door could be feet away or yards away. He held out the lamp, keeping it between his body and that advancing swirl of sparkles.

"Time to take back what b'long t'me."

(The child. She wants the child—wants his child.)

"You won't get it," he said.

The shape's breath, no longer exotic, steamed against his flesh.

"Time done come, Mr. Slug. De Beast be comin fo' yuh. An' ee awful 'oungry!"

("You won't get it!" he screamed.)

He threw the lamp toward the escalating animal sounds and lunged for the doorway. Behind him, the lamp exploded worthlessly, and the muddy chuckle rose again, tracking him as the Beast's roar erupted—and he slammed head first into the doorframe. He collapsed backward, reaching out. Finally, he grabbed hold of the frame and hauled himself into the hall, shouting.

Inches away, someone was screaming back: "Boo?"

The reverend's voice? He grabbed sightlessly and caught an errant arm. "Reverend, MOVE! NOW!"

Ahead, a curled line of bluish light—from the rose window at the top of the steps. He yanked the reverend in that direction, and the old man cried out.

"Ow, God, my hip!"

It's got him, Boo thought wildly; he tugged harder as the reverend went down, and then the Beast was on them.

Pastor Hatchel's leg gave out, and he fell. He threw the bedspread toward the roar of that creature as Boo Taylor's grip slipped off his bicep.

A tremendous weight crashed on top of him and got tangled up in the bedspread. He pushed and kicked blindly as a massive head, vicious, slavering, ripped at the fabric, trying to get at him. The thrashings and the heat and the stink of the thing were unworldly, and his mind was ablaze with the thought that it was going to get him, that it would tear through this flimsy cloth any instant and it's teeth would be on him and it would eat him alive. And then that horror came true as the blanket came flapping away from his face and teeth lunged at him, grabbed his heart and pulled. A sharp burn dug at his neck—the thing had ripped through his shirt and had a hold of his wongah, thinking it was a part of him, and it was whip-cording it wildly.

Somewhere beyond that immediacy came Royal Goody's hoarse shout: "Boo, are you there?" *Upstairs?* he thought crazily, *but how?* And then he remembered: Royal had the gun!

The teeth came free of the wongah.

"Shoot it!" he screamed. "Royal, it's right on top of me!"

Royal Goody wormed up to the last of the steps, the gun still locked in his right fist, adrenaline pounding through his veins as the sounds of battle escalated from the second floor—Boo shouting, Pastor Hatchel shouting, the roars of a Beast *(let me...touch you)* that was some sort of animal but was unlike anything so rational. He turned at the top railing, unable to see a thing because the only light was that slim bluish crease from the large window in the landing. He heard *(Royal? Bro?)* the violence burst into the corridor ahead of him. Boo shouting: "Reverend, move now!" The reverend shouting: "Ow, my hip!" Then that thunderous crash, shattering everything.

He dragged himself closer. "Boo, are you there?" he called out.

Someone screaming: "Shoot it, Royal, it's right on top of me!"

He could see nothing, only heard the savage snapping, shredding sounds of flesh being flayed apart. He fell to his elbows and aimed the gun into madness. He pulled the trigger.

Boo Taylor saw a flash of fire.

An instant later, a deafening explosion.

An instant after that, sharp flecks of plaster stung his face.

"What are you doing?" he yelled out.

Royal, beneath that thin line of light, yelling back, "I can't see!"

The reverend: "Godsakes boy, SHOOT THE DAMN THING!" The Beast's roars covering him.

Royal again: "I can't see...where?"

The old man screamed again. "Got my arm!"

The light. Can't see. Boo's brain slammed these fragment thoughts together *(light, can't see),* and he went charging for the thin line of light at the top of the stairs, frantic to remember the layout of the hall, praying he wouldn't trip over Royal Goody. He lowered his shoulder and went barreling full speed into glass and wood.

Royal heard the form rushing toward him, raised the gun and in the last instant did not pull the trigger. *(Can't see.)* Then, the form blew past him toward the window where glass was suddenly shattering. New light and a gust of wet air spilled into the hallway. Ahead, a huge black shape *(was that a woman?)* was wrestling *(no, some kind of animal)* over a shapeless peach-toned mass. Tufts of seafoam were flying everywhere. He lowered the gun and fired, missing. He fired again.

The jaws were clamped to Reverend Hatchel's left forearm like a vice lined with shards of glass. Hot drool mixed with his blood. He slammed his right hand at the animal's throat, squeezing and pushing away with every bit of strength he could summon.

From some distant place came the sound of a car wreck. He looked up, realized he could see again, and stared into two burning red eyes lost in a field of utter blackness.

A gunshot rang out. The teeth peeled away from his arm, the red eyes turned away. Then, another shot.

Sudden pain, shattering, a light far brighter than it should be. The wind consumed him, rain blasted over him. Boo was falling over, falling into the storm, his brain stunned useless by the impact, and a wide deck wobbled into view two stories below. He threw out his right hand for the window frame and small daggers of broken glass went ripping into his palm. He held on anyway as more glass slashed into his thighs near his groin, and he caught himself before he spilled completely through the window.

From behind him, shouts and gunfire and lunacy. Then a bloody, high-pitched shriek torn raw from another world. He spun himself around in time to see a massive dark shape collapse next to a shredded bedspread.

He sagged to the floor, bleeding and dazed.

Pain registered in his brain from a dozen outraged locations. In the dim light of the hallway, he made out Royal Goody, frozen belly-down and perched on his elbows. Farther away, Pastor Hatchel was kicking out from beneath a peach-toned bedspread that had been torn to pieces, goose-down fluttering around him like snowfall. The old man's wide-eyed shock was a comical parody of a minstrel act. The wall next to him was sprayed with a red-black splatter. The body of an exotically beautiful woman in a brown dress was sprawled beside him.

The reverend was puffing breaths. "Is that who,"—puff—"is that who I think it is?"

A chunk of the woman's head was missing. A viscous mixture of blood and tissue oozed into the carpet.

Royal still hadn't moved. A line of smoke feathered from the gun barrel. "I felt his hand, Boo," Royal said quietly. "How could she do that?"

Boo couldn't see Royal's face.

The reverend, still wide-eyed, was trying to push himself away from the dead body. "Could'a sworn it was some kind'a *bear!*"

Splintered bits of glass fell into Boo Taylor's lap, making the tinkling sounds of a small wind chime. He reached for his breast pocket. The frog was still there, still intact. *(Still alive.)* Hurricane Constance rained more glass and bits of wood over him. He shook his head but could not stop the ringing in his ears.

Murphy Ransome counted twenty rings before he hung up the phone.

..*eleven*

Waves rose to great heights and thundered havoc down on the beach, churning sand, altering coastlines. Boats strained at their moors, bobbing like toys in a bath. Sea creatures, answering to ancient wisdom, dove to the safety of deep water while, above, the wind battered trees and homes and buildings. At 3:24 p.m. Hurricane Constance officially made landfall on the South Carolina barrier islands, more than half an hour ahead of schedule and two hours ahead of high tide when the tidal surge was expected to breach the dunes and flood the eastern region of Sweetpatch Island. In the big house that dominated the southeast corner of the island, a woman lay dead on the second-floor landing, the blood and bits of bone and brain tissue already drying on the carpet. Wade Dutton's .38 was lying next to her head.

Further north, Boo Taylor was alone behind the wheel of his Tahoe. He had driven Royal Goody and Pastor Hatchel to the pastor's home, which was on relatively high ground near Mermaids Head on the western coast. Power was out across the island, a development the men registered on the drive north as dead traffic lights danced like puppets on power lines above the Tahoe's roof. Streetlamps were dark. Streets were abandoned, and rainwater ran high in the roadside curbs. At Savannah Road they detoured around a toppled oak, and a little farther on they had to drive on the sidewalk to avoid a collapsed billboard.

The wound on the pastor's arm was minor. Two small gashes and some bruising. Royal Goody had wrapped a strip of the shredded bedspread around the old man's arm, and the bleeding seemed to have mostly stopped. His hip was a more serious problem. With Royal aggravating his thigh wound, Boo had to carry the reverend down Sing Satterfield's stairs by himself—and later into the reverend's house, causing the old man considerable pain.

"How could she *do* that?" Royal kept asking. "Something in the air, or maybe that music. Some subliminal message or some *hallucinogen,* and don't you dare tell me it was something *different.* Don't dare tell me it was *real.* Jesus, I felt his fucking *hand!*"

Royal was alternately angry and hysterical, and Boo wondered if those were signs of shock. The reverend's niece, waiting for them and seemingly unfazed by their respective conditions, had calmly volunteered to walk the three blocks to the emergency shelter that was being set up in the elementary school where she would see about a doctor. Boo Taylor was bleeding from his left shoulder and the left side of his scalp where he had burst through Sing Satterfield's ornate rose window. A line of puncture wounds ripped across his upper thighs, and his already ruined right hand was cut deeply in several places. He felt bits of glass still lodged in his palm. Royal had wrapped Boo's hand for him in another strip of the bedspread. The wound bled through the cloth easily, and they had to change the dressing when they arrived at the reverend's house. Boo told them he needed to get back to MaeEllen's house to check on her, but he also wanted to get away from Royal Goody's escalating denials.

Now, driving east toward MaeEllen's house, the bleeding in his hand had ebbed somewhat. The pain in his left shoulder, however, had magnified. He was having trouble lifting his arm and everything below the shoulder was going numb. His denim shirt was ripped at the shoulder seam, and the sleeve was flapping and nearly torn away completely. The flap chafed at the lacerated flesh beneath. The skin there was turning purple. After driving some distance, he reached up with his right hand and ripped the sleeve the rest of the way off.

As he drove, fighting the escalating wind and rain, he brushed small pebbles of glass from his hair. He glanced at himself in the rearview mirror and decided he didn't like what he saw. MaeEllen wouldn't either.

Making the final turn onto Carriage Avenue, he made out the flashing lights in MaeEllen's driveway, and his heart sank.

He pulled in front of the house and stopped. Grunting through his aches, he pushed out of the Tahoe where wind and rain swept over him so hard they nearly knocked him over. He was no more than a half-dozen steps into the yard when a tall figure emerged from the storm, lumbering toward him and screaming. Without thinking, Boo threw out his right fist, connected hard, and the man crumbled.

Runners of pain laced through his hand. He hung over the man and rubbed his knuckles. "Sorry Murph."

Murphy Ransome was gaping up at him. His face was contorted in loathing so extreme Boo wondered if it would grow fangs.

Murphy, dabbing at his lip, said, "Where is she, you fucking creep?"

Wade Dutton was hurrying to them now, flapping like a plastic yellow bird in his policeman's poncho. His expression was unreadable. Behind that, MaeEllen Taylor and Bess Pope were holding on to each other on the porch, watching. Boo was dimly aware of Murphy yelling, of spit flying from Murphy's mouth, of the rain soaking Murphy's clothes. He waited for Murphy to get up, waited for the blow to come crashing across his nose, snapping the old fault line in the middle of his face, had no intention of preventing it when it came. Something had happened to Gussie. While they were in Sing Satterfield's house, something had happened to her.

"Quit yelling." he said forcelessly.

Murphy was still on the ground, still screaming at him as Wade's hands came up and grabbed Boo by the collar.

He was standing on the porch, gazing down on the lawn and wondering how he'd gotten there. Wade was standing beside him, his poncho snapping in the gale. Murphy Ransome was nowhere in sight; had he gone for shelter in Wade's police cruiser? And MaeEllen and Bess had moved inside where they hovered at the door, watching him. Boo seemed to know these things but could not remember them happening. A candle flickered at the window, and it registered with him that the house had lost power.

"He figured she up and run off with you," Wade was saying. Boo stared at him. Wade Dutton looked like the weariest man in the world.

"I wish she had," Boo said.

"Any ideas, Boo?" Wade was scratching the orange bristles of his scalp. "I tell you, I'm plenty scared."

"So am I."

Gussie hadn't arrived at home when she should have. The office at Taylor Dufette Realty was empty. Her car was gone. Circumventing protocol, Wade had already logged her as a missing person, had issued her description to the police and rescue forces throughout the island. No one had seen her since 10:30 that morning.

The revolving light on Wade's cruiser cast a red strobe across the storm. Boo found himself staring at the light. He was sore everywhere. The light was telling him he needed to lie down and sleep. Telling him he needed to close his eyes and drift away, wake up some time later after the hurricane had passed and Gussie was home and safe. Then Wade was tugging on his arm and he realized he had almost fallen asleep on his feet. He turned regretfully from the light. Wade was studying his wounds and his tattered and bloody clothes. "You wanna tell me where you been," Wade asked, "or do I even wanna know?"

"We broke into Sing Satterfield's house," Boo told him. "We killed her."

Wade's eyes blinked incredulity.

"It was Crystal Burne," Boo explained.

Wade Dutton bobbed at the waist and howled. When he straightened up again his face was twisted into a grimace. He stamped his foot. "God*dammit!* Goddammit, I *knew* somethin like that was gonna happen. You used my gun, didn't you?"

Boo nodded dumbly.

Another wince. "God*dammit,* Boo Taylor! You know how much trouble I'm in?"

"You want to arrest me?"

"I don't have fuckin *time* to arrest you! Jesus Christ, boy, you must *hate* me. You must hate me, cause you're ruinin my *fuckin life!*"

Boo rubbed his bare left shoulder with his bandaged right hand. He couldn't lift his left arm at all. "Wade, do you want to hear what happened or not?"

Wade stamped his foot again. "I don't got time for *that,* either! You stay here!" He shoved a finger at Boo's chin. Then he was bounding down the stairs. The wind took hold of his poncho and seemed to lift him into the air like a kite. At the bottom he turned and pointed again. "Don't fuckin *move!* Storm's done, I'm comin back and you're *damn straight* I'm gonna arrest you!"

twelve

The candle next to his bed flickered once...twice...Boo Taylor watched the flame, waited for it to wink out.

He stood by the bureau and stripped off his bloody, torn, soaking clothes, stripped off Royal's dripping wongah. He let them drop to the carpeted floor. When he heard the thump as his shirt fell, he bent down, picked through the soggy folds, and came up with the glass frog. Holding the frog in a hand wrapped in a rag, he pressed his remaining fingers to his temples. A board at one the windows had worked loose, and a pair of shutters was clacking rapidly like castanets, driving nails through his skull. He stood naked at the bureau.

He stared at the bed…remembering he was going to change into fresh clothes and go downstairs to sit with MaeEllen and Bess for a bit. Sip coffee and wait for word from Wade Dutton.

He walked to the bed…deciding what clothes he would take from the bureau. Figure out where he'd left his spare pair of work boots. Should he see if he could fix that loose board?

He drew back the bedspread and the sheet…thinking he would be downstairs in just a minute in his dry clothes and his spare loafers. He would be sitting by the phone.

He crawled into bed…remembering the phone was dead. But dead things came back, didn't they? So, he would wait. In a minute.

The sheets were warm and dry and soft. He bled into them. In a minute. He would go down in a minute. The shutters prattled ceaseless percussion through the room, through his brain. He stared at the ceiling, watching antebellum plaster shake and threaten to fall on him. Constance's tongue was continuing to toss the insignificant craft moored to Carriage Avenue, still tasting and only just beginning its feast.

The candle flickered, brightened unexpectedly. Then it went out.

❖   ❖   ❖

The child, the child, the child…is coming. It's coming, my baby, it's coming. Mine! It's my baby, and they (it/she/he) want to take it from me, but my child will not grow up without its mother.

I have no choice.

Eyes closed, they (it/she/he) had done something to her, dragging her down into this dark place where she could sense the movement through the lids of her closed eyes, could sense the movement through the mouth of a fierce beast, not knowing where she was being carried by those cold, hard hands. Dulling her to the sensations of being lifted and lowered and lifted again as if upon a wave. Dulling her to the fetid rot and mold she knew surrounded her, as she also knew she was inside some place—but it was removed from immediacy, it was a stuporous understanding because they (it/she/he) had done something to her. Dulling her to the world outside her flesh—but not dulling her to the iron-talon cramps that came and went like those waves, those cramps that were seizing her back, her groin her cervix. And she felt another one coming, those unseen muscles quivering with their own intelligence, signaling, warning, and then…

…it came upon her and even though her eyes were already closed she squeezed them as the pain squeezed her. Instinctively, the breaths puffed out of her, breathing through it, releasing, gushing out clouds of the pain. Puffing, puffing. Releasing as the iron talon took its time with her. Puffing, puffing. Holding her tight, a part of her and yet separate. (And in the middle of it, from out of the swirl of confusion, a gentle-sweet voice like a balm smoothing over the sharpest edges of the hurt: "That's it, honey, you doin fine…just fine…won't be much longer…

fine as wine, child ...fine as dandelion wine...") Puffing. Ruthless. Breathing, sending out cumulous bursts of steam. The grip slackened. Puffing. Releasing. Easing back. Puffing. Puffing. The cramp faltering, faltering...

...then gone. And then just the pain ghosting through her tired muscles. She panted, filling her lungs again. Sweat bubbled across her face, rolled off her face.

My child, my child. Panting. My child will have its mother. They (it/she/he) will not, will not have it. Never. My child.

Her eyes, unclenching. Arms shoved her cruelly, and she was on the ground, no longer moving. Through a blur of eyelash came sight of a screaming black skull, broad shoulders, emanating animal hatred. She felt the world beyond her flesh returning to her as the hurt ebbed and the dullness remained. She was lying upon cushions and blankets. The smell of rot and mold and piss more immediate now, like a poison. The angry howls of a wounded beast, somewhere near, whipping around the walls that surrounded her. Oh, the smells of decay, so strong, the smells of smoke and burning, and...somewhere very close...another smell? In her hand...a leathery rustle...another hand—not a talon, but gentle and delicate, like a loose bunch of sticks...another hand holding hers...

...Gussie was holding his hand in this dream, gently prodding at his wounds and crying over them. The touch of her fingers upon his ravaged flesh. The sad whisper of her voice. *"Your hand, your poor hand."* Her voice childlike in this dream, and laced with the unmistakable edge of guilt—but of course he was the guilty one, the one who had brought all this into her life. And she had no reason to blame herself. He would have told her so, but it was just a dream, and in this dream he was mute. A helpless lump in his bed.

"Look what's happened to you, Boo. Look at the scars..."

Mutely protesting her words. Savoring her touch.

"She hurt you, oh look how she hurt you."

She was crawling into the bed, stroking his bleeding scalp, the pulpy skin along his shoulder. Her hands were cold and damp. She had come through the storm for him. She was safe. She was pulling down the sheets, her hands slipping down to the cuts at his thighs. Stroking. Light fingertip swirls on his wounds. His heart quickened. Blood went throbbing through him, his cock lifting and hardening, her fingers finding him, circling and tracing gently up the length of him.

"You won't ever leave me again, will you?"

His voice coming to him, rolling up his throat like a steel ball, mouth opening. "No," he breathed.

"You love me, don't you?" Her voice, so childlike in this dream.

"I love you," he said.

He reached for her, feeling a damp blouse beneath his wounded hand, and in this dream the belly beneath was flat and childless. He groped for the buttons on her blouse as her fingers continued to run smoothly over the length of him, sending an exquisite ache through his abdomen.

"And you won't go there, will you?"

"...go there?"

"You'll stay here with me, and we'll have our own child. And maybe he'll let yo...live."

"But...what?"

Her wet hair, sliding down to his hip, fingers holding him snugly into place. Her tongue, warm, slipping like a wet muscle around him as her words purred with kittenish silkiness into his flesh.

"...we'll have...have our own child..."

Teeth raking him, taunting with their sharp threat. The dream was fading—now it was confusion intruding, the perpetual clatter of the shutter intruding, the storm raging outside his window. While inside, in this darkness, a frigid and damp hand clamping on him, her lips and her teeth eagerly stroking him, preparing him, the muscles of his abdomen aching and clenching with anticipation, eyelids working, fluttering open...

...eyelids working, fluttering, opening to fire-lit dusk: oil lamps and a fireplace blaze. She looked about her, at her slacks removed and bunched at her hip, at graffiti-streaked walls and ruined scraps of furniture and stacks of moldering books and knew at once where this dreamland (nightmare land) was. She looked down at her hand, saw the hand that was holding her own, the body that was settled next to hers. Then she looked up through the gloom and gasped...

He gasped, lurching away because in the bluish pulses of the storm he saw whose body was nestled over his in his bed. He tumbled to the floor, pushing away, the pain of her teeth upon his flesh, scrambling farther across the room and banging into a chair. "How did you get in here?"

Lightening scintillations through the rebounding shutters, he could see the shoulders sag in her classic posture of woundedness. If the light were better, he would see the classic pout on her lips, the baby-doll eyes fluttering sulky accusation. She made a move toward him, and he threw out a hand, pointing, warning her away. "Stay back!" And then, in the darkness, a flash of brilliance—pieces of a puzzle, pieces he'd been staring at all wrong for so long...in that sudden flash the pieces were turned to a new perspective and snapped into place.

Ate one up. Licked the other.

"You're a skin-stealer," he said.

In the aftermath of that brilliant moment, in the gloom of his room, he understood how incredibly stupid he had been...

...the ghost, this thing (not a ghost) was holding her hand. The ghost (not a ghost) was blind. The ghost (not...) was speaking. "Oh my, oh my, Miss Gussie, if you still ain't the prettiest!"

Thirteen

He was on his feet, slamming his limbs into dry clothes and awakening his wounds. Sandy Baker was sitting on the bed. He couldn't see her face. She was a dark outline against the blue-silver flashes at the rattling window. Her blonde hair—normally so straight and severe—was splayed out in dank corkscrews.

"You can't go there," she was pleading. "You don't understand; he's all through with you."

He moved to the closet now, keeping an eye on her, not trusting her as he yanked a shirt indiscriminately off a hanger. His brain was wobbling, understanding the dream was over, that this was reality, understanding it, and it was sharp as a crystal shard—and then it was all a blur, an impossibility, and this fuzzy darkness and the wild bellowing of the storm were all part of the delusion. Back and forth, each side tugging on him—reality or insanity—and neither one able to convince him.

Quietly, cautiously, she said, "He'll kill you. He won't let you out alive."

"Maybe," he said. "You set my house on fire. That's how you got there so quick."

"No, I *never!* Boo, that wasn't. . .I would never *hurt* you."

He pulled on the shirt and brought blunt stabs of agony through his shoulder. He welcomed the pain. The pain at least was certain and uncompromising. Grimacing, he knelt down and felt blindly for shoes in the closet while he kept his eyes on her. They had left the gun at Sing Satterfield's house, something that seemed like a good idea at the time, but now. . .if he had it right now, in his hand. . .would he?

"I *wouldn't* hurt you," she was saying. "I just wanted—"

"A child."

"*Your* child. I wanted *you*."

He tugged on the shoes, glared at the glimmering shape on the bed. When he rose upright again, too quickly, the blood rushed from his skull and his vision went bleary. He tottered. When his vision sharpened, he studied her shape again for signs of transformation, for aggression. But she hadn't changed at all. Still the passive seduction: quiet but voracious. He turned from her and, from the bureau, swept the glass frog up in his battered right hand. He dropped the talisman into his breast pocket.

"You killed her, didn't you?" she asked him.

"Yes."

He went to the bedroom door and swung it open. Bess Pope and MaeEllen were standing before him, each clutching candles as if they were weapons. The flickering light threw thick, anxious shadows across their faces. He shouldered past them, then stopped at the top of the stairs. "Call Wade Dutton," he said firmly. "Tell him I'm going to Chaliboque. Tell him Gussie's there."

MaeEllen stepped forward. "Boo, the phones are dead!"

"Then go out on the street and flag someone down!"

And then he was hurrying down the steps and into the storm.

fourteen

He was somewhere on an unprotected stretch of Atlantic Avenue, racing south, when the water began surging up to the Tahoe's axles. He slipped the truck into four-wheel drive and pressed forward, finding the road only by aiming between the stray cars parked along the curb, their hulks vanishing under piling swells. Power lines jigged loosely overhead. Corner traffic signs convulsed at mad angles. Rain and chunks of shrapnel peppered the side of the truck with such force that Boo Taylor's mind was lost in a perpetual roar.

Tailor's mother had a son

(He'll kill you.)

The sea had breached the dunes and was skidding across the road in streaks of foam. The power was still out everywhere. The only illumination was the Tahoe's headlights cutting an inadequate swathe through the first several feet of horizontal rainfall. The world beyond that was depthless shades of black and blue—he might very well be in the middle of the ocean.

and never had another one

(He won't let you out alive.)

An invisible wave slammed into him from the east. His head banged off the door as the truck's rear wheels left the road. For a panicky moment, the high beams were underwater and aimed in a slight downward trajectory, picking up the frantic flight of some wriggling sea creature. The undertow picked the truck up and drew it toward the ocean. Glowing, greenish water swamped the hood. The rear of the truck was being dragged with alarming ease. Then the wheels caught solid pavement again. He shoved the truck into second gear and floored the gas pedal. The grill bulldozed through the swell. He came to a road banking right and turned into it, up-shifting now as he headed in-island to higher ground. Behind him, the surf receded.

when that child died

(He's all through with you.)

The windshield wipers whacked madly, offering the briefest instant of clarity with each stroke but otherwise only managing to smear the blurriness a little, to reshape it into various grim psychedelia. Something like his brain, he thought—that indecision, back and forth, to and fro, off and on, reality-fantasy, waking-dreaming, lucidity-obscurity, sanity-insanity. His father's pocket watch swung from the rearview mirror in cadence with the blades. He wiped the sweat out of his eyes, breathed the stale-cigar air of the cab. He drove hunched over the wheel and squinting. When he reached a street he thought might be Polk, he turned left, heading south again.

without his own

(You can't go there.)

Then he saw a sign with an arrow. *Satterfield.* Names. Yes, he was on the right trail. The names had always marked the route, but he had always been too dense to read the names. Satterfield. *Sing. (can't go there)* Names were a part of the joke *(the lie).* Sing-singe; she sings, she singes; always singing *(you killed her)* always singeing—always *burning*, and hadn't that always been clear as Crystal? Seduced rich, awkward, nerdish Dalton Satterfield, stole some skin to draw him to her, stole his life, stole his name. *(Her grandchilds' names was Smith and Jones.)* The joke was always in the names. *(Boooooo!)* Even his own name was a joke.

He took the trunk of a downed palmetto at thirty miles an hour, cracking his head on the roof.

Queenie queenie had two daughters, hated one and liked the other.

He'd never met Sandy's parents. Her adoptive parents. Just stories. Not even photographs. The Bakers. Sweet old couple from a small town outside Chicago. A sweet old couple with the right name and suitably removed from their adopted little girl's Southern roots and too perfect for the joke.

He veered around an abandoned station wagon. A stop sign had pierced its windshield like a spear, and the red octagon was violently waving its warning at him.

It was Allen Noble who had introduced them. Had he used her full first name? He couldn't remember; at the time, he had no reason to think of it.

Sandy. Sandra. Cassandra. Cassie. *(Sandy, let me introduce you to one of our favorite clients. Mr. Robert Taylor, this is Cassandra Baker. Sandy's new to our firm.)*

Think Miss Cassie take a likin to you. Maybe she be your girlfriend, doctor's boy. She got nice light skin like you.

He drove through a block-long stretch of books and magazines *(Lester Meggett's eyes)* flapping up to the sky outside a destroyed bookstore, the Tahoe's wheels thumping over them, tearing them apart, because the joke was always there *(each one a way in, each one a way out)*. In Lester Meggett's house, the envelope lost amid a pile of beer cans and pizza boxes. Her name over and over. *(Sandy Baker, Cassandra Baker, Sandy Meggett, Sandy Baker Meggett.)* The dull slits of Lester's eyes hanging over the pouty, miserable face of a little blonde-haired girl. *(Sandy please spred your legs for me, please I stil love you.)*

The Tahoe's roof banged into a bicycle that was dangling from a swaying oak limb; in the instant before impact, he could see the pedals circling with fierce intent.

(I wouldn't hurt you. I just wanted...you.)

The gear knob was slick with the blood from the cuts in his palm. Scarlet spots dappled across his lap. He came to another stretch of water he identified as a swollen Soap Water Creek. He aimed for a space between two concrete pillars, hoping it was the bridge, and rammed the Tahoe forward. The water wrapped around him, sucking him under, and he lost speed. He down-shifted and kept bulling forward. The current slammed the rear bumper against the bridge rail. Metal shrieked against metal as he felt the tires trying to separate from the road again. He rocked in the seat, *c'mon, c'mon you sonofabitch, c'mon dammit,* and steadily picked up momentum. When he was ten yards past the midpoint of the stream, the tires settled and he was able to jostle the rest of the way onto clear road.

A short distance later, at last, he came to the entrance to the Sing Satterfield Wildlife Refuge.

A sturdy four-by-four barricade was padlocked in place across both lanes. Bolted in the middle, a reflectorized message: CLOSED. Beyond that, a muddy lane disappearing into darkness.

Granddaddy comin with the butcherman's blade.

(You can't go there. He won't let you out alive.)

The road on either side of the entrance dipped toward a steep, water-filled slough. Boo backed the Tahoe up until he found a relatively flat area of shrub about twenty yards to the right of the entrance. Rain and debris assaulted him. *"Shit,"* he muttered, shifting into first gear and bracing himself against the steering wheel. He gunned the gas, lifted the clutch. The truck lurched, barreled over an unseen dip and then crashed into an eight-foot wall of myrtle and bayberry. Leaves and wet branches exploded over the hood, covered the windshield. Boo was slammed forward, cracking his nose against his own knuckles, then slammed back into the seat. He heard the pop of something shattering. Salty blood leaked down his throat. He kept his foot on the gas, grinding forward as the branches fell away.

The truck burst free. He was in the vacant parking lot.

He dabbed at the blood that was collecting at his lip. One of the headlamps was broken and the passenger-side wiper was bent at a useless, outward angle. A bush was caught up on one of the axles, and he dragged it as he circled around the lot. He found the boardwalk that led to the welcome center and made the truck jump the curb, driving past picnic tables, past the lot where he had once walked with Gussie. It seemed impossible that it was not even nine months ago, seemed impossible that a sun was ever so glaringly bright and hot.

The path before him was barely wide enough to accept the truck, and the occasional wet branch slapped at its side. He made the bends and turns, trying to recall the route he had taken with Gussie that long-ago day, and then he was slipping into his boyhood, imagining the rutted dirt spur that bent around to Laylee Colebriar's shack, imagining the garden and the fields and the woods beyond that, twisting along the creek and leading to Pigg's Point. He passed a sign: PLEASE! DO NOT ATTEMPT TO FEED THE ALLIGATORS! where the trail became a swamp. He splashed through inches-deep water, took a right at the next fork and kept following that track until the headlights caught another sign—and it came to him now why the toy bridge in front of Sing Satterfield's house had seemed so familiar. It was, of course, another joke.

DANGER! BRIDGE IS UNSAFE, CROSSING NOT PERMITTED

Islands within islands. His father's watch rocked back and forth with the steady strokes of a pendulum.

He stopped the truck.

A minute later, he was pointing the flashlight at the humped footbridge. Pigg's Creek had spilled over its banks and was flooding muddy water in a powerful rush toward the west. The bridge, which had seemed rickety enough when the creek was at normal height, now looked suicidal. A small oak tree, swept up by the stream, had gotten tangled in the support stilts and the entire contraption was tottering precariously against the current. He stood next to the Tahoe, steadying himself against the storm. Rain battered him, soaked him, washed away the blood that was flowing from his many wounds. He had never imagined wind could be so strong and so loud—it was like standing in front of a great screaming mouth. The gale was lifting him, making his weight insignificant. He squinted at the bridge, at the sign hammered into the ground next to the roped-off entry: *Danger!* The wind would never let him cross; it would fling him into the floodwaters or simply tear the flesh away from his bones.

Boo Taylor leaned into the great screaming mouth and stepped forward.

When his shoe touched the first rain-slicked rung of wood, he slipped. He caught himself on the railing, pushed up, and steadied himself against the wind. He cradled the flashlight in his left arm, grabbing the rail with his right. Grunting, he heaved his body another step into the bridge. Then another, crouching low. And another as the span creaked under his weight and the bridge shifted. Another, moving faster now, then his right foot slipped again. The wind and the over-compensation of his left foot stole his balance, and he went slamming chest-first into the railing. The railing made a sharp cracking noise and gave way several inches under his weight. Rain covered him like a blanket and the wind caught him like a ship's sail, trying to launch him into the sky. Five feet below, a monster-version of Pigg's Creek thundered and foamed toward the Yamawichee Sound.

They're watching me. The thought pinging abruptly. And then a wolf's howl, shrill and wounded, was ice-picking through the storm. He glanced toward the opposite bank while he slowly, carefully, felt around with his feet. Finally, the relative solidity of a plank was beneath him. He eased his weight back to his legs. As his body shifted, the rail shifted with him like a spring. *Watching me; waiting for me.* The screaming wind was trying to pick him up. He started forward again, carefully pulling himself toward the middle of the span, trying not to rush. As he neared the bridge's peak the wind was at its fiercest and the leeward tilt was at its worst. The planks were coated with moss and as slippery as ice.

He pointed the light off toward the opposite bank, seeing nothing, but still certain someone was there, waiting for him. He went forward again, light as air, knees bent. A baby step. A soggy plank swagged with his weight but took it. He stepped again. A wind gust gave him an unexpected shove; he leaned into it, was able to keep his balance. Another short step. He listened to echoes from his boyhood: *You want to kneel down, maybe, Dew? Crawl the rest of the way?* His life kept insisting on coming around in its maddening circles. Another step, tottering frightfully again as the gale slapped something hard and sharp against his cheek, something substantial amid all the rain—just another stick, he guessed, but it stung like a wasp. More little baby steps, passing the crown and on the uneven down slope now. *More'n halfway there, Dew. Made it the first half, you can make the second half.* The tilt of the planks became less severe. He lengthened his steps, keeping steady hold on the flashlight with one hand and the sodden tree-limb railing with the other. And again—as he became sure he would reach the other side—that sense of being watched asserted itself. Only now, it was from behind. Someone back at the Tahoe. *Following me.* He felt a net coming down around him. The last several feet of the footbridge were under the rushing current. He splashed through it at a run, the water reaching his knees, and came at last to the other side.

He took the old trails now. Buried over the years under mounds of myrtle and sharp yucca and sumac, wrapped mummy-like behind the gauze of ropey vine. Buried now, invisible and dead, like ghosts, but he knew them anyway. He knew them as a fetus knows his mother's pulse; these trails, the veins were connected to him, leading him toward her heart. He knew the trails because this was the place of his birth.

Come join us, Boo. His mother's voice and those before her, lost beyond decades of growth. Wolves' eyes darting through the jungle leaves. He heard them in there, waiting for him. His escorts. Impatient. They had waited long enough for his return.

I'm here. I'm coming.

He pushed away tree limbs and sopping wet shrubs and dangling vines, aiming the flashlight ahead. *Who dat hidin in de swamp tree shade?* Was there only one voice out there, he wondered? It seemed there were more, but perhaps it was just the one, and just one Beast all along: the great dark granddaddy, master joke teller— one being, his life stolen *(the child stolen)* by angry, ignorant men, shadowing him now as he *(it, they)* had shadowed him all his life. Making sure he reached this destination. *I'm coming.* Like plunging backward into the womb, all this wet violence around him, the heat and the darkness, the contractions of the storm thrusting him away. What would he do if the Beast attacked now? If it leapt out from this next massive oak, or if it crawled up from behind and dragged him down? Or if it came from both directions, before and behind, splitting and becoming two daughters with one purpose? Yes, he decided, it would be like that. He had already felt them when he was on the bridge. One in front of him and one following. The trap was set. No way in, and no way out. And when they came for him, they could have him. He had nothing left to fight back with—and that thought brought peace. Nothing left. No place left for him in this world. His house, his money, his business were all gone. His friends killed off. Gussie married to another man—cruelest joke of all—and those two would be raising his child, not needing him, not needing the confusion and embarrassment and heartache his very existence made inevitable. He knew this; Gussie knew this. There was no place for him.

Come, be with us and sing your story to the dead.

Who was his mother, that voice beckoning like a wolf's song, like a heartbeat from the dead/living place just ahead? That woman hidden for all these years behind the veils of old, bloody gauze? *Tailor's mother had a son.* He was going to meet her and the granddaddy/grandmother Beast, not far away now at all, and find out who he was. Gale-whipped fronds slashed at his arms. A wolf's snarl erupted from his left, quickening him along.

I'm coming, he called out, hurrying now, *just please don't hurt my Gussie; please don't hurt my child.*

His shoes touched on sleek cobbles. Getting closer, now. The Yamawichee was a great sloshing colossus, invisible, on his right.

Tailor's mother had a son, had two daughters.

He slipped, fell hard on his right elbow, and got up slowly. The cobbles, like the planks of the footbridge were slicked with moss and rain, and he remembered falling on this very spot twenty-five years earlier, holding Gussie's hand as they escaped from Crystal Burne. Laylee Colebriar had been waiting for them that long-ago night. Miss Laylee, who had been more a mother to him and to Gussie than anyone had been. They had rushed to her, and she had protected them. She had protected two mother-less children in favor of her own great grand-daughter. And why would she do that? Why had she followed Samuel LaValle's daughter to the mainland instead of her own stolen child?

Hated one and liked the other.

And she had died for it.

He passed through the last of the groping jungle limbs. Wind streaked recklessly across an open space, catching his shirt and shoving him back. He bent his head and dug his feet in the mud, pressing forward. *Laylee, why would you do that?* He stabbed the flashlight's beam around and saw it. The corner of a gray stone slab poking like a crypt from straggling shrub. Peeling skin, graffiti-blotched, vine-ravaged. He craned his neck against the wind gusts to take in the great looming dead shape. Not dead: a red, ember-like glow burned at several of the eyes. Someone was screaming inside. Screaming his name, over and over.

Come be with us!

Laylee, why would you protect me and not your own?

Great wolf howls galed around him as he lurched toward the pulsing, not-dead house. His mother's heart—that long ago mother, Margaritte LaValle, the sickly woman with her sickly heart, married to his murdering great-grandfather. It was their home, and it was his home. It had always been his home, this place of grandeur rotting in the swamp. He swung the flashlight like a weapon, striking it across the pallid walls and saw the man standing at an upstairs window. Wide, rawboned shoul-ders. Seashell eyes. Blistered flesh. His arms were folded, and his face was all stony contempt. Boo wiped at his eyes, looked again, and the window was blank, the image stolen *(the child stolen)* back by the darkness.

He found the crumbled, window entrance. Still open. The piled rubble steps, grown over with weeds now, but still offering access to the house. He stumbled to the pile, began dragging himself up. *Why, Laylee, didn't you protect your own?* He was chest-level with the entrance when a lightening flash struck him from inside, and he caught a ghostly image of his fractured twin staring back, wide-eyed and startled—and another instant of brilliance rifled over him. Electric shock trembled through his veins, collapsed his lungs, set his brain on fire. He dropped to his knees. *(Nine-year-old boy running down sun-baked lanes, seeking out the old woman and crying because the first nail of truth had been beaten into him on the playground, but he had never he had never he had NEVER guessed the true black depth of the lie.)*

He knew.

(She knows things.)

Dems you own bone, boy. Dems you murrah bone.

(Your own bones.) (Your mother's bones.)

The boy knew.

"Oh, Laylee," he moaned. He clawed his way inside.

The patrol car, slipping in the mud, made a last, shivering turn in the trail and came to a stop. The rickety stand of the Pigg's Creek footbridge was caught in the beam of the car's headlights.

DANGER!

Before the bridge, Boo Taylor's badly dented Tahoe. Next to that, resting at an awkward angle, was a little red BMW. The BMW's diver-side door stood open. The engine was still running, and the interior light was glowing.

The brittle hand slipped out of hers. The old, old, old woman was limping blindly away. "You be still now, child. I'll be right back." From the throne, a black skull watched and smirked.

fifteen

He stood in the middle of a widening puddle. With his first steps inside, the world had become deceptively silent as the hurricane shrieks were suddenly muffled by the old walls, and all that was left was a distant, hollow ring. He wiped rainwater from his face. He played the flashlight around, picking up moldy corners, piles of junk (less than he remembered) and spray painted obscenities (more than he remembered). And of course the cracked mirror that had shocked the last, final truth into him. *(You like dat, boy?)* Light reflected back at him, stinging his eyes. His own shape *(twin)* a sopping, bloody mess sent sputtering from a womb. Frail and frightened as a newborn pup.

The flashlight played along the floor where tiny wolf-like tracks led deeper into the old house. He walked to one of the rubbish heaps and poked through it. Crumpled beer cans and whiskey bottles. Ropey shreds of a carpet. A flattened shoe. An empty picture frame. The light struck the whirling dust plume he stirred, rising like smoke from a fire. He picked the leg of an old table out of the mold and cobwebs, stirring more dust. The leg was thick and blocky at the top, tapering to a thin round handle near its clawed foot.

"Dat piddly thing ain't gonna hurt nobody."

He spun around at the voice. The flashlight slashed crazily across vacant walls. Nothing—the voice of the storm playing through cracks.

Or something that had moved on, something shuffling around the next corner. Something as sopping wet as he. Something old and tired.

He straightened up, gripping the table leg in his injured right hand as his mostly numb left held the flashlight. He aimed the beam at the floor and followed the trail of footprints further into the house.

He took the familiar corridors.

The old, frightened, sopping wet Beast slouched ahead of him. Dodging the light, keeping to the dark, wet places. Long, wobbly shadows. Hints of movement, just beyond the range of the light. The sound of his own breathing boxed in tightly around him. Hundreds of moldering tons sagging on ancient rafters. Another twenty-five years of decay: ceilings buckling and leaking rain, plaster walls crumbling. Margaritte and Samuel LaValle's ruined home.

"Tailor's mother had a son, and never had another one."

Yes, he knew the joke, now—Mamie Stuvant's joke was really the bitter testament of her existence. *(never had another one)* Margaritte LaValle had died giving birth, and that was a known fact. *(...already I sense his concern for the wretched state of my health...)*

But her child had died, too. Another in a string of miscarriages—and a fact, buried. A truth not found in Royal Goody's ancient texts.

(That child died, without his own.)

And so a lie was born.

Wiping at his eyes, rain and sweat bubbling over his flesh. His clothes clung to him heavily. His shoulder and hand throbbed and bled. His nose pulsed bluntly. The air thickened around him, became like the stagnant cloud over a swamp. He smelled rotting peaches and dog's breath, and beneath that the steady whiff of charred wood. He heard the scamper of tiny feet. The deeper squish of larger ones, still sliding stealthy beyond the range of his flashlight, luring him deeper...

"Why, that's good, Mr. Boo," the old thing was saying as it led him deeper into the house. *"You done figure that out, then maybe you know the rest of it."*

The rest of it. The rest of the lies, tumbling like block and brick around his great-grandfather as the cornerstone was suddenly stolen from beneath his palace. Walls crumpled. Pillars tottered. The child was dead; he needed a child. The king is dead; long live the king. He needed a LaValle child. A prince.

(...my fetal cargo is the legitimate treasure Mdsl V and her cousin truly cherish. Or rather, it is daddy's purse they covet and endeavor to secure by the rather old fashioned methods employed by the late kings of Europe for more political ends. SV's island barony requires a wealthy prince or princess lest it sink around him on its cottony foundation...)

It always came back to the child.

"Needed the Queen's money, boy. It always came back to money."

"He needed her family's money," Boo said aloud. "So he had to come up with a prince. Or a princess. Before anyone knew."

(...and the little frog told the guffer lady, "Why, I ain't really a frog. I'se a prince. This mean ol witch done come along and put a black whammy on me...)

Ahead, the wet and tired old shape, keeping just out of sight. And now, another shape, a younger one creeping up behind him, also staying at a distance. He flexed his fist tighter around the table leg, knowing he was being drawn deeper and deeper into a trap and falling further and further into his own exhaustion. He passed places where the floor had collapsed and the flashlight illuminated jagged, tumbled ruins. He came to the main hall. A ragged hole marked the place where he had once, long ago, gone crashing through the wall at the foot of the steps. He aimed the light inside and saw only a pile of plaster and sharp spokes of lathe. The whipping song of the hurricane reasserted itself, making strange, discordant echoes and a constant, low and playful hum. Wet, reptilian voices called to him:

"Now who's child you figure he done stole?"

"Hated one, and liked the other," Boo said, and gleeful titters rolled through the thick, fetid air, resounding off moldering walls, filling his ears. Laylee Colebriar, daughter of Joker and Sheba Tribbit, had accompanied Mrs. LaValle to Aiken. *(will be tending to YT who's fairly bursting herself...)* Bursting with twins. Laylee Colebriar *(queenie, queenie)* had two daughters.

"Ate one up, and licked the other!" A cackle of her old laughter. *"Oh, I had two daughters, sure enough. Twins. But they didn't look the same, now did they?"*

The light caught a skulking shape above, familiar, gray fur, tortured old eyes, shoulders hunched, wet and miserable—just a glimpse before it was easing into the shadows along the balustrade. An oil lamp had been placed on a table at the second-floor landing. It cast an orange glow over the upper hall, sending massive shadows capering down the walls.

The footprint trail began again. Soupy black splotches on a random track up the steps and risers. With the back of his wrist, he dabbed the sweat away from his brow and started up the stairs. Halfway up, a step snapped under his foot like dry kindling, and he rocked into the banister. His feet kicked loose several rails as the banister lurched under his weight. He was on the footbridge again, whipping his arms around, and finally catching his balance. He managed to keep a hold of the table leg, but this time the flashlight slipped from his grip. It went spinning end over end with one of the railings, spraying spirals of light through the main hall, and crashed on the floor. The light shone into the dust.

A merry, frog-like giggle seeped at him from several directions.

He took the table leg in both hands. His grip was greasy with sweat and blood. He glared up at the flickering lamplight, dim as a candle. Behind him, it was only darkness now.

Gently...very gently...he stretched to the next step.

From upstairs, the hurricane sounds swelled, all roars and whispers, swirling around in the air like solid objects and mixing and dampening the low, sad voice that drew him forward.

He reached the landing where he found a perfect, miniature footprint getting soaked up by the dusty floor. The lamp, set on a rickety looking table, was antique, with a fancy sculpted brass base and a glass chimney. A tiny blue-and-orange flame projected his own giant shadow on the walls. Thin wisps of black smoke threaded up from the glass and gave off a smell of burnt flowers. He moved cautiously around the lamp and saw three others, the flames all set low and barely lighting more footprints on the way toward the front of the house. The lamps were laid out like the sconces along Sing Satterfield's second floor corridor. Unlike Sing Satterfield's house, this place looked lived in. A stack of clothes on a chair. A towel draped over the railing. A jelly-jar glass, half-empty, on a table top. Someone was living here.

Samuel LaValle had stolen one of Laylee Colebriar's *(Eulahlah Jane Tribbit's)* little twin babies. And she let him do it. Had he threatened her?

"Oh, them children was twins, but they never looked it. One pale, one a little burnt. One stayed a bit too long out in that sun."

She had two daughters, hated one and liked the other. One little girl looked black, and one little girl looked white. One looked like her mother, one looked like her father.

(...Big J's lovely child was nearby, no doubt spying on my husband with adolescent notions of romance.)

"He raped you," Boo said. "Samuel LaValle raped you."

"Rape? Or master's privilege? He was a rakish man, 'nuff to charm a ignorant little nigger girl, leastways. But it wasn't rape, boy. S'pose I thought it was love. Figured he thought it was the same, though I suppose that was just the folly of a young girl's heart."

"But he stole your child."

"Was his own child, too, wasn't it?"

"And Joker found out."

"Yes, boy. Joker found out. But it was Sheba, full'a hate, brought the axe down."

One child consigned to poverty, the other to privilege. *(And the Lord had regard for Abel and for his offering; but for Cain and for his offering He had no regard.)*

Boo crept steadily past the low flush of the lamps and toward the turn ahead that would take him into the wind shrieks along the front hall. A desiccated floorboard screeched beneath him. He shuffled backward quickly to a solid spot.

Had a son and never had another one.

"Wasn't never s'pose t'be a boy-child. Sheba never saw that comin."

Behind him, nearly lost in the hurricane roar, a squealing step on the stairway. Someone back there—Sandy Baker following, little blond girl lost in her books, following, the Cassie/Sandy thing was still trying to claim him.

Carefully, he slid around the weak space in the floor, darting glances in front and behind. He followed the dim glow and the sporadic disturbances in the dust and turned the corner into the front hall. The sound of the storm was enormous. Another stack of clothes, old and threadbare, folded neatly and piled next to a small, weather-worn pair of shoes, more signs of someone living here. Ahead, more lamps leading to the end of the corridor—to the room around the next turn. Rain slashed in from between the boarded gaps at the windows on his right. Gales wept like women, filling his ears again with their sad, painful song.

Dems you murrah bone.

Those were your mother's bones.

"You're my great-grandmother," he said. "And those were my mother's bones they found in your shack. When it burned down. The bones Lester dug up; they put them there. You never died in that fire. You're still..."

The gray-furred shadow crept around that last turn. Boo shuffled his fingers nervously on the table leg, cords rippling through his forearms. The wails of the storm were making it difficult to think, and it seemed suddenly as if there really was a woman crying out in pain—not the shadow that was drawing him forward, but someone else. He kept moving, allowing himself to be pulled ahead, knowing there was no escape. Another cry.

"Gussie?"

Her voice came calling back to him. "Boo! We're here!"

He rushed forward, floor sagging with his steps. He swung the leg out blindly, and crashed into the room.

The skeletal shape was back at her side now, taking her hand as that second and thicker, more brutal skull shape slipped back to the shadows and dreamland demons danced about unseen but cast lewd shadow writhings on painted obscenities and (I used to paint pictures in the real world!) chanting hilarious bawdry and (pretty landscapes) clattering rotted log drums and (in watercolor) spraying a fine, boiling mist over the room. (The old woman is afraid.)

(...oh God oh God it's coming it's coming again.)

The contraction cramped through her muscles like an electric shock. She puffed, blowing through the hurt, blowing through the great clamping pull. The hurt was sharper now and longer, her tissue stretching, the pain coming to a fine white glow. Breathing. Puffing. She held the withered dreamland hand—little bird hand—in her own, and she was afraid of squeezing too hard, afraid that even in dreams, little bird bones snapped like dry twigs.

"You doin jes fine, honey. Gawd, you done this before, you know what you doin..."

She puffed, and a high-pitched groan leaked from her lungs when the pain peaked. The storm was filling up the room, screeching and howling—and through the pain and through the screaming demon wails and through the sound of her own cries she heard...Boo Taylor, somewhere...inside this dream house, calling... her name?

Her own voice, shrieking in competition with the storm: "Boo! Boo, we're here! We're here!"

A moment later, as the contraction at last eased, he burst from the dim hallway like some creature savaging its way out of a swamp—crouched low, filthy and soaked through with mud, hair matted, bright blue eyes wide and bright with fear, blood seeping pink ribbons down his left shoulder, his right hand (oh, I remember that, it swallowed them up like chicken bones!) wrapped in a blood-grimy rag and wielding a great club. But that second shape, that screaming black skull, was disengaging from the shadows and moving in on him.

❖ ❖ ❖

The storm reared back and let out a belly laugh. Seen through a dim, amber blush: Gussie, yes. Before the great roaring fireplace, hunched and raw on an old mattress, knees apart, heaving rapid breaths. Swaddles of sheets and towels and blankets. And beside her, kneeling before the king's throne...

(...the world, this house, shook under the force of the gale, wind streaming a hundred ululating voices through rotting eaves and fractured walls, making the antediluvian wood and plaster and block frame shudder like...)

...an old woman.

Older than he ever imagined a person could be.

A brown skeleton in a gray dress, sitting on its haunches, ancient and dry and long-since dead. Eyes milked over and blind. Skin cracked and loose like timeworn leather, thin as paper, dry as desert sand. Hair just a wispy hint of white cotton over a polished, coffee skull. The brutal contrast of pink scars around a delicate brown nose.

"Alive," he said.

"Boy," she answered, smiling, a raspy sing-song lilt. An ancient mummy's arm lifted, desiccated fingers reached up.

Those were your mother's bones.

"You're alive."

Off to his left, a dark shape emerged from the shadows, from the old throne, bellowing and charging. A broad silhouette in rags, wild hair flying. He turned, but the shape caught him under the ribs and drove him to the ground.

"Boo!"

Ancient floorboards splintered and gave way as the floor opened and swallowed him.

sixteen

(...everything gonna be fine, Miss Gus...fine as dandelion wine...fine as frog's hair...)

seventeen

Fire singed his arm. He jerked away from it, coming slowly toward consciousness, hissing at the sharp pain. He pushed up to his knees, then to his feet. His whole body throbbed. He shook his head trying to clear it, then staggered a few steps before falling back to his knees. A bank of flames was growing from a mound of debris and ashes were cascading around him like snowflakes.

We're here, boy...does you see us?

Angels, he remembered. Snowflakes were the angels coming down to earth.

He's comin now...granddaddy comin...gonna eat you up!

He reached out and placed his right hand on the wall to brace himself as he tried to get to his feet again. He was in the entry hall on the ground floor and his head was pounding. How had he gotten here? He tasted blood and dust. He felt a massive rustling in the darkness as winged things shuffled nervously at the intrusion. Then he remembered and looked up. A jagged hole in the high ceiling, broken bits of board pointing down. An oil lamp had fallen in with him, shattered, and caught on a dry pile of kindling and old refuse. The fire was spreading rapidly.

"Gussie," he breathed as he collapsed again to his knees. He could hear her up there, and she was in pain.

The child, boy...stole his skin...stole his child.

The winged things, angels, hiding in the dark. They lived here. They belonged here.

Does you get the joke?

She never left...was always here.

Lester Meggett, mindless puppet, leering at him over a scarred table. A dusty old skeleton *(dems you murrah bone)* was up there with Gussie, gone blind, withered from old to ancient in this dark ruins. Never left. Lester had always liked to dig up old bones.

You own bone, boy. You murrah bone.

Behind him, footsteps coming down the old and horribly sagging stairs. In front of him, a great mass shifting in the flames. Boo placed both hands against the wall and pulled himself to his feet. He took a wobbling step backward as a broad man-shape rose from the flames before him, scraps of garbage falling away. "Old man," Boo said, blinking, trying to clear his vision, taking another unsteady step. His body hurt everywhere. He wiped his eyes, looked up and saw a black skull screaming back at him. His knees buckled and he fell back against the wall. Laylee Colebriar's long dead voice was whispering down to him from the hole in the ceiling, her words woven amid Gussie's increasingly anxious grunts and groans. The thing crawling out of the fire toward him was made of the fire itself. "Old man," he said again. The thing was silent, a skin-stealer melting into something feral and mindless. Fire rippled up the walls and reached rain-soaked corners where an enormous hiss erupted, sending up plumes of steam to mix with the smoke.

Above, a sharp cry from Gussie.

"You can't have it," Boo said.

The skull glistened sweat, rippled flesh. A bearded grin drew back and made a yellow-toothed snarl as a flock of crows flapped to life behind the thing, scattering ash and smoke, filling the great hall. From the stairs, a small voice pleaded, "Please don't hurt him." A little blonde girl, weeping.

The crows shrieked outrage.

Boo Taylor braced himself against the wall then charged forward just as the Beast did the same.

❖   ❖   ❖

The brown, infinitely old skeleton twisted to comfort her. The gray skull turned to gaze blindness upon her. Fish went blind in caves, she'd read, their eyes milking over like these eyes, useless in the dark. "Won't be long now, Miss Gus." Another contraction, powerful, unrelenting. She breathed and groaned. Sounds of a furious battle rose up from the floor.

"What's happening to Boo?"

Root fingers stroked her hand. Paraffin-scarred lips twisted into a grim smile. "That sad ol man, he like a storm." The old voice was as ragged as broken glass. "Lot of thunder and wind and coldness. And tears enough t'make a flood. You got to breathe, child."

She closed her eyes, puffing, blowing. Below her, a crash. Boo Taylor crying out.

"His soul always been a tempest, but she never let him rest like he want."

"You—" breathing, breathing, the pain wringing her muscles "—you're like her, like Sheba, aren't you?"

Animal growls, shrieks from below. The walls shuddered under the force of the wind.

"Stole my baby, stole my life, stole me and put me here—course I ain't like her. Loved all my children, Miss Gus. Every one. Breathe, girl. Includes you; you always been like my own."

Her flesh was stretching now, ready to rip open as the baby shifted again and the cramp rifled through her. Steam and smoke were filling the air around her, the roar of the storm and a great hissing snake coiling through the room. Flames were shooting through gaps in the floor and screams echoed up from the room below, through the door, from the windows.

My child, my child!

Skin pulling taught, pressure building, pain slicing through her like a razor blade. The pain would not let her go, her chest rising and falling, the pain was twisting her apart.

"Is there blood?" she called out.

The gnarled fingers slid down to her thighs, pressing them apart. "You gotta make ready, Miss Gus. Baby's comin now, and when it happens it's gonna be quick."

In the middle of the great room, Boo Taylor slammed into a great shaggy weight. On impact, bones cracked. A magnificent pain rifled through his body. He had rushed into an equal but opposite of himself, a mirror in front a brick wall that took as much as it gave, shattered as he shattered, tottered as he tottered, pressed as he pressed. He groaned; the Beast groaned. The Beast was wearing a flannel shirt, with ripped-off sleeves, that was now on fire. Boo swung his mostly dead left arm around and dug into a pile of gray fur. His right hand, now stripped of the gauze, swung around and clapped against the Beast's ear. He pulled hair, and the thing howled into his face. Crows wings assaulted the air everywhere. The wings were thunder. The crows were screaming out his name. The room was black with them, a thick black smoke of feathers and sharp claws and sharp beaks, all shrieking as they caught fire. The Beast under him was a bull. The Beast thrashed and howled in pain. It brought up two bear-like arms and squeezed the breath out of him. Its yellow-green teeth slicked across his neck as it howled into his face. Boo's feet left the ground. He dug his hands into the thick pelt as the Beast tried to fling him off. Boo wouldn't let go, and the both of them toppled to the floor.

("Time to push, honey.")

The burning crows were circling now, spiraling upward with the flames and smoke and the steam. Bits of Sandy Baker flashed in and out between feathers and ash. She was on the stairway; she had followed him here. The rest of the room was ablaze, blasting his eyes with a ferocious light and baking him alive. The Beast's arms were pinned under his back, its great putrid weight bucking into him. The flames on its shirt blistered Boo's hands. In the growing firelight, Boo could see that the Beast was wearing thick work boots, was wearing tattered old jeans that were burned away at one calf. Jaws snapped at Boo's left shoulder, found the fresh wounds there and ripped into them. The pain was a blowtorch searing him alive. Screaming, Boo clamped his teeth on the Beast's ear and wrenched his head back and forth until a piece of flesh and gristle tore free.

("You got to push harder, now. Baby wants t'come, but he need your help.")

The roar of flame and storm and the dying crows filled everything. Somewhere above him, Gussie was screaming about blood. The stink of burning feathers was smothering. Boo kicked out, and the Beast fell away from him, bent, cupping a great furry paw to its ear, snarling. The Beast had a tattoo of a skull on its shoulder. Red eyes poured forth mindless rage. It screeched at him.

"BOY!"

Boo rushed it again, brought it down. Some massive piece of furniture wrapped in flames crashed next to them. Boo cannoned his right fist into the bearded face.

"YOU CAN'T!" the thing bellowed.

A heavy claw slithered up and grabbed Boo Taylor's throat. Boo reared his fist back again. The calloused, thick-fingered vice squeezed his windpipe, and he gagged. Just under his chin, the black skull was grinning at him. The vice tightened. Boo held his fist high, a mutilated lump that dripped blood. Then he rammed it down.

("Don't you quit, Miss Gus. He almost there.")

A feathered corpse thudded beside him. His knuckles were pulp.

"YOU CAN'T, YOU CAN'T!"

Another crow fell, careening off his back. Boo slammed his fist down again.

"You...boy...can't..."

He pounded at the Beast until the grip slackened. He kept pounding, and the claw slipped away.

("Almost there, honey.")

The great hall was an oven now. Stacks of refuse exploded all around him like mortars. Boo Taylor slammed his fist over and over into the heaping mass of animal beneath him.

"Don't hurt him!" Sandy Baker, dimly from the direction of the stairs.

His fist slowed, became too heavy to lift anymore as he gasped for air. He rolled off the Beast, gulping for oxygen, his skin roasting. His eyes stung. He searched the floor, staggering, thigh muscles straining to keep upright. Smoke rolled over him as ash and dead black lumps rained about him. He bent to the floor, came up with the table leg. He turned back to the Beast.

("Just a bit more.")

"Don't. . .hurt."

He raised the leg. The Beast, on its back, made small wet noises and lifted an open palm.

Boo Taylor slammed the club down. Blood splattered his shoes.

("Almost there.")

You can't. . .child. . .

. . .you!

Grunting, he brought it down again. The Beast hitched. The last of the burning crows plummeted to the floor, bursting open like rotten peaches.

(". . .almost!")

He brought the club down a third time.

Another involuntary flex of muscle.

(". . .almost!")

Boo Taylor dropped the table leg and tottered backward.

❖   ❖   ❖

"Why Miss Gus, that's a fine baby boy."

eighteen

The stairway was empty. He stumbled up it.

The heat was less intense on the second floor, but the smoke was worse. He hurried, bent over, coughing and trying to get in full breaths as he worked his way past the violence that was storming in through the front windows. When he reached the great throne room the smoke inside was so dense he could see nothing.

"Gussie!" he called. His throat was shredded raw.

Through the roar of fire and storm he heard a faint reply. Flames were rippling up through the floor in several places.

"Where?" he called.

Another faint shout.

He fell to his hands and knees, coughing, and scrabbled through smoke that was just slightly thinner near the floor. The floorboards were as hot as a griddle. He felt his way forward, scorching his knees and his palms until his hand brushed against a mattress and blanket. A gray plume hovered over it.

"Gussie."

Her voice, close, muted. "I'm here. We need to get out."

A hand swung out of smoke, and he took hold of it. Then she was bending toward him. She was pressing a towel to her face and another to her breast. White tears streaked from her eyes; her face was otherwise gray with smoke and ash. Her blouse was soaking wet. She looked utterly exhausted.

"Are you okay?" he breathed.

"I don't know. Boo, please get us out of here."

He leaned into her. "Put your arm around me. Where's Laylee?"

A muffled sob came from the towel at her breast.

"I don't know; I've been calling for her. She disappeared. Boo, please hurry!"

He pulled her close and lifted her, straining, dizzy and then coughing again as the smoke wrapped around him. He worked back toward the door, hunched, muscles ripped and throbbing. His blood felt like acid running through his veins. Gussie was hacking violently; her arm was tugging at the flesh of his neck. At the door, he slid carefully around the great hole in the floor. In the hallway the smoke thinned enough to see several feet ahead. He hugged Gussie closer and sidestepped along the railing, trying to avoid the rain that was slashing in from the front windows. The baby squirmed against his chest, and a pink, miniature arm waggled into view.

"You're all covered in blood," she said. "What happened to you? I was so scared!"

Huffing, "I fell through the floor."

"That was Henry Ray, wasn't it?"

He nodded. They came to the top of the stairway. He tried to peer through the smoke as he gently took the first step down. Fire filled the entire southern side of the lower floor. The upper section of the stairway was still clear, but it looked as if the lowest few steps might be in flames.

"Where is he now?" she asked.

The riser cracked beneath them, and he was certain the steps wouldn't take their weight. "Gussie, he's dead." He jiggled her up, trying to get a better grip.

"He was like Lester, wasn't he? She used him." Her eyes were drawn and red.

"I guess so," he said. *Maybe they wanted to be used.* He took another step, dared another look at the swaddled package at her breast. Gussie's arm was slipping on the sweat at the back of his neck. "Gussie, it's boiling hot down there. I'm gonna have to go quick. I'll try to keep you and the baby away from the worst of it, but you have to hang on tight. Okay?"

Her hand shifted at his neck, digging tighter. She nodded.

Boo started down, taking swift, short steps. Stairway treads splintered as he went. The heat rose up and he turned his back to it, shielding Gussie and shuffling down sideways. Halfway down his foot crashed through a rotted tread, and he stumbled, pitching deeply under the weight in his arms until his knee braced against the next step down. He groaned and struggled back to his feet. The flames roasted his back, and he bit his lip. In his arms, Gussie squirmed, tucked her head in close. He took the next step down, and it held as a section of the ceiling collapsed not far away. Planks of wood and chunks of stucco crashed to the floor. Boo took another step. Nearing the bottom, he could now see that the fire had in fact reached the stairs and was starting a run up the circling banister. The fire to the south was roaring. Blisters were rising on his back. "Hang on, Gus!" he yelled, and she clenched into him as he charged forward. They hit the flames. He lunged through them, the last risers dipping and splitting; he kept moving, on the ground floor now, holding his breath until they were at last through the fire.

He stumbled several steps away toward the corridor north.

Smoke was curling up from Gussie's hair.

"Okay?" he asked, gasping. Back muscles were popping under the strain.

Gussie peeked up at him. "Boo, you're on fire." She swatted at his head. The baby's arm waved at him again.

Boo staggered forward. "We're almost there. Can you hang on a little longer?"

"You're still on fire." She rifled her fingers through his hair.

He couldn't get his breath. The flesh on his back was molten lava, dripping away. Ahead, the corridor was dark and cool.

nineteen

He climbed over a collapsed wall of mossy brick at the old stable. He placed Gussie gently on the ground. One corner of the structure had long ago buckled over, but the rest of it was still holding up under a relentless beating from Hurricane Constance. Gussie was soaking wet from the rain. She was filthy with ashes, and she looked exhausted. "Are you gonna be okay?" he asked.

"I'm fine, Boo, but I need to get to a doctor."

"I know." His voice was a brittle croak. "Gussie, I have to go back. I have to get Miss Laylee."

Wind ripped through the trees surrounding them. Gussie propped herself up on one elbow. "Boo, look at you. You need a doctor more than me. You can't go anywhere."

"I have to."

"It's probably too late."

He bent to catch his breath. Bending hurt; breathing hurt; everything hurt. He understood his body was so far ruined it was beyond repair. *Of course it's too late.*

"They kept her there, Boo. All those years." She was crying. "All those years she was waiting!"

Boo lurched forward and knelt to her side. He put a blistered and bloody hand out, touching her. All those years. It was too awful to think about. "Boy or girl?" he asked.

Sniffling, Gussie managed a weak smile. She pushed wet hair out of her face and looked down at the tiny package gathered inside the towel. "Boy."

"Is he..." He tried to swallow. "Is everything...?"

Her smile widened, and she looked up. "Strong as his daddy. Even has all his fingers and toes."

The top of the baby's head popped up between a fold in the towel. Boo forced himself to straighten up. He looked off toward the burning house where biblical cataclysms raged and a cyclone of flames swirled high into the night sky.

"I forgive you," he whispered.

He glanced one last time at the son Murphy Ransome would raise. And then he was gone.

twenty

The baby's skin was warm against hers. It was the same skin as hers, alive, same blood pulsing through it, same cadence of heart. Even his hair was the same as hers—fiery red. In this dark shelter, she hugged this tiny, alive, and identical part of herself closer, and he let himself be hugged. Already, he was quiet and easy.

She saw a light bobbing through the storm. Footfalls crashed, a mild disturbance in the steady roar of wind. Aching everywhere, she brought herself up to a sitting position, cradling the baby in her lap. The earth around her was sandy and cool. The air was clean and fragrant. It smelled of rain and flowers and cinnamon.

Through a tumbled brick hole in the wall she watched as a yellow ghost lifted up high into the night. Wind and rain snapped at it, fought it as it worked its way against the force of the storm. The yellow ghost was holding a flashlight.

"Wade!" she called out.

The light swung around to point at her. She waved at it.

Then her brother was squeezing through the gap in the wall. He was blinding her with his flashlight. "Wade, put that down please; I can't see anything."

He did what she asked, and she could now see his face. Numb. Standing over her, dripping rivers from his great yellow poncho, from his red hair *(same as me)*, eyes wide as they went between her and the baby in her lap. His mouth hung open.

At last, he spoke. "Boo?"

Before she could answer, they both heard the sounds of someone approaching from the collapsed southern wall. Wade swung the flashlight around.

"Oh my God," he whispered.

A cane, gripped in the withered fist of a skeleton, poked its way into the stables.

twenty-one

Through the heavy rolls of smoke, Boo Taylor was able to make out movement on the upper landing. Someone up there screamed his name. The stairway was still standing, but its bottom half was engulfed in flames. He looked around for some way to get to the second floor without having to walk through that massive wall of fire and saw that a pile of rubble had collapsed against the northern curve of the steps. Plaster and heavy oak beams fallen from the ceiling. He scrabbled for it, dodging the still-falling bits of old roof, reaching the pile through swirls of smoke and flames. He climbed it, clawing up as the skin on his knees and fingertips were sliced open on broken shards of ancient stucco. He made it up far enough to reach the banister ahead of the flames. He hauled the wreck of his body over the side as his name was screamed again.

"Sandy, I'm coming!" he called out, not much louder than a rough whisper now, coughing as smoke filled his shredded lungs. He coughed, folding into himself. Broken glass tore through his throat. His stomach muscles cramped, became like rocks. Below him, the lower stairs finally gave way in a thunderous crash. Still coughing, he went on hands and knees the rest of the way to the top. He rolled over on his back and the coughing fit finally eased. The floor scalded his skin. The remaining pieces of his shirt hung in rags from his neck. He reached for the breast pocket, and the tiny glass lump was still there.

Another crash, somewhere not far. Smoke was billowing from the southern rooms like a black avalanche. A vast hole had opened up in the roof where flames and smoke were now rising up to clash with the hurricane. His eyes were swollen and burning. He wiped them with his bleeding fingers, and they only stung worse.

"Sandy!" he croaked again. "Laylee!" He tried to swallow but couldn't.

A thin pillar of fire, screeching, blubbering, raced across the windows of the front corridor. Boo pushed to his feet.

"Sandy, I'm here!"

The sounds coming from the fire were pitiful.

He stood, took a staggering step toward the windows, and saw a reflection in the flames. A man was in there, nearly lost in the smoke. He took another step, and the man took a smoky step toward him. Boo rubbed his eyes again. He was looking at a black man who was on fire. Wide, rawboned shoulders, dressed in rags. White seashell eyes, soulful, considering him, measuring him. Mauled and burnt horribly. *Stayed a bit too long out in that sun.* Boo and the man stood and watched each other, recognizing each other, as fire and smoke and storm crackled around them, heaven and earth reaching toward each other, trying to touch. It had been the way of things for uncountable centuries.

"I'm you," the man said.

He smiled, and Boo smiled at the same time.

"We were always the same."

The column of fire was whirling toward him and calling his name. Still smiling, Boo Taylor stepped forward to embrace the flames.

Hints: remember, in chess, kings cancel each other out and cannot occupy adjacent squares, are therefore all-powerful and totally powerless, cannot affect one another, produce stalemate.
—*Harlan Ellison, The Deathbird*

Epilogue
Final Lessons

iss Laylee, Miss Laylee!"

The little boy lumbered across the lawn on chubby legs, scattering gulls.

"Miss Laylee, lookit what I got!"

Well behind the boy, watching the boy, Gussie Ransome clutched her coat tight to her chin as a frigid wind blew in from the Atlantic. She stepped away from her car, following Savannah and Georgia who were following Jeremiah who was chasing after the boy, calling his name. But the boy was racing on ahead and ignoring them. Above, the gulls whirled and squawked their agitation.

Wind flung red hair across her face, and she brushed it back. Broad streaks of white streamed away from both temples. The streaks had appeared shortly after the boy was born. Her *Bride of Frankenstein* streaks, she liked to think of them. She refused to color them because she had long ago decided they were well earned.

The boy ran to a hunched silhouette in a wheelchair.

"Bobby Joe, be careful!" she called out, quickening now. *Careful, she's so old.* Anxious, she watched as the boy climbed into the old woman's lap, as the old woman shifted a bit to make room for him. A dark woolen shawl wrapped the old woman's shoulders, and a quilt covered her legs. The boy was presenting her with a box wrapped in gold. From this distance, Gussie could hear a cackle of delight.

The thing she had come to like most about Christmas on the island was the relative peace. The tourist crowds were long gone. The office was quiet; the rentals were vacant—because the holidays were for being at home. Being with family. On Sweetpatch Island, the native islanders emerged from their scattered shelters, sniffing the wind, assessing the change, like ghost crabs climbing from their holes at dusk, or the dead emerging from graves. They found empty streets and quiet beaches. A slower pace. Things as they remembered them. You could almost hear the collective sigh of relief. The regathering of thoughts. And you could recognize the faces you passed on the street, some of them you knew back to your childhood, a time when things, if not better, were certainly simpler. It amazed her that she could look back on that ugly Dutton childhood with something like nostalgia. Somehow she did. And some-how, around Christmas in particular, without all of those stranger faces cluttering the landscape, the *longing* for things and times lost, better or worse, was so acute she could be overcome with grief and joy.

MaeEllen Taylor was coming from the back porch, both imperious and matriar-chal in chinchilla, offering Merry Christmases and complaining about the cold. "Now they're saying it could even *snow*. Can you imagine? Can you even remember when it ever snowed?"

She took Gussie's hand and hugged her. The hand and the hug were warm. MaeEllen's eyes watered and glowed while chinchilla fur rippled in the wind. Hand in hand, they walked toward the old woman in the wheelchair, where Jeremiah and the girls had finally caught up and where the little boy was laughing at bits of gold paper dancing in the breeze.

A blind face turned to the sun.

A horribly scarred nose sniffed the wind.

Withered lips curled a grin.

"Miss Gussie."

The voice was the soft exhalation of ancient winds.

Gussie knelt next to the chair. "Merry Christmas, Miss Laylee. How are you feelin today?"

The grin widened. A brown skull tilted, focusing in on her voice. "Why, I'm fine as wine, Miss Gus. Fine as frog's hair." Purple lenses glinted a morning sun from that old, all-seeing but un-seeing face. So old. So old that all color had been drained from the woman and so she took on the colors around her. She was the gray of the sky and the steel-blue of the sea and the washed out hues of the dunes. Gussie blinked and the colors changed, became that of the children surrounding her.

Gussie leaned to kiss a leathery cheek. Blue-red-yellow sparks sizzled.

She was used to the old woman's magic.

The boy was in the grass now, sitting Indian style and tearing the paper off his own gifts. Caught up in his half-brother's joy, Jeremiah plopped in the grass next to him in an identical posture. Laughing, Savannah and Georgia did the same. MaeEllen drifted over to supervise.

"Got somethin for you, too, Miss Gus."

Laylee Colebriar leaned a delicate spine to a mound of presents all wrapped in Sunday funnies. She made blind swimming strokes through the pile. Finally, with infinite slowness, her old fingers lifted out a roundish blob.

Gussie took it from her, peeled off the paper.

"It's beautiful," she said.

A snow globe. Inside, a boy and girl in ice-skates, dancing face-to-face on a frozen pond. A large gray dog, perked tail, watching them.

"Lemme see!"

Gussie handed the globe to her little boy.

"You s'pose t'shake it up, boy!"

The boy gripped the globe in both hands, snarled, and gave it several hard jerks. Then he held it up and laughed as the cold stung Gussie's eyes and a tear rolled down her cheek and a miniature blizzard swirled over a tiny, plastic figure. The tear froze like an icicle just above her lip.

When she looked down again she found a brown root knotted up in her fingers. A hard, yellow fingernail was stroking the back of her hand. Gussie saw her reflection in the purple lenses, streaks of white flowing from red, a sad smile, sun glinting off a single drop of ice.

"He a handsome boy, Miss Gus?" the blind old woman asked. It was a standard question.

Gussie dabbed a knuckle at the frozen tear. "Looks just like his daddy." Her standard response. "Getting *ornery* like his daddy, too."

The root tightened.

I wish you could see him.

A bit of gold wrapping floated up to her face, did a somersault, then disappeared. The blind and ruined old face behind that purple glass was fixed up at her—and in the next moment she was flung up to the sky with the gulls, drifting on gray-white wings and borne by the unnatural cold toward the Atlantic. Vast continents beckoned beyond the horizon. Below her, her children laughed and an ancient woman cackled, not seeing her up here—her children because they weren't looking up, the old woman because those purple lenses were covering what was left of her once-lovely eyes. She circled up in this high, cold place, able to see across the island, north to south, east to west, the shell pile, the marshes, the beaches, the harbor, even the burnt-out hulk of an old mansion deep in the swamp; the island was its own little continent set adrift in the sea, peopled by its own unique race of island folk. Up here, everyone looked small and identical. Up here, the hardships and resentments below looked petty and irrelevant. Looked laughably simple. Up here, it all looked so beautiful—life, precious and fragile, miraculously clinging to a slim spit of sand and surrounded by great oceanic forces. Benevolent forces—if they could all only see it from up here, they would know this. Her bird-heart swelled.

Come be with us!

Voices calling to her—up here, so close to heaven, she could hear them, borne on their own wings, and she wanted to be with them. She was drifting in the place between heaven and earth. She had never realized how close they were to each other.

Come be with us, come be with us!

She rode the wind, touching feathers against those millions of wings surrounding her in this high place, letting the currents spiral her back down now, willingly surrendering to gravity, making a slow and pleasant descent as feathers gave way to flesh, as the land rose to her feet, as she hovered a moment longer before touching the planks of the pier.

She breathed in the cold salt air.

And walked out to the very edge.

The sea rose and fell beneath her in great heaves of steel-blue lungs. Creatures whirled in there, buffeted by the currents, drawing close as she approached, expectant. There was a gift waiting for her. Placed on the very last plank of the pier.

A tiny sack of burlap, wrapped in a red ribbon.

She bent to pick it up. From its weight, she knew what was inside.

"Mamma, mamma!" Her little boy was racing toward the pier. She felt a cold tear touch her face. Then another, swirling out of the sky, down from that wonderful chaos of wings. She looked up from the sack and glanced to the south where a smoky figure was now walking along the beach. Still far in the distance. Dark, with a silvery mist floating off his shoulders. He was working his way toward her, straddling sand and sea as he came.

She tugged at the ribbon.

"Momma, look!"

A little glass frog fell into her hand.

Another icy tear touched her skin.

The boy's footsteps reverberated on the pier. Gussie stared at the frog in her hand, cracks webbing through it, waiting for it to come to life. Another bit of old woman's magic.

"Momma look, it's *angels!*"

The cold wind was blurring her vision. A strong breeze lifted from the sea to carry errant strands of red and white south, reaching in that direction as she looked up again and raised her hand to the smoky figure on the beach.

After a moment, when snowflakes began to fill the sky, he lifted his own hand in return.

Acknowledgments

I would like to thank to the following people for their invaluable support: Leanne Campbell, Dick Yerger, Rene Hutchins, Fred Miller, Bill & Meg Maley, Mark Mossman, Sue Haldeman, Dana Shreve, Bonnie Piekarski, Bill Pease, and Daphne Wessells. Thanks also to Maryglenn McCombs and, from Hooded Friar Press, to Peter Honsberger, Rachel Fichter, and Bobby Dawson.

A special thanks to my wife, Leslie.

About the Author

Newark, Delaware, is Scott Fad's hometown. He currently lives in Landenberg, Pennsylvania, with his wife, Leslie, their two children, four dogs, three chickens, one cat, and a horse.